Frank Lee Benedict

My Daughter Elinor

Frank Lee Benedict

My Daughter Elinor

ISBN/EAN: 9783337047559

Printed in Europe, USA, Canada, Australia, Japan

Cover: Foto ©Andreas Hilbeck / pixelio.de

More available books at **www.hansebooks.com**

MY DAUGHTER ELINOR.

A Novel.

NEW YORK:

HARPER & BROTHERS, PUBLISHERS,

FRANKLIN SQUARE.

1869.

MY DAUGHTER ELINOR.

CHAPTER I.

WHERE THEY MET.

CLIVE FARNSWORTH walked up and down the long stone terrace which lay in the afternoon shadow, with no companion but his own thoughts, and society more dreary and dissatisfied he could not easily have found.

It was a pretty scene that spread before his eyes, if he had been in a mood to appreciate its charms. The flower-garden swept below the terrace, basking in the June sun; the green lawn sloped toward the avenue which made a pleasant drive to the road; the house standing on an eminence gave a fine view of the picturesque valley beyond, dotted with villages and country seats, a beautiful lake in the midst, and the blue mountains shutting in the landscape miles and miles away.

But the desert of Sahara would have presented as many attractions for him then; he was thinking his own dismal thoughts, and refused obstinately to see any thing pleasant even in Nature.

Perhaps you know the mood—Heaven help us, it comes upon most men soon enough after twenty-five. He was thinking what a poor, wasted thing his life was, how the hopes of his youth had shrunk to nothing in his hands, and how he had lied to his own soul in not having remained true to the dreams and aspirations of that season. He was twenty-eight years old; he had lived through the experience of a man double that age, and there was nothing to show; the sins of earlier years, which like other men he had called follies, pricked now and made the retrospect and the present still more barren.

Not that he was weak or given to crying out at each adverse blow of fate that the world had come to an end, but he was in one of those moods of discouragement and misanthrophy which the strongest must at times endure, uncertain whether to blame himself or life the most.

His new book had been frightfully belabored and picked to pieces in two hemispheres; he had been insane enough to become a candidate for Congress, and had gone through the disgusting details of an election, and the result had not been agreeable. He took his seat, and to his unbounded wrath and astonishment it was contested, and the case dragged nearly through the long session. He found himself ousted on the ground of his election having been illegal, and heard himself charged with more enormities than ten experienced rogues could commit in as many years, after the pleasant fashion in which political aspirants' characters are treated by our wise statesmen and magnanimous press.

These things of themselves could not have given him a sense of discouragement. He might have been roused to anger and defiance, but he had a strong will and could have found a certain enjoyment in braving the storm and by obstinate effort forcing public opinion to shift again in his favor. But he was dissatisfied with his life and at enmity with himself; hence those smarts made their edge felt with a keenness they could not otherwise have possessed.

So he walked up and down the stone terrace, and chafed under his dreary reflections after the manner in which he had spent a goodly portion of the weeks since he returned to his country place.

The people in the neighborhood decided that he was disappointed and misanthropic, and he had the weakness of caring when such things were said; therefore every now and then he forced himself to go out among them and endure the weariness of dinners and picnics and sailing-parties, and similar atrocities which ranked among summer enjoyments, as unfortunately the neighborhood of the lake was a favorite resort during the warm months.

Farnsworth saw one of the grooms leading his horse round to the front entrance, and felt savage with the poor man because he whistled cheerfully and talked kindly to Tempest, magnificently oblivious of the fact that the ignorant fellow's own troubles were certain to be as hard for him to bear as a poet's could be. A gallop along the shadowy roads in the late afternoon would be pleasant at all events, so Farnsworth went out and mounted his horse and rode away down the avenue. Clive endeavored to outstrip his tiresome fancies, and at a sudden turn in the lonely road he had taken, came face to face with two equestrians who had halted where two ways met, apparently uncertain which would lead them least astray in the world.

Farnsworth felt so delightfully uncivil that, though he comprehended their situation at a glance, I think his first impulse would have been to spur on and leave them to their own devices, although one of the riders was a lady and the other an elderly gentleman. But the elderly voice exclaimed—

"Why, it's Mr. Farnsworth! I say, my dear fellow, don't ride us down, but be Quixotic enough to halt a moment."

Clive looked and saw that it was the Honorable Mr. Grey, and wished him in Flanders, uttering words of pleasure at the meeting in the most approved and orthodox manner. He suddenly grew conscious that a pair of large gray eyes were turned upon him with a careless, absent glance, and it became apparent to him that a very stately young woman, who sat her horse like Diana herself, was the owner of those orbs.

By this time Mr. Grey had said—"I knew you had a den somewhere near — they were speaking of you at breakfast. We are visiting in the neighborhood." Then recalling his elaborate courtesy — "My daughter Elinor, Mr. Farnsworth."

And Clive bowed, and the eyes, which after that first slow glance of indifference had wandered away to the pretty view, came back and gave him another look not much more interested, and "my daughter Elinor" returned his salutation with grave civility.

"We were uncertain which road to take," Mr. Grey continued. "Knowing the selfishness of human nature, you can imagine how welcome you are."

"Are you stopping in the village?" Clive asked.

"No, we came last night to visit the Thorntons."

And Clive remembered that he had heard they were coming, and that he was invited to dine at the Thorntons this very day. He said something pretty and proper about his pleasure in welcoming them to the neighborhood, and with the usual brilliancy of masculine natures on such occasions, insinuated a hope that Miss Grey was condescending enough to admire the scenery. The large eyes looked at him again, and the expression had not altered. Clive Farnsworth was not accustomed to such glances from female eyes, certainly not three in succession, and to add to his annoyance, a voice considerably more indifferent than his own answered—

"It is very pretty. I should like it better without the houses and people at every turn."

"My daughter Elinor has a fancy for wild mountain scenery," Mr. Grey said suavely, perhaps to soften her words a little, which might have been susceptible of a double signification.

"A few miles up the valley one finds that," Clive said. "You will think it worth admiring, I am sure, Miss Grey."

"I have no doubt," she replied. "Mrs. Thornton has told me a great deal about her beautiful valley."

"Yes; she was born here, and so has a right to be enthusiastic."

"Naturally," replied she. "Papa, it is getting late."

"Yes—I forgot it in the pleasure of the meeting. Farnsworth, we shall see you soon? Oh, by the bye, you are of the dinner-party!"

Clive said he should have the pleasure of meeting them at that decorous festivity, and they rode away. As she bowed, Elinor Grey did vouchsafe him one smile, which lighted her face into such beauty that Clive turned his horse homeward with his judgment somewhat mollified. "Upon my word," he thought, "'my daughter Elinor' looks as if nothing mortal were worth a second glance—but she has a beautiful smile."

Even when he reached home Farnsworth remembered that smile, and went up stairs to dress with the accompaniment of an unusual pleasure—an anticipation; and it is something in this latter half of the nineteenth century to have such a sensation.

It was seven o'clock when he set out, and there being a path through the fields which brought Alban Wood within reasonable distance, Farnsworth bethought him that he could walk instead of getting out his trap. He took the precaution to put on a loose travelling-coat, that he need not make a spectacle of himself for the crows to laugh at by walking through the green lanes in full dress. It was a pretty ramble too, through his own woods, across a broad meadow where the sheep were feeding, and down toward the grove which made the boundary line of the Thorntons' place on that side.

Farnsworth found himself the last arrival, and had to endure the glare of all eyes—I speak advisedly, dinner being at hand—as he marched toward his hostess.

"I was in hopes you would be late," said she gayly, "for I should have had an opportunity of scolding you. That does you so much good I would not have cared for the dinner spoiling."

"Only some of the guests would have eaten me," returned Farnsworth. "Look at Mrs. Hackett!—this is an hour after her usual feeding-time—I am sure she would have devoured me."

"The consequences would have been most fatal to her, you cynic," said Mrs. Thornton.

Farnsworth did his duty by speaking to such people as could not be avoided from their propinquity, and looking about saw Elinor Grey at a distant window pretending to listen to what some man was saying, but in reality looking out through the twilight. She had on a black dress of a thin gauzy material that floated about her like a cloud, with a knot of silver flowers twisted in her auburn hair. She looked so different from any of the other women—Clive concluded that must be the charm. He had no opportunity to find out, however, for dinner was announced and he saw her led away by their good-natured host, while Mrs. Thornton whispered to him—

"Mrs. Hackett made a special request that you should take her in, so Tom has the pleasure of Queen Elinor's company; be grateful and be agreeable." And with the usual perversity of human nature, Farnsworth straightway felt indisposed to either effort.

At table he found himself nearly opposite Miss Grey, and she acknowledged his presence with another of those regal bows which were enough to annihilate any man; all the more exasperating because it was evident that indifference rather than pride was the cause. Every body devoured and remained stupid except Mr. Grey, who was the most captivating companion imaginable, and Clive sat fenced in by a heavy girl on one hand and Mrs. Hackett on the other. They both talked to him at once, having a weakness for celebrities. Through the din Clive looked over at Elinor Grey sitting like a fair statue of silence, and thought she seemed placidly amused at his plight. Mrs. Hackett was a golden idol—I mean she was so rich that she might have had a palace like Aladdin's if she had chosen—yet people said that once she had been a milliner's girl and carried a bonnet-box down the Bowery. She was a great woman now, and a determined lion-hunter, and read books—yes, and talked about them. I dare say that her opinions were as valuable as those of her neighbors, only her English was at times original; and though she had learned any quantity of long words, she occasionally twisted them in a marvellous manner both as to pronunciation and meaning.

"Do you admire Miss Grey?" she whispered.

"Of course you do! Why, they say the Emperor raved over her in Paris, and that Eugenie was quite vexed."

"Oh, of course I admire her," replied Clive, for she had announced the imperial admiration as if that settled the matter for all persons in possession of their senses.

"She is what I call an accidental beauty," pursued Mrs. Hackett.

"Accidental?" quoth Clive, inquiringly.

"Yes," replied she, seeming to push her words out like bullets, as she always did when she used long ones. "I say accidental as opposed to oriental, you know."

Clive was delighted, and he hoped that her whisper had been audible to Miss Grey even through the noise, for the champagne had begun to foam, and every body was talking at once; but the fair face gave no sign.

"The father is charming," continued Mrs. Hackett; "such manners—a second Richaloo."

Clive was dying to ask if that was any thing like Waterloo, but held his peace.

"He adorns his position," said Mrs. Hackett. "I was in Paris while he was ambassador, and it was worth while seeing him there; his daughter too."

Now the child of Pluto on Clive's other side —I mean the term to apply to her wealth, not her character—claimed his attention and chattered as young women will in all countries, upon every imaginable subject, and Mrs. Hackett joined in till Clive's head was dizzy with the avalanche of remarkable opinions and information concerning every thing under heaven from a description of Noah's ark down to modern spiritualism.

Clive saw Elinor Grey talking pleasantly with Mr. Thornton and the gentleman at her right—smiling at Thornton every now and then, and showing how the proud, still face could flash into beauty, the more desirable because it was not constant, but came rather from the soul than perfection of feature.

Occasionally the talk blended, and it happened that several times Farnsworth and Miss Grey exchanged words and even found an opportunity to differ upon some subject which could not be pursued because Mrs. Hackett grasped the various threads of conversation in her own hands and her voice rode triumphant over all other tones. But a brief difference of opinion is an approach to acquaintance between two persons of the opposite sex, and when the ladies rose from the table Farnsworth watched Miss Grey pass out of the room, and decided that she was not a statue but a woman worth studying, with heart and soul and warm womanly feelings, in spite of the abstracted glances the dreamy eyes gave ordinary mortals, and the firm repose which settled over her mouth when silent.

Mr. Grey moved his chair near, and Farnsworth was glad, because the ex-ambassador was as charming in his after-dinner talk as a human being can be, and besides, "my daughter Elinor" (he never spoke of and seldom to her in any other way) was frequently on his lips. Clive wanted to hear all he could about her, being given to odd conclusions, and having already a feeling that in the diplomatic triumphs of the past years her wit might count for as much as her father's shrewdness.

When they joined the ladies in the drawing-room Farnsworth took possession of an unoccupied seat by Miss Grey, and wisely went back at once to the subject on which they had politely differed at dinner, thereby avoiding the ice of commonplace questions and answers about things of which neither cared a jot, with which newly-introduced people, be they ever so brilliant, are wont to torment themselves and the sharer in the dialogue. And Elinor Grey could talk—when she thought it worth while to take the trouble. She demolished Mr. Farnsworth's theory with an energy which charmed him, because she flashed into beauty the instant she became excited. It happened that at some sentiment he enunciated she replied—

"Ah, you said that better in your last book; but it was not true there."

She had read his books—that was something, though as a general thing with the women he met it would have been a relief if they had not read them.

"But you need not belabor that unfortunate offspring," he said, smiling; "it has suffered enough at the hands of the reviewers."

"And so it ought," she replied coolly; "it was not true to yourself."

His eyes lighted so that she remembered if his "yourself" was as easily flattered as that of most of the literary men she had known, he would straightway be thinking that here was another devotee at his shrine, another romantic creature who had been making a hero of him. "I believe that was uncivil," said she. "I meant—"

"But it is so pleasant to say what one really thinks, and get a little off from conventionalities," returned Clive, suavely.

But she paid no attention. Straightway her eyes looked over him or through him into some dreamy world in which he had no place. That was unendurable! Clive vowed that before many days she should at least stay within reach when he talked.

"Will you tell me what you meant?" he asked humbly.

"And so make an enemy of you for life?" returned she, with her beautiful calm smile.

"Oh no! show that you think me worthy of your acquaintance by telling me the truth."

"That would be going back to Arcadian simplicity. But you would only defend yourself, and prove positively that whatever other censures might be pronounced against your work, mine certainly were unfounded."

"It was hastily written—"

"Just what I complain of," said she. "If a story be worth writing at all it is worth writing well ; if not, why begin it ?"

"I think I hardly know whether I consider literature my profession," he said.

"Oh! then I should write no more books till I was certain it must or ought to be. I don't believe in amateur authors any more than I do in amateur lawyers or physicians."

And one word led to another, till she told him roundly that his book was misanthropic, and that it was weak and youthful to be misanthropic. Finally she softened her strictures with a sweet smile, assured him that he wrote delightfully, and floated away from the subject, rather astonished at herself for the pains she had taken. They talked of all sorts of pleasant things—of Italy, and pictures, and Clive's last visit to Europe, where he ought to have seen Miss Grey, but did not, because she had gone to Rome when he reached Paris. People came and went about her, but Clive kept his seat, and was devoutly thankful when she refused to sing. He was sure that she had a charming voice, but it was one of his idiosyncrasies to hate women who did opera at parties.

Altogether the evening was the pleasantest Farnsworth had spent in a long time, and he felt that Elinor Grey was a new revelation in the way of womanhood ; bearing with a flutter unsuited to his years Mrs. Thornton's announcement that having once captured her, she would not release her under two months. He learned another thing too—Miss Grey's exact age—and according to our cousins over the water, it is a national failing to have a curiosity concerning the length of time every body of our acquaint-ance has trodden this mortal vale. In one of her flittings about them Mrs. Thornton chanced to say that something happened when Elinor was sixteen. "It was just before you went to Europe," she added. Now Clive knew that Mr. Grey had been ambassador two years at the court of St. James, and had gone immediately to France to serve his country for four more. So he did a sum in mental arithmetic, although as a general rule not much better at figures than I myself am, and discovered, since figures can not lie, that "my daughter Elinor" was twenty-two years old.

Mrs. Thornton was very anxious that her favorites should know and like each other ; consequently, with the usual fate of those trying to help people be agreeable, she managed to do the very thing that was wrong, and spoiled the evening for Farnsworth as completely as only a friend attempting to serve you can do.

She had glided up again to see that all was going well, and to refresh herself a moment after the oppressiveness of Mrs. Hackett. She sat down on a footstool at Elinor's feet, and being young still, and very small and graceful to boot, it was the kind of thing she did well and not too frequently—having that tact without which the prettier the woman the more like a fool she is doomed to act.

They were talking about the Marble Faun, and halted at the Falls of Terni for Mrs. Thornton to recall a pilgrimage she and Elinor had made to them when they were at Rome together. "And here is a sketch of hers," said Mrs. Thornton. "I made her bring a lot of things down stairs to show me this morning—she sketches like an angel. Where is the portfolio, Queen Elinor?"

"I hid it," said Miss Grey, quietly. "I didn't choose it to lie here on exhibition."

"And I watched you and brought it back," returned Mrs. Thornton, laughing merrily. "I did it for your special benefit, Mr. Farnsworth."

"I am your debtor forever," said he. "May I profit, Miss Grey?"

"Just one peep," pleaded Mrs. Thornton. "He really has eyes."

The matter was too trifling to be teased about, so Miss Grey allowed Mrs. Thornton to produce the portfolio in triumph from under an ottoman where she had concealed it. "There are only three or four here," said she, "but some day we will make her show you all she has."

Mrs. Thornton turned the sketches over to find the one of which she had spoken, and placed it in Farnsworth's hands. As she drew it out of the portfolio a water-color drawing came with it and fluttered into Elinor's lap. Mrs. Thornton seized it, exclaiming—

"What a lovely head! Oh, who is it?"

"A peasant girl in the south of France," Miss Grey answered.

"It looks like an American face," said Mrs. Thornton.

"Yes," said Miss Grey, "I made the study because she was the living image of a pretty

American girl I found once up near the Green Mountains."

Clive Farnsworth was holding the other sketch in his hand, and staring at Miss Grey like a man stupid from the effect of a sudden blow.

"Do look at this," cried Mrs. Thornton, giving him the portrait. "Did you ever see such a lovely face?"

"My American girl was prettier," said Elinor; "I wonder what has become of her."

Clive Farnsworth took the drawing Mrs. Thornton offered him. He only gave one glance—the paper fluttered out of his hand and fell again in Miss Grey's lap as if seeking protection.

"How careless you are!" exclaimed Mrs. Thornton in her pretty, brusque way.

Defending himself from the charge made a diversion, but Farnsworth saw Miss Grey looking at him, and wondered if she had noticed his trembling hand. He felt that his face must be pallid from that sudden sick feeling at his heart. Fortunately Mrs. Hackett came up at the instant and pounced on the portfolio, so there was no opportunity for any body to notice or think.

But the evening had turned suddenly black to Clive Farnsworth. Mrs. Thornton had sprung the mine in her effort to be agreeable. He remembered that he could not be ridiculous, and rush away like a second Lara with dishevelled hair, so he stood still for a few moments and managed to talk and appear to listen, till Mrs. Hackett's exclamations brought the whole party up to admire Miss Grey's wonderful productions. Then he made his adieus and departed, seeing, as in a dream, Elinor Grey's calm eyes, while through the hurry and blackness of his thoughts Mrs. Hackett's enthusiastic but slightly inappropriate exclamation came up—"Isn't she a second St. Cecilia?"—making him laugh a brief, bitter laugh.

His trap not having arrived, he started off through the fields again, and the quiet silvery night was a new pang, so that altogether he reached home a more miserable man than he had been during the gloom of the past weeks.

CHAPTER II.

MRS. THORNTON'S GENERALSHIP.

THE next morning the sun came out glorious, and the young day was so beautiful through its veil of golden mist that Clive Farnsworth left a portion of his weary thoughts in his bed-chamber, and took up life with more serenity than had seemed possible during the long watches of that sleepless night.

At breakfast came a message from Mrs. Thornton—he was to allow nothing short of an earthquake to prevent his joining their riding-party that afternoon. She wanted to show Miss Grey the glen at the head of the valley, and relied upon him to prove his claims to being a

genius by aiding her in the pleasant duty, or ever after to hide his diminished head and regard himself in the light of an exposed impostor. This command helped Farnsworth a long way on toward the reaction of spirits which the brightness of the morning had begun. Straightway the regal face rose before him, softened by its rare smile, and Clive again fastened the doors between him and the past.

That is a work at which we spend so much time in this life: we bolt and bar, and when every thing seems secure some ghost flings wide the portals, and there are the long, dreary corridors casting their grim shadows into our banqueting hall, and the cold wind chills us to the bone, withering our garlands, putting out the lights, and making confusion generally.

Farnsworth had secured the doors, and the remembrance of Elinor Grey's smile sent the sunshine across his soul. There were some orders to be given to the gardeners which took him out among the flower-beds; then the farmer came and insisted upon his marching off to a field of young wheat, so that the whole morning was spent in the fresh air. By the time he got back from the inspecting tour Clive was ready to sit down on the lawn and smoke a calumet of peace with Destiny under his favorite maple-tree. That is, he thought he was smoking the sour dame into complacency, whereas he was only blotting her from sight and dreaming of new hopes and a world into which she could not possibly enter.

The party were mounting their horses as Clive rode up the avenue of Alban Wood, and he had such cordial greetings from his ally Mrs. Thornton, and a look of such growing acquaintance from Miss Grey, that his horse became a winged Bucephalus at once—such is man.

The Thorntons had several guests besides the Greys; people whom the hostess charmed with her pretty attentions, and properly abused to Elinor in private for being there at all, after the habit of women in general.

They were all ready, the number increased by a few outsiders, and the array of fine horses and showy traps was good to see.

Mrs. Thornton was to drive Mr. Grey in her pony-carriage, having a great weakness for his spicy gossip, and flirtation with her not going much beyond that in spite of what people said. Farnsworth found himself assigned to Miss Grey by command of the little general.

"You are to make her admire the scenery the whole way," said she. "I will never forgive you if she does not come back enthusiastic."

"All visitors here are forced to be that at the point of the bayonet, Miss Grey," said Clive; "so be prepared."

"I am," she replied. "The garden of Eden was nothing to it—I assert that in advance."

"The worst of it is that the place is really beautiful," said Farnsworth.

"How do you mean the worst?" asked Mr. Grey.

"Because when one is dragged to see wonders, one likes at least to be revenged by not admiring."

"Monster!" cried Mrs. Thornton, allowing Mr. Grey to hand her into the low carriage. "Now, good people, let us be off. Tom, dear, don't come within a mile of me," she added to her husband. "That horrid horse of yours has a spite at my ponies—he always tries to give them sly kicks."

"She says that to keep me out of her way," quoth honest Tom, who loved the little witch with all his honest soul.

"And it is certain that I shall not miss you," said Mr. Grey, lifting his hat with a bland courtesy which made every body shriek.

Away they went, past the lake, and on up the narrowing road to where the valley was suddenly closed by twin cliffs, through which a mountain brook dashed in a triumphant cascade and fled laughing toward the tranquil lake.

There was no incident. I did not mean to delude you into the belief that some scene was at hand—that Clive rescued Miss Grey from the water-fall; or that they met face to face an old crone who prophesied impossible things, and made the past clear as a map; or that a pallid man suddenly started up from behind the rocks, and pointed a spectral finger at Elinor, with a shriek of "'Tis she!" or that some strange young woman, at sight of Clive, gave three perpendicular bounds into the air, like an India-rubber ball, 'and moaned with Pauline—"My husband!" I am sorry if you are disappointed, but nothing happened; and I can not pretend that there did, being as truthful as George Washington in his youthful days: Miss Grey did not even wet the point of her balmoral boot in the water-fall; neither the pallid man nor the mournful female made their appearance. If there were any such persons they were not up to time; or, what is more probable, were eating a ham-sandwich and having a tranquil flirtation behind the rocks. I have chronicled the expedition because it was the beginning of a knot of such golden days to Clive Farnsworth—the first of his summer idyl—which floated away through heavenly June, and so completely entranced him that he had no space to marvel whither it might lead or to know if he were awake or dreaming.

He did make rapid progress in his acquaintance with Elinor Grey, there was no denying that, and if she had thought about it she might have been astonished. But she did not do any thing so stupid. She was delighted to find herself in her native land after those years of absence; Mrs. Thornton talked of him as so familiar a friend, and the day was so lovely, that altogether she was beguiled into saying what she really believed upon such subjects as came up. Farnsworth talked remarkably well, too, and was not egotistical; and though Elinor Grey had lived in the great world, she had not met good conversationalists enough to take them quite as a matter of course. Above and beyond all, though he did not complain or moan, or act like a poet or a goose, it was evident to her perception that he was lonely and disappointed and that life was at a sort of standstill with him. Did ever any woman resist that? Why a man shall catch the sympathies of the oldest or the coldest of them with that chaff—I mean real, earnest women with hearts and souls under their armor.

Now you go and try it, dear Sir who reads—and get beautifully tripped up in trying, because I forgot to finish my last sentence. A man shall do all these things, even with his neighbor's wife—if he knows how. Perhaps it would be as well for you and me not to attempt it, but Clive Farnsworth did know how, or rather he did it unconsciously with a woman whom he felt could understand and sympathize with him.

The excursion was a success in every way. When they got back to Alban Wood they sat under the trees and ate ripe cherries and drank iced drinks before breaking up the party, and talked a great deal of brilliant nonsense which would probably be as flat as champagne opened yesterday if I tried to set it down. Mr. Grey and "my daughter Elinor" both admired the neighborhood so much that they talked almost seriously of hunting about for a nest somewhere within easy reach.

"Several places for sale," Mr. Thornton said. "There is Waterside—close by the lake."

"Never, with that name!" cried Elinor.

"You could do as you must with your own some day," said Tom—"you could change it."

They all laughed, but Clive thought Miss Grey's lip curled at the suggestion.

"Did my husband make a joke?" demanded Mrs. Thornton.

"My dear, I stumbled on it," said he humbly.

"Then I forgive you; but be careful, Thomas."

"Besides, there's no land to speak of," continued her spouse, following up his own train of thought.

"Now where has he gone?" asked his wife.

"His joke has led him out of sight of land," said Mr. Grey.

"There isn't any—I mean belonging to Waterside."

"That is no joke, certainly," replied Mr. Grey.

"Oh yes, there must be seventy-five acres," Clive said.

"Well, I meant no farm to speak of."

"Quite enough to be bothered with where a man only wants a place to live during the summer months."

"Well, that's true, after all," assented easy Tom.

"Notwithstanding you are both large land owners, you agree with Horace," said Mr. Grey.

"Indeed I have forgotten all about Horace," replied Thornton honestly; "but what did he say?"

"'Laudato ingentia rura; exiguum colito,'" quoted Mr. Grey, offering his snuff-box to Thornton with his indescribable manner.

"Oh, papa," exclaimed Elinor, "for shame —to quote Latin! It was Virgil said it, any way."

"Am I wrong, Mr. Farnsworth?" he asked.

"I believe you are," he said.

"And Elinor stands convicted of understanding Latin!" cried Mrs. Thornton. "Thank goodness, I have been better brought up."

"And all this while," said Tom, "I'm blessed if I know what he means, whichever old wig said it. 'Exiguum?' That's—"

"It sounds like something nasty to drink," broke in Mrs. Thornton. "Don't touch it, Tom.'

"It means—Let your neighbors be geese enough to own big farms if they like, stick you to a small one," said Clive.

"Virgil improved," smiled Elinor.

"Yes," said Tom; "beats old Anthon's notes all hollow! Well, it's true, any way; I know that."

Clive thought Miss Grey still looked as if she wished her father's lapse of memory had not led her into an avowal which might appear a pedantic assumption, but he was glad to know that she had read and cared for the classics—not being of Lord Byron's opinion that a woman must be ignorant in order to be interesting.

Clive rode home with spirits undiminished, and was even equal to entertaining several men who strayed up from the hotel at the lake; and one of them, an old artist, won Clive's downright regard by announcing that he had seen Miss Grey on horseback and that she was a queen. Tongues were unloosed at once, but Clive as soon as possible drew the name out of the conversation. It was not to be desecrated by unhallowed lips. Before the evening was over he lavished such praise on the artist's last picture—which he had seen at the exhibition while in town—that the shrewd old bird was in doubt whether he really admired it so much, or, intending to buy it, wanted to flatter him into a moderate price—being an old artist, acquainted with the pitfalls of the world and not wishing to walk blindfold into them.

The next day Clive had some business to attend to at the county town, but he spent the evening at Alban Wood and was rewarded by hearing Elinor Grey sing.

The morning after it rained. Clive stood in the breakfast-room window and looked out at the melancholy drizzle, so much more annoying than an actual tempest, and felt his high spirits droop as if the damp had got in them. He even looked drearily toward the stone terrace where he was accustomed to walk when his devils tormented him, and sighed to think that he might be brought to that before the day was over. He might have read—only when it drizzled he never could. He might have written—only that, printed author though he might be, he was not conscious of possessing an idea beyond the fact that the drizzle annoyed him and filled him with forebodings for his newly-acquired peace.

Fortunately, through wind and storm appeared a Mercury from Mrs. Thornton, and very sorely, I fear, had that Mercury periled his soul by the objurgations he lavished on his pretty mistress during the journey. Clive, recognizing his face, went out with alacrity to learn his errand, and received a dainty three-cornered note, in return for which he offered a supply of the root of all evil which made Mercury wish he had been shod with wings, that he might have grasped the reward the sooner—or at all events, he thought that thought in his own way.

Clive opened the billet and stopped to admire Mrs. Thornton's graceful writing—and, thank Heaven, American women do write pretty hands! All English women write so much alike that a man could not tell except by reading, whether the page was from his Dulcinea or his great aunt. French women make tracks like spiders. As for the Italians—well, I believe they do not trust much to letters for working their share of mischief. And Mrs. Thornton wrote—

"'It rains, it rains, and never is weary.' May my poetical quotation soften your iron will! I feel like Van Amburgh when the animals are hungry—with all these people on my hands. Queen Elinor has obstinately taken refuge in her room, pretending that she had letters to write—she just wants to avoid our stupidity.

"Will you please come over, in spite of the flood, and help me entertain my monsters? I promise that Her Majesty shall dawn upon you —she can't refuse, you know. I send this with my heart full of beseeching. My Bluebeard of a husband is looking over my shoulder, so be sure that you bring it back with you."

Then Tom had scribbled—

"'There's a trout baked in cream for luncheon—that's the way to bring a poet.' You must come prepared to stay over to-morrow."

Clive scrawled a rapturous, laughter-provoking answer, walked up and down, smoking like a Mohawk chief, till such an hour as he could decently set out, and was a new man.

After all, it was a delightful day. Some people from the hotel, rendered desperate by the infectious imbecility pervading it, made their appearance in wonderful mufflers and disguises, and the luncheon was perfect. If you have ever eaten a trout baked in cream you know that it must be the very dish which the gods called Ambrosia—if you never have, rush after some body that knows how to prepare it, else you will go down to your grave with one requisite sensation unexperienced.

They played billiards, they did charades, they danced, and when twilight came Clive so managed that he and Miss Grey sat talking in the pleasant old library, and added the crowning charm to his enjoyment: he persuaded her to sing to him in a half-voice, so that, as he honestly avowed, the rest might not spoil his pleasure by coming in to listen also, and she was guilty of that most exquisite flattery—singing some little verses of his own, written in the days when he had dreamed and been a boy, and life lay before him hazy and glorious in the morning light. As she finished, Elinor Grey looked at him and knew by her woman's intuition that she had sung him straight away into the land of vision—partly her voice, partly the spell of those old, old words coming back to him from his other self.

"I never knew they were sweet before," he said suddenly.

"I unearthed them this morning," she replied, "in a pile of Tom's old magazines—he saves all manner of things, you know, whether he needs them or not."

"And you thought them worth learning?" he asked softly.

"Yes, indeed; though the merit of study is small, they are very musical and cling to one's memory."

"Now I shall be able to remember that I have written one thing which procured me a great pleasure," he said.

And that naturally Miss Grey took as a pretty figure of speech; and having become much accustomed to such tropes and poetical flights, did not pay a great deal of attention. Only she thought that if he had it in his mind to turn Tom Moorcish, and take to personal compliment, he should be brought down to the actual without delay. She liked flattery as well as any woman—compliments had grown a weariness—the flattery must be the subtle, delicate perfume. She liked to think that a man confided in her—told her his aspirations and secrets—let her know the higher nature with which the world had nothing to do—but just now, as I said, she saw fit to bring Clive back to ordinary ground. So she made some inquiry concerning a mutual acquaintance whom she had not seen since her return—a man at that—and I leave it to the fiercest misogynist that ever wore boots if it is not an annoying thing to have a woman in the midst of a *tête-à-tête* inquire about the fortunes of any other of Adam's sons.

At once Clive began to pity him—there was comfort in the fact that there was reason. There had lately been some heavy trouble in his family—some reckless member thereof had even brought disgrace very near his pride.

"But you speak," said Miss Grey, "as if he must feel inclined to hide his face from the world on account of that sad story."

"I think he must," replied he. "Disgrace is horrible."

"He has done no wrong;—there is no stain on him."

"But to be sneered at and pitied—to know that people talk one over — that one's private affairs are on every body's lips — is loathsome."

"A terrible feeling if one has done wrong and is unwilling to atone," said Elinor Grey. "This man has the consciousness of having acted honestly. If he were vilified with all the power of evil tongues, that consciousness would be his support."

"A very slender one," Clive said.

And at once Elinor Grey went to the root of another of his weaknesses—he had a horror of being laughed at or pitied. Strong-made though he was, that feeling was powerful enough, as it is in so many of us, to stand between him and a right action.

"I see you think I am in error," he said.

"It is the creed, at least the rule of conduct, for half the world," she answered; "but I do think you in error. Let me hold my life on a secure foundation. If I had done wrong I would rather make expiation and live it down than go on to a hero's triumph with the knowledge that I had a miserable secret on my soul."

"But Moreland could have hushed that matter up."

"Yes, he could have wronged the innocent and helped the wicked; and during all time to come he could have known that any day the earth might fall in and show the ruin."

"You put it strongly."

"But truthfully, I think."

And Clive Farnsworth assented in a doubtful tone. At that moment Mrs. Thornton looked in at the door.

"They have gone," she said. "Good people, you will please to remember there are such sublunary matters as dinners, and mine is nearly ready."

They all went to their rooms, and owing to the turn the conversation had taken, I think Farnsworth was not sorry to have it so abruptly concluded.

When the evening was over and it was already past the time for reasonable people to be in bed and sleeping the sleep of the just, Mrs. Thornton sat curled up on a sofa in Elinor's dressing-room, and the pair were talking as two women will who can venture to be on really open, confidential terms. In their case a distant relationship proved an additional bond—an exception to general rules, I admit.

"I like your Mr. Farnsworth very well," Elinor said.

Now Mrs. Thornton would have been better pleased if she had not made such frankness; she wanted to see her differently disposed toward him than she had been to the numberless men who had paid vain homage at her maiden shrine.

"Don't say my Mr. Farnsworth," returned she; "I am married and proper, and will none of your foreign ways."

"Forgive me, daughter of Columbia," quoth Elinor.

"You see it is aggravating because I can't say 'my' when I talk about him," continued she openly. "Tom and I long ago pronounced him an unimpressionable brute."

"I believe Tom resents it if the whole world does not bow down under your chariot wheels."

"Of course. Tom is an angel."

"Don't," said Elinor, laughing. "You will

gain nothing. I declare to you I shall not repeat your compliments to him."

"Ill-natured thing! when they might be worth a diamond ring at least to me, if you represented matters properly."

"I should claim the ring for my trouble."

They both laughed, and could easily, for Elinor knew that the marriage of Tom Thornton and his wife had been one of those rare unions upon which the honey-moon had not set, although she had shone for a whole decade.

"But where were we?" asked Mrs. Thornton.

"You were lamenting Mr. Farnsworth's insensibility."

"Oh yes; but I forgive that, for he is the best friend—the sort of man one can be intimate with and be never misunderstood — you know how rare that is."

"Yes, indeed," returned Elinor, and her lip curled. "Generally, if one looks at the ugliest specimen of the race, he thinks one is subdued by his charms—all the while one is wondering if he will never discover what a weariness he is, and take himself off."

"And nowadays you look at the best of them as if they were a weariness," said Mrs. Thornton; "all but my Tom; you have the sense to appreciate him."

"Tom is never silly; then, dear, you are so hopelessly healthy there is no danger he can ever really trouble me."

"But you must marry sometime," announced Mrs. Thornton.

"Oh! must I!" retorted Elinor, disdainfully. "You say that in a matter-of-course tone, as if it were as unavoidable as being born or dying."

"But you couldn't be an old maid."

"It will not take many more years to decide that."

"Oh nonsense, at your age! But it would be horrible to be an old maid—with a hooked nose and a parrot."

"Unless I break it my nose won't have a hook," said Elinor, "and I might avoid the temptation of a parrot."

"Oh no, don't! If a woman could be born a widow, and always stay young, it would do very well. Oh, Elinor, it is nice to be loved! I don't often do the sentimental, but a woman is not half a woman till she loves and is beloved."

"I am not prepared to dispute it."

"Certainly you have been enough loved."

Elinor threw back her stately head.

"Yes, I know what that means—not worth the name! But you are too difficult—you seem ice. I wonder men run after you so, for you are not a bit of a flirt."

"Perhaps they like the ice."

"Nonsense! You don't deceive me. You are not cold at all—you have more heart than head, full as that is. I am not blind."

"I bow to your penetration."

"Now don't be sarcastic; you put things out of my mind."

"Not the men, certainly; you know the wise world says they are a fixture in every woman's mental vacuum."

"I'll not be called names, and I'm not a vacuum! And you haven't loved any body, Elinor?"

"Look at me!"

"Bah! Say that to a woman? A man might trust to appearance—we know each other better."

"Creditable to your sex, and candid. But at least you know that I am truthful."

"I do believe you are," said Mrs. Thornton. "It seems odd! But then the magnificent is your line. Now I couldn't be a Cornelia, you know! When I tell the truth it is something I am ashamed of, and I blush and stammer and look ugly."

"That is not to be endured," cried sarcastic Elinor.

"Of course not. But I do tell a lie so prettily! Even if I am found out, people forgive me for the grace of the thing."

"Oh, my dear, fulfill woman's destiny—go on fibbing to the end of the chapter, by all means."

"You do fly about so," said Mrs. Thornton, "and I want to know about your heart—"

"If I have one, I fancy it is well."

"And there's nobody in it?"

"Nobody but papa, you, and Tom."

"You are on honor now!"

"So be it, wise Portia."

"I am disappointed," exclaimed Mrs. Thornton piteously; and she spoke so sincerely one would have sworn she was telling the truth. "I thought you might have some tiny confession to make."

"I am sorry!"

"Oh no, you are not—your are glad—you proud thing, you! But I am disappointed."

In her secret soul the little serpent was uttering a pean of rejoicing. She had been dying to find out if any thing stood in the way of her plans running their natural course. By her plaintive earnestness she would have succeeded in convincing any man, but she overdid her regret and a sudden light flashed upon her companion.

"Aha!" said she.

At that exclamation Mrs. Thornton knew that she was suspected. She assumed at once the innocence of a dove, and looked only smiling wonder.

"Don't you get the least nonsense in your little head, Rosa," said Miss Grey, austerely.

"Then it must be empty—sense never will stay in it. But I don't know what you mean."

"Then I begin to think what you mean with your questions and your regrets, you little Jesuit."

"Hit a man of your size—Tom teaches me slang!" cried Mrs. Thornton. "Bless me, I'd as soon meddle with a young panther as you! Stop looking fierce. I'm married, and I won't be bullied and scolded."

"Very well! just you be discreet."

"As Harry Percy's wife, dear, and this time for the self-same reason—I don't know what you mean."

"'I do tell a lie so prettily,'" quoted Elinor.

"Oh, I never said so! Well, I hate being reminded of what I say—it's like having cold meat served to one. But I do say I wouldn't meddle with you for the world."

She hastened to change the subject, and saw at a glance that if she would avoid working confusion to her own stratagems she must remain tranquil, only bringing her hero on the ground and then leaving him to shift for himself.

She immediately flung a new dress she was contemplating into the conversation, and hid the enemy completely under its folds. They were women with brains, but in an instant they were miles away from dangerous ground. Before they were through they had pulled the contents of a great box on the floor to look at some wonderful lace. Their souls were so quieted by that intellectual enjoyment that they could go to bed in peace. (What the soul of Miss Grey's maid said the next morning, when she had to collect the scattered finery, I leave to female imagination.) They got away from the new dress and the lace at last, and had another long talk—Rosa to tell how happy she was, and Miss Grey to admit that Diana's throne was sometimes a lonely one, and that it tired one's hand always to carry one's sceptre.

So Rosa had hopes again, but she had gained wisdom from her little lesson.

"And you will give me the two months you promised?" she pleaded.

"You claimed two, you mean."

"It's all the same; and it always makes me ill to be disappointed—ask Tom."

"I am acquainted with your wiles where that unfortunate creature is concerned, but you must remember I am a woman too, dear, and know how hysterics are done."

"Oh, you venomous thing, I never have hysterics! And you will stay?"

"My dear Rosa, I'd rather be with you than any woman in the world. Unless I have to go somewhere with papa for a week I'll stay till—I haven't any more new dresses with which to excite your envy."

"And you have enough for Queen Elizabeth. I'm so glad!"

"You self-sacrificing person!"

"It looks so, but the truth is, I have a new supply too. Pinchon got them over for me. I am dying to see if they are not prettier than yours."

"Open confession is good for the soul," said Elinor.

"Not as a steady diet," returned her friend.

At that moment there was a sound at the door which made them both jump as if a battering-ram had suddenly been pushed against it, and Tom's voice was heard in injured tones demanding his spouse. He had sat smoking with Clive for a long time, and not finding his wife when he ascended to the connubial chamber, had fallen asleep by the table and nearly pitched into the lamp.

"It's almost three o'clock!" shouted he. "Elinor Grey, if you have foully assassinated my Rosa, at least produce her mangled remains."

"So that you can be certain nothing prevents your searching for a new blossom," said Elinor, opening the door. "Take your treasure, Mr. Tom."

She had on a dressing-gown of some wonderful Eastern fabric, and looked so gorgeous that Tom stared with all his sleepy eyes.

"Well, isn't she a beauty!" he ejaculated, turning to his wife.

"Don't stay here admiring strange women at this time of the night," cried she in pretended wrath, "keeping me up till all hours, while you smoke with dissipated bachelors!"

"I like that," said Tom, "when I nearly fell on the lamp."

"You are never to be trusted. If you had singed your whiskers I would have had a divorce. Good-night, Elinor, pet."

"Good-night, Elinor in a pet!" added Tom; and after a great deal more nonsense Miss Grey was left to the solitude of her bower.

CHAPTER III.

DAY BY DAY.

THE Greys being great people, of course everybody who might claim the privilege of their acquaintance delighted to do them honor, and the father won golden opinions by his affable manners, and "my daughter Elinor" queened it in absolute sovereignty. There was no resisting Mr. Grey. I do think he could literally have wiled a bird off a bush if he had possessed any ornithological tastes. He had a way of offering his snuff-box which would have subdued an enemy bent on following up a Corsican vendetta, and if he willed while talking to you that you should see black white, then white you saw it, if you were as obstinate as Diogenes or Mrs. Grundy.

The Thorntons had a succession of visitors, many of them agreeable people; the various country houses in the neighborhood were holding gala too, and the hotel at the lake was full; so that altogether the weeks were very sunny.

Clive Farnsworth went about in his beautiful dream, so lost that he did not know he was dreaming, but let the days float on like the measures of an Eastern poem. All of which is pretty and poetical, and means that he had fallen so helplessly in love with Elinor that he was ready to essay as many mad feats as Hamlet himself to prove the strength of his passion. He did not reason—he did not think. He kept the doors barred between him and the past; the summer roses had clustered so thick over them that it appeared impossible they could ever open; he just put every thing which had been and the whole world aside, and he loved her. This woman so completely realized his ideal that it seemed as if his ideal had only been a premonition of her. She was like a pure angel who wakened every thing good in his nature, and made any effort easy if her smile should reward him.

And so I might write for a month, and never say any thing worth reading. I will end where I began—he loved her.

With festivities the order of the day, Mrs. Hackett could not be remiss when there were distinguished people to entertain. She prepared her choicest dinners, and her most wonderful English, and did her part with a complacent state that was a delightful thing to witness and entirely baffles description. I suppose, left to herself, Miss Grey would have avoided society not precisely congenial, but for reasons of his own—not that he gave them; offering superfluous information was not in his line—Mr. Grey chose to be more than usually urbane toward the Golden Idol.

The truth was, old Hackett was a tremendous Bull in Wall Street—he was the meekest of elderly sheep at home—and Mr. Grey being a very extravagant man, and a very reckless one in certain ways, may have been caught by the prospect of being on friendly terms to make favorable future possibilities. The old Pluto might be said almost to hold the stock-market in his horny hands, and could send any stock up like a rocket or down like the stick if the whim seized him. But Mrs. Pluto held him in her hands naturally, so it was certain that if Mr. Grey wished to make ventures, here was the necessary support. He smiled on Mrs. Hackett, and when her spouse was visible, which was not often, offered him his snuff-box and made Pluto sneeze dolefully with the choice mixture, but looked the while as if the stock-market had no place in his world.

Therefore, since the Plutonian halls were to be frequented, Elinor Grey frowned upon Clive and Mrs. Thornton when according to the instincts of human nature they made a jest of the hospitality which they accepted. Indeed the house was a palace and the banquets were magnificent, only there was too much of every thing. One's eyes ached to look down the golden splendor of the drawing-rooms, and Mrs. Hackett in full-dress was so covered with jewels that she looked literally like a heathen idol in great repute among its worshipers. Elinor did not wonder that her father and all the world were willing to be entertained in that overpowering way, but it was very wearisome to her, and most wearisome of all the homage which Mrs. Hackett thought proper to lavish upon her.

In spite of herself she had to smile when Mrs. Hackett was anxious to know how the napkins were folded at the Imperial dinner-table, that her own might be arranged after the same fashion. And Clive Farnsworth immediately asked in a preternaturally grave voice of Miss Grey, if it was true that the Emperor used a napkin with gold fringe three inches deep, as somebody said. But Elinor would not laugh, and Mrs. Thornton was determined that she should, not wishing her to be so much better than her neighbors, and added—

"Yes, and they say one evening he got angry and threw it at Eugenic, and the fringe nearly put her eye out." And Mrs. Hackett sat open-mouthed.

"Dreadful!" said Clive. "Did you happen to see her, Miss Grey, while her face was scratched?"

"It was her eye," asserted Mrs. Thornton.

"I thought it was her left cheek," returned Clive.

"Those newspapers never get any thing straight!" exclaimed Mrs. Hackett. She looked so earnest and so anxious to know the exact truth that Elinor did laugh in spite of herself.

"I think, Mrs. Hackett," said she good-naturedly, "that it must have been in a Western newspaper if anywhere."

"Then you don't believe it?" she persisted.

"Oh, I fancy there is no doubt about the truth," said Clive.

"Ah," said Mrs. Hackett in a tragic voice—and they knew a quotation or something remarkable was coming—

"'Uneven lies the head that wears a crown!
I swear, 'tis better to be slowly born
And rage with humble livers in content,
Than to sit perked up in glistering grief—
And wear a golden sparrow.'"

The three listeners did not burst blood-vessels, but they were very near it. That was the style in which Mrs. Hackett always gave the poetical quotations which she studied from a book gotten up to save people the trouble of reading poems.

Elinor went away to a window and Mrs. Thornton and Clive had to bear it as best they might, while Mrs. Pluto sat up majestic, flushed with the consciousness of having done an impressive thing.

"How superb your lilies are, Mrs. Hackett," Miss Grey said, coming back from the shade of the friendly curtain as soon as it was safe. "They are favorite flowers of mine."

"A lily ought to be the signification of the word Elinor," said Clive.

Mrs. Thornton seized the opportunity and laughed long and wildly. She said afterward that it was all that kept her from suffocation.

"Now you have spoiled Mr. Farnsworth's speech," said Mrs. Hackett.

"I shall never forgive her," he returned, and took occasion to get rid of a little of his own laughter.

"I am afraid my garden will suffer," pursued Mrs. Hackett; "my head man has met with a misfortune—broken a limb."

Now Elinor had been six years away and had forgotten that there is a type of American women—thank goodness, the number grows less—who would die rather than say any thing but "limb" when speaking of the lower members of the human body; so in the innocence of her heart she said—

"Poor man! Was it his leg or his arm?"

Mrs. Hackett's face was a picture of distress and horror. Could it be Miss Grey who had used that word in the presence of a male biped? It must have been a frightful slip of the tongue, and the good woman tried to cover the bare leg to the best of her ability, till between her efforts and Elinor's look of wonder, Mrs. Thornton and Farnsworth were in a more pitiable state than before. It was agreed between them after that that the Idol had surpassed herself that day.

When they insisted on going before luncheon her feelings were actually hurt—the portly body was hospitality itself—but Miss Grey had the matter in her own hands this time and was determined to put an end to her companions' sport. Her father was busy with his correspondence that morning, she had promised to copy some letters, and as they were to be sent to town to catch the ocean steamer she really must go back.

"Oh, if it is a case of *belles lettres*," said Mrs. Hackett, "I can not say a word."

Mrs. Thornton felt confident that if they waited for any more sallies she must die outright, yet it broke her heart to tear herself away when the Idol was in such unusual high feather.

"You will come before long to see us, dear Mrs. Hackett," she said sweetly, as soon as she could command her voice.

"Of course, my love! I ever say that a day at your house is an Asia in the desert of life, and a mosaic in memory."

"She calls this beautiful house a desert!" cried Mrs. Thornton, laughing hysterically. Another stroke would finish her; but she must linger, though Elinor was making her furious signs to go, and Farnsworth felt like a torpedo ready to explode.

"I spoke allegorically," returned the Idol. "Of course I should not allow my house to be a desert when so much is expected of me, and I have a poet's love of the paradoxical. I play no minstrel's lute, Mr. Farnsworth, but poetry is quite the sustenance of existence with me."

"I am sure of that," he said politely.

Elinor would go now. "I promised papa," she avowed, and forced them away.

"Adieu, adieu," cried Mrs. Hackett, standing on the portico to see the last of them. "Fame, beauty, wit. The three Graces desert me at once—cruel sisters!"

It was dangerous to trust their voices; they waved their hands and drove off in haste. As soon as they were at a safe distance Mrs. Thornton relieved her feelings in a series of shrieks, Clive laughed till he was speechless, and even Elinor could not avoid joining in their merriment. Just as they were regaining their composure Mrs. Thornton pointed her finger at Clive, and cried in the Idol's tones, "Oh, cruel sister!"

Then it was all to do over again, and when they reached home she rehearsed the scene for the benefit of Tom and Mr. Grey, and spoiled every body's luncheon. After that Tom used to ask who were the three Graces, and give the reply himself—"Fame, beauty, wit, and Clive Farnsworth."

But Elinor must needs cast a cloud over my hero's day by reminding her father that she was ready to give him her assistance as amanuensis.

"Any time will do, my daughter Elinor," he replied, for according to his creed she ought not to have mentioned the fact that there was any thing to be done while a guest was present—if "ought not" could ever be applied to her actions.

But Elinor took her own way with perfect serenity, being well aware that the letters must be written, and not to be deterred from duty by such a trifle as the fact that it was disagreeable or that something else would be pleasanter. Indeed, she was a very inexplicable young woman, and somewhat given to making Duty a moral Juggernaut under which she crushed her inclinations, after the habit of young women with a great deal of imagination whose religious impulses assume an æsthetic tone.

"You needn't look so disconsolate," said Mrs. Thornton to Clive, when Mr. Grey had finished his regrets and allowed Elinor to lead him away. "You rudest of men, I don't think I am such bad company."

"I was looking disconsolate because I thought you were going to send me off," replied that insincere wretch.

"Say that to a woman!" cried she. "You, who write books and pretend to understand the sex! I ought to send you off for your palpable fib."

"Only you look your best when you are pardoning a sinner."

"How do you know?" asked Tom, stopping in the window to light his cigar preparatory to a saunter. "You never had the good taste to make love to her."

"I will, though," said Clive, "if you'll have the goodness to take yourself away."

"Now I'm not blind," exclaimed sapient Tom. "You have been going about in a dream ever since Queen—"

"Tom," interrupted his wife, "don't you grow poetical; it is not your style."

"I won't," said Tom; "but hasn't he?"

"I'll ask him—when you are gone."

"Why, one might take that for a hint!" cried Tom, apparently in great astonishment.

"One might," laughed Clive. "Would 'get out!' be more decided?"

Tom went off declaring himself an injured individual, and Clive said wonderingly, as he so often had—

"You certainly are two happy people."

"Yes, unbeliever! It does seem incredible, doesn't it?" returned Rosa. "We wake up enough every now and then to marvel over it ourselves."

Then she talked to him in the most charming way in the world; never asking a question as a woman of less tact would have done, but bringing Elinor into the conversation, and being as delightful as a Rose that had dwelt near the queen of the garden possibly could.

In the mean time Elinor Grey sat with her father in his room and had quite forgotten that lovers and admiration ever existed, in listening to certain hopes of his which letters lately received put in a state of sufficient forwardness to be mentioned.

Mr. Grey had made a brief visit from Europe at the time of the election, upon which trip Elinor had not accompanied him, having the Thorntons for inmates during his absence. The voyage had been made at the private request of the successful candidate, who was one of Mr. Grey's life-long friends, and during their consultation it had been decided that for the present he should retain his post abroad, as there were certain matters under discussion with several foreign Powers which no one could manage with as much skill as the artful diplomatist.

But what the President wanted was to have Mr. Grey in his Cabinet, and what Mr. Grey wanted was to be there, and they had both waited for a favorable occasion to bring about that desired result. The opportunity of enrolling him among the group of dignified counsellors had seemed at hand, and it was that reason which made Mr. Grey throw up his appointment and return home to the wonder of the uninitiated, although, in the eloquent speech he made at the dinner given him by the civic dignitaries of New York on his arrival, he had assigned as a motive his weariness of public duties and his desire to spend the years that might remain to him among the hallowed scenes of his native land, that happy home of the brave. He wanted quiet and repose, for life with him was past its prime—a life which he trusted had not been wholly valueless to his country; but he was tired, more than satisfied with the approval his fellow-citizens had bestowed upon his efforts, and now he would glide into that retirement which best suited his modest tastes, leaving political honors and the interests of the Republic in more competent hands.

His speech was very flowery, and brought tears to the eyes of the portly Alderman who rose to respond—at least the Alderman said tears, and it was well he did, otherwise the sympathetic drops might have been mistaken for the watery appearance that many years of public dinners had made habitual to his orbs.

The present holder of the office which the President desired to give his friend was a pig-headed man who had been accepted as a gift impossible to refuse from a powerful party, whom the august Chief had no desire to retain in his council, or, to put it less mildly and more truthfully, was anxious to thrust out of the donjon of State with the least delay. He had proved to be the tool of the party who offered him as an appropriate piece of furniture for the Presi-

dent's Cabinet, and had displayed so much opposition to the policy of the Administration that it did not seem he could longer in decency seek to retain his place.

Elinor was an ambitious woman, and her ambition took the womanly form of being for the man she most loved, and she worshiped her father. I think the life of this adored object had not been spotless; but that is somehow frequently the case with the lives of those who have most love and worship lavished upon them in this world. Perhaps there may be some grand law of compensation, hereafter to be made plain, which shall console the neglected good people for the present lack of idolatry—perhaps if the good people could engraft a portion of the graceful manners of the adored unscrupulous upon their varied and uncomfortable virtues, a different result might be obtainable even here. But we will not philosophize. Elinor Grey worshiped her father, and I am not telling you that he was unscrupulous or bad; perhaps I ought to say only that he lacked fixed principle and had therefore been somewhat discursive in his impulses and plans. I do not mean to rake up his past, whatever of folly it may or may not have hidden; it is enough that he was thoroughly charming at that age when Balzac declares a man to be most dangerous—fifty-two.

He had been very cautious to keep the enamel of his reputation without a flaw for prying eyes to point at, and it pleased him well to be faultless in his daughter's sight. He admired her above all women, and so conducted himself that he was a hero to her whatever he might have been to his valet; and really, unless one's valet developed literary tendencies and left his memoirs behind, I am at a loss to see the point of the threat held up to a great man that he can never aspire to heroship in that functionary's eyes? Just at present Mr. Grey had pressing need of twenty thousand dollars, for, as I have said, he was an extravagant man with divers weaknesses—and I may as well hint to you that a passion for cards ranked among them—and there being no other possible way of raising the money, he had decided that it must come out of the fortune which Elinor inherited from her mother.

Ask her for it? Good gracious, no! It was quite by accident that she discovered during the conversation how sore pressed he was, and begged him not to think her impertinent—she could be so charmingly humble, that proud creature—but would he borrow it of her?

He would and did: being very explicit to show what security he should give her, because it was right—which security was not worth a rush. But no matter; there was the Idol ready to make her Bull show him the way to realize speedily on some impossible stock which was a reality to a happy few in the commencement, and would prove a bright mirage to the unwary many who might later attempt to hold it. But he told her first of the probability there was of his being asked to become a Cabinet Minister, and Elinor only felt that the Administration was much more sensible than most of its kind, and was wise enough to strengthen itself with aid sought from proper sources.

She believed her father a happy combination of Brutus and King Arthur, and she got as near the truth as people ever do with their heroes. He was a wily, plausible man, and cold-hearted as a frog except where she was concerned. His tastes had been refined by luxury and self-indulgence until they were often a source of absolute pain. As for his honor—I am not prepared to say how he would have acted in a crisis; perhaps none might ever arise. In that case he would slip pleasantly through life, and go out with a halo around his head.

It was no wonder she made a hero of him. He looked so elegant, leaning back in his easy-chair, with his softest smile on his lip, his voice full of tenderness, and that wonderful manner of his which made the most trifling act of courtesy a chivalrous show of devotion.

"You approve of my accepting," he said, "provided the contingency should arise?"

"Indeed I do, papa! I wish sometimes you had not been so much of your life abroad, that you might have had a fair opportunity of occupying the highest position the country has to offer."

He patted her cheek softly, and showed her certain matters of moment which must inevitably arise during the next year or two, and he showed her also what popularity would be gained by the minister who took a certain course, which it was equally certain neither of his future colleagues would take.

"I understand — I see!" cried enthusiastic Elinor. "Oh, papa, I should be so pleased!"

"My ambitious daughter Elinor!"

"Only for you, dear."

"You give me the strongest reason why I should be ambitious too—at least do my best with such talents as I have," he said; and taking the hand that lay upon his knee he kissed it just as I fancy Richelieu might have kissed the fair fingers of his beloved and ill-fated child.

Elinor looked up at him with a tenderness which softened her face in a beautiful way. "It is so good of you to talk to me," she said.

He smiled down at her pleasantly. "Why, surely my daughter Elinor knows that her little head is the most capable of counsellors."

"You like to think so because you choose to believe me perfect," returned Elinor. "But indeed I ought not to be quite a commonplace woman after all these years of your companionship."

Then she had to kiss him again, and play baby to her heart's content, as only a really dignified, proud woman can do to perfection.

"Papa," she said, getting away to thoughts which naturally came into her feminine mind, "I think if we do go to Washington we must have a house and arrange our worldly belongings."

"Yes," he answered, "if I can settle those tiresome — that is — if you like, my daughter Elinor."

"Now, papa, you are thinking something you don't say! Please finish your sentence."

"So I did," he returned playfully.

"But not with your real thoughts. Oh, you bad thing, you are keeping a secret. Now I shall worry myself to death over it."

"It is nothing—indeed, I spoke carelessly."

"Just tell me, papa," she said in a wheedling voice.

"Now I shall have to, or you will be fancying all sorts of horrors, and it is a mere temporary annoyance."

He told her about the need he had of the twenty thousand dollars, and talked vaguely of a wonderful investment he purposed to make with a portion which might remain beyond his needs. And Elinor begged him to take it of her, and pleaded with such earnestness that it would have been downright unkindness to refuse. He allowed himself to be persuaded—oh, so gracefully!—and Elinor could not rest until the order for the necessary sale of stocks was written and she had placed it in his hand.

"There," she said, blushing charmingly, "put it out of my sight! I feel ashamed that it is not all yours instead of mine."

A man can afford to be in good spirits who lays such a sweetener of care in his desk, and Mr. Grey's spirits always sprang up elastic the moment the pressure was removed. "You look like a queen this morning," he said. "Ah, what shall I do one of these days when my daughter Elinor meets the true prince among her countless worshipers?"

"There is no danger," said she; "you have taught me too high a standard."

He shook his head in playful incredulity.

"The day will come," said he, "but the old gentleman will try to be content."

"Now, papa, in the first place you shan't slander yourself, and in the next—"

"Why, that we will leave to Destiny."

"With all my heart; and I hope she may keep away from us forever."

She hurried back to her dreams for him—the triumphs still in store—and he was content enough to listen, as Socrates himself might have been from her lips.

"And you are sure you will be quite set right by that stupid, stupid money, which belonged to you any way?"

"Perfectly," he replied. "But don't say that it belonged to me, or that I had any claim, unless on my daughter Elinor's love; it is pleasant to owe a favor to that."

"A favor! O father, you make me ashamed!"

"My peerless," he said, "it is true. I like to be obliged to you."

I dare say he believed what he said. I don't suppose he had the slightest recollection of the unpleasant apostrophe he made to his wife's shade fifteen years before, when she died so suddenly that there was no possibility of leaving him the fortune he considered his own. It had been so given to her that dying intestate the whole went to her child. And if any body could have seen Elinor the proud, with her arms about his neck, cooing like a dove, he might have gained a very different idea from that which a person must have formed on ordinary occasions.

Mr. Grey believed too that by a proper feeding of the Bull with the oil-cake of flattery, this money might open a golden harvest to him that should make his other assertion quite true. Perhaps if he could have seen through what fields he must walk during the next year or two, still with his eyes on that which held the golden fruition, he might have been less exultant.

But that is nonsense. If he had been permitted to see he could not have believed. It is the same with all of us. We are as deaf and stupid as the old owls were to Cassandra, until we sit howling under our ruined Troys.

CHAPTER IV.

AN UNEXPECTED DUTY.

It was only two or three mornings after that they sat over the breakfast-table, as animated a *partie carrée* as you could wish to see, in spite of the fact that one pair were husband and wife and the other parent and child, when the letters were brought in and made a diversion.

The others had finished the perusal of their epistles, and Mr. Grey looked up from the last of his pile and glanced doubtfully at Elinor, as a man always does glance at the feminine power of his home when he has some intelligence to impart concerning the effect of which he is not quite at ease.

Tom was busy with his newspaper and did not notice; any way he was a man, and probably would not have remarked the glance (as a sex we must have a thing mash our noses before we can see it); Elinor was occupied in feeding a Scotch terrier so ugly that he was picturesque; but Mrs. Thornton had her eyes at liberty, and seeing Mr. Grey's look she cried out at once—

"Elinor, he has something to tell you, and he doesn't know how you will take it."

Elinor poised a bit of bread in her white hand at a tantalizing distance from Dot's nose, and turned toward the table.

"What is it, papa?" she asked.

"One needs a mask in your presence, Mrs. Thornton," said Mr. Grey.

"Then I was right! I knew it!"

"Of course you were, dear lady. You don't suppose me foolish enough to deny?"

"Yet that Tom often will," cried she disdainfully, "when I can see through him without a lantern."

"Eh?" said the accused one.

"Oh, you may *eh!*" retorted she. "I do assure you, Mr. Grey, to this day he will try to deceive me, and think he is keeping a secret when I could read it if I only saw the end of his nose."

"What ails my nose?" asked Tom, coming out of his newspaper and looking vacant.

"Nothing, I am sure," said Mr. Grey. 'It is the noblest Roman of them all.'"

"But what is the news, papa?" asked Elinor.

"My old friend Mr Laidley is dead, and—"

"Has left you guardian to something," interrupted Mrs. Thornton.

"Oh dear," sighed Elinor; "it's a girl!"

"The old wretch!" apostrophized her friend.

Elinor dropped her hand and Dot seized the bread, giving a practical illustration in regard to the proverb about an ill wind.

"From whom is the letter, papa?" asked Elinor resignedly. "What does it say?"

"From her aunt. The young lady is still in Jamaica. Her father went there some months before his death. The letters have been rushing over all Europe since last March."

"Let her stay in Jamaica, then," said Mrs. Thornton.

"Yes, so she will for the present, but her aunt thinks— Just read the letter, my daughter Elinor."

And Elinor read it, and froze immediately. "I am very sorry for her," said she.

"Oh, of course, so am I!" cried Mrs. Thornton. "But she wants to stay with you, doesn't she?"

"After a time," returned Mr. Grey, with an apologetic manner.

"Ugh!" groaned Rosa. "And she'll be a nasty, stupid thing, you see."

"No, I believe she is pretty, and she is a great heiress," said Mr. Grey. "Just read the letter to Mrs. Thornton, Elinor."

And Elinor read it as if she were tasting something unpleasant, and Mrs. Thornton listened as if smelling something very nasty. You know the way women do such things.

The letter told how grief-stricken the poor girl was, and the aunt said how happy it made her to be able to have her brother's child with her, and what implicit confidence they both had in the dead man's choice of a guardian. Then followed a brief eulogy upon the virtues of the deceased, who had gone to be a seraph, and a hint that after a few months the writer thought a change would be beneficial to her niece, with a palpable meaning that she expected Mr. Grey to take his duties in earnest and receive her into his home.

"That woman has daughters of her own!" exclaimed Mrs. Thornton. "Now hasn't she?"

"I believe so—yes, three or four," said Mr. Grey.

"And they're ugly!"

"I can't be positive about that. I have not seen them since they were little children."

"Oh, I am sure of it! The heiress would stand in their way, so she must be set to torment poor Elinor."

"But she may prove a pleasant companion," said Mr. Grey.

Mrs. Thornton ignored the possibility.

"Never mind," said Elinor; "we needn't think about it for a long time yet. Don't look so troubled, papa."

"Mrs. Thornton quite fills me with evil forebodings," he answered.

"She will be a cat," said Rosa; "I know it!"

"I saw her years ago," added Elinor. "I remember she was a pretty child, but dreadfully spoiled."

"Poor Laidley has been wandering about for years in search of health," said Mr. Grey. "I dare say she has been neglected. Well, my daughter, I can't refuse my old friend's request. I hope it will not be the means of causing you any annoyance."

Elinor was softened and conscience-stricken, and began pitying the poor creature, but Rosa was not to be mollified.

"Let her go and be a seraph too," said she. "My dear, she'll be no end of trouble! She'll make love to your father—"

"Oh, oh!" expostulated Mr. Grey.

"There, Rosa," said Elinor, "your last restores my courage."

"She will," said Rosa; "girls are such deceitful things."

"Is she likely to rival me?" demanded Elinor.

Rosa admitted that it would not be very easy to accomplish that feat.

"And I shall be so charming that papa will not remember to look at her."

"I think I am to be trusted—after all these years," said Mr. Grey, very meekly.

"Men are never to be trusted!" announced Rosa. "There's my Tom—why, if I were gone, there's no telling the folly some woman would lead him into."

"Oh!" said Tom again, coming out of his newspaper. "What woman?"

"Any woman who took the trouble, you goose."

"What's wrong?" asked Tom.

"He hasn't heard a word!" cried the exasperated Rosa. "Tom, put down that newspaper! Here's Elinor over ears in trouble. There's an old monster must needs die, and his daughter's going to make love to Mr. Grey."

"Good gracious!" Tom exclaimed.

"Is that all you can say?"

"Well, just mark my words," returned Tom —"whoever she is, if she bothers Elinor she'll get the worst of it."

They all laughed at that, and Mrs. Thornton declared that Tom had given her a gleam of comfort.

"When you do have an idea, Tom," said she, "I will say it is really brilliant."

"She wants something!" cried Tom.

"No, I don't. The only misfortune is, you have one so seldom! There, take that scratch for villifying my character."

"And so you are chosen guardian, Mr. Grey?" said Thornton. "I am sure there's nothing unpleasant in being a pretty girl's protector."

"You atrocious wretch!" cried his wife. "And how do you know she is pretty?"

"His wife is so beautiful in his eyes that the claim of sex makes any woman pretty," said Mr. Grey.

"I forgive you for that," returned Rosa. "We never would have thought of it."

"I was just going to say it," said Tom. "But old Laidley was very rich—wasn't he?"

"Oh yes; the young lady has little short of a million," replied Mr. Grey.

"Richer than you even, Elinor," said Tom.

"It's like her impudence," added Rosa.

Elinor looked mildly contemptuous of Miss Laidley's golden charms.

"Never mind, Elinor," said Tom, "I'll show you how to treat her. My father was guardian once to two cubs, and how I used to punch their heads!"

"Thank you," said Elinor; "if I should ever wish that operation performed on the young lady's cranium I will bespeak your assistance."

"What is her name?" asked Rosa.

"Genevieve," replied Mr. Grey.

"How affected and sentimental," said Mrs. Thornton, not to be pleased with any thing concerning her. "She ought to be ashamed of herself."

"But she's not to blame," said Tom; "she wasn't her own godmother."

"I wish she had been," said Rosa; "she'd be an old maid now, and not want any guardian but a parrot."

"Oh, wouldn't she?" cried Tom.

"Don't slander the sex," retorted his wife. "Elinor, we'll call her plain Miss Jenny, just to punish her."

"But if she isn't plain?" demanded Tom.

"Oh, if you are going to be witty," vowed Rosa, "I'll go to bed with the headache at once."

"I remember Laidley very well," said Tom.

"He was an old college friend of mine," observed Mr. Grey. "I have not seen him these ten years. He was in wretched health then— and made me promise to act as his daughter's guardian if I should outlive him."

"College friends are always bores," said Mrs. Thornton. "Tom has several that come at the wrong time and take liberties with no better claim."

"Besides," said Elinor, "it is a woman's duty to hate her husband's friends."

"And I'll do my duty like a—like a—"

"Brick," suggested Tom.

"Like a Roman matron!" cried Rosa, menacing him with the tea-pot.

"I don't believe Cornelia herself had such a pretty cap, though," said Mr. Grey.

"Oh, you want to make me forget Miss Genevieve."

"That reminds me I must not forget. There

will be lawyers' letters to answer, and heaven knows what all. My long silence too must be explained ; so the troubles begin."

"If you will be the guardian to young women you must take the consequences," returned Mrs. Thornton.

"But, my dear lady, you don't accuse me of having sought this duty ?"

"Some achieve duty and some have duty thrust upon them," said Tom. "Shakespeare improved."

"And this is a case of duty thrust upon one with a vengeance," returned Mr. Grey.

"I do say it is uncivil of a man to fling his offspring in somebody's face and rush out of the world," exclaimed Mrs. Thornton.

"I exonerate poor Laidley," replied Mr. Grey. "He was as anxious to stay here as any man I ever knew."

"He used to write you such mournful letters now and then, papa," said Elinor.

"Only paving the way for this," cried Mrs. Thornton. "Don't think to soften my heart! I hate plain Miss Jenny, and that's all there is about it."

"If ever she sees her," quoth Tom, "she'll rush into a spasm of affection at once ; she always does with a woman she abuses in advance."

"I never abuse women, Sir."

"Oh no! no female ever does. Good gracious! to hear you and Elinor when you get fairly started—you don't leave a character to one of your friends."

"Pope said women had none," added Mr. Grey.

"And Pope was a misanthropical hypocrite," said Rosa.

"And as for me, Mr. Thomas," said Elinor, "I deny that I take away the characters of my male acquaintance at least."

"Though glad enough they would be to get rid of them," said Rosa.

"The very reason I leave them," said Elinor. "The worst punishment they could have is to bear them."

"Bring me an umbrella, somebody !" cried Tom. "Go it, lovely women."

"I think, Tom, you had better make your peace," said Mr. Grey.

"Oh, Elinor knows I am getting the bay filly in training for her," observed Tom artfully.

"You are a love !" cried Elinor. "Tom, I have always thought Rosa treated you shamefully."

"O Judas !" said Rosa.

"But when that beautiful creature is at stake, dear, you can't blame me."

"Give her a lace collar," said Tom ; "that'll bring her round."

"I am not to be bribed," returned Rosa. "Besides, she gave me the last one she had only yesterday."

"Now I am curious to know why ?" queried Mr. Grey.

"Because collars are so unbecoming to me," said Elinor. "Don't say women never tell the truth."

"I do think those little what-you-call-thems in your neck are ever so much prettier," observed Tom.

"Oh yes, just because she has a neck like a swan," replied his wife. "For my part I am willing to be disfigured—in Brussels Point."

"I'm off," cried Tom, pushing back his chair in great haste. "If she gets fairly started on that subject she will discover she needs a new set of flounces at least."

"And those are 'airy nothings' which cost a man dear," said Mr. Grey. "Thornton, I'll walk with you over to the fields ; I am sure you are going there."

"Of course he is," said Rosa. "One would think he had his soul planted among his grain, and was anxious about its coming up."

Nothing more was said concerning the new trust that had devolved upon Mr. Grey, nor did he give the subject much more thought than the others, beyond taking the necessary steps toward the fulfillment of his duties.

After a little more idle banter between the merry husband and wife the two gentlemen started on their walk, followed by a parting injunction from Rosa.

"If you stray near Mr. Farnsworth, bring him to luncheon. I wish to upbraid him for not coming yesterday."

"I dare say we shall get over to his place before we come back," Tom said. "I'll give him your orders, and tell him of your dire intents."

But they did not reach his place. Thornton was so busy tormenting his guest by showing his improvements on the land that had lately fallen into his possession, telling how this promising wheat-field was once a sterile plain and that luxuriant clover-meadow formerly a morass, after the fashion in which the wisest people will inflict their visitors, that in his eagerness and Mr. Grey's state of polite boredom, neither remembered Rosa's commands until it was too late to go. When they came out on the road, and Mr. Grey stood panting somewhat after the exertion of climbing several fences, to say nothing of the hill which had been the last grievance, along the ascent of which he had left a good deal of his breath and patience, Clive Farnsworth's house became visible in the distance, looking very stately and picturesque among its lofty trees. The view being one that Tom expected all his guests to admire, Mr. Grey looked languidly through his glass, and rather than be bored further by going into raptures, asked if that was Farnsworth's place he saw.

"Yes, that's his," said Tom. "Bless me ! I forgot Rosa's message entirely ; we were so interested about that new ditch."

Mr. Grey looked blandly at him, with a secret pity and indignation hidden under his smile, and mentally repeated the pronoun in utter rejection of any share therein.

"I suppose you don't care to walk over now,"

continued Tom; "though there's a short cut through the fields, if you will."

"Thank you, no; perhaps we had better go back," replied Mr. Grey, not anxious to try any 'short cuts,' that morning.

Tom captured a village boy who had strayed away thither on some unlawful errand, no doubt connected with the stealing of strawberries or unripe cherries or some similar wickedness, who at the sight of the two gentlemen had seated himself innocently on the fence, and was gazing up into the sky with as much intentness as if he had been an embryo Herschel on the lookout for wonders or worlds. He was a miracle of leanness and precocious wisdom, this boy, and listened readily enough to Mr. Thornton's proposal that he should carry a message over to the house on the hill, when he saw the gratuity that accompanied the request. Tom scribbled on the back of a letter—

"Rosa wants a poet for luncheon. Come and be eaten or abused, for want of a better. Dont fail, you reclaimed hermit."

The boy put the paper in his pocket and cantered off as if he had reindeer blood in his veins. When he came near the gates of Farnsworth's domain it seemed good to him, before fulfilling his errand, to stop and collect a store of round pebbles out of the brook that flowed through the grounds and crossed the road in that spot. So it chanced that Clive, returning homeward from a morning ride, encountered him; that is to say, the boy jumped into the road at his appearance, thereby endangering his own neck, for at sight of the shirt-sleeved apparition the horse gave a tremendous bound which might have disturbed a less secure rider, then sidled with his back feet and pawed the air with his front hoofs, in a manner that appeared to afford the lean boy extreme delight, as if the exhibition were gotten up for his express amusement.

"Hallo!" exclaimed Clive, somewhat irritated, as was natural.

"Hallo!" returned the boy easily, apparently thinking the salutation had been meant for a friendly greeting which he was bound by politeness to return in the same spirit.

"Don't you know any better than to spring out before a horse in that way?" demanded Clive. "It's a wonder you weren't killed."

"I don't die easy, I don't," replied the boy.

"Why, he does it just like a circus, don't he?" continued he, in opened-mouthed admiration of the prancing horse.

Clive checked the unsatisfactory Franconi style of performance which had gratified the youngster and looked at him, somewhat amused by the creature's coolness.

"What is your name, my lad?" he asked.

"Don't you know? Why, I thought everybody knew me," replied the boy. "I say, what's yourn?"

"Don't you think you deserve a thrashing?" asked Clive.

"Some folks says I always do," answered he.

"But I shan't get my deservings jist at present."

"I don't know," said Clive; "I feel somewhat inclined to prove that I agree with 'some folks.'"

"In the first place you can't ketch me," said the lean boy; "in the next place, I've got sumpthin' for you."

"What may it be?"

"I know," said the boy; "but you wouldn't tell your name, so how can I tell you's you."

It was useless to do any thing but laugh, and impossible to avoid that undignified proceeding. The boy looked in size as if he might be about fourteen; his face might have been any age it was so thin and care-worn, and the hard mouth might have been learning reticence for half a century, although the sharp eyes had a certain good-natured twinkle in them that seemed to speak of uncontrollable propensities for mischief rather than downright wickedness.

"A perfect Flibbertigibbet," said Clive involuntarily.

"That's in Walter Scott," exclaimed the boy; "I've read it. Oh, ain't he slow! The Slave Girl of Moscow is worth twenty of him."

"Where do you live?" asked Clive.

"To hum, mostly — when I'm there," replied the boy, taking a handful of pebbles from his pocket, tossing them in the air and dexterously catching them on the back of his hand. "I was a going there now for a change, when Tom Thornton he stopped me."

"Who?" demanded Clive in astonishment.

"Tom Thornton, I told you," answered he, giving the pebbles another toss. "Dern it, I've dropped one."

"That's not very respectful, my boy," said Clive.

"'Cause I said Tom? Lord, this here's a free country, this is! You rich folks thinks everybody talks behind your backs as if you had crowns on your heads; but they always says Tom Thornton and Old Hackett and Puggy Hamlyn, and most ginrally they call you Pompey the Great Farnsworth, 'cause they think you're stuck up."

"Since you are certain about my name, suppose you give me whatever Mr. Thornton sent by you."

"That's what I come for," replied the boy, counting the pebbles. "I say, your trees ain't a going to have no harvest-apples on 'em this year."

"Have you been up to examine them?"

"Yes; there ain't many orchards about that I hain't; last year yourn had lots," said the boy in an injured tone, as if he considered the probable failure of the present season in some way Farnsworth's fault.

"I suppose you had your share," Clive observed.

"You bet I did. The deacon and old Granny Cumber said if I stole I'd go to Tophet, so I stole right off—I wanted to plague that old tortle that keeps house for you. I go to Sunday-school, I do. I can say hymns like split if I'm a mind to—it kind o' pleases Aunt Prudence. When I'm out with the railroad men I can swear like blazes—that pleases them. Ye see that's turning to account what Saint Paul says—I'm all sorts o' things to all sorts o' folks." He cocked up one eye, and looked so preternaturally wicked that Clive was silenced between his face and this novel application and delivery of the Apostle's text.

"Here's the paper Mr. Thornton sent," continued the boy, reaching it toward him.

"And here's a half-dollar for you," said Clive.

"No," replied the boy, "he paid me."

"Take this too," Clive said, somewhat astonished at this trait of honesty after his confessions.

The boy pocketed the money indifferently, stood waiting while Clive read the scrawl, then he said—

"You don't want any thing more, I s'pose?"

"No, there's no answer needed. Would you like to go up to the house and get something to eat?"

"If you'll make 'em give me some bread and milk, I do. We hain't got no cow this summer, an' I miss her like a mother—that's so."

"Where do you live?"

"Down not fur from the depot. Uncle Josh he tends depot. I'm there a good deal to keep things straight myself, when I ain't off on a ingeine or about loose. I ain't much good, you know—I hate old Josh wors'n the devil. I say, you hain't got the sequel to the Black Rover of the Perary, have you."

"I don't think I ever heard of the book," said Clive.

"Didn't you? Some folks never reads. The newsboy down to the depot has got it, but he hain't the sequel."

"Perhaps he will have sometime," said Clive. "Go up to the house and find Mrs. Sykes and say I told her to give you some bread and milk."

"She wouldn't believe me; I know her of old—she comes to see Aunt Pru. She's awful stuck up 'cause she's housekeeper up to your place. I fired a spit-ball right in her eye the other night to prayer-meetin'. She was a prayin' 'like all possessed,' and it brought her up with a ring."

"I am not surprised you don't care to encounter her after that exploit."

"Oh, she didn't see me—I was behind the post. It's good fun to go to prayer-meetin' sometimes. Was you ever there?"

Clive was forced to admit that he never had been. "Do you go to school?" he asked.

"Not now. I went last half to the deestrict, but the marster'n me we don't agree. He's got his niggersyncrasies an' I've got mine, an' they don't hit off. But I'm mostly at sumpthin'—I lamped it awhile."

"What's that?" asked Clive.

"Why, lamped it, of course; what else would it be?" returned the boy. "On the railroad, you know. Then I kind o' helped old Josh, the hunks; but the more you do fur him the less thanks you git. Then I newsed it—"

"Newsed it?"

"Yes—sold papers. I say, you don't speak English much, do you—been hammerin' so long round furrin parts?"

Clive, convicted of ignorance, decided to ride up to the house before going over to Alban Wood, perhaps to be certain that his toilet was irreproachable. He told the boy to follow, promising that he should have the treat he desired.

Mrs. Sykes, who greeted the lean wizard with many shakings of the head and doleful groans, to which he responded by inquiring with an air of great interest "if she'd been eating sumpthin' that hurt her," informed her master that he exulted in the name of Tad Tilman, and added the information that he was noted far and wide for his wickedness, and was an unfailing source of grief to his worthy relatives. The boy, sitting on the door-step of Mrs. Sykes's apartment, to which Clive had 'ridden, listened with much composure while the good woman detailed his numerous misdeeds, setting her right when she erred with a kind of consciousness of modest merit that amused Farnsworth as much as it irritated the housekeeper.

"He's been a subject of constant wrastlin' in prayer to his aunt and uncle," said Mrs. Sykes in conclusion, "and the deacon has done his furthermost, like a Christian and a shinin' light as he is, but they hain't wrastled the Evil One out of that boy yit."

The boy treated Clive to another twist of the thin visage of a nature so irresistibly ludicrous that it forced him to leave the room without delay. Tad sat on the door-step and quietly disposed of his milk and bread, while Mrs. Sykes took advantage of the opportunity to tell him what a dreadful creature he was, and what judgments were certain to be in store for him if he persevered in his present course.

CHAPTER V.

IN AUGUST.

Two months passed so swiftly that they seemed like two weeks; those months without much incident which do fly so rapidly and yet are so long and golden to look back upon through the mist of after tempests.

Elinor Grey had remained quietly at Alban Wood, though her father during the time had been obliged to absent himself on brief journeys. The pleasant old house was declared by all sojourners to be the coolest and most delightful of resting-places during midsummer heats.

It was the middle of August now. The fields of stubble lay red and brown in the sun; the quail piped in the meadows; the exquisite haze settled every afternoon over the mountain-sides and changed the scene into new beauty.

It had been a delightful summer to Clive Farnsworth; a new waking to life from the gloom of that despondency in which it had found him. Of late even the ability to write had returned to him; that incomprehensible faculty concerning even which a veteran author shall be able to give you no explanation; which comes and goes as it pleases, and is so difficult to be restrained by any wiles that it is not wonderful writers are often careless and lazy and wait vainly for the spirit to move. But the power had come back to Clive in its most bewitching form; the vision was clear and distinct; his characters lived before him as real as the men and women he met daily, and the plot arranged itself with as much accuracy as if it had been a decree of fate. He was writing a tragedy, and each day he read to Elinor the scenes he had brought into shape on the preceding night; and of all the pleasure any writer ever had, that of reading his productions still fresh in his own interest to an appreciative woman is the most enjoyable.

They had taken to long walks now, and there was nobody to remind Elinor of the intimacy which had grown up between her and this man. There were no visitors at the Wood, her father was absent, and Rosa moved about as innocent as a dove and kept a watchful guard on careless Tom, that he should not so much as look significant. Clive had shown her his favorite walks. The grove on the hill which separated his place from the Thornton's became their almost daily resort, and the most beautiful to Clive, for it was there he read to her his tragedy.

There was to come a break now: the first reminder that he had been wandering in the enchanted garden, and that he had not yet discovered any spell which could make it a reality; that it was still doubtful whether it might not vanish from his sight and be no more found in this world. Elinor was going away. Only for a fortnight; but sometimes a week is more important than ordinary years.

Clive had ridden over to the Wood one morning, and as soon as he entered the room where she and her friend sat busy with a pretty female pretense of work, Mrs. Thornton exclaimed—

"Oh, isn't she a wicked creature? She is going to-morrow."

Clive felt as if she had suddenly thrown cold water in his face, and his disappointment was so visible that Rosa added—

"It is only for a fortnight—that is some comfort."

Clive recovered himself and said properly—

"It may seem so when the last week is almost over. But is not this sudden, Miss Grey?"

"Oh no; I told Mrs. Thornton I should have to steal time to visit an old cousin of papa's. He wants us now, he writes, and papa is to take me up on his way from town."

"But I had settled on Saturday for my breakfast, or *fête*, or whatever you please to call it," said Clive.

"And why hadn't you told us?" inquired Rosa.

"I wanted a little surprise. I was going to tell you to-day, and send out the invitations."

"It must wait till Elinor comes back," returned Rosa.

"That would not be fair," rejoined Elinor, "though I shall be very sorry to miss it."

"As it was to be given to show Miss Grey my old place," said Clive, "I am afraid it must wait."

And I am afraid that Miss Grey was so accustomed to being first in people's thoughts that she rather took that as a matter of course.

"Say two weeks from to-morrow—Thursday fortnight," urged Mrs. Thornton; "that will bring it the day after the false creature's return."

"If that will please Miss Grey?"

"I shall be delighted," said Elinor. "But it is cruel of you to make my dull weeks still duller by the anticipation."

So it was arranged, and while they were yet talking and Clive was teasing Mrs. Thornton by pretending to make a vast secret in regard to his preparations, Tom burst in like a hurricane after his usual fashion.

"Has the world fallen in two?" demanded his wife.

"I haven't heard," said Tom; "I'll send up a boy in a balloon to inquire. How are you, Farnsworth? I say, the Idol is driving up in great state. I hurried in because I want some fun."

"I must tell her about the postponement of my breakfast," said Clive.

Rosa put up her lip, contemptuous.

"Has the Idol been in your confidence?" she asked. "Dear me, Elinor, I suppose he is going to show us Dagon."

"No, Mrs. Pluto has sent down to get him the bottle-imp," said Tom. "What is it?"

Clive explained, and added—

"I was obliged to tell her because I found she meant a dinner on Saturday."

"A dinner in August!" cried Mrs. Thornton.

"She ought to be broiled on one of her own gridirons," said Tom.

"Hush," said Rosa, "there is her carriage. Elinor, don't look so aggravatingly virtuous and superior, else I'll bite you."

"I was wondering if I mightn't go away," she said. "Tom will be sure to make me laugh."

"I'll be as grave as a judge," promised Tom.

"I do believe it makes you uncomfortable to be wicked, Miss Grey," observed Clive.

"Indeed, it does seem a shame to laugh at any body so kind-hearted as Mrs. Hackett."

"Nonsense," said Rosa; "don't every body laugh at us and every body else? Don't be goody, goody! Laugh now and wear a 'golden sparrow' of remorse to-morrow."

They all laughed, but she checked them, for a servant opened the door bearing in his hand the Idol's card.

"Yes," said Mrs. Thornton, "at home, John."

When the Idol was heard rustling through the hall she rose to meet her and did the delighted. The Idol exclaimed, kissed her, greeted Elinor warmly, and said—

"Why, you have quite a levy, Mrs. Thornton. How is your good spouse? And how do you do, Mr. Farnsworth?"

"We are all well, and you are just in time to mourn with us. Have you any sackcloth?"

"I could get it," said the Idol, who always took things literally; and I defy an angel of mercy not to laugh at people who do. "But what is it, and what is it for?"

"There is going to be an eclipse of the sun," said Tom.

"Total?" she asked.

"Yes, but transitory."

"He means that Miss Grey is going to leave us," explained Mrs. Thornton.

"O no, that would be too cruel!" cried Mrs. Hackett, really distressed. "And dear me, Mr. Farnsworth, your party—ah, I forgot."

"It is no secret now," said Clive; "I have had to tell them about it."

"It seems you were admitted into his mystery," remarked Rosa.

It pleased the Idol to think she should have been. "Only by chance," said she. "He told me because I had set the same day to give a little pleasure to our Accidental beauty."

Elinor frowned down Tom's face of fun—Clive had told them about the twist she gave the magnificent word Occidental.

"You are all only too kind, Mrs. Hackett," said Elinor. "It is well I am going away for a little; you would spoil me utterly."

"You can not gild refined gold," said the Idol, with a gracious inclination of her head, "nor can you add to the perfume of the lily by the supplication of a moment."

"Ah, Mrs. Hackett," said Tom, "you beat them all when it comes to poetry."

"But mine are only stolen gems," she replied; "Mr. Farnsworth has the true blossoms in his garden."

By this time she had her metaphors in a state of hopeless confusion and was proportionately content.

"How is Mr. Hackett?" Rosa asked.

"Quite well. He has been in town since Monday."

"He is so devoted to his business."

"Yes, I often reproach him for it," said she. "I say to him—what is wealth? For my own part, my idea of bliss is to be a shepherdess with a crook."

And on the instant Tom, sitting by Elinor, seized her pencils and began an elaborate sketch of the Idol in that costume, at which Elinor gave one glance and dared not look again.

"'As You Like It' and the 'Forest of Ardent,'" pursued Mrs. Hackett. "Think of it, Mr. Farnsworth!"

"He would answer for a 'melancholy Jacques,'" said Rosa.

"Is he ardent enough?" asked Tom in a thoughtful voice, as if he were meditating deeply upon the matter.

Elinor privately threatened him with her needle, and he revenged himself by sliding the caricature toward her on the table under cover of a book.

"So for two whole weeks, Miss Grey, we are to lose you?" continued Mrs. Hackett.

"If you are good enough to consider it a loss," Elinor replied.

"She is very meek, knowing how we shall regret her," said Rosa.

"Even Courts have had to do that," returned Mrs. Hackett; for the chief ground on which she based Miss Grey's right to admiration was the fact that the newspapers said the Emperor had praised her appearance.

Yes, it was absurd, as you say, but I think the chronicles of our time report similar instances—dear, blessed republican people!

"Have you had a lawsuit, Elinor? asked Tom.

"Ah, you know what I meant, Mr. Thornton," said Mrs. Hackett. "You have not forgotten that letter."

"Oh yes," said Tom; "stupid of me! one of the triumphs of our accidental beauty."

"So you like my little title for her?" asked the Idol complacently.

"Nothing could be better suited," said Tom.

"As opposed to oriental, you know."

"Precisely," said Tom, with an overwhelming bow.

"Mr. Farnsworth ought to show himself a poet laureate on the occasion of Miss Grey's departure," said the Idol.

"Beautiful lines of Tennyson," said Tom, quoting Bon Gaultier's wicked parody—

"'Oh, who would be a poet laureate?
Oh, that would be the post for me!
With plenty to get and nothing to do
But to deck a pet poodle in ribbons of blue,
And whistle a tune to the Queen's cockatoo,
And scribble of verses remarkably few,
And at evening empty a bottle or two,
Quaffingly, quaffingly.'"

"'Tennyson?" queried the Idol, for whom the mention of the name was enough. "Beautiful, of course! But I want our American Laureate to wreathe a chaplet."

Clive was not so well pleased. He objected to Mrs. Hackett's making him ridiculous whatever she might do with herself.

"I want our children of genius to assert themselves," said she. "I am truly patriotic, Miss Grey."

Elinor bowed and said that her sentiments were praiseworthy, and Mrs. Thornton, dreading a grand spread of the Star-Spangled Banner and a flutter of the Eagle's wings, immediately asked some question which changed the conversation. Mrs. Hackett was given to worshiping the immortal bird in theory, and running mad after foreign pomps and vanities in daily practice. I suppose she is a solitary instance, is she not?

"When do you go to Newport?" Rosa asked.

"Indeed, I ought to be there now. I shall go and return for Mr. Farnsworth's *fête*. I wish I could persuade Miss Grey to accompany me."

But Elinor showed the impossibility and expressed her regrets in a civil way. The Idol had lately returned from a trip to Saratoga, and she expressed her sorrow that Miss Grey had not appeared there.

"People were so disappointed," she said. "But I told them you were as fond of retirement as Marie Antoinette herself; and were buried in the country, lost in Ethiopian dreams."

Mrs. Thornton upset her basket of worsteds, and she and Clive were very busy hunting the stray balls. Elinor bore it like a martyr, but Tom cried out with his blankest look—

"Are you going to be a Colonizationist, Elinor?"

"No, no, you mistake," explained the Idol patronizingly. "I did not speak of actualities—I referred to an old poem; whose was it, Mr. Farnsworth?"

"I really forget," Clive said, diving behind a great chair in search of worsted.

"At all events," continued she, "it is about fancy and retirement—unreal, you know—an Ethiopian dream. Ah! Mr. Thornton, you men of this generation do not read enough; you are too busy thinking of the vile dross."

"I only wish one had enough without thinking," said Tom, catching her expression as she spoke, for a last touch to his caricature.

"Oh, don't let us be mercenary," she exclaimed; "let us be light and airy and fanciful."

"And Ethiopian," added Tom.

"By all means," said the Idol.

"How well that would suit the Accidental Beauty," said Tom.

Elinor gave him a beseeching look, but Mrs. Hackett was blissfully unconscious.

"That is what I told them at Saratoga," pursued she; "I told them that I too was weary of the vortex of pleasure, and loved more and more my Ciceronian shades."

"She means Plutonian," whispered Rosa to Clive, and they both had to hunt for more worsted before they could venture to resume their seats. She went away at length, and Clive was heartily rejoiced; he could not endure to have this last day desecrated.

It passed as pleasantly as the others, not that any thing more definite came of it; perhaps in a certain sense it was the more enjoyable on that very account.

I may tell you that those had been pleasant weeks to Elinor Grey herself, and perhaps her heart had gone nearer his than it had ever been drawn toward that of any other man, but there had been nothing to make it necessary for her to rouse herself or think, and she had drifted on in the sunshine.

They sat under the trees on the lawn, they drove out when the summer twilight cooled the air, and Tom kept them all amused by his high spirits. It was not farewell either that had to be said when they returned, for Clive was to stay all night, and they were to see Elinor to the station the next morning.

"I don't like even this break," Mrs. Thornton said, as she and Tom sat on the piazza, and Clive and Elinor walked up and down in the moonlight. "Things so seldom go on just the same after any change."

"No dismal auguries," said Clive.

"She would be vexed in a moment if any body else croaked," said Tom rashly.

"Croaked!" repeated she. "You said once I had a voice like a dove, you monster."

"And somebody talks about the low complaining of the dove," said Elinor, "so perhaps it is part of the old compliment, Rosa."

"That suggests a fretful dove," replied she.

"The natural transformation women undergo," added Tom. "First they are innocent doves, then turtle doves, and then fretful ones. Elinor is an example of the first, my Rosa of the last."

"Any thing is better than being innocent," cried Rosa; "that means you don't know any thing. I used to hate it when I was a girl, because I knew I wasn't innocent."

"That is a confession," said Tom.

"No matter," retorted she, and curled her head down on his shoulder, pretending to be cold and sleepy, and watched Clive and Elinor, who had pursued their promenade and stood at the end of the porch looking across the moonlit garden.

"After all," Clive said, "I believe Mrs. Thornton was right—even brief partings are dismal things."

"And one gets into such idle, dreamy ways in this Castle of Indolence," replied Elinor. "I think it will do me good to be roused by a little change."

"Only the dreamy ways are so pleasant."

Elinor agreed to that, but made a movement to resume their march, and Rosa mentally vituperated her for spoiling the pretty picture they had presented standing together in the yellow radiance.

"I shall expect you to have reached the last act of the tragedy by the time I get back," Elinor was saying as they passed the place where Rosa and Tom sat.

"Bah!" thought Rosa, "haven't they got away from that tragedy all this time?"

"I am afraid I shall lose my inspiration," said Clive.

"Oh, you are so far along in it now that you must not stop," she replied. "I have fully made up my mind to see it played next winter, and you must not disappoint me."

"Suppose it shares the fate of most tragedies?" asked he.

"You will have done the work, and done it with all your power, so you need not be discouraged. But it won't fail."

"I shall be certain of success now," said he. "I believe in your prophetic instinct, you know."

Rosa heard that too, curled up on Tom's shoulder, while he yielded to a pleasant doze.

"Prophetic instinct!" quoth she, in high scorn. "If he can't do better for himself than that I'll break up the sitting and go to bed."

"I shall be anxious for the last act," Elinor continued. "You have not told me any thing about that."

"Then you will remember to think about it?" Clive asked. He had been on the point of saying "me," but recollected himself and wisely added the neuter pronoun.

Elinor gave him one of her beautiful smiles, but that was not an encouragement, although agreeable, for he had seen her smile at other people in the same way. "Of course I shall remember it—when your heroine is my namesake."

Clive thought of a thousand graceful things he might have said to any other female, but somehow they sounded weak and overstrained when he wanted to offer them to this woman. She looked so grand, so unlike any body unless some vision of ancient poetry, wrapped in a scarlet shawl which became regal drapery as she folded it about her, her great eyes mournful and soft in the moonlight, and so womanly and gentle with it all—how could he say any thing worth her hearing?

They stopped again when they reached the limit of their promenade, and talked for some time. Rosa gathered heart and allowed Tom to dream in peace, smiling to herself. But she might have listened; Elinor was still talking to him about his play, and bestowing that subtle flattery which only a woman can do; and having faith in his genius, meant every word. Then perhaps they did both yield a little to the influence of the scene, and talked somewhat dreamily about life and hope and the silver mist setting over the garden, but not going very far, because as they walked back and neared Mrs. Thornton Elinor was saying—

"Oh, the first night—I shall sit in a stage-box and be sternly critical."

"I'd like to box your ears!" thought the exasperated Rosa. "You are the most aggravating she-leopard I ever knew, and that Clive's a muff."

She gave Tom a push and roused him without mercy, and he with a propensity common to human nature desired to show he had not been asleep but hearing every word that had passed.

"It's just like her!" said he.

"Why, I vow you are clairvoyant!" cried Rosa, and laughed. "Good people, moonlight is pretty and I am pretty therein, but I am going to bed now that I may be pretty to-morrow. I shall have a cold in my head if I stay here any longer."

Of course they all went in, and she was .. ciless in ordering every body away.

"I'll have some sort of revenge," thought she. "Horrid things! My nose aches with the cold. I know it's red."

But she relented when she remembered Elinor was to go the next morning, and the consequence was that they sat there and talked till some preposterous hour. That was one of the pleasant things about Alban Wood—people never got to bed.

The next morning was gorgeously beautiful —the only part of an August day in which one is willing to be alive—and the train would be at the station early enough to make a punctual breakfast necessary. So it was pleasant to the last—very pleasant.

Tom drove them over in his new trap, and Rosa insisted on sitting by him. "He is so careless," said she; "and I feel safer where I can watch him with these new horses."

Now Tom, who was the exquisite whip only the owner of American trotters ever is, looked aghast and irate at this abominable slander, and Rosa pinched him slyly. What she meant he understood just one hour and a quarter after— it takes that length of time for a female plot to get through a masculine head.

There were not more than five minutes' space for last words. The express came shrieking up and halted; there stood Mr. Grey on the platform ready to receive his princess and utter and return hasty greetings.

"Bring her back in just a fortnight," cried Rosa, "or I'll never forgive you."

"I could not keep away from you any longer if I would," replied Mr. Grey.

Clive handed Elinor up on the platform—she diappeared—the engine shrieked again, and they were gone.

A flower had fallen from the bouquet Elinor carried and lay at Clive's feet; he committed the old, old folly that will always be new and always pretty—hid it in his vest and turned to join his friends.

"I feel as if she were gone forever," said Mrs. Thornton dolefully.

Clive's very thought. A sudden gloom swept over him which took the brightness out of the morning sky. They drove round by his place and deposited him at the gates, and he walked slowly up the avenue, to learn what existence would be like deprived of Elinor Grey.

CHAPTER VI.

AT EASTBURN.

THOSE were not exhilarating days which Mr. Grey and "my daughter Elinor" spent with their venerable relative; but similar visits are among the penalties all lives must undergo, and they endured the sojourn with such philosophy as could be summoned. Still and uneventful gh the time had slipped by, until Elinor rose one morning and remembered that the next but one would be her last day.

Her father and his cousin were going off upon some expedition, and Elinor would have the hours between the inhumanly early breakfast and late twilight entirely at her disposal. She meditated several things, then woman-like sprang at something entirely different and proceeded to act upon her newest impulse. She was only two or three hours' journey, thanks to a portion being by rail, from the little village, nestled among the hills, where she had once spent several quiet weeks years and years ago. She had always wanted to visit it again, and she had determined not to go back without carrying her wish into execution.

This day was the most favorable opportunity imaginable, and as soon as she was left to her own devices Miss Grey ordered a vehicle to take her to the station for the first train, not being in the least helpless or fine when she really desired to do any thing, and equal to a good deal more than a brief journey without a protector.

She had always remembered that village with so much pleasure, having spent some weeks there the summer she went to Europe. Aunty Olds, the mistress of the farm-house where she lodged, had been a sempstress in Mr. Grey's establishment when he was at one time settled in New York during Elinor's childhood, and had petted her so much and sent her occasional letters since, written in wonderful English, that Elinor remembered her pleasantly and had promised her a brief visit when she came within reach of her. At the railway terminus she found a conveyance to carry her on without delay, and it was still early in the morning when she reached the village and drove along the one street it could boast, marvelling to see how exactly the same all things appeared. Perhaps the maple-trees had gained in their spreading branches; Mrs. Olds's house maybe looked somewhat grayer as she walked up the yard, but there was no other perceptible change.

The good woman was in a state of such exstasy at her visit, and so full of grief that it was to be so short, that Elinor would have been repaid even if it had cost her some trouble. She had to hear every thing that had happened during those long years, as far as Mrs. Olds's experience was concerned; an elaborate account of Mr. Olds's death included, with particular mention of the different sorts of "doctor's stuff" he had taken and how wickedly his children behaved because the farm and every thing appertaining thereto was left to their step-mother. Elinor was properly sympathetic and indeed sufficiently interested. The incidents narrated by a quaint body with any individuality are not half so wearisome as the affairs of our every-day friends, be they potentates or high-priests. After she diverged to the history of the village, and Elinor remembered the pretty girl whose beauty had so impressed her artistic tastes and

who had been her companion in daily rambles among the hills.

"And Ruth Sothern?" she asked. "What has become of her, Aunty Olds?"

The good woman shook her head.

"Oh, I hope she is not dead, or married to some man that has allowed her to work her beauty all away."

"Either one or t'other would have been a blessing," replied Mrs. Olds.

"What has happened to her?" Elinor asked.

"Deary me, deary me," exclaimed Mrs. Olds; "I do say I felt sorry for her. But la! you couldn't say so here to this day; folks hain't no mercy."

"But where is she?" asked Elinor. "Does she live up in her grandmother's house?"

"Bless you, no! she hain't these three years and more. Old gran'ma's dead; there aint nobody in the house now. Ruth she rented it to Miss Jinkins, but she went out West to live with her son and there hain't ben nobody there these three months—"

"Do tell me about Ruth," Elinor interrupted, fearful lest she should hear a long narrative about Mrs. Jenkins and her expedition instead of the story of the poor girl.

"Oh dear, 'taint to tell," said the old woman. "Not but what such things happen often enough, as I used to know when I was young and lived in towns; but away up here—it did seem as if the Devil must be sharp to hunt up a poor gal 'way here."

Elinor waited. The good woman must tell the tale in her own way if she told it at all; any attempt to shorten it would only put her ideas in hopeless confusion.

"It was all that fellow getting hurt and staying there—what was his name? It wasn't Johnson—my head is just like a sieve for all the world, But he did stay and stay, long after I thought he might better ha' gone, but 'twant for me to say so. Wal, he went, and fall came and Ruth's grandma died sudden, and there was Ruth all alone—oh, my dear!"

"Poor Ruth!"

"She stayed shet up there, but oh, it wasn't long afore folks began to talk, and I wouldn't believe it—"

"You good heart, you."

"Yes, but oh deary, I had to! It come along a'most to March, but it was dreadful cold weather and we'd had a terrible fall of snow. In the middle of the night who should come a pounding at my door but Miss Jinkins's little boy — he'd stay ever since gran'ma died. 'Git up, git up!' says he. 'Ma's afeard Ruth'll die afore morning.'"

"I slipped into my clothes and paddled away through the snow and got up there at last. I don't never want to see another such a sight. There was the doctor and Miss Jinkins, and Ruth a screaming and raving on the bed, and oh, my dear, afore daylight her baby was born and died, and I just knelt down and prayed that she might die too;—but the Lord didn't see fit to have it so."

The old woman broke off to cry a little, and Elinor cried too with her womanly sympathies thoroughly roused, having passed that age when girls are such severe judges of their own sex.

"What became of her?" she asked at length.

"As soon as she got well she went off, leaving Miss Jinkins to live in the house."

"Did she never come back or write?"

"Never. You can guess where folks said she was gone, but I al'ays told 'em I guessed their thoughts was blacker'n Ruth's life."

"And the man?"

"Oh la! no more of him of course. Some said she'd gone to him, and some said she was a doin' worse, and Miss Jinkins stayed there till three months ago."

"And have you no idea where Ruth is?"

"Yes, I have, my dear, and I'll tell you. Jest about the time Miss Jinkins went away I had to go to Luckey's Mills on some business, and there I see Ruth Sothern. She cut down another street—she needn't ha' ben afraid of me—but it was Ruth. She's a workin' in the Mills, and may be a doin' better than them that wouldn't speak to her."

"How far is it to the Mills?" Elinor asked.

"It must be thirty miles and more. There's a railroad though into ten miles of here." And Elinor discovered that she could return that way and still reach home by the time her father would arrive.

"Mrs. Olds," said she, "I am going round by Luckey's Mills to see Ruth."

"And it'll be the blessedest thing you ever did," replied the good creature. "Tell her the house is empty, and jest to come back and live in it and farm her little lot and let folks talk, instead of working herself to death in them dreadful mills."

She gave Elinor some luncheon at once, that she might start, and disregarded her own disappointment at this hasty departure, in her sympathy for the unfortunate girl.

"It'll be like a new lease of life to her," said she. "And who knows, Miss Grey, how you may help her on? I jest believe the Lord sent you to-day, for he never forgets."

"The Lord never forgets!" They were simple words, but many and many a time when troubles gathered about Elinor Grey, and her burden seemed harder than she could bear, those words came to her mind and gave her new strength.

"But you'll come to see me agin, Miss Elinor?"

"Indeed I will; perhaps not till next summer, but I'll come then and stay two or three weeks."

"That'll be better'n a pictur-book to me all winter," said the old dame. "You always do remember a promise, so I know you'll come."

Elinor was in haste to be gone, and it was not until she was seated in the train and

whirling away among the picturesque hills that she reflected whether her visit might be wise. That it would have been considered Quixotic and highly improper by the generality of guides for young women did not trouble her in the least. "I am sure it will do the poor child good," she thought. "She'll not be afraid of me after the first moment, and the little thing will be glad to speak freely for once in her life of secrecy." She was so busy with her reflections that she was surprised when the conductor shrieked in an unearthly voice, "Luckey's Mills."

Miss Grey found several mysterious-looking vehicles at the station, and entering one she ordered the driver to take her to the Mills, and was rattled through the busy town with so much noise that she might have believed she was travelling at high speed. But the Mills were silent and deserted; a workman told her there had been some accident and business couldn't go on for a week. There was a clerk in the office, he thought, and being an Irishman he showed her the way with the greatest alacrity—any thing was better than keeping to his wheelbarrow. So Miss Grey, "familiar with courts," as Mrs. Hackett was wont to remark, stepped into the office and confronted the inky gentleman who ought to have been busy with the accounts but was munching peaches instead. He was so much abashed by her sudden appearance that he swallowed a peach-stone, and being a nervous, hypochondriacal man, for days after fancied that he could hear it rattling in his aggravated interior every time he moved. He found voice to answer her inquiries; rubbed the peach-juice from his mouth with a red silk pocket-handkerchief, and told her where Ruth Sothern might be found.

She was not at the boarding-house for the Mills. He went to the door and pointed out a little cottage up a lane and informed her that the young woman made her home there, then stopping to draw breath he became suddenly conscious that he had done for himself and the peach-stone and recollected what an immense one it was. At first he thought it must be in his throat and he choking to death without having known it. He stood before Elinor with his face so changed and disturbed by the horrible fear, and the convulsive efforts he made to swallow, that she was inclined to think him mad.

"I am much obliged for your kindness," said she, turning to go.

"Not at all, not at all," returned he, clutching at his throat to ascertain if the mountain was perceptive to the touch. "It's gone! its gone!" he added in a tragic voice.

"What is it?" Elinor asked kindly, confirmed in her opinion that those wearisome lines of figures on the pages of the open ledgers had proved too much for his brain.

"Oh, nothing, nothing—nought, nought—as Hamlet says," replied he, for he taught the "district school" in the winter and was conversant with elegant literature.

"He must be mad," thought Elinor, and got out of the office with all speed, leaving him to marvel about her and to fancy a hideous pain at his vitals.

Miss Grey walked up the grassy lane and knocked at the door of the little cottage, which looked very home-like and pleasant with its porch covered with woodbine and bitter-sweet. It happened that Ruth Sothern was alone in the house, and sitting in the room into which a door gave entrance from the porch. She rose and opened it and found herself face to face with Elinor Grey. She knew her at the first glance, retreated a step with one heavy, sobbing breath, and stood irresolute.

"My dear little Ruth," said Elinor, seizing both her hands lest her next impulse might be to run out of sight, "I am so glad to find you! I came on purpose. Have you forgotten me?"

"No—no—I remember you," she replied in a hurried, breathless way, like a person that had been running till almost exhausted.

"And I hope you are glad to see me," said Elinor. "I had not forgotten you in all these years. You look exactly the same—you look so young."

"How did you know where I was?" asked Ruth, eying her with sudden keenness, in doubt apparently how to act.

"Mrs. Olds told me, dear," replied Elinor softly. "I came from Eastburn."

The impulse was strong again in the girl's mind to run out of the room, but Elinor laid her hand on her arm. "Are you not glad to see me, Ruth?"

"You know then—they have told you?"

"I know that I pity you very much, dear—isn't that enough?"

Suffering had not made the little creature bitter, nor had it given her that hard strength it does some women. She melted at the voice, and retreating to the table sat down and hid her face on it, sobbing drearily. Elinor knelt by her and whispered comforting words out of her great heart, for she was a true woman in spite of her imperiousness, her pride, and her legion of great faults. After awhile Ruth could look up and even smile in a wan, hopeless way. "I haven't cried in a good while," said she; "but it came so sudden—you are so kind."

"Then you are glad I have come?"

"Oh so glad! I'm so lonesome—oh, I'm so lonesome!" And the complaint, like that of a child, was very touching.

Elinor kissed her and put back her hair, and when she had quieted her said—"I have a long hour to stay with you, Ruth; can't you take me to your room so that we can talk?"

Ruth led the way up to her chamber; the prettiest, daintiest room, in spite of its plainness. There were books on a row of shelves, a few pots of flowers in the windows, a bird singing in his cage among them, and that indescribable air of purity which Elinor's womanly instincts comprehended at once. That little room showed certain unerring traces of the character of its occupant, and the cheerful, well-assorted colors, the attempt to brighten its simplicity, betrayed the love of beautiful things and the warm imagination which might have helped to lead her into trouble.

"What a pretty place it is," Elinor said, sitting down near the window.

"I tried to make it so," replied Ruth; "I'm always here out of mill hours."

"Is the work hard?" Elinor asked.

"Not very, now I am used to it. Oh, I shouldn't mind if it was, though I'm lazy by nature; but any thing to make the time pass."

"And you like to read," said Elinor, glancing at the shelves of books. "I am glad of that, it is such a help."

"But it's novels and poetry, I am afraid," returned Ruth; "I am such a simple creature and always shall be."

Elinor thought it would not be she who would give the poor creature a lecture as to the bad effects of romance and poetry on the mind; let her read both and forget the real world if she could.

A sudden red burned in the girl's cheeks, and she added in a shy, frightened way—"But that isn't all the truth. I did try to study—sometimes I do now. I thought—I thought—if ever he should come back he need not be ashamed because I was ignorant."

The last words burst from her with sudden violence; she could not control herself if the every-day restraints were in the least forgotten, and now she was down at Elinor's feet with her face hidden in her dress, sobbing piteously—"But he won't come—he won't come."

Whoever the man might be that had wrecked her life the girl loved him yet, and Elinor Grey recognized there a different and in some respects better nature than her own, in that it could forgive. She felt that in a similar strait she should be full of bitterness and scorn, with a mad desire in her soul to prove a very Medea to the deceiver. But she could sympathize with and pity the girl all the more that she loved him still. And now she wanted to make her talk and tell her poor story, that she might know how it would be best to act, for Elinor had no mind to solace the girl by an hour's visit, and leave her with her daily life more desolate than before.

"Do you know where he is, Ruth?" she asked.

"Not now," she replied, without lifting her head. "Once in a great while he writes to an address I sent him; but he doesn't know where I am; and I haven't heard, oh, in so long."

"Did he promise to come back, Ruth?"

"No, no! Oh, don't think he was a bad man. Miss Grey—he wasn't bad! He pitied me so—he couldn't take me then—he wasn't wicked—you must not think that!"

If she could have seen the lightning which flashed from Elinor's eyes, and heard the mental wish she breathed that he stood there at the moment, Ruth might have doubted whether

Miss Grey was prepared to consider him so leniently.

"Will you tell me his name?" whispered Elinor, her soft hands resting on Ruth's head and giving her a feeling of repose by their touch.

"May I show you his portrait?" asked Ruth. "I found it among some papers of his. Sometimes it's such a comfort to me—sometimes it breaks my heart—but oh, the hardest of all—my baby, my baby!" She gave way to such a passion of weeping that Elinor was almost alarmed.

"I know I ought to be ashamed," she sobbed, "but I can't help it. If I could have kept my baby! Perhaps if he never comes it would have grown up and hated me—but so many years first—and it would have been all mine—and I'm so lonesome, so lonesome."

Elinor reminded her in whose care it was, and tried to speak the words that sounded so weak.

"Yes, I know," moaned Ruth; "I say it to myself; but I miss it—I'm alone."

When she was quiet again she rose and went to a drawer kept locked and took out a miniature. "It's so like him," she said, looking down at it; "but he must be altered. It's more than three years ago, and I have never seen him since."

Elinor held out her hand for the picture and Ruth gave it to her, sinking down in her former attitude with her head resting on Miss Grey's knee. Elinor looked at the picture—grasped it hard in her hand and stared at it as if unable to believe the evidence of her senses—then she dropped it with a gesture of loathing and horror. It fluttered down on Ruth's shoulder and she seized and hid it.

Elinor Grey had received the most sudden and violent shock she had ever felt, and she sat absolutely stunned.

"He was very handsome," Ruth said softly, "and so gentle and tender. I pitied him at first—I think that was the way—I had to nurse him after his hurt."

Elinor was relieved by the sound of her voice. It was something to be called back to the present; to be obliged to concentrate her thoughts upon this child—in so many ways she seemed a child still; to have a little time before reflecting on this terrible blow which might well shake her faith in all things.

Ruth told her story with the pathos of deep feeling, and Elinor listened with such pity as she had never known for any human being; the while an under-current in her mind rolled toward the man who had worked this misery with such scorn and anger that she would have been startled at her own powers of hating could she have had leisure to reflect.

"And you love him yet, Ruth?"

"Look at me!" cried she, with sudden passion. "I'd rather to-day meet death at his hand than be a queen. I'd suffer tortures just to see his face! I know it is wicked; I can't

help that—I love him! I can only feel like his wife waiting for him to come—waiting."

"And you thought he would come back?"

"He never told me so—he didn't lie. Oh, he was not bad! He was young too. We didn't either of us think, but just floated through those blessed weeks. Don't despise me—I was so happy! He could not marry me; when he had to go he told me so. That woke me. I waited for him—waited and loved him—I loved him!"

There were no words possible; there was nothing to be said. Useless to argue, to say what another would have done. She had expressed the whole—she loved him.

"If you could read his letters—he suffered too. I did think he would come—yes, I did. It made me study—I tried to grow like the women in books—I wanted him to find me so altered and improved that he need not be ashamed. I couldn't help but feel I was his wife—I do yet. I know what I am; but oh, in God's eyes—He is so merciful!"

And Elinor Grey felt that if the man were there present she could have set her foot upon his neck and crushed him. The girl looked so young, in spite of every thing Elinor could scarcely believe she was only a year the elder. The brilliant loveliness of her earliest youth was not gone; the pink still dyed her cheeks; her great brown eyes were soft and beseeching—she was such a fairy of a thing after all her suffering.

"And I have suffered," she said. "Sometimes I thought I must die; but I dared not pray for that, it was too wicked. I came away from the old home—I couldn't endure the old faces. I wanted to be lost. I have work—I couldn't touch his money, you know. I've seen the months grow into years and here I am, and still I keep saying—to-morrow—to-morrow!"

She accepted meekly the consequences of her sin—she did not rebel under her misery—she could believe it right that she should be barred out of the world—but she could not root the love out of her soul or even make an effort to struggle against it.

Elinor could not give her hope—what was there to offer? She did the kindest thing she could—gave her gentle words and made her feel that at least to one human being she was not a Pariah and an outcast.

"Nobody knows me here," Ruth said; "I came back six months ago. I was in Massachusetts before that. But some day they'll find out my story, and then—"

She broke off with a shudder: Elinor held her fast in her arms, her eyes flashing as if she had the whole world to battle and was prepared to defend her.

It was like having new life given to the desolate creature, that privilege of talking freely after those years of self-restraint and concealment. It was pitiful to hear and think of the record of the long, long months, with their

C

varying feelings from brief hope to the apathy of despair, and back through the aching round, but never once maddened, as would have been the case with many natures, by sudden desperation, when to rid herself of existence seemed the easiest way and the best; submitting patiently to her fate, doubting neither heaven or her love, acknowledging always the justice of her punishment.

Another trait in her character came out by chance. In speaking of the time she lived in Massachusetts, during one of her bitterest seasons of suffering, when she did wonder why she was left here since life was ended, she told how mercifully she was shown the way out of the gloom by having work given her and being made to remember that even her blighted existence might be of use. An infectious fever had broken out among the people employed in the mills, and this girl, weak and childish as she looked, had labored day and night in the hospitals, shrinking neither from danger nor fatigue. It was not till long after, that Elinor heard the full account from other lips, for Ruth only incidentally mentioned the occurrence, and knew that she had shown a courage and devotion equal to that of the women whose names go down in history linked with the remembrance of heroic deeds; but there was no one to chronicle the fortitude of this outcast but the angels up in heaven. Ah, perhaps when we read their records written in letters of light we may understand more plainly how poor our judgment was here.

"It was such a comfort to me," Ruth said, "to know that I could be of use—that I was permitted to be. And O, Miss Grey, some of them blessed me when they were dying! I could not feel that I was all alone after that."

Elinor had to go away at length, and though for a few moments Ruth clung to her with the sensation a drowning man might have as he felt the last spar slipping from his hold, she was able to control herself and to take in Elinor's words of hope.

"I shall not leave you for long, Ruth," she said; "I can make no arrangements now, but I promise that you shall see or hear from me very soon."

"A letter from you would do me so much good," the poor girl said humbly.

"You don't understand, Ruth," she replied. "In some way I mean to change your desolate life; but I can't yet tell how."

"Why should you be so kind? I have no claim on you—"

"Hush, dear. There, keep yourself quiet and trust me. I shall not forget."

"I know you will not. But I mustn't think!"

She was crouching on the floor at Elinor's feet; as she spoke she closed her eyes, sitting quite still, with the palms of her hands pressed tight together. The youth and brightness had gone out of her face. Elinor could fancy her sitting thus in her loneliness until the posture had become habitual. The picture was too painful. She rose to go, and knew that it was better to make the parting brief.

Ruth did not weep now. Elinor thought that the wildest passion of tears would not be so sorrowful to witness as that pale, silent resignation which she had forced herself to learn, and which was as foreign to her nature as it would have been to that of an impulsive child.

They parted, and Ruth went back to her little room and was alone with the familiar suffering, all the more dreary that she was so well accustomed to its every phase.

Elinor was soon on her return journey and reached the farm about the time her father and their host returned. Mr. Grey was quite astounded when she told him of her day's expedition, omitting any mention of Ruth in her account, and praised her courage as much as if she had been Madame Pfeiffer just returned from one of her impossible voyages.

Elinor Grey had the whole night before her to think and reflect, and it was not a quiet one. The next day they were preparing for their departure, and several times Elinor pleased and somewhat surprised her father by the energy of the compliments she lavished on him. "I do believe you are the only true man in the world, papa," she said; "with the others, the fairer the outside the worse they are in reality."

"Solitude has made you misanthropic," he replied. But Elinor persisted in her opinion and revered and worshiped him more than ever.

CHAPTER VII.

THE END OF THE FÊTE.

DURING that fortnight Clive Farnsworth led quite a hermit's life, and very impatient he had grown of it. It was difficult to settle to any thing. He could not have written a line only that the desire to obey Miss Grey's slightest wish was an anchor with which to stay his restless thoughts. He had few visitors; every body had gone to Newport or sought some other place of summer gayety. Even the Thorntons, two days after Elinor's departure, were seized with a desire to make an expedition, and fled to the White Mountains, trying in vain to carry the moody Clive with them. Yes, two very doleful weeks they had been, and time had appeared absolutely to stand still.

It was the first break in Clive's dream; a favorable opportunity for numerous ghosts to flit out of the past and torment him, and the unquiet shades did not hesitate to come. The lonely marches on the terrace had to be resumed, and many and many a night the stone flags resounded to his tread until the gray dawn put out the watchful stars. There was no possibility of sleep, and Clive knew too well the torture of attempting to woo slumber under such circumstances to be deluded into the effort even by bodily fatigue. Sometimes in those gloomy vigils he almost determined to go away and never see Elinor's face again; but he could not do that, and tried to quiet himself with the old sophistries wherewith men have sought to soften their sins to their own consciences since the Flood.

But time had moved on notwithstanding; the last days of waiting began to shine. The Thorntons were at home again, very much weather-beaten and in wonderful spirits; the whole neighborhood was gradually returning, and Clive commenced preparations for the second of September. That was to be the day of his *fête*: the Greys would be back on the first. Clive was determined that the festivities should be in a style worthy of her in whose honor they were to be given, and he was one of those fortunate beings able to carry his conceptions into execution.

It did come, the day that was to bring Elinor near him, although Clive had felt in regard to it somewhat as he used when a child looking forward to a holiday. Before sunset he made an excuse to ride over to Alban Wood to consult Mrs. Thornton about some arrangement for the morrow, and his subterfuge was so apparent to the crafty little woman that she was delighted to see him properly punished—the Greys had not arrived.

"Can any thing have happened to delay them?" queried Clive anxiously. "The trains on those cross-roads are such traps to keep people waiting in all sorts of horrible places."

"Yes," said Rosa, provokingly calm; "you men of influence ought to protest against it. Fancy Queen Elinor detained for hours in some out-of-the-way den, and Mr. Grey forced to eat a country inn dinner."

"What a tease you are, Rosa," said Tom.

Clive did feel that he would have liked to suffocate her—a little.

"We have had a telegram, Farnsworth," pursued Tom. "They'll be here this evening."

"I could have told him that if he had asked," said Rosa. "I didn't think he seemed anxious."

"Then all my plans for to-morrow are at stake," said Clive reproachfully, trying, as the wisest men will under similar circumstances, to make it appear that such were the grounds for his anxiety.

"Oh, of course that is the reason," retorted Rosa.

And she teased him and snubbed him, as the children say, and scolded Tom about some little matter concerning which she was profoundly indifferent, and made herself almost disagreeable, though she looked very pretty and mischievous the while. At last Clive was glad to take himself off, which was just what she wanted.

"You are too wicked," said Tom, when he had gone. "The poor fellow wanted to be asked to stay."

"He's a stupid, my dear, and you are another," explained Rosa complacently. "Ten to one

Elinor would have been offended at finding him here."

"And now she'll snub him because he isn't," said Tom. "Oh, gentle women, ye be 'rum critters.'"

But Rosa proved to him satisfactorily that being a man he was not capable of forming an opinion, and as she began to grow restless for the hour to send to the station, she tormented him till he was almost cross. Having effected that result she made love to him and smoothed him down, just as when a girl she used to worry her pet cat and rub his fur the wrong way till he emitted electric sparks, and then coax him into equanimity.

In the end she was punished. The Greys arrived, and Elinor had a terrible headache and would go straight to bed, and was no more mindful of Rosa's desire to sit with her than Rosa had been of Farnsworth's wishes. But she never remembered that it was a case of righteous retribution, and would have been vexed only Elinor did look so pale and tired that her heart softened. "There's something the matter," thought Rosa. "She looks as she used to when she was a little girl and had been in a great passion over somebody's injustice and had her feelings hurt too."

The day came to an end and Clive walked up and down the terrace; but he vowed that it should be his last forced march for some time—the sun would shine to-morrow. To-morrow came and literally the sun did shine, however it might be about the fulfillment of Clive Farnsworth's metaphorical allusion.

It was a glorious day, and by three o'clock the grounds were a pretty sight with the striped tents spread here and there and the gay groups flitting about. Hosts of people made their greetings, and Clive had time to be expectant until he hated every thing and every body, and compliments were drugs and the whole crowd a set of unnatural monsters, whom, if he had been Prospero, he would have ruthlessly annihilated by an earthquake. All because the Alban Wood party did not appear, though Mrs. Thornton had promised that they would be early. The troops of guests began to grow impatient for breakfast; and Clive saw it and exulted, and was sorry the repast had not been a dinner that it might be completely spoiled. But the carriage did drive up the avenue at last, and Farnsworth was on the steps to receive them.

Rosa came first, and as he helped her out she whispered—"I am so sorry; it was Queen Elinor. I thought she never would be ready."

Clive turned back to assist her majesty, and stood petrified at the first glance, while the words of welcome absolutely froze on his lips. Miss Grey was looking at him very much as she might have looked at Caliban had he suddenly appeared prepared to play the gallant. But oh, she was so courteous! She replied to Clive's awkward words with graceful speeches, and all the while transfixed him with those solemn eyes.

"You have made a fairy scene," said Mr. Grey; and Rosa and Tom joined in the compliments till Clive wished them dead at his feet and himself a howling Dervish in an Indian jungle.

He gave Elinor one imploring, wondering glance. She saw it, and her eyes began to burn and a cruel smile answered him. She complimented him too, very prettily, and every word stung like a hot needle, and Clive felt as if he had been neatly flayed alive in about ten seconds. After that pleasant exercise she left him and became the centre of a group at once. Everybody that knew her and everybody that wanted to were constantly surrounding her, and she was in her most brilliant mood, charming all beholders, and the very soul of amiability.

Clive Farnsworth wandered about a miserable man, but had no leisure to speculate as to what this change toward himself might mean, for there were scores of eager people expecting to be amused, and he was host. He was so miserable! There was a blur before his eyes which confused the throng into pink and blue clouds—only he could see Elinor Grey distinctly wherever she moved, brilliant, radiant. At least he could feed the menagerie and so get on toward the evening. The bugle sounded recall to the wanderers, and they poured in a stream toward the gayly-decorated tents.

Every body knew that the *fête* was given in Miss Grey's honor, so Clive had to go up to her again and offer his arm. She was seated by him at the table. The airy sweep of her draperies touched him as he sat, the delicate violet perfume which always pervaded her dress dizzied him with its subtle fragrance. She was in a gayer mood than he had ever seen her; she talked and laughed with the men who hovered near her chair instead of finding seats; she was elaborately civil to Clive, and nearly drove him mad with every word.

He must speak—it was impossible to be dignified or proud—he was too sorely hurt. "What have I done?" he managed to whisper.

She looked at him in smiling surprise. "Given a lovely *fête*," said she.

"You have not tasted a morsel, Miss Grey," interrupted her neighbor on the other side.

Clive had noticed and been quick to interpret, but he would make one other offer—if he could gain the least consolation! He selected a bunch of rare grapes from a dish near and offered them to her. "You know the Arabian proverb?" he said, with a miserable attempt at playfulness.

She took the grapes. "I do, replied she," and I believe in it." "The purple cluster dropped on her plate. She gave Clive that double glance only a woman can give—the mouth smiling for the benefit of the lookers-on—the eyes fairly menacing as they shone on him through the contracted lids.

Indeed it was a dangerous moment. There was an impulse in Elinor Grey's mind to sit there and tell the truth to the whole assembly and let him writhe under the very fullness of scorn and obloquy. She could not trust herself; she could not remain another second. She rose from her chair, took the first arm which offered, and left Clive in the desert. The breakfast was over 'at last; the groups spread through the grounds again.

The gorgeous sunset burned to its full glory and faded into a pearly twilight; a few stars shut up in the cloudless sky; the band on the platform erected down by the bowling-alley began to play, and exhilarated as people always are after being fed, the real pleasure of the entertainment commenced.

Clive went about doing his duty. He danced—he talked; he could see Elinor Grey dancing, and again he wished that a friendly earthquake might swallow the whole crowd. As the twilight deepened the colored lanterns cunningly hung among the tree-branches began to blaze, and the scene was as pretty as possible. When Clive saw other people admiring and happy he felt as if he was standing in the dark and looking into some enchanted land whither he might not enter.

But he would speak to Elinor Grey—she should tell him what had come between them. He could wait no longer—his love, his hopes, his anguish—he must pour out the whole. Just as he was growing desperate enough to have snatched her away from all astonished beholders, and really thought he saw an opportunity of getting near her, Mrs. Hackett seized his arm and took that occasion to deliver a long-winded compliment which she had carefully prepared several days before. Clive had recently escaped from three damsels who had fired a battery of small exclamations at him, and now the Idol rustled up in her purple draperies and wonderful decorations, looking like some huge tropical bird.

"I would come back from Newport," she said; "I only reached home last night. I could not miss this day."

Clive said it was kind of her, and mentally called her dreadful names and periled his soul by the wishes he silently breathed in her behalf. The Idol looked about to be certain that there was a sufficient audience within hearing to make it worth while to sound the grand trumpet, shook her plumage and waved her fan.

"I call it the Peri's offering to the queen of the fairies," said she. And a young gentleman near, who wanted to be invited to the Idol's balls next winter, cooed admiration. Unluckily he did it at the wrong moment. The Idol fixed him with her glittering eye, took in his full proportions, and registered a vow that she would not forget him, and that after her return to town he should never cast his shadow athwart her ball-room and coo in the beginning of one of her best speeches. She recovered herself and continued impressively—

"Paris has truly cast the golden apple at Venus's feet this day"—she waved her hand toward Miss Grey to point her words—"and Troy may as well burn itself"—indicating the house—"since it can never surpass this golden rain."

There was a good deal more in the same style, but Clive managed to get away without doing her mischief, and left her to listen to the praises of her satellites, while several Boston people who never visited New York and looked upon it as a second Gomorrah, and consequently did not care for the Idol's favor, laughed among themselves and congratulated each other that gold did not rule in Modern Athens.

By the time Clive was at liberty, Elinor Grey had disappeared. He sought her vainly among the crowd, and was constantly being stopped to hear or say pretty things or bid farewell to people who had had enough and were going home. At least a moment to himself, that he must have; and Clive passed behind the dancers and down the platform steps into the shrubbery. Fate had led him in the right direction, whether kindly or not he could have the rest of his life in which to ask, for as he turned into the first side-path, he saw Elinor Grey seated on a rustic bench looking away through the night.

The moon had come up, the broad white September moon, and her rays trembled across the branches of the late-flowering shrubs and quivered at her feet. The shorn turf gave back no sound under the tread, and Clive was close to her before she saw him. "Miss Grey," he said hurriedly, "I have been looking for you everywhere."

She surveyed him with the level glance which had so annoyed him at their first meeting, but there was something worse than indifference in it now. "I came here for a moment's quiet," returned she. "I suppose Mrs. Thornton wishes to go. I am sorry you should have had so much trouble on my account."

"She is not going yet," he answered, scarcely knowing what he said. "I wanted to see you—to speak with you—"

She looked coldly surprised, and checked his words. "A privilege you can claim as my host," said she.

Clive gave himself no time to think; he was too wretched to be angry. "Will you tell me how I have offended you?" he asked, in a voice sharp with pain.

"Have I been so lacking in courtesy that you could think me offended?" she returned. "I must beg you to pardon me."

"Oh, Miss Grey, you know the courtesy that cuts like a knife," cried Clive; "worse than a man's blows."

"Surely to-day's triumphs might satisfy even a man's vanity," said she. She was merciless. Feel? Yes, if he could feel he should be stabbed home.

"Will you tell me what I have done?" he asked. "Another woman I might accuse of coquetry, but Elinor Grey is above that. There must be some reason. You are so changed; and we parted friends—if I may use the word."

"Yes, friends—you are right," replied Elinor Grey. "Go on, Mr. Farnsworth."

"How can I?" he exclaimed. "How can I question as I would of a friend—it is more than that. You are crushing my heart under your feet, Elinor Grey, for I love you!"

He had not meant to speak those words—he did not know what he had meant—but the avowal was made and his passion burst out in hot utterance that would not be restrained. She did not interrupt him; she sat motionless, not so much as looking at him.

"Answer me," he pleaded. "Say something—tell me that you hate me if you must—don't sit there silent!"

She looked up now—looked him full in the face. "Mr. Farnsworth," said she, "I have been in Eastburn."

He gave one heavy breath that was like a groan, and stood mute. Strange, all day while racking his thoughts for a clue to her altered manner, he had not once thought of the miserable secret and the barred-out sin.

"I need give you no other answer," continued she. "I have seen Ruth Sothern. Now you come to me with words of love on your lips—you dare to love me! For what woman do you take me, Sir, that you venture to throw the insult of your love in my face?"

He did not speak.

"I did trust you—I did call you friend—I believed you honorable and good—and I find you a man the very touch of whose hand is contamination to any woman. I had no mind to come here to-day; but I kept your secret. You were very near hearing it told before all those people."

"I wish you had," he groaned; "I wish you had! What are they to me? Oh, Elinor Grey, if you could know the suffering, the remorse—"

"Remorse, when you could have atoned for your sin?" returned she. "Don't treat me to a rhapsody from a French romance, Sir! Suffering? You talk to me of your suffering when I come from the sight of that poor girl whose life you have destroyed!"

"And my own with it," he groaned.

"Yours? Oh no! such sins are venial in a man; the world pardons them. I am unwomanly, unmaidenly, no doubt. I ought to have shrunk from your victim and come back to accept your hand with smiles. The fault is in my nature that I can not act like the world. I can hold her by the hand and feel no shame—the very air you breathe is pollution to me."

She looked grand in her scorn; and though her language at another time might have seemed overstrained, it was natural in that excited state of feeling.

"I deserve all that you can say," he answered. "You can not loathe me more than I have loathed myself."

His pale, wretched face did appeal to her womanly impulses, but she would not permit herself to be softened. "Why did you speak such words to me?" she cried.

"Because I tried to lie to myself," he said. "I tried to accept the world's creed; to say that one error should not blight my life."

"And you can't do it!" she exclaimed vehemently. "Oh, don't make me believe you as miserable as the common herd—leave me my faith in you—earn your pardon of God."

"What can I do?" he asked.

"Claim your wife—she is your wife in the sight of Heaven. Right her in the face of men and angels—save her from more agony. If you knew what she suffers!"

"And make myself a jest and a by-word—put myself beyond the pale of society—be a laughing-stock—"

"Be an honest man who feared God and dared to atone for his sin."

"I have wanted to; will you believe me? Oh, don't think my sin has not burdened my soul. But marry her? It would make her as miserable as I should be."

"No, for she would have your heart to rest on. Mr. Farnsworth, be true to yourself—do this. She is young yet—she loves you so! Who is to ask of the past—if you will think of that? But if the whole truth known would bring her suffering as your acknowledged wife, think what it will be for her to meet it alone."

"Have I not thought? Do you believe I am the sort of man that sins without remorse—and that one sin for which I had most abhorrence, the meanest that ever stained a man's soul?"

Elinor was conquered; her loathing and her scorn gave way to womanly pity. "You are not base, you are not vile," she exclaimed; "you will redeem this one error. I tell you, it is your only hope of peace. Think of going on toward age with the blighting of a human soul on your conscience—what a mockery fame and honor would be. Save yourself and her. Decide now. Mr. Farnsworth, if ever Almighty God pleaded with a sinner, I believe he is pleading with you."

In his remorse, his doubt, his agony at the sight of the heaven of which the power of loving which might never be shed on him, Farnsworth groaned aloud and flung himself on his knees with his face hidden on the bench. He felt Elinor's hand laid softly on his head.

"Friend," she said, "my friend, pray to him. Oh, do not mind the weak philosophy men put between themselves and the Father; pray, and he will hear."

"He has seemed so far off," answered Clive. "I said he could not hear—that it didn't matter."

"And so we all do, and think ourselves brave. Mr. Farnsworth, be a true man, and own him and obey him. Oh, my friend, you will go to Ruth—you will give her back her happiness."

"I loved you so," burst from him. "I loved you so! Don't be angry."

"I am not angry. I beg your pardon for insulting you as I did. I am so hard."

"And if she should ask me if I loved her?"

"She is so good, so trusting, she will never ask. She will take her happiness and be content. And you will love her—you did love her."

"I thought so; I didn't know you then."

"Only don't think of that. Will you go?"

"My life can't be more dreary," he said; "why should I hesitate?"

"And it will brighten—believe that. You would never be loved as she loves you; not one woman in a thousand is capable of such devotion."

"A child—an untaught—"

"No, no; she has studied—she is so graceful—so thoroughly lady-like and gentle. Only go and see her. You can make of her what you will. Any man might be proud of her love."

"I wanted yours—forgive me."

"But think if I had loved you—oh, my friend, the misery for both. It would always be the same. No woman worth loving would marry you if you told the truth. If you concealed it, and she found it out after—why then Heaven help all if I were that woman."

"Could you have loved me? I ought not to ask; but see—never again in this world can we talk so—give me a little comfort."

"No, you ought not to ask; I ought not to answer even if I could. Be glad that I have had no time to think; you are going to Ruth."

"Other men and women don't judge like this," he exclaimed. "The whole world would say I had done my part in placing her beyond the reach of want—that any thing more was Quixotic and absurd when I could not even plead love as a cause."

"It is true," she replied. "Possibly some men might sneer if they knew it—some women maybe. Does that alter right? Do these decisions satisfy your conscience? Have you had peace?"

"God knows I have not."

"And never will have except in following the right. I believe the Bible—I am glad and thankful to own that I believe every word—and if the Bible teaches any thing it teaches the doctrine of expiation: we must atone to make repentance availing."

"Oh," he said bitterly, "I know your High Church doctrines. I am not prepared to go to such lengths, unless I become Roman as well as Catholic, and set up for canonization."

"You would be sorry after, if you said harsh things," she replied softly. "I do believe, and it is blessed to be able. I don't mean to preach to you, Mr. Farnsworth, but indeed, I don't know how to urge you except by asking you to seek the Father's help."

"I beg your pardon. I know how poor and weak it all is; I thought I was more of a man."

"And in what you call your weakness you

are nearer true manhood than ever before. I must go now; we shall be missed."

"The last time," he said sadly—"the last time."

"And you will go to her—you will begin the new life."

"If not, I shall never see your face. You need not be afraid."

"You will think it over — you will go Good-bye now; you are a better man than you knew, oh my friend."

He took her hand, held it for an instant in both his, and then hurried away. Elinor Grey sat still for a few moments, leaning back in her seat, pale and exhausted from the excitement and emotion. She closed her eyes, and at length two great tears trembled on the lids and rolled slowly down her cheeks.

"I am glad he is not here to ask me again if I think I could have loved him," she said brokenly; "I am sure now."

Presently she rose and went her way, and came upon Tom, who vowed that he had been searching everywhere for her. "Most of the people are gone," said he, "and Rose and your father are in a fever."

So they went away too, and Clive Farnsworth was not to be found that they might say their farewell, but Mrs. Thornton talked of every thing except that on the way home. She felt certain that a consummation had been reached, but of what nature she could not imagine, and though burning with a desire to know if her wishes had succeeded, she possessed too much tact to give Elinor an inquiring glance.

CHAPTER VIII.

CLIVE FARNSWORTH'S JOURNEY.

For two days nobody in the neighborhood saw any thing of Clive Farnsworth, though every one was talking about the *fête* and pronouncing it a success, ready to lavish a due meed of praise upon him when he should emerge from his modest seclusion. On the third day Clive, marching up and down the stone terrace, saw the Alban Wood carriage pass, and even at that distance through the break in the trees he could distinguish Elinor Grey seated therein. He called at the house, certain of finding nobody, left his regrets at not seeing them, with the news that he had been summoned away from home very suddenly and was then on his way to the train.

Clive Farnsworth had gone.

When the party returned from their drive Rosa picked up the card on the hall-table, and seeing his name exclaimed—"Mr. Farnsworth has been here. Too bad. I wanted to see him. I mean to send and order him back to dinner." She noticed the hasty lines scribbled underneath, read them, and cried out—"Why, he's gone!" and stared at Elinor in wrath and consternation.

"Gone?" echoed Tom. "Where?"

"Goodness knows where—to the moon for his wits, I hope," returned the exasperated Rosa.

"What does he say? Let me read it," said Tom, taking the card from her hand. He read out the brief lines. "What can have called him away so suddenly?" he queried. "It must have been some business about his oil stock."

"Business!" repeated Rosa in high disdain, and glared at Elinor once more, and only by a strong effort kept herself from being rude and telling her lord and master that he was somewhat less than three removes from an idiot.

"He is different from men of his craft in general," remarked Mr. Grey, "if he is in the habit of attending to business punctually."

"Oh, there is a good deal in Clive, if he does write poetry," said Tom, after the sapient fashion in which ordinary people are wont to speak of such a trifle as genius."

Elinor Grey's heart had stood still for a second and then given a great bound of exultation and joy. He had gone to redeem himself—to fulfill her belief in him—and she rejoiced. Tom's voice recalled her to herself.

"What do you say to this, Elinor? Come down to reality, my queen—Clive Farnsworth is gone."

They were all looking at her. She was a little pale, but there was a beautiful smile of triumph on her lips which no one there could have interpreted. "I am less surprised than you," said she, "for I knew that he thought of going."

"Indeed!" returned Rosa sharply. "And pray why didn't you say so instead of letting the news come like a thunder-clap?"

"I thought a surprise would be a pleasant variety," said Elinor.

"Humph!" quoth Rosa.

"We shall miss him greatly," observed Mr. Grey. "He is a charming man—I scarcely know his equal—eh, my daughter Elinor?"

"He is one in a million," she exclaimed with sudden energy. "He is brave and true and noble beyond ordinary comprehension."

"Bravo!" cried Tom, and stood open-mouthed.

"Could she have sent him off?" thought Rosa. "She couldn't speak out like that if she loved him. But what does she mean? Oh, the aggravating thing."

"My daughter Elinor does not praise by halves," said her father, laughing.

"Because I feel strongly," replied she. "I like Mr. Farnsworth—I admire and honor him."

"And I agree with you thoroughly," returned Mr. Grey.

"And you'll drive me mad among you," continued Rosa in thought. "I'd like to shake her till I got at the truth." Then aloud, and with such elaborate acid sweetness—"Tom, dear, unless you are quite stunned and senseless, perhaps you would have the goodness to ring the bell."

"Certainly," said Tom, "but I'm blest if I know what I've done wrong to make you so very polite."

"Done," said she, giving vent slightly to her irritation, "just what men always do—nothing. As for Clive Farnsworth, he's the greatest idiot and the rudest man I ever knew; to dash off in this absurd fashion, nobody knows where, and Elinor standing there, like a Roman what-you-call-it, to sound his trumpet."

She swept away in high state, and scarcely spoke to any body except Mr. Grey for the rest of the morning, during which she was consumed by an inward fever. That night she did appear in Elinor's room as playful and caressing as a pet kitten; she wanted to get at least a conjecture with which to steady her mind. She started "around Robin Hood's barn" with a vengeance, and emerged from under the folds of numberless contemplated dresses to exclaim suddenly, "And why did you send Clive Farnsworth away, my love?" And Elinor left her more perplexed than ever, acute as she was, insomuch that the little woman went to bed in high dudgeon and would not allow the name of the absent to be mentioned in her presence for three whole days.

Clive Farnsworth had gone after that brief delay, which was not of reflection or purpose, for he was incapable of either. Two days of chaotic thought alone in the darkness; the world had reeled quite out of sight and borne Elinor Grey with it. He would go back to the little village where she had found that poor girl in her humble innocence; beyond that he did not attempt to look or plan.

It was still early in the morning when Clive walked toward the brown cottage standing beyond the village, with the maple-trees waving about it and the late summer flowers withering in the neglected yard. He knew that Ruth was not there, still the impulse first to visit that haunt had been stronger than he could resist. The doors were locked, but he gained admittance by a back window, went through the kitchen and passed into the little sitting-room. Old Mrs. Jenkins had left the dwelling in perfect order, and it had not been closed long enough to make it seem dreary and deserted.

Clive flung open the shutters and set the outer door ajar, and the warm sun streamed in over the home-made carpet and lighted the room into cheerfulness. It was so little changed it might have been yesterday that he had sat there and watched Ruth tending her flowers under the windows, or hastening in, her face aglow with happiness at the mere sound of his voice calling her name. There was the comfortable lounge in the corner where he had liked to lie in the luxurious idleness of returning strength; the table near it, just as it had been placed that his books might be within easy reach; yes, even some stray volumes that he had left still lying upon it. The room was homely and simple, and yet possessed a grace of its own from the art with which Ruth had beautified it in numberless little ways.

so that its plainness would have been pleasant to the most fastidious taste. Over the lounge hung a water-color drawing. Clive remembered it at once. It was a sketch he had made of Ruth and bidden her hang there that he might have it to look at when her light duties called her away from his side. He crossed the room and stood before it. The soft eyes beamed down on him with such gladness; the rosy mouth half parted in a smile welcomed him with a host of dimples.

The sweet, beautiful, innocent face—how it wrung his heart. He remembered that the peculiar way in which the hair was dressed had been a caprice of his—twisted in a knot at the back of the head and falling over the left shoulder in soft brown waves, separating here and there into glossy curls. A face which gave no evidence of great strength of intellect, but of a vivid fancy, a love for the beautiful, an appreciable nature which in proper companionship might be taught to admire and sympathize with aspirations that it could not comprehend; and beyond all, the large brown eyes made the chief loveliness of the countenance. Their expression was that which we only find in eyes of that color, a half-beseeching, half-eager look like those of an animal; and a woman with those brown eyes has devotion to the man she loves as the chief attribute of her nature.

There Clive Farnsworth stood and looked at the girlish face while the past came sweeping back and brought before him the minutest detail of that season which had seemed a brief episode in his life and was in reality life's turning-point upon which all after-existence must hinge.

Three years ago—more than three years—for it was in the month of May when Clive Farnsworth first saw that quiet village. He was young still, and his youth had been a passionate, restless one with impulse for a guide. He had been the spoiled favorite of a wealthy uncle, who humored his boyish whims till it was no wonder he grew selfish and ready to believe that his own inclinations were the most important things the world held.

He had a brilliant career at college, and graduated very young; he had published his book of poems and been pronounced a prodigy, and his uncle's pride and exultation in this heir to his name and wealth knew no bounds. Then had followed the tour in Europe, and the elder Farnsworth's companionship had been no restraint. Every error was a youthful indiscretion, and he believed to the fullest extent in the miserable old maxim—*Il faut que jeunesse se passe.* So he stood complacently by to see Clive's youth fulfill itself, and was thoroughly satisfied that his plan was the only good one; having faith in himself because he was a sceptic in regard to most things; pluming himself on the possession of a bold and vigorous mind because he accepted Voltaire's sophistries and dogmatic declarations.

It was fortunate for Clive Farnsworth that his

instincts were delicate and refined. Excess in any form would have disgusted him at once. He loved pleasure as he did champagne, on account of the excitement, but he wanted his cup wreathed with roses, and his ideal and his youthful dreams went with him and kept him from sinking to darker depths. But those years left their effects—it could not have been otherwise; the aimless, purposeless life, in spite of its brilliancy, would of itself have eaten like canker into his soul. They had returned home, and after a winter in town, during which Clive had disgusted himself with a new book, and tried to believe himself in love with a woman not worth it that he might be misanthropic as youth likes to be, he was glad to get away from the whole world for a season.

He started, and a mere chance as he believed it—not having grown wise enough to know that the commonest incident in the commonest life is under guidance—the reading of some descriptive newspaper paragraph, led him into the neighborhood of the Vermont hills. Early in the season as it was, he was charmed, and the fresh keen air was like new hope and strength to his fretted soul. He came to Eastburn, and the still loveliness of the little hamlet so fascinated him after the feverish whirl of the past years that he settled down there in transitory content.

He found a horse which was easily trained into tolerable riding order—a vicious young brute that pleased him by his wickedness, because he was fond of ruling whatever did not like to be subdued—and he splashed about the muddy roads at all hours. Only a few days elapsed before returning one bright sunset from his ride, the vicious colt became frightened at a loaded wagon, and in the first instant managed to dash himself and Clive with such force against it that he broke Clive's arm and completed the thing by stumbling and sending Clive, powerless with the sudden pain, quite over his head. The wagoners stopped and picked up the senseless rider and carried him into old Mrs. Sothern's house, which was close at hand. Clive came to his senses to find himself lying on a bed in a strange room, a gentle hand bathing his forehead, and one of the loveliest faces he had ever beheld gazing anxiously into his own.

That was the beginning.

A physician was sent for, who after a deal of manipulation announced that his shoulder was dislocated and proceeded to set it with such skill as he possessed, and luckily for Clive Farnsworth it was equal to the occasion. But he could not be moved, or he would not be, and had very soon so charmed the old lady's heart that it was agreed he should stay there and be nursed. He was able to use his right hand, and he wrote to his uncle, giving a careless account of his accident, wherewith the old gentleman was forced to content himself, being held fast at home by the leg—that is, he was suffering from a sharp attack of his enemy, the gout, and

there never was a man whose self-indulgent life rendered him a more lawful prey to the insidious tyrant.

Clive trusted too much to his strength, and was very ill for a week from his imprudence. There he lay delirious with pain, and Ruth Sothern watched him morning and night. He talked about all manner of foolish things, as we do in delirium, and very often lay and babbled French or Italian or some other foreign tongue which had grown familiar in his wanderings, and it was just as well that Ruth knew no language but her own, for somehow when he talked English there was nothing unpleasant to be heard. Indeed, the recollection of her face as he saw it when waking from his swoon haunted him most, and he said such wild things, and uttered such rash vows, that poor Ruth grew accustomed to his love-making before he was conscious of putting forth any powers to please. Then followed the delightful weeks of convalescence, and the delicious idyl that drifted into midsummer.

I am not seeking to palliate Clive Farnsworth's sin—it is the one of all others which I hold in the utterest abhorrence—but I will free him from the stain of deliberate wickedness. He was as entirely without thought as herself; then they were so wholly left to themselves; night after night, when he was restless and in pain, she must sit by him and soothe him; read poetry to him; perceive that her hand on his forehead had a magnetic influence which lulled his feverishness; grow accustomed to have his nervous fingers play with her hair. It was not at all strange—God help them both.

It was not long before Clive wakened from his dream; and when summons after summons came, calling him back into the world, he realized his sin and cursed himself and fate. But Ruth Sothern's summer vision only deepened to new richness, till at last the blow fell with cruel suddenness. Clive was obliged to go away. His uncle's health was failing; he prayed him piteously to come back in one breath and in the next threatened, ill as he was, to hunt him up and discover what insanity held him there. Clive could not hesitate longer; he had to go, and here the blackness of his sin began. He did like other men, pitied her, execrated himself—but never once allowed his conscience to be heard when it commanded him to set her right before the world at whatever cost to himself. The bitterest pang was that she believed in him so entirely; his will was so completely her law that his decision was like that of fate. Could he ever forget how her first cry of anguish rang in his ears? "Going away? You can't leave me, Clive, you can't leave me!" And when he showed her the necessity—the humble resignation, the attempt at smiles harder to bear than thrusts from a dagger, the beseeching look in the tearless brown eyes which showed the agony worse than death. For years Clive Farnsworth had been pursued by that picture; countless nights he had wakened from sleep to the echo of that plaintive cry, "You can't leave me, Clive, you can't leave me!" And he had left her, lying to his own soul to the last, for he knew that he could never go back.

In her girlish ignorance the poor creature did not comprehend the fullness of her misery and suffering until he had been gone for weeks. Even then she did not send him word—she could not bring herself to name it—he might come back—she was always waiting.

For nearly a year Clive was closely occupied with his uncle. He made that an excuse to himself. When he knew the worst he silenced conscience by the thought that it was too late, he could not help her now. If he were to marry, her the mere fact of her humble birth and training, all else concealed, would be enough to kill outright the sick man who was so proud of his lineage and blood which had borne honors and titles in the old world beyond the sea. That was his first excuse, and when months passed and that obstacle was removed by the death of his unwise guardian, conscience and remorse were not so strong as his fear of the world.

The world's opinion looked very small just then—expiation might not present itself pleasantly—the new wound might ache and throb—the path might be rocky and sterile—but any thing would be a relief which buried remorse and left him to feel that his soul was no longer cramped in that desolate hell.

The sunlight streamed in at the open windows; the song-sparrows flitted past with joyous trills of melody, and Clive tried to bring his soul out of the darkness and make it see the day. He flung himself in a chair, and leaning his head on his hand sat quiet, not so much lost in thought as resting from the excitement of the past days.

There was a step on the moss-grown threshold; a figure paused an instant in the open door and a pair of eager eyes looked wonderingly into the room. An instant's hesitation only; the wonder changed to an ecstasy of happiness, and before he could turn or look up Ruth Sothern was at his feet, her hands clasping his knees, her voice crying out—"You have come back to me! Clive, Clive, you have come back!"

It was so sudden, so unexpected, that he could not stir, and she called his name again, as a spirit just landed on the Hidden Shore might call some loved one seen standing afar off in the brightness—"Clive! Clive!"

The surprise, the joyful shock had proved too much. She writhed at his feet, still clinging fast to his knees, in a hysterical spasm which was pitiful to witness, sobbing brokenly—"Clive—come back—Clive!"

He had to raise her, to hold her fast in his arms, to address her by endearing names, frightened out of any thought beyond the exigencies of the moment. At length she laid her head down on his bosom, and then came a blessed rush of tears which partially restored her composure.

"Speak to me, Clive," she whispered. "Let me hear your voice—hold me fast—oh, it isn't a dream!"

"Ruth, my little Ruth," he said softly, pityingly; and he knew now that however his solitary vigil might have ended had he been left to fight his demons unaided, the matter was settled. He knew that with the pronouncing of those words he had bound himself irrevocably.

"Say it again," she pleaded. "I am your Ruth—your own little Ruth. Oh, it isn't a dream—make me sure it isn't a dream!"

"My little Ruth, my poor lamb!"

Her face lifted itself imploringly toward his; all that was purest and best in Clive Farnsworth's nature was fully roused as he pressed his lips to hers and gave life back to her in that tender, pitying kiss. "I was afraid it was a dream," she murmured, closing her eyes like a tired child with a smile of ineffable content. "Sometimes I used to see you so plain—to hear your voice—and it was dreadful to wake up in the dark. Oh, my Clive, my Clive!"

I should lie if I attempted to say that Clive Farnsworth did not sit there with death in his heart; but after the first dolorous pang, he put every thought of himself aside and would hear and see only her and her happiness.

"You love me still?" he said. "You love me, Ruth?"

"My heart grew fast to yours—I couldn't tear it away," she answered, flinging her arms convulsively about his neck. "I knew you loved me—I knew you would come back."

No thought beyond—no reproach—no question. He had come—he loved her—it was enough.

"I haven't been here before, Clive; I didn't know why I came to day; I couldn't help it. Are you glad I did, Clive—glad to see me in the old home?"

"Very glad—best here," he answered.

"It was so long to wait; oh, so long! But I knew you would come. I tried to make myself believe I didn't expect you, but I knew you would come."

"Will you forgive me that I waited so long, my Ruth?"

"I'll forgive you any thing when you call me that and look at me so kindly. Oh, the dear eyes—the old look—my Clive! my Clive!"

He held her close to his heart; she wanted no other assurance.

"It doesn't seem long now," she hurried on; "sitting here it seems as if all these years had been a bad dream."

"And you are happy? Say you are happy."

"Happy? Oh, Clive, I haven't any words—I am only afraid I shall die."

If they might both die then and there, perhaps it would be the choicest boon Heaven could grant, Clive thought sadly. But there was no room in her heart for any chill from his reflections to strike; it was too full of happiness.

"Do I look the same, Clive?" she asked.

"Have I faded and grown old? Am I much altered?"

"It might be yesterday we sat here for any change there is in you," he told her, and she was content.

"I don't think I'm quite an ignorant thing, Clive," she said humbly. "I have tried so hard to study, and tried to like it—for your sake—that you wouldn't be ashamed of me when you came back."

It smote his heart more deeply than any reproaches could have done to see the evidences of faith sustained through those years of falsehood and desertion. He could not remember so bitterly then the sacrifice he had brought upon himself, and the world looked further and further away in the presence of her restored bliss.

"You will tell me if you have missed me some time, but I'm tired now, Clive." And she leaned her head back on his shoulder, then raised it quickly to ask—"But did you miss me—did you think of me?"

"There never was a day or night in all these years that I did not think of you and curse myself," he fairly groaned.

"No, no," she pleaded, unable to support the thought of his suffering; "you could not help it. I always told my heart that. We won't talk about it, darling. You are here; I can't think of any thing else. Let me rest, Clive—I'm so tired—just let me rest."

He sat there and held her in his arms, and she lay quietly reposing in the only haven this world had for her, uttering broken words of gladness at times or catching his hands close in hers to be certain that she was not dreaming. She went to sleep at length, nestled upon his breast, and Clive laid her gently down on the lounge and sat watching her. With the features relaxed in slumber he could see how they had changed: she was more lovely perhaps; the face was singularly young, and the mouth had kept its childish smile; but the change was there, the waking and development which trouble and weary expectation must bring. And sitting there Clive Farnsworth realized more and more that there was but one course open to him. He would not think of the future as it concerned his own heart; he could make her happiness complete at least.

She woke very soon, refreshed by her sleep, and smiled up in his face. "You are here," she whispered. "I was half afraid to wake. How good you are to me."

"Don't say that, Ruth; you break my heart."

"But I will say it. How pale you are, Clive. Are you always so now?"

"Time doesn't stand still with any body but you," he replied, trying to speak playfully.

"But you are grander than ever. There's nobody in all the world like my Clive."

He must endure it—these loving words—the caressing way in which her restless fingers twisted themselves about his—the thousand unconscious tokens of tenderness; not only endure, but keep her from feeling the chill at his heart or ever suspecting the bridgeless gulf which lay between their souls.

"To think of my coming here this very day I couldn't think of any thing else since she came Oh, I haven't told you about Miss Grey." She told him then of her visit and her kindness, and Clive listened and answered that he knew the lady.

"You know her? I am glad. She said she would not forget me—that she would come or write."

"And after that you longed to see your old home?" Clive asked, not anxious to pursue that branch of the subject further.

"Yes, indeed. I couldn't bear to think of it standing empty and lonesome. There was no work in the Mills—"

"What?" interrupted Clive.

"Oh, I didn't mean to tell you. Don't be angry, dear. I am so sorry I mentioned that."

"Have you been working, Ruth? Didn't you receive my letters regularly?"

"I couldn't take the money, Clive—don't scold me—I couldn't, dear. And work was good for me—it wasn't hard. See my hands—they are as soft and white as they used to be when you kissed them and said such dear, foolish things about their beauty."

The fair, dimpled hands—Clive kissed them again with a more poignant pang of shame and self-loathing.

"I am glad I did not know it," he said; "I should have gone mad."

"But you are not angry, dear? It wasn't wrong?"

"You are more an angel than a woman, Ruth," he said slowly. "Heaven make me half worthy of your love!"

"Worthy, my King Clive? I always thought of you when I read stories about Marshal Saxe and their brave, handsome men—only I knew they weren't half so handsome or brave."

He let her talk her pretty folly till he saw her begin to look tired again, then he made her lie down. Poor child, it was the first time after all those years that she had not been under the excitement of expectation—night and day waiting; no wonder she was weak and exhausted now that the strain was removed.

Clive had to speak of other things. There must be no delay; he could not trust himself. There was a nobler reason too—he could not lose any time before giving her every right which could atone for his wrong. He asked her if she would go away or be married there in the old house. He tried to speak quietly, dreading the effects of any more agitation upon her, and shrinking from it himself. She began to weep at that question, and it was difficult to calm the over-tried nerves.

"I will stop as soon as I can," she kept saying. "Oh, Clive, I am too happy! I don't deserve it."

Through the pleasant afternoon Clive Farnsworth walked down into the village and found the old pastor, who at first did not remember him, and when he did ventured on no word of reproach or reproval; there was that in Clive's face and voice which taught him this was a matter beyond his attempts at counsel. Ruth had wished it, therefore Mrs. Olds was bidden likewise to come up to the cottage.

The first step toward expiation was taken. Clive Farnsworth stood in that quiet room and pronounced the solemn words which bound him for life to the heart that had so trusted him.

CHAPTER IX.
MRS. HACKETT'S MANIA.

Mrs. HACKETT was seized with a mania, and a mania is a good thing to have, no matter on what subject, when one has leisure; the more ridiculous it is the more amusement one gives one's friends and so becomes a public benefactor.

Certainly in that way Mrs. Hackett had done her duty as became her station ever since she had a station to adorn. To be fashionable was not a mania with her; that was the one grand purpose of her life. She had floated up gradually to her present height. Had she looked back she might have recalled many rebuffs in the early part of her career, when Pluto was beginning to grow rich and she to blossom. How unmercifully she had been snubbed, and how patiently she had toiled under the smarts until the day came when great men awoke to the fact that old Pluto was their leader, and their elegant wives discovered that it would not do to slight Mrs. Pluto, since her husband could work such detriment to their spouses if he saw fit. But to do the Idol justice she bore no malice; indeed she had literally forgotten that she had not always been exhibited upon the dazzling pinnacle on which she now stood, and her faith in herself was really sublime.

It was just when one of the numerous Nicaraguan colonization schemes chanced to be the rage; and she heard a great deal about it, for among his countless plans Pluto was interested in some Central American canal and railway bubble which formed the basis of the other undertaking. Mr. Grey himself had been dazzled by the ship-canal speculation; it did show wonderfully well—on paper; and he talked so much beautiful sentiment about the colonization movement that between his talk, the excitement among business men, and the eagerness of a lot of restless people going about in search of doing good on a grand scale and in a noisy way, the Idol herself became interested and at last took a fine fever. She cared nothing for the railway and canal, she averred—gold was dross—but here was a Paradise opened to the sons of toil, and she meant to drive them all into it whether they would go or not.

I will say for her that she gave liberally, and somebody among the societies in which she interested herself pocketed the funds. But she was not satisfied with ordinary measures; she wanted to immortalize herself. She determined to write a pamphlet for private distribution which should be spread far and wide, read among her own set with admiration, and dazzle the fancies of the poor who were to be aided. It would be a splendid beginning to her winter's campaign. Indeed, the more she thought of it the more probable it seemed her work would bring her such praise that when she returned to town a crowd of distinguished citizens would give her a triumph like that of Cornelia—she meant Corinne; but no matter, it was something Roman—and in default of a Capitol would bear her with loud acclamations to her Murray Hill mansion. She was so much in earnest, too, that before leaving for New York she wanted to send all the laboring people in the county seaward, and be certain that they were on their way to the tropical garden of Eden. She was untiring in her efforts. She talked incessantly about the Land of Promise; she drove from village to village and tried to inflame the working classes; she went boldly into people's houses and waved her flags, and sometimes met with unpleasant rebuffs. The children of toil being free-born American citizens too, and poverty not appalling their energetic natures, she was frequently recommended to mind her own business, and was even told by one virago that "she didn't want no stuck-up Yorker a comin' to put fleas in her boys' heads." "They are so blind," said the Idol when she repeated the story; "but it only gives me new zeal. I have hung out my banners—I shall march to Birnam Wood."

I am afraid that wicked Tom Thornton suggested the idea of the pamphlet: she snatched at it like a Pythoness at an oracle from her god. She was soon hard at work. A young gentleman glad to secure himself comfortable quarters for a few weeks was only too happy to act as her amanuensis. "The double labor is too much for me," she told her listeners. "My thoughts seethe and burn, and often I am forced to pace the floor while I utter the words."

"It's quite like inspiration," said Tom Thornton.

"I assure you it is," replied she in all seriousness. "Actually, I felt yesterday almost nervous; like those people who say they are impelled by the spirits—only I know there can't be any thing in that, for our set has never noticed it, though I believe 'the Emperor was quite interested in Mr. Home."

"Ah, with you it is unaided genius," Tom told her; and she believed it.

She was very busy; for, although the youth managed to be tolerably grammatical in the structure of his sentences, she would have her grand words put in, and she jumbled up Paradise and ancient Rome, the Goddess of Liberty and the old-time nymphs and dryads, and flung them recklessly about in a very sensational manner indeed.

Rosa said the Idol was the only amusement she had now, for every body had grown stupid, except Mr. Grey—and he was always writing letters—and Clive Farnsworth gone off in that absurd fashion and never sending a line.

The Greys were soon to take their departure; they had several visits which must be made, and Elinor wanted to have them over and be settled. She was tired and dreamy and in no mood for playing any body's guest, but the penalty of having too many friends must be paid, besides it was due to her father that she should assist him in every way possible. She was sitting with Mrs. Thornton one morning, listening to her lamentations and plans for the winter, when Tom rushed in waving a letter in the air. "He's done it!" cried he. "I never was so astonished! You'd never guess, either of you."

Elinor comprehended in an instant. It was news from Clive Farnsworth at length—he was married.

"Are you out of your senses?" demanded Rosa. "Tell me this moment what has happened."

"I'll give you three guesses, and a diamond ring to a pen-wiper that you're wrong every time."

"I am not a Yankee," said Rosa. "I dare say you have no news at all. Go off, and don't disturb us when we are quiet."

"All right," said Tom; "good-bye, fairy *Fainéante*." He turned toward the door; Rosa's indifference was gone in an instant.

"Tell me what it is, you wretch!" She sprang toward him and tried to snatch the letter, and Tom dodged about among the chairs and tables and she after him, being very much given, that absurd pair, to every species of improper and inelegant performance when there was no one near who could be shocked. Elinor took that opportunity to grow very cold internally, and very calm and self-possessed in outward appearance. She had quite prepared herself by the time Tom threw himself on a sofa and begged for mercy.

"Then tell me," said Rosa.

"Clive Farnsworth is married!" shouted Tom.

"I don't believe it!" shrieked Rosa. "It's just some stupid story. Who wrote it?"

"He did, and I suppose he ought to know."

"He isn't—he shan't be!" snapped Rosa. "Give me the letter."

"There it is in black and white," said Tom; "read and be convinced, Mrs. Obstinacy."

Rosa looked fairly dazed; took the letter and read it slowly and wonderingly. The epistle was brief and apparently written in haste. He wrote to say that he was married and on his way South. He must snatch leisure to ask his dear friends to remember him and to pardon his reserve—he never had any faculty of telling things about himself.

"I never heard the like," cried Rosa, and flung the letter on the floor and looked over at Elinor.

Miss Grey sat placid.

"Were you ever so astonished, Elinor?" exclaimed Mrs. Thornton.

"Many times," said Elinor.

"Did you know of this?"

"Partially."

"And I thought he was in love with you," said Rosa, divided between wrath and disappointment.

"And a fine romance she wove," added malicious Tom.

"I am sorry it should have been wasted," returned Elinor.

"You are a pair of traitors!" exclaimed Rosa. "I'll never have any faith in human nature again."

"You told me yesterday I was not human," said Tom, "so that doesn't apply to me."

"I tell you now you are a—a—"

"Howling Hooshier," suggested Tom.

"I don't care," said Rosa, "it's too bad."

"Elinor," said Tom, "you ought to be ashamed to thwart my Rosa. What do you mean by such conducts as those, young woman?"

"I beg her pardon," replied Elinor. "The next time she wants me to marry any body she must say so."

"Say so!" repeated Rosa in an annihilating tone.

"It's rude to repeat people's words," said Tom; "I read it in a Guide to Polite Society."

"If I had so much as looked it you'd have hated him at once," pursued Rosa. "Elinor Grey, you'll be an old maid; and that's what you'll come to, with all your mind and your money."

"I am resigned, dear."

"Ugh! Think of having one's maiden name on one's tombstone, followed by 'aged seventy-six,'" shuddered Rosa. "Bless me! marrying Tom was better than that."

"Thank you, love," said Tom.

"I am not your love. I hate the world. I mean to make a Trappist of myself."

"They are all men," suggested Tom.

"You don't think I'd go among them if they were all women, do you?" retorted she.

"But where was he married, and to whom?" asked Tom.

"Not a word does he say," replied Rosa, looking at the letter again. "Not a word! There never was a woman so tormented by the people about her, I do think."

"'Died of curiosity' will be on somebody's tombstone in capital letters," said Tom.

"Not on mine—for Clive Farnsworth," replied she. "He's made a fool of himself, that's one comfort."

"That's good. How do you know, when you never even heard her name?"

"I don't wish to hear it. But I know he has—men always do when they get married."

"My love, I can't be impolite enough to contradict."

"Oh, I'm sick of politeness—this is what comes of it. I mean to go and be a Nicaragua colony or something."

"Elinor," said Tom, "you have a great deal to answer for. If I am at charges for a straight-jacket through your means—"

"She wouldn't care," interrupted Rosa. "See her sit there like a statue. Bah! I am glad I'm not ice."

"Oh, good heavens, so am I," cried Tom, brushing his hair on end so that he looked dreadfully frightened.

Rosa fairly drove him out of the room, and he went off laughing. She came back and sat down opposite Elinor.

"This is your fault," said she. "Now don't deny it."

"You will not let me speak."

"Don't tell fibs. That man loved you—I'd stake my life on it. You sent him off."

"I think not," replied Elinor.

"Now he has gone in a fret and married some dunce," continued Rosa, not heeding her words. "I don't think I ever can forgive you, Elinor Grey."

"Let the verdict be, 'Recommended to mercy,'" said Elinor, finding it very difficult to sit there and jest, but bearing it as women will bear small tortures with a fortitude a Comanche might envy.

"The next time—"

"Ah, the next time don't make plans, you wicked Rose. Do you want to lose me that you are anxious to marry me to the first-comer? Just think. I could not visit you half so freely; why, it would spoil all our enjoyment."

"That's why I wanted you to marry Farnsworth," said Rosa. "Every thing would have been right then."

Elinor did not care to pursue the subject. She was meditating a flight, and wondering what excuse would be sufficient to procure her an hour's solitude without risk of exciting some suspicion in Mrs. Thornton's mind. But Rosa kept talking, and kept leading the conversation back to the theme uppermost in her thoughts, so that Elinor was actually glad when Tom's voice was heard in the hall in animated greeting to Mrs. Hackett.

"The old cat!" gasped Rosa, unable to bear any more. "Tom called her a whale. I wish with all my heart she was in her native element."

"Married!" the Idol was exclaiming as Tom opened the door and disclosed her a statue of astonishment on the threshold—"Mr. Farnsworth married!"

"Now we shall have to listen to her verbiage," muttered Rosa. "That miserable Tom, not even to give one the satisfaction of telling the news one's self."

"Married!" repeated the Idol in a voice like that of Constance before her first incredulous wonder changes to wrath—"married! You strike me dumb. My dear Mrs. Thornton — my charming Miss Grey—how are you both? how

sudden this is! Were you not astonished? Tell me all about it."

"Really, I can only tell you that Mr. Farnsworth is married," said Rosa. "The happy pair have gone South, and after awhile I suppose they will appear."

"I hope Genius has found a fitting mate," said the Idol, seating herself and spreading out her draperies.

"And speaking of genius," said Tom, "how does your work get on?"

"Ah, do not apply the word to my poor efforts," replied the Idol, who began to think herself an author of long standing. "I have been wrapped in my task all the morning, and came here for a little relaxation; the flow of reason's soul invigorates one after mental labor."

"Are you nearly ready for the printer?" Rosa asked.

"Nearly; I am anxious to make the closing pages—the prologue, so to say—impressive."

"I am sure it will be," said Tom.

"You are too kind. But oh, Mrs. Thornton, it is a thankless task to try to show people what is for their good."

"Indeed it is," replied Rosa, giving Elinor a reproachful glance which delighted Tom.

"But what new instance of moral turpitude have you met, Mrs. Hackett?" Tom asked.

"Only yesterday I heard that a young mechanic down in the village—Brainard, I think—I remembered him because he had done various things at the house—"

"I know him," said Tom; "a fine young fellow."

"Well, he is lately married," continued the Idol, "and yesterday I had to drive to the village and I went to see him and show him what an opening the Nicaraguan field would prove to a young couple like them."

"And what did he say?"

"I was quite overwhelmed by his impertinence, though he did not mean it for that. The climate,' said I, 'is paradisaical. Then I sought to bring it down to their comprehension. I said it was so warm that clothing, except of the simplest and most inexpensive sort, was unnecessary."

"And that was an important point, I am sure."

"One would think so, in these times. But the wife, a pert little thing, said that she preferred to stay where people wore clothes, and her husband had read in the newspapers of the way the natives went about."

"And she didn't approve?"

"I was quite shocked, and came away. But we shall succeed; I am sure of that."

"What name do you give your pamphlet, Mrs. Hackett?" asked Elinor, from the necessity of saying something.

"Indeed, I am undecided. Several have occurred to me. I want something alterative and attractive."

Tom's face was a study. "Yes," said he,

there's every thing in a name, Miss Capulet to the contrary notwithstanding."

"Oh, I care nothing for her or Miss Martincan either," said the Idol, supposing him to speak of some literary woman, and being determined to show her ability to quote names too.

Mr. Grey entered at that moment, and when the Idol had finished her elaborate greetings and been charmed into a more perfect state of self-complacency by the diplomatist's honeyed words, Mrs. Thornton said—

"We were speaking of Mrs. Hackett's book."

"The theme of all tongues," returned Mr. Grey.

"You overwhelm me," said the Idol. "And ah, do not dignify it by the appellation of book, Mrs. Thornton; it is only a brief effort."

"At least we may hope that its complete success will induce Mrs. Hackett to pursue her literary labors," said Mr. Grey.

Elinor looked almost reproachfully at her father; in her present mood such talk was more distasteful than usual to her. She hated to think that he was like the rest of the world even in the most trifling matters. But Mr. Grey was wise in his day and generation, and certain actions of his during the past week had made him more than ever interested in the grand canal project, so that he was desirous of attracting attention toward the country in every way possible. If Mrs. Hackett with her money or by making herself ridiculous could serve any purpose in that direction, of course she must be fooled to the top of her bent.

"Who can tell?" the Idol was saying in answer to his remarks; and she looked as if countless poems and scores of romances were seething in her brain.

"At all events we may hope," he said. "Have you found a name yet?"

"I am still undecided," she answered.

"You mentioned several to me the other evening," said Mr. Grey, "which sounded effective and poetical."

"The difficulty is to choose."

"*Embarras de richesses*," said he; and she, half catching the French words, replied hastily—

"Oh, very *embarras* indeed."

Tom Thornton was silently and sweetly choking in the corner.

"I thought of the 'Golden Gate,'" continued she.

"Pretty," said Mr. Grey.

"'A Haven for the Weary.'"

"Beautiful sentiment," said Mr. Grey.

"Ah, I fear you are a sad flatterer," returned the Idol. "You praise all my efforts."

"My dear lady, you must make them less perfect if you wish to be depreciated."

"I am more and more interested every day," said she, "in this grand scheme. Dear Miss Grey, I wonder you are not a little more—what shall I say?—enthusiastic in regard to it."

"I am afraid my philanthropy will not bear so long a journey," said Elinor.

"But the distance makes half its charm," replied Mrs. Hackett. "Every-day plans, to be carried out just about us, look so prosaic; this distance lends a charm like—like a hazy mountain-top in the blue expanse."

She got the metaphor somewhat confused, as she always did, but I wonder if she was not animated by the feeling which governs so many philanthropists?

"It is a wonderful country," said Mr. Grey.

"Yes," added Tom Thornton, "and my opinion is that this grand railway project will prove a grand fiasco."

"My husband has great faith in it," said Mrs. Hackett majestically.

"Oh yes, and of course he is not going to burn his fingers," replied Tom coldly.

"I believe Mr. Grey shares his opinion," continued she.

"At a safe distance," returned Tom.

Mr. Grey did not look uneasy, he was not capable of any such weakness, but he gave a slight push to the conversation. "But what interests Mrs. Hackett," said he, "is the plan for sending out emigrants."

"That is my object, of course; and as Mr. Ritter said in his lecture the other night—the lecture you would not attend, Mr. Thornton—'a more noble enterprise never dilated the human soul or indented the human mind.'"

What the man might have said no mortal could tell, but that was the way she heard it. Tom used to say there must be a twist in her tympanum.

"And so it is," continued she, "and the destiny of the American people must bear them to the furtherest limits of this broad Continent, until they sink into the Southern sea."

"Yours is a thorough Monroe policy, Mrs. Hackett," said Mr. Grey.

"I hold it the only true one," replied she, like an oracle. "I believe it to be as irremediable as the irremovable hills."

Mr. Grey took a pinch of snuff.

The idle talk went on, and Elinor found it more and more difficult to keep her thoughts within listening distance. She felt colder and more tired, as if exhausted by fasting and a long walk in a wintry wind. Other thoughts came up—every thing present slipped far away. She was roused by her father saying gently, "My daughter Elinor!" She came back with a start, perceived that the Idol was uttering poetical farewells to her, and managed to give discreet and coherent answers.

She got out of the room in the departing one's wake and went straight to her chamber, sending her maid off with an intimation that she was busy, for Rosa's benefit, if that restless female should be prompted to follow her. She sat down in the old listless, weary attitude, and the world, life, and all things looked very poor and faded to Elinor Grey.

She tried to be thankful that the girl she had pitied was restored to happiness; she tried to be glad that this man in whom she had believed had redeemed himself—that he was as far removed from the common herd as she had thought him. But her attempts at thankfulness and exultation were miserable failures, and sitting there in her loneliness, Elinor shed some bitter tears. She was not of the order of women who cry so easily that they are ready to baptize every incident with the sacred dew; indeed, weeping was usually a very tumultuous business with her, involving so many dry sobs, and so much expenditure of nervous strength, that she had a dread of the recreation. But she wept easily and quietly now, and after a time she cried the bitterness away and was ready to reproach herself for her ingratitude and selfishness.

Nevertheless the world looked a poor place, and her life seemed more and more empty. Before that she had been healthy enough in mind and body to outgrow the restlessness and the morbid cravings which torment people in early youth, to take existence as it came and enjoy it with a certain zest. Now she began to wonder in a profitless fashion why she was living, and pleasant things were a weariness to her, and people's attentions and kindness only an added bore.

The feeling went with her through her round of visits, but her new fickleness of manner and her caprices only made her more charming, people said. She had been a little too cold and evenly statuesque before; now if she had seasons when she would not talk, or was haughty and imperious, she atoned for them by showing especially witty and brilliant when her mood changed. But the sense of solitude and dreariness remained. It followed her like a shadow to town, where it was now fitting that reasonable people with a proper regard for their duties to society should establish themselves.

CHAPTER X.

AT A BALL.

THE season commenced brilliantly, for it was one of New York's grand speculating eras. Every body was growing rich, or was dazzled by the speedy prospect of so doing, and Murray Hill blazed into splendor in consequence.

Mrs. Hackett had finished her pamphlet, and it had been flung about liberally in all quarters. The favored farmers in the country had a fair opportunity to puzzle their brains with its high-sounding paragraphs; specimens were sent to every newspaper to which the word Nicaragua not having become a horror and a bore would be likely to give the merits of the work due consideration; and countless copies, elegantly bound in crimson silk, were distributed among the Idol's very broad and somewhat eccentric circle.

Every body read it, and every body ridiculed it in private and gave Mrs. Pluto her meed of praise to her face. It was well and safe so to do, because great as Pluto had been for years he was now a more potent Bull than ever Bashan produced. He had only to point his finger at the wildest scheme—it took shape and rolled a new fortune into his coffers. No wonder Society was willing to go down in the dust at the Idol's feet, for it was gold-dust.

She was not precisely greeted with a Roman triumph on her return, but it came very near it, and I have not the least doubt that the Mayor and the whole Corporation would willingly have arrayed themselves in togas, and bound as to their temples with garlands, have gone out to meet her and cast laurels in her path if it had been hinted to them that an ovation of that nature would be acceptable. The Idol rose lightly to her new eminence, believed in her literary fame, and sometimes spoke in the nominative plural when discussing authors.

It would be expected of her under the circumstances, as she was fond of saying, that her entertainments during the winter should be numerous and unique in their magnificence; it would be expected, and she was prepared to do her duty. New furniture for the drawing-rooms had come over from Paris; a wardrobe which in its variety of dresses must have filled Queen Elizabeth's shade with envy if she had been anywhere about; the conservatory enlarged into an absolute flower-garden, and all things in keeping.

The Idol gave the first grand ball of the season, and stood clothed in rainbows, like an overgrown and matronly Iris, smiling and content in the midst of her guests. And there Elinor Grey met Leighton Rossitur, one of that odious order called "the rising men of the day." But Mr. Rossitur was not odious; he was polished and agreeable, with a well-shaped head which was given to plotting, and a nature fiery enough to need all the restraints the head could give. He was poor, and he was ambitious, and his position of under-secretary of something connected with Washington affairs would have poorly supported his claims in the world if it had not been for the perquisites—"pickings and stealings," the servant girls call such things when applied to their class—which of late years are so abundant to the initiated and wise holding any office under our easy-minded Government.

Mr. Grey was already acquainted with him, and the greeting he brought procured him the reception of a friend. Astute Rossitur congratulated him, on the strength of rumors growing into matters of belief among the Washington set, that the coveted Cabinet appointment would soon be offered. The present Minister differed with the President, and it was known from Maine to Georgia, of course. Indeed, one energetic Western newspaper had announced that in the height of a little disturbance in the family the belligerent Secretary had throttled the illustrious Head of the Republic in the presence of the assembled Cabinet. Naturally the English journals caught at that and announced a new instance of Yankee bar-

barity. The House of Congress had been indulging in a Bacchanalian revel and had burned the President in his bed. There was no doubt of the truth of the story, and Britannia groaned over the enormities of her transatlantic cousins, and wondered they could not have remained content under the rule of the sapient George, and so have been an enlarged garden of Eden, like Canada and India and Ireland, even to the present day.

Mr. Grey looked smilingly impassive in return for Rossitur's congratulations, but he gave what would have been a sure sign of pleasure to any body who knew him—he took Mr. Rossitur by the arm and led him through the labyrinth to the place where Elinor was holding her little court, very much bored by her adorers because one of her gloomy moods held her fast.

Elinor's first sensation was that of absolute repugnance as she looked at the pale, aristocratic face, which had no youth in it although it was young still, with lines that might have come either from dissipation or intense thought. Fortunately for Rossitur, his active life made most people ascribe them to the latter cause, and the face was handsome enough to win the generality of feminine opinions in its favor. Elinor Grey looked at him and felt such unreasoning and unreasonable aversion that I believe actually her impulse would have been to turn her back and never look in his face again. But as one can not well indulge in such honest little ebullitions of feeling she did the next best thing, was courteous and scolded herself for her absurd nervousness.

He talked with her, he danced with her, and he did each well. Miss Grey forgot her ridiculous internal shiver, and probably if he had left her after that first dance would have forgotten all about Leighton Rossitur. But he did not—he was at her side many times during the evening, and was sufficiently unlike the jaded men of society to be a relief; an unutterable boon where keeping aloof the Youth of New York was concerned.

For the Youth was there in full force. The Idol was good-natured and really liked young people, so there the Youth was, more marvellous than usual as to its white ties and the parting of its back hair. It danced and it smiled, and the worst thing was, it would try to talk. It always will — oh, why? For the Youth of New York is a genus by itself. Boston has nothing like it; neither London nor Paris ever furnished the model, although it is travelled and is quite foreign in tastes. Nowhere beyond the limits of Manhattan Island has the race been discovered. It is suckled between Harlem and the Battery, fed with the pap of mild learning at Columbia College, and is only seen to full advantage at Saratoga or within the bounds of its native isle. It came about Elinor in a wearisome train. It was slightly afraid of her; but she was a woman to be known, and the Youth would do its duty and

be seen dancing with her, and after it would avenge itself over a broiled oyster at Delmonico's by declaring that she was dreadfully overrated.

Leighton Rossitur gazed at Miss Grey's pale, still face, with the far-off look in her eyes rather too apparent for the occasion, and wondered what subject he could touch that would bring her within reach as they walked up and down between the pauses of a waltz. His fates led him to choose the only one which would have served his purpose; he talked about her father, and Elinor listened. But though the subject proved a success, Mr. Rossitur, as was natural, did not care to sound those praises for any great length of time, and he cast about for something nearer his own interest which should still keep her within reach.

"Do you enjoy this sort of thing?" he asked. "I know that is stupid, but I can't help it."

"I suppose I did once," replied Elinor, and it seemed to her just then as if the time must lie far back.

"I don't know," he said slowly; "yes, I suppose we all did. Ah, now I see the trouble, Miss Grey."

"Do you? Then enlighten me, I beg."

"Your soul doesn't rest in your heels," said he. "Look at that couple yonder. The youth is evidently fulfilling his mission, and the young lady has been dancing ten years to my knowledge—was dancing while you wore bibs—and isn't tired yet."

"Poor thing," said Elinor. "But you need not laugh."

"Not I; on the contrary I am filled with pity for her ill success and admiration of her fortitude. How many years ago the opening season must have been a forlorn hope; and yet she perseveres."

"It is very easy to sneer," replied Elinor; "but if girls are taught that husbands are absolute necessities, what can you expect?"

"That they should gyrate until they get them, if there is no other way, by all means."

He thought Miss Grey's eyes were going off again, and what he had said did not sound so witty as he had expected.

"I think society must have been pleasant in the old days," he continued, "when the French world was most brilliant, for instance. Then flirtation had a purpose; a woman had a political end to gain by every smile or repartee."

"It made a little excitement, certainly," replied Elinor.

"And some women need a purpose," he said. "If you could have come with one to-night you would not be enduring boredom as I am forcing you to now."

Elinor laughed. "Pray go on, said she; "I really believe you will make amends."

"Encouraging, at all events."

"Are you sure yours was not an instance of

'How much we give our thoughts a tone,
And judge of others' feelings by our own?'"

she asked.

"I was dreadfully bored the early part of the evening," he answered; "then you came, and I was interested in watching you."

"Such a pretty little old compliment."

"No, it was a rudeness in fact, considering my thought."

"Then you shall tell it to me. Nobody ever is rude—do be peculiar."

"I will remember your hint when I study a style."

"But tell me what you thought?"

"I looked at you, and—"

"Dear me, was I doing any thing very improper?"

"No, you were dancing and smiling, and being quite decorous in every way; but I looked and thought—'What a pity that lady has left her soul at home. She considered it too precious to bring, and her eyes are looking back after it.'" He stopped, then said quickly, "I do beg your pardon. Was that rude?"

"It was very pretty," said Elinor.

"And it's original. I declare to you I did not read it in a book."

"If I find it in one I shall know the author stole your idea."

"And wasn't it true?" he asked.

"Rather exaggerated, that is all," she replied. "I believe I was absent and preoccupied."

"That is not the word. If you had been preoccupied your eyes would have had a different expression."

"Your skill at reading eyes and faces is appalling. Pray how did I look?"

"As if you wanted something to occupy you, some pleasant, engrossing thought; as if the 'halls of mirth,' as Mrs. Hackett says, looked a little empty and dreary to you." He had come very close to the truth—she began to look at him now. "But I am talking stilted nonsense," said he.

"We must talk nonsense, you know; I don't see that the sort makes much difference."

"But isn't it a pity that— Oh, Miss Grey, here come three men from three different directions; please waltz with me before they can get here."

She let him whirl her away. He was more agreeable than any body else would be; at least he was different.

"They rush so frantically along," said he, looking back, "that I'm afraid there will be a collision. There, now they discover that you have vanished—blank amazement on every face. Oh, see that one with the marvelous tie stare at the ceiling. Can he think you have been transformed into that frescoed damsel?" They waltzed until the pursuers had flitted off in search of other prey, then he advised her to get a breath of air in the great conservatory in which a few people were walking up and down.

"But what did you begin to say when those men appeared?" she asked.

"You are very good to remember that I began to say any thing."

"Which you don't mean, of course; it is the sort of answer all men make."

"I'll tell you why I made it. I was trying to think what I meant to say, or to make up something if I couldn't recollect."

"You said, 'Isn't it a pity that—'"

"And then the invaders stopped me, the Goths."

"But you are to remember what it was; I'll have nothing substituted."

"I know what it was. I was thinking it is a pity one must always talk nonsense with people at first; so often one sees something in a stranger which quite drives the nonsense away, and one wants to speak real, earnest things in reply to what is in the new face."

"Probably the new face would be very much astonished."

"I know you would laugh at me. Admire the sweetness of my nature: I gave you the opportunity after having had time to make up something else."

"And I think it is true, too," said Elinor, "if I did laugh and if it does sound a little—"

"Like Owen Meredith or some one of that school," she added.

"No; not even that. We keep finishing each others' sentences."

"And since you have said 'we,' how can I beg your pardon for being uncivil?"

"You can't; but to punish you I shall not conclude."

"That is because you have forgotten. I saw your eyes going off. Please come back, Miss Grey; it is lonesome."

He said his odd things gracefully, and all the while his face looked pale and earnest, and even when he laughed the faint twin lines between his eyes never disappeared. Elinor looked at him again and discovered the fault in his countenance—his eyes did not laugh. Whether there was something cold and secretive in his character from which her instincts had at first recoiled, or whether it was because his nature really was so deep and serious that this talk was the merest society work rather a bore to do, she could not decide.

"You will tell me sometime," said he quietly.

"What shall I tell you?" she asked, but feeling a little guilty.

"What you were thinking—I know you were making up your mind whether to call me endurable or to hate me outright."

"Which do you prefer?"

"To be hated; there is nothing so odious as indifference."

"I can imagine your having a stronger feeling toward any one who ran counter to your wishes or plans," said she.

"You fancy me a good hater? Do you agree with Dr. Johnson?"

"No," she replied; "and I can think of no greater self-torment than to be hating somebody."

"Nor I," said he. "You see you did me a

little injustice, Miss Grey. I never even bear malice."

"I did not mean to be rude."

"I do not think you were. I ought to have said—'As if Miss Grey could be.' You were very good-natured to form an opinion or to think me worth one. But don't fancy me going about cherishing fell designs toward those who rouse my enmity, and making a modern Corsican of myself."

"I did make an absurd speech," said she; "but you might be generous enough not to laugh."

"I imagine that is the only vengeance I should ever seek under any provocation," he replied. He was very playful and said a number of amusing things, but beneath there was a singular anxiety to remove the impression from her mind, which had been only a passing thought after all. There came an interruption—a new invasion of the Goths—and this time Elinor had to yield.

As they entered the ball-room the Idol in her magnificence bore down upon Leighton Rossitur. "I am doomed," he whispered in Elinor's ear. "Pity me—remember me—'it may be four years and may be eleven,' before we meet again." And indeed, the Idol was an overwhelming sight swooping down upon one devoted man. To say that she looked like a ship under full sail would be trite; a whole fleet would not be a comparison; nothing could apply but some immense noun of multitude. Gorgeous and bedecked, she was reflected in countless mirrors till she seemed no longer one Idol, but the entire collection from Abou Simbel or some other heathen place with more idols and a more unpronounceable name.

"You are not to stand here lamenting our princess," said she, tapping Rossitur's shoulder with her fan in gigantic playfulness. "You are too rare a visitor in town to be allowed to hide your light."

"I am content to watch your shining," said he.

"No compliments," returned she with another sportive dash of the fan.

"No wonder you are weary of them," he replied. "And what an insatiable woman you are! Not content with ruling society, you must needs go and dim the sheen of all our our authors' laurels."

"I never meant to," she returned with sweet humility. "No, no; I leave the bays for broader brows. To benefit my kind was my leading-star—not fame. But come, a score of lovely young ladies want to converse with you; you are growing famous, you know."

"Mrs. Hackett is always surprising one with pleasant news."

"Yes, yes; we shall yet see you classic in the senatorial halls," said she. "What does Byron say?—'A pedestal—a bust—and a worse fame!' How misanthropic he was—glorious soul."

Rossitur was willing to compound for a waltz

with Hecate to escape from the present infliction. He allowed her to lead him whither she would. And he did his duty; watching Elinor Grey afar off, and revolving many things in his busy brain.

Mr. Grey had met the Bull prowling disconsolately for a few moments about the gorgeous halls and looking stolidly miserable and astonished at his own magnificence, as if he felt inclined to bellow. Mr. Grey had swept him off to admire a picture, and had whispered a few questions about certain stocks and schemes, and looked radiant after the Bull had softly lowed a hopeful response.

The night culminated and waned as all such nights do, and after supper Leighton Rossitur found himself near Miss Grey again—found himself there in the most accidental manner possible, as he had been trying to do for the last half-hour.

"What is 'pleasure's twirl?'" he asked.

"I don't know," said Elinor.

"Nor I either; but Mrs. Hackett said it was an 'entrancive thing,' and I think it must be that which has brought me near you again. I had no idea I could find you a second time in this mob. That woman must know ten thousand people at least, and I should think they were all here."

"But she is so kind-hearted that one has not the cruelty to laugh at her vagaries."

And Leighton Rossitur thought—"Now shall I give her an opportunity to lecture me, or shall I do the scorn for people who court wealth and then sneer?" He compromised like a modern statesman. "I do laugh about people," said he, "and am sorry after." And he said it so honestly; and Miss Grey liked people to be honest. They stood talking for a few moments, then Mr. Grey came up.

"I am quite ready, papa," Elinor said; "it is dreadfully late."

"How long do you stay in town, Mr. Rossitur?" Mr. Grey asked.

"Only a week," he answered. "You know I am not a free man; I come and go under orders."

"I know," said Mr. Grey, "that you are taking the right course to be one who gives orders long before you are my age. I like to see a man have an aim and follow it."

"Miss Grey looks approval too," said Rossitur, his lips smiling and his eyes as cold as ever.

"Who would not?" she asked. "Look about at these saltatory disciples."

"They certainly have an aim," said Rossitur.

"And don't let us be severe, my daughter Elinor," added her father. "Perhaps you would do us the favor to dine with us to-morrow, Mr. Rossitur? We have a few friends engaged—let us have the pleasure of adding you to the list."

Mr. Rossitur would be only to happy. So much for saying the right thing in the right place; it had served his turn before.

"We are enduring the weariness of life at a

hotel," said Elinor; "it is a real favor to help us in our desolation."

"What would satisfy you?" he asked.

"I want papa to settle in Washington and take a house: I think I would rather live there than here; I should be quite content then."

So would Mr. Rossitur, and her words sent him off in high spirits. He held his position under the Cabinet appointment certain to be offered Mr. Grey before another fortnight, who in his acceptance of it would not desire to make any changes so late in the Presidential term—at least, not in Rossitur's case. He thought that the confidential relations which would thus be brought about between himself and Mr. Grey would be a satisfactory aid to the pursuance of the daughter's acquaintance. He blessed the obstinacy of the present incumbent and his propensities for recalcitration, and was glad to know that the President had every intention of taking immediate advantage of the new breach which had occurred between him and the pig-headed honorable, the pig-headed having put himself in a position where he must resign his office to give a decent appearance to his going out.

Elinor and her father went in search of the Idol to make their farewells, and she was overpowering in her modest depreciation of what she felt to be one of her grandest efforts. "You are too beneficent, Mr. Grey, to say that you have enjoyed yourself," she gasped in return to his pretty speeches. "But if my poor efforts have succeeded in giving a passing lightness to a mind briefly to be oppressed by new political emoluments—you see I repeat those far-spread bird-whispers—happy am I—too richly rewarded." Then more smooth words from him, and Elinor began to be impatient with the good woman and to reproach herself therefor.

"I have so regretted our dear Thorntons," said the Idol, as she took Elinor's hand.

"Yes, Rosa hoped up to the last moment she should be well enough to come to town, but she wrote me yesterday that her influenza was worse than ever."

"The brightest blossom must have its blight," said the Idol; "this has been mine in my evening of roses."

"But your guests have had no opportunity to think of any thing but the pleasure you gave them," said Mr. Grey.

"Thanks. Your praise is my guerdon," said she, bringing out the word as if it had twenty-four letters at least in it, and putting in an extra vowel according to her wont.

And Elinor on her way home recollected Leighton Rossitur, and took the trouble to ask her father who and what he was. After she was alone in her room she recalled several odd things that he had said—queer, contradictory speeches—in keeping, she thought, with his face, which had no business with that smiling mouth, else was belied by the cold eyes. She remembered too the feeling of repulsion which had come over her when she first looked at him, although while listening to his animated conversation it had passed from her mind. She remembered it and doubted if her impression in regard to him was favorable notwithstanding his pleasant talk. When his hand touched hers in the dance, the light grasp of his gloved fingers had something unconsciously hard and firm in it. "That is the way he would hold to the least whim," she thought. "And he could hate—in spite of all he said. Yes; he was so anxious I should think he could not." Then she forgot him altogether, and sat for a long time by the fire looking down into the glowing embers and thinking how strange it was that she should be so solitary—she whom people courted and envied. She did not allow herself to understand why her thoughts were gloomy, but there she sat and dreamed instead of going to bed like a sensible, practical young woman. To her credit let me add that her maid was never kept up on such occasions. Elinor Grey had her faults, swarms of them, but she was not mean, and she never made a dependent suffer for her caprices or enjoyment.

CHAPTER XI.

AN OVATION.

DURING the week that Leighton Rossitur remained in town he had frequent opportunities of meeting Miss Grey, and he made the best possible use of them toward establishing a basis for an acquaintance which should give him the advantage over other men when she made her appearance in Washington. When she was in his society and listening to his conversation Elinor liked him; but somehow whenever she remembered him in her quiet hours—she had very few just then—the first feeling toward him would come back, and she found it so impossible to analyze, that on their next meeting she was more cordial by way of atonement for the crooked thoughts she had indulged. Leighton Rossitur was—now let me see what he was—at once very artful and rashly impulsive, with hot passions and a clear brain. He never forgot himself and his own interests except when one of his insane fits of temper seized him; at such times he was capable of ruining the dearest plan he had at a blow, and in or out of temper he would have made a bridge of his mother's coffin to cross any gulf which blackened between him and his wishes. He liked to plot and scheme; it was ingrained in his nature; but his manners took their color from his impulsive qualities and were absolutely fascinating. (Forgive my employing that ill-used word of all work.) He wanted political position and he wanted money, and he did not intend that any trifles should stand in his way toward procuring both those desirable aids for carpeting the rugged path of this world. He could love—burn and pant; but in the height of his fever he could have wrenched his heart away from its idol if it had been to serve his ambition. He would have known that he must suffer, and suffer bitterly perhaps, but he would have known too in the first moment that the pain would pass and that if he allowed his heart to stand in the light of his reason he should curse himself after, whereas the heart would find a new aim.

He met Miss Grey at somebody's dinner-table the night before he left town, and had the good fortune to be seated next her. "I had quite made up my mind that you would not come," he said, when he had an opportunity to speak with her.

"Why so?" Elinor asked. "People don't usually accept invitations and stay away."

"No; but it is my last evening in town, so I was prepared for a disappointment."

"If you were prepared, no great harm could have come of it."

"I was trying to put the matter in a decorous way. But I should have been so disappointed—I may say that, mayn't I?"

"Certainly you may, and I shall believe as much as seems good to me."

"Ah, you had better believe the whole. It's so nice to believe. Nobody does believe any thing nowadays, and it is pleasant to believe things."

"Do you expect me to believe that you are in the habit of going through the world with unlimited faith in every thing you meet?"

"I suppose you will not, and yet I have a great deal of faith. I know it is antiquated, and one ought to be ashamed of not being *blasé* and misanthropical, but I can't help it."

"If you are in earnest you are to be praised for not adopting the modern creed."

"And I am in earnest. I suppose I get laughed at, but as I don't know it, what matter?"

"And if you did, what matter?"

"Still less. I am afraid my self-esteem overbalances my vanity. I am not afraid of the world's laugh."

Fear of this world had been one of Clive Farnsworth's chief weaknesses; that thought came into Elinor's mind and at its heels another—why should he be in her mind at all?

"Do you think I am wrong?" Rossitur asked.

"I think you right," she replied. "You have touched the chief of my pet insanities."

"I am glad. Now I shall care less than ever."

"When you are certain that the world and not your judgment is in fault."

"That of course." He talked quite eloquently; it sounded to Elinor fairly like an echo of her own thoughts, and she liked him better. It was very pretty and he was very sure of his ground. He had overheard Miss Grey express some opinion upon the subject a few nights before, and knew where he stood. "I don't want to go away to-morrow," said he suddenly.

"Do you find town so much pleasanter than Washington?"

"But you see Washington doesn't hold Miss Grey."

"Unfortunate capital!"

"It is all very well to laugh. Still, I am glad to go back to my work; nature or habit make me more content when I am busy."

"And you are ambitious too."

"I don't deny it. I don't believe you blame me for that."

"I can't pay you personal compliments, but imagine me offering a tribute to ambitious men in general."

"Among whom you would be if you had been a man; as it is, yours is all reserved for your father."

"The pleasantest sort, I am sure, and one of the advantages my sex has."

"The very pleasantest. Sometimes it is dreary work being ambitious for one's self with nobody to share the feeling."

"It would be unless the motive were stronger than the desire for personal distinction."

"Yes, I know what you mean—one needs to remember it too. Then sometimes the work is hard, and one forgets both the aim and liking—and looks about at other men enjoying ease and luxury."

"Would they content you?"

"I hope you believe they would not. But it is very nice to be rich," he continued, laughing. "Now you know I am not, and to a certain extent money is power. I don't set up for a Diogenes—I am rather fond of luxuries, and wouldn't be a Spartan if I could help it." She liked him for such frankness; she looked at him and thought, if he was really as open and honest as his conversation sounded, how much she had wronged him in her judgments. "Some men sell themselves under such circumstances," said he.

"To a party or an heiress," replied Elinor. "I do not know which is the meaner."

"Really, I have often wondered—one wonders about all sorts of things. There's that Miss Jones we met last night—they say she wants to change the family escutcheon—which was a saddle—for a good old name."

"You see Miss Jones has an ambition."

"Yes, but if I were she I'd take my saddle and ride out in search of a better aim."

"Then you don't approve of the buying and selling?"

"It is just disgusting;" and he began to laugh.

"At what?" asked Elinor.

"Why, I quite forgot you were an heiress; but being a Grey on one side and a Courtenay on the other, a reputation for a beauty and a wit, I don't see in what direction you are to ride."

"Wait till Cuba and Mexico have each an Emperor," returned she, entering into the jest, fearful that he was troubling himself lest his idle speech about heiresses might not have been civil.

"That will do," said he; "and I shall be

President and flutter the Monroe policy in your imperial faces when you come over."

"I shall bring in the plea of being an American citizen."

"Oh, you would be sure to outwit me in some way."

"Being a woman," said she.

Of course this talk had been in fragments, wide apart, but it is easier to set it all down together. The ladies were leaving the table now, and Leighton Rossiter did not get near Elinor again till the party was about breaking up. "I shall not marry Miss Jones," said he.

"Has she asked you?"

"No—not exactly; she has spoken to me twice."

"What did she say?"

"Once she asked me if I didn't adore Verdi —that was when I was introduced."

"And you assented."

"No, I hate Verdi. His screaming operas ruin the voices of half the women."

"What did she say next?"

"She said she adored blonde whiskers like Colonel Audley's—that Englishman—and as I only wear a mustache and it's almost black—"

"It was not encouraging."

"But you know every man thinks Venus de Medici would come off her pedestal and marry him if he asked her."

"Most men," replied Elinor; "but I do not fancy that those who think so talk like you." And he saw that he was leaving exactly the impression he had desired —an agreeable consciousness to carry away.

"Now I must say good-bye," said he. "Think of it!—I start by the early train."

"Hadn't you better wait and ask Miss Jones to reconsider the subject of blonde whiskers?"

"I would in a moment—if I loved her. But you see I like sensations; and I've never been in love yet. Miss Jones's money wouldn't stop me—some men it would. That is just as cowardly and mean as marrying for it." He had touched the right chord — Miss Grey's own creed. "And you will come to Washington?"

"Probably."

"Oh, it is certain; they need your father and must have him. I am glad, glad." He said it boyishly. How young and frank the mouth looked with its smiles; his eyes were cast down so that they sent no shadow over his face, and the narrow lines between them strengthened and ennobled the whole expression. He took his leave, and when the next night came with its ball, Elinor looked about among the men and fairly regretted him. There were enough of them agreeable and cultivated, but it was the old, old model slightly altered to suit individual characteristics, and Leighton Rossitur had been in every way different. On the whole, Elinor went through her duties in a rather fatigued manner, and I am afraid disappointed people very frequently. Many a man of the world looked at her pale face, with its lines of force and its capabilities of passion, and realized that she could feel, and hated her because he knew that he had no power to rouse the slightest stir in her fancy. As for the Youth—indeed, I don't believe it approved of Miss Grey, although it pranced about her a little, just to tell that it had pranced in her neighborhood. On the whole it preferred Miss Jones, who adored Verdi and went into ecstacies about blonde beards, and did not take its little breath away by glances of indifference or forgetfulness.

The Thorntons came to town and established themselves for the winter, and it was understood that if Elinor and her father removed to Washington, the conjugal doves were to make them a visit. "And we are charming to have as guests for a little while," said Rosa. "One mustn't have too much of us—we are like preserved peaches or Indian pickles."

"I am the peaches," added Tom, "and she is pickles—of the most exasperating sort." The Doves were as happy and full of spirits as ever, and pecking at each other constantly in a playful way which would have been dangerous for most matrimonial birds to attempt, but which answered perfectly in their case. They were at the Clarendon, too, so the old intimacy was pleasantly resumed.

One morning the Idol descended upon Elinor and Rosa as they were promising themselves a quiet day. Mrs. Hackett loomed larger and more important than ever; the Colonization movement was going on at a rapid gallop, and the directors assured her that her literary labors had done much to bring about that desirable state of affairs. There were numerous dolefully good people engaged in the work now; any number of restless women whose homes did not offer a sufficiently broad scope for their talents; the men connected with the railway scheme were favorable; and Mrs. Hackett had done what in her lay to make the undertaking fashionable, which would give it the certain stamp of success. That morning there was to be a grand convocation of the directors, and persons interested in the matter were desired to be present. Unfortunately for the meeting, as far as Fashion was concerned, it was to be held in some impossible locality, to consult the convenience of "energetic sons of toil," the notice said, who might wish to present themselves and perhaps be excited into putting their names down upon the list of emigrants. The Idol had promised to be present by way of representing the Goddess of Fashion, and had been rendered complaisant in regard to the unhallowed quarter by a private hint that a small tribute of admiration and gratitude would be offered her in the guise of certain extra ceremonies which might read well in the next day's Herald. She had checked her chariot wheels at the hotel for the purpose of inducing Rosa and Elinor to go with her, and as Tom consented to accompany them they went, Rosa to see the fun and Elinor because she was really glad to oblige Mrs.

Hackett, in regard to whom she could not help having qualms of conscience.

There the directors were on the platform—fat, sleek men; lank, long-haired men; men with their hair brushed straight back from their foreheads and with beaming, philanthropic expressions for the world in general, as if they felt their smiles to be sunshine and would do their duty in diffusing them for poor human nature's benefit. There were several women of the strong-minded order seated on prominent benches, looking very severe and manly, and a group of flowing-tressed males hovering about them, as flowing-tressed men always do hover about females with virtuously short locks and a mission for setting the universe to rights. There were the eager women who craved work in the Lord's vineyard—in prominent places; there were sensation preachers who looked much better there than in their pulpits; here and there a keen business man who had leanings toward the railway scheme; and then the ordinary flock of mortals. Not a large one, however. It was humiliating, but after all the efforts the audience was sparse. A few "hard-handed sons of toil" congregated near the doors and looked wonderingly about. Sundry of the order of *gamin* had sacrilegiously intruded, and were making audible remarks expressive of their desire to learn what species the row of strong-minded women belonged to, in spite of the vigilance of the attendant policemen who thumped the smallest boys unmercifully and looked as majestic as Trojan veterans; and a band of Sunday-school children had been procured for the occasion. The eager women always rushing about the Vineyard are never at a loss to produce a set of the most precocious little hypocrites. As the Goddess of Fashion entered the directors met her in a body and led her to a high place in the synagogue, while Tom and the two ladies followed, feeling they had not quite understood where they were to be brought. At the same moment the Sunday-school children struck up a melody composed for the occasion, which began with—"I long for Nicaragua," sung to the refreshing air familiar in such establishments, "I want to be an angel." They sang loud and clear, and at a signal from their leader the troop filed past the seat on which the Idol sat enthroned and pointed spectral fingers at her, chanting—

"And she'll lead us there, and she'll lead us there!"

Elinor and Rosa were ensconced behind the Idol, and to their great joy quite concealed from observation. The children filed back to their places. The applause was deafening and the Idol wept tears of delight. One of the directors made a speech in which he called her a variety of names, beginning with Helen of Troy and ending with Miss Nightingale, and the strong-minded women commenced to shake their heads and mutter among themselves—a good thing might be overdone.

There was not much business transacted be-

yond proving that the society needed money, and Mrs. Hackett headed the contribution-list with a sum which made the eyes of the sleek men water. Suddenly one of the strong-minded women bounded to her feet. "I should like to observe a remark," said she, and was frowned down by the women of the Vineyard, and one of the lank men said that the business would be transacted solely by the directors, although they were glad to have all friends present. The row of strong-minded women groaned in concert, rose from their seats, and in solemn majesty paced down the hall. At the door they paused. The leader—a gaunt, bony woman accustomed to public speaking, the head and front of Womens' Rights battlers, to whom the darkest isms were transparent as moonshine—elevated her spectacled nose and exclaimed in a thin, sharp voice which seemed to belong to somebody else, "We retire! We came here thinking to be illumined by the light of the far-visioned Present; we find ourselves in the gloom of the Past, and hear the rattling of the chains which bound our foremothers. We will none of them! We renounce you—you and your pitiful scheme which will disappear like a bubble of Lethe—you with your slavish worshiping of vulgar wealth and imbecile fashion—with your antiquated prayers and mummeries which offend Nature!" The troop groaned in concert and swept out, followed meekly by the long-tressed men, leaving a general confusion which could not be quieted for some moments. When order was restored one of the chairmen requested such sturdy sons of toil as might be present and desired information to come forward, or if any wished to put their names down among the adventurous band who were about to seek a broader life in golden lands—here he bowed to the Idol in token that he quoted from her pamphlet, and she, forgetful of dignity in her agitation, nodded her head in return like a Chinese mandarin strung on wires—why now an opportunity offered. The women of the Vineyard drew near the directors' table—they would at length have a little occupation to busy their restlessness; the regular meeting was over—they could talk and ask questions.

Near Elinor was seated a little fat, puffy woman in rusty black, who had been making notes with a stumpy lead-pencil on soiled slips of paper, stopping occasionally to refresh herself with bonbons from a flat reticule on her arm, and at intervals emitting from an inquisitive nose which looked as if afflicted with a cold of long standing a series of short sniffs that grew alarmingly loud and frequent when she was pleased or dissatisfied with what was going on. Against the end of the bench leaned a green umbrella which she guarded with a watchful eye and never forgot in her busiest moments. If any body near so much as stirred, out went one dust-colored hand and grasped the umbrella as though she thought hostile designs were entertained toward it by the whole world. If any person got in her way she made a weapon of it and poked the offender in the back with its point, and when not occupied with her notes she clasped her hands about it and leaned her chin on the crooked handle, easily surveying the throng from that resting-place. Indeed the umbrella was so evidently always uppermost in her mind, so much a part of herself, that at length an observer came to feel a certain interest in it too, as if it had been a fat baby in a faded green dress or a familiar spirit shut up in whalebone stays. It was a rakish, dissipated-looking old chap as far as its garment was concerned; it was puffy and ill-shaped as if from overfeeding, with the air of an umbrella accustomed to late hours and unwholesome atmospheres. But the crooked handle, which looked like a beak, had a sternly-virtuous, sanctimonious air, and seemed to regard with suspicion the entire universe, with a certain self-complacent expression added which completed the charm. Nobody could watch the dumpy woman and her associate long without forming any quantity of odd speculations in regard to it; in other society the monster might have been only an umbrella, but in her companionship it became a marvel and a mystery, and one felt that she would not have been half the woman she was without its presence.

Tom had pointed her out to Rosa, and now the short woman shoved nearer him along the bench, after the fashion of boys at school. "Got a penknife?" demanded she, in a wheezy whisper. "I've worn the point off my pencil."

Tom politely offered to sharpen it for her.

"Just give me the knife," said she; "I shan't steal it. I always like to do things for myself."

"A very praiseworthy spirit," said Tom.

She sniffed in high disdain, and muttered something about men in general, not complimentary to the race. "You see I'm taking notes," said she, leaning coolly over Tom and addressing Elinor and Mrs. Thornton in the same wheezy whisper, which could be heard further than one of Rachel's. "I suppose you think it's odd for a woman—I write for the daily papers and I have to make a report of this meeting. How those women did act!" and she sniffed violently. "It made me ashamed. I'm not strong-minded myself—I'm a Presbyterian."

There was no necessity for any body to speak; indeed, she gave no opportunity if any one had felt inclined. "That's a beautiful bonnet of yours," said she to Mrs. Thornton. "I've a great love of pretty things—I am fashion editor for one of the papers."

"She looks it," whispered Tom.

She wore a plaid cloak over her black dress, a red scarf about her neck, and she had on a green bonnet with yellow in it. "That's Mrs. Hackett, isn't it?" said she, pointing to the august lady.

"Yes," said Tom.

"I'm going to speak to her. I want to tell her I'll see she has a proper notice. Here, you know her, don't you? Just give her a nudge and say I want to tell her something."

Tom complied at once, and the Idol turned about, still complacent from the effects of the triumph.

"How do you do?" said the stumpy woman—she looked like one of her own fat pencils, squinting horribly and sniffing with renewed energy—"How do you do? I'm Mrs. Piffit—I write for the papers—I came here to take notes. I just wanted to say I'd see you were properly noticed."

The Idol glared, divided between wrath, horror, and a wish to be properly noticed in the papers. The stumpy woman was quite regardless whatever she did; she wet the end of her pencil in her mouth and fell to work at her slips of paper, sniffing and blowing desperately. In the mean time the chairman had repeated his invitation to the sons of toil without effect; not a man walked up the aisle.

"What's the matter?" asked Mrs. Piffit, suddenly becoming conscious of the stillness, and speaking quite aloud to the assembly in general. "Won't they come? Of course they won't! Ugh! Men — nasty, dirty brutes! Hmf! hmf!" She sniffed as if she smelled something very unpleasant, and dashed at her notes again to make up her lost time.

"You are very industrious, madam," said Tom.

"Am I?" she snapped. "Why don't you go to Nicaragua?" She turned to Rosa and added—"Is he your husband? I don't like men! As I was coming down in the car a nasty brute set his foot right through my dress skirt—look at that!" She pulled up the article unhesitatingly, displaying several petticoats of different lengths and marvellous colors. "That's what men are!" said she; let her skirt fall, sniffed twice, and set to work again.

Now the chairman's voice rose anew, bland and persuasive: "Let no one hesitate to come forward," said he; "it binds them to nothing."

"Let them come for information," said one of the Vineyard women.

"That's Mrs. Stoles," said the stumpy lady, not pausing in her task, and still speaking aloud. "She's always talking, and never says any thing—that's the worst thing about women. She's a Unitarian too; and what do they believe? Hmf! hmf!" And the Vineyard woman heard her and shook with impotent rage, but was silent.

"Will any one come?" asked the chairman.

"He! he!" tittered Mrs. Piffit, and her laugh was as remarkable as her sniff—sharp and cutting. "Men, you see, men — nasty, dirty things! My dress is ruined—hmf! hmf!"

But this last appeal proved more successful; in response to a loud voice which might have belonged to either sex exclaimed from the door, "I'm just goin' up mysel'. Stand out of the way, Patsey McGuire. Come along, me darlint, follow your moder; shure, we're in the land of liberty and the flag of the free."

Up the aisle marched an immense red-haired Hibernian, dragging a child in each hand, two more clinging to her skirts, and a larger girl following with the youngest bud of the hopeful family in her arms. The boys had on old men's hats, and one had trowsers and no shirt, and the whole group were a picture of misery and destitution. One of the little girls kept losing her shoe, which was much too large for her, and impeded the family progress by hunting for it between their legs at unexpected moments. "Be quiet, Biddy," said the matron. "Shure, we're goin' up to see the land o' goold along wid their worships and their leddyships. And just look at the grand leddy"—and she pointed out the Idol—"wid her feathers like a paycock—it's a duchess she'd be this minute av she had her jew—and oh, Phalim, my darlint, av ye ax her sweetly for a dime I know she'll give ye a dollar. I see it in her smile, Phalim."

She was near the table before the bewildered policemen had decided whether she was a fit subject for emigration or arrest, and there she stood before the astonished directors, courtesying low and talking volubly. "And how do yer honors do?" said she. "I've come wid me little family to see the land o' goold. Hand me the baby, Kathleen. He's a fine boy, yer honors, on'y eight weeks old, and I'm a lone widdy woman, av ye'll plaze to consider. Phalim, ye spalpeen, why don't ye ax the leddy for a dime and git a dollar as I towld ye."

"My good woman," said the chairman, "we don't want to send out females unless they have husbands to till the ground or follow mechanical pursuits."

"Purshuits, is it? I'm ready for any. Ye said ye wanted populators—"

"Cultivators," interrupted Mrs. Stoles.

"Cultivators or populators, it's all wan, me leddy, and I'm ayther quite convenient, me leddy."

The crowd about the doors began to laugh, and the woman exclaimed angrily, "Don't stand gaupsy, ye bla'guards! Patsey McGuire, spake up like a man."

And Patsey, a shambling, knock-kneed Irishman, stepped into the aisle, and rubbing his shock of hair between mirth and confusion, called out, "Shure, yer honor, Biddy O'Nale is as dacent a woman as ye'd find, barrin' she likes a drop now and then—"

"Hould your tongue, Patsey," interrupted she; "ye needn't to mintion that. Shure, every body has their little weaknesses, as their worships and their leddyships knows."

"Go and sit down!" thundered the chairman, enraged at the ridiculous turn affairs had taken.

"I jist stepped up wid me little family, yer honor, to see the land o' goold, and I'm a lone widdy woman and this is my youngest on'y—"

"Go and sit down, I say!" he repeated. "If you don't, I'll give you in charge of the officers."

"It's a purty free country that won't take a lone widdy woman when she wants to go," howled the woman, suddenly changing her smiles into a most virago-like aspect. "Och, down wid the aigle—it's a dirrty birrd any way! Here, Kathleen, yez take the baby!" She threw the squalling innocent at his sister and looked ready to attack the eagle or take the chairman as his substitute.

"She's drunk," Mrs. Piffit's voice remarked, aloud as usual. "Nasty, dirty thing—hmf! hmf!"

"Drunk, is it?" cried Biddy. "Who called me that? Och, was it you, ye little woman whom I won't mintion perticlar, in a plaid cloak and yaller flowers, that's allays prowlin' about the newspaper offices, wid never a penny fur—"

"Policeman, take that woman out!" cried the chairman.

"Why, I wonder if she could mean me?" said Piffit meditatively, and sniffed very much.

So Biddy O'Niel was carried shrieking and fighting down the aisle, and her brood followed, a mournful chorus with melancholy howls.

It was difficult after that interruption to conclude the meeting with proper dignity and effect. "It's a failure," said the stumpy woman, rolling up her notes, stuffing them in her reticule, and menacing Tom with her worn pencil —"a failure. I expected it. Tell Mrs. Hackett I'll see she's properly noticed."

Elinor and Rosa began to be very anxious to beat a retreat, but it was some time before the Idol could be released from the eager throng of directors. Mrs. Piffit kept her station close to the party, and suddenly astonished Rosa by opening her reticule and taking from it a bit of chocolate which she held toward her between her dirty thumb and finger. "Have one?" said she. "I get 'em fresh because the people want notices." Mrs. Thornton declined the proffered refreshment with a coldness which affected Piffit no more than it did the wooden pillar against which she leaned.

"It was beautiful," the Idol was saying; "so impressive. Hope on, gentlemen — we shall succeed. I see the golden light shine from the Elysian fields."

"She talks a good deal of poetry," said Piffit, sniffing. "I have to write it for the newspapers, so I never do. Where's my umbrella? Oh, it's under my arm."

They got the Idol away at last and departed; but as they stood on the steps of the building, waiting for the carriage to drive up, out rushed stumpy Mrs. Piffit dragging the chairman of the meeting with her. "Now do it quick," said she, shaking him and sniffling till her bonnet fell off and hung to her neck by the strings.

"Mrs. Hackett," said the confused man, "let me present Mrs. Piffit—one of our illustrious literary ladies—"

"Written lots of biographies for the newspapers," interjaculated the stumpy woman.

"Mrs. Piffit is a correspondent of several of our journals—"

"Yes, now you know me," said Piffit. "How do you do, Mrs. Hackett? I spoke to you before, but of course I didn't call your name—not being introduced it wouldn't have been proper."

"Mrs. Piffit wished to say—"

"Yes, yes, I'll tell her," said the stumpy woman, nipping him in the bud again. "I'll see that you are properly noticed. Very remarkable your pamphlet was—next one I'll help you if you want me to. I write every thing—plays, religious memoirs, translations, any thing. I'll notice your friends if they'll just give their names." She made a dive at her reticule to get out her pencil and notes, but the carriage drove up and Mrs. Hackett, for once left quite speechless, was glad to allow Tom to hand her down the steps. "Three—oh, there's four of you," called Mrs. Piffit; "if there hadn't been I'd have just asked you to leave me at the office, Mrs. Hackett; but I suppose there's no room outside for that gentleman. Always in the way—men! I'll remember the notice."

The carriage drove off, and the last they saw of Mrs. Piffit she was arranging her bonnet with one hand and holding fast to the director with the other, while the worthy man stood a picture of abject and hopeless misery, mechanically clasping the green umbrella which she had placed in his arms that she might have greater freedom in shaking him.

CHAPTER XII.

IN THE SHADOW.

CLIVE FARNSWORTH took his wife South. She was weak and suffering now that she had time to rest. He took her away from every thing connected with the gloom of the past years, and strove to bring the color back to her cheeks and the light to her eyes.

I should employ a word feeble and inadequate if I said that Ruth was happy. If one believed the Romish doctrine of purgatory, and could imagine a soul, purified by its pains, suddenly removed from the darkness into the light of the higher shore, I think it would be the fittest comparison. During the first days there was almost the fear of dying of her own happiness; but that passed. She leaned upon him and rested in the full sunlight, and her heart throbbed with new freedom and her beauty developed to its prime. She had not a thought, not a suspicion, as a woman of another type might have had. Clive loved her—he had claimed her at last—he was all her own. She worshiped him; his will was her law, his slightest wish her delight. She lay on his breast and prattled like a happy child reposing after a day's pleasure, with hosts of lovely fancies and dainty ways to keep her from appearing puerile and tiresome.

Clive Farnsworth went through the varied forms of agony which must have beset a man of passionate impulse and vivid imagination. Sometimes, instead of the self-loathing, he thought that God had dealt more harshly with him than he did with other men. The new faith taking root in his soul would lose its strength, and he fought in the darkness against fierce doubts or yielded passively to impious whisperings which seemed like the audible promptings of the Devil himself. Through the wearisome round of changeful feeling and back again—oh, the dreary circle! And all the while the days went on and the bright Southern sun mocked him with its splendor, and Ruth clung fast to his hand and leaned her head upon his shoulder. But delicate and sensitive though she was, no chill smote her heart. She was so entirely happy there was not room for a doubt to come near. He had claimed her the moment he was permitted; his love had been like hers. Besides, he was so tender of her. Here it was that the real strength and goodness of the man's soul showed itself and made him a hero, at least in my eyes. He not only schooled his face, but the very pulsations of his heart, lest she should be disturbed. When faith deserted him, and he was in the darkness with his demons, he clung unwaveringly to that one resolve and acted upon it.

The days went by rich with Southern beauty. They wandered about in a quaint old Florida city; they drifted over the bay when the sunset slept gorgeous upon the waters; they explored wild haunts and gloomy lagoons where the dank luxuriance of foliage made an oppressive splendor—always together—and to Ruth each day appeared more perfect than its predecessors. She loved beauty, she was quick to comprehend and sympathize with his artistic tastes, so that the hours spent in those rambles were the most endurable Clive found. Among other lessons he must learn to live in the present moment, and his whole life long he had been a wild dreamer, wandering in ideal regions, so that the task was much more difficult than it would have been for another man.

"I could stay here forever," Ruth said one day when some business letter which had followed him reminded Clive that sooner or later they must go back to the world. "I had forgotten that we must go away some time—hadn't you, Clive?"

"I had indeed, my little one. I just live in each hour as it goes by, and never think of the one that is to follow."

"Because we are so happy, so content. O Clive, do you believe other people have such happiness?"

He smiled down at her, but had no need to speak.

"No other woman ever had, at least," continued Ruth—"for she had no Clive."

"But she had her Clive, little one."

"It's not the same at all. There's only one real Clive—and he's mine. The rest are make-believes. Oh the poor women!"

"My foolish Ruth."

"But you like it—you are glad to know it!"

"I like you to tell me you are happy—over

and over again. You can never say it often enough, my little one."

"And I think I say it and sing it all day long. O Clive, do you think I improve?" Her words had made her remember her lessons. Clive had chanced upon a good professor of music, and was having her natural talent for the accomplishment made serviceable.

"Indeed I do; you will sing the things I like—sweet old ballads—and your voice is like one of your native wood-thrushes."

"And you'll write songs for me to sing?"

"I'll coin my heart in bits to give you a moment's happiness!" he exclaimed passionately. It sounded like the cry of love, born out of his pity and his remorse that he had only pity and tenderness to give.

"I must study so many things too," she went on; "I'll try not to be stupid. I wish I wasn't a lazy little thing. You will teach me, Clive?"

"Whatever I can, little one."

"I'd like to know every thing you do, darling. I shall want to be able to understand those great old Greek books you used to be so fond of; but I know it's no use; I haven't any application. But I'll try to learn little things. I'm not very awkward and savage, am I, dear?"

"Look in the glass, you foolish child."

"Yes, I know; I am handsome now, but that's because your beautiful eyes shine on me —the dear, good eyes!" And she had to spring up from the footstool where she nestled at his feet and kiss the beloved eyes, over which the white lids shut with a dull, heavy pain. Then she was back in her favorite attitude— her head resting on his knee, so that she could look in his face. "I want to learn—I'll try very hard. Where shall we live, Clive? I haven't had time to think. It seemed, till you spoke about that letter, as if we should dream on here forever."

If they only might—if he need never take up life again. But he knew that could not be. He must work too; real, earnest employment would be a greater help and safeguard than any thing else.

"Where would you like to live, Ruth?" he asked. "Would you wish to go away over the ocean into Italy or Spain?"

"It would be very lovely, but I am so afraid of the sea. Only I'll go anywhere you please, Clive."

In certain ways a plan like that might be more agreeable than existence elsewhere, but Clive felt that it would be in a measure shirking his duty—he must be a dreamer no longer.

"I think, Ruth, we will go and live at my old country place," he said, turning resolutely from the impulse which came over him.

"I should like that best of all," she replied.

"And you must encourage me to work, Ruth, and not think, as some women do, that it comes between us."

"I never will; I'll try not to be foolish. You will talk to me. If I can't follow all your beautiful dreams, I should like to think I know

them and feel their power, though I may not understand."

"It shall be arranged for your happiness, little one."

"You are so good. Don't let me grow selfish. O Clive, what will I do when I am mistress of your fine house? I'm such a shy thing. Why, I shall not know how to be waited on. You know I have done things for myself all my life."

"You will be very quiet and not think about it."

"Well, one thing—promise me one thing."

"Yes, in advance."

"Don't make me have a maid as they do in the novels. I should be so afraid of her. I'll wear what you tell me, I'll try to be dignified, but I know the lady's maid would kill me outright."

"Then we will dispense with her and avert the danger," he replied with a smile.

"Oh dear, I hadn't thought. And people will visit us and invite us; and oh, I shall have to sit at the dinner-table. Now I am beginning to be afraid."

Would people visit them? There was a question. Clive Farnsworth knew, if one whisper crept hissing among his friends, exactly what must follow. He turned from the thought with an inward shudder. He would do the best he could; that possibility must be left alone.

"How will I get through it?" Ruth was saying. "Why, I don't know any thing. I never went to an opera, and in books people talk so fine."

"My little one, you need not be afraid; people are not so wonderful after all. Be perfectly natural. You are graceful and pretty; you talk better than half the women. There's nothing to be afraid of."

"Just think though, Clive. I shouldn't know the names of the things on the table. Oh dear, I'm afraid I shall be horrid. You see, may be I'm not awkward, and I have read stories enough not to be quite a dunce; but there are such lots of little matters—I declare, it frightens me to think."

It was very weak and contemptible to share her fear, and yet he did; and though the troubles of which she spoke might be very trivial, they could have stings.

She was graceful as a bird, and with her woman's quickness she learned readily, but of course in her humble life she could not help being ignorant of many things, absolutely nothing in themselves, and yet matters of importance since we are accustomed to remark that a man is ungentlemanly if he is ignorant of them, just as we would if he were rude or coarse. It seems contemptible; but when Ruth at first occasionally forgot and put her knife to her pretty mouth instead of her fork, it did annoy Clive as much as if she had done something absolutely wrong; and it would any of us. Small, miserable as such fancies of which that is an example may be, they will disturb those accustomed to what we call the habits of the world if noticed in any person connected with us, and there is no good in denying the fact. But Clive had patience and she was very quick. She was fortunate in having for teacher a gentleman at heart instead of polished manners without that accompaniment.

"And you think I need not be afraid? I shan't make you ashamed, dear?" Ruth asked.

"I can't have you afraid, my child; don't even think about such petty matters. Be yourself, your real, lovely, lovable little self, and you will do exactly as you ought."

"If you tell me so I shall believe it," she replied. "I won't think at all, only—"

"Only what, Ruth?"

She turned her face shyly away, and he could see the blush roses deepen in her cheeks.

"Only that you love me, Clive. I shall not be afraid then."

"That is the wisest conclusion of any," he replied; "the very wisest, my little one."

She sheltered herself closer to him, her nervous hands playing with a ring on one of his fingers, and closed her eyes to feel her still happiness to the utmost. Clive Farnsworth meanwhile sat looking through the open window out on the beautiful bay which billowed softly in the sunshine, dotted with sails that shone golden in the distance, as if they had been the pinions of fairy barks wafting favored voyagers away from the dullness of earth; sat there and looked out over the bright waters until some movement Ruth made brought him back from mournful thoughts, and he remembered that he had already been giving way to the old habit of dreaming, against which scarcely an hour before he had cautioned himself.

"It is a lovely day," Ruth said.

"Too lovely to waste in the house. Get ready, and we'll go out in the boat; there's just a pleasant breeze."

That was one of their favorite amusements. Clive had procured a sail-boat on their arrival, and as he managed it well, they enjoyed the trips without danger of some romantic incident such as being run down by a schooner or drowned in a sudden gale.

"I can not believe it is December," Ruth said, as she sat on her pile of cushions in the boat, which was scudding merrily before the light wind.

"December?" echoed Clive. "It is not possible."

"Yes; I have been counting."

He did not know the time had gone so rapidly. Had he gained any more courage? he asked inwardly. But Ruth was unconscious of his self-questionings, and went on with her own thoughts. "You are as much surprised as I was. We have been so happy and so quiet, that is the reason. Will the days always be so bright, Clive?"

"My little one, when you know that everybody must have some cloudy seasons!"

"I don't believe they will come near us," she answered confidently. "Any way, I should not be afraid—I have you."

"And they shall not come near if I can guard you," he replied. But he was very tired that morning, very tired—in a mood when her pretty words and her sweet evidences of affection made him impatient, and self-reproach following, caused him to be more gentle and guarded than ever. He allowed the boat to float toward a shady cove in a sweep of the bay, furled the sail, and they drifted into the retreat where the great trees clad with vines and long floating moss made a sort of bower. In the distance the city shone in the light, but about them the stillness was unbroken save by the lapping of the water against the white beach, the rustling of the vines, or the peculiar, sharp shiver of the great bunches of mistletoe which hung with their pearly berries on each decaying trunk.

"This place looks more lovely every time we come," said Ruth; "I think the fairies must have made it just for us."

"And it will disappear when I carry their queen away," replied he.

"But we will come back some time, Clive?"

"Oh yes, and find the bower prettier than ever." He drew the boat up on the sand, lifted her out, arranged her cushions at the foot of a great oak and placed her on them, throwing a crimson shawl down as a carpet to her feet.

"You pet me so," she said, with her eyes a little moist. "I believe you think I must not touch the ground even."

"Not if I can keep you in the clouds, my child."

She made a pretty picture seated on her soft throne, with the bright draperies at her feet, the tree branches waving overhead, and her countenance radiant with happiness. It was hard for him to look and feel its beauty with his cultivated tastes, and feel too his heart aching under; his thoughts in spite of himself going away to another face which might have watched him as that sweet girl did, might have been the recipient of as many tender cares with a delight in the giving, only that by his own act in the past he had ruined the future. But he would not think. It was not wicked only—it was weak. Here his wife was; here his thoughts should centre; and he came resolutely back.

They had brought books and a basket of luncheon, as they often did on such excursions, which even at that season were enjoyable in the climate of our new world's Italy. Clive would not think, he could not talk just then, so he took up one of the tiny blue and gold volumes from the basket. "Shall I read to you, Ruth?"

"Of course. Is it Tennyson?"

"If you like."

"Yes; read 'The Lord of Burleigh,'" said she. It was one of her favorites; in her glad humility she liked to trace a resemblance between herself and the lowly maiden so well beloved by the lord of high degree. Clive sat by her and read the pretty romance of which she never wearied. "It is like you and me," she said—"our history—only it must not end the same."

"Heaven forbid, little one."

"No, no; you must not kill me with your gifts and my new splendor. After all, Clive, he was not like you."

"Lord Burleigh?"

"Yes. You would not have let her die; you would have shown her your wealth was only an evidence of your love; if she could live under the happiness of that, the weight of grandeur needn't have killed her."

He looked earnestly at her; child-though she was in many things, her intuitions were so true, her fancies so poetic. Oh, he must be more than ever watchful lest some perception of the truth should thrust her beyond her childishness and leave her stranded on the bleak rocks, a desolate woman.

The talk wandered a little, but he led it back to books; it was a rest to him. He had brought Shelley, whom she scarcely knew yet, and he told her the story of his life, with its errors and its searchings after light, and about the woman who loved him so and had such genius too; and then stopped suddenly, because he remembered the other woman—the poor abandoned first wife—whose memory casts the darkest shadow upon this poet's records. When Clive saw the tears in her eyes he remembered how the dew had softened his when he first stood beside that grave, years back, as he was passing out of his wayward boyhood. How far away that time looked! what gulfs lay between! Oh, if he had died then and been buried under the grand arch of the Roman sky, how much sin and misery he would have been spared.

Ruth's voice dispelled his reflections. "I like you to tell me such things," she said; "your way is so much prettier than that of the biographers and all those people. Nobody talks like Clive. I never shall forget how you told me that story of Hawthorne—all those years of waiting—and the beautiful light which came at last." Ay, there was patience—there was a life of waiting! Oh, the grand soul! One is glad to think, though the fame came at length, that he went away from its fullness to a broader existence than his nature could have found here. "But I like to hear your own poetry best," said Ruth, "and you won't read it to me."

"My little one—that rubbish."

"It is not rubbish," said Ruth indignantly; "it is beautiful. I want you to write more."

"I lost my verse-making ability a great while ago," he answered.

"But you will write. I know your last book by heart. O Clive, I looked to see if—if—"

"What, dear?"

"There was any trace of me in it. But it sounded sad, and it was bitter. Poor Clive, you were unhappy when you wrote it. Now you must write another. I shall be so proud; you will read me bits here and there as you write."

Clive Farnsworth remembered the last time he had read an unfinished work to a woman; it was his tragedy which he read to Elinor Grey, feeling thus he read it to a mind equal in powers with his own, able to appreciate, and whose suggestions were precious — the poor, unfinished tragedy which had been put carefully out of sight and would never be completed now. Yet he must write or plunge into politics—occupation of some sort he must have, and that soon. This season of absolute quiet had been necessary, but it must not be indulged too long, or it would unfit him in its turn for actual duties.

They spent several hours in their retreat, then took to the boat again and drifted homeward through the late afternoon. While Ruth went obediently and diligently to her music, the actual labor of which she hated, Clive picked up the newspaper that had been brought during their absence, and began listlessly to read. Among other items he came upon one which gave him a start. It was a notice that the Cabinet appointment had been offered the Honorable Mr. Grey, and it was certain that he had accepted it and was soon to take up his residence in Washington, accompanied by his daughter, whose triumphs in the fashionable world were as well known as her father's in another field; and so on through long paragraphs of disgusting fulsomeness. You know what a thrill the sight of a name will sometimes give one. Clive's hand shook till the newspaper fairly rattled. Separated by the width of a world from that woman and never to come any nearer in this life — the old sorrowful truth that we write poetry about and read in novels and laugh over and sneer at, as we do at so many things sacred to our hearts, but retaining its truth still, always interesting, always new, and shall be while human hearts beat. Clive Farnsworth threw down the paper and leaned on the window-sill, gazing into the twilight. He was thinking of Launcelot as he leaned over the casement, "sick of love and life and all things." Not that there was any similitude in his fate to that of the false knight, but the measures of the poem were yet ringing in his ears and ringing themselves up with his reflections, as such things do in the minds of people who read romances and dream dreams, until sometimes the records are like a new pain added to the actual sorrow.

CHAPTER XIII.

COMING HOME.

It was almost spring before they reached New York, and Clive had no inclination to make a long stay there. During the last weeks in Florida he had begun to write; the feverish necessity had full possession of him once more, and he was glad to feel the old power and quickness of thought return, because before that he had been haunted by the idea that he should never be able to write a line, never have a plot or an idea for the simplest story or poem again; and nobody but one accustomed to literary exertion can imagine what a desolate sensation that is or what a weight of peevish discontent it brings. The Thorntons had gone to Washington, and Clive was not sorry; he wanted time still before he saw any one sufficiently intimate to expect revelations. They passed a few quiet days, but when they were about ready to leave, Mrs. Hackett saw Clive one morning as he passed through Union Square, down which she was dashing in her carriage, and having unfashionably long sight, notwithstanding the eye-glass which hung to her chatelaine, she stopped her equipage and began beckoning to him in a frantic way.

At first she could only exclaim and roll out immense words of astonishment. "I had not heard of your arrival," she said.

"We are only here for a day or two," he answered, "on our way to my place."

"Oh yes—we—happy poet. Accept my tribute of orange flowers, late as it is," she cried ecstatically, making a movement as if to fling a flowery spray upon his forehead, but it was only a glove she had forgotten was in her hand, which landed on Clive's hat. "Wedded bliss," she went on, taking the glove from him with beautiful unconsciousness; "how sweet thou art. You surprised us all so, naughty poet; you Apolloites love mystery."

"But I did not mean to make one, I assure you."

"I must see her—take me to her. What is she like? A muse, a Clytie? And I thought it would be Miss Grey! May I call to see her? She worships you, of course."

"She is a very dear, sweet child," said Clive, "who knows nothing about the world—"

"A wood nymph—a Neraid!" cried she, plunging the wood nymph into the water without mercy. "Beautiful simplicity. Ah, if we need not be so artificial! I shall doat on her."

"You are very kind," said Clive; "but you must let me congratulate you. I have heard of your success."

"Thanks, thanks; a trifle. You know I seek not Corinnian laurels—only to serve my humble meed. But the world is ungrateful. No matter—speak no more." She was so very tragic that Clive wanted to get away, and pleaded an engagement. She told him that as she came back from Stewart's she should call on his wife. "The world's silken fetters bind us," said she, "and even you and I must leave our Gregorian dreams when—"

"Shopping is concerned," said he.

"Cruel poet, to speak so frail a word! But —val! val! I have been wandering with the classic poets since we parted. Oh, sweet age of Augusta, if we were but there! I only dream of Pope's Æneid now, so val! val!" She drove on, and after some thought Clive discovered that she meant to be Latin and say vale. In some of her researches among lexicons the Idol had picked up the word, and immediately fancied herself a proficient in the stately language.

Clive postponed his business and hurried to the hotel to prepare Ruth for the visit, and laughed more than was good-natured about the Idol, in his wish to allay his little wife's nervous agitation and put her at her ease. Presently the Idol appeared; the moment she caught sight of Ruth she swooped down upon her and embraced her. "My joy is mute," she cried; "I am a swanless voice"—getting very much astray in her excitement—"I greet you—I greet you, beautiful bride of our Columbia's nightingale—val! val!" Clive had her settled in a chair at last, and Ruth forgot her nervousness in her wonder and a vague fear that this was some mad woman instead of the expected guest.

"She is seraphic!" gushed the Idol, in an audible aside to Clive; "she is Raphaelitic! Oh, for a word to canonize her loveliness! She is the nine muses personated—a real emulation of genius."

They had to sit still and let her talk, and for a quarter of an hour she mingled praises of Ruth, admiration of Clive, Virgil and Venus, her own triumphs and fragments of news, in a way which was as incomprehensible to one of her listeners as if she had talked Sanscrit. "But duty calls," she said at length; "I must obey—merciless as the trumpet which summoned Hamlet. Will you dine with me to-morrow? Grant me that boon out of the joyousness of connubiality."

"Unfortunately we are obliged to leave town to-morrow," Clive said; "our arrangements are made and we must go, sorry as I am to decline your invitation."

"The loss is mine. Alas, it is a painted cup from which we drink! And to-day I dine out—at Count de Sariettés. I court not foreign dignitaries—I am a true Columbiad, as you know—but duty, duty!"

"Always your watch-word, I remember," said Clive.

"It is a chime of silver bells with which I clasp life's burthens! Dear lady, we shall meet soon. That cruel poet must not keep you concealed to waste a violet."

Ruth looked as dazed as if she had been under a shower-bath, but managed to say that she hoped to meet Mrs. Hackett again.

"Yes, yes, in sylvan shades, away from the glare of men. Oh, I know the poet's Forest of Ardent."

Ruth looked so utterly helpless that Clive thought what a pity it was Rosa Thornton could not be there.

"But why leave the giddy twirl of town's vain delights, my poet?" demanded the Idol.

"I want to work," he answered, "and I never can here."

She clasped her hands in ecstasy. "I would not detain you; take my good wishes for a guerdion;" and she flung an imaginary something at him. "I rejoice. I speed your flight, although it leaves us in darkness! How you will cull gems from flowery fields, and golden ore from the dark mines of your new happiness! Go, Apollo, you have your Cynthia with you."

She rose to take her leave, and after overwhelming Ruth with another embrace, prepared to sail out under a closing period of great impressiveness—"Toil, my poet; gasp, sigh, beat about in the furnace of genius and bring out the bays! You have your muse beside you—happy pair! I shall dream of you and pine for you in the midst of Fashion's hollow temple—oh, val, val!" She swept from the room and would not allow Clive to accompany her down stairs, feeling that she could not equal that burst of eloquence, and unwilling to dim its shine by ordinary conversation.

"She isn't mad, is she, Clive?" Ruth asked in a whisper which completed the scene, and made Clive laugh more heartily than he had thought would ever be possible again.

"She is one of the people you were to be afraid of," said he.

"O Clive, every body can't be like her!"

"No, dear; I think she stands alone. But you need not fear the others any more."

"If they all talk as fast as she does I shall never have to say any thing, that is one comfort," continued Ruth. "But, Clive, there must be some people like those in books."

"I am a little afraid you will have difficulty in finding your ideals clothed in flesh and blood."

"But there are, Clive. Miss Grey—she might be a queen, and she is so gentle. O Clive, my heart warms when I think of her." Clive did not turn away or fidget with his books or give a grand start like a hero in a novel; he sat quiet as we do in real life under such stabs and answered in appropriate phrases. "I should like to see her again. I wonder if she knows we are married?" pursued Ruth.

"Undoubtedly."

"I can't remember if she said she was acquainted with you. Clive, she was like a beautiful white angel coming to me that day."

"My little one, you are on forbidden ground. Don't think of that time."

"Only to be thankful; I must be thankful, Clive."

He was silent then.

"I wish she knew how happy I am," said Ruth thoughtfully; "she would be glad. Clive, might I—do you think it would be wrong if I wrote to tell her—"

"Wrote to Miss Grey?"

"Yes; would it be wrong? I should like her to know how grateful I was for her visit—to tell her how happy you make me—might I, Clive?"

She went up to him and put her arm about his neck; it seemed to him that he should suffocate. He had never experienced a feeling so horrible in all his suffering from her loving ways. Holding him fast, she, standing there in the place which should have been that peerless woman's! It was horrible agony, and after

the first blindness Clive recognized that it was a more horrible sin. He could not move—could not take her arm away—he must not yield even in thought to that wickedness. In that instant he grasped at the only help which offers in a need like that—the help which we sneer at in our modern philosophy—the Almighty Father's. Let me tell you, if you ever stand in a similar crisis, modern philosophy is as weak a stay as the old forms of infidelity; if you have any hope of passing the danger, it is in putting away the cold, abstract idea of a Great First Cause and calling on Him who loves us and died for us; and if you say that sounds like a Methodistical tract, why I can only say, God aid you when such need of him arrives. Clive Farnsworth did call; his soul fairly shrieked in its agony, and was heard. He learned then that Nature is not God; that Humanitarianism is the wretchedest lie ever palmed off on human souls eager to grasp at delusions; that there was no strength in his boasted intellect and will to support him; that it was something extraneous and yet within him; his and yet not of him; the blessed help of the Crucified.

"Shall I write to her, Clive?"

It seemed to him that he had been a world away and was brought back by the sound of Ruth's voice. "If you like, dear; yes, by all means."

He had some business which called him out, and he was glad to be in the fresh air; he felt sick and weak from that tempest. He had never before realized that there could be such black possibilities to his nature. He had been brought to the pass where he could understand how men are led on to murder, to the fiercest and lowest crimes; and it is a terrible hour to any soul when some turn in life sets it face to face with such knowledge. The next day they left town. It was not a long journey; the greater part of it beside the beautiful Hudson, which charmed Ruth even in its wintry desolation. At length they took a cross-road and were soon at the village station which Clive had left months before smitten by such trouble. He had dreaded this return—dreaded the drive along the familiar road—the places he had last seen with Elinor Grey—the arrival home—the burden and the pain. He thought about it during the journey—he was prepared to be very wretched—and nothing happened as he expected, which is usually the case in this world. There had been some mistake and the carriage was not at the station, nor was there one to be seen, the village in the winter being so dull that hack-drivers retreated with their equipages to parts unknown. The forenoon had been warm and bright, and with the inconsistency peculiar to our climate the mercury had without warning dropped as many degrees below zero as the length of the thermometer would permit it to go. When they entered the waiting-room there was scarcely a glimmer of fire in the diabolical close stove, and Ruth looked half frozen in spite of her wraps. There was nobody to send in pursuit of a stray carriage, for Clive had no servant with him; the usual loungers were not visible, and the long, shambling, unsteady-kneed station-keeper had few suggestions to offer, and those few of the vaguest sort: "There's Jameses livery-stable open in the village—if he haint tuk his cattle over to Newburg. I heerd he was a talkin' that way."

"At least try and make your fire burn so the lady won't freeze," said Clive wrathfully, "while I go and see."

"Yaas, coal is poor stuff anyhow. I often says—"

"Sit down, Ruth, and keep your furs well about you," said Clive, not noticing the man, who opened the stove-door and finished his sentence to the interior, hitting the black lumps aimless thrusts with the poker, which wedged them closer together and rendered a blaze more hopeless than ever.

"Are you an idiot?" cried Clive, exploding at last, and snatching the poker out of his hands, uncertain whether to attack him or the fire.

"I'm not cold, Clive," said Ruth; "don't mind me."

The man had retreated at Clive's energy, but now his dim eyes made out who the impatient gentleman was. However, before giving sign of recognition he must wave the national flag a little and make the eagle scream by asserting his rights as an American citizen, free-born, and one of the rulers of the land. "We don't want no British lordin' doin's round us," said he, with a twang which only a son of Massachusetts could have accomplished, "and this is the land of the free, 'n we hez fires ur we hezn't jest as—"

"Look here," interrupted Clive, "you stop your impertinence or you shall not keep your place twelve hours."

Massachusetts dropped the star-spangled banner and allowed the eagle to soar away, and stood the meekest of men. Then he began to do surprise, recollecting that Farnsworth was quite able to make his threat good, and remembering how lavishly he flung current coin about during his sojourns in the neighborhood. "Ef it ain't Square Farnsworth!" cried he, opening his mouth very wide and apparently divided between astonishment and pleasure. "Deary me! I want tu know! I never knowed you—what with your bein' so wrapped up, and yer musty-touch longer'n ever. Deary me! But the minit ye got mad I knowed the grit. Why, how du ye dew, Square?"

Clive was ready to laugh at his own absurdity, so he answered civilly that he was well.

"I want tu know! Ben tu furrin' parts, and that's yer wife? Deary me! Wasn't suspectin' of ye afore summer. I didn't mean no harm o' course; I like to be perlite. I'll fix the fire. That ere scape-goat of a nephy of mine ort to be here, but he's never arcound 'cept when he ain't wanted. Can't I run and git a carriage myself? Set down, Square; draw up, mum; be tu hum. Glad to see you back, mum, though mebby's it's your fust visit—"

"Go and find a carriage, my good fellow," interrupted Clive. "Never mind the fire; we are in a hurry."

Massachusetts buttoned up his coat and departed, and once at a safe distance he unbottled his wrath. "Why, yeou overbearin', outrageous, artisocratical cuss!" he exclaimed. "I guess I'm good as yeou be any day, yeou furrin-haired, ornary critter! But never mind! I'll hev a leetle of it cout on ye. I'll take yeour money anyhow."

He had scarcely departed before the lean boy who had often encountered Clive after bringing the message in the preceding summer, made his appearance, stretching his mouth in a grin of satisfaction at the sight of Farnsworth, then suddenly puckering it into shape for a whistle of surprise, which he with difficulty repressed, on seeing Ruth. He flew at the fire and attacked it vigorously, muttering uncomplimentary remarks about old Josh and his laziness, glancing at Clive over his shoulder, very anxious to be recognized and addressed. Clive remembered him, and thought he looked more lean and forsaken than ever, and spoke to him so kindly that the boy was in a state of ecstasy which he expressed by thumping the bars of the stove-grate with vigor. He was much pleased with Ruth's appearance, and when she smiled upon him and said something kind about his pains with the fire, he mentally vowed allegiance to her on the spot—from which he never faltered—and immediately informed her that "he wasn't a bad hand at fixin' flower-beds if she liked to muss among 'em, and he knowed where lots of wild flowers growed." He was so extraordinarily upon his good behavior that his uncle would hardly have recognized him, or if he had would have considered his conduct only an additional proof of the utter depravity of his nature, having the habit of charitably taking for granted that any show of improvement in the lad was a cloak assumed to cover some design of unusual darkness and guilt.

By the time the fire began to display signs of vitality a carriage drove up and Massachusetts opened the door of the waiting-room. "Here we be, Square, all right! Lovely day—a leetle cold, mebby. This way, mum, this way—wife, I s'pose, Square? Yes, he'arn yeou was married—yes."

His graceless nephew got close to him and whispered audibly, "I say, the fool-ketcher's round this mornin'; you better look out or he'll be after you."

"The wust boy that ever growed up as I may say under the droppin's of the sanctuary," said Massachusetts, in his prayer-meeting whine. "Don't notice him, mum; he's a sore affliction tew me and tew his aunt. He makes a pair of Jobses of us indeed."

"A precious bad job you be," muttered Tad.

Clive thrust some money into the man's hand and led Ruth on toward the carriage, regardless of his exclamations — "'Taint no matter. I ain't one as duz fur money—"

"Oh, my eye!" cut in Tad.

' "Glad tew see yeou, back, Square," he continued, darting a vengeful look at his nephew. "Like tew see the real supporters of the country a rallyin' reound."

"O, Lord!" said Tad.

"Yeou wicked, onnat'ral, pervicious young varmint!" exclaimed the uncle. "Yeou're past bearin' with."

"Go it," said Tad; "cuss in your turn—it's swearin' when I do it, but its religion with you —call me a devil, do."

' "Drive on," shouted Clive, anxious to get beyond the sound of their voices; and the carriage rattled away, leaving the pair to pursue their interchange of compliments at their leisure.

Clive was so fretted by the delay and the worry and the man's insolence and the fear that Ruth was perishing with cold, although she assured him she was not, that he was carried over the familiar road without remembering to look out and be thrilled by old sights. The carriage turned in at the gates and they dashed up the avenue where the leafless maples sighed and moaned in the wind, and Ruth, silent and breathless, gazed at her new home which seemed so stately and grand. Long before the Revolution the dwelling had been built by one of Clive's ancestors, and it had been remodelled and added to according to the caprice of after-possessors, although with sufficient taste and judgment to leave it a very imposing mansion; and most wonderful of all in this land of change, was the fact that a lineal descendant of the original proprietor claimed it still.

"Home at last. Welcome home," said Clive as he lifted her from the carriage. The noise of the wheels had brought the housekeeper and half a dozen servants to the door, and in the bustle of their apologies and his desire to deposit Ruth close to a good fire, Farnsworth's actual arrival passed without any strong emotion whatever.

CHAPTER XIV.

ELINOR'S WINTER.

ELINOR GREY found a temporary relief from the loneliness and weariness which had taken the zest out of her life in the interest of arranging their new home and settling every detail so that it might be in keeping with her father's fastidious tastes. They had leased a commodious house which was fortunately vacated at that time by some foreign diplomat recalled to his land of guttural voices, and as it was partially furnished the task of getting comfortably established was not unpleasant. Only Elinor did wonder that any woman could have borne life while obliged to walk over such carpets as displayed their huge patterns in the drawing-rooms, and shuddered as any blonde would have done over the yellow gorgeousness which had been Madame's boudoir. But the great furniture boxes which had accompanied them over the sea were brought on and unpacked, and the dwelling was soon sufficiently complete and luxurious to satisfy even Mr. Grey, whose requirements in that line were not slight. That done, Elinor sat down and let the world revolve about her as it was very happy to do, and tried not to feel the tired, desolate sensation creeping slowly back, and the dull, dissatisfied ache troubling her heart. She took her fancies sorely to task for their folly; she repeatedly told herself that there was no reason in such complaints, that she was ungrateful and stupid; and did her best to please her father by making their home the centre of all that was bright and agreeable; but it was hard work notwithstanding.

"It must be because I am growing old," said Elinor; "it must be that," and she convinced herself for the moment that she had found the real cause, and looked upon her age as something immense, with girlhood wholly faded out of sight. Certainly there was nothing fresh or exhilarating in the round of Cabinet dinners, where the elderly fellows paid her lengthy compliments and their wives looked stately as became their station; the receptions at the houses of the foreign dignitaries, where mustached murderers of English made loud lamentations because duty had cast them on America's savage shore; and outside the rush and whir of the native set gathered from the four quarters of the land, always noisy, always rushing after something new, but at least possessing the virtue of good nature. Yes, it was tiresome, but it must be borne, and Elinor was sensible enough to bear it gracefully.

Leighton Rossitur placed himself among the chief in her circle, possessing the advantage of previous acquaintance, and the greater one of being an unusually agreeable man, and knowing how to make the best use of the facilities offered by his connection with her father.

Elinor speedily disgusted an Englishman with a handle to his name and a pair of very long whiskers, an impediment in the way of pronouncing the letter r, and a general resemblance to Lord Dundreary in dress and manner, who had been attracted by her appearance and was condescending enough to feel something within his dilapidated bosom which he called his "hawt" quite upset by her, "yaas, by Jove!"

"My daughter Elinor" had seen lords and baronets enough to lose the republican craving after every thing that owns a title; and finding unmitigated and unadulterated Dundreary conducive to boredom, she rather ignored his magnanimous intentions in her behalf. It was some time before he could admit such an idea: he thought it must be Yankee shyness, or he tried to think that, wondering all the while that any woman not a daughter of Albion could be so smilingly frozen; then he pulled his whiskers and stood in petrified astonishment as the truth forced itself upon him.

E

"She must be mad, you know," he remarked in confidential intercourse with a brother islander connected with the legation; "quite mad. It's something incomprehensible, by Jove! They wouldn't believe it at home—aw—now weally. What would Lady Mary say?" And his compatriot, a jolly young fellow, delightful in many ways as a well-born, well-bred young Englishman thoroughly healthy in mind and body can be, told the whole story to Elinor, being a great ally of hers, and they laughed more than Lady Mary would have approved, and Dundreary did not recover from his stupefaction during the entire season.

"But it's all a bore and you don't care about it," said Leighton Rossitur one evening as he led her away from a group of men of which she had been the centre, to the disgust of numberless damsels who sat partnerless, wondering if they had been invited to General's Mansfield's ball for the express purpose of ornamenting the walls and looking at that Miss Grey flirt in an outrageous manner. "It's all a bore and you don't care about it," said Leighton Rossitur in his abrupt way, which was odd and graceful and he knew it, as they stood waiting for space on the crowded floor to make two turns of the dashing waltz which the military band played with such spirit.

"What is a bore?" said Elinor.

"Every thing—every body. Do you include me?"

"I have not said a word. You shall include yourself if you like."

"But I don't like," said Rossitur. "Just say you don't, please."

"Very well—I will just say it."

"But you will think— Why, those eccentric mortals have changed to that glorious galop—it is no time to think."

They flew down the room to the exhilarating measures which would have made a dancing dervish of Saint Augustine if he could have heard them, and when they were both breathless, Rossitur begged her to sit in a shady corner which he espied, noting, with his quick eye for seizing the advantage, that there was nobody near except a deaf old woman who always would go to balls, people said, whether she was invited or not, and who always sat in shady nooks staring vacantly at the crowd, and occasionally asking questions of those who came within reach as to what a group of persons at an impracticable distance were saying, declaring she had missed the point of their remarks. Rossitur persuaded Miss Grey to sit down there, and while they rested he talked. He had reached a standing-place from which he could talk to her about himself, which was a great length gained. He told her of his wishes, his aspirations, and showed nobly; and she liked to listen, and they talked longer than was discreet, considering that other people had eyes and tongues too; nor was that unpleasant to Mr. Rossitur.

The old deaf woman leaned over suddenly and almost put Rossitur's left eye out with one of her ostrich plumes. "What was that?" she asked in a mysterious whisper.

"What does she mean?" queried he, not afraid of her hearing, since the last trump would scarcely have been audible unless Gabriel had blown an extra blast directly in her ear. "Has she been listening to me? She couldn't hear, though."

"What did you say it was?" repeated the old lady, her plumes shaking on her eager head. "What did General Mansfield say?" Rossitur looked and saw the General standing a quarter of a mile off, more or less, talking to a lady, and, by his bent head, evidently talking in a low tone at that.

"Did he say we'd have a war with Mexico?" questioned the old lady.

"Or Bagdad," shouted he in her ear.

She nodded, quite satisfied, but of course not having understood a word.

"I thought so," said she, looking as wise as a magpie, and retired into the chaotic domain of her thoughts.

Rossitur went back to his conversation. "Do I bore you?" he asked at last. "Am I the most egotistical man you ever met?"

"You ought to know you gratify one of the chief weaknesses of female nature by talking freely about yourself."

"Do I? You see I am absurdly impulsive; but one can so seldom talk honestly. I have unconsciously fallen into the habit with you, and it is very nice. Some day you will be tired of it, and I shall be alone again." That would have been sentimental and foolish, only he said it as if half laughing at himself.

"But you will have your ambition still," said Elinor.

"Without any sun to shine on it," he answered in his gravest voice. "Don't grow tired, Miss Grey."

"I am not yet, at all events; we will not anticipate unpleasant possibilities."

"It is better not," he replied. He knew he had gone far enough for that moment, and he had the wisdom to stop. "May I ride with you to-morrow?" he asked. "I know you go out on horseback every fine day."

"If I ride, certainly; but how do you know it will be fine?"

"Because you have promised me a pleasure."

"Now you are going back to your pretty speeches."

"Was that a pretty speech? Dear me, it is habit—comes of being naturally poetical."

"They have finished that galop," said Elinor. "Please to take me into civilized society again."

"How ungrateful! Never mind; I see Dundreary lying in wait for you; I shall be avenged."

"Oh, then take me the other way."

"But see; the next dance is a quadrille," said he, glancing at his card. "Just shock propriety by standing up with me."

"Treachery; when I have no chaperon but a male one, and am on my good behavior."

"But it's so nice to reward one's virtue by doing wrong."

"I can't have the pleasure unfortunately, for I am engaged to—let me see to whom—General Mansfield," she added, looking down her little tablet.

"And he really is too pleasant an elderly body to disappoint."

"He is not an elderly body. Take me to him."

As they rose, the deaf old lady, who had been sitting upright as a post since her last attack, caught Rossitur by the arm. "Isn't the President coming?" she asked.

"If he had sent me an intimation of his august designs, I'd tell her," said he. "What shall I say?"

"Poor soul! it is of no use to say any thing."

"Did you tell her he had gone to Utah?" exclaimed the deaf female, who was watching them suspiciously.

Rossitur shook his head.

"What did you say so for, then?" she demanded with acerbity.

"I think she is inclined to be belligerent to-night," said Rossitur.

"Don't laugh. I wish she would stay at home; it is painful." Elinor nodded and smiled at her.

"Did you say supper?" cried the old lady, jumping up with alacrity.

Elinor shook her head in her turn.

"Did you say they weren't going to have any? Never heard of such a thing! Why, the General ought to be ashamed."

It was a hopeless task to attempt to enlighten her mind, so they left her, but as they turned away they could hear her mutter—"No supper! The President gone to Utah? I won't be a Mormon, for one! Supper—Utah—President—" Her voice was lost in the distance, but there she sat shaking her head till the feathers on it nodded like the plumes upon a hearse, as if she were the funeral of her own youth, and waiting till a break in the crowd should permit her to pursue her journey.

Elinor went through her quadrille with the gallant old General, who was stately enough to have danced a minuet with Madame Maintenon, and so simple and natural, in spite of his martial honors, that she liked him exceedingly. At its conclusion a Western Congressman assailed her, and when she declined to dance he girned at her—the old Scotch word alone will express his look—and remembering that he had a vote and that she might chance to want it for something sometime, with the customary duplicity of her sex she talked so agreeably to him for a few moments that he was appeased and afterward pronounced her — "Considerable shakes. She looks very stand-offish, but she's good grit and she knows what's what." Artful Elinor had praised his maiden speech, of which she had never heard a word, and was unconscious he had made until he told her. I don't exactly know how the recording angel manages about the little lies even the best women tell, but I know it is ten to one he will be proved in the wrong somehow, and they will slip gracefully past Saint Peter in spite of him.

Dundreary came and "aw'd" at Elinor, and his English friend came and ridiculed him in order to do his duty in the amicable relationship. After they had departed a French tiger connected with the embassy tripped up on his toes and put his sticky mustache nearer her face than he ought, as French tigers will, and fancied himself fascinating when he was only silly and insolent. I think she suffered next from a hard-breathing Austrian, who spoke many languages and made them all incomprehensibly Teuitch. Then a waif from the Youth of New York pranced about her; a knot of dismal old Senators followed, and Elinor did her duty bravely. Meanwhile numberless women, who found society a waste peopled with unappreciative monsters, glared at her and abused her, and liked her when she talked to them notwithstanding; and Elinor went through the round and felt herself a slave.

At last Leighton Rossitur could come back, and they had a few more pleasant moments and another little talk, and Elinor in secret admitted that what enjoyment the evening possessed she owed to him. Night after night it was the same, and she was learning to depend more and more upon him to make such festive scenes endurable, and wise Rossitur knew it and bided his time and kept sufficiently composed to weave his plans and carry them out. He rode out with her the next morning and made himself a delightful companion. Looking at him with his radiant face, Elinor remembered their first meeting, and wondered that she could have deemed his an unpleasant countenance, and thrust that earliest intuition further into obscurity, as we all do such warnings, in order that we may blunder on to annoyance and trouble. When she returned home she was in unusually good spirits from the effects of the fresh air and that agreeable talk, and her father being out, she had a long season to read and be quiet before it was time to dress for dinner. At least she told herself that she was going to read—that she never had leisure now except for novels, and it would not answer. She could not easily settle herself to any thing, however, and began various little tasks and finished none of them, and wasted a long half-hour over a stand of hyacinths in full bloom, intoxicating her senses with the delicious perfume until she felt like one of Tennyson's lotus-eaters. Straightway on becoming conscious that she felt thus, she rushed to the other extreme, with the usual inconsistency of dreamers. Back came the loneliness, and she sat down by the fire to pity herself or call herself bad names, according to the changes of her mood. Again Leighton Rossitur's face rose before her, and she was glad to think about him; he was genial, open, and clever; yes, she was very glad she knew him. She would not call herself desolate any longer since she had her father to pet, and this man told her how precious her sympathy was to him, and how much he needed her counsels to keep him straight on the crooked paths of political life.

In those days Elinor Grey turned resolutely from thoughts of the past summer, and flattered herself it was because in her strength its records had become of no importance, and was willfully deaf and blind to any thing which might have undeceived her.

Her maid looked in with an intimation that Miss Grey was still in this sublunary sphere and must dress for dinner, at which there would be eight guests, according to Mr. Grey's habit of a Tuesday.

"Yes," said Elinor; "I had forgotten about it;" and she felt Tuesdays and dinners and eight people bores that ought to be swept out of existence. "Never mind—I'll wear any thing, Coralie." But Coralie looked so horrified that the woman rose in Elinor. "No, I'll not," said she; "I'll wear that new dress that is between moonlight and silver; and cut those lovely white hyacinths for my hair; one must make sacrifices. Not an ornament. And I'll look well, Coralie; make me handsome, please."

Coralie told her in voluble French that she was spared the trouble; and, after her mistress was dressed, vowed that the attire had been an inspiration, nothing less. The gown was a wonderful shade. I don't know how or why, but there was a moonlight look about it which was entrancing. Miss Grey looked at herself in the mirror and put away her visions, like a sensible woman, until she should see if her toilette was perfect. "It's all stupid, Coralie," said she, "and one is a slave; but one needn't be a fright, you know."

"Je crois bien que non. To look well—voilà, le grand devoir d'une femme," cried Coralie.

By way of fulfilling her devoir to the utmost, Elinor changed her mind about the jewels, took up an odd ornament—a narrow black onyx necklace, exquisitely cut, with a knot of pearls to clasp it—hung that about her throat, and, while Coralie uttered ejaculations expressive of her admiration and delight, turned away satisfied. She was gorgeous—that is what she was, and I will write it—she looked like a picture, as a woman can who has a genius for dress, and the woman who has not ought to curse her stars and seek a speedy death.

Elinor went down to the library and found her father, and the pair secretly admired each other as relations seldom can do, we not being yet near enough the millenium for lions and lambs and other unpleasant beasts to dwell amicably in the same fold. Mr. Grey was unusually complacent and sunny. He had received news from Wall Street that day; the Bull was carrying his burdens bravely and putting out the eyes of the envious Bears with the dust he raised. Besides this cause for content-

ment, there had been a Cabinet meeting, and a plan Mr. Grey had at heart for his country's good had been smiled upon; if it succeeded, he would be rewarded by new popularity. Naturally, with every thing so well disposed, he could throw aside the cares of State and the private ventures, and be prepared to enjoy himself.

"I almost forgot to tell you, my daughter Elinor," he said, after she had asked about the proceedings of the conclave, and learned that his opinions had been received as they ought; "Mr. De Forest is quite ill, and can't dine with us."

"We ought to have had somebody," she replied; "you know you hate a gap at table, papa."

"Yes, I always expect some Banquo to step in and take it. To guard against such intrusion I did an impertinent thing by Mr. Rossitur."

"You, papa?"

"I, my daughter Elinor. I met him as I came away from the White House. I told him of De Forest's inconsiderate attack, and begged him to take pity on us."

"Did he accept?"

"He was good-natured enough to say that he looked on De Forest's quinsy as a special interposition of the gods."

"I am glad," said Elinor; "he is very agreeable."

"And thorough-bred," added Mr. Grey. "Nine young men out of ten would have stood on their dignity and been sulky."

"But Mr. Rossitur is not at all a common man."

"Indeed, no; I have great hopes of him. I do not know any man who could have satisfied me so thoroughly in the post he holds." In the distance, Mr. Grey saw where, if his plans were successful, exigencies might arise in which Leighton Rossitur could be very useful; but he did not say that, the palace of Truth having been left in too ruinous a condition by long-forgotten generations to be a habitable domicile in this age. He paid more compliments to the absent, not repeating what he had said—he never bored you by saying a thing over and over because it was good once—and Elinor was encouraged in the opinions she had formed.

The guests arrived, mostly Mr. Grey's set of men; one woman whom Elinor chose with rare discretion as a support, neither too young nor too old, and who lighted well; and Leighton Rossitur. "I have been wondering for what unknown good deed the Fates are rewarding me," he said, as he made his salutations. "So much happiness in one day is bewildering."

"Does your conscience reproach you with not deserving it?"

"You ought to know that undeserved things are always sweetest." He had no opportunity to talk to her then. Dinner was announced, and General Mansfield came to lead her away. Rossitur wished the venerable hero had been asleep for twenty years under a monument reared by a grateful country, of such weight that there would be no possibility of his getting out and straggling along to dinners to be in the way of younger men. This Elinor Grey bewitched him to-night. As he stood by her, the delicious fragrance of the hyacinths fairly dizzied his brain. First he could only sit at table and watch her, peerless and cold, with such flashes of beauty kindling her face when some chance word animated her. He looked at her, and he drank several glasses of rare wine which Mr. Grey had brought back from the South of France, and felt his spirits rise to the occasion. Seizing the opportunity he talked, and talked so well that the gray-beards listened, but he was careful not to overdo it.

Looking at Elinor through the warm light, with the hyacinths clustering in her hair, and her complexion more pure than ever from the silvery sheen of her dress, it seemed to him that the scent of the blossoms and not the wine exhilarated him, and he yielded to the spell as his sensuous nature loved to yield to such emotions, kept above the region of coarseness by his delicate perceptions.

Miss Grey was glad to see his success among those men whose opinions could be priceless to him. Presently, with a woman's tact, she gave him another opportunity, and by artful prolongings of the conversation made it appear that he was obliged to answer, so that the gray-beards could not censure him as a forward youngster, but admired his brilliancy, and after they had gone, remembered Leighton Rossitur and prophesied great things of him.

Satisfied with her small triumph, Elinor made a sign to her lady companion, and they retired to sip coffee in feminine solitude. When the dreary little interlude was over and it was time for the men to follow, Miss Grey went up to her own room a moment—what for, do you think? To take the hyacinths out of her hair and replace them with two other odorous clusters which she cut remorselessly from their stems, not to be deterred by their piteous quivers, which sometimes, when she was fanciful, would have touched her like complaints of her cruelty. She had a passion for flowers, and she would scarcely give away a blossom to any body, but to-night she had willed to sacrifice that sentiment, and if she wore natural blooms they should be perfectly fresh. All of which was a very pretty specimen of female nature and speaks volumes.

Leighton Rossitur coming into the drawing-room, found her more fascinating than ever, and the heavenly odor of the hyacinths stung his senses with such delicious keenness that it was well the gray-beards were there, and well that he had before long to go off to some stupid person's stupid reception, else he might have been rash and said or done, Heaven knows what. "I am glad I have to go," he observed, with an abruptness which was entirely different from other people's efforts in that line, inasmuch as it had a purpose and was made the support for pretty speeches he could not have uttered so effectively in any other way.

"Your candor is charming," Elinor replied with a laugh.

"The scent of those hyacinths bewilders me," he replied. "I couldn't trust myself near you another moment. I feel like one of Tennyson's lotus-eaters."

The very sensation she had experienced that morning. How odd it was this man seemed so frequently to have a clue to her feelings, or thoughts in common with hers. She was liking him to-night and had been pleased at his success, yet as this idea came over her she was dissatisfied. "You shall have a cup of strong coffee to take away the effects," said she, "and get your brain steady."

He took a cup from the tray a servant presented. "The worst remedy in the world," replied he; "it goes with perfumes and Eastern dreams and white flowers and silvery dresses and all sorts of bewildering things."

"You will be able to dance the whole night then."

"It is cruel of you to disappoint Mrs. Ames; I know she expects you and will consider her evening a failure."

"I was at her last reception; she must have a little conscience, I should think."

"Not a trace of one, I fancy. You are quite sure you won't come?"

"Quite. I am not going out when I can have General Mansfield all to myself."

"He that ought to have been a memory ages ago," said Rossitur. "Oh, I am so sorry."

"That he is not a memory?"

"No, that I asked you to ride to-day."

"You have my thanks. Why, if you please?"

"Because if I had not I could have asked to join you to-morrow."

"But I am not going to ride. I am going to the Capitol library to hunt for a book papa wishes to consult."

"And I am obliged to go there to copy something—it isn't a make-believe. Now I can live till then. Good-bye. I wonder if the hyacinths will make me dream?"

After every body was gone and Elinor Grey had bidden her father good-night, she looked about a little to see whither this acquaintance with Leighton Rossitur was leading. She speedily decided that she was tired and could not think; besides, though he sought her constantly, and talked freely, he had so conducted himself that she could console her mind with believing she was his friend and that he was glad to stand on such ground; and she did not try to think any more.

CHAPTER XV.

MRS. PIFFIT APPEARS.

ABOUT this time the Thorntons came on to make their promised visit, and Elinor had less opportunity for thought in the quiet house between coming home from balls and going to bed, which was very well for her, many things considered. Still, although she was glad to have her friends there, the dressing-room chats and the mysterious midnight conclaves with Rosa were not always so acceptable to Elinor as they had been during the moonlight summer nights; but Elinor did not reason about it. When, as often happened, it was much nearer dawn than midnight on their return from what Tom called saltatory expeditions, and he in his marital cruelty insisted on driving his female dove into her nest without loss of time lest she should be fit for nothing except crossness on the morrow, and Rosa was forced away pouting, Elinor could not be sorry, but she told herself it was only because she liked to see Tom thoughtful and tender of his blossom after these long years of marriage.

One morning when Mr. Grey had gone to his post and Tom was teasing his wife and Elinor with endless last words before getting out of sight as a discreet man does remove himself from his womankind at such seasons, faithful old Hungarian Henry, who made the house a paradise by his punctuality and ruled the servants with a rod of iron, opened the door and approached his mistress with a puzzled and ruffled look which gave him a ludicrous resemblance to a turkey-cock. "I beg your pardon, Mademoiselle," he said, "but there's the strangest woman in the hall. She wants to see my master, and if he is out she insists on seeing you; and she has seated herself and will not go away on any terms."

"What is her name?" Elinor asked.

"I beg pardon, but I could not catch it. There she is; says she has a letter, and vows she will stay."

"Shall I go and look at her?" Tom asked.

"No," returned Elinor, "I'll go. Some petitioner—"

"Let her come up," interrupted Rosa; "I know she'll be fun. Strong-minded women that sit down in peoples' halls and won't go away are always fun."

"Very well," said Elinor; "show her up, Henry."

"But, Mademoiselle, she is very odd," expostulated Henry.

"So much the better," cried Mrs. Thornton. "You can stand outside and keep watch, Henry, if your mistress is in danger."

Henry bowed low and departed, but he looked disapproval—he must consult his conscience so far. Presently a loud wheezing and sharp exclamations could be heard from the hall. "This way, eh? I know she'd see me! Comes of foreign servants — pah! Why can't people be Americans?"

"Piffit, I'd stake my life!" whispered Tom.

Henry threw open the door, and Tom's prophecy was verified. In trotted Mrs. Piffit, wearing the plaid cloak, a new and wonderful bonnet on her head, and the green umbrella under her arm. "How do you do, Miss Grey?" she began at once, squinting and sniffing with all her might. "Which is Miss Grey? I'm so short-sighted. Nasty foreigner wouldn't let me up—hate foreigners—wonder you have them about."

"Did you wish to see me, Madam?" Elinor asked politely, rising and going toward Piffit, who had caught her hoop against a chair, and in her efforts to dislodge it, was displaying a great deal of ankle, a drab worsted stocking, three petticoats of different lengths, and a long yellow string which held her together somewhere.

"Yes, if you're Miss Grey. Caught my hoop—hateful things—"

"Let me help you," said Elinor.

"No, its all right now," replied Mrs. Piffit, giving the chair a vicious push against a mosaic table and settling her draperies with a pull. "Yes, you're Miss Grey. Remember you—saw you at the meeting—great failure. I'd have noticed you though."

"May I ask your business with me?" Elinor asked, very courteously, but desirous of recalling her visitor to some sense of what was proper under the circumstances.

"My business isn't exactly with you," returned Mrs. Piffit, squinting horribly; "it's with your father. I've got a letter of introduction—from Mr. Holly, the editor."

"My father is at the Department," said Elinor.

"So the men told me," replied Mrs. Piffit. "Always like to find out things for myself—servants lie so—foreigners worst of all—wonder you have 'em."

"I have no doubt you will find my father there," continued Elinor.

"It's no matter," said the unheeding Piffit; "I'll tell you about it. Sit down—don't let me keep you standing." She seated herself as she spoke in a large easy-chair, leaned her umbrella against the arm, pulled the flat reticule from under her cloak and laid it in her lap. By this time, with much squinting and sniffing she became conscious of the presence of the Thorntons. "Your friends, Miss Grey—saw them with you at the meeting. Introduce me, please."

"How do you do, Mrs. Piffit?" said Tom, before Elinor had decided how to act, rising and making a grand bow; "I am happy to meet you again."

"You're very polite," said Piffit, and suffered a smile to soften the disdainful sniff she could not help giving when any thing masculine addressed her. "How is your wife?"

"Thank you," said Rosa; "I am quite well."

"I suppose you think it's odd, Miss Grey, for me to come like this," said Mrs. Piffit; "but you see I've a letter for your father—from Mr. Holly—"

"The editor," added Tom.

"Every body knows that," she snapped. "I thought I'd like to tell you all about it, Miss Grey. He's in hiding—but I'll find him—I'll expose him as sure as he's a nasty, dirty man."

"Mr. Holly?" Tom asked.

"No; he's well enough—for a man—pays regularly. Can't you understand?" cried Piffit wrathfully. "Of course you can't—men never can! Why her husband—he ought to be ashamed of himself—let me catch him."

"I think you have not told us of whom you are speaking," said Elinor, wisely deciding that it would be absurd to treat the woman as she deserved.

"Haven't I? I've been so hurried—only got here last night," said Mrs. Piffit. "What nasty places these Washington hotels are. I'm at the National—say it's the best, and as she pays my expenses—she couldn't do less, you know."

"I should think not indeed," responded Tom.

"Oh, yes," retorted Piffit; "that's just like men—as long as a woman pays they don't care what one nor how much. I don't do such things for money, Miss Grey—any body'll tell you that—but I'm always ready to help my sex and be after those men." It was true that Piffit was only too happy to have an opportunity of plunging into a quarrel of any description if she could hear of one anywhere within reach. "I want to do my duty," said she; "I'm a Presbyterian."

"But who is this man?" Rosa asked.

"Why her husband, to be sure. Of course, if she wasn't what she ought to be I shouldn't interest myself in her."

"What has he done?" Tom inquired.

"Oh, done! Every thing atrocious he could, what men are always doing—the brute! Now he's got the money she'd laid away, and here he is in Washington—we heard that day before yesterday. But I'll find him—I'd do it if he was fathoms deep in hiding." She crossed her hands over her cloak—the shortness of her arms prevented her folding them—squinted defiantly, and sent out a little cloud of steam in her energetic sniffs.

"I think he is not hidden here," said Rosa. "I should have discovered him if Miss Grey had any recreant husband secreted."

"Oh, that's a joke," returned Mrs. Piffit. "He, he! I like a joke as well as any body. Of course, I didn't suppose he was here, but I wanted to see you, Miss Grey, because I've the letter for your father—you might just hand it to him." She clutched her reticule, opened it with a snap, and began turning over the heterogeneous contents—papers, bits of sticky candy, several worn pencils, a pair of spectacles, a black stocking, a shoe-lace, and at last a ruffled night-cap, which she thrust hastily under her cloak with a glance and a sniff at Tom. During the whole operation she kept muttering, "For your father—introduction letter—from Mr. Holly, the editor. I'll find him as sure as he's a nasty man—in hiding indeed!—Oh, here's the letter!" she exclaimed, fishing it up from the bottom of the chaotic heap. "Here it is—it's all right."

She laid the letter on the table beside her and began cramming the other articles back in her reticule. "I'm very orderly," said she; "always my way—one thing at a time." She snapped the bag together and hung it over her arm and snatched the letter—she always snatched and always jerked. "Now, Miss Grey, if you'll give this to your father—an introduction—from Mr. Holly, the editor—I'm Mrs. Piffit, the writer—every body knows me—you'll tell him about it."

"Perhaps if you have a letter for my father you had better send it to his Bureau," said Elinor; "he transacts all business there."

"Of course I have one—here it is!" cried Mrs. Piffit. "No, you take it—that's better. I hate those Bureaus—so many understrappers about—unless you'd go with me? May be if you are not busy you'd put on your bonnet and step round."

Elinor politely pointed out the impossibility of her "stepping round" that morning.

"Then I'll leave it here," said she; "he can read it, and I'll come in again. I shall stay a week or two, I think. I must find him. I thought I'd like to go into Congress and get up an article for the paper, you know; and there's several things I want to learn about. What made the Senate drop that bill for homesteads, and why doesn't the President go ahead with his policy?"

"They haven't told me," said Tom, on whom her eye chanced to fall, "so I don't know."

"Of course you don't—they don't—he don't any more—men!" She brought out the last word with a sniff of such energy that she fairly lifted herself out of the chair.

"That is the trouble, I suppose," said Tom. "But after all, Mrs. Piffit, you must admit the world without any men to make blunders would be a dull place."

"I never admit any thing," snapped Piffit; "a Philadelphia lawyer taught me that. I don't want any thing of the men—only that brute who's in hiding. And I'll have him—just wait."

"I think it scarcely possible that my father can assist you," observed Elinor.

"Oh no—that isn't it—the letter wasn't for that. Mercy, Miss Grey! of course the Honorable Secretary doesn't know any thing about such creatures. The letter was an introduction, you know—from Mr. Holly, the editor—I'm Mrs. Piffit, the writer."

"So well known and justly admired," said Tom.

"I don't know about that," replied she, suffering from a chronic difficulty of agreeing with any male. "I try to do my duty—I'm a Presbyterian—I was a Presbyterian before I was a writer—been a writer a good many years though. Done every thing—translations, stories, fashion articles, memoirs—for the papers."

"I am well acquainted with your literary efforts," said Tom.

"Humf!" sniffed she, a little softened, but unable entirely to lay by her animosity to his species. "Sorry I didn't know your name that day, Mrs. Thornton; I'd have noticed you. Meeting was a failure. How Mrs. Hackett does dress! I like pretty things. I make my own bonnets. I'm a fashion editor, and get all the new patterns."

Mrs. Thornton bowed.

"I'll notice you now, if you like," cried Piffit, suddenly.

Quick as a flash she had out her spectacles and adjusted them on her eyes, making herself look like a gray cat-owl. She squinted about the breakfast-room, apparently taking notes. "Blue and silver," said she; "pictures—bust in the corner.—Tell well in an article.—Found the beautiful and famous Miss G. seated in her boudoir. The Honorable Secretary was out; but with her noted grace she received us in an elegant *demi-toilette*.—That sort of thing, you know—French words always tell."

"Excuse me, Madam," said Elinor, "but I must request you to leave out any mention of me or this visit in your letters."

"Of course—if you like. Such popularity is tiresome—I find it so myself. Only think, somebody wrote about me and called me a ' roly-poly of cantankerousness!' It was a man—I think I know him. I never bear malice—I'm a Presbyterian—but just wait till he steals another play from the French, and won't I be after him !"

"Quite right, too," said Tom.

"Of course. You men always like to hear each other abused," retorted she. "Do you want to be put in a letter?"

"Heaven forbid!" cried Tom. "No, no; stick to the man in hiding, Mrs. Piffit."

"I will. Won't he wish himself somewhere else when I find him! No matter where it is—if it's in the House of Representatives I'll point him out."

She snatched up her umbrella and levelled it at an imaginary culprit. "Nearly lost it in the cars night before last," said she, her thoughts diverted into a new channel by the sight of her constant companion, which she patted affectionately. "I got up for a drink of water, and while I was gone a great nasty man got my seat. I went back—'Anyhow, give me my umbrella,' said I. 'It's mine,' said he. But I told him what he was and who he was and what his father was before him. How the people stared!—'I'm Mrs. Piffit,' said I, ' and I'll put you in the papers.' "

"I suppose he was cowed then," said Tom.

"Yes; showed his umbrella—old, torn thing—pretended he hadn't noticed mine—wanted to keep 'em both. I will own, Miss Grey, I'm foolish maybe about my umbrella. Steal my trunk, but leave my umbrella. I don't mean you, you know—Secretary's daughter, of course not—but those men that are always prowling about and ready to take whatever they can lay their hands on."

"But you haven't told us the name of the miscreant who deserted his wife," said Tom.

"Presume he's got a dozen," said she. "But I'll find him. Hiding, indeed! His wife does needle-work and has music scholars — hard-working woman—and he's got her money and

skylarking about here. I'll find him! She cried so, poor thing, I told her I'd come on ; and I took my umbrella and we started."

"Is the wife here too?" asked Tom.

"No, no; can't you understand? Of course you can't—men! She, poor thing, she's only fit to cry at home. But I'm after him! Tell him Mrs. Piffit is coming." She shook her finger at Tom and swept him a shower of sniffs as if she thought he had the runaway somewhere concealed.

"I'll tell him if I see him," said Tom ; "I'll advise him to give himself up, because you are determined."

"I should think I was. Let me get at him—only let me !"

"It would be shameful that your kindness should be wasted by not finding him."

"Oh, I wanted to come to Washington—never been here before. I've letters for lots of people—several Senators."

"From Mr. Holly, the editor?" asked Tom.

"Only two or three are from him—Mr. Grey's is—for Mrs. Piffit, the writer—I'm Mrs. Piffit. But I've any quantity—every body gives me what I ask for. I wanted to write some articles, and I want to know what the President means."

"It is due your position as a writer that you should," said Tom.

"Nonsense!" sniffed Piffit. "You only want to laugh at me—men always laugh. But I want to know, and I'll ask him; and I'll tell him what the newspapers expect."

"So you ought—who knows better than you—I'm not laughing," returned Tom, in spite of Elinor's frown.

"I want to call at the White House," said Mrs. Piffit. "I dare say one of the Senators will go up with me. Oh, maybe you'd go, Miss Grey. It's kind of nervous business, you know."

"My time is so fully occupied that I shall be unable to do so," replied Elinor.

"I suppose you've lots to do. Fashionable life is tiresome—I've some fashionable friends. I like to know what's going on among such people on account of my articles."

"I think, Mrs. Thornton," said Elinor, "that we shall have to plead our engagement; it is getting late."

"Oh, don't let me detain you," cried Piffit. "I've had a charming call! So glad to have seen you, Miss Grey, and your friend. You're sure you'd rather not have a notice?"

"Quite sure, Madam."

"Just like me—modesty in the great is so lovely. Be sure and give the letter to the Honorable Secretary, Miss Grey. I've several letters to leave. Oh, I must remember the one for one of the Senators from New England. I'm so hurried—haven't a moment to spare." She picked up the reticule, took her umbrella under her arm, and prepared to go.

"I hope we shall meet soon again," said she.

"And I hope you will discover the hidden wretch," said Tom.

"Oh, my!" wheezed Piffit; "I've just thought—I've a little article I'd like to show you, Miss Grey; just hold that." She planted the umbrella across Thornton's knees, then snatched it off with a sniff as if it had been contaminated by the momentary contact with a pair of masculine legs, looked about in search of a resting-place for her treasured friend, and finally laid it on the table. "An article I want to show you—"

She paused suddenly. Her eye had caught sight of the night-cap which had fallen into the chair. She dashed at it, crowded it into her pocket, and squinted ferociously at Tom as if she dared him to own that he had seen it.

"An article," suggested he.

"Yes, for Miss Grey. She'll be interested. Where did I put it? Didn't I leave it on the table at the hotel? No, it must be in my pocket." She drew aside her cloak and plunged her hand into the mysterious recesses of the cavern, and brought up the ruffled border of the cap. "I guess I haven't it," said she, somewhat confused. "No matter—another time when I call. Good-bye, Miss Grey—good-bye, ma'am—so glad to have seen you; day to you, Sir. Oh, my umbrella! Haven't I dropped any thing, have I? So short-sighted—good-bye." And Piffit, sniffing prodigiously, wafted herself out of the presence.

"I think," said Tom, "that we have seen Mrs. Piffit in her full glory."

"And I beg we may be spared another infliction," replied Elinor.

"Nonsense," said he. "You have no reverence for writers."

"I don't fancy Mrs. Piffit," said she. "I asked about her after we saw her at the meeting. It is not only that she is vulgar and pushing, but she is ill-natured and malicious."

"And tells downright fibs if she is a Presbyterian," added Rosa. "They say her friendship is not to be depended upon, with all her boasted attachment to her sex."

"Prejudice," urged Tom. "I approve of Piffit—I am glad to have seen her—one hears of her everywhere. There has not been a literary quarrel in ten years that she was not at the bottom of. She is always hunting up recreant husbands and exposing undutiful wives and trying to help persecuted children. Piffit forever! say I."

"At a distance, then," observed Elinor.

"If she were good-natured one could pardon even her restless meddling with every body's business, but she is downright wicked and meddles because she loves mischief," pursued Rosa.

"Injustice of the sex," cried Tom. "I approve of Piffit! I haven't laughed so heartily in a month."

"I hope at least we have seen the last of her," said Elinor.

But they had not. Mrs. Piffit was not to be so easily set aside and her claims disregarded, and whatever was to be seen she meant to see. Only the next day Tom went up to the gallery

of the Senate Chamber to hear a speech from one of the most noted of the Conscript Fathers, and there was Piffit. Fortunately she did not perceive him, and the speech was over before she created any sensation beyond that which her remarkable appearance always excited wherever she went, and of which she was profoundly unconscious. Tom saw her and watched her with silent delight. She was seated on an adjacent bench, spectacles on her funny little nose, diligently making notes, while the flat reticule hung on her arm, but for once the green umbrella was invisible. If people got in her way she nudged them unmercifully; one man inadvertently standing so that he obstructed her line of vision, Piffit bounded on her seat and thrust the point of her lead pencil in his ear without remorse. "Get out of the way," she said, quite aloud; "I'm Mrs. Piffit, and I'm taking notes. Can't you be quiet? What do you come here to make a disturbance for? Ain't you ashamed of yourself? I'll put you in the papers if you don't sit down and be quiet."

The unfortunate man, being fresh from rural seclusion, looked woefully abashed, and faltered out that he had not meant to disturb any body.

"You did," said Piffit; "you always do. I know you—men! The miserable retreated amid a general titter, rubbing his ear dolefully, but Mrs. Piffit continued her task perfectly unmoved. Occasionally she lifted her voice without pausing in her work and said in a general way, "I'm taking notes—for the papers. That Massachusetts Senator promised to get me a seat on the floor—it's a shame! What can you expect? If women were Senators it would be another thing; but men—hmf! hmf!"

The speech was concluded, people were leaving the benches, when suddenly there was an outcry and a disturbance, and Piffit's voice rose shrill and clear — "My umbrella! Where's my umbrella? Somebody's stolen it! Call the police! Stop that fat man!"

"Hush! hush!" said her neighbors. "The ushers will come and put you out."

"Let 'em. I'll put 'em in the papers!" cried the undaunted Mrs. Piffit. "Where's my umbrella? I will have my umbrella! Which of you took it? Here, you; come back, the whole lot of you, or I'll put you in the papers. I'm Mrs. Piffit, the writer, and I will have my umbrella."

Tom passed with the crowd into the lobby, but before he could proceed further out rushed Piffit, her bonnet falling back and her strips of paper rustling in her hand. "Stop 'em!" cried she. "Police! President! Senators! I tell you I will have my umbrella. Somebody's got my umbrella!"

The unsympathizing crowd stared and laughed; at length somebody called out, "You didn't have no numbrellar; I saw you when you came in."

"No more I didn't. Now I remember. Oh, where did I leave it? Has any body seen a green umbrella with an ivory handle and a brass ring round it?"

"Saw it going round the Capitol," suggested somebody, "and I thought it was a balloon."

"Men!" sniffed Piffit, too frantic to be at all mindful of any thing but her loss. "I had it—oh, I had it when I was talking to that Senator from New England."

"Do you suppose the Senator stole it?" asked one of the knot that had gathered about her.

"He was a man before he was a Senator," retorted she; "men'll do any thing—hmf!"

A sudden light broke upon her. She thrust the crowd right and left, sped back into the gallery, dove down among the benches, leaving her hoop on the top, and presently emerged flushed and triumphant—in her hand the green umbrella, which she flourished above the heads of the assembled Senate. "Left it there myself," said she, appearing in the lobby again. "Remember now, I hid it under the bench so there couldn't any body steal it."

"So the New England Senator didn't have it?" demanded some one. •

"He didn't have the chance—men'll do any thing. Ho! ho!" and she clapped her hands in a new frenzy. "Stop that man—that one going down stairs!"

"Now she wants another man," said one of her admirers. "He hasn't your umbrella."

"Stop him!" shrieked Piffit. "He's in hiding—he's stolen his wife's money—I'm after him—I'm Mrs. Piffit—stop him somebody."

The words stolen money caused some eager person to catch the departing innocent by the coat-tail. "Come back. Here's a woman says you've been stealing."

"He's in hiding. Hold him!" cried Piffit. "Let me get to him! Why, get out of the way, why don't you?" She pushed along and finally hooked the struggling stranger with the handle of her umbrella.

"Let me alone!" said he. "Never saw you in my life—you're mad!"

"You're in hiding!" cried Piffit. "You've stolen your wife's money—you've got to go home—oh, you brute!"

The man turned about. It was the unlucky creature whose ear she had stabbed with her pencil. "I've borne enough from you," cried he. "Who are you, anyhow?"

"'Tisn't the man," said Piffit. "Let him go. I've no doubt he's run off from somewhere, but 'tisn't the one." There was a general shout, and Mrs. Piffit beat a hasty retreat, holding her umbrella before her like a truncheon.

For the next two weeks she was seen and heard of everywhere. She assailed Congressmen without mercy, she worried the Senators, she made the round of the newspaper offices, she went up to the White House to find out the President's policy and demand assistance to hunt the recreant husband who was in hiding. She was forever thinking she had found him and making disturbances without regard to place or time, hooking unfortunate men with the handle of her umbrella and then abusing them because they had deceived her, trotting about from morning till night with her roll of dingy papers in her hand, presenting letters, claiming acquaintance with people, and distinguishing herself in every possible way. "I'm Mrs. Piffit" became a by-word at the departments and bureaus, and Mrs. Piffit in person was more dreaded than an army would have been. Meantime she wrote her letters to any paper that would publish them; she forced her acquaintance on any woman she could, and ruthlessly scribbled lies about her as a return. But, however occupied, she never forgot the grand purpose of her coming any more than she did her green umbrella. She hunted for that wretch everywhere. There was not a spot in Washington from the East Room at the White House down to a restaurant in which she did not sniff, seeking for him, and wherever she went the green umbrella went too, and she informed whoever would listen that she was Mrs. Piffit, the writer, and had come after a man who was in hiding, and meant to find him if he was above ground. She heard of him at last in Georgetown, and thither she went, astonishing the quiet old place out of its propriety by shrieking like a mad woman in one of the principal streets where she chanced to espy her victim. She was down upon him in an instant, poor drunken creature, sick and weak from his long revelling. She turned his pockets inside out, boxed his ears, maltreated him generally, narrated his misdeeds to the wondering crowd, told them they were no better than he, and wound up with—"I'm Mrs. Piffit, the writer; and I said I'd find him, in spite of all the Senators and Congressmen, and I have!"

Her victim was too maudlin drunk to do any thing but cry, so she boxed his ears again, pushed him into a carriage and drove off wheezing—"I've got him! Where's my umbrella?"

She actually took him back to New York; and he confessed after, that ten years in a penitentiary would not have been so horrible as those brief days, but not in the least did his sufferings move Piffit. She carried him back to the weeping wife, put an account of her own philanthropic deeds in the newspapers, and sniffed more outrageously than ever. What the little pale music-teacher, who received her penitent spouse so much after the fashion in which the Prodigal Son was greeted, may have thought, I can not tell, but it is believed that she would have lost less money if she had waited for her wandering husband to spend what he had purloined and return, for Piffit had done her philanthropy in a generous way where Piffit was concerned, and the flat reticule never disgorged when once it closed over its prey.

------◆------

CHAPTER XVI.

AFTER THE CONCERT.

ABOUT this time Mr. Grey went on to New York for a few days. The newspapers said there was some important political secret connected with the trip which would doubtless soon be laid before their readers; as they always do say whenever a prominent man lifts his eyebrows, hinting that the mystery is quite plain to them in their capacity of public guardians, but that they are silent because the moment for any thing beyond oracular murmurs has not arrived. They said these things as usual, and Mr. Grey led Elinor to suppose that his journey was connected with some old, half-forgotten investments somewhere, which promised to prove valuable if looked after, but indeed his attempts at business explanations were never clear. Whatever the motive was, he did go to town, and had a dinner given him by the civic dignitaries, and made one of his admirable speeches which pleased every body and meant nothing at all. I have no doubt he was serving his country in some way—Elinor knew that was always his first wish—and perhaps Mrs. Hackett's Bull of Wall Street could help him serve it; at all events, he had more private talks with him than any body, and the Bull's voice might be heard bellowing amicably in the Secretary's apartments. There was a rush a few days later down in Broad Street after certain new and mysterious stocks of the Bull's backing, and both in Close and Open Board dishevelled men elbowed each other and shouted themselves so hoarse that when night came they had no voices left to exult over their triumphs.

Mr. Grey was not long absent; he came back flushed with victory of some sort, but held himself more grandly placid than ever. It was reported in Cabinet circles that he had been doing something wonderful, though nobody knew what, and he was more courted and popular than ever. Elinor accepted the patriotic efforts as a matter-of-fact, naturally, but she learned too that her father had found time to look after the stupid property, whatever it might be. She received the impression that it had been sold greatly to his advantage, and thought no more about it.

Talking that night with Tom and Rosa she did not hesitate to avow her horror of speculation, and her father agreed with her. "You and I, my daughter Elinor, will never be dazzled by Wall-Street Eldorados," said he.

I dare say he thought he never would be again. What was going on now was scarcely speculation. Gigantic certainties looming in the close future were not speculative ventures. Mr. Grey could coincide with his daughter's opinion in the blandest manner.

"I'm not so grand and virtuous," admitted Tom. "I should not hesitate to buy and sell to any extent, only I am notoriously a fool about business, and so unlucky."

"Yes, indeed," added Rosa. "He is a goose, Mr. Grey, and I wouldn't trust him within a mile of Wall Street."

"Very fortunate for him that he has so wise a little wife," replied Mr. Grey. "For my own part, my life is too busy for me to think about such things."

"And you have too much regard for the dignity of your position, papa, only you never will pay yourself compliments," said Elinor.

"I have no need while my daughter Elinor does it so charmingly," he answered, looking at her face bright with filial pride and affection. He loved her so. Much as he craved the world's admiration, that daughter's was even more necessary to him. He could not have borne to know her faith disturbed.

They went to a ball given by some embassadress with an unpronounceable name. Lent would come in early that season, and Washington is socially the dullest city on the continent during Lenten gravities, so that people were crowding all the amusement possible into those last weeks. Leighton Rossitur was at the ball and made himself pleasant to Elinor, but nobody knew that he was any more agreeable than the rest of the troop which revolved about her. Miss Grey was a terrible flirt, people said, but a very general one; women added that she had no heart, and only wanted every man in the world at her feet to keep him away from the rest of her sex.

Rossitur looked at her that night after overhearing similar remarks from envious Eves, and knew that they lied. He looked at the broad, low forehead full of intellect, the luminous eyes, the delicate nostrils, and the proud, sensitive mouth, and thought what idiots the talkers were not to be able to read that language, then was glad that only he could do so. Elinor Grey could love, and she should love him! Had he come near the moment when he might venture to speak? She did not love him now—he was not silly enough to deceive himself—but she admired him, she had hopes for his future, and she was lonely; he knew that and how to make use of the knowledge. Perhaps some time those proud pulses had quickened under another man's glance—it made his blood boil to think of the possibility—but if it were so, if the memory of some girlish romance filled the heart of the woman with a vague sadness for her beautiful dream, Rossitur saw that it would be a help to him if he employed it rightly; it would have left a stronger need of companionship and sympathy. Could he but choose the moment when the lonely feeling was most powerful and tell her of his love, his devotion which was willing to wait to earn her affection—if she would trust herself to him and share his ambitions and be his guide—that very loneliness might incline her to listen and to yield. One day, if she married him, it would be in the man's nature to hate her if he thought that every heart-beat was not for him, and he might make a daily torture out of the suspected dream; but he did not think himself capable of such meanness. He could only think how he loved her.

He was recalled to his senses, and forced to remember that a ball-room was not the place to indulge in sentiment, by some reckless pair revolving against his toes, and not satisfied with that punishment, looking penknives at him for being in the path. With speed he got away from Scylla and tumbled into Charybdis. Moving toward the spot where he saw Elinor Grey standing for the moment disengaged, he fell into the clutches of the old deaf lady who always went to balls and never had any name that anybody remembered. "What is that Senator Jordan says?" she asked.

As usual with the person to whom she thought she had been listening, the Roman stood at an impracticable distance, trying to look like Cicero in a dress-coat.

"Did he say the Congressmen ought to be impeached?" Rossitur nodded with all his might, and tried to extricate his sleeve from her bony fingers. "Or was it the Queen of England?" whispered the old lady, like an inquisitive starling. Rossitur nodded again—there was nothing else to do—smiled a ghastly assent, and consigned her to the lowest place in Hades. "Don't deceive me," said the old lady. "I'm a little hard of hearing to-night."

Rossitur gave another tug at his sleeve; she only held it more firmly. "You old jackdaw!" he thought, and one can not blame him for his rudeness, because he saw Elinor Grey led off to dance just then by a dangerous Bostonian who had a rent-roll as immense as his dignity, and that was beyond comparison.

"In the Constitution, is it?" demanded the old woman. "Oh, I didn't know that! It's all right then." She released his arm and sat down quite satisfied, repeating, "It's all right then—in the Constitution! Why don't they have supper? I want my supper! Aren't they going to have any supper?"

Rossitur cruelly wished that a set of South Sea Islanders were at that moment supping off her ancient bones, and hurried away to where he saw a patient man holding Miss Grey's bouquet. The patient man meant to reward himself by dancing with Elinor as soon as she was at liberty, but being bashful and generally stupid, as most patient people are, he had not proffered his claims in advance, but stood there a model of modest humility. Wicked Rossitur, with malignant designs, halted at his side and talked to him as smilingly as possible, till he saw Miss Grey approach on her partner's arm, then he stepped directly before the patient man and had taken possession of Elinor while the bouquet-holder was getting his breath in readiness to say something. The consequence was that patience met with the return it usually does in this weary world—the bashful man was thanked for his kindness and deserted—not even the bouquet left as a future hope. Rossitur for a crowning wrong carried it away.

"I do think this waltz belongs to somebody else," said Elinor.

"I hope so. May he wait as long as I have."

"And I ought at least to speak to that poor man," continued she; "he has held my bouquet half the evening."

"Reward enough for him," said Rossitur. "Besides, why does he come to such places if not to hold the nosegays? I thought he was hired for that special purpose."

Every way the patient man got the worst of it. When will people learn that certain of the virtues became exploded theories of beauty centuries ago?

"To-morrow is your concert," observed Rossitur.

"Yes; so tiresome. What made people get up this rage for morning entertainments public and private, I wonder?"

"That I might have the pleasure of seeing you the oftener," replied he.

"A view of the matter which had not occurred to me."

"I dare say not. Women and republics are ungrateful."

"But I am very anxious about my concert," said Elinor.

"You just declared it tiresome."

"That was only one of the silly speeches one makes."

"Shall you sing?"

"You know I will not. They are all professionals except Mrs. De Lucy and Mr. Jervis."

"They always sing everywhere—they will do it."

"But Mrs. De Lucy has been very kind in helping me. You know I give the concert to let that poor little Miss Borden have a fair hearing. She came out in New York and was badly treated. She ought to have had a success."

"Oh, yes; the agents or somebody did all manner of dreadful things."

"They sacrificed her to Madame Villeneuve—she had some hold on them. Now I mean Miss Borden to have a success to-morrow, so that she can give a course of concerts here."

"Don't let her sing too much, then."

"Only twice—a ballad and an aria. I have great hopes of her."

"Of course you will make her a success."

"That is pretty of you."

"Yes; it did sound like Mrs. Hackett."

"I am sure I have worked hard enough," said Elinor. "I have made love to every body, from the President down, for a week past."

"Be easy in your mind. I heard some people talking to-night; they said it would be a triumph, and your dear friend Mrs. Ames added—'Oh, yes; just because Miss Grey takes the girl up you'll all go mad over her! I wouldn't make a concert-room of my house for any body.'"

"Dear Mrs. Ames," said Elinor; "as if anybody would go if she did!"

"Oh, oh! Can you say spiteful things?"

"Indeed I can! How mean it is. I always hate myself after."

"And are good-natured even to poor me by way of making amends. I am glad you nipped dear Mrs. Ames; you'll be pleasant all the rest of the evening."

"I shall go and talk to Mrs. Reese."

"That will be doing penance. But her name is not Reese any longer."

"Pray what is it?"

"Ever since she came back from Paris last autumn she has put on her cards—Reesé—with such a heavy accent."

"What a wholesale calumniator you are."

"Yes, I hate petty dealings where gossip is concerned."

But he did not want to talk that idle, foolish talk. His heart was panting and burning; he wanted to hold her fast to him—to drain her very breath with kisses—to make her love him or kill her outright with his passion. But he restrained those private insanities and did only what was decorous: people can not be Romeos or Othellos in modern dress, at least outwardly.

Elinor Grey went home that night more restless and tired then ordinary, and was heartily glad when Tom shrieked at Rosa, who had paused at her door for last words which would inevitably prolong themselves into a chat over the fire if she was left to herself—"You come this minute, you absurd last rose of summer, else to-morrow you'll look one of several summers ago, very badly preserved."

"I only want to tell Elinor—"

"Not a word, not a syllable! Elinor is a discreet damsel and wishes to seek maiden slumbers." He caught her up in his arms regardless of her flounces.

"You'll tear my lace, Tom," she pleaded.

"No matter; duty before lace."

"Oh, you monster, you hurt me! Oh, I'd like to bite you," cried Rosa. "Good-night, Elinor. Isn't he a griffin?"

She was carried shrieking along the corridor, and the next morning Tom vowed that she had bitten him, and threatened to appear at the concert with his arm bandaged and to tell the whole story when questioned.

Elinor went to her room and shut herself in with her discontent, glad at least to be relieved from any other companion. There was a letter on the dressing-table which Mademoiselle Coralie probably had forgotten to give her on its arrival. Elinor broke the seal, wondering why people would write letters, and inclined to vituperate the inventor of the art. She broke the seal and glanced down the carefully-written pages to the signature. It was from Ruth. "From Ruth Sothern," thought Elinor in surprise, and had another quick thought which made her dizzy: not Ruth Sothern now—Ruth Farnsworth. Then she sat down and began to read the letter. She was so tired that she felt dizzy still—very, very tired she kept saying to herself, as if making excuses to some one else.

It was a sweet, touching letter, like the pretty creature who wrote it. She told Elinor how she loved her—thought of her—talked of her to Clive. She told how happy she was; she painted her daily life—her bliss ineffable—and Elinor Grey read on and on till suddenly she dashed the letter down and buried her face in her dress, afraid of her own emotions. She was so proud, and for the first time in her life shame as connected with herself had drawn near—shame and humiliation. In that hour Elinor Grey had to stand face to face with her soul and acknowledge the secret which she had put away, denied, covered up, refusing to believe that it was hidden somewhere under her subterfuges. She loved Clive Farnsworth—loved him after all, in spite of all! She was jealous of this girl—his wife. Every detail of his tenderness, so artlessly described by its recipient, burned into her heart like fire and roused sensations which she had not dreamed could ever find a resting-place in her soul. Proud Elinor nearly went mad, and fought there with her shame and her horror and her agony until the cold light peeped in through the curtains.

A black, stormy vigil, but she found the one way out. When in the bleak chill dawn Elinor Grey knelt, weeping silently, the fever and excitement gone, she knew that she had lived through the worst—that she could never be exactly the same woman again—and she felt strange to herself in this new position. It would be a long time before her pride recovered from the shock; she thought the old arrogance and haughty self-reliance never could come back, and she did want so to conduct herself that this trouble should be at least purifying and ennobling. She could look at the matter more rationally. At first she could not bear her thoughts—she had been afraid to see her own face in the glass—but she was able to think at last. She knew that Clive Farnsworth could be nothing to her henceforth; that with God's help she should have no more to fear from her heart's weakness; but she was tired and worn; to take up life again was an effort of such magnitude. If she could find some new thought strong enough to engross her powers—some aim. She cast desolately about, but nothing offered, and yet life must go on.

By this time it was clear day-light, and Elinor crept into bed and tried not to think any longer, because she knew that she must sleep. She could not be like a heroine in a play, going about with pallid cheeks and disordered tresses; she must sleep and get strength and be ready to meet to-morrow which had already come. And when several hours after Coralie tapped at the door, according to orders if the non-ringing of the bell proved that her mistress had overslept herself, it seemed to Elinor that she had not really lost consciousness once, had dozed and dreamed, but always miserably aware of her own identity, and she wished that her commands about the knocking had been less imperative. She forced herself to get up, and she felt very cross and nearly snapped at faithful Coralie, which was unheard of with her. She was not perfect, and she had been born with a hasty temper, but when it did get the better of her it was where equals were concerned; she would not nip people who were forbidden to answer, as petty people of both sexes do. She was penitent under the inclination and told Coralie that she believed she was growing an ill-tempered old dragon, and Coralie expostulated till she was purple in the face. But Elinor would not listen to her asseverations, and found a sense of relief in calling herself unpleasant names—it is next best to miscalling other people—and then she rose sternly with a purpose in her soul. She did not dash pearly drops of water upon her fevered brow with a jewelled hand as the young women do in novels; she always took off her rings when she went to bed, like a sensible person. It was more than that. She marched into the adjacent bath-room, and without giving her resolution time to falter, stood under the shower and pulled the wire with a desperate jerk, and let such an infant Niagara down upon her devoted head that Coralie shivered with sympathy in the outer chamber. Presently Elinor emerged fresh and nearly frozen, and went through the duties of getting ready for sublunary gaze with her emotions chilled into quiet, as I think the fiercest and most hissing that ever desolated the bosom of a tragedy queen would have been by that barbarous treatment.

There was not much to occupy her although she was to have a concert that day; but Hungarian Henry was a host in himself, and would have managed any quantity of festivities without bustle. But to gratify the feminine weakness of liking to feel of use, Elinor and Rose made a pretense of arranging flowers, and Tom teased them, and Elinor was conscious of a wish that the world might split in twain and her expected guests land in some distant bourne where concerts are not, but controlled herself. And Rose laughed and Tom teased, and Hungarian Henry came and went on tiptoe and awed the domestic staff by the mere lifting of his finger; and Elinor could not be a five-act melodrama, but had to go and dress after rushing up and down a veranda at the back of the house till Rosa pulled her in-doors with the pleasant information that her nose would be redder than one of her scarlet geraniums by the time she was ready to receive the people. Care and trouble, cark and fret, can be thrust aside for intervals of leisure, but a red nose can not when once the color gets seated, so Miss Grey put by her doleful reflections and stopped making what Rosa called "a private menagerie" of herself, and went up stairs to get inside of a heavenly blue dress that would have made Dido postpone suicide till she had excited the envy of the female portion of Carthage by wearing it; if she had owned the gown and it had been becoming to her complexion.

By and by the performers appeared, professionals and amateurs, and Elinor solaced herself by a little talk with an operatic woman, who said so many witty things that Miss Grey was inclined to think it would be much jollier to be literary or artistic or theatrical, or something compromising and disreputable, than a Secretary's daughter and have to entertain people who were proper in the world's eyes. Then poor little Miss Borden must be consoled and soothed out of the nervousness which threatened to make her voice shaky, and the amateur singers had to be flattered and thanked and told they were—not Mario and Grisi, that would have been too mild—but seraphs and other heavenly birds. The people had begun to come, and Miss Grey departed to take her station and to say and hear pretty things till she wished herself deaf and dumb, and then to be stunned by the pianoforte banging and the operatic carollings, until at length little Borden was led forward, and stood there innocent and pretty, and sang a mournful old ballad in the freshest and sweetest of voices that made Elinor Grey's heart swell and her mood change into one of nervous excitability which caused her to long for a hysterical cry.

Watching her as he always did watch her, Leighton Rossitur knew that she was in an unusual state of mind, and he wished that it was in his power to take advantage of it. At convenient opportunities during the music, or the intervals of eating and drinking delicious abominations with which people corrode their vitals on such occasions, Mr. Grey sunned Rossitur in his smile and paved the way for making him useful, as he had contemplated, and every body said how rapidly Leighton Rossitur was rising and how far he was sure to go. And Rossitur being to the full as astute as the elder man, understood more than it was intended he should, and in his turn looked forward to possibilities where the honorable gentleman might be forced to serve him. As was natural, they were mutually satisfied, and paid each other a great many compliments, and told a great many lies, as people must who go about the world burdened with plans and looking forward to possibilities. But all the morning Rossitur kept aloof from Miss Grey. He could not understand what he read in her face; he wanted some clue so that when he did talk to her he might touch the right chord. Let those men blunder about her if they chose; they were making hideous bores of themselves, Rossitur was certain of that, for though Miss Grey smiled and talked, her eyes were leagues away and her soul was with them. Let them blunder, he was glad to have them. Why, even that sensible Boston man could not see that if he had ever had a ghost of a chance it was lost by this morning's work; and that political leader—he was worse—written down a diabolical enormity from henceforth, in the hugest possible capital letters. Rossitur was very glad, and he allowed them to bow and chatter and make blind geese of themselves, but he stood aloof and forced Elinor Grey at last to wish that he would come and help her. He was watching; he saw when she remembered and wanted him; he went up and stood behind her chair, and whispered, "You look as if you could not endure another moment. They are going at last."

Was he always to read and comprehend her thoughts? Was there really some mysterious sympathy between them which gave him this power? But Elinor had no leisure to indulge in fancies and grow transcendental, for people were rushing about her and taking leave, and it was all confusion and talkee, talkee. Rossitur helped her. He said queer things, he made the leave-takers laugh, he covered her bewilderment and confusion, and she was dimly conscious of a sensation of rest in having him there, as if her mind had suddenly found a prop to lean against.

It was late; every body declared the time had flown; and away they scampered dinnerward. Mr. Grey and the Thorntons were to dine out—Elinor had been previously excused —and as the heathens who had invited them lived a Sabbath day's journey off, according to the habit of people in the city of magnificent distances, it would soon be time to go, for life, as Tom Thornton said, was a pilgrimage. Rosa had to rush and change her dress, lest waifs of the concert people should be at the dinner and think she had only one gown. Mr. Grey retired to some retreat favorable to a doze, and Tom went off to solace himself with a cigar, declaring to Rosa that he would rather be an ostrich in the desert than lead a life like that, and Rosa told him he was worse than any ostrich in or out of a desert.

"I feel as if I had been one and had fed on rusty nails," said Tom, departing.

Elinor looked about and saw that the last of the crowd had actually disappeared; only Leighton Rossitur was standing by her chair.

"I won't speak," he said; "I ought to have gone; but you look so tired."

"I believe I am tired," replied Elinor.

"But you can rest while the people go to that dinner."

"Yes. Are you going?"

"Neither there nor anywhere; I am going home. But I wish you would let me be rude and ask to stay a few moments while you sit here quiet."

"You may stay if you can endure my stupidity."

"What do you mean to do?" he asked.

"Get up to my room, I think."

"But you are mistaken. You will think you are going; instead of that you will sit here looking at that flower-stand until some of the servants venture to disturb you."

"I dare say you are right."

"Let me prescribe, will you?"

"Certainly; I am too stupid to resist."

"There is a fire in the boudoir—please go and sit by it and rest for a long hour before you attempt the exertion of mounting the stairs."

"The advice is so in keeping with my indolence that I agree to it with pleasure."

He gave her his arm and they went through the long suite of rooms into the pretty apartment Mr. Grey had himself made a fairy nook in order to be worthy of his Elinor. Rossitur drew a low chair to the fire and she sat down. He placed himself near—doing every slight thing for her comfort in a noiseless, gentle way which was indescribably soothing to her irritated nerves, and would have been a lesson to most of us male awkwardnesses. He talked to her a little, but he did not make her talk. He prophesied a success for Miss Borden, and Elinor had the young thing's interests much at heart, and had shown the greatest possible wisdom in her choice of the people gathered for the occasion. To-day, little Borden is Signora Clementi, you know, wife of the old violinist, and has been landed in London and encored in Paris, but she may thank that morning concert of Miss Grey's for the opening, and, what is odd, she knows it and says so.

After a while voices rose in the hall; the party were starting for the dinner. "Where is Elinor?" they heard Mrs. Thornton ask.

"I think she has gone to her room," Mr. Grey replied; "she is lying down, I dare say."

"Oh, we won't disturb her," said good-natured Rosa.

Hungarian Henry stood by and held his tongue; he knew very well where his mistress could be found, having been about the rooms like a mustached ghost, putting out lights. But he was the discreetest of mortals, and since his young lady did not choose to appear he would, if questioned as to her whereabouts, have unblushingly asserted that he saw her start for her chamber, or the moon, half an hour before—blessed Henry!

There was stillness again; they had gone. Elinor leaned back in her chair with a delicious feeling of repose, and a stranger feeling that she owed it to Leighton Rossitur.

"You begin to look better," he said. "You see what an admirable adviser I am."

"It is very pleasant to be advised, too," returned she; "at least when the advice goes with one's wishes." She tried to be playful and smile—it was an effort.

"If you feel that you must talk and entertain me, I shall go away," said Rossitur. "I don't wish to kill you outright."

"Indeed I am very glad to have you stay. It isn't exactly proper, is it? You know I have not quite got beyond young-ladyhood with its necessities for chaperons and guardians."

"Luckily we are in America. It is all very well for foreigners to abuse the privileges young ladies have here — don't the foreign young women wish they could enjoy them!" returned Rossitur.

But Elinor did not answer; her thoughts had wandered. After a moment she said, "I beg your pardon ; I am very rude."

"Oh, don't say that. May I tell you what I was wishing ?"

"Yes ; if it was kind and good-natured."

"That I knew where you had gone, and so might not jar on your fancies by a wrong word."

"Nowhere, had I ? I believe I was not thinking—just going about in a circle."

"I know the feeling," he answered. He was silent for a little, then he added, "You are very lonely, Miss Grey." At another time he would not have ventured upon that speech ; but he could do it safely now.

"I ought not to be," she said slowly.

"You torment yourself by thinking that. Tired and lonely—they may not be romantic ills, but they are very hard to bear. If you only had some one thing on which to concentrate your mind, what a help it would be."

Here he was repeating her very thoughts again. She was too weak, too near crying, to remember that his conversation was going over to new and untried ground, to a landing-place which once reached can never leave any man and woman upon the ordinary terms where they stood before.

"It would be a help," she said ; "but where to find it? I am very wicked to say life is empty when I have my father who loves me so, but I think I am losing the old energy and will."

"And life will grow more empty," returned Rossitur, in a low voice which seemed like the mournful echo in her own soul ; "more and more dreary unless you find some object, something whereon to lean and rest."

"And where to find it ?"

"You are very proud and self-reliant, but that would make such rest all the sweeter ; an ordinary, weak woman could never comprehend its happiness as you would."

"You tell me this but you don't show me any way," said Elinor. She forgot that she was talking to Leighton Rossitur ; it seemed that she was answering that inward voice which tormented her so.

"May I tell you of a way ?" he asked, forcing his tones to be low and soft ; keeping back the eagerness which began to quicken them.

"If you could," she said ; "if you could."

"If some man loved you—a man whom you could trust entirely—who had a future in which you could share—who from the first moment he saw you had made you his guiding-star—had loved you—had thought only of being worthy to tell you so ; if you could listen and be patient and let him strive to earn your affection, you would find rest, Miss Grey."

He had spoken very rapidly now ; his voice was low as ever but full of a sudden passion. She had no space to interrupt him if she had wished, and she did not wish ; just then such words, such promises, brought an added feeling of quiet. Rossitur had chosen the moment well.

"I love you, Elinor Grey ! I had not thought to speak—it is stronger than I ! Let me tell you—don't be angry. I am not patient, but I could wait so patiently to earn your affection. Failing that, I would be your friend — the one person to whom you could talk freely, could trust and lean upon."

Elinor Grey listened ; she had no mind to interrupt him. "I think you ought not to say that," she answered ; "I don't believe I am half worthy such love."

"But I have given it—I can not take it back ! You will not despise the gift ?"

"Despise it ? I am grateful—I thank you."

If she could be interested in him ; if he could make her love him ! Ah, here was a way out of danger and pain, which would annihilate the past as completely as if she had gone into another world—a hope indeed. She was not thinking of Clive Farnsworth ; she could keep him from her thoughts now that she knew such memories were a sin ; but here was more than forgetfulness proffered—a new interest in life, a hope for the future always growing stronger and more sweet.

"If you could feel even a sense of rest in such love, tell me, would it not be pleasant ?" he asked.

"Very pleasant ; so much more than I deserve—I who have so little to give."

He had known before that Elinor Grey did not love him, but those words were a blow as they would have been to any man. He would not heed—he had passed the limits—he would dare every thing now only to establish the weakest link between himself and her, trusting to time and his own power.

"No matter how little you gave ; a look would be more precious than the full love of another woman. Oh, Miss Grey, they call me cold and ambitious. I am ambitious ! no man would have a right to love you who was not. But I need you to keep me right, to keep life noble and pure ; my heart needs you more than all, for it has found its idol."

Elinor tried to rouse herself and not go drifting down the stream of such sweet words.

"I am wrong," she said ; "I am treating your love unworthily by listening with such selfishness merely because it is pleasant."

"If you listen I am content. If you can give me the least hope, you raise me up from the darkness into heaven."

He was very handsome and noble now ; his whole face was aglow ; he looked a man whom any woman might trust, proud of his affection.

"Do you indeed love me so ?" she asked, almost wonderingly.

"Have you never suspected it ? Could you not see ?"

She shook her head. "You may know how selfish I am—I have not thought. You made yourself pleasant—a friend to whom I could talk. I have learned to expect your kindness; I missed you if I did not see you; but I have been very selfish and blind."

"You give me the sweetest reward! Think what your words mean."

Elinor sat upright and forced herself out of the dreamy bewilderment. "I must not allow you to deceive yourself," she answered; "they meant literally what I said, and I have been very, very selfish."

"You must not say that; you make me so happy. I have longed to know if you remembered me, separated me in your thoughts from the crowd about you."

"I have done that, perhaps more than I was conscious."

"Then I am quite satisfied."

He was so humble, but so manly; so strong in his humility that she felt a keen pang of self-reproach.

"I am not worth this," she said sadly.

"You are worth the love of an angel! Don't pain me by underrating yourself. Where is there a woman like you, with your noble mind and your generous heart?"

"It is very sweet to be so praised, Mr. Rossitur," she said.

"Will you tell me that I may hope?" he pleaded. "Only say one word—only don't forbid me."

"I must be honest, Mr. Rossitur. I am tired and confused, but I must not let you go away thinking things for which you would afterward have a right to reproach me very bitterly."

"I could never do that! All my life long I should hold myself honored by the thought that you had tried to love me."

"Perhaps I must not even promise that."

"But let me love you—let me strive to win, to earn your affection—I will ask nothing more."

"That would be unjust to you, Mr. Rossitur."

"Let me decide that; I am quite content. May I love you—may I hope?"

"But if you found that your love and your noblenesss had been wasted—if I could not return them—"

"I gave you my answer. I should be proud to think I had loved you," he answered.

"Oh, this must not be!" she cried. "If you talked to me of esteem and admiration, I should not feel ashamed to listen."

"If you can only say that you begin with those!"

"You know I can. But it must be a disappointment to you. I only wonder that you are not angry with me and yourself for lavishing your love on a woman who can reply so coldly."

"Ah, Elinor Grey, can not you imagine a love strong enough to be humble? I don't think I am a good man, but I love you so I can't be selfish. If my affection can give you a little rest—if it would ever soothe a lonely hour to think, 'He loves me,' I shall be repaid."

F

"And it would," Elinor replied; "I shall acknowledge that. It would please me, too, that in your hopes of success you thought of me. But all this is terribly selfish, and I am ashamed."

"Oh, Elinor, Elinor!" he cried, "let this be! Share my hopes with me—talk with me—think of them! My whole soul is at your feet and will not come away! I can not remember my disappointment—I can only feel your words. Let me love you!"

Elinor leaned back in her chair and shaded her eyes with her hand. "I want to be honest," she said; "I want, if possible, to tell you exactly how I feel. In this moment I am so softened by your love that I could yield—I could engage myself to you—but it would be misery for both."

"I do not ask you to bind yourself—"

"Nor must you be bound."

"Too late. I would not change it if I could."

And once she had had thoughts of this man —had doubted him! What a wretch she was, and what miserable cheats her boasted intuitions were.

"I don't see where we are," she said slowly; "for both our sakes we must see the ground clear now. I tell you fairly it would be better if you could go away and learn to think of me as a friend—"

"That is impossible! Don't torture me."

"But if you stay, what shall I answer?"

"Tell me I may wait—that I may try to teach you to love me. No matter how long a term you put, I shall be content. This binds you to nothing—I must love you—at least it will be kinder than sending me away into the dark."

"It may not be in the end. I can not feel this right, Mr. Rossitur."

"But you can not help my loving you; that admitted, is it not a kindness to show you think my love worthy of consideration?"

"But this might go on for years."

"Then set a time when I may come for my answer. From here till then I will tease you with no love-making. We will be friends, but friends in the truest sense, who talk with their hearts open. Will you consent, Miss Grey?"

"I can not think it fair—"

"These are the vainest scruples! Or, Elinor, if you could content yourself with being loved you might marry me to-morrow."

"I would not do you that wrong. No, Mr. Rossitur, if I ever do become your wife I must love you. It might be safe for another woman to marry with a less motive, but not for me."

"You have taken one step when you contemplate the possibility."

"Do not deceive yourself; believe exactly what I say. You must understand me thoroughly or I should be wretched."

"I do understand. Will you let me wait? May I come again with this question?"

"But when?"

"You shall decide. Months, years—Elinor, I can wait."

"But there shall be a limit. I am doing wrong, Mr. Rossitur: it must be wrong."

"At least you shall not answer me now—in July."

"July?" repeated she. "If I could be certain it was right."

"Is it pleasant to you? Are you glad to think that if you can love me my heart is yours, waiting?"

"It is such a rest—you can not know."

"Then it is right. I don't care for the past. I am not afraid that any man will come between us."

"I should never marry you if there was a shadow," she answered. "I am not a young girl, you know, Mr. Rossitur. It is fair to tell you that once my heart went very near another, but he never knew it, nor did I know it till such thoughts could be only a memory."

"I thank you for your confidence; it does not trouble me."

It did not. He was certain of victory; he liked to triumph, and would find a pleasure in driving the old dream away: it would be a sort of revenge on the man.

"If between now and that time you can turn your heart from me," she continued, "I ask you to do it. Will you promise?"

"I promise."

"And yet I feel that I am treating you unfairly."

"Think of me as the truest and most devoted of your friends. Learn to call me by that name, will you?"

"My friend!" she repeated. "It sounds very sweet."

"And sometimes when we are alone may I call you Elinor? The name comes so naturally to my lips."

"I only ask you to do nothing that you shall afterward regret. In the worst I could bear people calling me a flirt, but I could not bear you to think you had been humiliated before the world."

"I understand. I should not care for that."

"I think it would not be doing right by you to repeat this conversation even to my father at present," she said. "I may tell him—"

"I should be glad he knew."

"That would seem to you like a hope. I will be honest."

"I can't praise you—I haven't any words. Perhaps, Elinor, another man would think it necessary to remind you that he was poor—to assure you that your wealth had not influenced him—"

She interrupted him with a disdainful gesture.

"You would despise him for it," he went on, as if he had not observed her movement. "I am not afraid of your money: probably I shall never think about it."

"Nor I, unless to be glad, if—"

"If you could learn to love me! Finish the words, Elinor."

"Don't make me say any thing that I could regret."

"Not a word, not a syllable," he said. "I wont talk to you any more about it. You shall rest now and forget every thing except that you have a friend to whom you can go when the world looks empty and dark."

"You are so good to me!"

"So good to myself, you mean, Elinor."

He had been gentle and cautious—not even touching her hand as a man with less keen perceptions would have done. Indeed, if Leighton Rossitur could always have been what he believed himself in that honr, Elinor need not have feared to trust her future to him.

"I have been unconscionable," he exclaimed; "a brute to forget how tired you were."

"No, I am rested."

"And is the loneliness gone?"

"Quite gone."

He gave her one of those beaming smiles which made his face so young.

"It is I who have no conscience. I have let you stay here and make me dreamy and content, quite forgetting you ought to be away eating your dinner like a sensible man."

"Please let me stay. I don't want any dinner! I won't be romantic—I ate all sorts of things to get the taste of Mrs. De Lucy's singing out of my mouth. Oh, you are laughing! I am glad to see it. Now mayn't I prescribe for you again?"

"Certainly. I am not half so strong-minded as I seem. I like to be directed."

"Let me ring for that old Paragon and you shall have a cup of tea, and then let me sit and read or talk—if you are not utterly weary—the people will not be at home for hours."

"You are so good to me," she repeated. She felt very childish, this proud Elinor.

Rossitur just gave her a look—it was better than any words. He rang, and when Henry, who never allowed any sacrilegious under-servant to answer the boudoir bell, appeared, Miss Grey told him to bring some tea.

"You shall have some of my orange pekoe, Mr. Rossitur," said she, "as a reward for keeping me company in my solitude."

So Henry tripped away and fulfilled her orders. Henry adored his mistress, and never thought any thing about her beyond what she said, though a long pilgrimage in this dreary world had made him fearfully wise: and having served as confidential servant to great people of all sexes and nations, he considered human nature a wretched failure in general, but Miss Grey sat on a throne in his imagination. He came back with the tea and a priceless little equipage of old Dresden which was a fit accompaniment to the nectar.

Rossitur would not let Elinor move. He poured out a cup for her and sweetened it just enough: most men are crooked abortions when they attempt such pretty little tasks. Elinor drank her tea and felt revived, and Rossitar sat there for a long time, talking about agreeable things, but never once betrayed into the weakness of going back to the old subject. He made her laugh, and he laughed too as blithely as a boy, and glided to graver topics and led her to talk about his hopes and feel an interest in them, knowing that here was his strongest ground, the surest way of teaching her woman's nature to feel an interest in himself.

At last he went away, making her promise that she would go at once to bed and have a long night's rest. "You are sure you are better?" he asked.

"Much better, thanks to you."

"And you won't be lonely? You will remember your friend who is thinking of you, longing to help you."

"I will remember my friend."

He took her hand—the fair, beautiful hand with so much character in its carefully-modelled proportions—looked longingly at it, then laid it softly back on the arm of her chair as if it had been some sacred treasure. Elinor Grey was a woman to appreciate that delicacy. It was one bit of acting that night—he knew it would please her—but it was acting in which his feelings so mixed themselves that it was natural enough he should have thought it real.

CHAPTER XVII.
A NEW INMATE.

THE Thorntons brought their visit to an end before Elinor or her father were resigned to losing their sunny faces, but Tom was, or fancied himself, called back to town. It was not oftener than once in six months that Tom was seized with a mania for thinking he had business which required immediate attention; when it did happen, Rosa declared that he fluttered like a pigeon tied to a stake, and imagined himself performing remarkable feats because he beat his wings insanely and made a grand outcry. Some news he received at this time excited the semi-annual fever; go he must, and Rosa would go with him, inventing numerous subterfuges, which Elinor pulled to pieces one by one. "At least acknowledge that you can not stay away from that troublesome Tom," said she.

"I believe that is the truth," returned Rosa, apparently in great surprise at the discovery. "I suppose the reason I did not recognize it, is because truth is a stranger to me."

"You are a foolish dove," said Elinor.

"Yes; but you envy me having some one to be foolish over, you tyrannical woman, afraid to share your sovereignty."

"Perhaps I do," replied Elinor; "I mean to be an exception to old maids in general—I will always own that I would have married if I could."

"Don't say such horrid things," cried Rosa. "I won't have my friends called names!"

"Except by yourself."

"Of course I will call them all the wickednesses I please. The truth is," continued Rosa, "I ought to stay and watch you. Here are troops of men about—which is it to be?"

"I could not venture to decide until you pronounce judgment, dear."

"Oh, you satirical, deceitful puss. None of the foreigners—I won't have that."

"I promise."

"Not the politician—his nose turns up."

"He shall never have a legal right to turn it up at me, love, I assure you."

"Well, not the high and mighty Bostonian, either—he walks as if he had a cork leg."

"I am warned, Cassandra. Are there any others?"

"Hosts, and you know it; don't be aggravating. Let me see. No, I do not believe I should like Mr. Rossitur, though he is so graceful and witty."

"I will tell him when he asks me," said Elinor. "But you will finish the list and leave me still unprovided for."

"There's nobody fit to have you," said Rosa.

"'Praise from,' etcetera."

"And you're a provoking panther—so you are," moaned Rosa. "I can't let you marry any of them; but I must do my duty, and see you safe in the hands of some human tiger-tamer."

"Then you had better stay."

"Don't urge me—I am torn by conflicting emotions," replied she. "No; I must go. Tom needs me, and somehow I'm not quite well—I am dolefully conscious of a back and painfully aware of a shoulder. I'll go to town and keep Lent."

"And get quite strong again."

"Oh, there is nothing the matter to speak of. And Elinor—it won't be Mr. Rossitur?"

"I think he is safe, Rosa."

"I can't tell why—I like him—I don't like him. He seems all sincerity and frankness; I don't know what it is. He laughs with his mouth, and his eyes look so watchful and cold all the while."

Elinor remembered her old feeling in regard to him; she did not wish to hear it repeated by Rosa.

"Don't have intuitions," said she; "and never mind any of the set—troublesome creatures."

"Just wait till you come to me in the summer," returned Rosa; "we will leave this matter till then."

"Postpone it for ten summers, if you like."

"The provoking thing; she doesn't care," exclaimed Rosa, apostrophizing a bust of Clytie. "She wants to put me out of temper—I'll be angelic just to disappoint her."

Elinor was glad to get away from the discussion. The opinion Rosa had pronounced concerning Rossitur gave her a feminine desire to contradict; but though, woman-like, she would have defended him warmly, it made her think of that first evening, and she could not forget it, until, meeting him, his genial manner served to put the fancy out of sight again.

The days and weeks got by, and Lenten dullness took the place of the late festivities, but people said that it was much less quiet than usual, and certain it is that a moderate person would have been very well satisfied with the gayety which still reigned.

One day there came a telegram from New York; Miss Laidley had arrived there and was in a state of bewilderment at not being received by her guardian or some of his friends; and her guardian was equally astonished that he had not previously been made acquainted with her intentions. That morning's post brought a package of Jamaica letters which explained the matter and showed that the affectionate aunt had duly written. The epistles had been delayed and must have come by the steamer which conveyed the young lady herself. Hungarian Henry was dispatched to town to smooth all earthly ills from Miss Laidley's path, and as one of Mr. Grey's friends would be returning from New York in a day or so, the Paragon took a note to him, that he might proffer his assistance to the heiress, and she feel herself treated with due consideration. Elinor saw that her father was afraid she was annoyed, so she received the tidings good-naturedly, gave orders for rooms to be put in readiness, and only hinted that if the young lady was so delicate she wondered at the aunt's allowing her to come North at that season.

"She says Miss Laidley's spirits were affecting her health, and there was a good opportunity for her to come on," replied Mr. Grey.

"I am afraid she will find it dull; she is in mourning, too."

"Poor Laidley has been dead a year," said he; "a little amusement will do the poor thing good."

Elinor thought, what was a year; nor indeed had so much time as that elapsed; but she said nothing, deciding to wait until she saw whether Miss Laidley might be inclined to rush into society, in which case she would reserve to herself the privilege of setting her down in her own mind as an unnatural monster.

The next day but one Elinor heard a bustle in the hall, the pulling about of heavy trunks, and she knew that the guest had arrived—her precious freedom from restraint was a thing of the past. She indulged in a long sigh and went down stairs, meeting Hungarian Henry, who bowed low before her and informed her that he had seated the newly-arrived in the breakfast-room. Elinor went in and saw a slight figure clad in voluminous black draperies cowering over the fire, although the room was like a hot-house.

"I am very glad to see you, Miss Laidley," said she cheerfully, determined to make the wanderer feel at home, and touched by the forlorn attitude which her entrance had disturbed. "You are here safe at last. The letters missed, which must account for any seeming neglect."

Elinor walked up to the visitor and extended her hand with her most winning smile, and Miss Laidley, with a little cry of astonishment, rose and held out both hers. "I am so glad to see you, Miss Grey," said she; "how nice you are to receive me so cordially." .

"I suppose you are half frozen," returned Elinor; "sit still by the fire and take your bonnet off. Was the journey very tiresome?"

"I didn't mind it," replied Miss Laidley; "I am used to travelling." She threw aside her bonnet and heavy cloak, and Elinor looked with natural curiosity to see what this stranger was like who was to be placed in such close companionship with herself for a year to come. A tall, slight figure, a face with lilies and roses, a profusion of houri hair, all made up a pretty girl. Elinor looked, and was too much softened by the astray, melancholy expression, which she had not yet put aside, to form judgments, and in her turn Miss Laidley looked and kept her sentiments to herself.

"I am glad you are here safe," repeated Elinor.

"And I am so glad to be here," replied Miss Laidley.

"Please to give yourself a home feeling at once, Miss Laidley," continued her hostess; "we must forget that we are strangers."

"Thank you. I have thought about you so much, Miss Grey, that you don't seem a stranger. I was so disappointed when I arrived at New York. I knew the letters must have failed. I didn't want to come on at all, but Aunt Gordon was uneasy about my health."

"Your guardian's house seems your natural home—if you can be content," said Elinor. She became conscious that she was fibbing a little in her desire to be hospitable; it did not seem natural that this stranger should be quartered there. "I trust your health will improve," she hastened to add.

"Oh, there is nothing ails me; only Aunty fidgets. I am a nervous, absurd thing, that is all. I have had so much trouble, you know—poor papa." She began to cry a little in a becoming way, and Elinor comforted her, and that went far toward establishing an acquaintance, for it was Elinor's nature to be kindly disposed toward any one who needed consolation. When Miss Laidley had cried enough she dried her eyes, and in five minutes was smiling and talking gayly. "You look as I expected, Miss Grey," said she; "only you are more beautiful."

Now Elinor knew that on ordinary occasions she was not beautiful; to-day she was paler than usual, and her eyes were black. She gave Miss Laidley due credit for her sincerity; and not being softened any longer, owing to the disappearance of the melancholy expression, she commenced passing judgment in her mind.

"I hope you won't hate me for being your father's ward," said Miss Laidley, after an instant's pause which Elinor had not filled up with a return compliment. "It must be odious to have a young girl forced in on you."

"I hope we can make it mutually pleasant," replied she. Were they to come to pin-thrusts already? Miss Laidley had spoken of herself as a "young girl;" did she mean that Elinor was so near spinsterhood that she ought to hate her?

"I am sure it will be delightful for me," exclaimed Miss Laidley. "I shall love you—I always know the moment I see a person—something here never deceives me;" and she laid her hand on her heart.

"You are very good to be favorably impressed, Miss Laidley," said Elinor.

"And you must love me a little — now won't you? I may as well tell you in the beginning—I always own it—I'm a ridiculous thing—just like a pane of glass. I say everything in the most heedless way. Aunty always scolds me, but I can't remember." She looked very pretty and artless; Elinor was sorry to decide that she was a cat. "But you'll keep me straight, Miss Grey," continued she; "you look very sensible."

"She means I am ugly," thought Elinor. "Come, this is quite refreshing."

"Promise in advance to love me," said Miss Laidley. "I've told you all my faults—and I am good-tempered. Now tell me about yourself."

"I am afraid I can not be so frank; I shall leave you to find out my faults."

"I don't believe you have any. How you will help me. Only do love me, though I'm not a bit intellectual. And call me Genevieve, won't you?"

"It is very pretty name," said Elinor, evasively.

"I am glad you like it. Papa called me Eva and Evangel—dear papa!" She shed two more pearly drops, then talked again. "You see I have been absurdly petted and spoiled; I'm a perfect child. Just remember that, and so excuse me always, won't you?"

"I will think of it if occasion should require," replied Elinor.

"You are so kind. I fancy I could be afraid of you, but I won't; you look very stately though."

"I hope you won't find me very formidable."

"You are delightful. I can remember seeing you once—I was a tiny thing—I recollect you as tall and grave and queenly."

Elinor did a little subtraction very rapidly. Miss Laidley was two years and six months younger than herself; the airs of extreme youthfulness and the implied gap of immensity between their ages was a good beginning.

"Do you recollect me?" asked Miss Laidley.

"Oh yes, enough to make me feel that I am welcoming an acquaintance."

"Say friend—I want to be such friends with you! Was I pretty, dear Miss Grey?"

"Very pretty."

"And terribly spoiled?"

"Terribly."

And Miss Laidley clapped her hands and cooed; and she did it very charmingly.

"The infantile style is becoming to her," thought Elinor. "Now I wonder if it is natural, or if she is an artful little animal. She isn't little though; it's only that she's so slight and willowy."

Miss Laidley had burst out again. "And your papa, tell me about him. Oh, I know he is fascinating; all the world says that. Will he like me?"

"Yes, I am sure he will," Elinor answered confidently, feeling certain that Miss Laidley could make herself agreeable to any man.

"You must tell me what will please him—won't you?"

"Just be yourself; I am certain he will be charmed."

"Ah, you have complimented me at last," cried she with another coo. "I do love compliments, and I always own it; Aunty scolded me for that too. Oh dear, she's very severe; but I love her. She's so strict with her daughters; but they are not a bit pretty."

"You must have been a dangerous rival, then," said Elinor.

"I was in mourning, you know; but still they were jealous. Oh, I didn't mean that—I told you how heedless I was—I am very fond of them all." She went on to tell how happy they had all been together—the sort of sentiment in which the aunt had indulged in her letter.

"You must have grieved very much at leaving them," said Elinor.

"I was heart-broken. Only toward the last it wasn't so pleasant. Cousin Josephine had a lover and they were engaged, and the stupid fellow must needs be struck with little me. I was so sorry. I couldn't help it, you know."

"Did they think you could?"

"I'm afraid they did. Aunty looked so black and Josephine cried till her nose—oh, I can't give you an idea how her nose looked."

"I trust it has resumed its natural appearance before this, and that she is reconciled to her lover," said Elinor.

"Dear me, I'm afraid not. He went off to Cuba. You see I was lonesome and used to walk in the myrtle grove a great deal; and he had no business to come there, but he would—"

"Dare danger."

"Yes—oh no, I didn't mean to be dangerous. I never thought at all—only about poor papa. But one day the great goose went down on his knees to me, and Josephine found him."

"That was unpleasant."

"Oh dear, I wished myself in heaven. There was a great scene. I said I hadn't expected it—that I didn't care a pin for him; but she sent him off. He met me once after, and tried to be nonsensical, but I wouldn't have it—you can understand how I felt." Elinor thought she understood the matter with tolerable clearness. Miss Laidley must flirt and tease somebody; if a woman's heart was broken and a man's faith violated, she could only cry and say, "I didn't think."

"But how I am gossiping," she exclaimed.

"I told you how heedless I was. Indeed I wasn't to blame, and I love them all very much. I know I shall tell you every thing; you are the sort of person one can't help being confidential with; magnetism, isn't it?"

"I am not a professor," said Elinor.

"Oh, you are laughing at me. I dare say I am silly.' But I can always tell—I feel it here—in my heart. And you must talk to me. Oh, have you any secrets, Miss Grey?"

"Not one, unfortunately."

"Such a pity. I always have a hundred at least; a little mystery is so nice. But you have hosts of admirers, I have heard, and they say you love nobody, and are like—like—Diana. Who was she?" She did and said nonsensical things in a very bewitching way. Elinor had not fully decided whether she were only weak, selfish, vain, and with a certain quickness of wit that answered instead of intellect, or whether there was more under. "Shall we go up stairs now?" she asked. "By the time we get dressed my father will be home."

"I shall be so nervous; I hope I won't be afraid," returned Miss Laidley. "I must look a perfect fright too. Do tell me if my eyelids are red."

"'Twin white rose leaves,'" quoted Elinor.

"How pretty; I wish I could say such pretty things."

"Unfortunately it was not original."

"Oh, you read? They say you are so intellectual; and I don't know any thing. I shall try to be like you. No, it wouldn't do; I should be ridiculous. I must be an absurd little canary-bird to the end of my days."

Elinor gathered the wraps and they went up stairs. Miss Laidley was in ecstasies with her two pretty rooms.

"You can have all the retirement you wish," said Elinor.

"Thank you—so good. But I don't like to be alone much. You'll let me sit with you, won't you?"

"You shall have as much of my society as you choose to take," replied Elinor, but she groaned inwardly at the prospect of having her privacy intruded upon. "I hope you will be happy with us, Miss Laidley."

"Happy as a bird—only for thinking of dear papa. But I won't be gloomy; I promised Aunty I would not, and I must obey her now poor papa is gone."

Elinor thought of the myrtle grove, of the young man down on his knees, of the unfortunate Ariadne with her swollen nose, and the mother's rage—it all joined prettily with this last bit of dutiful sentiment.

"And your father," pursued Miss Laidley; "of course I shall consult him and do what he wishes."

"It will be unnecessary trouble; only amuse yourself and my father will be quite content," said Elinor, and she had some difficulty in saying it smoothly.

"But I shall need his advice and yours; you must keep me straight, Miss Grey—I am so heedless."

Enough of this for once was what Miss Grey thought, but she said — "I believe, then, I must begin by advising you to dress. I see they have brought your boxes. Will you have my maid?"

"Oh, mine is with me—my old Juanita—the most faithful mulatto; she doats on me."

Miss Grey without more ado rang for the faithful Juanita and she appeared, a shrivelled middle-aged woman with great gold hoops in her ears, and wild eyes that made her look like a gipsy, and a complexion so peculiar that it was not easy to decide whether she were yellowish-brown or brownish - yellow. She chattered Spanish and she talked volubly in English; she kissed Miss Grey's hand, flew at her young mistress and embraced her as if they had been separated for a year; and Elinor went to her own room feeling that there never were mistress and maid more completely suited to each other, and wishing devoutly that their stars had led them in any direction except to their present shelter.

When Elinor was dressed she tapped at Miss Laidley's door, but the young lady was not ready.

"Presently, if she please, Senora mia," said Juanita. "My young lady not quite ready, bless you."

"She will find me in the library," said Elinor.

She had not been sitting there long before her father came in, scrupulously dressed for dinner—a compliment he always paid his daughter.

"You have heard of Miss Laidley's arrival, I suppose, papa?" Elinor said.

"Yes, my daughter. Won't she be down to dinner?"

"She was not quite ready to appear."

"I know you made her feel at home, my Elinor."

"I tried to, papa. I think she will accommodate herself easily to new scenes."

"I hope you will like her. I am very selfish for my daughter Elinor, I am afraid; I ought to be thinking of her likes, poor young stranger."

Elinor went and kissed him and told him what a blessed darling he was, but just then the door opened and Miss Laidley appeared. She was dressed in black, but her neck and arms were uncovered, and her beautiful hair was relieved by white flowers; Elinor would hardly have known her. She stood for a second by the door in the loveliest attitude of timidity.

"Now I know why she wasn't ready," thought wicked Elinor; "she did not wish the effect of her entrance spoiled." If Elinor's thought was correct, one could not blame the creature; she did the thing perfectly. I can give you no idea of what it was like, unless you saw Laura Keene in the days when she charmed all New York. Mr. Grey admired the attitude to the full and went forward to meet her. "I need no introduction to my ward," he said. "My dear young lady, I am delighted to see you."

Miss Laidley threw back her head a little, held out both white hands, and smiled at him like an Undine. "I am glad to see you too, Sir—I am a little frightened—I know you will be good to me, though." Then the white hands sank in his in such a confiding way, the blue eyes looked so trustingly up, and with his antique gallantry Mr. Grey kissed the dainty fingers and thought her bewitching. He told her how grieved he was the letters should have been delayed—what a pleasure her arrival was—asked her to feel at home, and was very agreeable. "We will at least study your happiness," said he.

"You are so kind. It reminds me of papa." She struck another attitude—it was 'prettier than the first—and the great tears filled her blue eyes.

"My poor child," said Mr. Grey, "we have grieved with you; don't think of those sad things."

"I won't—I didn't mean to—you won't notice my foolishness," said Miss Laidley, brokenly.

"I honor you for your tenderness to the beloved memory," returned Mr. Grey, but he looked somewhat helplessly toward Elinor, not being much accustomed to young women who were of the melting order. But Miss Laidley gave Elinor no time to come to the rescue; she dashed away her tears, glided out of the drooping attitude, and smiled brightly on her guardian. He made proper inquiries after her aunt and family, and said how much he would like to see them again. He always remembered them as a hungry pelican and her brood, but he did not say that. "I suppose you found the sea voyage very tiresome."

"Oh very; I was horribly sick. I did think I should die, and I didn't want to, you know."

"We couldn't have spared you, I know," said he.

"But there were some pleasant people on board," she continued; "Mrs. Jameson and I quite enjoyed it when we got well."

"Many ladies?"

"Oh no; only two or three." She said it with such devout thankfulness in her voice, quite unconscious though, that Elinor smiled.

Dinner was announced, and Elinor, all the while thinking how silly it was, felt a pang when her father offered his arm to Miss Laidley. No more pleasant tête-à-tête dinners to which he had led her with such charming courtesy; this girl would always be there now. The coming year looked very long as Miss Grey regarded it on her progress into the dining-room. "And if she doesn't marry, she may stay with us after her majority," she thought. "Oh, Rosa Thornton shall find her a husband; she must have a husband."

But the dinner was gay; Elinor did her part, and her father talked, and Miss Laidley said any quantity of heedless things, but was never silly. In his masculine blindness Mr. Grey hoped that his ward might prove an agreeable companion to Elinor after all. "I suppose Washington is dull now," she said.

"Very," replied Mr. Grey; "but we must try not to let the time drag on your hands."

"Oh, if I consulted my own wishes I should stay shut up in the house," she answered.

"But that would not be wise, my dear young lady—"

"No, I promised Aunty I would go out. She made me promise to get some things in New York; and I wanted to obey her last request, you know; I must not be selfish."

"You could never be that, I am sure," said Mr. Grey.

"I am in half-mourning, any way," she continued, turning to Elinor. "I got all lavenders and whites—lovely things. I shall be heartbroken, I know, at going out; but I won't be selfish and make every body miserable by my gloom."

"Your sentiments do you the greatest credit," said Mr. Grey, for he had a horror of mourning or being reminded that there were such unpleasant things in the world as sorrow and death.

"Then I shall say my guardian insists on my not staying shut up," returned she.

"I do indeed; I can not permit it."

"It weighs on my spirits so; I get miserable."

Mr. Grey inwardly vowed that go out she should; he could not endure having a lachrymose damsel in his tent.

"But I wouldn't dance," she added to Elinor; "unless it might be in the most private way."

"You can easily go to the little reunions people give in Lent," said Mr. Grey. "My dear young lady, you must allow me to insist that you do—and you must dance."

"I shall obey you; I mean to be good." She smiled at him artlessly, and Elinor could have boxed her ears. It was plain to her that the girl only wanted to force her father to urge her to go out, that she might have an excuse if blamed; and she was a little monster, just as Rosa Thornton had predicted.

When people learned that the other heiress had arrived she had any number of calls, and did what Elinor expected. She told every body how loth she was to stir out, how any approach to gayety jarred upon her feelings. But she averred that she could not be selfish; she had promised her guardian not to make a nun of herself; besides, it would be wicked of her to sadden her kind friends with her sorrows.

Elinor found that Miss Laidley expected an opening festivity of some kind in the house in honor of her arrival. Not that she said so; she only accidentally admitted that some of the callers had asked when there was to be such, and that she had not known what to say. Elinor complied, and gathered a set to look at the heiress, who was more than a little dissatisfied because it was not a ball, and told people how saintly dear Miss Grey was; how she admired her: only she did hope she would not be perverted to Romanism. Naturally it was not long before Elinor heard that a report was prevalent that her reading of Doctor Pusey and keeping of Church days was fast leading her into the bosom of the Scarlet Woman, but she did not trace the story to Miss Laidley, and deigned no contradiction.

"Dear Elinor insists on having a little party for me," the young lady said to Mr. Grey. "I know you want to make me happy. I can not thank you enough. If you see me looking sad, remind me of it; don't let me seem ungrateful."

Mr. Grey praised and flattered her to her heart's content, and went away thinking what an affectionate little thing she was and what a pretty picture she made with the tears in her blue eyes. The disconsolate one shut herself in her room and ordered old Juanita to spread out the numberless new robes which had come on from Madame Pinchon, that she might decide which would be most becoming and would utterly annihilate Miss Grey. She tried to make Juanita own that their hostess was handsome in order that she might be vexed, but Juanita was too wise, and then Miss Laidley scratched her, metaphorically, for disappointing her.

After the evening, when she was so quiet that Elinor was surprised, the invitations began to be frequent, and Miss Laidley sighed and wept a little, but declared that she could not hesitate about making the sacrifice for her guardian and her beloved Miss Grey. So Elinor said to her father—"I must ask Mrs. Copeland to go out with us; I believe I can't play chaperon quite yet." And Mrs. Copeland was quite happy to oblige the young ladies, but Miss Laidley said artlessly—"Dear me, Miss Grey, how stupid I am. I never thought but that you could be chaperon to both of us."

"I wonder if I have gray hair and wrinkles?" thought Elinor. "Little gnat, either you are very shallow or you are too pert for any woman's politeness to endure long."

It was not a great while before Elinor discovered Miss Laidley's drift at least in one direction. She had been quiet at first because she was watching people. The myrtle grove affair was evidently the sort of amusement in which Miss Laidley delighted. The unscrupulous way in which she spoiled married womens' flirtations and took possession of other girls' lovers, was something good to see; and all the while she was so innocent that every body except the deserted ones was deceived. She bewailed her successes without reserve, was pained and had not meant any harm—a poor little thing who was grieving for her dear papa, and would not go out only that she had no right to make her guardian's house dark with her sorrow. She told Elinor things which made her listener's hair stand on end, although she was not a prude, nor given to suspecting other women of wickedness; but Miss Laidley was so childish about it, one could hardly believe she comprehended how wrong it was, and she cried if any body looked disapproval.

Leighton Rossitur was a good deal at the house, and Miss Laidley was dying to discover if Elinor cared for him; failing in that, she left him out of her guerilla attacks until such time as she might have exhausted the field which was plain before her. "She is one of those creatures to whom the French words she is fond of using so well apply," said Rossitur one evening to Miss Grey. "She is *gracieuse, caline, enfantine*; I hope she hasn't claws."

"I think she is only thoughtless and childish," said Elinor good-naturedly. "She is very pretty, and seems very amiable."

"She is too selfish to be otherwise unless opposed," returned Rossitur; and with his usual discernment he read Miss Laidley very correctly. The terms on which Miss Grey and Leighton Rossitur stood were exceptional enough, but he was faithful to his promise; there was no love-making. He proved a delightful companion during those weeks. No Bayard was ever more chivalrous and devoted; but he never endangered his position by a moan or a sentimental look. Whenever he could see Elinor alone he talked as he would only to the person whom in the whole world he most honored and respected. He needed her approval to every hope; with it all he made it apparent that he regarded her as a devotee might some guardian saint worshiped in secret. He was always shielding her from annoyance or weariness, but so cautiously that people did not talk. He made himself necessary to her in numberless ways, and day after day Elinor felt how rapidly she was learning to trust him, to lean on him. Willingly would she have gone further if it had been possible; but when she tried in thought, there came such an ache in her heart, such a loathing and horror of the very idea of loving any man now, that she had to get away from the thought. She must think of him as her friend—the truest and most devoted woman ever had. In that light it was a pleasure to think of him; it rested her in her solitary hours, and kept from her the loneliness and desolation. But the instant she tried to go beyond this there was a recoil so violent that it actually affected her physically—the touch of his hand in the dance would make her shudder.

Dangerous work for a woman so organized to try to love any man; and Elinor becoming conscious of it, reposed wholly on the friendship, conscientiously endeavoring not to do the least thing which could make him feel that he had been trifled with if the term of probation should close and find her no nearer him than now.

CHAPTER XVIII.

THE IDOL'S SUCCESS.

ABOUT this time Mrs. Hackett, the golden Idol, being in need of change, made her appearance in Washington, with two maids and a man, and an express train full of baggage, as was befitting her state and dignity. The colonization movement had proved a failure, and the Idol wearying of it, the scheme was likely to die a lingering death and be buried ignominiously. Mrs. Hackett had found doing the public benefactress tiresome business. Vulgar people had actually besieged her doors; odorous specimens of the Great Unwashed in the way of foreign poor had stood on the steps of her mansion and desired to be sent to the land of gold without delay; altogether it was more than she bargained for. So she came away to the Capital and established herself for a few weeks.

I am inclined to think that she had hoped to be invited to take up her quarters in the Secretary's house; and Mr. Grey, with a recollection of the need of keeping the Bull tranquil in his Wall Street pasture strong upon him, hinted to Elinor that he supposed such invitation would be agreeable. But that sacrifice Miss Grey felt would be a work of supererogation. She compromised for any number of dinners, and courtesies of every other description, and Mr. Grey was glad to yield, conscious that to make the house a temporary shrine for the Idol would be terribly overpowering.

Mrs. Hackett was feasted to an extent that would have been dangerous to anybody but a golden Idol with a digestion to match, and the wheels of her pedestal rolled from the White House itself to the dwellings of statesmen and Conscript Fathers, and the retreats of foreign dignitaries. It was a little odd to observe, that while the foreign dignitaries and their trains were never weary of crying out against the blind Yankee devotion to wealth, how cheerfully they too prostrated themselves before her. It was rumored that one or two licked up gold dust enough, through the aid of the Bull himself, to purchase some gorgeous sets of jewels which their titled spouses sported the succeeding summer at Newport and alluded to as "cherished heirlooms—family gems which once crowned the brows of queens," and that sort of thing. But the Idol amid all the worship was faithful to her old friendships.

There was no man whose flatteries were so pleasant as those of Mr. Grey, and she admired Elinor more than ever. She at once took Miss Laidley to her heart because she was the Secretary's ward and Elinor's supposed friend, styled her, "a gushing young flower," and petted her exceedingly; in return for which and numberless presents, Miss Laidley adored her in public and called her dreadful names behind her back and then said—"I didn't mean it. I am so heedless."

The Idol speedily recovered from the little shade which had been cast over her spirits by Nicaraguan horrors, and was radiant. "My dear Miss Grey," she said, "this visit has revivified me! Communion with these exalted spirits who rule our happy land has pyramided my soul into purer airs."

"I am glad you are enjoying it," Elinor replied.

"Enjoyment is too feeble," cried the Idol. "As I said to the illustrious head of the Republic last night—I thrill with rapture and scintillate with delight."

"Oh how beautiful!" cried Miss Laidley, who was sitting on a footstool at the Idol's feet.

It was one of Elinor's reception-days, and the Idol had asked to come and spend the whole morning—making it her reception too—and Elinor could not refuse. It was early yet and people had not begun to appear, so the Idol was seated in gorgeous array and pouring out her overflowing heart to her young friends.

"It is absolute poetry!" cried Miss Laidley. 'Scintillate with delight!' Oh, mayn't I say it? I do so like pretty phrases! I'll give you credit for it, darling Mrs. Hackett."

"Foolish child!" cried the Idol. "Oh, gushing youth, how sweet thou art!"

"Now that's prettier than the other," said Miss Laidley. "I don't know which to treasure up among so many poetical gems."

"Your partiality for me blinds your eyes," said the Idol. "But, dear child, if any lucubrations of my poor brain can be worth your repenting, I shall be flattered and proud."

She was so good and kind, in spite of her absurdities, that Elinor returned Miss Laidley's mischievous look with the first frown she had ever bestowed upon her. Miss Laidley only made a mouth like a naughty child and continued—

"I mean to write down all of them I can remember. I know one thing, Mrs. Hackett—if you'd make a book of such sentences it would be a priceless treasure."

"I have so little leisure for literary effort," replied the Idol; "nor can I think my Lavaters would make an aphorism."

"I am sure they would," said Miss Laidley confidently; and not knowing Lavater even by name, she was dreadfully puzzled to understand what the Idol meant under that confusion of terms.

"Perhaps. We shall see when returning summer invites me to sylvan shades; where I hope to greet you and our peeress Miss Grey."

Gentle Laidley did not wish Miss Grey to have even an ungrammatical compliment when she got none, so she put out her claws a little way from under the velvet.

"Is Elinor going to be a peeress? What lord is there in her train?"

"I applied the term to her charms, my love," said the Idol. "I knew a child of genius last summer who spoke of her as Elinor the peeress."

"Oh, who was it?" demanded Miss Laidley, hoping that she might get on the track of even the smallest of Miss Grey's secrets. "Who was the child, dear Mrs. Hackett?"

"Ah, I must not whisper old tales," replied she. "I meant Childe as Moore employs the word."

"But tell me who it was," urged the damsel.

Elinor did not wish the conversation to turn on those days or that one name. "I think Miss Laidley is surprised that I should have had a compliment," said she, laughing.

"Oh, now she is scolding me!" cried Baby. "Don't let her, dear Mrs. Hackett! I am afraid of her—she is so superior."

"Miss Grey was only dallying with a jest," said the Idol.

"What a lovely death's-head!" exclaimed Miss Laidley suddenly.

She might have been applying the term to Elinor, only she had seized an ornament hanging to the Idol's chatelaine. It was a marvellous little work of art cut out of a ruby, and had cost goodness knows how much, but the Idol took it off the chain at once. "Wear it and love the giver," said she.

"No, no! I didn't mean that. You are too kind! I haven't the strength to refuse," cried Miss Laidley.

"Pain me not," returned the Idol. "It is but a gloomy type for so fair a flower to sport; but wear it and think of me."

To desire herself remembered in company with a death's-head, although a ruby one, was not flattering, but her intention was kindly, and Elinor looked on in wonder that any creature so young and rich could be so mean and such a rapacious swallower of gifts from every quarter available.

"You give me so many things that I am ashamed," said Miss Laidley. "One of these days I must search all Paris for something worthy of your acceptance."

"Speak not thus," said Mrs. Hackett; "give me your sunny smiles. I could ask no brighter coronet."

She was terribly stilted and not seldom horribly ungrammatical, but Elinor vowed that henceforth she would not hear one so good-natured laughed about.

"You are the darlingest duchess!" cried Miss Laidley. "Oh, mayn't I call you Duchess? The title just suits you."

"Gushing child! Call me what you will," said the Idol.

After that Miss Laidley often greeted her by the lofty appellation, and in private she named her Duchess Dumpty. She hung the ruby to her own chatelaine and did an immensity of baby talk over it which had ceased to be graceful to Elinor, but with which the gullible Idol was enchanted. "The irradious flower of youth!" cried she. "Ah, Miss Grey, to you in your Elizabethan puressness, to me in my world-worn experiences, how sweet this fragrant artlessness is."

"Oh, do you think Elinor Elizabethan?" cried Miss Laidley. "My, she isn't an old maid yet?"—with an almost imperceptible lingering on the particle.

"My child," exclaimed the Idol in horror, "Miss Grey is at the axis of maiden loveliness. I applied the term to her stateliness, her queenly mien."

Elinor would not give Miss Laidley the satisfaction of supposing she thought the words maliciously intended, else she could have dealt her a delightful stab; besides she must be polite in her own house, and the creature was not worth an answer.

"Oh no," continued the Idol; "Miss Grey is my cynosure—my dream of perfection."

"Oh, now I don't know what you mean in the least; you are too poetical," said Miss Laidley, wishing she had kept her malice to herself since it only resulted in praise of Elinor.

"Miss Grey has been a toast on titled lips," pursued the Idol loftily; "a monument of admiration in imperial halls."

"Dear me, a monument!" said Miss Laidley innocently. "Wasn't it very tiresome, Elinor."

"In metaphor," said the Idol.

"I'd rather have been in white tulle," said Miss Laidley.

"Be sure she was in whatever Venus's taste might have chosen," said the Idol. Present or absent she was faithful to her friendship.

"Oh, don't praise her any more," cried Miss Laidley, in her most naive way. "Praise me now."

"Lovely blossom—transparent dew-drop of purity," returned the Idol, quite moved by her artlessness.

"I'd rather be that than a monument," said Miss Laidley. "What if I should call you so, Elinor?"

"I think you may keep to my name unadorned," replied Elinor quietly, but Miss Laidley understood the tone and knew that it would be wise so to do.

"Hark!" said the Idol, assuming a tragic demeanor, as she was fond of doing. "The roll of wheels. The world is rushing back to disturb our Ethiopia."

"I am going to repeat that too; it is beautiful," exclaimed Miss Laidley, and she was as good as her word.

"I fear we shall be thronged," said the Idol. "I have told my friends, dear Miss Grey, that I was to be with you this morning—so sweet of you."

"On the contrary I am very much obliged to you for coming," said Elinor; "it turns out a real favor, for Mrs. Copeland sent me word last night that she could not be here, and I am too near Miss Laidley's own age to be chaperon and hostess too."

If Miss Laidley could have bitten her it would have been bliss to her feelings, but she could not venture to speak even.

"Always thoughtful, always Vesta's self," cried the Idol. "I hold myself honored that I can do you the least favor."

"I mean it too," said Elinor; "and I beg

you to believe, Mrs. Hackett, that I am grateful for your friendship and admiration although they do overrate me."

Miss Laidley thought it would be well to be cautious; evidently Miss Grey did not mean her to make sport of the Idol with impunity. "Somebody coming at last," said she, and felt relieved.

While she was arranging a new smile, she thought how she would revenge herself by talking of "Duchess Dumpty;" and that Elinor, grown odious, how could she worry her? It was difficult to find a way, skilled as Miss Laidley was in the art of annoyance. The horrid thing had no secrets—she cared for no man—how could she touch her? A little martyrdom might be effective. If she could make people think Elinor tyrannized over her—that would be delightful and punish her properly for her dignity and reserve and fling a new halo of interest about herself. She was frank enough to own the thoughts; she was not in the least ashamed of them, and kept her lies for other people.

Callers came and went, and said languid stupidities and drank more chocolate than was wholesome, to pass the allotted time. The Idol loomed magnificent, and Miss Laidley was like a streak of sunshine—April sunshine—because occasionally she would do a little grief, stretch her hands toward imaginary guardian angels, slip in wickednesses about Duchess Dumpty, and sly stinging words at Elinor when an opportunity offered. Fortunately men are not a rarity in Washington—indeed, I think I don't go too far in saying there are more than I see any need of, if it is a paradise for women—so the feminine ranks were not left to their own resources. Plenty of men came who ought to have been in their seats or at their bureaus, but men would go where Elinor Grey was, and that made sister-women want to be near her.

Leighton Rossitur found his way before the morning was over—about the time he thought Elinor would begin to wish for him—and his appearance had never been more welcome.

"Ah, Mr. Rossitur," said the Idol, "only think how fleeting life is!" It was useless to inquire what caused the thought. "I am thinking of that fair bud of Murray Hill whom we all admired."

"Oh yes; poor Miss Jones," said Rossitur. "I was shocked to hear of her death; very sudden, was it not?"

"Very. She caught cold; guitar in the head followed—was neglected; tubbercils formed on the lungs, and she went to the stream of Lethe—though was it Lethe or Tempe where the ancients sent their lost?" she asked.

Rossitur was silent because Miss Grey was close at hand, but a grave Congressman, who probably knew about as much of ancient lore as the Idol, replied that he thought it was both.

"It may have been," said Mrs. Hackett. "And she has gone! So it is we cry to our loveliest, val val; and they fade away."

Lethe and Tempe had recalled her classical studies to her mind, but she instantly apologized for her indulgence in learning. "It was a lingual lapse; I would not be a pedanter; I employed the sweet Latin phrase thoughtlessly. I have been wandering with Augusta, Mr. Rossitur."

Wickedness must gain the day if it lost him Elinor, and Rossitur could not help replying that he hoped she had found Augusta an agreeable companion.

"The poets of her age, you know," pursued the Idol—"sweet-singing Æneid and eclogic Homer."

Elinor had to smile under Rossitur's eyes, but she shook her head, and he did a bit of penitence a few moments after. "I didn't mean to," said he; "please forgive me."

"But we won't laugh at her," returned Elinor; "don't let us be like these people."

"You have said 'we,'" whispered Rossitur. "She is safe as far as I am concerned. Are you sure I am your friend still? I have scarcely seen you for three days."

"And I have missed you," answered Elinor; "does that content my friend?"

Some one was coming up; he could only reply by a look, but it had such patient devotion in it that Elinor was absolutely pained.

"Oh," thought Miss Laidley, "if I only knew whether she cared for him!" She was talking sweetly to two men, but she saw Elinor all the while, and her head was clear enough to pursue a train of reflection entirely removed from her conversation. "He has no eyes except for her," she went on, between a smile and a repartee for her admirers; "and he is so handsome. I wish I knew. Bless me doesn't he even remember I am here?"

Rossitur's polite indifference had caused Miss Laidley to think a good deal about him of late. If the strongest passion his heart would ever know had not had full possession of the embryo statesman, and he had desired to win the heiress and her cargo, he could not have pursued a wiser plan than this which he followed without any regard to her. She had begun to think about Leighton Rossitur; it was quite probable if something new did not divert her attention that she would make a romance in her mind and adore him as the hero; for live a romance in some form she must. If she could only have been certain that Elinor cared for him she would have rushed into love and absolutely made Rossitur carry off herself and her money. For she thought incessantly about her money, delicate and refined as she looked; she loved it and she was miserably avaricious except where her own vanity could be gratified.

The Idol had agreed to stay and eat a quiet dinner after the fatigues of the morning, and Elinor asked Rossitur to come back and help her through.

"That will be delightful," said the Idol overhearing; "quite Lucullian."

"What does that mean?" asked a woman

who came up at the moment to take leave, and who having conceived a hatred for the Idol longed to deal her a blow. "Lucucullian? What is it? Any thing like culinary?"

The Idol glared. This woman—this Mrs. Tallman—had on several occasions made herself odious to her. It was unusual and insupportable to the Idol to have her pedestal shaken by such thrusts. "I addressed a responsive soul," returned she loftily; "Mr. Rossitur understood."

"Have you any thing culinary in your soul, Mr. Rossitur?" asked the undaunted Mrs. Tallman, not flinching under the Idol's gaze, but returning it audaciously even and eager for a fray.

"I have a liking for culinary triumphs, at all events," said he.

"And I believe," said the Idol with great majesty, "that Mr. Rossitur at least "—she emphasized the words — "perfectly understood when I referred to the banquets of Lucullus."

"We shall all have to provide ourselves with classical dictionaries," retorted Mrs. Tallman, determined not to be put down.

"If we could be more classical in many ways it would be an improvement," said the Idol, and feeling that she had the best of her adversary she turned away.

Mrs. Tallman took her leave, vowing revenge in her soul, for she had an old grudge against the Idol which the triumphs of this Washington visit had only increased. Elinor could have made a little moan over the unpleasant things which she was forced to do and the disagreeable people she was obliged to meet. This very Mrs. Tallman—certainly it was a mild species of torture to be obliged to send her cards for receptions, to endure her loud voice and her overpowering manners—but it had to be done. Mrs. Tallman's husband was seated where he had a vote, and there was a measure coming up before the House in which Mr. Grey desired to secure the Californian's voice on the side of the Administration, so Elinor must be civil to his wife. But she must allow herself the privilege of saying that it was hard, and she was at times inclined to think that however glorious a republic may be in practice, and however noble democratic principles in theory, any position would be more pleasant than that made by political honors.

"An odious woman," said the Idol, who was seldom harsh in her opinions. "She quite takes my breath away. Ah, Miss Grey, greatness has its ills, and the most golden crown will droop a thoughtful brow."

She was convinced that she had been quoting poetry, and assumed an inspired attitude at once. She was more stately in mien and overpowering in language for the rest of the morning in her desire to make the difference between herself and a woman like Mrs. Tallman duly felt, and was wonderfully supported by the reflection that she had gained the advantage in, this little tilt of words without having compromised her dignity. Indeed she enjoyed the entire day and evening without alloy. After dinner she played écarté with Mr. Grey, and they sent Elinor to the piano, whither Rossitur was bound to follow.

Genevieve Laidley had one of her silent demons in possession of her—she was watching. But finding that a waste of time—for her quick ears were not rewarded by a stray word, or her eyes, which Elinor fancied shone in the shadow like those of a cat, able to intercept so much as a tender look between the pair at the musical instrument—she grew tired and turned her attention to her guardian; hung over his chair and helped or hindered him play, and there being no one but the Idol to listen, did not scruple to say pretty, sweet things to him, and she was so innocent and child-like that he could not help feeling pleasure and taking them for gospel.

"Gushing youth!" murmured the Idol, gazing pensively at her cards and holding a knave by the heels in doubt whether to play him at that juncture. "How sweet thou art!" continued she, modestly placing Jack on his feet once more and sending forth a queen instead.

"We shall spoil this child," said Mr. Grey. "But if she will be so charming, how can we help it?"

"I am so glad you like me!" cried Genevieve, clapping her hands and cooing. "Don't ever see my faults; I can't bear that."

"You will have to adopt some first," said her guardian.

"Ah, you are very kind; you won't see them. Elinor is so superior and so intellectual that she discovers them—only she is much better to me than I deserve."

They called from the piano for her to come and sing, but she declared that she was cold, her voice was frozen, and whispered, "I'd rather stay here. I'm a lonesome little thing. Mayn't I stay?"

The Idol took a portion of the request to herself and gave a rapturous assent, but if she had caught the glance at Mr. Grey from the blue eyes with their yellow scintillations, she might have discovered that her opinion was of little consequence.

"Stay," said her guardian, "and make it summer for us."

"I'll stay if you tell me such pretty things," said Baby.

The Idol, still occupied with her cards, delivered a brief eulogium on Mr. Grey's powers of compliment, and Genevieve cried — "Oh, if I could have said that!" Then she made a delightful little grimace at the unsuspecting lady which nearly upset Mr. Grey's composure.

By and by Elinor came away from the piano, leaving Rossitur absently running his fingers over the keys, recalling stray fragments, and stood by the fire looking at the card-party.

"Oh, that's a little German thing," cried Miss Laidley. "Play it, Mr. Rossitur."

"I can not," he said.

Miss Laidley flew to the piano and set him

unceremoniously aside. She played and sang, and her voice, neither strong nor sweet, had something bewitching in it. Rossitur told her that it was like listening to some Rhine nymph, some dangerous Lurely, to hear her.

"But I am not dangerous, said she; "any way not to you."

"No; I have escaped so far," returned he.

The blue eyes shot out their odd light again. "It was Lurely's fate, maybe, only to be powerful with those who were not worth putting in danger," said she.

"Wherein you differ from Lurely," replied Rossitur.

"You say so, but you don't mean it. You think me an absurd little thing that couldn't be dangerous to you."

"I didn't think you had even honored me with a look," returned he, laughing.

"I don't think I have," said she; "but I know where your eyes are always turned. I am not so blind as these people."

"Don't you make any mistakes, Lurely," said Rossitur.

"Do you never think she is a beautiful snow-queen animated by a spell, like the people in fairy-stories?" continued she.

"Now whom do you mean?"

"Elinor!" called Miss Laidley, "Mr. Rossitur says you are a snow-queen animated by a spell." She gave him a delightfully wicked look.

"Miss Laidley supplied the last," said he, laughing. "I said that only such comparison was befitting Miss Grey's pure serenity."

The party at the card-table laughed too, and Miss Laidley whispered—"Oh, now I hate you—hate you!"

She rose from her seat and darted toward the fire. "Get away, snow-queen," said she; "I am chilled to the heart."

She curled herself up on a rug close to the blaze, which fairly illuminated her. Rossitur followed, trying to make up his mind about her. Was she a heedless child—was she a little mischievous devil—was she after all one of those passionate souls sometimes put by mistake under such slight forms and babyish graces?

"This has been an evening of sweet commune," said the Idol, when it was time to go.

Elinor had kept her from being ridiculous for half an hour, to Miss Laidley's chagrin, but Mrs. Hackett could not take her leave except on the swell of some sublime sentiment. "I feel etherealized and subtleized," said she; "my spirit has been panoplied in purer airs and bathed in Parhelian groves. Farewell, dear friends! I quaff greetings to future symposias." She waved her hand and glided away and Elinor followed her to the dressing-room. As soon as they were out of hearing, Miss Laidley sprang up from the rug and did the Idol to the life and convulsed the two men.

When the Idol's voice was heard in the hall the three went out. "This was unnecessary," said she; "dear Mr. Grey, never disturb your laurel-earned repose for me."

"My dear friend, I always want to see you to the last moment," said the bland hypocrite.

"The last moment is what he thinks the best," Miss Laidley whispered in Rossitur's ear; then she darted at the Idol and kissed her as a fly does sugar.

"Beautiful Spring!" said the delightful Idol. "How to find a fitting emblem for her. She is like the fair goddess who poured ambrosia for Mercury—Phœbe, was it not?"

"No, I won't be—it isn't a pretty name," said Miss Laidley.

"After all, I think it was Aurora," said the Idol. "Phœbe drove the chariot of the sun. Mr. Rossitur, I pass your hotel—let me set you down."

"Yes, be his Phœbe," said Miss Laidley.

Elinor looked so vexed that neither Mr. Grey nor Rossitur ventured upon a smile.

"Farewell again," said the Idol, embracing Elinor. "I must tear myself away. Parting is such sweet strain that I shall say farewell forever, as Hamlet hath it."

"He ought to have been vaccinated for it," whispered Rossitur to Miss Laidley, and she did a little impromptu waltz of delight.

Mr. Grey would lead the Idol down the steps to the carriage—she would keep stopping to make speeches, so that the proceeding was as long and as fatiguing as a royal progress, but she was very happy with it all. When she had gone Elinor went away and Miss Laidley started for her own room, but she had to come back several times for things she had forgotten, and on each occasion she talked a great deal of pretty nonsense to Mr. Grey, who was still standing by the drawing-room fire.

CHAPTER XIX.

INDIANA.

It was a dismal morning, and Spring after promising a speedy arrival seemed to have been seized with a fit of the sulks, as a pretty woman often is in the midst of her smiles. Elinor and Miss Laidley sat in the breakfast-room, where Mr. Grey had left them. Elinor had a great longing for the privacy of her own chamber, but when she made a move to go, her companion said—"I shall go too. I can't be left alone to-day; I shall be wretched. Oh, you sweet Elinor, don't leave me." Elinor remained. If she must have Miss Laidley's society it should be endured there; she would not have the young lady fall into the habit of invading her private haunts. So they talked; and Miss Laidley was sufficiently amusing, there was no denying that. She made sport of every body and every thing, and mimicked people delightfully; but when Elinor could not help warning her how dangerous it was to indulge in such pastime, she cried—"Oh, I don't mean any thing—I am so heedless." She talked about Mr. Rossitur, and was disgusted because Elinor discussed him as coolly as she would have done one of the overpowering foreigners or a Prancer strayed forth from the Youth of New York.

Soon Henry brought the letters and a new French novel that Rosa Thornton had sent from town. "Now you read to me, like a dear!" cried Miss Laidley. "It's About's new book. I wish it was George Sand—About is so dreadfully moral. Will you read, love?"

"Certainly," replied Elinor; "but I must write a note first. Oh dear, there isn't a scrap of paper here."

"I am going up stairs to get some *chocolats*; I'll tell Coralie to bring down some," said Miss Laidley.

"We can ring," replied Elinor, somewhat astonished at Miss Laidley's proposal, for she was the most indolent creature breathing; but the reason for this unwonted effort appeared.

"Thank you," said she, "but I can't trust Juanita to get my boubons. She steals them—the greedy thing! I hide every box I have—the horrid old magpie!"

"Then please ask Coralie to bring down my writing-desk," said Elinor, covertly smiling at this new trait of meanness in the heiress.

Indeed Miss Laidley never scrupled to save her money at other people's expense, but she did it gracefully. She used Elinor's carriage and Elinor's saddle-horses without mercy, and had more than once kept Miss Grey at home—but she was always going to be provided with them. At her request her guardian had ordered some Centaur to send scores of steeds for her to try, but none of them suited, and the probability was none of them would please her as long as she could be provided without cost to herself. She went away carolling one of the quaint German ballads she affected—the only things she sang well—and Elinor listened as long as her voice was audible, and then fell to reflection concerning her, and was sorry to feel herself harsh in her judgments.

Miss Laidley appeared at length, bearing the writing-desk herself. "The heavy, horrid, beautiful thing!" cried she, setting it down on the table.

"Why did you bring it?" inquired Elinor. "You should not have troubled yourself."

"Oh, Coralie wasn't in your room. I shrieked myself hoarse, and then I went in and got it. Now write your note like a darling and read to me."

Elinor was soon ready to begin the book, and Miss Laidley coiled herself up on an India shawl with her head on a pile of cushions, the box of *chocolats* by her side, and prepared to listen. "This is delightful!" cried she. "I am warm to my very soul."

She had so little vitality that she was always frozen. Elinor looked at her basking in the fire-light and thought of all sorts of odd stories—of Lamia, of a white snake that one of Dumas's heroines wore about her wrist—and pretty as the creature was she felt as if she were a serpent, and, innocent as she looked, would bite venomously if her repose were disturbed. Elinor read in a clear voice and with her perfect accent and Miss Laidley reclined *croquante*, but at length the warmth and the unexciting nature of the pretty story, so unlike the French novels which she perused in private, lulled her into oblivion. Elinor looked up from her book, and seeing the graceful head flung back with the fair hair straying over the cushions and the blue eyes closed, thought what a picture she made and decided that she might pause in her task of trying to amuse the Princess Monchalante. She drew her writing-desk toward her and began turning over its contents. She came upon Ruth's letter crumpled small under some papers, and was shocked at her own carelessness. She thought she had burned the sheet on that black night when its reception caused her such suffering. It was very careless, wicked of her, for the letter was one that might have made Ruth's secret at least suspected by any person who read. Elinor was glad to remember that the desk closed with a secret spring—she would burn the letter now. She sat holding it in her hand and thinking of so many things which the sight of those little pages brought into her mind. She fastened her reflections upon Leighton Rossiter at last—oh, should she ever be able to love him and be at rest? She reminded herself of every noble trait in his character; she made herself feel how she trusted him, how helpful he was to her; but trying to get beyond that, to contemplate other possibilities, the old horror came back, and the touch of his hand seemed on hers filling her soul with dismay. Ought she not tell him now just how she felt? He might be forming too much hope. It seemed so doubtful whether she would ever be able to care for him except as a friend, to get beyond that dread of the very idea of feeling her hands in his and he with a right to speak words of love.

Looking up suddenly she became conscious that Miss Laidley's eyes were partially open and watching her. Elinor believed the creature's first impulse was to feign sleep that she might still watch, but if so she relinquished it, seeing that she was discovered. "What are you thinking about?" she asked, lifting her head lazily. "You look like a sibyl."

Elinor flung the letter in the fire and sat looking at it burn.

"What is that?" demanded Miss Laidley. "An old love-letter? Oh, why didn't you read it to me? You never will tell me the least secret."

"I have repeated so many times that I have none to tell," replied Elinor.

"You don't trust me. I don't believe you love me a bit!" said Miss Laidley piteously.

Elinor was quite certain that she did not, and being in no mood for uttering fibs, she remained silent.

"It's wicked of you," said the girl, "when I love you so much."

"I hope we like each other very well," returned Elinor.

"Oh, you cold thing—you Northern heart! I am glad my blood is warmer; I can love my friends."

"But, my dear Miss Laidley, real friendship is a thing of time. It doesn't grow in a night like Jonah's gourd."

"I don't know any thing about Jonah's gourd—it's in the Bible, isn't it? I never read the Bible—Aunty made me hate it when I was a child—I had to learn verses for being naughty."

"Perhaps if you were to read it now you would feel differently."

"No, I shan't! Don't prose at me, that's a dear. Poor papa got quite Methodistical while he was sick; just weakness, I know, but it gave me the horrors."

Could she realize what she was saying?

"Oh, Miss Laidley," Elinor began, but not very well knowing what she ought to say, and saved saying any thing by an interruption from her companion.

"You will call me Miss Laidley—it's wicked. Poor little me—making a stranger of me."

"I say Genevieve sometimes; I forget from not hearing you called by that name."

"I mean to ask Mr. Grey to call me Eva; formality kills me," cried she; "freezes me outright. "I am a child—a baby—I won't be held responsible for every thing I say and do as if I was a grand creature like you."

"Baby Genevieve," said Elinor, laughing.

"There, I like that. I wish your father would call me so."

Elinor wished that she would leave her father's name out of such conversation; she did not relish the idea of hearing him address his ward by affectionate epithets.

"What is that old song?" continued Miss Laidley. "It was meant for me. I want to be called a star, an elf, a bird."

"Shall I call you a blue jay?" asked Elinor.

"Now you are laughing at me. I don't like it; I am a foolish little thing and can't answer. Besides, I'm nervous this morning; I'd cry in a minute and make a dreadful scene."

"Please don't," returned Elinor.

"Yes I will; I want to cry! Oh, my papa—my dear papa! I feel as if I was choking—my hands are like ice—oh, oh!"

She looked very pale and her eyes fairly dilated: she could work herself into a nervous spasm; she did it sometimes from pure love of excitement.

"I am afraid you are not at all well—let me get you something," said Elinor.

"I won't take a thing! I shall have convulsions! I mean to die! Oh, I am choking!" cried she.

Elinor knew very well that she could control herself if she wished, but any remonstrance would only make her worse. "Lie still a little while, Genevieve, and it will pass off," she said soothingly.

"Then pet me. If you pet me I'll try. Oh, my breath! See my hands twitch!"

She caught Elinor's hand in her icy fingers, and she looked such an uncanny thing, shivering and shaking, with her face deathly pale and her eyes shooting yellow gleams, that Elinor felt absolutely uncomfortable. Miss Laidley insisted on holding her fast, on lying with her head in Elinor's lap and being sung to, and if Elinor hesitated to obey her caprices she began to beat her clenched hands on the cushions and to moan piteously. At last Elinor got away from her and rang the bell. By that time Genevieve began to shriek in spite of herself. Miss Grey sent for Juanita and the mulatto rushed in, saying—"Oh, Senora! Lord bless! Juanita's darling! Come to mamsey—poor lamb." She was accustomed to such scenes and knew what to do. Genevieve would not be carried up stairs, so the mulatto flew off and brought some drops and coaxed her to swallow them, and Elinor had to hold her head, and at last she tired herself out and went fast to sleep.

There Elinor sat in a very uncomfortable posture and held the girl, and presently she woke and began to coo and laugh. "I feel well now," said she. "Oh, you darling Elinor, to hold me all this while. Now I want to dance! Elinor, let's have luncheon and eat lots of brandy peaches—there's some that have the meats put in to flavor them—it's like drinking refined prussic acid." After luncheon she wanted to go out, and Elinor was glad to get her into the air; any man would have thought she was going mad, but women are able to cope with prussic-acid loving damsels.

That evening they were invited to the rehearsal of an amateur concert which was being gotten up as a proper penitential amusement for Lent. Miss Laidley, after dining off soup flavored with some horrible East Indian compound with which Mr. Grey was fond of making a small purgatory of his interior, olives, indigestible sweets, and a glass of champagne with a little strong coffee added, was able to go to the rehearsal, and looked more peculiar and attractive, than ever, and was as gay as a bird.

The Idol was at the rehearsal, and Mrs. Tallman was present, and they were both interested in the affair, which was to be made subservient to some charitable design. There had been a great deal of discussion and not a little disagreement as to the particular purpose for which the proceeds should be employed, and at this rehearsal they were to come to some definite conclusion in regard to the matter. Elinor thought the infliction of the concert would be quite Lenten mortification enough without submitting to this rehearsal, but the Idol had begged her piteously to come, desiring to have her opinions strengthened by the presence of as many allies as she could bring. Mr. Grey reserved himself for a card-party, like a sensible man, but Mrs. Copeland appeared at dinner prepared to chaperon the young ladies to any extent.

The rehearsal was in the hall which had been hired for the concert, in order that the performers might accustom their voices to its proportions. Mrs. De Lucy shrieked till she was black in the face, Mr. Jervis roared, and the rest of the band screamed in turn and flung their arms about, and every young woman with a voice suited to the mildest efforts essayed grand cavatinas from Ione or Traviata, and every man thought himself Mazzoleni or Carl Formes, and every body abused and laughed at every body else, and every thing went the way usual with such performances.

Several prominent women interested in a proposed fund for erecting a statue of the Goddess of Liberty in the grand entrance of the White House were there, and clustered about the Idol, who was chief mover in that idea, and wanted the concert proceeds to be made a nucleus for future bequests. A little apart sat Mrs. Tallman, enforced by her friends, most of them Western people; for her plan was that the money raised should go to help some remarkable society in Chicago. Mrs. Tallman—Indiana Tallman was her full name and she was fond of being so called—was the wife of a California politician, and she was rich and held a certain sway. She had seen the light somewhere toward the setting sun, and concerning her early course the historic muse is silent. She commenced her career in Washington some years previous as a widow, and very soon took possession of the wealthy son of El Dorado. People said that her first husband had been a tavern - keeper; people said she had been a school-teacher; people said she had been several things which I shall not set down here; and how much of either story was true, nobody could tell. At present Indiana Tallman was a woman past forty, a little too raw-boned for elegance, but still imposing. Having passed her childhood on Western prairies and being nourished on corn-bread had saved her from the gaunt appearance which she would have presented had she been reared within the shadow of Plymouth Rock and fed on codfish. She was well educated—possibly the teaching story had some foundation; she had all the insolence of these last years of ease and power plated over her native brass; she had a tongue which spared neither friend nor foe; she wanted to shine and be a whole constellation by herself, and she was greatly admired and reverenced by her own set as was meet. Behind her back she was familiarly known as the "Banger," owing to a certain rush and confusion with which she moved, expressive also of the force which she carried into any plan that might chance to engross her attention.

Now the Banger—I like to call her that, it is so sonorous and it does her no harm; every body has a nickname in this abandoned century; you and I have, only we don't know it, and are too busy inventing titles for our friends to find it out—now the Banger—that other sentence evaporated in a parenthesis—Indiana the Banger, had conceived a bitter hostility to the Idol. It was an old wound and had rankled in her mind as ancient wrongs did in the breast of Juno. It had been fanned into new fury by the sweep of the Idol's garments as they made a high wind in the Capital, and she was as determined on revenge as Saturnia was on annihilating that wretched prig Æneas and all his Trojan crew. Only the winter before, Indiana the Banger had ventured into New York for a few weeks, and armed with letters from many Washington notables had striven to disport herself in the sacred precincts of Murray Hill. But Murray Hill is peculiar. Murray Hill can endure a certain degree of coarseness, but Western coarseness makes Murray Hill shudder through all its breadth. The Banger was not a success; I may go further—she was even snubbed. Nobody cared for her money, because she was not going to live there; nobody cared because Honorable was tacked to her name; what was that to the wives of men who were Bulls and Bears and divers other kinds of wild beasts? It is hard to assign reasons for Indiana's failure; it always is hard to assign reasons for a failure or a success in New York; but the fact was there. The Idol disliked her because she talked loud and long and knew hard words and pushed people about, and the Idol turned her back on her and the rest of Murray Hill turned the rest of its back.

No wonder that Indiana, meeting the Idol on ground familiar, felt her soul burn to avenge those former slights. She could not venture on snubbing her—the Idol was too potent even in a strange territory for that—but she abused her; she laid ambushes for her; she tormented her a great deal, and the Idol never appeared quite at ease when she knew that Indiana the Banger was listening to her gorgeous sentences. In dress the Idol had the advantage, for though the Californian was rich there was a bottom to his coffer, but the Bull's coffer was like the deep, deep sea, and the Idol could dash at its treasures with the hugest possible bucket and leave no trace of diminution. Indiana fought manfully; she counted that the Idol never wore more than six different colors at once, so she wore nine, and all the Western people thought that she had conquered in the way of gorgeousness. But this matter of the concert brought about an opportunity for a pitched battle, and that was what Indiana craved. The Idol had no fancy for battles, but she had started the Goddess of Liberty project and could not retreat, when to her wrath she saw Indiana array herself and her Western host against her and dash with gauntleted hand a rival project into the arena. The conflict had raged for days; it had deferred the concert, but now the performers were tired of being kept in obscurity and vowed that they would sing, no matter to whom or what the results of their piping was paid.

Elinor had heard very little about the affair, and though her name was down among the directresses would have kept away from the rehearsal if she had known that the Idol desired her presence as an aid to victory in the strife which her prophetic soul told her the Banger would have. And Indiana glowered like an angry giantess at Miss Grey from the place where she held her court, and Miss Grey, unconscious of having giving offense, greeted her with a pleasant smile.

Mrs. De Lacy sang; Mr. Jervis sang; the the nervous young lady sang—at first she had to be coaxed to begin and then she had to be coaxed to leave off; the pale young man with the tenor voice sang, and his voice cracked like a reed in the middle of the first howl; the foreign gentleman who condescended to be Carl Formes sang, and jerked and pulled himself till it seemed that he was going down into his boots after his voice, and when he found it the voice sounded very wheezy and hoarse, as though the boots were wet and it had taken a heavy cold.

When he was lifting the voice up (it did not seem to be his, but one that he was trying to use for that occasion) the deaf old lady who never had any name that any body mentioned, and whose invitations Washington said were sent round the corner, made her appearance armed with a huge trumpet which looked like a sea-serpent. She had on a white opera-cloak and a bonnet with blue feathers, and she stood still in the middle of the aisle and levelled her trumpet at the amateur Carl as if she were going to blow things out of it directly at him. Several busy people tried to make her understand that it was not the night of the concert, and to hint at the tops of their voices that she had no business there. The old lady smiled and nodded, not hearing their shrieks or the groans of impromptu Formes any more than she would have done the songs of May breezes or the report of a percussion cap cracked directly on the top of her bonnet. "What does he say?" she asked, her voice one instant a yell and the next a whisper, and the yelling when she thought she whispered. "Tell him not to shake his fist at me—I'm disturbing nobody." She subsided into a seat at length and was tolerably quiet; occasionally she would stretch out her trumpet and tap somebody in the eye or on the nose, as it happened, and whisper, "What did he say? What is Congress doing?" But on the whole she was discreet, and the very bass man stopped at last and returned his borrowed voice suddenly to the boots, where it wheezed and grunted a little and then was still.

They all sang, and they all looked very purple and wretched when they were through, and afterward the young women that were to do the piano-forte and the young man who was to be flutist, and several other young men and women who were to be a variety of things, wanted to rehearse and were condemned to silence from lack of time. So they made a quivering knot of themselves and bemoaned their wrongs, and audibly expressed a conviction that perhaps if they were not needed they had better retire from the affair altogether. As nobody asked them to stay they persuaded and softened each other and determined to be magnanimous and

G

do their duty regardless of the slights of the envious and the stings of the proud.

At last somebody said that it was really necessary to decide what the concert proceeds were to go for. Tickets to the amount of hundreds of dollars had been sold—to what end?

Then uprose a gentleman who had the Idol's project at heart, and he explained it in glowing language. He said it was a noble aim, worthy of the heart and brain from which it emanated—and he waved his hand toward the Idol—and declared that the White House needed a work of art like that. He told them how the goddess would bend benignly over the troops of noble Americans who sought those beloved halls; and here he was interrupted by the Banger, who said—"If a statue bends, it breaks, and then it tumbles—I hope none of the troop of noble Americans will be crushed under it." The eloquent gentleman was embarrassed; he tried to recover himself, but the group about Indiana tittered so audibly that after stumbling over a few fragments of the broken statue, he sat down in utter confusion.

"This is not a meeting," said Indiana, seizing her opportunity; "we are all acquaintances—we have come here to consult—I shall venture to be strong-minded enough to do my own talking. I dare say some persons may be shocked; but I am not a delicate Eastern lady: I am a true, earnest daughter of the West, and I shall speak a few words." Her friends loudly admired; the Idol assumed an attitude of careless ease and looked as blind as a bat and as deaf as an adder, but Indiana vowed that she should hear. "In the first place," said the Banger, "this is a Washington concert, gotten up by people who may call this their home, who, as men, serve their country here, or if women, do their duty in their natural sphere. I do not think that a plan ought to be proposed by a lady from any sister city, however distinguished she may be—in her own little circle." Indiana paused for breath; Elinor, seated behind the Idol, laid her hand softly on her arm and kept her silent. "I have a project," said Indiana, "not my own indeed—I am not so ambitious of a little brief notoriety that I thrust my crude efforts upon statesmen—but this is a project which is worthy of the highest praise."

Somebody asked to hear what it was.

"Oh, that horrid woman!" whispered the Idol. "My dear, she will get her own way! I would rather give fifty thousand dollars."

"Sit still," returned Elinor. "If you will promise not to answer her or seem to hear, you shall defeat her yet."

Elinor whispered to a gentleman and told him what to say when the Banger's plan was offered, and told him to propose a third use for the money and to carry the day before the enemy could recover.

The Banger said—"I want—we want—most of us want—to help that society for the relief of orphans in Chicago. Let us be informal—all those who are in favor can hold up their hands. Don't let us be too fashionable—we are not on Murray Hill."

But up rose the gentleman to whom Elinor had given an idea, and he showed how preposterous it was for them to send the money to Chicago when a society for distressed something in Washington needed it so much. In fact he carried his point, and when Indiana was exulting because at least her enemy had not triumphed and had made her friends vote for the distressed something, and it was too late to retract, up rose the gallant knight and said he begged them all to thank their dear and admired Mrs. Hackett, who had proposed this scheme which was so favorably received.

Indiana could have flown at the Idol and maimed her for life; but she had to endure it. Then up rose the Idol, and on her way out she collected her wits and dealt a last blow.

"Dear Mrs. Tallman," said she, "what a mellifluous speech you made—what a colleague your husband must find you." Away she sailed and left Indiana foaming at the mouth, from which burst in smothered accents the one word —"Trollop."

The deaf lady had sat with her ancient head turning in vacant surprise from one group to another, understanding nothing that went on, evidently at a loss to know where she was or what people meant, and looking more dazed than usual. Suddenly she started up when she saw the groups dividing, rapped one man fiercely with her trumpet and grasped another by the arm. "Are they going to have supper?" she cried. He nodded and tried to get away. "Show me where!" she wheezed. "I want my supper—I will have my supper?" She held her trumpet extended to impede further progress till she should have discovered where the supper was.

"She'll stand there all night," said one of the performers.

"No," said the tenor whose voice had cracked; "I'll show her down stairs. She'll think I am taking her to supper."

He was a good-natured youth, like most tenors whose voices crack, and he went up and offered his arm and she levelled her trumpet at him, but concluded to be led away, whispering faintly, "Supper? Are they going to have supper?"

Indiana stood crest-fallen among her coterie; she had expected a triumph and it had been a miserable failure. Every body said the Idol decidedly got the best of it, and Indiana raged like one of the buffaloes on her native prairies to think that her enemy would return to the inaccessible haunts of Murray Hill and she be unable to sate her soul with vengeance.

The Idol was so grateful to Elinor that when she called next day to express her feelings she was quite unable, and it really seemed probable that some of the huge phrases she gasped out would suffocate her. "I have no words," said she, over and over again. "If all my sensibility were coined into spoken intellectuality, it would be as weak to express my emotions as river billows are the ocean's swell."

"I would not think of it," said Elinor; "the woman was rude and impertinent."

"But your kindness—I thought of that. Your illumination of genius—a real emulation! My darling Miss Grey, you were perfect before in my eyes, but now you are constellated into paradisaical brightness."

Miss Laidley's appearance soon put an end to the compliments and gratitude; she had not patience to listen to the chanting of Elinor's praises and changed the conversation, finding that her little sneers and sly hits had no effect upon Miss Grey.

The Idol had set her heart upon taking both her favorites back to town with her for a visit during the brief season of renewed life between the close of Lent and the general flitting of the Idol's world toward the country. Elinor proved easily how impossible it would be for her to think of any thing of the sort, and the Idol was forced to admit the validity of her excuses, so she centered her persuasions upon Miss Laidley, and the fair Genevieve made hasty but clear comparisons of the two fields. She knew that before long Leighton Rossitur was going to town; he had said so only the other evening. The Idol would hymn her praises to all Murray Hill, and feast her with lofty honors, and New York would be less dull than the Capital. "I can not refuse you, dear Mrs. Hackett," said she, at the close of her compendiums but precise mental statements. "If you will be troubled with a foolish little thing like me I shall be very happy to go."

"Darling child," cried the Idol, "you rejuvenate my soul! How my friends will envy me the beautiful ray of sunshine I bring back."

"And you will pet me—you will be good to me!" exclaimed Miss Laidley, in the tone of a child who had been suffering for six months from the fiendish cruelties of a step-parent and was about to be carried away by a fairy godmother.

Elinor perfectly understood, although the meaning was lost on the Idol.

"Your lightest wish shall be my law, lovely one," said she; "your smile my guerdion."

"I will go—thank you so much—if my guardian is willing," said Miss Laidley with sweet humility, "and if dear, wise Elinor thinks it right."

"Oh, your guardian will not refuse," said the Idol.

"I am sure my father and I both desire Miss Laidley to consult her wishes in all things," added Elinor.

"Of course," returned Genevieve. "It makes no difference where I am now, there is no one to miss me, no one to regret. Oh, papa! papa!" She raised her eyes to heaven, she stretched out her hands to the imaginary guardian angel, and she looked very pretty and very forlorn.

The Idol was moved almost to tears, and if she could have thought her adored Miss Grey guilty of a fault she would have considered her a little cold just then. She lavished endearments on Baby, and very soon the young lady was as gay as a sky-lark. Elinor could not help feeling a sense of relief in the temporary quiet and solitude she should have, for the companionship of a Baby who was a sylph, an Undine, and a scratching little puss all in one, had become somewhat wearing.

Miss Laidley was stricken with grief at leaving her, and went through a farewell scene which would have done credit to a veteran actress, completely fascinating Mr. Grey, and even blinding Leighton Rossitur, who had come to say adieu. (Men are such asses. We have been since Adam ; we shall be up to the last man.) Elinor bore it all — the pathos, the shower-bath — and knew that she appeared a very stony, inhuman woman, compared to this sensitive fairy ; but histrionics were not in her line and she could only utter a few civil commonplaces. When left alone she felt as if she had disposed of a hooded-snake or got rid of a chameleon who might any time turn into a monster, of any impossible thing most unlike the fair, childish creature who had been swept away on the Idol's lofty pedestal.

CHAPTER XX.

CLIVE'S BOOK.

HAVE you forgotten Clive Farnsworth ? He was sitting in his library, an almost gloomy room in spite of its cheerful furniture, and darker, from its deep-set windows and old-fashioned ceiling of carved black walnut, than the haunt of a studious or melancholy man ever ought to be. It looked out on the broad stone terrace too, and Clive had long since taken to his solitary prowlings up and down the slow-talking flags. The terrace was dreary enough with the garden stretching below in its winter desolation ; though the days had begun to be bright, they had little real warmth and comfort, "for the spring comes slowly up that way."

Clive was busy with his book. It was almost finished, and he would soon lose the society of those ideal people who had been such realities to him. He had bent all his energies to his task, and had tried to make the work a good one. There was no Elinor Grey and no Clive Farnsworth in it. He had kept his gloom as much aloof as possible, and had written conscientiously day after day, but he was very doubtful of the result.

He had been writing all the morning and was dreadfully tired, and now he sat there with the pile of manuscript before him, and leaned his arm on the table and wondered where his energy and his brains had gone.

Soon the door opened and Ruth came in, so bright a blossom in her tasteful dress, with

such life in the brown eyes, such happy smiles on her lip. "Clive, dear," she said, "I know you must be done work ; any way you ought to be. I don't disturb you, do I ?"

It would have been a relief to growl, to answer coarsely like Lord Byron, but Clive had been faithful to his determination even in the smallest things. "You never disturb me, and your seat is always ready here, you know," he answered, smiling, and pointing to the ottoman by his chair, the place where she often sat while he was at work, trying to study or watching him. "But I am through writing for to-day."

"Such a tired old darling," she exclaimed, going up to him and laying her hand softly over his eyes. "I ought to have interrupted you two hours ago."

"Such a bright young blossom," returned he, not shrinking from the touch of her fingers, though she had not the power to soothe him by the pressure of her hand, and so only made the pain and irritation more acute. "Has something happened, or is it that you look brighter than usual because my eyes are tired ?"

"I have had a letter from Miss Grey," said Ruth ; "a dear, sweet letter. Will you read it Clive ?" She held up the envelope—Clive involuntarily stretched out his hand, then remembered that he could not trust himself.

"You shall tell me about it," he replied ; "my eyes won't bear any thing more in the way of manuscript."

"You bad old fellow to work so hard," cried Ruth. "And to be so patient — how can you ?"

"I feel so cross and irritable this moment that I could snap like Ponto," said Clive.

Ruth laughed ; he often made that confession and she never believed it, and saying so did a great deal to relieve him. Indeed, I do not know a better remedy than to avow the crossness ; sometimes you can laugh and it passes away.

"Shall we go and walk ?" he asked.

"I wonder if we mightn't ride ? The sun shines warm and this wind must have dried the mud. Do you think you would freeze, little one ?"

"No, indeed. I am longing for a gallop."

"Then go and get on your habit and I will order the horses."

"Yes, this minute.—Oh, the letter."

"That will keep."

"You naughty thing, to consider women's letters of no importance—but I can scold you another time." She ran away to change her dress, leaving the letter on the table. Clive glanced at it, and resolutely shoved it out of sight under the papers, and walked up and down among the shadows till Ruth came back in her plumed hat and trailing skirt to say that the horses were coming round. They mounted and rode away through the keen air, and Clive felt the irritation and fatigue gradually leave him, and could talk gayly with her.

"It is perfectly delightful," she said, "and not in the least cold."

"What did some American woman write about a gallop? 'The queen in my soul puts on her crown—'"

"That exactly expresses it," cried Ruth. "I remember the poem."

"And the crown is very becoming to your soul, and that little hat to your face," said Clive.

"As if you could speak for my soul—"

"I am looking straight in your eyes."

"You do tell me the sweetest things. They say other men don't compliment their wives."

"Perhaps they are not worth it, little one." He did say pretty things to her always, and though sometimes he felt a pain the while, he was not insincere; and he was determined to keep watch over himself in every trifle.

They came back from their ride, and Clive read aloud for a while; then they dined, and he helped Ruth with her French and praised the daily improvement in her voice as she sang, and she was as blithe as a bird. She had set her heart on not hearing a page of his book, not so much as an outline of the plot, until it should be finished. That trifling thing showed how entirely satisfied she was; how perfect his self-control, how vigilant his care had been.

With her quick intuitions and her vivid fancy, if she had been troubled by a shadow, if she had been smitten—even no more than to make her restless—with a vague fear, she would have wanted to read it page by page, to keep herself constantly in his mind, to know that she was prominent in his written thoughts, by way of an assurance to dispel the suspicion.

So Clive had written with that sense of loneliness which it is hard for a writer to bear—which made Molière read his plays, as he wrote, to his old housekeeper; but in his own case Clive knew that it was better, though he missed the gratification. Ruth would have given such unqualified praise—every line would have been perfect. Once that might have been agreeable enough, but since that period Clive had known what it was to read his productions to a woman whose intellect could grasp every half-expressed thought, whose critical judgment had weight, who could understand, too, every dream, because she might have been a poet herself had fate so directed her life. Oh, that poor unfinished tragedy—hidden away carefully where he could not by any chance stumble upon it and receive a shock—where no one would ever find it during his life-time. How sadly he thought of it, with an absurd pity such as he might have felt for a beloved child that he had in some insane fit shut up in the dark, and could not let out although its lamentations hurt him cruelly. Never to be found during his life—he thought of that when he concealed it; he often had since, and wondered who, after his death, would come upon it, and what would be said of his strange whim. For it would be found long before the ink had paled or the paper grown yellow. He was strong and well—but he was not to have a long life. Ah, that would be as God pleased; how glad he was that he need not reproach himself for the belief. Perhaps Elinor Grey, coming to soothe Ruth in her loneliness, would search among his treasures at the little wife's request, and discover and recollect those incomplete pages; would recollect the long summer afternoons when he read to her under the shadow of the maple-trees, and standing with the manuscripts in her hand, would look back upon his memory, softened and touched. It might easily be; some way it had become a settled idea in his mind that she would find it. If so, she, and she alone, would understand some words written at the close of the last half-finished page—a few words and two dates, nothing more—the day on which he had read the opening scene of the tragedy to her, the day on which he had read the last. She would understand, she alone, and, standing there at such time, would acknowledge that he had redeemed his faith, had striven up out of the dark; and that would be reward enough for his poor life.

So Clive was alone in his work, and they never sat in the library in the evening.

To-night Ruth was tired with her long ride, and Clive told her that she must be put in bed like a naughty child.

"I have not the energy to stir," she said.

He took her in his arms and carried her up stairs as he often did in sport, and when she was in bed he sat and read to her until she fell asleep. "But you won't go back and work?" she urged, as he took up a book.

"Not a line. I am not sleepy, so I shall go to my den and smoke while you dream."

She held fast to his hand as children will to some one watching them; very soon she was in a sound slumber, and he could steal away without fear of disturbing her. He went down into his library and sat over the smoldering fire and smoked. He did not however at once enjoy his meerschaum and think about the chapter he would write to-morrow. As he passed the table he stopped to arrange the papers, and Elinor Grey's letter peeped out and stared him in the face. He looked at it, half turned away, but took it up and read it—a letter full of friendship and kindness, with no allusion to the past; many good wishes, and a fitting mention of Ruth's husband, whom she had met. That was all he was to her now—Ruth's husband!

Clive had a weary hour of it, and cursed his own folly in reading the letter; then remembered that he must become accustomed to more than that. He must meet her and behave as people are expected to in modern days, and above every thing, his heart must not struggle or throb—he was Ruth's husband! Those words reminded him that he had more to do than that which should be simply decorous and proper—he had to do right, to be faithful even in thought to his vow, lest through mental wanderings he should be led into actual wrong.

And it is hard to do right. Almost any of us are capable of some one grand effort, but to live up to it day after day when the excitement is gone and life as dull as a muddy beach from which the tide has gone out — it is very hard then. The agony of a great sorrow brings a certain strength—it is the little stings which are unendurable. A stab with a dagger bright and sharp is quickly over, but to be stuck full of pins and needles, to be made a human pincushion for petty sufferings to be thrust in, is a martyrdom beyond that of Saint Lawrence.

Clive had a return of the agony that night—a fierce stab from the dagger which had before drunk his blood. It was a change, any way, from the dull aches of the past weeks, the added feeling of self-contempt because he cowered under the details of the life he had accepted; and a change of torture is a species of relief. After awhile he smoked and got back somewhere near tranquillity; and when he thought he could sleep, he went to bed. Just as he turned on his pillow, and congratulated himself upon the fact that he was beginning to doze, the dissipated moon, newly risen, looked in through the curtains and assured him that he was doing no such thing. He would get up and shut out the diabolical planet with her wan stare; but Ruth stirred in her sleep, murmured his name, and took possession of his hand; so he lay there and watched her in the ghostly light, and never closed his eyes until it was day.

They are very long and very dreary, those night watches, but we can bear them; we can bear any thing if we only try in the right manner. Youth goes, life itself goes on the current of those wakeful hours, and very rapidly too—I am not sure but that is the one ameliorating thought.

Clive Farnsworth woke and went about his duties like other men—the world and the work of toil or pleasure must proceed, though Hamlet may have been wandering with his father's ghost all night, or Othello may know that Desdemona lies strangled in the next room.

They lived there, the husband and wife, almost as much alone as if they had been encamped on some western prairie. The people owning places in the neighborhood who could lay claim to Farnsworth's acquaintance were of the order who flee the country in autumn and do not return until late spring has warmed the earth. There were two or three dismally quiet and correct families who avoided the dissipations of town life and remained stationary on their broad acres. These people had called soon after Clive brought his wife home, had been called on in return, and had offered the newly-wedded a few precise, uncomfortable dinners, where Ruth could not eat she was so busy swallowing her yawns. There was the rector, to be sure, and he was a very agreeable man; but his wife was a thorn in his own side and the sides of his whole parish; and he was always busy, going about among the poor and keeping watch that his lambs did not stray off into dissenting chapels or frighten themselves with Calvinistic horrors. Good as he was, he was always reproaching himself for his sins, and wore a mental hair-shirt with which he scratched himself unmercifully. So he was not much to be counted on as a companion; once in a while he would stray up of an evening without his wife, and he and Clive had a pleasant chat. But when he thought about it after, and remembered how much he had enjoyed the glass of wine and cheerful talk and a game of backgammon with Ruth, he was afraid that he was too fond of pleasure, and put an extra quantity of rough hair into his shirt. He need not have done that, however, for his nuptial hyena scratched him enough to atone for more sins than his quiet nature, cooled by fastings and a perpetual Lent, would lead him to commit during his whole life.

But the result of it all was that Clive and Ruth were left very much alone in the great house to which the Presbyterian preacher often alluded in his sermons as " the gilded halls of feasting and wicked revelry." Ruth was very happy in that solitude, and she had time to grow accustomed to the change in her destiny, to accept her place as mistress with a very pretty dignity, and, more than that, time to adore Clive to the fullness of human possibility. She read, she studied hard, love supplying the power of application and making the work pleasant, and was so quick to learn every necessary trifle, as women are, that very soon she might have appeared among the most exclusive of her husband's friends without fear of being commented on save for the unusual quiet and ladyhood—is there such a word?—which characterized her.

She saw Elinor Grey's letter on the library table that morning and said to Clive, "Oh, the letter, dear. Won't you read it before you begin work?"

"The letter?" Clive repeated, somewhat deceitfully, to give himself an instant's breathing-space.

"Miss Grey's, you know—"

"Oh yes; I did look at it last night while I was smoking," replied Clive, pulling his inkstand nearer and picking up his pens. "A very charming letter, as you said."

"I love that woman, Clive."

He had drawn his paper toward him; he looked a little abstracted, as was natural.

"You want to work," said Ruth. "I am going to read; I'll be as quiet as a little mouse." She fidgeted him sometimes by her very stillness; to-day particularly he would have given so much to be alone; it was almost impossible to write knowing there was a human creature within a mile. But he was patient and quiet. When he looked up from his work, after he had succeeded in working, he was rewarded. Ruth had dropped her book and was gazing intently at him. "I am so happy!" she whispered. "I was waiting for you to look up, that I might say so."

"You might have jogged my elbow even to tell me that," Clive answered.

"You are such a dear boy to want me always with you. Not a bit like those horrid men we read about that had so few pretty thoughts they must keep them for their books."

"Aren't you afraid of my growing outrageously conceited, little one, with all your praise?"

"No, indeed! you are too proud for that. My Clive is perfect."

"Forgetting that you have just admitted I owned one of the seven capital sins."

"Oh, you wickedness—I never did! Clive, please, since you have stopped, read this little bit of Metastasio."

And Clive read the mellow old measures about the *beate gente*, and made a little rhymed translation which pleased Ruth so much that she must needs write it down; and Clive was impatient. She went away at last to feed her pigeons, and Clive found that he could not write any more that day. Elinor Grey's letter had disturbed the groove into which he had slipped during the quiet of the past weeks; he must devote himself to getting back, and must learn to guard against similar shocks.

He could not write that day or the next, so he went out with Ruth into the sun and they galloped over the hills, and he essayed many healthy exercises, as was sensible, instead of giving himself up to moody feelings and miserable pains, as his inclination prompted. He reaped the benefit of his discipline in fresh spirits and the ability to resume his task with a certain forgetfulness of himself which made the companionship of those dream-children more pleasant.

But the restlessness of those days and the dark thoughts it had created left certain effects which betrayed themselves in a conversation with the rector, who chanced to stray into his library before Clive had become thoroughly settled. Ruth was not there, else he might have been silent through a fear of disturbing her; and though the rector could not help him much, and was flattered exceedingly by this glimpse of a soul struggling toward the light, when he had come for easy talk and a little enjoyment, I think it did Clive good.

The rector was an excellent man, but he was no logician; he knew it himself and deplored the deficiency more than he need to have done: his life was a better lesson than a whole quarto of arguments could have been; and his companion felt that. Besides, Clive had reached the point where, humanly speaking, he could help himself. He had lived enough and his soul had sufficiently grown so that he was no longer afraid of being weak in the possession of a simple, child-like faith. It sounds very grand, no doubt, to be able to bring up endless fine theories and showy sophistries; to say that the thinking soul demands this and the bold mind will have that ancient superstition flung aside; but it is a grander thing to have the intellect and soul so developed that they can say to the heart—"Lead me—help me on to faith—I am not afraid of being weak—not afraid of being a child in this."

Clive gave his restlessness vent and felt better, suddenly reminded that there was nothing new or wonderful in it, that doubt is not sufficiently original to be a matter of triumph; and he glided away from the subject, leaving the rector to compose his mind on simpler themes.

The good man liked to talk about his choir-boys and the new painted window at which the dissenting preachers lifted their hands in holy horror, and the growing faithfulness and attention among his flock, whom he was trying hard to make understand that religion was something for every-day use and practice. He liked his painted window, and it made him think of heavenly things to see that row of white-robed boys chanting with their fresh young voices, and he liked flowers on the altar, and a thought-inspiring cross, and a variety of matters which I like and hope you do. He loved and reverenced his Church, and was glad to do every thing which kept her seemly and beautiful. He avoided making a guy of himself in a black Geneva gown, and was particular to honor the Church days, and had learned that in spite of new creeds and isms, religion, if it is to be an all-permeating power, must address every sense. He knew too that each seeming trifle which has come down to us as a symbol of Catholicism, helped to widen the minds of his people, and tended as much to remove them from the chill errors of schism and dissent as it did to keep them from slipping into the cold forms and fetters of Romanism.

Clive brought him back to tranquillity by a long talk about pleasanter things than weary old doubts, and was a little ashamed to perceive that, with all his intellect and his growing fame, this humble parish priest had a broader soul than his, since he was willing to acknowledge his own littleness, and was not afraid of being weak or narrow-minded by yielding to faith.

The days went by, and Spring drew nearer and thawed the brooks into good nature, hung out red tokens on the maple-trees, and sent warm whispers down the wind to say that she was coming. Clive was busy, and occupation is the surest safeguard against any trouble. If he could not write, if his books grew pages of dull hieroglyphics, and Homer and Sophocles had neither sound nor poetry to his ear, and modern bards and schoolmen were dryer yet, there was enough to occupy him without. Perhaps the first impulse might have been selfish; but to be busy with other people, to look persistently away from the pain and admit that life does not hinge upon one feeling, will bring thoughts which are not selfish and have their reward.

So it was that gradually Clive became the master of his sorrow, instead of allowing it to grow into a grim tyrant which would have dwarfed his powers, checked his mental growth, and warped and distorted his nature in every way. And Ruth was like a flower in the morning sun, she so rapidly developed new graces and new charms. As he waxed stronger, the bitterness and the mad yearning by degrees lessened; it ceased to be such constant effort to appear gentle and kind.

He would never love this child, but he would grow very tender of her, and in time the old wounds would cease to throb, and— We are such poor creatures, there is a good deal left in life after we think that every thing is lost. A good deal left, and it is well perhaps that we are poor creatures.

Ruth was occasionally frightened anew when she had time to think how the weeks were passing, and to remember that the neighboring mansions, standing silent among their great trees and broad pleasure-grounds, would soon be inhabited, and that as Clive's wife she should have to meet Clive's friends and encounter a segment from that mysterious circle called Society.

"But you have not been frightened yet by any one you have met," said Clive, when she was one day confiding her doubts to his guardianship, by way of relieving herself of their weight.

"No—I believe not. But then old Mr. and Mrs. Sherman are so commonplace, even if they are stately, and old Miss Livingston is deaf, and Mr. Walters is so good-natured—"

"Oh, pause in your list," laughed Clive; "the catalogue of names is like enduring their actual dullness."

"But they have all been good-natured to me, Clive."

"I should think so, my little brown thrush."

"But when the people come up from town, and the hotel at the lake is full, and there are picnics and dinners and dances and—"

"Horrors innumerable; why then, little one, you will take stupidity in large doses instead of small ones."

"But if I should do something very outrageous and make you ashamed?"

"I am not afraid of it; you are a small princess by nature."

"And you are a darling old boy to assure me. I don't believe I shall be afraid with you by me."

"And we need not dine or picnic ourselves into fevers," said Clive; "you had forgotten that."

"But I must not think that I am separating you from your old friends, Clive; I should be miserable."

"People that eat one and picnic one are not necessarily friends," replied Clive.

"Perhaps I can't explain what I mean. I must not stand between you and old associations. You have loved me, given me a place here; I must be a part of your life, not selfishly drag you off into a new path."

"You don't know how to be selfish, little one."

"If your petting does not teach me; I am so afraid of it sometimes."

He remembered what he tried as much as possible to forget—the necessity there was for doing nothing which could cause comment about her. They must see people and live among them; every thing must go on as it would if he had married the dullest and richest girl in his set, whose antecedents could be traced back to the Mayflower or Virginia cavaliers or good old Knickerbocker blood which grows scarcer and more diluted than one could wish. "Yes," he said, "we can not be hermits, and my Ruth will look like a violet among all those tired creatures coming back from unlimited Germans and late suppers."

"If they'll only be good to me and not stare."

"Of course they will stare at any thing so pretty."

"You absurd boy. But, Clive, I don't intend to think; I mean to let every thing go its way and enjoy myself."

"The very thing you ought to do." He knew her well enough to be certain that this would be. She was perfectly happy; so unconscious of self that little things would not disturb her as they might have done another. She enjoyed amusements so much in her quiet way that she would never be on the lookout for slights or whispers; she was so satisfied that she must be worthy since she was worthy of his love, that she would undergo scrutiny with composure.

And Ruth had laid her happiness as an offering just where she had laid her sorrow, and it was made holy.

CHAPTER XXI.

TELLING THE SECRET.

AFTER Miss Laidley's departure, Elinor Grey's home life fell so much back into its old routine that she might have forgotten the young lady had not occasional letters, full of affectionate phrases and elaborate accounts of her pleasures, arrived to remind her that the present quiet was a respite which must terminate whenever the fair Genevieve's caprice changed. The epistles, written in the daintiest and most illegible of hands, were so replete with encomiums of the Idol, that Elinor became confident they were written for that lady's eyes as much as for her own, but she knew that one part was real— the impression made by Mrs. Hackett's wealth.

It had not required a long acquaintance with Miss Laidley for Elinor to discover the respect which she had for money, and her lip curled over many little exhibitions of character which the writer unconsciously betrayed. Her greed of receiving presents appeared to have not in the least declined, and Mrs. Hackett had certainly taken the surest means of reaching her heart, for she loaded her with costly gifts; and Genevieve wrote that she was absolutely ashamed to take them, but dear Mrs. Hackett would hear no refusal, and she, Miss Laidley, intended when she came back to consult her sweet Elinor's perfect taste in regard to sending to Paris itself for some token which should be worthy of the Duchess's acceptance—if such could be found.

"That last touch was worth a new bracelet to her," thought Elinor, throwing aside the letter. "I am sure Mrs. Hackett paid her in diamonds." Miss Laidley was always going to send to Paris for something for somebody. Elinor knew that the assertion meant about as much as the old promise given to children of treasures they are to receive when Mamma's ship comes from the moon.

But as the weeks went on Elinor had graver thoughts to occupy her than those connected with this affectionate creature who signed herself a variety of childish names and had numerous pretty French and Italian phrases at command to break the tedium of dull, cold English. Graver thoughts indeed, and more under the influence of reason than they ought to have been to be very romantic, considering that they centered upon a member of the opposite sex.

Elinor knew that her heart was no nearer Leighton Rossitur than it had been when he first addressed her, and she was perplexed and troubled how to act. He had been a great help; she had the kindest, truest regard for him; she acknowledged that his society and the consciousness of his love had done much to enable her to come out of the gloom; but she feared that she should never go beyond this; if not in his case, certainly never in the case of another. She decided that it would be wrong not to tell him this frankly, but she was confident it would have no effect; besides, as he kept to the strict letter of his promise, and never "made love," it was difficult to speak of these things which gave her more and more uneasiness.

There was an opportunity at last, but it was not easy to improve it as she ought. Rossitur was going to town for a week upon some business connected with the Department; he was intrusted too in certain private matters of Mr. Grey's which were better arranged by another, and Rossitur desired to see the Bull on his own account, for confidence between them was an old bond, and had helped them both before now. The evening previous to his departure he spent with Elinor. "I dread to go," he said; "I don't like to make any change, lest nothing should be the same after."

Elinor remembered the time that another man had spoken similar words; she remembered what followed, and she suffered most at the idea that she did still remember. If any way to forgetfulness might be found—if marrying Rossitur could be the means, she would not have hesitated at that moment. The impulse passed, and Leighton Rossitur did not know that in spite of his penetration he had lost an opportunity which might be long in recurring. "At least you will miss me a little," he said, by his very voice rousing her from that mood.

"You are quite certain that I shall," she replied.

"Not so certain as I could wish. Oh, Miss Grey—Elinor—I may say so now—haven't I kept my word?"

"You have been every thing that was gener-ous and noble, Mr. Rossitur," she answered, remembering that she ought to tell him what had been in her mind.

"And you don't know how hard it has been to keep silence. If the time only comes when I may tell you how hard, I shall be more than repaid, Elinor."

"It is that which makes me seem so wicked," she exclaimed impetuously; "your patience, your kindness. Oh, my friend, I don't know how to say it—but if you could go away and not think of me any more."

A sudden light blazed in Rossitur's eyes and he grew very pale. The mere thought of losing her now filled him with fierce rage, but he answered quietly—"I can't go—you know it."

"And if the time passes and I can't—and I am unable—"

"And you can not love me," he added; "don't try for gentle words, Elinor—that was what you meant."

"Yes, it was. I have wanted to talk to you about this; I am afraid of myself—oh, I am wicked to let you go on loving me when there is so little hope of a fit return."

"Neither you nor I have any thing to do with that," he answered; "that is beyond our control—I must love you."

"If any one could advise me," exclaimed Elinor in her distress; "but in this nobody can."

"Nobody?"

"Yes, you could; and yet how absurd that is."

"Let me advise you, Elinor," he said, putting aside his anger and his sudden fears. "I am your friend now—not the man who loves you. Surely you can trust me—you have promised, you know; put the other man out of sight—forget him completely."

"And what does my friend advise?" Elinor asked, inquiringly, softened by his gentleness.

"That you should not allow yourself to think—"

"That would be unfair to the man who loves me."

"But I, your friend, shall be content, Elinor. When these weeks are over do not think about your lack of love; if you are certain you can trust that man, marry him."

"Oh, Mr. Rossitur! And if I never loved him and he knew it?"

"Never mind the possibilities. You would not like to be alone again, Elinor; without vanity I may at least believe so much."

"I would not lose my friend for the world."

"You see? I am not afraid, and I promise you that the lover shall be as patient as the friend."

How could she put in words that which she really feared? She could not understand the feeling herself. She only knew that when she thought of him as her friend his presence was a pleasure to her—when she dreamed of the possibility of being his wife she was filled with unutterable horror. There was no language in which she could express a sensation which it was impossible for her maiden purity to comprehend, but of which her soul warned her with all its force. "I can not explain," she said, "but one thing is evident—I ought not to trifle with you; I must not let the time go by and leave you deceived up to the last."

"You are not deceiving me, Elinor. I was to wait until the summer; you are not to think at all."

"I do believe you would be noble enough not to blame me," she replied; "but that does not satisfy me."

"It must. I would sooner go away from you forever, Elinor Grey, than know that I was tormenting you." That was not heart-felt, but it sounded so grand that he could not resist saying it.

"I don't know how to act," returned she sadly.

"Only be quiet and don't think; it is all you have to do."

"I can not rid myself of the responsibility in that way. And oh, Mr. Rossitur, if I were willing, never marry me because I am grateful for your affection and afraid of my own loneliness. It would not do. I am not gentle, not good enough; it would be black work for both of us."

"Trust to my friendship now, Elinor; trust to that love later. I shall never change; you know me thoroughly. I am a better man just from the influence of the past weeks. I shall grow better and stronger—you need not be afraid."

"It is myself, my own weakness that I fear. Mr. Rossitur, every day shows me some new trait in your character that heightens my respect and esteem; but I told you the truth when I said that I was not worth such love."

"My pearl of women! You must let me judge of that."

She was gaining nothing by this attempt at explanation; she was only more softened by his goodness, and placing herself on less certain ground. "I know I ought to end this," she said; "I ought to answer now."

"But you have no right; you gave me till July; I won't have your answer now. It is your friend talking to you, Elinor—we won't mind that other man."

She would marry him at last, he was certain of that; he had never failed in any thing on which his whole heart was set. There was a peculiar charm in this present aspect of affairs, so unlike any experience he had ever known. He loved her—he would win her. It did occur to him that he might kill her with his love if every pulse was not his then; but he would not think; he believed himself capable of a great deal that was noble, as we all do till we are tried. "Promise me that you will not fret about it while I am gone," he said.

"And that will not be honest."

"Let me judge; it is what I wish. Promise me, Elinor."

This was all she had accomplished by the effort which cost her so much. He had gained an advantage, yet she was no nearer loving him than before, and by an additional step had made it so much harder to go back if time should prove it necessary.

"Do you give me your word, Elinor?"

"I will at least try to be more of a woman, and less horribly selfish."

That was very unsatisfactory; if once she thought of things in that light, he was lost. "You promised to regard me only as your friend," he said; "to find a comfort in my love."

"You tempt me so," she answered, smiling, but nearer tears than she liked. "I am inclined to be selfish and weak, to float on in a dream; and you aid me."

Let her float on. If she could only remain in that state of mind until the time came for a decision, her conscience would not allow her to retract. With her overstrained ideas of right, she would marry him through a fear of having trifled: he should conquer any way. "Only miss me," he said; "I will be importunate then."

"You know I shall do that everywhere I go."

"I am quite satisfied, then—quite. If you tell me when I come back that the week seemed long—am I very selfish?"

"You make me ashamed of myself, Mr. Rossitur. You are very noble, and very generous."

He thought he was, himself; and it was true, if his virtues did not fail when the decisive moment came, as yours or mine would have been very likely to do. "So there is an end to all these doubts and fears," he said; "tell me that I have succeeded in dispelling them."

"While I listen to you, yes; but indeed, Mr. Rossitur, I must not forget. I must be just to you and to myself."

"I am going away now, so I can say nothing. A hope of gaining your love will make me happy, and my happiness will give me power to keep you at least quiet and content: there is nothing to fear."

"A wrong to you is what I dread most—do believe that."

"I believe—I know it. But, if you can trust my love, it is enough; you need not fear for my happiness."

So she had gained nothing by the interview, and she recognized the fact very sensibly after he had gone. Still there was little to do but follow his advice—avoid thought as much as possible. She did miss him, even more than she had expected; and a woman has gone a long way when she misses a man. If lovers could know that a little wholesome neglect, apparently brought on by uncontrollable circumstances, is a capital aid toward winning a woman in Elinor Grey's state of mind, it strikes me they would not trust to uninterrupted teasing and attention. Elinor missed him; and as his absence was unavoidably lengthened into a fortnight, she had ample time. He wrote to her, and his letters were exactly what they ought to have been; the friend wrote, and the lover peeped through here and there in the most delightful way. But Elinor did not answer those epistles; she had warned him that she should not, and she persevered in her resolution, although sometimes she was sorely tempted. If she did write, she should be certain to say something that she would regret. She could guard her tongue and her actions; but she knew what an instrument of mischief a pen is in a woman's hand, and she avoided that danger.

She had never told her father of the story Rossitur had whispered weeks before; not that she was given to keeping secrets from him, but she was so anxious to be strictly honorable in her conduct toward this man. She did tell him, however, during Rossitur's absence. It came about from the fact of two of Elinor's adorers laying their distressed cases before Mr. Grey himself, instead of appealing directly to the young lady—a very upright and manly sort of proceeding, we all say and think, but it is blatantly asinine, nevertheless. Elinor had to tell her father that the pining ones need not come to her, and was very glad to be relieved from having to say unpleasant things to them.

"It becomes alarming, my daughter Elinor," said Mr. Grey, laughing a little, as the best of men will at others' disappointments. "I have sent so many despairing swains away during these last five years, coming, I think, from every quarter of the globe."

"But I can't help it, papa. I do not flirt, and I would be in love if I could."

"And when I think of it," returned he, "it is a little odd you have never cared."

"You are in no hurry, papa?"

"I am not anxious to be left alone, my daughter. No, I think even to have said 'your ladyship'—as I might three separate times, only you were hard-hearted—would not have been any compensation."

"I shall just stay with you, papa."

"Ah! ah! young ladies' promises! No, my daughter Elinor, you shall marry the man toward whom your heart goes out. I shall love him for your sake, and resign myself to growing old gracefully."

"You will always be young, papa. You should not be the most agreeable man in the world if I am to have a husband."

"My Elinor knows her flattery is exceedingly pleasant."

"And papa knows I mean it."

"And my daughter is a foolish puss, in spite of her dignity," said Mr. Grey. The purest feeling that man had ever known was his affection for his child; and these past years had made her a companion so congenial that it would be very hard to yield her to another. "I only stipulate that you shall give me fair warning, my daughter," he said; "I must have time to grow familiar with the idea of losing you."

Elinor thought that she ought to tell him the terms on which she stood with Mr. Rossitur, and she found it very difficult. "Papa," she said

suddenly, "if I should marry, it must be a man who has your full approbation."

"My daughter Elinor could not love a man who would fail to have it," he replied; "I know too well what your judgment is to have any fear."

"Papa, do you like Mr. Rossitur?" she asked abruptly.

He was a little startled, but his composure was not easily shaken. He only showed that he had been surprised by opening his snuff-box and taking a pinch of the odorous mixture in a dainty, graceful way. "I like Mr. Rossitur very much," he answered in his deliberate voice; "but what has your question to do with the subject, my daughter Elinor?"

"I should have told you before, papa, only it was not my secret; though I have been quite troubled at keeping it from you."

"Oh, it is a secret of Mr. Rossitur's? But that has nothing to do with our subject either."

"Oh yes, it has. What a goose I am at making explanations. Papa, he would insist on loving me—he would wait six months for an answer."

"And what will the answer be, my Elinor?"

"Indeed, if I could decide I should be so glad. I believe I have a cold heart, except for you. He was so noble and kind I could not send him away; and yet I think I ought to have done so."

"My Elinor is so wise that I need not tell her how dangerous such compromises usually are."

"I know it, papa, and I want to do right; I told him frankly I could not love him. Since that he has acted like the truest and most patient of friends—not a word or look that could disturb me."

"Then I see no way but for you to wait till he comes to receive his answer, my daughter."

"But is that right, papa?"

"It is simply unavoidable. I know very well you will not trifle with him."

"That you may be sure of, papa."

"Mr. Rossitur is not rich; he will be a distinguished man if he is persevering and works hard," continued Mr. Grey. "I can only say that you must decide for yourself, my Elinor."

"But, papa, if I don't love him?"

"Perhaps you will discover before then."

"I never shall—I am certain of it; I shall never love any man. He would be satisfied—he is so good—he would take me with my cold-heartedness; but I can not think it would be just to him."

Mr. Grey did not quite understand. Men of fifty do not easily comprehend all the workings of a young woman's heart and mind—not men of his stamp, at least. But Mr. Grey talked very prettily about gratitude warming into love, and a girl's friendship being often *l'amour sans yeux*, and so rather helped Rossitur.

"I have told you, at all events, papa," she said; "whatever happens, you at least will believe that I have tried to do right."

"But you must be very careful. I know

how sensitive you are, my daughter Elinor. If you desire it, when the time comes I must give you up to Mr. Rossitur; but if it should be otherwise, you must not have a doubt with which to torment yourself."

Elinor explained every thing, and was consoled to find that her father did not think she could have acted in any other way. Certainly, ambitious as he was and eager to employ every aid in self-advancement, Mr. Grey had no mind to make use of his daughter's happiness. Besides, there was no man already in power whose alliance could benefit him particularly; there was a good deal more to be hoped from this aspirant for dignities.

Mr. Grey appeared very noble and disinterested, and, at the same time, gratified his affection for his child, being in no haste to lose her, and loving her so well that he did not think any event in life could arrive which would make him admit even the possibility of sacrificing her to his needs. Elinor had a sense of relief in confiding the matter to him, and gained a refuge from her doubts by remembering that he approved of her conduct.

In the mean time Leighton Rossitur was detained in New York, and, as was natural, he often visited the house of the Idol, where he was always a welcome guest. Miss Laidley was in her best looks, and made quite a little Circe of herself; and Rossitur could not help being pleased with her, although he was in love with another woman. He was not fearful that any report which could go back to Miss Grey would cause her an instant's reflection; he knew her pride and generosity too well. As for the fair Genevieve's peace of mind, I do not suppose that he once thought about it. Indeed, he had no intention of having a flirtation; but the little thing was very bewitching, and the Idol's house was pleasant, and Rossitur did not hesitate to sweeten the pangs of life in every way that offered. But it was all very unsatisfactory to Miss Laidley when it was over. She could not be certain of having made an impression on his heart—had not so much as discovered whether that uncomfortable bit of property belonged to Miss Grey.

If he had loved her, gone mad for her as men had done, it is highly probable that she would not have cared a fillip of her ear-ring for him; but as it was she did care a great deal, and in a stormy, impetuous fashion which would have astonished the wisest physiognomist that ever looked for people's characters in their faces. If her fever had no other effect, it deepened her detestation of Miss Grey into tolerably strong hatred to be indulged by a pink-and-white creature in this latter half of the nineteenth century. It was bad enough for Elinor to be beautiful and stately, and what Genevieve called "deadly superior;" to have no secrets, and be ridiculously truthful; but to have, in addition, the fear that Leighton Rossitur loved her, was more than Miss Laidley's equanimity could endure. She would have liked to stick her unconscious rival

full of pins and needles, literally or metaphorically—both, if that had been possible. She praised her wherever she went, and made it clear all the while that she was a sweet little martyr, and that Miss Grey was jealous and tyrannical.

She did not try that dodge much with the Idol, for the Idol was true as steel to her favorites, and actually believed in the people whom she liked—oh, marvel of the age! But Genevieve prowled about her, and poked her here and tripped her up there, and tried to discover if she were acquainted with the least mystery concerning Elinor. She was at length rewarded by Mrs. Hackett's telling her what she knew about the affair with Clive Farnsworth, although that was very little. "He was a glorious creature, my dove," said she, "and I thought he flung his noble heart at our beautiful princess's shrine. I must have erred, else he felt the blight that preys upon the rose, for he wedded another—the fairest floweret."

"But was there nothing odd about it—no secret?" Miss Laidley asked.

"His marriage was very instantaneous—"

"No, no—he's of no consequence now. But did not Elinor care for him—are you sure?"

"It could not have been, my perfect. Our statuesque Elinor could not have loved in vain."

"So he married nobody knows whom," said Genevieve.

"Some little country blossom—a treasure. But indeed I think Miss Grey told me that she knew her formerly."

"I think it is very odd, at least."

"Perhaps so, now you make me cogitate. But not if Miss Grey was acquainted with her; our princess never errs in judgment."

"I'd like to pull your turban off and stamp on it," thought Miss Laidley. "You old parrot, chanting that horrid thing's praises!"

Genevieve was fain to leave the subject, since it resulted in Miss Grey's charms being loudly extolled. She did the only ill-natured thing she could—she insisted upon it that Mr. Farnsworth's marriage was a very mysterious affair until the Idol thought it was too, and said so to Rosa Thornton, who, womanlike, began to be infected with the same suspicion. If she had known that it originated with Miss Laidley, she would have held it in contempt at once, for she had conceived an aversion to that pretty creature, who cordially returned it. The consequence was that they were very sweet to each other; and Rosa wrote to Elinor that the Laidley was the most abominable little cat among all the cats she had known, and cats seemed to comprise the greater portion of her female acquaintance; but the Laidley was the worst. After that they kissed each other when they met; and Miss Laidley said very innocently to every body that Mrs. Thornton was a lovely woman—how beautifully she flirted—how lucky Mr. Thornton did not care; she was so open about it, and let Mr. Norton kiss her hand in the conservatory at the Idol's house; but Miss Laidley did not mean to mention that—she was so heedless—there was nothing in it, of course, but people would talk. And of course Rosa heard it, and she and Tom had a hearty laugh; but it did not make her dislike Miss Laidley any the less, and she called her worse names in the next letter she wrote to Elinor. She was glad that pussy had not arrived when she left Washington; now she need not invite her to Alban Wood. Artful Rosa decided that she must make the Idol ask Miss Laidley to sojourn with her in the country, so that Elinor would be free to go where she liked.

Rossitur's stay in town was over; after he had gone, Miss Laidley took the edge off her feelings by breaking an engagement between two happy young people, carrying a disgusting Cuban, who chanced to be of importance at the time, away from a married flirt, and performing several feats of a similar nature, the most wonderful of which was flirting with Jack Ralston, and keeping Jack's wife, who was jealousy incarnate, blissfully blind and complaisant — a thing no other woman ever succeeded in doing.

Tom Thornton told Elinor the next summer that he never saw any thing to equal the way in which the Laidley turned poor young Greyson's head, and drove his affianced so mad that she broke the engagement in her frenzy; while Tom regarded the performance with an artistic eye, his opinion of Miss Laidley was best not put in words. Of course Greyson made an ass of himself and brought his heart to Miss Laidley, who did not wish the gift and had never expected it. She sent him off quite insane between penitence and wrath, and she went weeping to throw herself on the Idol's bosom and deplore the harm she had unconsciously done. The friends of the young pair were not dumb, and every body knew the story, but somehow Miss Laidley managed to preserve her credit—she had not meant to do mischief. After that she attacked the Cuban, and, though she had a veteran coquette to contend against, she was successful. The Cuban actually laid his sequins and his slaves at her feet, and she did a bit of virtuous indignation, and told the Idol that she considered it an insult to be persecuted by a man who had been so talked about with a married woman.

When there was no more deviltry to be transacted she began to find town very dull in its after-Lent awakening, to grow weary of the Idol's long stories and sesquipedalian words of compliment. She wrote a beautiful letter to Mr. Grey—some business matter was the pretense—wherein she depicted so vividly the woes of a solitary canary-bird pining for her parent, who had gone to be a seraph, and hinting that nobody could soothe her loneliness but her guardian, that Mr. Grey answered begging her to return, and told her how they had missed her. Neither of the letters were shown to Elinor; Mr. Grey mentioned having received a business note from his ward, but for some reason, probably undefined in his own mind, he kept the contents to himself.

Miss Laidley told the Idol that her guardian desired her to return; she must bring her visit to a close, though it broke her heart to leave her darling Duchess; but she must be obedient to him who stood in the place of her lost parent. The Idol admired her angelic virtues, wept over her, and made her promise to come back and go up to the Castle in the country, which looked exactly like a square tea-tray decorated with four pepper-boxes.

Under the protection of old Juanita and one of Mrs. Hackett's men-servants, Miss Laidley journeyed back to Washington, and got up a respectable little flirtation with an entire stranger on the road, to relieve the tedium of travel. She descended upon Elinor more blooming and excitable than ever, and upset the whole house in the most innocent manner possible, causing the servants to consign her mentally to a hotter place than the kitchen furnace, and making Elinor wish that the Millennium would come.

Mr. Rossitur was unusually occupied at that season of the year; indeed, he rather kept out of the fair Genevieve's way, finding that she expected the town episode to be followed up. Miss Laidley in her heart believed that Elinor ordered him out of her reach for fear of danger. She thought virtuously that such wickedness deserved to meet with righteous retribution, and constituted herself an avenging angel to administer the punishment. Having such resolutions in her mind, made her more affectionate than ever to her hostess; she did the martyr with increased sweetness for other people's benefit, and swooped down on the unwary Mr. Grey like a beautiful pigeon-hawk.

CHAPTER XXII.

A SCENIC EFFECT SPOILED.

I BELIEVE I have quoted somewhere what wise old Balzac said about fifty-two being the age at which a man is most dangerous to women. I never was fifty-two, and am therefore unable to speak from experience, but observation has taught me that if a pretty girl wants to make a puffy, pulpy, disjointed idiot of a member of my ill-used race, she ought to select a man of that age to do it in perfection.

Now Mr. Grey was a wise old serpent, and had been *un homme galant*, and knew a good many things about women men never know about each other; but Miss Laidley's type was not familiar to him, and he was completely deceived by her pretty innocence, her appealing helplessness, her solitary condition, and the entire trust she had in him, which was expressed with such artless freedom. He was not to be deluded into making a blatant idiot of himself, but he was a good deal more fascinated than he would have liked any body to perceive.

Elinor did not observe Miss Laidley's performances at first—puss was exceedingly wary. She had ways and means of knowing when Mr.

Grey was alone in his library—old Juanita was the most faithful of waiting-women—and she was always going in by accident, or to seek advice, or to ask him to comfort her because she was a lonely little thing, who would never be wise enough to remain unguarded in a wicked world. When Elinor did discover what was going on she was filled with wrath; and not aspiring to angelic amiability, she gave way to her temper, and Miss Laidley had an unpleasant morning. Not that Elinor betrayed the real cause of her irritation; she was quite a match for any woman when it came to the necessity of employing high art; and the Laidley had not the satisfaction of knowing that her success was noticed. In the midst of her rage Elinor would be civil; but there was an opening, and she improved it. Miss Laidley chanced to amuse some callers with a reproduction of the Idol the very day on which Elinor discovered her machinations toward the Secretary, and she read her a lecture which was worse than being scalped.

And Elinor would not quarrel; she only would do her duty. She told Miss Laidley that she had talked so much about duty that her, Elinor's, mind was infected too; and she had to say, that to accept a person's hospitality and presents, and then laugh about him or her, was the most contemptible thing of which any woman past twenty could be guilty. She frightened Miss Laidley by vowing that if it happened again she would write to Mrs. Hackett and let her know how her kindness had been returned; she begged to be understood thoroughly in earnest. She conquered, and Miss Laidley had to cry and beg, and wound up with a hysteric fit from passion. Elinor gave her a dose of very bitter medicine, spattered her new dress mercilessly with water, and brought her out of it.

"I mean it all for your good," said she, sweetly; "you know that. But, my dear Genevieve, I can not permit you to abuse my friends; I want you to remember it."

Miss Laidley did a war-dance in private, and pulled old Juanita's hair, and called Elinor certain names which would not look well in print, but which are sometimes not strangers to the lips of pink-and-white creatures who look too ethereal for an earthly thought.

Elinor could not be sorry that she had given way to her temper, and she vowed inwardly that, with all her craft, the creature should not trouble the peace of her home. She had the highest respect for her father's judgment, but she did know what unheard-of things men will do, and she had no intention that Miss Laidley should carry proceedings far enough for her to be forced to acknowledge that her father had foibles like common men.

Miss Laidley was more wary than ever, because she had sworn vengeance, and meant to sting Elinor's very soul. Indeed, she felt that she could almost marry Mr. Grey for the satisfaction of torturing her; perhaps she would

have said quite, if it had not been for the recollection of Leighton Rossitur and her unfinished romance. She did show her hand, however, crafty as she was. A few days after the explosion in regard to the Idol, she suddenly fell at Elinor's feet, and sobbing as if her heart would break, cried out—

"Forgive me, Elinor, forgive me! Your coldness tortures me."

"I have not been cold," replied Elinor; "I have treated you just as usual."

"But I feel the difference — here—in my heart. Only say that you forgive me. I know how wrong it was to speak so of Mrs. Hackett; I know you meant it for my good; I should be called ill-natured if I indulged in such thoughtlessness. Only say that you forgive me."

"If you want my forgiveness, Miss Laidley, you have it."

"Darling, perfect Elinor! And don't be icy; you won't, dear? That nearly kills me, for indeed I am a good little thing."

"I am willing to think it was only thoughtlessness," replied Elinor kindly enough, but not to be deluded, "unless you force me to believe otherwise by continuing the practice."

"I never will say a word against any body," sobbed Miss Laidley. "You are sure you forgive me, chérie? You will, I know you will, because you are better than other women; you are perfect—"

"If I am not amiable when my friends are attacked," said Elinor, not thinking it necessary to thank the young lady for her encomiums.

"I am thoroughly ashamed. I can't think how I came to let my tongue run away with me; I am so heedless. But I shall be careful now; you have made me see how wrong it is, and I thank you so much for doing it—oh, so much!"

She did such exaggerated gratitude that Elinor knew how venomous she was at heart. Miss Laidley made the mistake of employing too much art; her penitence and her thankfulness might have deceived a man, but they only left her little game more apparent to her listener, and she was on her guard.

Elinor did not say a word to her father, and she hoped that he was too much occupied to bestow any thought on the small serpent. But one day, when weeks of preparation led Miss Laidley to believe that she could venture on striking what she would have called her grand coup, make a smiling idiot of her guardian, and have the pleasure of telling the story far and wide, she rose up like a young Napoleon in his might.

Elinor was out, and Mr. Grey had returned earlier than usual. The Laidley heard him go up to his room. She knew his habits, and was certain that he would presently descend to the library. She stood before the glass and made her wavy hair look more picturesque than ever; she could at any time grow pale by working herself into a nervous state; she would have artistically darkened her eyelids till they seemed heavy with painful thoughts and unshed tears, had she not remembered that she might have to shed real ones, which would disturb the lines; and down stairs she crept with the velvet tread of a panther.

When Mr. Grey opened the door of his library a few moments later, he saw a figure crouched in a graceful attitude on the floor with her head buried in her hands, and heard a broken voice sob—

"O my father, my father! Come and take me—your lonely little Evangel—O my father, my father!"

The diplomatist was absolutely startled by this paroxysm of suffering. He closed the door softly and stood uncertain what to do, but the slight sound he made was enough to disturb the mourner, who sprang to her feet, uttering in a tone of passionate bitterness—

"Who is it? Can I never have a moment's peace?"

"My dear child," he said, going toward her, "what is the matter?"

"Hélas! it is my guardian," she gasped, putting out her hands with a gesture of confusion. "Let me go, Sir; I did not mean to intrude; I thought I was alone in the house; let me go." She ran straight to him, and almost fell in his arms.

"You must not go," he said, greatly touched by her grief. "Tell me what has happened—what troubles you?"

"Nothing—nothing! Let me go; let me go!" and she clung tight to his hand with both her trembling fingers.

"Are you ill, dear child? Have you had bad news?"

"No, oh no. There is nothing the matter. I was lonely—foolish. Oh, I was thinking of papa. I would not have had you found me for the world; I did not dream of your being near."

"My dear little Genevieve, you know I am your nearest friend now," he said, somewhat fluttered, as masculine nature will be by the trembling pressure of two white hands.

"The kindest, dearest friend ever a lonely, heart-sick creature had," she murmured, looking up in his face through her tears. That appeal was irresistible.

"You can talk to me if you really consider me such, you can tell me every thing that pains you," he continued.

"Oh don't: you will make me cry again; don't speak in that gentle voice. I thank you so much. I am so sorry to distress you." She tried to check her sobs, but they would burst forth in spite of her efforts, and very lovely she looked in her agitation.

"I am grieved to think you suffer," he said; "I can not bear it; you stay too much alone."

"No, no; I am best alone. Nobody understands me, nobody cares for me—but you," with the softest lingering inflection on the pronoun.

"Poor child, if I could help you in any way, you must know how ready I should be."

"I do, I do; I am not ungrateful. Say you believe I am not."

"How could I think it? But where is my daughter Elinor?"

"She is out. Don't tell her how you found me; it would only pain her. Oh, dear Sir, I am such a foolish child. You are both too kind to me; but when I see you happy together, it makes me wretched. Once I was loved and petted, and now I am alone—all alone!"

She flung up her snowy arms with a despairing gesture as they do in novels, and fresh tears gushed from her eyes; then she clung to him again with that mute expression of confidence, and Mr. Grey was very much moved, and quite dazed between her grief and her entire trust in him.

"I must go now," she said mournfully. "Forget this, dear friend. Promise me that you will forget it. I will come back presently, and you shall see me gay and smiling—the thoughtless child I seem to the world. I will not throw back the disguise again." She began to sob more violently than ever, and he held her hands fast as she made an effort to withdraw them.

"You must not go yet," he said kindly; "you must have no disguises with me, but let me soothe your grief."

"Only you can," she whispered; "you are so good to me; I can not thank you, but oh! if you could read my heart!"

"Your confidence will be my best reward," he answered; "I can not let you go away to weep alone."

"Thanks, a thousand thanks. May I stay? I shall be better in a moment. May I talk to you?"

"I shall be very happy if you can, dear child."

"Yes, call me child—call me Evangel."

He did call her so—a pretty little Evangel she was likely to prove to the worldly man of fifty-two, who ought to have been dangerous, and was near being a goose for once.

"My lovely Evangel—the loveliest man ever had!"

"Ah! the word is so sweet!" she sighed, lifting her eyes to heaven. "I was alone—I was in the dark—and you came to me like a guardian angel, bringing such precious words of sympathy."

"But you must not be lonely," he said; "I can not permit that. Remember how much I want to make you happy."

"I do—I do; I bless you for it. There is not a night but I recall your kindness in my prayers. Oh, I am not ungrateful."

"You are every thing that is gentle and lovely," said he; "but it makes me feel guilty to see you suffer. I fear that I have been careless of my precious trust."

"No, no; don't think that. You have been all goodness, all kindness. I have no words to utter what you have been to me."

"But we must find some means to keep these

gloomy thoughts away; you must be made content and happy."

"You are only too good to think it worth while," she answered, with a fleeting smile. "Are you busy? do I disturb you, Sir?"

"Your presence here is always a pleasure to me," he said, "and no business could be so important as my ward's happiness."

"Thanks—oh, a thousand thanks. Then sit down, and let me sit by you—I'm such a foolish little thing, you know. See, I am quite composed and happy now," and she turned her angelic eyes upon him and smiled again.

He permitted her to lead him to his favorite seat; she nestled on an ottoman close at his side, and, in her childishness, laid her head down on his hand, which chanced to be resting on the arm of the chair.

"Now I am quiet," she said, in a voice which might have made Mr. Grey think of Lurely, or the wind spirits of German legends, or any other dangerous and devilish and beautiful thing, if he had not been for the time under the influence of her spells. "Now I am quiet; I can rest here—I can rest."

"Rest, my pretty Genevieve," he replied; "this shall be your place as long as you choose to keep it."

He was bewildered, and he was a good deal fascinated, but he was not prepared to be quite a smiling idiot. Lurely saw that she must go further, she must do something that would upset him completely; she might never have another opportunity like this.

"At rest, at peace," she murmured; "ah! if I might always be as happy as I am now!" She raised her blue eyes to his and smiled; her soft hair floated over his sleeve. I'll be hanged if she would not have made a fool of Solomon himself.

"If it were in my power to make you so, you should be," he said.

"I know that," she answered; "oh, don't think me ungrateful."

"I think you every thing that is lovely and charming," returned he, "and yet a child at heart."

That was very pretty and it was pleasant to hear, but Lurely wanted more than that, much more. She had not been singing her siren's songs for so little return; she wanted to dizzy his brain with her notes till she could carry him down an unresisting captive, and bang his head against the sharpest rocks, in order properly to avenge herself upon Elinor; and bang his head she would, no matter what sort of song she had to sing.

"Yes, yes," she sighed, "you only think of me as a child to be petted and coaxed out of crying; you forget that I have a woman's heart."

Bless the creature, what did she mean? Had he not been deceiving himself? Did this lovely girl care for him in earnest, despite the difference of age? What was he to think—what was he to say? He had no fancy for being

a dunce; he had known from the first how absurd he should have considered thoughts like his in another man; but indeed, when it comes to having a pink-and-white creature lay her head on the arm of the sagest Solon of fifty-two, and look up in his eyes, and be the very soul of childish innocence and truthfulness, it is somewhat difficult to think at all.

"And I shall always be a child," Lurely sang in his ear; "I need to be petted and loved—it is sunshine and life to me; I fade, and freeze, and die without the warmth."

And the statesman was more bewildered than ever.

"I shall never marry; nobody will ever pet me as you do, so I shall stay here always—always," sang Lurely. "Oh, mayn't I stay? Won't you keep your little Evangel? When darling Elinor marries some great man, I'll stay and be petted; oh, mayn't I?"

He was more bewildered and dizzy still, but, before he could speak, Lurely suddenly cried in a changed voice—

"I forgot. Perhaps I ought not to say such things. Oh dear, I am such a foolish girl, wearing my heart on my lips with those I trust; but they are so few now. Oh, my poor, lonely little life—only you—I have nobody—no one in the world left but you!"

Without the slightest warning she went off into a fresh paroxysm of anguish more poignant than the first, more painful to her audience of one from its unexpectedness, when he had thought her lying on his arm and singing herself into quiet.

"Oh, my lonely life," she sobbed, snatching her hands from him and flinging them wildly about. "Oh, my heart! I freeze—I die! Oh, papa, come and take your poor Evangel—father, father, come! Is there no one to hear? Are the angels deaf? has Heaven no mercy?"

"Genevieve, Genevieve!" pleaded Mr. Grey, nearly frightened out of such wits as he had not lost before,

"Let me die," she moaned; "I only ask for death! O Heaven, be merciful, and give me rest in the grave."

She threw herself on her knees, looked up, and seemed ready to soar away, but Mr. Grey's voice checked her heavenward flight.

"My dear child, you frighten me; be calm, I entreat."

"Yes," she shrieked, "one friend left—one! Oh, my only friend, don't grow tired of me—don't hate me; don't let another take my place." She caught his hand in her frenzied pleading; she had changed her attitude, and was leaning on the ottoman. "Promise me," she repeated, with passionate sobs; "promise, if you would not see me die here!"

Oh, Mr. Grey, Mr. Grey! Lurely had conquered, and you fifty-two! The words were on his lips—he actually was going to be, not a smiling but an agitated idiot, and ask Lurely if she could be content always to stay there, if she could be his wife, his darling, his— Goodness knows what he might have said : an elderly fool is much worse than a young one.

But at that instant the door opened and Elinor Grey walked unsuspectingly into the room, not knowing that her father had returned, and stood petrified by the tableau. Mr. Grey saw her and felt his senses come back; no, he felt as if somebody had slapped a lump of ice suddenly on his head.

"Is Miss Laidley ill?" asked Elinor in the lowest, quietest voice, but one which would have sent the wildest dream whizzing away from a man when heard under such circumstances.

Miss Laidley called her a dreadful name between her teeth, went off into a new spasm of sobs dictated by different sensations, and rushed frantically out of the room. Once within the privacy of her apartment, she gave way to her emotions without restraint. She had made herself nervous in order to play her part well, and now, enraged by this defeat at the moment when victory was within her grasp, she was ready to have spasms in earnest. She fairly danced up and down; she flew at the bed and pulled the blankets off; she caught some china ornaments from the mantle and dashed them on the floor; she must break things and dance and storm or she should fly in pieces. She moaned and shrieked and belabored Elinor in terrible apostrophes, and when Juanita came up and tried to get her in bed she flew at the long-suffering mulatto and nearly took a brown fragment out of her with teeth and finger-nails; but it did more to restore her than a quart of red lavender could have done.

When disappointed Lurely dashed past Elinor and flew out of the room in that high-tragedy way, the wise princess said coolly—

"Has Miss Laidley gone quite mad, papa?"

Mr. Grey was a good deal confused, and it took several pinches of snuff to revive him, but somehow the sight of Elinor had restored his senses; the remembrance of her would steady his head during any future scene Lurely might attempt.

"I am afraid the poor child is ill," said he. "I found her here a few moments ago, crying as though her heart would break."

"What occasioned her grief?"

"Upon my word, I hardly know. She was weeping for her father, and I did my best to soothe her; but I absolutely thought she would burst a blood-vessel."

"Oh no," returned Elinor quietly; "she often makes those scenes. She told me herself that she did it on purpose, by way of having a little excitement when she was dull."

"Oh!" was all Mr. Grey said, but he said it in the voice of a man who had just tumbled out of the clouds; and he took another pinch of snuff.

"She has them only twice a week, as a habit," continued merciless Elinor, "and she has had two without this one, which must have been for your special benefit."

Mr. Grey lingered over his pinch of snuff.

When any woman who has a claim on a man, be she sister, daughter or aunt, interrupts a tender scene and remains beautifully unconscious that it was tender, but talks about the woman who did Pauline in that mild voice, I would counsel the man in whose home the speaker rules, be he President of the United States or Emperor of France, to follow Mr. Grey's example—take a pinch of snuff and say nothing.

"Yes," said Elinor, still unconscious, "this is the third. Juanita will be obliged to you for playing audience, papa dear, and so sparing her, for Miss Laidley pinched her on Tuesday till she was blue instead of brown. She didn't pinch you, did she, papa?"

Mr. Grey was a little red. I do not suppose he had been guilty of coloring before in a quarter of a century. But he laughed.

"To tell you the truth, my Elinor, I was utterly at a loss what to do; I am not much accustomed to young ladies fond of scenes. But, really, I did think her in earnest; and she cried bitterly."

"Oh yes," said Elinor, "she is fond of crying in pretty attitudes. I saw her do so on Mr. Ames's shoulder last week."

"My daughter, are you not a little severe?"

"I think not, papa; but I fancy Mrs. Ames would have been if she had seen it."

The dream fled forever. Mr. Grey stood self-convicted and full of disgust. A girl that would cry on the shoulder of old Ames (he was good five years younger than the gentleman who mentally called him thus) was only to be set down as an artful, ridiculous creature who deserved severe punishment.

The opportunity was so favorable that Elinor related a few more of the young woman's performances; and Mr. Grey disposed of nearly the whole contents of his snuff-box, and the tip of his nose looked angry for the rest of the evening. Elinor did not believe that her grandfather could have been in any real danger from Lurely's arts, but she did not choose his sympathies to be played upon and future risk incurred; therefore she made these little statements, and did not weaken their effect by a word of censure. "I suppose she is only thoughtless," was what she wound up with, well aware that the remark would complete her triumph.

"Thoughtless!" exclaimed Mr. Grey, more sharply than he often spoke. "A girl who makes trouble between engaged people, and wants to distress men's wives, is not to be let off on that plea. I am shocked with Miss Laidley; I desire you to tell her from me that my ward must not allow her conduct to make her the subject of such stories." He was very indignant, as was natural, to discover that an innocent young Una with half a million instead of a lion for a dowry, who seemed to consider him Jupiter (excuse the confusion of comparisons), was a deceitful Lurely that had come near rapping his august head with great force against jagged rocks. That was what Miss Grey gained by having tact and being sensible; nine women out of ten would have gone into a passion and played directly into Lurely's hands.

The Laidley wearied herself with her tossings and bouncings, and had to go to bed, and was sick the next day from the effects of the medicine she was obliged to take. Elinor was sweetness itself, and watched over her so patiently that Lurely knew she was found out and had been again thwarted by her enemy. She lay in bed and snapped at Juanita and was pettish to Elinor, who smilingly disregarded her petulance. She wished that the ceiling might fall and mash her conqueress's face, or that she could plead insanity and poison her, or do something like some woman in a sensation novel; but instead of that she had to lie still and content herself with being as disagreeable as possible.

The need of excitement was stronger than ever after this defeat, and Miss Laidley buzzed about like a humming-bird and threw off the slight restraint which her mourning had at first seen to her. She could not bear to stay alone with Elinor; Mr. Grey was as kind and gallant as before, but she knew that it would not answer to sing Lurely songs in his ear or get up private theatricals for his benefit any more, because Elinor in her wickedness had done nothing to make it useless. She might have meditated until she could actually have brought herself to marry Mr. Grey for the express pleasure of making Elinor's life wretched, but that thought of Leighton Rossitur still stood in the way. Therefore, as she must have excitement after her agitation and disappointment, Lurely, accustomed to enamoring victims, fell into her own trap. She thought about Rossitur, she dreamed about him, and finally she was in love with him with all the force of which her nature was capable. She could exert so much strength for a time in any feeling, that it looked worth a great deal more than it really was; but indeed this was a stronger emotion than she had ever known. Rossitur's indifference, the desire to thwart Elinor, carried her far along; and her passion for romance, her wish to live a true volume novel with every page fuller of incident than the wildest effusions of her favorite authors who crowded four murders, a duel, a suicide and a conflagration into a single chapter, did the rest—Miss Laidley was in love.

Mr. Rossitur was so much occupied that he had no opportunity to think about her—little opportunity even to visit Elinor. The duties of his place pressed heavily upon him at that time; and he did not shirk labor, although he hated it. Besides his duties he had many things to employ his mind, and was engrossed with plans that promised to ripen into glorious successes.

After that conversation with Elinor, Mr. Grey gave himself more freely up to the confidence he had been inclined to place in Rossitur; and he was convinced that she would marry him, although in his intercourse with Rossitur he appeared perfectly unconscious of any knowledge or perception of the secret which had been confided to him. In his heart Mr. Grey trusted no man; he believed that each had his price and would betray his grandfather if there was enough to be gained by it; but he had need of a person like Rossitur, and he grew more bland and slipped into an intimacy highly satisfactory to its recipient, while Mr. Grey was at ease from feeling that a community of interests bound his ally to him, the hope which glittered in the distance in regard to Elinor, being the strongest proof of any.

As for Rossitur himself, he knew that in the end he should succeed—that Elinor would marry him. He was glad to like and be liked by Mr. Grey; but deeply in love as he was, he did not lose his clear-sightedness. He meant that the Secretary should give as much as he claimed, and the wave that carried him up must raise Leighton Rossitur also, which was a natural enough determination on his part, seeing that he belonged to a world which is not quite ready for the thousand years of peace and purity, in spite of latter-day prophets.

Rossitur managed to see Elinor alone sometimes, notwithstanding the vigilant watch Miss Laidley maintained at this period, for he possessed a good deal of that young female's art in finding out things and turning them to personal advantage. He joined Elinor in her rides when the Laidley had refused to go because she thought from some remark of his that he would have no leisure to ride for a week; and there would be a pleasant morning beyond the reach of eyes and ears.

He stood out more and more noble in Miss Grey's sight; nor was his conduct acting. He was in earnest; he believed in himself; and it was true that he was young enough for life yet to receive the stamp which must decide the future. Any important action now would help him very far along in one direction or the other. If two ways opened before him and he chose the right, he might redeem and outlive his faults, overcome much in his character that had a twist in it, and go on to honorable success.

As the rides and the quiet talks took their course in spite of Miss Laidley's vigilance, so did Rossitur's manner, when he met her, leave her in a state of delightful uncertainty which fanned her fancies into new fervor. He became a hero to her in downright earnest; she was feverishly impatient to know whether he meant to play his part properly. She thought it was because he had so little opportunity that there was such slight progress, and she blamed Elinor therefor, adding another wrong to the list of injuries which must be repaid, for, like all mean, crafty people, Miss Laidley believed in vengeance.

In the mean time the days and weeks swept by without much incident, and Spring asserted herself in the most determined manner. Congress continued its session until late in May. Not that any thing of importance was done, but the venerable body was always going to do something to cover its reign with glory, and, while waiting to achieve that desirable consummation, squabbled and made itself ridiculous in the old fashion. It fell to pieces at length in a crumbly, mouldy way; the members separated till autumn and went their different roads to delight their individual constituents with an account of the heroic acts that would have been performed if so many villains had not possessed a vote and a voice within the august halls. Washington dropped dead at once; there was not even the ceremony of dying; you could only say that it became a heavy, senseless, ill-smelling corpse in the spring sun. The hotels emptied simultaneously; schemers and pleasure-seekers rushed away as if the familiar haunts had been plague-smitten. The season was over, and those who had succeeded in their plans, men or women, went off triumphant, and the disappointed took their moans whither they pleased, or if not that, wherever they were obliged, meeting with no more sympathy than has been the portion of the vanquished since the days when the old Romans originated the requiem for them that from ages of repetition has grown as wearisome as the sight of the defeated themselves.

Miss Laidley had the satisfaction of thinking that she had sent her share of injured men and enraged females into obscurity. Indeed, many a girl who had believed that this season would prove her last in the business of husband-hunting, and thought she saw the nuptial-ring close to her finger, had to go home a disconsolate and unwilling Vestal, blaming Miss Laidley for the discomfiture. Poor things, it is melancholy to think of them—that return must be so doleful. To have ill-natured cousins sneer, to hear Papa fret over the expense, and to find Mamma deaf to entreaties for new dresses, must be hard to bear. The dilapidation, not to say ruin, of wardrobes, is one of the horrors of a Washington trip. No woman goes away with a whole gown; and, in addition to the mortification of defeat, to find Papa obdurate and Mamma displaying a stony disregard of the devastation, must be frightful, as they sit like so many Mariuses among the wrecks, not of Carthage, but of silks. But Miss Laidley cared nothing for the sorrows of these Ariadnes grieving in seclusion; she would not have been moved if their united moans had come up in one grand howl. Women have missions in this century, and Miss Laidley's mission was to make all the trouble she could for her own sex, and work the severest havoc possible among the opposite one; and she performed her mission very thoroughly.

At last there came pleading letters from the Idol. She was going up to her Castle early that year, and she longed for the companionship of her young favorites; she must have them both, her princess and her rosebud, or her Castle would be a dreary prison and her state a brilliant mockery. Elinor could not think for an instant of going; she had no intention of leaving her father so soon. She wrote a kind letter to the Idol, but held out no hope of a visit, as the only weeks she could give that neighborhood

were promised to Rosa Thornton. The Idol besieged Miss Laidley, and Lurely was willing enough to go, because she was very dull, and, when she was in that mood, would have gone to purgatory for a new sensation. It offered her an occasion to be unhappy; she could depart and mourn over Leighton Rossitur—that would be the next best thing to having him make love to her, which he had not begun to do —from lack of opportunity, Miss Laidley saw fit to believe.

She wavered a little, undecided whether to wait and win him or to end her novel in a tragic manner by marrying somebody and have him come after it was too late and tell her that he loved her all the while, but was forced to be silent under the pressure of some dismal secret, connected perhaps with Elinor Grey. In that case they would be delightfully wretched, and that idea pleased her. She fancied herself a pining wife, and Rossitur soothing her lonely hours. She pictured him unable longer to bear his burden and sorrow, and one day when they were rowing in a boat on some beautiful lake, suddenly seizing her in his arms, and having poured out his passion in burning words, proposing that they should die together. Sometimes he rescued her from danger—saved her life—and consequently, by every law of transcendental philosophy, her life belonged to him. Sometimes the imaginary husband was a grim tyrant with jet black beard and eyes, and a complexion pallid as a vampire's; and she, unable to endure his cruelty, allowed Rossitur to carry her off in a chariot drawn by four horses, hotly pursued by Bluebeard, who fired pistols in the air and cursed horribly. Not seldom she had a duel, and husband and lover lay at her feet weltering in blood. Occasionally she confessed every thing to Bluebeard, and implored him to save her from the yearnings of her heart. Sometimes she went down, down, to where only laudanum or a pan of charcoal could aid her; but in whatever manner she ended her novels (and she composed enough to have made a library), she was always lovely and pitied and picturesque to the last.

She decided to accept the Idol's invitation, and thought that it would be well to join her before she left town, in order that a dazzling wardrobe might be procured for the summer. It occurred to her how many beautiful dresses and costly trinkets the Idol would force upon her, and she could be practical in the height of her romance. Indeed, she often left Bluebeard and Rossitur lying on the ground with nobody to stanch their wounds, while she diverged to a mental discussion of the ways and means most likely to soften the Idol to that degree where her gifts would nearly fill the huge Saratoga arks, and leave Miss Laidley's pocket as little touched as possible. When she thought of that she began to be eager to go; and recollecting that Elinor would be quite alone and very dull, she was more anxious than ever.

She yielded gracefully to the Idol's prayers,

and made a great merit of leaving her friends who were so kind to her. Still she must not be selfish in any way; she must show her dear Duchess how grateful she was for the love bestowed upon a solitary little creature whose heart was not in the amusements of a vain world, but had followed her dear papa when he mounted on seraphic pinions. She wrote a letter so moving and sweet that the Idol wept over it, praised her in endless sentences to her entire world, and rushed out to buy vanities enough to have stocked all the booths at a fair, to give the lovely blossom on her arrival, as a sign that her virtues were duly appreciated.

Miss Laidley departed, and not having an opportunity to make a scene with Rossitur, occupied herself on the journey with a vision in which she died of a broken heart, and in her last moments, pride yielding, she allowed him to be sent for, and breathed her final sigh in his arms, and he went mad directly and stabbed himself, and that wicked Elinor immured her conscience in a convent, and was properly punished for her sins by a hollow-cheeked Abbess who, as a sequel, suspecting Elinor of heresy, ordered her to be put to death. She was smothered between two feather-beds, and the whole troop of nuns sat on the top mattress and chanted the Lamentations of Jeremiah, while the Abbess and three priests marched in solemn procession about them and cursed the departing soul with book, candle and bell. · She elaborated the closing scene greatly, and exulted so much over Elinor's groans when a fleshy sister, whom even fasting and penance had left a heavy weight, seated herself directly on Elinor's stomach, that she fell asleep thinking about it, and dreamed that the sister had planted her bulk upon her chest instead of her enemy's, and woke to find that some lurch of the train had bumped her ruthlessly against the edge of the window; and she blamed Elinor for the pain—the nasty thing absolutely caused her bad dreams.

CHAPTER XXIII.

PLAYING WOOD-NYMPH.

CLIVE FARNSWORTH's book was now finished and had gone out of his hands. The ideal men and women with whom he had been living had disappeared forever among the shadows, and, after the first feeling of loneliness was over, would never be any thing to him again. Even the half-pleasurable, half-uncomfortable work of reading the proof-sheets was at an end, and Clive ceased to be tormented by the sight of puffy, distorted envelopes at inconvenient hours. The book was finished and published, and it was a success. The reading public happened to be in the right mood, and the work struck a responsive chord—Clive was sent up like a rocket.

The book and its reception made Ruth so happy that Clive felt it would have repaid him for his labor without other reward. "My life is full of new pleasures," she said, "and they all come from your love."

"If I can only keep it full, little one," he answered, "I shall satisfy my dearest wishes."

"Because you are an unselfish old darling. I believe you care for the fame and the praise only because they please me.

"And they do please you?"

"They make me so proud, so glad—oh, you know, Clive."

Clive could hear such speeches now and suffer no pang of self-reproach. He knew that he was trying to do his duty, and he believed that it would grow easier as time went on.

Ruth's days had many interests beyond or rather growing out of her love, because that affection permeated every feeling and action. Her happiness made her more and more alive to the beautiful; and though Clive was a poet, her quick eye helped him to discover new charms in their walks and rides. She was busy superintending the planting of her flower-gardens, and with her customary thoughtfulness remembered Tad Tilman, the bad boy, who had offered his services on the day of her arrival, and who had often since made visits to Mrs. Sykes and endured her fiery sermons, in the hope of catching sight of the mistress of the mansion. Tad had conceived an admiration for her that in an Italian peasant would have been like devotion to the Virgin; but this twig of a Protestant tree, brought up in an atmosphere of such piety that he regarded religion as a species of jail, and its devotees the jailers, only waiting for a favorable moment to give small sinners like himself over to the Devil, would not have dreamed of the horrible sin of finding such a comparison for his respect.

Tad was skillful and willing, and he and Mrs. Farnsworth devised several flower-beds which the cross Scotch gardener or his underlings were not to approach; and Tad, at Ruth's suggestion that they should attempt the cultivation of wild flowers, ransacked woods and morasses and the banks of the lake for tiger-tongues, spring beauties, lady-slippers, wild geraniums, cardinal-flowers—or, as he called them more musically, Indian plumes—and every other species of delicate or gorgeous-hued blossoms which fill our forests and fields, that could be expected to bear transplanting from their native woods by dint of care and sufficient of their proper soil to make them forget their exile. Tad's chief enemy, the deacon, would not have recognized him had he seen him working so cheerfully, his brown face lighted up with a childish pleasure that was new to it; and he breathed freely in that garden from the consciousness that its mistress absolutely considered him a trustworthy creature: and Tad was very proud of her confidence.

Mrs. Sykes could not understand the change at first, and, whenever she caught the boy alone, shook her head and groaned over him and looked warnings in the old fashion, till Tad began to worry her as much as ever in private. He would make diabolical faces at her behind Ruth's back, or stand on his head, or secretly hold writhing fish-worms toward her, until she decided that his pretense of goodness and industry only concealed darker designs than he had ever before meditated, and pondered much whether it were not her solemn duty to expose him to her lady, particularly to mention the enormity of standing on his head or showing how the deacon rolled up his eyes and snorted while engaged in prayer.

Ruth took Clive away from his books and forced him to be idle, and did him a world of good. "You have written until the lines have come in your forehead," she said; "I want you to sit still and let me kiss them away. If I did not watch, you would be at work again just from habit. Come out and be foolish, like a dear old boy."

And Clive allowed her to make him as idle and content as was in her power, and to regard her happiness as best of all.

"Every thing here is so lovely," she used to say; "Clive, I walk about in a garden of Eden the whole day long."

Besides her flowers, her books, and other new sources of enjoyment, Ruth was glad to let the old rector find her work; and she helped his poor so unostentatiously that he was delighted with her; and she never grew stately remembering that she was doing good.

The days and the weeks went by, and the trees again cast broad shadows across the lawn; the flower-gardens were gorgeous masses of purple and white and glowing scarlet; the house was redolent with the odors of hyacinths; the birds trooped back to their old haunts, and from the first break of day the air was filled with the joyous songs of thrushes and orioles; the woods above the dwelling was the pleasantest dream-haunt imaginable, and Spring flushed into full beauty.

People began to stray back from town; the adjacent country-seats showed signs of life; the hotel commenced to furbish and brighten in expectation of what a little more time would bring. Pale, weary faces, with a long winter's business or dissipation written on them, met Clive and Ruth in their drives, and called at the house in a languid fashion and were called upon, wondering at Ruth's freshness of bloom and taking pleasure therein.

Before long the Thorntons returned and fluttered into their dove-cote, and were so glad to be in the country again that they abused each other for having stayed so long away, and were as merry and happy as of old. They made acquaintance with Clive's wife, and were delighted with her; but Rosa could not forget that Clive had married in an odd manner, although she tried not to think about it.

More new-comers called, and were charmed with Ruth; but those faint whispers spread—he had married in an odd fashion. She was lovely —they were glad Farnsworth had brought her among them—a new house was acceptable, for a bachelor's establishment had been only an occa-

sional good; still—it was odd; but nobody had leisure to think much about it because there was no one to set the ball in motion. Clive was pleased to see the impression Ruth made, and she scarcely recollected her fears of strangers in the friendliness and good-nature of her new acquaintances. "I think the world must be full of charming people, Clive," she said; "I am not frightened in the least. I think I like Mrs. Thornton best of any body, however."

Clive agreed with that sentiment, still the two houses were not on such terms of intimacy as might have been expected. There was a slight restraint between Rosa and Farnsworth, and neither could speak. She felt a little sore because he had not married Elinor, although confident it was no fault of his. But he ought to be pining now, and in a state to make further efforts to soften the princess's obduracy, instead of being bound and fettered and looking tranquil and matrimonial, therefore she could not exactly forgive him. On the other hand, Clive knew that Rosa had been as well aware of his love for Miss Grey as if he had made a direct confidence; she had been his tacit ally from first to last, so that it was somewhat awkward for him. Owing to these causes they held aloof from one another, though there were calls and frequent interchanges of civilities, and Rosa was ready to decide with Tom that Farnsworth's wife was a duck. But there was something odd —Rosa must think that, although she held her tongue even where Tom was concerned, being a woman in ten thousand, whose worth could not be estimated by mountains of rubies.

Genevieve Laidley made herself so bewitching to the Idol that she fully succeeded in her money-saving intentions, and exulted thereat as much as if she had been an Israelite with a long beard instead of a pink-and-white seraph. The Idol called her Angel, as a pretty diminutive of Evangel, and expressive of her character; other people called her Angel too, and believed in her, and she was radiant under their satisfaction. She had not grown tired of her romance with Rossitur for the hero; she dreamed about him, was mad for him as she always was for any new thing, but it did not prevent her weaving numerous episodes into her novel; and she was more unscrupulous than ever about giving pain, because of her own restlessness and suspense. She was greatly occupied with the selection of countless toilettes, and it was too late for gayeties; but she found occasions for doing mischief.

Young Greyson had become reconciled to his betrothed, and had softened her into a renewal of the engagement. The Angel fluttered her wings in Greyson's face once more and drove him wild. The end was that poor little Sophy married a horrid brute out of spite, and Greyson went off to South America, and the Angel composed her plumage, feeling that she had done a meritorious work. By the time Greyson sailed, a howling monomaniac, and poor Sophy was selecting her bridal finery with death in her heart, the Idol was ready to go up to her Castle; and

Genevieve, having six new dresses at least for each of the coming summer days, and having completed her duty in every other way, was prepared to accompany her and be amused and petted to any extent.

The neighboring places were the abode of festivities, the hotel had begun to fill with guests when the Idol and her Angel illuminated the Castle by their presence, speedily followed by relays of visitors, according to its mistress's hospitable habit.

The Angel was secretly anxious to see Clive Farnsworth; there was an undefined feeling in her mind that it would be pleasant to vex Elinor by engrossing his attention to an extent which would make her arrival a matter of indifference: if the new wife could be teased into the bargain, so much the better. He was a man of note, too, and the Angel admired the poems he had published during his callow years; they were full of passion and gloomy sentiment, and she often wept over them and knew the most doleful of the sonnets by heart.

If something romantic could happen by way of beginning the acquaintance. Miss Laidley did not fancy seeing him decorous and stiff, seated in the Idol's reception-room, with his wife beside him, where only proper things could be said and done. If she could meet him by chance, as people meet in novels; if she might be in some danger, chased by a panther or a mad dog, and he could save her life or do something preposterous and impossible! But there had been no panthers in that neighborhood since any body's recollection, and it was not probable that one would stray thither for her benefit, and the season for mad dogs was still distant, so the Angel cast about in her mind for romantic ways and means of encounter without those valuable accessories. She seldom walked—she could waltz ten miles in a ball-room without stopping, but walking hurt her—she was so delicate, and she could not ride because she was an arrant little coward and was much more afraid of a horse than she was of the Devil. Indeed, she had rather an admiration for the latter personage, when she believed in him at all; sometimes after reading Byron's Cain she thought she should like to see him. On the whole, she preferred Mephistopheles to Lucifer, and could quote whole scenes from Faust. When she was younger she had tried incantations on nights that she felt nervous, to see if he would not appear; he did not come, so she consoled herself by drawing a skeleton with phosphorus on the wall of old Juanita's room and frightening that yellow familiar out of her senses.

But she was not thinking about Mephistopheles now, although the Devil was in her mind still—she was bent on knowing Clive Farnsworth in some poetical way that should at once establish a bond of sympathy between their souls. The Idol's garrulity in regard to her friends' habits had made the Angel acquainted with Clive's wanderings in the wood back of his house, and she discovered that it was not far from the Idol's domain. She prepared to support fatigue and the perils of solitude—strayed out of the grounds and lost herself in Clive Farnsworth's "forest" in the most picturesque costume that could be devised.

She had not much difficulty in finding the spot of which the Idol had spoken, but unluckily Ruth was there instead of Clive, and the Angel's moans brought her to the rescue. The Angel, in looking about in search of her victim, had stepped into a spring hidden among the leaves and was wet to the ankles, and between fatigue and rage she screamed in downright earnest. "Help me out—help! I'm drowning!" she cried.

Ruth, who had caught sight of her among the trees, ran forward at her appeal, pulled her out on dry ground, pitied her, and said she supposed she had lost her way.

The Angel told her who she was and where she came from, and cried bitterly as she surveyed her ruined costume, and had three minds to fly at Ruth and pinch her as she did old Juanita, because she looked so fresh and dainty in her simple dress.

"I am very sorry," Ruth said; "my husband had a note from Mrs. Hackett yesterday; we are going to see her this morning. She called on me last winter. I am Mrs. Farnsworth, if you will let me introduce myself."

The Angel was more enraged, and wept fountains.

"You are tired and frightened," Ruth said, touched by her distress. "I wish you would forget we are strangers and come down to the house; it is only a little way. You shall have a pair of dry shoes and we will drive you home; won't you come, please?"

Shoes—she, the Angel, whose feet were smaller than a real seraph's, coolly advised to put on that odious creature's shoes as if they would fit her! Miss Laidley suddenly drew herself up with great dignity and looked at Ruth as though she had been a fiend trying to tempt her. "I will go back the way I came. Goodness knows I never dreamed whose woods I was in—never!"

Ruth was too full of sympathy to observe the tone or words, and continued her entreaties, thinking that the pretty girl was shy as well as tired, and having a fellow-feeling for shy people.

"Don't mind my being a stranger," said she; "I know your friend Miss Grey, and I feel as if you were an acquaintance from that."

"Thank you," replied Miss Laidley, in the sweetest, most insolent voice; "but I am not romantic—I do not claim acquaintance with strangers in a wood. I don't know who you are, Madam."

"She is really out of her senses between fatigue and fright," thought Ruth. "I am sure she does not mean to be rude, for Mrs. Hackett wrote to us that she was the dearest little creature." Having given Miss Laidley the benefit of this charitable reflection, she repeated, "I am Mrs. Farnsworth—"

"Oh, oh!" screamed the Angel, and jumped up in the air with a vigor very unlike the customary languid grace of her movements. "A snake—it has bitten me—I'm killed, I'm killed!" A harmless little brown-and-gold reptile, not much larger than an overgrown worm, crawled away among the bushes, much more frightened than any body else by the sensation he had produced, but Miss Laidley continued to scream in spite of Ruth's assurances. "The wood is full of them!" cried she. "I shall die —I shall die! Oh, you horrid woman, you did it on purpose; you keep them here, I know."

To Ruth's great relief, Clive at that instant appeared among the trees, and she called to him to make haste. When Miss Laidley heard who it was coming she stopped shrieking and took a hasty survey of herself. Here was a plight to be in; this was a pretty culmination to her romance. Her shoes were covered with mud; she had torn her gown in her leap; her petticoats were draggled; her face soiled and tearstained, she was certain; and here was Clive Farnsworth to see, and worse still, that horrid wife of his to look on and prevent her making the best of the catastrophe.

"Clive, Clive!" repeated Ruth. "Do come."

"What is it?" returned he, approaching near enough to be astounded by the sight of a stranger in their private haunt.

Ruth ran out to meet him and give a hurried explanation. "It is Miss Laidley; she came out to walk, and lost her way. She stepped in the spring and a snake frightened her; she's almost out of her senses, poor thing."

The ridiculous side of the adventure struck Clive; he smiled involuntarily, and Miss Laidley saw him. She turned sulky at once and stood drooping, dripping, and silent. Clive put by the smile for another occasion and hastened up with proper condolences, and reiterated his wife's invitation to seek shelter in their house.

The Angel's first impulse was to give them both what women call "a bit of her mind;" then she burst into fresh tears and thought of running away; but she was too tired for that. She perceived straightway that Clive was thinking more about his wife than her, and was amused in spite of his politeness, and on the instant she conceived a hatred for him as vivid as her admiration had been, and sympathizing Ruth came in for a full share in the aversion. She dried her eyes because she felt that for once tears were not being shed in a becoming manner; and after pouting like a great school-girl for a few seconds, allowed them to lead or half carry her down to the house. She could not recover her spirits enough to make the most of misfortune; she was cold and tired, and looked a very pale, stupid young thing in whom they were both disappointed.

Clive persuaded her to drink some brandy, and treated her with great courtesy, but was evidently not impressed. As a crowning injury, Ruth took her up to her dressing-room and provided her with fresh stockings and boots, and the boots were so narrow they hurt her feet—she would never forgive that; angel though she was, that insult would rankle forever in her mind. Ruth tried to talk, to be kind and agreeable, but Miss Laidley would not respond—she was beyond doing theatricals—she could only shiver and sulk, and the brandy made her sick. Clive had his phaeton brought out, and they drove her back to the Castle, and she did not recover enough to attempt the least histrionic effort during the ride.

So it came about that the Idol, standing at a window, saw Farnsworth's trap approach the entrance, and to her utter amazement beheld the Angel lifted out limp and miserable. In great haste she ran into the hall, and between her alarm, her pleasure at seeing Clive and his wife, and her eagerness to know what had happened, she nearly choked herself with fragments of gigantic sentences. The Angel fell into her arms and went off in hysterics, so she had to leave Clive and Ruth to their own devices while she summoned assistance and saw the creature carried to bed. That done, she came back, kissed Ruth, admired Farnsworth, bewailed her pet's misadventure, and was so stilted and unintelligible in her excitement that Ruth's suspicions concerning her sanity were confirmed. "Such joy to greet you!" she exclaimed. "Oh, my poor Angel — that type of purity — half-drowned in a wretched spring! Sweet lady, I bid you val, val! Oh poet, I see new foreheads on your bays—oh this fearful contretemps—life is a cataplasm of horrors! My lovely Angel—the dearest child — the sweetest heaven-breathing blossom, my Apolloite—that such a fate should desolate her!"

Clive thought of the rumpled young woman who had sulked like an ill-natured, overgrown baby during the drive, and bowed.

"Ah, fairest nymph," continued the Idol, "I joy to felicitate your success—this triumph— his Apolloites, I mean—alas, my Angel—indeed, I am bewildered! But stay and lunch with me—I will see my floweret—I shall be more calm anon."

They would not stay; and the Idol felt, glad as she was of their visit, that she was in no state of mind, under the circumstances, to give them a proper reception.

"You must depart? But we shall meet soon, soon—I exult to be again in sylvan groves—yes, yes, we shall meet! I long to show our Cynthian Phoebe the beauties of the vale—to be her Cicero, as the sweet Tuscan tongue hath it. I know a bank—a shadowy moonlight— nay, nay, I can not quote—memory is a cosmos in this bewilderment. But return anon—forget this ill-omened visit—not that—you have my thanks—so kind to my Angel—I can not express my gratitude—alas, alas!"

They got away with speed, and when they were at a safe distance Clive laughed long and loud at Ruth's bewildered look and the utter absurdity of the whole affair, beginning with the moment when he saw Miss Laidley stand, a soiled Dryad, pouting at his wife.

"The poor girl," said Ruth, "don't laugh, Clive."

"An Angel with blackened stockings!" cried Clive. "The most commonplace, red-nosed little damsel I ever saw—not even wit enough to make the best of the matter; she'll drive the Idol mad at last, I prophesy."

"Really, I could not understand a word Mrs. Hackett said," returned Ruth. "I am very sorry it happened; poor Miss Laidley looked so mortified and troubled."

Clive shrieked again. "It will do her good; she's a ridiculous, romantic little serpent," said he; "she will hate us both forever. But only to see her—"

"Clive, don't make me laugh so!"

"With one foot in the air—oh, the Angel!" shouted Clive. "And the Idol moaning and upset. It is the best thing I ever saw, altogether." He laughed and jested unmercifully till they reached home, then both he and Ruth forgot the Angel, who was only a silly little girl to them.

But the Angel did not forget. She lay in bed for several hours and was petted by the Idol; she slept awhile and woke with her feet and her back aching, and anxious to do the wickedest thing she could in order to punish Farnsworth and his wife for her misfortunes.

CHAPTER XXIV.

A MODERN ANGEL.

FROM that adventure of the Angel dated whispers in regard to Clive Farnsworth and his wife which people were ready to hear—no, that is not exactly what I mean; they are always ready to hear gossip—to which their minds were prepared to give credence because the marriage had already been pronounced an odd affair.

Whispers and hinted words spread abroad; every body repeated them, though no one could have told from whence they came; they spread and grew as such venomous things will, and turned into hydra-headed serpents which the whisperers themselves did not recognize as the monstrous growth of their idle talk. For some time the reports were too vague to do any great harm, and so varied that nobody could settle upon any one of them as a truth.

Clive had not intended to weary Ruth with gayety; he wanted to go out enough to avoid any appearance of singularity, but had no mind to make his house a caravanserai for temporary prowlers to stray over, or a convenience for visitors with nothing to do added to their original capabilities as bores. People were perfectly civil as yet; calls were made, Ruth was stared at with more eagerness than ever; good-natured women thought she looked too innocent for the changing reports to have any foundation in fact; still the tide of gossip went on, while she and Clive pursued the even tenor of their days, without a suspicion of the storm which might break over them if something did not dissipate it.

For a time the Thorntons heard nothing; they were known to be real friends to Farnsworth, and Rosa was supposed to have a tongue when her favorites were attacked; they were therefore left in ignorance for a season and then only heard enough to be troubled and uncertain how to act.

More gossip, more stories, or the old gossip and the old stories altered and enlarged till they would not have recognized themselves. Ruth had been an actress—Ruth had been a model for artists—then both were lies. She had loved Farnsworth, and had to go into an insane asylum, and he had brought her back to her senses by making her his wife. Very soon that was all nonsense—perhaps it was remembered that marriage was more liable to disorder the brains than to set troubled reason straight. He had only seen her twice before their wedding; she had fallen in love with him through his poetry and been in the habit of writing him letters which so charmed him by their simplicity that he had sent for her photograph, fallen in love with it, and the rest had followed in due course. Next it was that he had proposed to Elinor Grey the preceding summer and been rejected. In his despair he had rushed off to the White Mountains, tumbled down a precipice and broke his neck, and Ruth, picking berries in a thicket, discovered him in the ravine, carried him home and nursed him, and he sat up and had his neck mended and married her out of gratitude. But whatever yesterday's tale might have been, that of to-day gave it the direct lie; and there was no step taken by any body. And Ruth appeared at intervals at dinners and picnics, and was more noticed on account of the reports.

About this time Mrs. Piffit decided that she needed a little country air, and thought that the Lake House would be a desirable resting-place, and that the proximity of her acquaintances, as she called them, Mrs. Hackett and the Thorntons, would make it still more desirable. She made great preparations in her way. She went about to the shops where the people wanted newspaper puffs and bargained for pretty things in return for paragraphs, and being as she said a Fashion Editor, she was able to compose a variety of remarkable toilettes.

She appeared at the Lake House with her trunk, the flat reticule in her hand, and her faithful friend, the green umbrella, under her arm, dressed in her worst clothes because she was an economical soul, and very dusty and tired from her journey. She stood in the hall and shrieked for the proprietor. Waiters rushed forward in abundance; a knot of idle men came and stared; no one would answer but the proprietor. She thumped on the floor with the green umbrella and ordered the crowd to bring the individual, as if she were a detective disguised in petticoats of unequal lengths, who had come to ferret out a murder and meant to arrest every soul present unless the object of her search was produced without delay.

The courteous host appeared and in his turn stared in astonishment at the new-comer, who with ridges of dust on her forehead, spectacles on her nose, and a mingled air of dilapidation and ferocity, was more odd than ever.

"How do you do?" snapped she. "I am Mrs. Piffit, the writer—I've come to stay at your hotel. Are you the proprietor?"

He mildly said that he was; but Piffit chose to have the verdict of the guests and the waiters before she believed, standing in front of the host and menacing him with the point of the green umbrella.

"It's all right, then," said she, sniffing violently; "always want to be sure I'm right—been cheated enough since I started! Nasty railroad people—I'll expose 'em—I'll put 'em in the papers—wouldn't give me a pass! Told 'em what they might expect, and I'm always as good as my word."

The hotel-keeper tried to say something civil about being sure of that, but she shook the umbrella and cut him short.

"You don't know any thing about it," said she; "never saw me before in your life. Just like a man—ugh! How do you do? I'm Mrs. Piffit, the writer, I've come to stay two or three weeks at your house."

The host tried to falter a remark about being glad to hear it, but she shook the umbrella again.

"That's my trunk they're bringing in," she cried. "Where's my bonnet-box? Here, you porter, I want my bonnet-box! It's got S. P. painted on it, and a blue string tied round the handle. If you've lost my box I'll have the law of you." Luckily it was at this moment brought in and set down beside her trunk and she mounted guard over them. "Come here, Mr. Proprietor," continued she; "I want to speak to you."

"I'll have you shown to a room, Madam—"

"I tell you I want to speak to you. Why, come here, I say!"

She reversed the umbrella, seized him by the crook and drew him toward her. Somebody among the lookers-on tittered and Mrs. Piffit heard it. "Send those waiters away," cried she. "Drive those people out! Why, I never saw such a set in my life! I'll put the whole lot of you in the papers if you don't take care—staring at a body like a show. Men, ugh!"

The waiters dispersed, the guests moved away more slowly. Piffit took offense at one man whom she recognized as an old enemy—the person she had assaulted in the Senate chamber. "You're a pretty fellow," sniffed she. "I've seen you before—never forget a face. Saw you in Washington—knew you'd run away from somewhere."

The unfortunate wretch, being a meek man

in poor health, was quite upset by this new attack. "I believe she's mad," he whispered to those near.

"What are you saying?" demanded Piffit fiercely.

"I'm not saying any thing," groaned the unfortunate. "I dont want to say any thing—I don't want to see you even; but you're always falling over me wherever I go."

"You do," cried Piffit; "you're always saying things—you do it on purpose I believe you're in hiding this minute."

"Now did any body ever hear the like?" moaned the dyspeptic, appealing for sympathy to the landlord and such by-standers as were left. "I don't know what she means—I don't know who she is."

"You do," retorted she. "I'm Mrs. Piffit, the writer. I've told you so forty times. Don't tell lies—its wicked. Men are all wicked—don't tell me—ugh!"

"I don't want to tell you," moaned Dyspepsia; "I don't want to speak to you."

"You do," snapped Piffit again. "You're always stumbling around just to be spoken to. What do you mean? Why, I won't stand it—I'll put you in the papers—I shan't take a dare from any man."

She flew at him and opened the green umbrella directly in his face, and he retreated, declaring that he would go to Kamtschatka to get away from that woman, and actually departed from the neighborhood by the next train.

The landlord tried again to induce Mrs. Piffit to retire to a private apartment. "Wait a minute," said she, shutting up the umbrella and tying its fat carcass together with a string. "See here first—always best to have things plain." She pulled him toward her, and then pushed him away and said in one of her stage whispers, blinking horribly with each word, "I'm Mrs. Piffit, the writer—I've got letters for every body, from Mr. Holly, the editor. You must give me a good room cheap—then I'll notice you."

The landlord assured her that she should be made comfortable; wishing devoutly that he could fling her and her trunks out-of-doors, but not venturing upon the step.

"I want things settled," said she; "that's my way. I write for all the papers—East and West—I can do any thing I want to—I'm Mrs. Piffit. I expect to pay—never eat at any man's expense—but allowances for what I write I do expect, and nobody can say that isn't fair."

The landlord was only too glad to permit her to settle matters in her own way, and saw her on the road up stairs preceded by a waiter and a porter carrying her luggage. She sniffed satisfaction at the appearance of her room, and was so elated by her success, the battle with the dyspeptic man included, that she spoke somewhat loftily to a full-skirted Hibernian who entered with fresh water and towels.

"Are you the chambermaid?" she asked.

"I'm the young lady that decorates the

apartments," replied the Hibernian, with a loftiness equal to Piflit's own.

"I just want to say I'm going to stay here two or three weeks—I've seen the proprietor and he knows who I am. He expects you to take great pains with my room."

"Then it's himself that'll tell me and save ye the throuble, ma'am," said Ireland, with a grand toss of her head, flinging the towels about and setting the ewer down with violence.

"It's no trouble," said Mrs. Piflit; "any way I never mind trouble. Now—is your name Bridget?"

"Me name is Eugenia Honora Arabella Dunlavy, ma'am, and I don't like to be called out of it by sthrangers."

"Oh!" sniffed Piflit, somewhat taken aback by the young woman's fierceness and the array of grand names. "I write for the papers—I always notice people that take pains."

"Oh, I thank you, ma'am," replied Eugenia Honora, "but the papers in Ameriky is bla'guards I'm towld, and I won't be made paragrums of by any body. I'm a respectible young woman that was born in County Clare of a high family, and have had misfortins and pitfalls, but I'm not to be paragrumed in a frae counthry."

Piflit sniffed anew and busied herself taking off her bonnet, and Honora watched her with a belligerent aspect till Mrs. Piflit grew a little confused. "I don't want anything more," said she meekly, for Piflit was easily cowed, like most of her kind.

"I thought mebby ye'd more histories to give of yerself, ma'am," said Honora. "Av I've yer lave I'll rethire, for I've a grate dale of sinsitiveness, and mnynial employments is what I wasn't brought up to, born in County Clare, of a high family that had misfortins."

"Yes, it must be unpleasant," sniffed Piflit, rubbing her nose and feeling afraid of Honora's keen eyes.

"Ye may well say unplisant, ma'am. I couldn't tell ye what I endure av I discoorsed a week. A young lady of a high family that ought to be at the queen's coort av me mother had had her rights, and compilled often to do mnynialities for them as would never be ladies av they thravelled through all the hotels in the land."

"I should like to lie down; I'm sleepy," said Piflit, looking very wide awake and very wretched.

"I'll lave ye to yer slumbers, ma'am, and I'm glad to see ye're one as can appreciate the faylius of a young lady born of a high family, that's foorced by disasthers to sarve Yankee trash that never had a grandfather even."

Eugenia Honora swept out of the room, and Piflit vowed that whatever other person she might trample on, Eugenia should be left in peace and treated with the respect due to a female gladiator. Mrs. Piflit had come with her flat reticule full of letters for people living in the neighborhood, as she always managed to do wherever she went. Persecuted editors and literary men gave her the epistles to get rid of her, as she was quite capable of invading their sanctums and of sitting squinting and sniffing resolutely in the easiest chair to be found, eating surreptitious luncheons out of the flat reticule and covering her chin and dress-front with the fragments until she looked as if she had begun to crumble and would soon be in bits generally. There she would sit until she got what she wanted, and nowadays people seldom kept her waiting. They quarrelled with her and endured her malevolence, or they consented to her requests without listening and hustled her away.

Mrs. Piflit arrayed herself in early summer attire and blossomed like a rose of Sharon—whatever that may be. She had a partiality for checkered things, as was natural in a stumpy woman, and was great in bonnets which had a weakness for leaving her head and dangling on the back of her neck whenever she shook herself into an excitement. If she chanced to be much engrossed in talk she would push the bonnet forward by a dexterous rap on the crown with the umbrella crook, so that often, for a whole day after, she went about with Piflit, her mark, legible upon her head decoration. She made acquaintance with every body in the hotel who could be induced to tolerate her, and as there are scores of people who would give their little fingers to be noticed in letters from places of summer resort as the charming Miss So-and-so, or the elegant Mrs. 'Tother, Piflit succeeded in having listeners to her endless conversations. She went about the neighborhood distributing her letters of introduction with her own hands; whenever it was possible following the astounded domestics into the presence of her victims and volubly announcing her title and estate and offering notices in all the papers if they were desired.

Her legs were short, in fact they were too short, else her body was too long, so that when one saw her rise suddenly she seemed to have turned into somebody else, or at least in her hurry to have appropriated some smaller woman's underpinning. But brief as the legs were, they did Piflit good service, and carried her about briskly, unless she could stumble into some luckless person's vehicle. She had no hesitation in asking an entire stranger to give her a seat, and several times when some lady's carriage stood at the hotel door Mrs. Piflit, sallying out on an expedition, would espy it and ensconce herself therein, greeting the exasperated or astonished owner when she appeared with, "How do you do? I'm Mrs. Piflit, the writer. Saw you at breakfast—thought I'd just ask you to give me a lift as I'm going your way. How do you do?"

The flat reticule was always on her arm, and, no matter how bright the day, the green umbrella in her hand, and once or twice, in her anxiety to make coachmen stop when she wished, she poked its point through long-suffering people's carriage windows. She was always mortified thereat and offered amid a refreshing dew of sniffs to pay for the damage she had caused, was greatly relieved when the offer was refused, and promised a notice on the spot.

It was not long before she assaulted the Idol's Castle with the green umbrella and carried it triumphantly over the draw-bridge, past opposing guards, and into the Idol's presence. Now the Idol had her weaknesses—she did love to have herself and her glory scribbled about, and she tolerated Piffit because of the letters which Piffit read to her with so many sniffs as to be almost unintelligible and sent broadcast over the country, signed S. P., which ill-natured people declared stood for sniffing puffy.

Mrs. Piffit appeared at Alban Wood, once, twice, even thrice, but Rosa had heard of her proximity and was on her guard: Alban Wood was an enchanted forest of which she could not obtain the clue. On her last visit she encountered Tom in the avenue as she was puffing and muttering toward the gates, and he amused himself with a little talk. After that, Piffit said he believed that his wife was crazy or drank too much, she was not certain which, and had to be kept in confinement. When somebody denied both suppositions, she vowed that Tom was a brute and so jealous that he kept watch among the trees to see who visited his wife, and that she, poor thing, dared not say her soul was her own—just like a man—ugh!

As might have been expected, the Illustrious had not failed to obtain a letter of introduction to Clive Farnsworth, and as a sop to please literary vanity she had written several notices of his book and had them cut out of the newspapers and safely stowed away in the flat reticule to exhibit to his gratified eyes. She hunted up the note, and one day when some luckless individual was going to drive past Farnsworth's place, Mrs. Piffit boldly demanded "a lift"—she wanted to visit her fellow-author.

In her most gorgeous attire she mounted the steps of the mansion and pulled the bell unmercifully. She always rang a bell till somebody came, no matter how long the interval might be, in a series of characteristic jerks, so that the sound dying out between the pulls, wretched people inside the dwellings thought that a whole regiment must have invaded their privacy in quick succession. Clive's man opened the door and naturally could make no more of Mrs. Piffit than other strangers could; he stared helplessly while she poured out her account, thrust her letter in his hand and shook the umbrella at him as a warning to make haste. He took the epistle in a dreamy sort of way, and showing her into the nearest room, departed toward Clive's library. But Mrs. Piffit never waited—time was too precious. She trotted along in his wake, and before the bewildered domestic had made Clive understand what was the matter, Piffit appeared on the threshold, dropping abbreviated courtesies and exclaiming between a shower of sniffs and winks—

"How do you do? I'm Mrs. Piffit, the writer—you're Mr. Farnsworth. How do you

do? I've brought a letter of introduction for you—from Mr. Holly, the editor. Oh, you've got it! Thought I'd follow your man and explain myself—always my way—servants make such blunders. How do you do? You're Mr. Farnsworth? I'm Mrs. Piffit, the writer—with a letter —from Mr. Holly, the editor."

She stopped suddenly with a loud sniff, as if she had been a machine and something had broken with a creak.

Clive rose and advanced toward her, knowing her very well by sight and reputation, and determined that Mrs. Piffit should never force another entrance into his house. "I am pleased to see you, Madam," he said very civilly, but in a way which put her half a mile off and confused her somewhat, as quiet dignity always did. "Pray be seated."

In her excitement she did not notice the chair he was offering. She whirled round three times, caught the umbrella in her crinoline; settled herself on a pile of books which untidy Clive had just pulled down; skipped up as the foundations gave way; wavered between a table and the piano-stool, and finally came to anchor on an ottoman, plump on the crown of Clive's hat.

"How do you do?" she repeated, puffing violently and blinking to such a degree that Clive thought she must have six pairs of eyelids at least. "I concluded I'd make you a call—know how busy literary people are—wouldn't drag you out."

At that instant the hat crown gave way with a subdued murmur of complaint and Piffit bounced into the air. "Good gracious, what's that?" snapped she. "Is it a cat? What do you have reptiles about for? It might have bitten me. Hate cats—ugh!"

"Take this chair, Madam," said Clive, settling her before she could do any more mischief, for she had nearly upset an inkstand on his writing-table by the flourish of the umbrella.

"Yes, this is better. But what do you have a cat for? You're not Mahommed — nasty things."

"I believe it was my hat," said Clive politely.

"Oh dear, oh dear! How sorry I am. Was it a new one? Don't say a word; I'll make Genin send you another. I will—he often wants notices. A hat is a hat in these days."

Clive begged her to think no more about the disaster, as it was not of the slightest consequence.

"Yes, I believe you're rich," said she; "different from most writers. I'm not rich myself—but I'm not a beggar either—he! he! How much have you made out of your new book?"

Clive civilly replied that it was too soon to know.

"Yes, may be so. But keep a sharp lookout on those publishers—rascals, the whole of 'em. I know 'em—ugh! They never try any of their tricks with me! 'Pay me,' I say, 'or I'll expose you! I'm Mrs. Piffit, you know—I'll put you in every paper from Maine to Georgia.' That's the way to do it! I'll go and see yours for you, if you want me to."

"Thank you, but mine are very satisfactory men to deal with," replied Clive.

"Yes, they have the name, but I don't trust any man too far," responded Piffit.

"A very wise rule," replied Clive. "I believe, Mrs. Piffit, you are said to have a sort of animosity for my sex."

"I have—I shan't deny it. Exceptions, of course, there are—I dare say you'll be one—but men in general—ugh!" She made a high wind of sniffs and shook the umbrella in the air as a warning to the offensive race in general that it was found out and had better keep out of the way.

"I am flattered by the exception in my favor," said Clive.

"That's pretty—I don't care much about pretty things as a rule; I always say, talk to me right out—no shame. I hate lies. I'm a Presbyterian—been one a good many years. Do you profess?" Clive was a little at a loss to understand her meaning, but she did not wait for him to solve it. "I suppose not—men are so careless—writers in particular. I'm very cautious what I write—morality, morality, I say."

Clive applauded the sentiment and mentally recalled a performance of the lady's which had come to his knowledge, wherein she wrote anonymous letters to a female friend and injured her in every way in her power.

"I hope you aren't a Churchman," continued Mrs. Piffit; "they're only Papists in disguise—I've written a letter about it. They say this parson here is terribly High Church—got candles on the altar and a painted window—it's ridiculous, it's wicked. I'm going to talk to him about it before I go away. I've got a tract I want him to read—a beautiful thing by Elder Simmons, called the 'Illuminated Road to Perdition'—that's the lighted altar, you know. Want to read it?"

Clive declined on the plea of occupation.

"Yes, I suppose you're busy. I know what it is—am at it early and late myself. Thought I'd come up here and have a little rest and see what the fashionables are doing—I always like to be posted. I'm a Fashion Editor—often make my own bonnets from the plates—made this one. But la, you don't know any thing about such matters—men never do—ugh!!"

"At least I know enough to admire the bonnet you wear," said Clive.

Piffit winked and gave the wonderful structure a rap on the crown which settled it neatly on her apex. Her bonnets were a weak point—she was somewhat mollified by this compliment, for she had been going out of her confusion into a spiteful stage on account of Farnsworth's cool civility.

"Your book is a success," said she; "it's beautiful. I've written half the notices that are in the papers—always like to be obliging. May

be I've two or three in my reticule—wait a minute."

She composed the umbrella on a neighboring chair and opened the bag, searched a little among the heterogeneous contents—in the brief interval Clive caught sight of pamphlets, pocket-handkerchiefs, a corset-lace and some bits of chocolate—and pulled out several dingy slips of newspaper somewhat soiled with candy.

"Here they are," said she; "keep 'em."

Clive took the scraps a little unwillingly—laid them on the table without reading, and thanked her politely for her good nature. Mrs. Piffit sniffed; matters were not conducted in a way to please her.

"How is your wife?" demanded she sharply.

"Quite well, thank you," replied Clive.

"Of course my call is on her too," said Piffit; "may be she isn't named in the letter, but I'd like to see her—never call on gentlemen, of course. I'm very particular."

"Unfortunately my wife is out," replied he; "she drove down into the village and will not be back for some time."

"Well, she can call on me—owes a call now, you know. I'm very au fait in matters of etiquette—being a Fashion Editor, you know. I've written a Guide to Polite Society—ever read it?"

Clive was obliged to confess that, although familiar with Mrs. Piffit's newspaper effusions, he had not read the work in question.

"I don't think much of it," said Piffit, "but it sold—had to put in lots of nonsense to'please people. I gave it to the smokers, I tell you," and she emitted the sniff suspicious.

"I am sure all such feel self-condemned when they read," said Clive.

"Oh, I don't know—men never feel condemned—that's their way. I'm sorry your wife's out—wanted to see her. Look's odd to visit a man, too—hope she won't be jealous."

Clive begged her to feel at ease on that score.

"Lots of women are jealous," said Piffit; "never was myself. My husband was an exception to men in general. I wore mourning ever so long, widow's cap and all—didn't mind the expense."

Clive recollected to have heard how Mrs. Piffit and her deceased spouse quarrelled before he sailed down the river Styx, but he said that he had no doubt her matrimonial relations had been most delightful.

"Never was a happier couple," returned Piffit; "I shall never marry again—never!"

Clive thought that highly probable—certainly the whole world could not produce a second man willing to be yoked with Piffit—but by the sniff and the little titter Clive knew that, in spite of her hatred to the race, Piffit would not be too obdurate if a husband presented himself—and had a squint ready for such offers, like the weaker members of her sex.

"Haven't been married long, have you?" continued she. "Literary men always quarrel with their wives—hope you'll be an exception."

"I will try to deserve Mrs. Piffit's good opinion," said he coldly.

"Sorry your wife's out—always like to see poets' wives—how they do dress generally—hate a woman that hasn't good taste—yours has, I've no doubt. Very much in love, weren't you? Wrote oceans of poetry about her, didn't you? Was it a long engagement? Tell me all about it. We writers are public property, you know—people expect to read every thing about us in the papers."

Clive's patience was nearly exhausted. "I have no ambition to see my private affairs in print, Madam," said he, "nor to be put there in any way other than where my books are concerned."

"Oh, you mustn't be touchy," said Mrs. Piffit. "Writers are almost always irritable—never was myself. There's Mrs. Tweetum—writes under the influence of opium—I wouldn't say so because she's a particular friend of mine. Every body knows how Howland drinks, and Mrs. Jay treats her husband abominably. But I never talk scandal—I think it's wicked—I'm a Presbyterian."

"An excellent rule whether one is a Presbyterian or not," said Clive.

"Hope you don't take opium? Writers are so apt to seek stimulant—don't do it. What's in that little bottle?"

"Red ink, Madam, but I never drink it."

"Oh, of course. Do you write with red ink? Eccentricity of genius—we all have them. Now I can write with any thing—habit, you know—done so much for the papers. Mrs. Tweetum always talks about wanting space—space. I should think she did—such absurd stories as she writes."

Clive felt confident that she would go away and declare that he wrote poetry with blood from his wife's veins, and tell Mrs. Tweetum that he had pronounced her work abominable trash.

"She's immoral, you know," continued Piffit; "that's what she is. I wouldn't give a book of hers to my daughter, if I had one. People tell dreadful stories about her, but I never listen—she's my friend."

"I think, if you please, we will not discuss our co-workers," said Clive gravely.

"Oh, of course not. Dear me, you began it," cried Piffit, commencing to give sniffs defiant. "I never talk about any body. I'm a Presbyterian—was one before I was a writer—hope I know my duty."

Clive bowed.

"I must go; wanted to see you, being in the neighborhood—I'm at the Lake House. Bring your wife down, now do. That letter will be proof that I'm myself—you know Mr. Holly's writing—or you can telegraph. No, that's expensive; don't do it."

"I am quite satisfied as to your identity, Mrs. Piffit," he answered.

"Well, then call and bring your wife. Writers ought to know one another. I don't write novels—haven't time; always busy with the newspapers, you know."

She shoved her reticule further up on her arm and grasped the green umbrella and glared at Clive, divided between a desire to keep on friendly terms with a lion and a wish to give vent to her spleen. She compromised by a shower of winks and sniffs of such energy that any body outside the door would have thought the author had developed a taste for mechanics and was getting up a model steam-engine in private. "I must go," said she; "had a pleasant call. Sorry your wife was not at home; tell her to run down and see me—it's only a step. Come with her if you can, but if she's alone, just let her ask for Mrs. Piffit, the writer—every body knows me."

Clive was civil to the last, but he did not promise that her visit should be returned, nor did he ask her to honor his house with another call, and Piffit remarked the omission and went into a silent fury which made the green umbrella shake ominously in her hand.

"I am going to see my friend Mrs. Hackett," said she; "I owe her a visit. She's very fond of me because I'm intellectual. I like to see people appreciate talent. Do you know the Thorntons?"

"Yes, Madam."

"Friends of mine too—met them in Washington at Secretary Grey's house. Charming girl, his daughter—not so young though, I fancy, if the truth was known—can't be, you know. But how they do talk about the Thorntons! Some say she takes too much and that he beats her—it can't be true of course."

"Certainly it can not. Let me advise you, Mrs. Piffit, not to repeat such stories."

"Oh, I never repeat any thing—I'm a Presbyterian," said Piffit, emitting the sniff pious and looking inexpressibly wicked. "They've gone off somewhere all of a sudden—looks queer. He can't have taken her to an asylum? I'd help her in a minute if he abuses her—always help women—noted for it."

Clive told her very decidedly that the Thorntons were his friends, people universally respected and beloved, and that to hint such suspicions would inevitably disgust the whole county with any new-comer.

"Of course," said Piffit; "thought you ought to know what people say, being a mutual friend—want to do my duty. So glad there's nothing in the stories. Well, good-bye. I've had a pleasant call. Now come down and bring your wife, do. Don't go to the door—I can find my way—always like to help myself."

But Clive chose to ring and have a servant show her out. His opinion was that if left to herself, Mrs. Piffit would peer into every corner of the house before she departed.

"Too much ceremony," said she; "republicans shouldn't ape foreign manners. Good-bye—come soon—good-bye." She shook her umbrella at him frantically, partly because that was her way of shaking hands, but more to gratify her feelings as the next best thing to giving him several hearty pokes with it.

The moment she was gone, Clive gave orders that by no artifice or force must Mrs. Piffit again obtain entrance; and Piffit having an impression that he would do this as strongly fixed upon her as if she had been clairvoyant and overheard his command, trudged down the road under the shadow of her umbrella, snorting with rage and composing newspaper paragraphs and inventing stories which should present Clive Farnsworth and every body connected with him in the blackest colors to the world.

As the green umbrella appeared like a huge parachute near the gates of the Idol's Castle, Genevieve Laidley walking about, followed by faithful Juanita, espied it, and watched its progress as it bobbed up and down, with great delight. The Angel often strayed through the shrubberies to that gate which was only a secondary affair, and was not guarded by a lodge and a vigilant porter like the grand entrance, over which loomed a gigantic pepper-box that made an arriving guest feel as if he must be a cruet of some sort being driven into a proper place in a castor. The Angel said she walked for exercise and was gaining strength from her exertions, but she could not disport herself even in the grounds without the care of a sheep-dog—she was so modest, so keenly alive to decorum, the admiring Idol declared to all her friends, and there being more to gain by belief than doubt in the case, people gave credence to the statement. Juanita was a sheep-dog of the most faithful and intelligent breed; she never barked unless her young mistress gave the signal, and the Angel often left her deaf and blind near the gate while she strolled into the grove beyond and did not stroll alone. Some victim was sure to have been warned of her angelic intention and to appear in an accidental manner to share her ramble. Heaven knows whom she had expected this day; it might have been some stranger first encountered in a romantic fashion and straightway transformed into a Prince of Como or a wandering troubadour, whose improvisations would be sweet to her for a time, provided she could make a mystery of the affair.

But for whomsoever she waited on this occasion, she had waited in vain; neither prince nor troubadour appeared, and the Angel had been solacing herself by a little pecking of Juanita, when the approach of the green umbrella attracted her attention. Presently Mrs. Piffit's wheezes were audible behind the parachute—it seemed as if she propelled the machine by her puffs, and the movements of the monster were irregular and eccentric, as though the gas-works were out of order. The Angel ran to the gate and opened it, exclaiming—

"Why, it is dear Mrs. Piffit! How glad I am to see you, dearest, sweetest of good-natured souls. Oh, did you notice the dress I wore at the hotel hop last Tuesday? Did you say I was perfection and the other girls horrid guys?"

"Pf! pf! pf! Ugh! ugh!" steamed Piffit,

touching a spring somewhere about the parachute which caused it to collapse and revealed her smoking and dusty "Pf! pf! Ugh! ugh! How hot it is!"

"Come in and rest; here's a lovely shady seat," urged the Angel. "How tired you look. You poor love, if you had let me know you were coming I'd have made the Duchess send a carriage. I am so glad to see you. Did you notice my dress, you dear creature?"

"Of course I did—said I would—always keep my word. Besides, you're one of my favorites." She waddled along to the rustic bench and the Angel sat down by her, beaming with tender interest and taking mental notes that she might be able to amuse her friends with a correct reproduction of the authoress in a state of fatigue.

"So sweet of you, dear Mrs. Piffit; I declare, I don't know how to show my friendship for you. I'm going to make the Duchess give you a beautiful present—I shall have one for you too, when I get a box from Paris—you're such a good creature."

Piffit liked presents almost as well as the Angel herself, though she was not so accomplished in the art of procuring them. She smiled till her double chin came out in a fresh crease and she appeared suddenly to have developed a third.

"But where have you been, dear Mrs. Piffit?" demanded the Angel. "That is not the road from the village."

"Been?" repeated Piffit, glad of an opportunity to uncork her rage—"been, indeed—you may well ask! I've been where I don't want to go again in a hurry, I can tell you."

"Bless me, where was it? Do tell me quick."

"I never heard such talk and such goings on in all my life," cried Mrs. Piffit, as usual, when excited, regardless of the fact that her listener could not have the most distant idea of whom or what she spoke. "Never" in all my life! Why, I thought of myself, a lone woman sitting in the room with that man—and all I could have done would be to put up my umbrella—and what's an umbrella, I ask you?" she added, slandering her favorite in her wrath.

"Alone with whom?" demanded the Angel eagerly. "What did he do—what did you want an umbrella for? Oh, tell me about it, dear Mrs. Piffit—I'm such a childish little thing. Was he very wicked? Oh, what did he do?"

"He better not. I'd have punched him with the point of it if he'd so much as winked," snorted Piffit, giving the umbrella a flourish.

"O my, did he wink? What did he mean by that? Who was it? Tell me; you'll drive me mad."

"That nasty Farnsworth man, and that's who it was!" and Piffit sneezed twice.

"And he winked at you? Oh, what did he mean?"

"I tell you he didn't dare—I'd have punched him! I would as sure as my name is Piffit, if he'd been twenty authors and I'd been twenty unprotected women."

"Then what was it? Tell me, dear, though I can't understand if it is any thing wrong—I'm such a baby," cooed the Angel.

"I'd like to have heard him say a wrong word," cried Piffit, with another war-horse snort; "I'd have liked him to try it! But his looks were enough—his talk about women! I know he's as wicked as he can live—all men are—ugh!"

"Are they, dear Mrs. Piffit? Oh, you frighten me—I've such a dread of wicked people."

"Sitting up there as if he was King Herod," pursued Piffit; "and all because his trumpery new book is praised. Can't other people write, I'd like to know? Haven't I been filling the papers for years?"

"And beautifully you write too," said the Angel. "But tell me about Mr. Farnsworth, like a dear."

"Bless me, there isn't much to tell. He has a great opinion of himself. Wait till his next book comes out—I'll be ready, I bet you!"

"But I thought you had to put your umbrella up," cried the Angel in an aggrieved tone. "I don't understand you at all—I can't see that any thing happened."

"Of course not. Do I look like a woman that things happen to?" snapped Piffit. "No, indeed! But I could read his mind, and I tell you he's bad—bad—worse than that fellow in hiding—ugh!"

The Angel started and glanced about with a sudden fear, but there was no one to be seen except the trusty sheep-dog seated at a discreet distance chewing some sort of brown bark after her habit.

"And you think he is wicked?" she asked innocently.

"I'd swear to it in a court of Justice," exclaimed Mrs. Piffit, bringing the point of the umbrella down on the grass with great violence. "He abused every other author—he said the most horrible things about Mrs. Thornton. Oh, he's got a forked tongue indeed!"

"Did you see his wife?" asked the Angel.

"No, he said she was out. I wanted to see her—tell all about a woman the minute I set eyes on her."

"And they say such dreadful things about her," sighed the Angel.

"I know it. I believe 'em—I believe 'em all!" cried Piffit viciously. "Let me find out the truth, that's all! I'm Mrs. Piffit, the writer. I'd show up the President and all Congress in a minute!"

The yellow gleams began to shoot from the Angel's eyes. Here was a way to vengeance—set Piffit on fire and let her illuminate the neighborhood. The Angel had been obliged to be cautious, although she had done a reasonable share of mischief; but she was not satisfied. Here was a favorable opportunity, and if the stories came back to her she would be believed rather than Mrs. Piffit. The Angel

thought of her attempted romance that ended in a fiasco so mortifying—she thought of Elinor Grey, and that stung her into new bitterness. Besides, she was unusually irritable and wicked that morning on account of the non-appearance of the Prince of Como. Every thing conspired to make this the occasion for striking the blow she had held in reserve for weeks past lest some harm should come to herself.

"His wife!" she repeated. "Oh, Mrs. Piffit, there's worse than you know—worse than I can understand. Juanita heard it—found it all out. Oh, I couldn't even listen—but she'll tell you."

"What is it? what is it?" exclaimed Piffit in a frenzy. "Call her here, quick! You yellow woman! what's your name?" She flourished the umbrella and shook as if she would come in pieces.

"Juanita," called the Angel, in her most seraphic voice, "dear old Juanita, come here, please."

The sheep-dog approached, alert and watchful. "Please to want me, young Senora, bress her?" she demanded.

"Tell me all about it!" exclaimed Mrs. Piffit. "All that wicked woman's doings. I dare say she's worse than he if that's possible. Where did he pick her up? Who was she? Why don't you tell?"

Juanita seemed puzzled, and rolled her eyes till she looked like a Chinese Joss, but her mistress made Mrs. Piffit's hurried remarks somewhat more intelligible.

"All those things you heard in Washington about Mrs. Farnsworth," said the Angel with sweet childishness. "Tell Mrs. Piffit. I shan't understand half of it, I know; I am so glad."

"Don't know noffin," said Juanita cunningly. "Let lady tell her story."

"They say she's been all sorts of things," cried Piffit, and she poured out a long tirade of gossip, whereat Juanita chuckled.

"I can't understand half," sighed Miss Laidley. "Now, Juanita dear, you know what they said."

Juanita had been primed that she might be in readiness for an occasion like the present, and seeing by the yellow light in her young mistress's eyes that she meant her to speak, the sheep-dog barked furiously. The story was dreadfully confused; the Spanish interjections and words of no human language—probably hereditary cries which had come down to Juanita from long-armed apes—made the tale more difficult to comprehend—but Piffit understood, enough. When questioned as to the source of her information, Juanita was more broken still, and seemed about to take refuge in the monkey cries altogether if too sorely pressed, but Piffit was not particular about the source.

"The abandoned wretch!" cried she. "Oh, the villain! Why, they ought to be burned at the same stake."

"It is horrible," sighed the Angel; "I never heard of any thing so wicked, but it's all Greek to me. Dear Mrs. Piffit, never mention this."

"Oh, I won't, I won't," gasped Piffit.

"If my name should get mixed up with the matter," said the Angel sweetly, but firmly, "I should sue the person for slander, and I'm very rich."

"I shan't say a word," asseverated Mrs. Piffit; "I never talk about people. But this will get out—such things always do. Why, there won't a soul visit her."

"Dear me, I don't think people ought," said Miss Laidley plaintively. "I can't understand; but what a wicked thing she must be; and she's not a bit pretty, is she, Juanita?"

"Not bit," declared Juanita. "Pretty? no, indeed!"

"She's a wretch and he's worse," said Piffit.

"Oh, I don't know," sighed the Angel; "a bad woman is worse than a bad man—more odious."

"So they are," assented Piffit.

"Every thing is certain to come out," observed Miss Laidley; "such things never can be kept quiet long."

"They ought to come out," cried Piffit, emitting two sniffs, the first in the cause of virtue, the second for religion. "Why, it would be countenancing sin. What would the world come to—innocent women exposed to meet such people? It'll come out, and she'll be treated as she deserves. Let him write another book! A pretty fellow—oh, the animal—I wish I had him here!"

She gave the inevitable shake to the umbrella and looked all eyelids and chins.

The Angel felt that she had done a good morning's work in spite of her disappointment, and now she wanted to get rid of Mrs. Piffit. "I must go back," she said, looking at her watch; "I had no idea it was so late. There's a clergyman coming to call on me; dear Mrs. Piffit, I am so devoted to good people! I can't ask you up because the poor Duchess is in bed with neuralgia."

The Duchess never was in better health in her life.

"I couldn't stop this morning," said Mrs. Piffit, eager to get back to the hotel and find listeners to her tale of horror; "I must go this minute; so good-bye."

"Good-bye, good-bye, dear," cried the Angel. "Write a notice about me soon, now do; and forget this dreadful story, oh, promise."

"Of course," said Piffit, "of course."

The Angel bade her another affectionate farewell and pursued her way to the house, pensive and sweetly melancholy, and the sheep-dog followed, chewing bark and rolling her eyes more hideously than ever.

Mrs. Piffit elevated her umbrella and steamed off, but alas, in this world the virtuous and good often meet with misfortunes in the pursuance of duty, and Piffit, bent on the righteous errand of exposing without delay the iniquity of Clive Farnsworth and the woman who might be his wife—but that was doubtful, or if she were, was rather worse than if she had not been—was overtaken by an evil fate, probably at the instigation of some demon who took offense at her being an epitome of all the cardinal virtues.

The way was long, the weather hot, Mrs. Piffit dumpy and suffering more from a desire to relate her story to numerous listeners than from the heat. She remembered that there was a by-path through the fields, leading to the village, which would materially shorten her journey if she could find it, but she was uncertain where it began and her short sight made the search for it rather unpromising. It chanced that out of the plantations appeared Tad Tilman, who had intercepted the Angel in her homeward walk to deliver a letter, for Tad was mail-carrier in general to those who had secret missives to send, and was now returning, whistling as he walked, and into the hands of the bad boy fell the doomed Piffit. He saw her standing where several roads met, squinting at various stiles and gates which gave admittance to the fields; and knowing very well who she was, stood still to enjoy the peculiar appearance she presented and to copy her squints and sniffs on the spot, as a means of amusement to his evil companions and the older people who ought to have been ashamed to encourage his wickedness and were not. Mrs. Piffit heard him approach, twisted her eyes into new shapes to make out who or what he might be, and, having apparently satisfied herself, exclaimed loftily—

"Here, you boy, show me the right path. It'll be the first time you've been out of mischief to-day, I'll warrant."

Immediately the demon who desired to annoy saintly Piffit whispered to the bad boy to mislead her, and he yielded incontinently to the appeal of the demon.

"Bless me, ma'am," said he, virtuously, "I ain't never in mischief, I ain't; who's ben a takin' away my character?"

"Nobody," sniffed Mrs. Piffit; "I don't know you—never saw you before—don't want to again; but you're a boy—that's enough for me. Always in mischief—ugh."

"I wish you wouldn't say so, ma'am," said Tad sweetly, "I really do; most of 'em are, I know, but I aint a common boy by any means. I'm a Sunday-schooler, and a prayer-meetinger, and a reg'lar straightforward chap every way."

"Don't talk," said Piffit; "words prove nothing. Show me the way if you want me to believe you—hmf! hmf!"

"Of course I will—I'm a goin' myself—I always like to help folks when I can, jest like George Washington and the cherry-tree."

"Oh here," said Piffit; "don't mix things up that way—you ain't mad, are you?"

"No, ma'am, oh no; I'm a Sunday-schooler."

"Well, well, show me the path—shorter isn't it through the fields?"

"Oh, ever so much," replied Tad, in his softest voice; "my, yes; ever *and* ever so much."

"I'm glad of it—I'm tired. Come, get along—don't stand there—you don't think I want to stand here all day, do you?"

"Oh my, no, ma'am. This way—follow me —over the stile; here we be—it's all right."

"Glad of it," said Piffit; and thinking herself now sure of her way, she added hastily, "As you were going I shan't pay you for showing me—you won't have earned it—can't expect money when you don't earn it."

"Oh dear, no; I don't want nothing. Why, it's a pleasure to me, it is," said Tad; "shan't I carry your umberelly for you?"

"No—get away," snapped Piffit. "Want it to keep the sun off."

"Oh, yes; of course. Let me take your ridicule, ma'am."

"No, carry my own things. Why, what do you mean? Look here, boy, don't try tricks on me; I'll—I'll umbrella you in a minute. Do you know who I am? I'm Mrs. Piffit, the writer."

"Oh—oh—my!" exclaimed Tad. "Ain't I happy to help you! Why, ma'am, I've heard your name ever since I can remember. Wal, Thaddeus, my boy, you are in luck—a showing the way to *Mrs. Piffit—the* writer! I do believe, ma'am, it's all 'cause I've been good and a Sunday-schooler, instead of stealin' apples and a misbehavin' like common boys. But rccly, this seems too much reward, even for me —*Mrs. Piffit—the* writer—oh my!"

"I hope you're a good boy—I hope so," said Piffit, mollified by his expressions of delight, but squinting closely at him to see that he was up to no tricks.

"I be, ma'am, indeed. I wish you had time —I'd ask you to go round by the deacon's; he'd tell you, or the school-master."

"Yes, yes; well, I'm in a hurry. Much further? Don't see any thing of the village? Why, what's that ahead—woods?"

"A grove," said Tad magnificently; "when we get through that you'll see the hotel beautiful. Here's a fence; I'm afraid you'll have to climb it, there's no steps—folks ought to be ashamed."

"A fence? They said the way was clear. I can't climb fences. Now look here, you boy—"

"Oh! oh!" shouted Tad in tones of fright, "here comes Mr. Gleason's red bull full tilt. Oh, get over the fence—he hates petticoats and umberellys—hurry, hurry!"

Piffit bounded forward, clambered and fell over the rails and landed on her back, while her umbrella sailed off like an immense bird.

"Oh, you're down, ain't you?" exclaimed Tad in wonder and pity. "Be you hurt? Ketch hold of my hand."

"Stop my umbrella—get my umbrella—if I lose it I'll have you sent to jail! Oh, you young villain!" howled Piffit, scrambling up from her reclining posture.

Tad ran after the umbrella and captured it, muttering, "She wears one blue garter and 'tother's yellar. She'll be so melted down by this you could put her in a quart measure. Wal, Gleason has got a bull, and if that had ben Gleason's field, he'd have ben in it. I mistook—that might happen to the deacon."

He restored the umbrella to its owner, who cut short his lamentations over her fall, warned him to attempt no tricks with her, and followed him through the wood. It was a hard scramble. There was a great deal of underbrush—brambles twined lovingly about Piffit's ankles—saplings swaying in the breeze snatched at the umbrella she had put under her arm, and with every step the ground grew more damp, threatening to end in an actual marsh. Mrs. Piffit began to vituperate Tad; he was chanting

, "Oh beyond Jordan we will dwell—will dwell,"

in a voice so loud that her wheezing accents were quite lost, and with each instant her fatigue and ill-temper increased.

They came suddenly out of the wood; alas! the predictions of the soft path were realized— another step forward sent Piffit ankle-deep in damp black mud, and as she emitted a cry of fright and wrath, the bad boy stopped his chanting, and pointing to something white far in the distance, remarked coolly—

"I said you could see the hotel from here— there 'tis; looks pooty, don't it?"

"Where is it? Where am I?" shrieked Piffit. "Oh, you dreadful boy, you've misled me. I'll have you sent to jail—I'll have you hung."

She got her spectacles out of the reticule, adjusted them on her nose, and by their aid could see the hotel far away and the blue lake gleaming peacefully beyond it.

"You've led me right away from the village," she cried.

"You didn't say you wanted to go to the village," returned Tad, apparently in great surprise; "you said you wanted to walk through the fields. Dear me, why didn't you tell me?"

Mrs. Piffit shook the umbrella at him in speechless wrath.

"Why, it's good two miles to the village," said Tad. "I ain't a goin' that way myself; you must keep through the marsh, down through the blackberry patch, cross the brook and the ploughed field, and then you'll come out to the willer bushes—there's such lots of yellar worms there— and over the stone wall into the road, then you'll know where you be."

"You little villain! You thief—you murderer!" screamed Mrs. Piffit, making frantic dashes at him with the umbrella, which he danced to and fro to avoid, holding his sides with laughter.

"Why, stop," said he; "what are you at? Asking me to take you for a walk and then trying to eel-spear me with an umberelly."

"I'll have you hung," shouted Mrs. Piffit. "Who are you—what's your name, you young villain?"

"I'm Jim Foster, the deacon's son," said Tad. "Oh, don't tell dad—he'd kill me—don't!"

"I will. I'll make an example of you—oh dear, oh dear!"

She jumped up and down, and each bound

only sent her deeper into the mud—she brandished her umbrella—she kicked—she screamed —she was a whole mad-house in herself.

"I do believe you're a crazy woman," shouted Tad, apparently seized with sudden terror. "Help, help, somebody! Here's a poor Sunday-school boy set on by a crazy woman. Help! help!"

He rushed whooping and shouting away, and neither prayers nor imprecations could induce him to return. He disappeared from Mrs. Piffit's sight, and she, with a fresh howl of misery, sat down on a moist stump in the midst of the marsh and sobbed and shrieked till she was on the verge of apoplexy.

A good half-hour after she was discovered by some sportsmen and rescued from her wretched condition. She reached the hotel at last—her clothes ruined, her umbrella wet, and she speechless with fatigue. To make the matter worse, she sent for the deacon and told him what his son had been guilty of, and the deacon having but one heir, and he a blind boy, went into a great rage at the slanderous charge, and they berated each other in the hall in a Christian way that was intensely edifying to the sinners who collected to listen.

CHAPTER XXV.
THE WORLD'S VERDICT.

THE whirlwind which had been for weeks gathering about the home where Clive Farnsworth had thought to make a shelter for the woman who loved him, burst in its blackest fury.

There were no longer mysterious reports and vague rumors which made new-comers curious to see the husband and wife; people listened and talked openly, and were only too ready to believe that the woman must be shunned as a moral leper and the man condemned or else forced into putting aside the creature who had deluded him into palming her off upon his acquaintance as worthy of their notice. In a few days it would have been impossible almost to trace the stories to their original source, though the Lake House was the fountain-head of new gossip, and Piffit's tongue ran riot. She grew bold from hearing other people talk freely, and she went about like Alecto, with her serpents hissing, to work the mischief desired by the Angel up at the Castle who had sent her forth upon her errand. The Thorntons were absent; there was no one to attempt to stem the tide, and it increased daily in fury and blackness.

I could not exaggerate in my description; you all know how scandal spreads through any circle, and in the idleness of summer repose people are able to give their whole minds to the business, and it is the one thing they do thoroughly. It increased until Clive Farnsworth, familiar with the world's ways, knew that the plague-spot had spread, although not a soul had breathed to him a suspicion.

I

He felt the danger in the brief, cold courtesies offered himself and his wife by those who at first had been eager to claim her acquaintance. Several of the more decided neighbors gave entertainments to which they were not invited. Groups of women exchanging salutations at the church doors, who during service had been waiting to see the groined arches fall upon Ruth's sacrilegious head, separated abruptly when she came out with Clive, hurrying away with chilling bows which were worse to endure than words of actual insult. He was furious with the people, half insane to think that this trouble which menaced Ruth was of his causing, but it was necessary to be calm and keep her from suspecting that any thing was amiss. He only told her that the Thorntons being absent there was no one for whom he cared particularly, so they two would have a fortnight's quiet, and Ruth was glad. What was to be done after, how she was to be kept from a knowledge of all that would hurt her, he could not tell, and there was no one to help him to a decision.

The first thought in his mind was to select some man who might so much as have smiled at the gossip or allowed his wife to talk, and shoot him like a dog. It was a natural enough impulse; and if Clive had been younger or had possessed less judgment, he would inevitably have done it. Fortunately he remembered that by this he should ruin Ruth utterly. He might have the satisfaction of shooting half his acquaintance, but each murder would involve the woman that loved him in blacker desolation.

Ruth did not observe that any thing was changed, he kept her thoughts so pleasantly occupied that she had no leisure. Two or three times in their drives they encountered a female magnate severe in virtue, who took the initiative toward ostracising the pair, and whirled past in sublime unconsciousness of their approach; and Ruth once said innocently, "Mrs. Hamlyn's dashing new carriage raises so much dust that she did not see us."

"For which she will moan when we tell her," laughed Clive, and felt his heart-strings crack under.

He gave every moment of his time to Ruth: he read to her—interested her in new studies—wandered with her in the woods—petted and watched over her, till this new trouble brought her closer to his heart than any thing in the world could have done.

And the people talked—oh, words full of infernal malignity, breathing the essence of every thing that is vile and devilish—they talked! As is ever the case, the story most prevalent had not a shadow of truth for its foundation. They said that Ruth was a girl whom he had discovered in some Southern city, a young adventuress who was determined to have position, and had entrapped him into a marriage; they said she had been on the stage and failed, and he had sought to console her and been led into this last folly. This was the chief basis of the tales, more of which I need not repeat, but indeed if the female accusers and judges could have been told the simple truth, they would have called Clive a fool so much the more, and have been as resolute to trample Ruth down.

To be sure, there were exceptional cases—two or three there are in every large circle. There was Jack Ralston's wife—every body knew what she was while her first husband was alive. Every body knew that old Sackville had actually instituted proceedings for a divorce which an apoplectic fit cut short, and having no time to alter his will she came in possession of his millions in spite of his infuriated family. She went into decorous mourning, and gained new consideration with each fold of crape—after the contents of the will were known. When a season sufficient to satisfy morality had elapsed—like the woman in Scripture—"she tired her head and painted her face and looked out of her window," and caught Jack Ralston who was sauntering by.

Jack was lazy and had run through his money; his relations were potent in the land, and they held Jack's wife up. There had never been a suspicion since nor any cause, for she had found her hell. She loved Jack with a fierce passion and was jealous as a fiend, and Jack insulted and tormented and made her life miserable. She was an exception to the old rule, but the Ralstons must not be offended, and she was an exemplary wife now. People forgot the old horrors in the pleasure of laughing at her present distress. She was staying at the Lake House and was one of the fiercest of the Furies, and would have been ready to go up and set fire to Farnsworth's house and bury Ruth in its ashes.

The good-natured Idol herself was infected with fears and went with the current. Mrs. Piffit told her stories, other females told theirs, and the Angel was constantly harassing her mind in secret.

"I can't understand it, dearest Duchess," she sighed; "I'm such a baby; but she must be a horrible creature."

"How should you understand, my lovely blossom?" returned the Idol. "My love, I am shocked—shocked; I can not endure to credit these tales. He is such a glorious Apolloite, and she the most idolizable young thing."

"Oh, my!" cried the Angel. "I don't think she's a bit pretty—such a bold look—did you never notice it?—something wild in her eyes. I don't know what it means, but every body says such women always look so."

"Perhaps there may be; I had not observed it," said the Idol. "My heart blinded my judgment. I was prepared to take our poet's wife to my bosom;—I was ready to believe her the purest Cynthia of every moment."

"But you can't visit her, darling Duchess; every body is cutting them. You can't fly in the face of society."

"No, dearest, no; the fetters bind us."

"If she is bad you can't wish to go near her."

"As you say, if she is—no, no."

"And she is; there is not a doubt. I can't understand, dearest Duchess—I am such a child —but she is terribly wicked."

"I fear so, I fear so; but my heart aches," said the Idol; for she was a kindly soul, only—she must do like the rest of the world.

"My aunt would never let me meet a person like that," pursued the Angel; "she is so particular—she sheltered me so carefully; why, she never allowed me to read the newspapers even! I am like a babe in the woods."

"Sweet, innocent floweret! No, she must not come near you; lovely blossom, you must not inhale the atmosphere of her presence."

"I couldn't, you know, if I liked her ever so much," continued the Angel. "A young girl must be very circumspect—above all, an orphan like me; and my guardian trusts me so entirely, dear Duchess, I must not be unworthy of such confidence."

"My love, his trust shall not vibrate even," returned the Idol, very much troubled, but seeing no way out of the difficulty only to push Ruth down. Struck by a new thought she added—"But she knows Miss Grey; she told me so."

"I don't believe a word of it. Remember how particular Elinor is—how proud—the haughtiest woman I ever met."

"Not haughty, yet; a concatenation of Vestal purity and Junonian grandeur," exclaimed the Idol, solacing her distress with the largest words she could recollect at short notice.

She must be nipped for that ponderous praise of Miss Grey—nipped on the spot.

"Dear Duchess—mille pardons—un instant," cried the Angel, darting on the Idol and rubbing the poor lady's left eyebrow violently. "There was a spot of black—you hadn't put it on well—it's off now. I'm so glad I saw it before any body came in."

The Idol was confused by this exposure of one of her toilet mysteries, but she did not go into a rage as another woman would.

"It must have been false; she never knew Miss Grey," asserted she with new energy, by way of forgetting the spot on her eyebrow.

The Angel would have liked to assail Elinor, to hint that she was odd and capable of knowing strange people, but it would not answer; besides, she had her own reasons for not wishing to mix her enemy up in the matter.

"Perhaps they will go away," said she; "it is the only thing they can do. To see her at church on Sunday so brazen and unconcerned, I declare, it made me shudder. Why, if I had told a fib I should expect the roof to fall on me —but I never tell even the smallest, dear Duchess; truth is so beautiful."

"You are a transparent well of veracity," cried the Idol.

"I don't want to think about the creature," pursued the Angel; "a young girl's thoughts should be like white lilies."

"Charming sentiment—true poetry!" exclaimed the Idol.

"Was it? Oh, I am very glad; I am very, very shy, you know—often I keep back such fancies for fear of being thought unnatural—but I can talk freely to you."

"And I love to read that melodious soul, with its gushes of unwritten music," said the good Idol, ready to worship her.

"Sometimes after I have said my prayers at night," continued the Angel, almost in a whisper, "I think of that woman and feel contaminated. I can not understand—à Dieu ne plaise that I should—but the first day I saw her, something in my soul shrank from her; for all she was so bland and smiling, I felt as if an evil influence was near—had come like a shadow between me and the sun."

"You are so pure that your spirit intu—intuinted you," cried the Idol, so much impressed by this information that she was more convinced Ruth must be vile and wicked.

"Perhaps," said the Angel. "Oh, I do abhor wickedness! I have been so carefully shielded; my darling papa was so loving—and now he is gone—O father, father!"

"But we all love you," exclaimed the Idol, ready to weep when the fair creature flung up her arms and gave vent to the little burst of melodrama; "we will shield you and treasure you, my white dove."

"I know it, darling Duchess—you most of any," returned she, coming gracefully down from tragedy to pathos. "Often I think my father is near—I seem to catch the rustle of seraphic pinions—I grow calm, stilling my heart with the reflection that my guardian spirit is not hand." Then from pathos she glided into tenderness. "I love you so, my Duchess—no one can pet and help me as you do. What a heavenly turquoise that is," she continued, examining a wonderful ornament in the Idol's head-dress—a butterfly made of various shining stones with a large turquoise laid on his back as if to keep him from soaring off his perch.

"Wear it for my sake," said the silly Idol, and disarranged her head decoration without scruple, to get at the butterfly.

"Don't, don't!" cried the Angel, when the ornament was safe in her hand. "Don't disarrange your hair. Oh, you have taken it out—the darling beauty! I can not accept it—I won't indeed—let me put it back; you overload me with treasures."

"Though I piled Ossa on Pygmalion," cried the Idol, "and the mountains were solid masses of gems, they would be weak to express a tithe of my affection."

"Like Milton," sighed the Angel, "but a great deal smoother. I can not refuse the little love! I adore the beautiful in every form, you know."

"You are perfect," replied the Idol, and believed it.

"Let me arrange your head-dress," said the Angel, adjusting it with her skillful fingers and resisting an impulse to set it awry and run a pin in her friend's head. "Voila, bien—the butterfly will not be missed; you are so grand you don't need ornaments."

"Artless flatterer," smiled the Idol.

"No, it is my heart, my foolish heart, that will speak. I love you—I must express it! The influence you have over me—why, often I catch and repeat your very phrases, don't I?"

It certainly was true, and thereby convulsed by-standers with an effort to hide their appreciation of her satire, while the Idol was touched by such proofs of her love.

"Now I must go and write a long letter to my sweet aunt," said the Angel, who usually found excuses for getting away, if condemned to much of the unrelieved society of her hostess.

"Always thoughtful — always P-cu-rity's self," returned the Idol. "But forget not that we go to dine in festive halls."

"Oh no, I'll be dressed in time. Good-bye, sweetest—I shall give you six kisses—I could devour you. I wish I was a butterfly to rest on your head-dress."

"Rest in my heart, you Nymphalian blossom," said the Idol with majestic tenderness, which was ridiculous in expression but thoroughly sincere; "your place is ever there."

The Angel flew away to her room along with her newly-acquired butterfly, laughing heartily at the Idol's absurdity. She lay down on a pile of cushions, devoured chocolats and read Mademoiselle de ——, which she had procured as she did numerous books that must be read in secret, through the instrumentality of Juanita, and looked like some fairy princess indulging in Oriental indolence. She was an innocent little thing, protected by an unseen guardian, who wanted her thoughts to resemble white lilies, and so she read a great many queer books to keep them whiter by contrast.

A fortnight passed; a very long one it had been to Clive, waking each morning with the fear that before the sun set he might see the light die out of Ruth's eyes and know, however patiently she should bear, that she had been stabbed to the heart by some cruel hand—see in every glance how she suffered more for him than herself.

The Thorntons returned from their impromptu trip and the abominable slander was brought to them. They were terribly at a loss how to act, as the best people are in such circumstances; because to do any thing the step taken must be so unusual they are frightened to go to sea without the aid of the old corks and life-preservers, with the landmarks and buoys kept in full sight. Rosa could not help believing there was something amiss, but she could not think that pretty Ruth was a bad woman—she was inclined to lay the brunt of her censure upon Clive. Neither she nor Tom would talk; they would not listen; but when left to themselves, the Doves looked disconsolately at each other and were sorely perplexed. Tom wanted to rush off and tell the whole story to Clive, not having faith in any portion of the gossip himself; but how to tell a man such things was the difficulty—nobody ever did tell the victims—there could be no old landmarks left in sight if he put out in that direction—but Rosa settled that part of the matter.

"You shall not stir a step," said she; "a pretty thing to tell him. He'd go to shooting people right and left and ruin her outright—I know what duels do for women."

"It's an infamous lie, the whole of it, I'll swear!" shouted Tom. "There isn't a man believes the stuff. Oh, these carniverous old women—they ought to be gibbeted in rows."

"So they ought," said Rosa; but she could not be entirely free from the influences which education and example force upon her sex. "But O, Tom, I don't know what to think—if there should be any thing wrong—the marriage was very odd."

"Odd!" repeated Tom in wrath. "Because two people are sensible and don't choose to make a spectacle of themselves—because they consider marriage something too holy to have the ceremony performed in the midst of a crowd, she with her bosom as bare as if she was ready to go to bed instead of the altar—"

"That'll do," interrupted Rosa.

"It makes me furious," cried Tom. "I'd like to tell them what they are, those tabbies—I'd like to tell them the reason men give for their being virtuous."

"Bless me," said Rosa; "do tell."

"Do you think any fellow would try to tempt such a set of vicious, sour—"

"There, you can stop again," interrupted Rosa. "Oh dear, oh dear, I don't know what to think."

"Don't think!" vociferated Tom. "If I were a woman I'll be hanged if I'd take a verdict from my own sex. I tell you that little wife of Farnsworth's is sweet and pure and good."

"Oh, you men! Of course you want to uphold a woman that is pretty, no matter if she is a fiend."

"Sweeping; sounds like Pifflt; and isn't true," said Tom.

"Don't laugh," returned Rosa; "I don't know what to do. How can I fly in the face of the whole neighborhood? Besides, she'd be snubbed."

"If you would let me tell Clive."

"You lunatic!" shrieked Rosa. "He'd kill you and himself and every body; and don't I tell you that would ruin her? Probably, if he didn't fight, they'd say he was afraid, and if he did they'd say if the stories hadn't been true he would have paid no attention."

"What will you do? You are afraid the gossip may be true, or you are afraid of your neighbors—"

"I am not afraid of any body," interrupted Rosa, a little sharply, because there was justice in Tom's thrust.

"Then what is it?"

"People tell the stories as facts," said Rosa. "Now I don't wish to be deluded into receiving a bad woman if she is Clive Farnsworth's wife."

"Beautiful!" cried Tom. "My dear, you had better begin to weed out your acquaintance forthwith."

"Don't be rude and wicked—I am troubled."

"There are no facts in the case," said Tom; "it's all slander; there are too many different stories. That old hag, Jack Ralston's wife, and Mother Pifflt have done the mischief."

"I believe so," replied Rosa; "and Tom—I don't know why—I suspect that cat at the Idol's —an Angel, indeed."

"That girl is a born devil," said Tom.

"So she is; but you needn't swear."

"Thank you; I've no respect for the Devil that I should hesitate to take his name in vain. That's another sweet humbug—women faint at your wickedness if you say hell, but the most pious of them will call on the Lord and his dwelling-place in any trivial conversation. Don't you be a darling little goose."

"I wish I knew what to do," sighed Rosa.

"Go and see Mrs. Farnsworth and be good to her."

"But suppose—"

"Hang supposes! My dear, if you can endure the female Ralstons, and the Angels, and the imps generally, poor little Ruth Farnsworth isn't going to contaminate you."

"I am not afraid of being contaminated, Tom; but people have stopped visiting her. The women all vow she shall not be forced on them."

"The little dears! Upon my word, it is enough to make a man sick to see how women like to pull another woman down."

"I don't want to pull any body down," returned Rosa; "but I'm not an Atlas—I can't hold up a mountain. I can't carry Clive Farnsworth's wife into society on my shoulders. If people won't receive her, they won't."

"I'd like to bring the matter home to somebody," growled Tom.

"Oh, you never can such things."

"And when you can't, they are usually lies. I wish Elinor Grey would come. I'll be sunburned if she wouldn't do something."

"O, Tom, Tom! Elinor certainly told me she knew her. I had forgotten it—I'll write this very day."

"Write and get her here; it's time, any way. Up in some unheard-of place near Vermont, isn't she?"

"Yes; I have her address. Heaven knows what took her there; I'll write this minute."

"In the mean time, let me talk with Clive."

"If you don't promise to stay at home and be quiet, I'll have a hysteric fit like the Angel," cried Rosa.

She was in earnest and Tom had to promise.

"I don't know," said Rosa, struck by a sudden thought; "Tom, I don't know whether Elinor told me she knew the girl—"

"Call her a creature, oh do," returned he in a parenthesis.

"Don't put me in a passion. Or did Ruth say so? Now I think of it, the Idol said something about her palming herself off as Elinor's friend—but there, she said so much that I am dizzy."

"My duck," counselled Tom, "you write to Queen Elinor. If she doesn't know Mrs. Farnsworth, the young woman is a liar, and probably the rest is true about her. But let me tell you, Rosa, pet, if 'my daughter Elinor' does know her and like her, she will light on these people like a hawk on so many June bugs—all of which is inelegant but most particular true."

Rosa decided that the one thing to be done was to write to Elinor forthwith; while awaiting an answer at least she would do nothing to help the scandal.

"I'm going to bed with neuralgia, Tom," said she, "and I'll lie there till Elinor comes. She will help me out."

"She will pull your hair, I'll bet a ducat. Elinor Grey is a trump. But what am I to do? Clive will be expecting us over."

"Meet him accidentally; say I'm sick—dead. Good heavens! I don't know what to say or do. I wish I was a baby or a rubber doll with a big scream in it—how I would deafen you."

In her distress and bewilderment, Rosa sat down and cried so bitterly that Tom had to kiss her, and coax her, and make fun of her, and pity her, and be a dear old goose generally, till she could put the whole business out of her head for the time.

CHAPTER XXVI.

THE QUESTION SETTLED.

As the weeks had borne Elinor Grey toward summer, she longed more and more to get beyond the confinement of brick walls and to enjoy the quiet and freedom of the country. She did not wish to go to the Thorntons at present; she had promised Rosa a visit in July, but before that she wanted some time wholly to herself, for in July she was to make that decision which was of such importance in her life. After Miss Laidley's departure, Rossitur was a great deal at the house again, more gentle and devoted than ever, but careful to avoid the slightest action which could seem to show overconfidence on his part or any trace of masculine vanity like an assurance of success.

But Elinor wanted to go away, and the desire grew stronger when June came and the period for doubt and hesitation grew so brief. She resolved to fulfill her promise to the old woman away up among the New England mountains. She would go and lodge there for a while and be left entirely to herself, and see what counsels her solitude and the influence of the pretty spot would bring forth.

Mr. Grey thought it well for her to leave the Capital without further delay, and as it was meet that the annual visit to the old relative should be made, he decided to accompany her

there; after spending a few penitential days he would leave Elinor safe at Eastburn and return to his duties, which did not permit a long vacation at present.

Elinor told Rossitur where she was going, and he was not sorry. He reflected wisely that the quiet and the solitude would be favorable to his cause. It was arranged that when she went down to Alban Wood, Rossitur should appear in the neighborhood for a season. While that matter was being settled, he did not startle her by any words about the question which would have a right to be on his lips when they met—he was only her kind, knightly friend, anxious for her comfort and happiness.

Elinor and her father started on their journey, and the purgatorial visit to the old relative was duly paid. When the necessary days had expired, the Secretary betook himself again to Washington, stopping in New York long enough on the way to have a long interview with the Bull, who was rushing and bellowing as usual about Wall Street.

Elinor took the train to pursue her morning's journey, having duly apprised Mrs. Olds of her arrival. She had dispensed with the services of Coralie, feeling that the elegant damsel would be out of place in the good woman's modest dwelling, and productive not only of ennui to herself but absolute grief to Aunty Olds, and a daily provocation to her mistress. She would not permit her father to be bored by accompanying her, assuring him that she was quite capable of making the journey alone, but he would not hear of that; so she resigned herself to Hungarian Henry's guidance as a compromise, and sent him back at the first stopping-place where they encountered a return train.

The past year had worked a change in the little village she was seeking, and Eastburn in name had vanished from the face of the earth. Some enterprising man had started manufactories of some sort in the neighborhood, and a new village was growing up which, as well as the old hamlet, must needs bear the euphonious appellation of Plympton Mills, in order that the cognomen of the enterprising man might receive its due meed of celebrity. A branch railway had been established, and Elinor was whirled off among the hills and in due course arrived at the busy station, disgusting in its newness, with the great factories stretching along the pretty river, and every thing so changed that she almost feared she had made some mistake in spite of Mrs. Olds's warning letter, written in intricate sentences and with many capitals. But once beyond the atmosphere of the factory and walking up the well-remembered path into the little village, she found every thing the same, and the sudden quiet, the sight of the old brown houses embowered in forest-trees, gave her a feeling of repose and content.

Mrs. Olds was expecting her; she and her dwelling were prepared and in holiday attire to greet the guest. A happy woman was Aunty Olds as she shook Elinor's hand and chattered like an ancient blackbird, trying vainly to express her delight.

"I told you last summer I should come," said Elinor.

"And you always keep you word; you always did as a child," replied Aunty Olds. "I am so glad to see you. But, deary me, who knows if I can make you comfortable—a great lady like you, with your par at the top of the tree! But I'll do my bestest. Sampson couldn't do no more you know, Miss Elinor."

"Just don't bother about me," replied Miss Grey, "and I shall be as happy as the day is long. I am tired to death, Aunty Olds, and I want to rest and run wild in the woods."

"Bless your heart, so you shall. Seems to me you look a little pale, and—not but what you're as harnsome as ever."

"Oh, you wicked Aunty Olds, to flatter me."

"Oh, law, I ain't one to flatter, and you must ha' got used to bein' told you're harnsome, Miss Elinor—I sort of take to that name, you know, but I'll say Miss Grey if you'd ruther."

"But I wouldn't. How pretty the old house looks. What lovely flowers you have out there; and oh, you naughty old woman, I believe you have scoured every nook and corner ten times over."

The door into the great kitchen was open—a delightful, old-fashioned kitchen, with the yellow-pine floor shining like amber and the tins like looking-glasses, and a general appearance of immaculate cleanliness, and, better still, a look suggestive of delicious country dinners.

Aunty Olds followed Elinor as she went to look about, and she shook her head with a vain effort at humility. "'Tain't nothing to brag of," said she; "I try not to be at sixes and sevens, but that's about all."

Elinor's praise delighted her, and she smiled till her face shone like one of her tin pans as she repeated—

"'Tain't nothing to brag of. But, deary me, let me show you your room, Miss Elinor, and you shall get your burnit off and I'll have one of the men go down after your trunks."

Elinor assured her that she had attended to the luggage, and at that moment it appeared on a wheelbarrow, not of sufficient magnitude to frighten Aunty, for Elinor had sent her arks, which every woman nowadays must possess, straight on to Alban Wood.

She went into the little sitting-room and sat down to rest while the boxes were carried up stairs, and after that Aunty Olds showed her the upper room prepared for her reception—the tidiest, homeliest old room, which charmed the eyes tired of splendor and luxury. A great square chamber, lighted by square windows, curtained on the outside with woodbine and fragrant honeysuckle and morning-glories in pretty confusion, and their white draperies within. A home-made carpet woven in green and white stripes covered the floor; there was a lounge with soft feather pillows, and willow rocking-chairs, and shelves for her books, and a white toilet-table. When you stood in the middle of the chamber you perceived that it was no longer square, but had an eccentric jog large enough to have made another room, and in that recess stood an old-fashioned bed, with high posts twisted and carved sticking up in the air, which looked to one lying in it as if they were astonished arms that the bed was holding up.

Elinor was pleased, and admired every thing from the carpet to the china bowls of June roses, which filled the chamber with their fragrance and delighted Annty Olds's heart.

"So here you be, Miss Elinor," said she, "and glad I am to see you, if only you can put up with my doin's, and I won't bother you any more than I can help; and I've got the neatest little gal to wait on ye too."

She was as good as her word, and Elinor settled down in the quiet which was unusually welcome to her. The blessed woman feasted her upon viands so delicate and well prepared that they might have restored the palled appetite of an epicure. She slaughtered spring chickens without mercy; she made the most marvellous pies and boiled puddings; cream and maple sugar flowed as freely as if the old house had been an improved Canaan, and Mrs. Olds's one trouble was that Elinor did not devour from morning to night, and Elinor herself had a fear that she should be killed from over-abundance.

The weather was charming, the roads in good order, and Elinor procured a saddle-horse from some worthy who trained animals for the New York market, and galloped about among the hills or wandered in the woods, hunted wild flowers, rowed up and down the little river in a light skiff, and drank great draughts of sunshine and strength with every new day. The entire freedom and seclusion were delightful to her; nobody to trouble her with calls or attempts at acquaintance; nothing to do but walk and ride and grow strong in body and mind.

Aunty Olds, keen-sighted New England woman that she was, knew very well that Elinor had many grave thoughts to occupy her, and she never wearied her with talk or intrusiveness. She was very happy if Elinor came into the kitchen or sat on the porch at the back of the house while she churned or picked over strawberries or found some work for her busy old fingers, but she was never troublesome. Of course she had to talk about Ruth Sothern as she called her still, and she wept tears of pleasure as she related the incidents of the marriage in the brown cottage.

"Oh, my dear, I was very glad. He looked so good, so patient; he never could have been bad—never. And she was like a bird—I can't tell you how she looked. And they went off, and it was so sudden the people here knew nothing about it, for the minister he held his tongue and I jest made it my business to make a lot of visits—I never do visit much, but I says to myself this is the time—and everywhere I went

I would manage Ruth's name should be spoken, and then I said kerless like—'La, didn't you know she was married to that man?' I didn't tell no fibs, not approachin' even, but they jest chose to think she'd been married all the while, and it was not my business to say she hadn't."

She told that story many times, and always in one long sentence without pause or stopping to take breath, although in general she was not a rapid talker; but that matter was too wonderful and a source of too much satisfaction to be treated like ordinary affairs.

Elinor listened and was glad, and oh, so softened and thankful to know that she could be glad. The days went by without incident, without the slightest interruption to the quiet, and though they passed rapidly, it seemed to her, as she looked back, that she had been months there in the stillness.

June was carrying her soft breezes, her purple skies, her gorgeous moonlights into the full glory of summer, and Elinor remembered that her season of quiet was almost at an end. She was not frightened now when she looked forward, and she resolutely regarded the matter. She had promised herself that before she left Eastburn her decision should be made, so that when Leighton Rossitur came to her for an answer there should be no hesitation and no trifling.

There was a little interval just here between his letters, and Elinor found herself missing them sorely—found herself wondering if he were ill, and perplexing herself about the delay. She was not sorry to be anxious, she did not try to hide the feeling from her mind; she believed that it was a sign her heart was softening more and more toward this man who had shown her every good impulse of his nature. At last the expected letter came—a long, long letter. He told her frankly that he had not written for several days because the love had been uppermost in his heart, and each time he began to write he could only give it utterance. Those unfinished letters lay in his desk—perhaps some day she would read them—but he dared not dwell upon that hope. He could write to her now—his last letter—because the period for her departure to Alban Wood was so near that no later epistle could reach her in her solitude, and at Alban Wood they should meet. Yes, he could write—he, her friend—and he begged her for the last time not to have any fears about making her lover happy. If she could trust herself to him, could be content in his affection, it was enough—bliss to the man whose after life would have no ray of sunlight if she left him. And in the midst of the sweet words of friendship a bold, passionate burst of love which would not be restrained—left unfinished, and without comment or apology—and the letter continued.

Elinor Grey received that letter as she was leaving the house for a morning's ramble. She laid it in the tiny luncheon basket Aunty Olds had provided and set out. She took a path that led through the fields back of the house and struck into the wood which crowned a height overlooking the river. It was Elinor's favorite haunt, and she sought it that morning intending to read her letter there, and to remain while she reflected upon it, knowing that when she returned, her decision in one way or the other would be formed. She walked slowly among the leaf-strewn paths; the trees murmured musically overhead, the thrushes sang their gladdest songs, and the whole grove was vocal with the melodious notes of orioles, bobolinks, cat-birds, wrens, and the hosts of songsters which are formidable rivals to those of other lands, in spite of the oft-repeated assertion that America can not produce such. The sunlight stole through the branches of the tall beech-trees and tinted the fern moss, lighted the white-birches into pearly purity, made the sycamores lift their quivering leaves to its rays and turned the pine tops into golden spires, for the wood was a collection of various species of trees, as the second-growth forests of our country usually are.

Elinor came out on the summit of the hill—a smooth, grassy level, with great moss-covered rocks forming commodious seats, and a knot of pine-trees in the centre, standing up like sentinels to guard the spot. In front the cliffs stationed their precipitous rampart close from the water's edge, garlanded with vines and ferns, and a mountain brook dashed down them, laughing and singing to the stream below. She seated herself under the pine boughs and looked miles and miles over the beautiful landscape spread beneath; lofty peaks rising here and there; miniature lakes peeping out between them; the river appearing and disappearing among green fields until it was a silver streak in the distance; the magic haze of summer beginning to soften every rugged feature into new loveliness, and overhead the clear, warm blue of the sky with fleecy white clouds sailing slowly about the horizon.

Elinor drank in the full beauty of the scene, and at length, with every feeling elevated and quickened, she opened Leighton Rossitur's letter and read it. She read it very slowly, and sat holding it in her hand, gazing still across the landscape, but seeing its loveliness no longer. She read the letter a second time, dwelt upon every sentence, noted every word, folded it up, and remained looking out into the distance.

Repose became irksome in her earnest thought; she rose and walked up and down the grassy level, thinking, thinking, but observing every trifle about her, as we so often do in moments of serious reflection, in spite of the seeming paradox. She counted the white violets peeping from among the moss, in an unconscious way; saw a spider spinning a fanciful web in a juniper bush—a peculiar spider that had a long, slender body dotted with silver specks, weaving a web which looked like a ladder of lace, and as earnest in his task as if it was to be admired by the whole world. She noticed a robin's nest in a hollow sycamore, and watched the busy owners feeding their second brood, which had just hatched and was clamorous for nourishment. The pair looked at Elinor with their beautiful black heads on one side and their eyes full of wisdom, and talked a great deal about her, and at length half made up their minds to be friends, and hopped to and fro on the grass, devouring the crumbs which she threw to them. Finally the father of the family flung up his head and swelled out his red bosom and opened his golden bill, and sang a delicious aria; in the midst of it a steel-colored cat-bird alighted on a sapling near and began to mimic him and to imitate every other bird which had sung in his neighborhood that summer, and made a whole opera of himself to the robin's disgust.

Elinor walked up and down and remarked each trifle, and nothing so slight connected with that scene and that morning that it could ever fade from her mind. Many and many a time in after years she would close her eyes and recall that spot and see the white violets as plainly as she saw them then, and hear the songs of the birds and the solemn whispers of the pine-trees, which seemed quite conscious of her thoughts. See, hear and remember to her life's end. Elinor Grey had made her decision.

She remained in that lonely spot and watched the noontide hush which steals into a summer day, as if all nature were dozing in the warmth. The robins slept, opening round eyes and uttering querulous murmurs at every stir in the branches; the cat-bird flew off into a thicket with a parting shriek of triumph, so unlike his previous melodious carols that it sounded as if some bird-demon had unexpectedly taken possession of him; even the spider ceased his work for a time; the breeze died away—everything was still except the subdued laugh of the brook as it bounded over the rocks. She stayed and watched the calmness of the late afternoon deepen into the glories of sunset. A great lake of molten gold suddenly spread out in the west, broke into billows of crimson and white and purple, and streamed away into the blue of the upper sky, until the eyes ached and the senses grew tired from the very excess of gorgeous beauty. She waited and saw the first pearly tints soften the glowing waves, and then turned into the wood paths which began to look dark and mysterious already.

Elinor Grey had made her decision and there was no faltering in her mind. She would marry Leighton Rossitur. She did not love him, but he was more to her than any man in the world now; his love for her was so great that it would be cruel to close her heart; his generosity so noble that he was willing to be content with such feeling as she had to give, and it might be that time and his companionship and devotion would do the rest. She did not deny to herself that she had once thought it would be dangerous for her to marry with no stronger regard, but every thing seemed very different now. With all her pride and self-reliance she needed and craved love—surely never again would any man love her as Leighton Rossitur did—and,

more than she knew, she was moved by the fear of giving him pain and the dread of not having been honest and generous. The compact had been that she was to consider herself entirely free, but now at the close she could not do so; she could not bear the idea of his suffering or the torture of self-reproach lest she might have trifled and been acting wickedly all through. She thought more of his friendship than of any thing else—she could not dwell upon his love—she believed that he would continue her friend, patient, unwearying, and would help her more and more.

She had made her decision, and there was a great stillness in her mind; the contrast to these months of restless thought made her try to believe that it was the new content in having yielded to his supplications. A great stillness; but in the very midst of saying to herself that it was content, she surprised her composure by bursting into tears, and sitting down in the gloom of the wood she wept, not in the old, tempestuous fashion, but very sadly. She could not explain her feelings to herself; she was not unhappy—her mind was more composed than it had been for weeks—she was not thinking of Clive Farnsworth; she came out and faced her soul boldly and asked that question—but no, there was not an emotion which would cause her a pang. Yet she wept; quiet, silent tears, with a strange ache at her heart as if she had buried something beautiful and beloved under the shelter of the pine-trees, and was going away from the grave, never to return. She did not despise herself as being weak; she sat there and cried till the tears ceased of themselves, then she rose up softly and went down through the shadows, still with that inexplicable feeling as if she were going further and further from the grave under the whispering pines, where she had buried something inexpressibly precious, that was to be lost and forgotten forever.

Aunty Olds was standing in the front door as Elinor entered the yard, and she cried out—"Land's sake; of I hadn't begun to think you'd had a happening of some sort. I was gettin' real oneasy."

"I am here safe," said Elinor, smiling pleasantly at her; but Aunty saw the signs of recent tears in her eyes, and her kind old heart was troubled to know what sorrow could come near Miss Grey in her grandeur.

But with rare delicacy not a word did she utter, only was more anxious than usual to see Elinor eat, and quite in despair that she could not be persuaded to go beyond milk and bread. "Any how you shall have it with lots o' cream," said she. "Massy sakes! 'twon't do to live like a sparrow."

Elinor talked cheerfully to her, and the good soul was greatly relieved to hear her laugh.

"Law sakes!" cried she suddenly. "I forgot your letter—my memory is gittin' so treacherous. I'd forget my head if it wasn't fast to my shoulders, I guess."

"I had my letter this morning."

"Yes, I know; but the postmaster he sent up another arter you'd gone out—said it got mislaid, and he's a feather-pate anyhow. I laid it away so it would be safe. Now let me see, where did I put it? Oh forlorn, what a goose I be."

She stood bewildered, pushing her cap this way and that as if she thought it might be hidden in the crown. "Did I lay it in your room? No, 'cause I remember I was too busy to go up."

She began to search in every unlikely place for a letter to be put; in books, under the pillows of the settee, in the corner cupboard, and exclaimed and vituperated herself, and Elinor laughed at her trouble, being certain the letter could be of no great importance, as she had received one from her father on the preceding day. "I said to myself I'd lay it away safe," continued Aunty Olds, "and the dear knows I have."

"The man is bringing in the milk," said Elinor, who sat where she could look into the kitchen; "go away, you blessed old blunderer, and I'll find the letter."

"I declare, I wonder you ain't real mad," cried Aunty. "Mebby it's dropped behind the table."

Down she went on her knees, regardless of the creaking joints which did not approve of such treatment, but all she got for her pains was a bump on the head as she incautiously raised it. The knock seemed to quicken some organ into activity, for she exclaimed suddenly, "Law me, I knew all the while; why couldn't I say so? I put it on the top shelf in the pantry right in a big chany bowl—dear suz!"

She flew off as nimbly as if she had been sixteen instead of nearly sixty and brought the letter, which Elinor at a glance recognized as one of Rosa Thornton's rare epistles, for Rosa hated letter-writing. Mrs. Olds went away to attend to her milk pans and Elinor sat down in the door to have full advantage of the waning light.

It was a more hurried and incoherent letter than usual, ordering Elinor to come on at once and leaving her in doubt whether some dreadful thing had happened. But there was a postscript and it said—

"Tom declares I haven't told you what was the matter, and no wonder, for I have cried till I am sick. We have been away for a fortnight on a visit to his old dragon of an aunt, who would have come to us if we had not—but no matter, I can abuse her when you get here.

"My darling Queen Elinor, the whole neighborhood is in a blaze about Clive Farnsworth's wife, and I want you to come. Did you know her? Oh, hurry, and tell me what to do—get a balloon—come by telegraph; I vow to goodness, I shall go mad if you delay.

"I do believe that little cat Laidley is at the bottom of it. I have not the slightest reason for thinking so, but I do—it's borne in on me, as the ism people say, and when I'm most unreasonable I am generally nearest the truth.

"Come quick, before Clive hears the talk and murders everybody—he may murder the Angel, though, if he wishes—she's a nastier cat than ever. Do come! I am holding Tom fast to keep him from telling Clive—he's just like a mad turkey—oh, do hurry—Tom says you can settle matters."

Confused as the letter was, Elinor comprehended that danger menaced the poor child that she loved. What was expected of her she did not know, but apparently she could render some assistance. She did not need time to think; she did not hesitate about making the journey alone or allow any other absurd scruple to interfere.

"Aunty Olds," she called, "what hour does the first train leave in the morning?"

"Four o'clock," shouted Aunty from the recesses of the pantry; "its a Repress, or whatever they call the thing—stops to water at the station."

Elinor went into the kitchen and met the old dame coming from the pantry. "I must go away by it," said she abruptly.

Aunty dropped two milk pails, which were fortunately empty, and sat down in the nearest chair.

"Nothin' the matter? Law, tell me quick!"

"No, no; but I must go a few days earlier to my friends than I expected. Don't be sorry, that's a dear soul—I am going on business—to do a little good if I can."

"Then I hain't a word to say," replied Aunty, and picked up her pails. 'It's like losing my eyes to lose you, Miss Elinor; but law, you know what's best, and you've ben good to the old woman."

Elinor consoled her, promised future visits and hurried away to get her properties in readiness. Mrs. Olds did not cry over her, nor make loud lamentations, because she was a sensible New England woman, but Elinor knew how grieved the lonely soul was to lose her. She left any quantity of keepsakes and a golden reward that would please Aunty's New England heart when she had time to think about it, and wonder whether she ought to take so much more than her wildest fancy could have supposed would be offered.

Elinor started on her journey and discovered that she could reach her destination sometime that evening or in the night. At a junction, she had leisure to telegraph to Tom to meet her, and so pursued her travels without fear or annoyance, as any woman may in this happy land, where the best places everywhere are given up to them and every attention shown, which truth compels me to admit they usually receive with a most annoying amount of indifference, and an air of "you-couldn't-do-less"—which makes one long to read them a little lecture.

The dispatch reached Alban Wood in due course, and for the rest of the day Rosa and Tom were in a state of feverish excitement. They had the horses out in the middle of the afternoon, although they knew it was simply impossible she should arrive by any such hour.

From then till midnight they amused themselves by driving to the station to meet about six trains, and the last one brought her, and they carried her home in triumph.

CHAPTER XXVII.

TO THE RESCUE.

THE next morning they were up to an early breakfast—even lazy Tom, who had forbidden explanations or talk on the previous night because Elinor was tired and Rosa ready to be hysterical between delight and the worry of the past days. The first thing was to tell the story or the stories, for there were three entirely different, of which each had eager supporters; and some people believed the whole number in their anxiety to be right, regardless that one tale flatly contradicted another.

Elinor could safely and truly say, "There is not a word of truth in these reports. Ruth Sothern was my friend—I know every thing about her. She is as lovely and good a creature as ever breathed, and the man or woman who declines to visit her can't visit Elinor Grey." She opened quietly, and was in one of her grand rages before she had half finished.

"Bravo!" cried Tom. "What did I tell you, my duck?"

"Rosa Thornton!" exclaimed Elinor, and her great eyes began to flash and her face to grow pale, as it used when she was a young girl and some one had roused her to passion by an act of injustice. "Rosa Thornton! You dare not tell me you have believed—"

"Oh don't. I haven't said a word. Ask Tom. I went to bed to wait till you came. Now don't, Elinor—I don't mind other people—but don't look at me so. Tom, tell her I haven't done any thing, or she'll fly out of the house and never speak to us again."

"No, no, Nelly," said Tom; "she has only been in doubt and afraid of Mrs. Grundy."

"I could not suspect her," replied Elinor. "But oh, Tom, this shall be stopped—I say it shall!"

"Then it will," returned Tom; "I told Rosa you would do it. Just women's talk, and all it needs is for a woman of influence to come out and turn the tide."

They told her every thing, and Elinor suspected, with Rosa, that the Angel had a large share in the mischief, though she admitted that the idea was very ungenerous.

"The Idol will say what you say," continued Tom, "and believe what you tell her, and we'll get a lot of the best people in the land here and make much of Ruth Farnsworth, and drag her chariot wheels over the gossips' heads."

"I am so glad it is not true," cried Rosa.

"She never was South till she went as Mrs. Farnsworth," said Elinor, "I know her whole history from her childhood; there is not one word of truth in the whole matter."

"You see I wanted to go to Clive," Tom began, but Elinor nipped him as Rosa had done.

"You see you had better mind your own business," said she, "and Mr. Farnsworth had better mind his. Ruth must never know there was any slander; he mustn't know it; and in a month people will forget they ever believed or heard it."

"And Elinor," cried Rosa, "it's all very well to be Christian and forgiving, but if we can catch that little serpent of a Laidley, we will so sit upon her and so mash her flounces and so show her up for what she is, that she'll be glad to go off to Jamaica and live among her fellow-serpents."

And although Elinor would not assent, she could not say No to the proposal, for she feared that if she did find the young snake's trail at the bottom of the stories, she should be as ready to sit upon her as Rosa herself.

"I saw her out driving with Mr. Rossitur yesterday," said Tom.

"Oh yes, he's here," observed Rosa; "I forgot to tell you—came three days ago. Was it because you were coming, you wicked thing?"

Elinor would not confess or be confused, although she was touched by this eagerness on his part. She suddenly remembered that the next day but one would exactly end the season of probation.

"What is the order of the day?" inquired Tom, not caring about Leighton Rossitur, or rather doing the contrary, for he did not fancy the man, in spite of his agreeable manners. "What are you womenkind to do in the way of mischief this morning?"

"I am going to beg the carriage," said Elinor; "I want to call on my friend Mrs. Farnsworth."

"I'll drive you over," returned Rosa. "But I won't go in, for you will have oceans of things to talk about, not having seen her since her marriage. I will call on Mrs. Hamlyn and two or three women and tell them where you are; a good beginning, is it not?"

"My Rosa will be your lieutenant, General," laughed Tom.

"Then I'll go back for you and— What shall we do next, Elinor?"

"You shall drive me to the Castle."

"It is spoken!" exclaimed Rosa, tragically.

"To hear is to obey," added Tom.

"Mind you remember that always when I speak," said Rosa.

"Yes; but I didn't exactly mean that; you were to hear and obey."

"That will do, monster! You never know what you mean—you never mean any thing—"

"And men are always mean—ugh!" sniffed Tom, à la Piffit, whereat they all laughed, it being a habit of theirs to have a great deal of nonsense and fun when they were together, and to do and say things which would have shocked staid, proper people and sorely puzzled those who were not quick to understand badinage—and I use a French word because I don't know of an English one that answers as well—do you?

As soon as a respectable hour arrived for morning calls in the country, the gray ponies were brought round attached to the loveliest new basket carriage, and Elinor delighted Rosa with her praises and declared that the little loves were prettier and their tails longer than ever. Rosa loved and petted her ponies as she had done her kittens when a child, and indeed the pretty creatures were not much larger than the childish pets had been. Tom watched them off, and then made preparations to go to the trout-brook, which was being so diligently fished that it seemed probable this season would exterminate the race of speckled beauties in those particular waters.

Mrs. Thornton drove up the avenue and brought her ponies round the front of Farnsworth's house with a grand flourish and sweep; and Elinor had no time to think, which was as well, considering whom she was to meet for the first time since these changes of the past twelve months. The tiny tiger sprang down with an alertness that might have excited the envy of his jungle namesake, and made the house echo with his thumps on the knocker, which he could only reach on tiptoe, nearly upsetting himself with every blow, to Rosa's infinite amusement. The servant who appeared in answer to the summons, though a large man, was quite appalled by the little tiger's ferocity, and replied meekly, in response to the cards thrust in his hands, that his mistress was at home, and solaced himself with a grin at the tiger's numerous buttons, for buttons were the tiger's one weakness; whereat the tiger trod on his left foot and caused him to execute an involuntary pirouette and twist his insolent British flunkey's face into a spasm of silent agony. Satisfied that he had done his duty thoroughly, the small tiger went back to the ladies and announced that Mrs. Farnsworth was to be seen, and stood hat in hand while Elinor emerged from the basket, and really believed himself of the utmost assistance as well as ornamental.

Elinor ascended the steps, and the tame tiger attended her obsequiously and made a private grimace at the footman; with two bounds was in his seat again, and Rosa lashed the ponies as women will at the most uncalled-for moments, and the little equipage dashed off like the chariot of Venus—Cupid sitting behind, however.

Elinor was not kept waiting long enough in the reception-room to have time to wonder if she should see the master of the house. A light step was heard—a glad voice—and Ruth was in the room, and Ruth's two arms were about her neck, and she was crying, "Miss Grey, my Miss Grey! I am so glad, so glad!"

There was a little interlude of embracing and half-finished sentences, according to female habit, after which they stood apart and Elinor said, "You are prettier than ever, Ruth."

And Ruth, half weeping, half laughing, replied, "And you are beautiful as you always were—like a white angel to me—I told you that long ago." She took her visitor away to her special nook—a tiny room off the library fitted up by Farnsworth expressly for her—a little wilderness of beautiful ornaments and Indian furniture and flowers and birds, only an orderly wilderness, as any spot where Ruth reigned must always be. She seated Elinor in the softest of low chairs, and said how glad she was, and broke off to add—"Clive is out; he will be too sorry. Oh, when did you come?"

"In the middle of the night. My first visit is to you," replied Elinor, unconsciously becoming much more at her ease since Ruth's last announcement.

"It was very good of you to think of me at once, Miss Grey."

"If you don't call me Elinor I will go away. Remember, everywhere and always, I am Elinor to you."

Ruth could have no idea of her visitor's meaning; she only thought it was another exhibition of Miss Grey's sweetness and friendliness; but there was more than that in the request: Elinor wished in every way to impress upon people that she and Mrs. Farnsworth were on the most intimate terms.

"Now sit down, you little bird," said she, "and tell me that you are as happy as the day is bright."

"So happy—I couldn't make you believe—there are no words. Oh, Elinor, my husband is perfect, my home is fairy-land; I am only afraid of dying of my happiness."

There was an instant's pang at Elinor's heart, but it was no sentiment for which she need blush; she only had an impulse of vague envy at this girl's bliss. Straightway she called up Leighton Rossitur's image and remembered that she too might be loved and petted and be the fairy princess of a knight noble as Sir Galahad.

"That was what I wanted to hear—I am satisfied now," said Elinor.

Ruth told her how each day passed; showed her home; told of her studies, her amusements; and the constant recurrence of Clive's name, his connection with the slightest detail or pleasure, proved how completely he had fulfilled his vow.

"For a few weeks past," said Ruth, "we have been very quiet. Clive said the Thorntons were away and we would rest. Everybody has been so kind—dear Elinor, I have not been a bit afraid of people."

Clive had heard or felt the hideous reports which were abroad—Elinor knew that at once.

"But Mrs. Thornton is the most delightful of any body after you," said Ruth. "She has been at home so little that I have not seen her much, but I like her."

"She will come for me by and by," said Elinor; "she is delighted with you."

"I shall grow terribly vain," laughed Ruth. "Clive spoils me completely, and every body seems determined to help. I am so happy, oh so happy! I want to say it to you over and over—the Heavenly Father has been so good to me, Elinor." There was no allusion to the past, no oppressive thought of it in Ruth's mind even at this meeting. Many women, knowing the whole story, though ready to pity and love Ruth, would have interpreted this as a sign of hardness or recklessness, but Elinor Grey perfectly understood that her husband's care was so entire and her trust in God so perfect that there was no space for remembrance, as there was no stain on her soul to be obliterated, no thought to be deplored. Elinor said to herself that the most overwhelming answer to the slanderers would be to show them Ruth as she looked at that moment sitting in her loveliness among her household gods ; no human being, however willfully perverse or blind, could believe evil of her after that.

"I want to tell you every thing in a breath, and I finish nothing," laughed Ruth, after she had been pouring out her eager revelations.

"I see you are happy," replied Elinor, "and we are too near each other in heart not to understand every word and look."

"I have longed to see you. I asked Miss Laidley about you—oh, the poor thing, she lost herself in our wood, and Clive laughed—he was quite wicked—but we took her home and did every thing we could." Good grounds, Elinor thought, for the Angel to hate both husband and wife. "She is a pretty little thing," continued Ruth ; "just like a child. We haven't seen much of her or Mrs. Hackett, but we shall now ; we can not stay shut up any longer, I suppose."

"No," said Elinor ; "make up your minds to that. Mrs. Thornton is to invite a set of my friends to visit her for a week or two, and I shall have you crowned queen of the summer ; so be prepared."

"If they don't frighten me," said Ruth. "But indeed I am afraid I must be a bold thing, when I thought I was shy. You see while I talk, or people talk to me, I look at Clive, and he looks back as if I was perfection and talking pearls and diamonds like the girl in the fairy story ; and I know if he is satisfied I can't be very silly, though all the while I know it's his love and goodness that makes him feel and look so."

"Only every body that meets you shares the feeling," said Elinor ; "so be ready to be petted and loved on all sides."

"But I can't be stately and grand like you."

"But you can be a lovely little May-queen ; and I am only an icicle, people say."

"It is not true," cried Ruth indignantly ; "you are the best, the dearest, the tenderest—"

"Stop and get your breath," interrupted Elinor ; "you need not flatter me, May-queen ; I am proud and conceited enough."

Ruth denied that too, and grew prettier than ever in her mirthful vehemence. She looked the fit mistress of that charming haunt ; the morning sun stole in, brightening the tiny gems of pictures, making the flowers give out new fragrance, and rousing a cardinal-bird whose cage set in the open window into a burst of such passionate song that Ruth and Elinor could only be silent and listen.

"He sings all night," said Ruth, when he ceased for an instant, drawing a deep breath in her sensitiveness to every thing beautiful. "Clive says his song is more like that of a nightingale than that of any other bird."

"So it is ; it has the same human ring at times," replied Elinor. "And what a beauty ; what vivid, flame-like scarlet, with that bit of black on his head—the beauty."

"We brought him from Florida with us," said Ruth. "Oh, Elinor, what a visit that was —those first weeks ! Only I am happier now because I am not so bewildered and dizzy—oh, I can't explain."

"But I can understand."

"I thought then I could be no happier," continued Ruth, in a voice which grew almost solemn with tenderness ; "but every day increases it. I go farther and further into Eden, and every new path is more beautiful—every new pleasure brighter." She paused, fearful that she had appeared foolish or romantic. "I forget, you see ; I talk to you as I do to Clive," she added, after an instant's hesitation.

"You always must," replied Elinor, "as you do to Clive." She repeated the name involuntarily—as it passed her lips she remembered—but straightway came the thought that with this pure creature for a bond between them she had no fear to call him thus, and that checked any tremor or pain.

Ruth wanted her to go and see the flower-garden, and while they were wandering about she recklessly plundered the choicest rose-bushes for Elinor's benefit. "You must take them away to remember where you have been," said she, "and to remind you that you must come again before they wither."

"I don't need them for that. Ruth, this white rose with a blush in it is like you."

"That was what Clive said. I shall tell him —he will be so pleased. But look at these pansies ; I do think the common flowers are the prettiest after all.—Oh, there comes a carriage."

It was Rose's equipage coming round the sweep with the importance of a triumphal procession. They went to meet her. She alighted for a little and they all sat on the veranda and talked gayly, and Rosa rushed into one of her enthusiasms for Farnsworth's wife, and would have been ready to fly at and peck her slanderers' eyes like an enraged dove if she had encountered any of them.

It was time to go, and they were half an hour at least in separating, as women who like each other usually are. Starting and coming back— off resolutely this effort, and stopped by another word from Ruth. After they were in the basket there was so much to be said, after the very last of the last words, that the long-tailed ponies grew impatient and the tiger from his perch swelled his chest till the buttons were more conspicuous than ever, and thought sagely what very silly creatures women were, the best of them, with so much talkee, talkee!

"Oh, the lovely little thing!" cried Rosa, as they drove out of the gates. "And where now, my Queen Elinor."

"To the Castle; I want to see Mrs. Hackett; I can't wait for etiquette or any other nonsense," replied she.

Recollecting that the wild animal near the back of their heads had ears even if his claws were hidden, and that he had been spoiled by Tom, who always called him Cupid, till nothing but the incessant promise of unlimited thrashings by the same good-natured master kept him in decent subjection, they began to talk French, and Cupid, having his auricular appendages wide open to no purpose, was intensely disgusted, and wondered "what the dickens they mean by that sort o' gibberish." Rosa related the incidents of her visit to Mrs. Hamlyn, and described that virtuous great lady as much impressed by hearing that Miss Grey had gone to spend the morning with her darling friend Mrs. Farnsworth—so much that she dropped the subject and never hinted at the scandal till she should have time to see what turn affairs were about to take.

They reached the Castle and found that the Idol was in presence, ready to receive chance guests at the foot of her pedestal. She was so charmed and excited when she saw her visitors that she burst into long phrases of delight and broken sentences full of capitals, and seemed ready to explode like some sort of gorgeous fireworks. "Miss Grey! Our princess—oh, the pleasure! Darling Mrs. Thornton to bring her —welcome always, doubly welcome with this sister rose! I would have flown to you had I known you were here! When did you arrive? Summer has come indeed!"

"We were out driving and called on the way," said Elinor.

"A boon—a relic!" cried the Idol. "And my dear Angel is out—breathing freshness and freedom in the seclusion of the park. I will dispatch Mercurris—I will—"

"No, no," interrupted Elinor; "I dare say she will be in; besides, I want to see you."

"I shall be selfish and restrain you to myself," said the Idol. "But whence came you so delightfully matinally?"

"From Mrs. Farnsworth's," said Elinor; "I had to rush off and see her the moment I finished breakfast, for she is one of my real friends; I rank her with Rosa here."

The Idol looked aghast and bewildered, and seemed to totter on her pedestal.

"Yes, indeed, and I am horribly jealous," said Rosa, "only Mrs. Farnsworth is so sweet that I can't help loving her too."

"She—did you tell—old friend—such tales," gasped the Idol.

"What is it?" asked Elinor sweetly, while Rosa leaned back in her chair and refused to help the poor Idol, who had not been in the least to blame.

"Has not Mrs. Thornton informed you?" questioned the Idol. "Such horrible reports— the whole neighborhood aroused—I am blind, stupefied. I was so grieved. I adore our Apolloite; I was prepared to pour oceans of love and admiration at the feet of his Dryad."

"Nor could you bestow them on a more lovely woman," said Elinor quietly. "I knew Ruth Farnsworth when we were young girls—I was the elder considerably. She has lived all her life near an old lady with whom I have just been staying. She is a dear friend of mine whom I wish you to like as much as you do me."

Elinor delivered her effective little speech in the most composed manner, and the Idol looked as if a thunder-storm had jarred her pedestal and made her temple shake to its lowest foundations. "Thank heaven, I have been cautious!" she exclaimed. "But you know—Mrs. Thornton has told you?"

"She has told me that very absurd, very impossible, and very wicked stories are in circulation, Mrs. Hackett," said Elinor. "But Rosa has been absent, so I want you to tell me from whence they spring, because I know you have a good, kind heart, and could not sit by to see an innocent woman injured."

"Never! I am not a Tartarus," gasped the Idol. "The vile wretches! Your friend?— O heaven, that I did not shield her on my heart."

"The harm done can easily be counteracted," said Elinor, "if a few women like you, Mrs. Hackett, will be firm."

"Immutable as the cliffs that guard our valley," answered the Idol. "One word from you, idolizable Miss Grey, crushes the foul calumnies at my feet."

"Let us see if we can not discover from whence these reports have proceeded," said Elinor.

"My dear lady, every body has talked—indeed, I can not hold myself guiltless," said the honest Idol, full of remorse.

"I am sure you have not been unkind," replied Elinor.

"Indeed my heart was lacerated—I told Mrs. Thornton so."

"We all know you are goodness itself," said Rosa; "but let us find out who started the stories."

"It is so difficult to trace slanders to their source," said the Idol, meditatively. "There was gossip at first—only enough to make that fair flower more interesting—but of late—"

"Never mind the stories themselves," Mrs. Hackett," interrupted Elinor, not having the pleasure that so many good women even appear to find in dwelling on the details of disgusting reports; "who first told you?"

The Idol hesitated. "I would not recriminate any one willingly, dear Miss Grey," said she, sorely perplexed.

Rosa looked at Elinor: she saw the sensitive nostrils begin to dilate, and the overpowering light come into the great eyes; she really wanted to save the Idol from an explosion. "Dear Mrs. Hackett," she said hurriedly, "in a case like this it would be wrong to hesitate."

Elinor Grey lifted her head, and her voice took the clear ring Rosa knew so well and knew too what it portended.

"A pure, good woman is vilely slandered," said she, "and that woman is my friend. Mrs. Hackett, I can only say to you what I said to Rosa Thornton here, what I would say to my own sister if I had one—the person who can help to set this slandered lady right in the world's eyes and refuses, shall never touch my hand or meet so much as one glance of recognition."

The Idol fluttered, and appealed, and agreed with her, and said, "I honor and love you more than ever." And so she did, for she was a good old Idol, in spite of her follies. "I do believe, Miss Grey, the worst stories have come from the Lake House and from that Mrs. Piffit. She told me."

"And Jack Ralston's wife has helped her," said Rosa.

"But who told Mrs. Piffit?" demanded Elinor.

"Ah, who can tell?" sighed the Idol. "Perchance she invented the tales out of Tartarean wickedness."

Rosa was going to say something bitter about Miss Laidley, but Elinor checked her with a sign; she did not wish to bring her name into the matter if it could possibly be avoided.

"At all events, Mrs. Hackett," said Elinor, "I may be assured that you take my word these stories are false?"

"You may indeed! I will go to that lovely creature to-morrow—I will honor her in every way," cried the Idol.

"We must be very careful that neither she nor her husband ever know there has been any gossip," said Elinor. "If you, the wealthiest woman in the county, and women like Mrs. Thornton and Mrs. Hamlyn, only say that you will not hear such stories—that Mrs. Farnsworth is your friend—the slanders will die speedily."

"Always thoughtful, always Palladian!" exclaimed the Idol. "I will perform my part, nor shrink though seas should fail and suns should fall."

The occasion was one of tragic magnitude, and the phrase sounded so well that the Idol thought she must be quoting blank verse grand enough to meet the exigency of the case. "I must dispatch messengers for my Angel," she said, coming gracefully down from her height. "She will be desolated else."

She was saved the trouble, for at that instant the Angel flew into the room on snowy pinions with blue decorations. At sight of Elinor she paused, threw up her arms, cooed with delight, and did a lovely tableau of astonishment, old Juanita having told her who was there.

Miss Grey waited till the tableau was over; then the Angel cried—"Elinor! Elinor!" and as Miss Grey rose she flung herself upon her and enveloped her in voluminous draperies, and could only repeat — "Elinor, darling Elinor! You have come back to your poor Evangel at last!"

Rosa Thornton sat with a look of intense disgust on her face, and a huge desire in her soul to sit upon the Angel then and there, and smash her puffs and her frills and her furbelows and her floating ribbons, beyond the possibility of restoration. But the Idol was greatly affected and exclaimed—"The lovely floweret! Such tenderness! Such seraphic sweetness!"

The Angel retreated from Elinor and looked at her to be certain that she was there, then clasped her hands and did another tableau, while Miss Grey said several cordial and proper things. The Angel saw that her scenic effects were wasted, except on the Idol, and as she could get them up for her benefit at any time, she subsided upon an ottoman and usurped the conversation as she always did.

"You darling Elinor! How could you be wicked enough to stay away so long? And you have scarcely written to me—I would be vexed if I could."

"Sweet Angel," sighed the Idol.

"I thought I wrote quite often," said Elinor.

"Oh, I am exacting, I suppose. But the dear guardian has written—such sweet letters!"

She hoped that would annoy her guardian's daughter, but it did not in the least; she being certain the Angel would never again deceive him in any manner.

"Our Blossom will always be a child, loving and artless," said the Idol, and straightway Rosa Thornton looked absent, to repudiate any claim of having a share in the Blossom, and Miss Laidley saw it.

"My dear Duchess," said she, "everybody is not so affectionate as you. Plenty of people can see I am only a foolish little girl, though you like to call me Evangel."

"What a pretty name," said Mrs. Thornton with an innocence quite equal to the Angel's best efforts; "I thought your name was Jenny, Miss Laidley."

She looked so sullen on the instant and pouted so very unbecomingly that Rosa was perfectly charmed with her own success. "My name is Genevieve," said she shortly, and not at all in a seraphic tone.

"My love, my dove, my peeress Genevieve," broke in the Idol. "Whose sweet poem is it—Mrs. Hemans?"

"Oh, the Duchess calls you Evangel, because—because—why does she?" pursued Rosa, beating the Laidley all hollow at her own game.

"I am sure I don't know why," returned the damsel, no longer an angel, but a commonplace, ill-tempered-looking girl, as she was the moment any body found the spell to disperse her airs and graces.

"But she must know why," persisted cruel

Rosa, doing the Angel's most mellifluous voice to perfection, anxious that the Angel, turned into a pouting girl, should recognize it, and longing to be as insolent as she could and be lady-like—"she must know why, and I want to know why; so ask her, please, because I'm such a curious little thing and always want to know why people are called names."

The Idol never could perceive raillery, therefore she said honestly—"I call her Evangel because she is so lovely, so earnest, so truthful."

Whereto Rosa Thornton responded by one word, pronounced in an entirely different voice; she only said—"Oh!" but the little monosyllable spoke volumes, of which Miss Laidley understood every page and line.

Elinor did not feel in the least sorry for her, still she did not choose to assist Rosa in tormenting her, so she said, "We must go, I think; we are forgetting the time."

"Not till after a slight repast," pleaded the Idol; "grace our midday board with your presence; a frail meal such as my Angel loves—flowers—fruits of the vine—oh stay."

"Fruits of the vine?" repeated Rosa. "Good gracious, Miss Laidley, the Duchess is slandering you—she means you have a weakness for champagne."

"No, she didn't!" snapped the Laidley, giving way to her ill-temper till she was rude and ready to cry from wrath.

"Mrs. Thornton does but jest, my precious," said the Idol.

"There are some jests scarcely civil," retorted the Laidley.

"I beg ten thousand pardons," exclaimed Rosa; "I had no idea of offending you, Miss Laidley. I retract—I don't believe you have any weaknesses at all. Come and see me soon and let me learn to consider you a lovely, artless, truthful Evangel."

If it had lasted much longer the Laidley would inevitably have flown at Rosa and scratched, and that abominable Rosa would willingly have borne the pain for the satisfaction of exposing her to the Idol and showing the marks to the whole neighborhood. But the Idol, taking Mrs. Thornton's words *au serieux*, said with ponderous gayety—

"You see, my Angel, she did but dally in sportive phrase. She loves you as we all do—she appreciates you."

One more thrust—Rosa could not help it, although Elinor was begging her to stop as plainly as eyes could speak. "Mrs. Hackett is right, sweetest Miss Laidley; I do appreciate you—oh believe it—appreciate you thoroughly." She made one of the Angel-gestures and the Idol was charmed, and the Laidley nearly bit her tongue off to keep from calling her mischievous assailant bad names.

"Flee not," cried the Idol, as the two callers rose. "Tarry, I pray, and share our meridian draughts."

"It is long after noon now," said Rosa, "and my husband will be expecting us. Come soon, dear Mrs. Hackett, and bring our sweet Evangel with you."

"Oh yes—briefly, briefly. I long to commune with you and Miss Grey—we shall come briefly, briefly."

"Good-bye, Genevieve," said Elinor.

"Oh, good bye," replied she crossly, quite forgetting her late tenderness.

"I don't think you are well, Miss Laidley," said Rosa, with an appearance of the kindest interest. "You look pale; don't, please—it is not your style at all."

"I am not in the habit of studying effects," replied Miss Laidley.

"No?" returned Rosa, in a tone beautifully modulated between an interrogation and an exclamation.

"Artless pet," said the Idol. "She is all heart—all soul."

"Why, then she is two people," cried Rosa.

The Idol looked a little confused.

"Come, Rosa," said Elinor; "the ponies will be so wicked from standing that you can't manage them."

"Oh yes, I can," replied she, with the sweetest laugh and a glance at Miss Laidley which the young woman understood; "I can manage any thing wicked—I like to—and I always conquer."

"Such spirits!" exclaimed the Idol. "Dear Mrs. Thornton drinks surely from the fount of Helicon."

The Laidley breathed an inward prayer that the ponies might run away and send her to a fount expressed by the first syllable of the Idol's word with another liquid letter added.

"I am so happy that you came," continued the Idol. "So blest that we spoke of sweet Mrs. Farnsworth; my mind is clear from doubt as a Peairan spring."

Rosa Thornton, looking covertly at Miss Laidley, saw her start as the Idol pronounced Mrs. Farnsworth's name. Having seen that sign of confusion she was ready to go, and followed Elinor out while the Idol sent a volley of farewell explosives after them.

"Adieu! We meet to part—life is so—val! val! We shall meet briefly, briefly. Remember us—love us—oh, val, val!"

The instant the ponies dashed off at a reckless pace, Rosa began to laugh. "I think I plucked a few of the Angel's best feathers," cried she. "The little serpent! Elinor, I saw her start when the Idol mentioned Mrs. Farnsworth's name."

"Really she is not worth minding," replied Elinor.

"Oh, isn't she? I don't agree with you. I want something to do—I shall take up a mission. I mean to worry that Angel and turn her into a spiteful little cat and make her show her true nature every time I meet her."

"Let her alone, do, I beg. I was afraid she would cry."

"Bah! She would have liked to scratch. What fun it was, and how well I did it. I caught her voice exactly. And to see that dear, blind old Idol so unconscious!—How Tom will laugh."

She exulted greatly, and declared that it was delightful to have an opportunity to be wicked after the worry of the past days.

"And now where, Elinor?" she asked, as the basket turned into the high-road.

"I am going to see Mrs. Piffit."

"Upon my word, you do mean to kill the hydra outright. I declare, Elinor, you are a good girl, and you are the bravest creature, and—"

"And in praising me you will let those vicious ponies run away and break my precious neck," said Elinor.

"Not I; my ponies know me. I wish I could quote poetry—but no matter, the meaning is, they know I would give it them if they didn't behave with decorum."

"Do stop using Tom's phrases. That wretched man will teach you a whole vocabulary of dreadful expressions."

"Slang, you mean, only you can't bring your royal lips to say it. But, my princess, it is so jolly, as Tom says."

She was in immense spirits, and said the wittiest things all the way down to the village, and Elinor had to laugh until she almost forgot her errand. But it was a bootless one, for when they drove up to the private entrance of the Lake House and sent the tiger in to learn if Mrs. Piffit were visible, he came back and said that she was not—she had gone out.

"Another time, Elinor," said Rosa; "you can think about it all night, and you will be prepared to give her a more horrible—there, don't frown, I'll change the word—lecture, to-morrow."

"Wait an instant, Rosa," said Elinor, who had not been listening. She remembered that it was due to Mr. Rossitur that he should have some sign of her presence and some sort of message, and here was an opportunity to send it without trouble.

"What now?" questioned Rosa.

"I should like to let Mr. Rossitur know that I have come to your house," said Elinor unhesitatingly.

"Nonsense! He'll find it out soon enough. It's none of his affairs any way," cried Rosa rapidly, not having changed in her feelings toward that gentleman. "Besides it isn't proper to leave messages for young men. I am astonished at you—setting up for a statue of propriety as you do. I couldn't permit it. Tom wouldn't approve—Tom's very particular, and I always obey Tom—I promised at the altar."

She said it all as fast as possible and in a voice like Mrs. Piffit's, and Elinor could not interrupt for laughing.

"You absurd goose, you are quite mad to-day," she said. "But nonsense aside, Rosa, Mr. Rossitur is one of my best friends—"

"I hate people's best friends," interrupted Rosa.

"And he has come from Washington and probably brings letters for me from papa."

"Say no more—Elinor *victrix*—which is all the Latin I ever knew, and I thought for a great while that meant victuals—Le Rossitur shall be informed of your arrival—it shall be done in a proper manner—my matronly card shall loom upon his astonished vision. Cupid, hold the ponies steady."

She gave Elinor the reins, pulled out her card-case and pencil, and said—"Now what shall I write?"

"I thought you had decided on something proper."

"Yes, dear, in theory—somehow I can't reduce it to practice. That's always my trouble—my theories are perfect. Let me see! Shall I write under Mrs. Thomas Thornton—Elinor Grey her pa—"

"Give me a card," cried Elinor, cutting her short.

She took the case out of Rosa's hand and fortunately found one of Tom's own pasteboards. "This will do exactly," said she, and wrote a single word under the name in her peculiar chirography that nobody could mistake who had ever seen a page thereof.

Rosa looked over and read aloud—"July!" She stared at Elinor with her eyes like saucers and repeated—"July!"

"So you have read once, said a second time," returned Elinor calmly.

"Then perhaps I'd better sing it now," cried Rosa. "But what on earth does that mean—Ju-ly?"

"Send Cupid in with the card and let him give it to the man in the office," continued Elinor.

"Cupid, indeed!" retorted Rosa. "My Cupid shan't help where that man is concerned. July! Tell me this instant what it means, Elinor Grey, or I'll have hysterics and shriek till the ponies run away and the whole village rushes out."

"It means that Mr. Rossitur knew I would be here in July—it shows him that I have come—it is better than writing notes or being foolish. Now are you satisfied?"

"No, I am not; but I suppose you must have your way. Here, Cupid, carry this card and tell the book-keeper to send it at once to Mr. Rossitur's room."

While the tiger was gone, Rosa sat playing with her whip and Elinor Grey looked unconscious. When the ponies were off again Rosa was greatly occupied with them, and her taciturnity was in such contrast to her recent high spirits, that Elinor said, "There you go, from one extreme to another, as Tom says."

"I am not thinking about Tom," replied Rosa curtly.

"What then? what is the matter?"

"Ju-ly!" cried Rosa, lengthening the word as if it contained a dozen syllables. "July! That is the matter."

"Oh, July!" replied Elinor in her turn. "Yes, dear, but don't take it to heart."

"Don't tease—I won't have it. Oh, Elinor, are you in earnest?"

"Now, Rosa, don't be a goose. I have said nothing—done nothing."

"I don't know," shivered Rosa. "I feel something in the air. Well, I shall say nothing myself; warn me in time—do it gradually—that is all I ask."

Elinor laughed at her a little and changed the conversation, and Rosa soon recovered her spirits and discoursed volubly till they reached home. She gave Tom a glowing account of the morning's work, and he was particularly delighted that she had so routed Miss Laidley.

"It will all be right," cried he. "Just let the Queen get at Piffit. I saw Clive this morning; he looks worried. Never mind, it will all be right now."

Rosa had left him and Elinor at the luncheon-table and was standing by the window and saying to herself—"July! July!" She did not like it at all; but she would hold her peace even to Tom for the present; and may be there was no danger to be feared—Elinor was odd.

CHAPTER XXIII.

MORE HISTRIONICS.

THE door had no sooner closed upon the departing visitors than Miss Laidley burst into floods of tears and flung herself on a sofa, calling dismally for her disembodied parent to fly down and take her away from a world where she was not appreciated. "O father, father! come and take your Evangel—your lonely child—father, father!" Her piteous cry did not bring a seraph, but it roused the Idol, who had been kissing her hand to Elinor from the window; and the Idol, startled by this unexpected outburst, hastened toward her, exclaiming, "My sweetest, what is it? Are you ill? Tell me—speak!"

The Laidley, who had been only a commonplace, sulky girl under the transforming spell of Rosa Thornton, now turned into an angel again with drooping pinions and a wail. "O father, father!" she moaned, clutching at invisible shapes in the air, shaking her wavy hair about her face, and making various hasty preparations for a scene; "Father, come!"

"Oh, my Blossom, not that appeal," said the Idol, who was always so touched by the pathos of that special adjuration that she was completely at the Angel's mercy. "You are not alone—I am here. Sweet, tell me what it is?"

The Angel moaned more piteously; at length between her sobs she gasped, "Mrs. Thornton was cruel to me—cruel!"

"She did but jest, love; it is her way. I was fearful she might wound your sensitive nature," returned the Idol. "She does not know you as I do; she does not understand how frail a breeze will chill your soul. But weep not; smile, only smile, my Angel."

But the Angel could not smile yet; she had a good deal more sobbing and sighing to do. She had made a strong effort to keep from giving way to her temper under Rosa Thornton's persecutions to a degree that might have astonished the Idol; now she must cry, as she always must after a fit of rage. Moreover, she had been rendered nervous by the few words spoken in regard to Mrs. Farnsworth; into the bargain she had not indulged in a scene for several days, and she must perform. She went through her best act and did not omit a single point, and each successive one "brought down" the Idol till her eyes were swollen from weeping sympathetic tears, and she looked a damp and miserable Idol generally, and was very absurd in her distress, but honest and patient as ever.

The Angel shrieked for her parent to appear and save her until he must have come unless absent in some very distant sphere on important business, or a very hard-hearted seraph indeed. Finding no response from that quarter, she appealed to her aunt to rush from the orange groves of her southern island and carry her little Evangel back to their fragrant shades. She called herself several scores of pretty names expressive of desolation, she assumed numberless attitudes, and the effect of her histrionics upon the Idol stimulated her to new efforts. "Bid that cruel woman come back!" she cried at length. "Let her come back and look at her work—I am dying—dying!"

She fell upon the cushions, rigid and still, and the Idol fluttered about her, first on one side, then on the other, pitying, soothing, trying so many things in such rapid succession that she seemed, as she always did at such times, not a solitary Idol but a dozen, bobbing about, running against each other, and occasionally, when she was quiet for a second, melting again into one huge Idol with her draperies wide enough for the whole twelve. "I am dying," moaned the Angel. "Let me die! Let me die!"

But the Idol would not permit that on any account, and she was so distressed that if there had been any observer of the scene he certainly would have pitied her while he laughed at her absurdity. "Die not, my Angel! Live—live for your friend who loves you so! Sweet Blossom, disolate not my heart with such frenzied words—Promethean pangs in the vulture's breast!" she cried, getting the comparisons twisted as usual and pouring out the great words from force of habit. "Look up—one smile—I shall die with you!" She blubbered outright and made a noise like a sea-calf, and sat flat down on the floor and pulled the Angel into her lap, and was really beside herself.

The Angel was appeased—she had distressed somebody. She lay quiet for a few seconds, then slowly opened her eyes and gave the Idol one of her heavenly smiles. "I will live," she whispered; "I can not leave you—my one friend. I am better now. Oh, how grieved I am to have distressed you—I am so weak, so foolish."

K

"You are all soul, all ethereal nerves," returned the Idol. "But my sweet pet is better?"

"Much better—you soothe me. She was so cruel—how could she treat me as she did?"

"Dear child, forget it; Mrs. Thornton would not have pained you for the world. She is so full of life and vigor that she disremembers how fragile your spirit is."

"I forgive her," sighed the Angel, in a voice like that of an early Christian martyr heaving her last breath—"I forgive her. She is cold and hard; but you love me—you understand me?"

"You are fettered in my heart," vowed the Idol.

"I know it—ah, it gives me new life! I am so nervous, so excitable. The unexpected meeting with Elinor was too much for me—I thought she seemed cold—and I love her so fondly."

"She reciprocates your affection," asserted the Idol. "She was anxious to see you, but you know she is always Palladian in her mien."

"Yes, yes—cold—ice. Oh, darling Duchess, nobody loves me truly and understands me, except you."

"Sweet Angel, you console me by those words. Be calm, my sweet. Oh, what can I perform to make you happy?—I would dare Titanish feats! Listen, sweet—you remember my emerald necklace? Will you accept it and wear it for my sake?"

The Angel's heart gave a great bound. Here was consolation beyond her wildest expectations. Why, that emerald necklace had made her miserly soul sick for its possession—it was worth countless shekels of silver and shekels of gold.

"I can not take it," she sighed; "no, no! I only need your love—I am content with that. Feel my heart beat; I appreciate your goodness so."

"You shall wear the necklace—it must be yours," persisted the Idol, who would have given all the emeralds and diamonds she possessed—and she had as many as if she had been a modern queen of Sheba—to restore her favorite to happiness.

"I can not, I can not! There, I am better now."

"And you will accept the poor gift?—Give your fond Duchess that pleasure, my loveliest."

"Since you insist—you are so good," returned the other with the voice of an angel and the instinct of a Jew pawnbroker. "I can not refuse—you shall not be pained."

She sat up and dried her eyes, and looked very lovely with her hair straying over her shoulders, and smiled at the Idol, who was in ecstacies at seeing her willing to live a little longer. Although the Laidley was well acquainted with the Idol's generosity, she could not be easy in mind until the emerald necklace was absolutely in her possession. She often promised people things herself and forgot to give them; the Idol never did hesitate to fulfill her offers, but she might where a necklace, which would have made an empress cry with envy, was concerned. So the Angel said—

"If some one should come in! We will go up to your dressing-room, darling Duchess, till we are both more composed."

The Idol supported her up stairs, and after they had arranged their disordered plumage before the mirror, she cooed—"I am happy now. Dearest Duchess, do me a favor—don't ask me to take the necklace."

The Idol flew at once to her jewel-casket and upset things recklessly, snatched the gorgeous decoration and fastened it about the Angel's neck. "Wear it," she cried; "never even speak of it or you will pain me."

The Angel looked in the glass and saw the stones gleam and burn. She had done a good morning's work—she wished she could engage Rosa Thornton to come every day and hurt her feelings.

"You make me dumb with delight," said she, and nearly strangled the Idol with embraces. "But see how you have scattered rings and bracelets and every thing else. Oh, you careless Duchess—sowing the floor with diamonds!"

"What are gems compared to seeing you smile again," returned the Idol. "I would fling the whole worthless store into the lake yonder, if it could soothe my Angel."

The careful Angel collected the ornaments and arranged them in their places—the only task that was always pleasant to her—and she managed so well that the Idol put several costly rings on her fingers and made quite a pyramid of pins and ear-rings in her lap, and the Angel cooed and expostulated and took them all, as she usually did.

"But what had they been saying about that Mrs. Farnsworth?" she asked suddenly.

"Oh, love, so glad you reminded me. It is all an error—a black Tartarean! She is Miss Grey's friend. We must visit her—love her."

The Angel went into an inward fury at once. "But the stories must be true," she asserted; "every body repeats them."

"They will have to cease," said the Idol. "No, dearest, I am quite convinced—so will all our circle be—Miss Grey is her warrant—her Medusian shield. Let us think of it no more."

"Did they mention me? You said I never had believed the stories?" demanded the Angel.

"Oh yes; but they dreamed not of blaming you."

Miss Laidley breathed a sigh of relief. "You were mistaken in thinking Miss Grey did not know her," continued the Idol.

"I never said so!" cried the Angel in dismay. "Somebody else told you! Oh, dearest Duchess, you never told Elinor I said that?"

"No, no; we said nothing of you."

"But it was not I—just remember."

"It could not have been," said the Idol, convinced that she must be in error. "Who did say it?"

"Oh, Mrs. Piffit or Jack Ralston's wife—they are so wicked."

"Yes, wicked indeed. Of course it was one of them."

"And we'll go and see Mrs. Farnsworth and pet her and love her—we both liked her," said the Angel enthusiastically.

"We did, we did," cried the Idol, forgetting that the liking had been confined to herself. "You are so good, so pure—you will be glad to aid in dispersing these evil reports, will you not, my dear Angel?"

"It will make me happy. Dear Duchess, I have cried myself to sleep night after night thinking and grieving about her; Juanita can tell you—Juanita knows."

"I am certain you have—sweet soul."

"And if that Piffit woman should try to blame me—"

"My love, she would not dare."

"Oh, she is so wicked. It would be just like her to try and throw it all on a lonely, helpless thing like me."

"I am your guardion," cried the Idol, swelling into dignity; "I am your Athenian palladium," for only a jumble of the hugest words could express her resolve. "I know that you have scarcely seen Mrs. Piffit except in my presence. No, love, you are innocent; no one could dream of blaming you."

The Angel was satisfied; if the lies must come out, let Piffit be crushed; she would float airily aside and be among the warmest of Mrs. Farnsworth's supporters and wound her in some other way. It was long after the luncheon hour; and her feelings soothed, the emerald necklace in her possession, to say nothing of the lesser treasures, the fear of exposure having been removed, the Angel commenced to undergo certain earthly needs, ethereal as she was. "The selfish monster that I am!" she cried; "you have had no lunch; you will be ill with one of your headaches. Oh, my dearest Duchess, let me order something sent up."

"Yes, yes; and you must take sustenance too."

"I am not hungry; I never am; but I can't let you be made ill by my selfishness," said the Angel.

She rang the bell and ordered a quantity of good things, ostensibly to please the Idol, and when the tray was brought up she vowed she would not touch a morsel, and ended by devouring brandy peaches, fresh strawberries and cream, a rich paté, stomach-destroying pickles, and various similar delicacies, which pink-and-white seraphs with peculiar organizations are wont to crave. The repast over, she insisted on the Idol's lying down; she would go and rest too. They both needed repose after the morning's excitement, and toward sunset they would go out for a drive.

She kissed the Idol, left her safely deposited on her gorgeous couch, and flew away to her own apartments intent upon her private affairs. Old Juanita was there, chewing brown bark, squatted by the open window and nodding lazily. "Get up, get up you brown bête," cried the Angel, and Juanita rose submissive. "I've got the necklace at last!"

Juanita surveyed the treasures with delight, and the Angel locked them carefully up. "Get out that lavender dress," said she; "be quick."

"My, bress her! Tear labender all to pieces 'mong de trees," cried Juanita.

"I don't care—the old Idol gave it to me. Get it quick! I will look pretty—you'd better hurry!" And Juanita knew she had.

The Angel made a charming toilette, and grew good-natured and frolicked with Juanita, who was jubilant at command, for her young mistress had a witch-like control over her, body and soul. While she dressed, Miss Laidley told Juanita what was to be said and done if Piffit betrayed the source of her information; promised her a silk gown if all went well, and Juanita was prepared to lie to any extent.

The Angel was too lovely and fairy-like for a creature of common earth when her toilette was complete. She arranged a black-lace shawl over her head as a finishing touch, and surveyed herself in the mirror with gratified eyes. "Sit here," said she; "I am in bed and asleep—you couldn't disturb me for the world, because I have been crying about poor papa."

Juanita nodded intelligently and squatted down in the window again, solacing herself with a fresh bit of brown bark.

Owing to the luckiest chance in the world, there was a private staircase which led from Miss Laidley's room into a passage never used, and from the passage she could step at once into the thickest of the shrubberies. She often made use of it when she wanted to meet the Prince of Como or a troubadour and to indulge in a little romance. She departed and sped through the wood, saving her draperies in a miraculous way. She had told Leighton Rossitur she was going to walk there that afternoon, and she felt certain that unless he had heard of Elinor's arrival he would be somewhere near. She was not mistaken in her hope; when she reached a lonely summer-house, there he sat.

In the height of his love, with the decisive moment so close, Rossitur, like nine people out of ten, men or women, could see no reason why he should not shorten the lonely moments by an hour's flirtation with Miss Laidley instead of moping in his room.

The Angel did a little astonishment, but not too much, then said—"You had no right to come here. I did not think, when I mentioned my walks, you would join me."

"Please let me stay; I am tired and lonely," said he, not in the least deceived by her artlessness, but quite willing to utter pretty speeches to any female creature so lovely.

He made himself as charming as ever he did to Elinor Grey, because he was a born flirt and trifler, and in one respect he resembled Miss Laidley—he was in earnest for the time, which is the great success of success in flirtation, as in every thing else. He had a volume of Owen Meredith in his pocket and he read to her out of the passionate songs—he quoted the Queen of the Serpents and applied it to her—he uttered half-earnest, half-playful speeches, and made his features and voice wholly earnest — he pleased himself with her smiles and her witcheries, and she could be very bewitching. They had a long talk, and Miss Laidley's romance grew a more serious matter as far as her feelings were concerned.

He had been jestingly reproaching her with her numberless coquetries, and said abruptly—"You have heard who came last night?"

The Angel thought he meant Miss Grey, whose name she had been careful not to mention; she was deceived by his question into supposing that he was aware of Elinor's arrival and had come to the summer-house instead of visiting her.

"Oh yes—Elinor?" she answered. "She came to see me this morning."

Rossitur gave a start and allowed Owen Meredith to fall on the grass and stain his blue-and-gold dress. "Miss Grey here?" he exclaimed.

The Angel felt something rise within her as if seven devils had taken possession of her soul. "I thought you meant her," she faltered.

"No; poor Walters—your victim," he replied, making a grasp at self-control and Owen at the same time. "When did Miss Grey come?"

"Oh, last night," said the Angel. "Now I suppose you will go and flirt with her. Dear me, you won't stand much chance here, I warn you."

Rossitur was a furiously jealous man, like all people who are capable of great latitude in their own actions; Miss Laidley's words kindled his mind at once. "What do you mean?" he asked.

"I won't tell. Oh, you will find out! Yes, I will, because I like to tease you. No, I don't like to—I did not mean that—I am too much your friend, Mr. Rossitur."

"There is no reason why I should be teased," he answered unconcernedly. "I think, like you, that Miss Grey is an icicle."

"At all events, she did love Clive Farnsworth," cried the Angel. "People here know that; they were engaged last summer."

Rossitur had never heard a whisper of this—he felt his blood turn to fire. "But Mr. Farnsworth is married," said he, resolutely controlling voice and features.

"He was not then. They quarrelled, and he went off in a rage and brought this girl—such horrible stories as they tell of her."

Rossitur had too recently arrived for the gossip to reach his ears, and he avowed his ignorance.

In her rage at the emotion he had displayed at Elinor's name, the added provocation of having herself given the news, the Angel poured out the whole story. Of course she did not say a wrong word or appear conscious of what she was telling. She told it as pink-and-white creatures do tell such things; and if the man who listens can read character, he knows that the narrator, in spite of her childishness, is a little devil or a sort of mermaid, according as her veins are filled with blood or water.

Now Rossitur understood Miss Laidley. He knew that she was of the mermaid species—sensuous in thought,. but never to be guilty of going beyond romance and respectable mischief; because in spite of her warm fancies she was physically weak, and the mermaid chilliness in her veins counteracted the other instincts. He listened and he was filled with fierce rage. Elinor Grey had loved Clive Farnsworth! His first impulse was to find the man and murder him; then he remembered that it was a thing gone by; he had almost conquered—he would wholly. He put aside his anger and was only anxious to get away from the mermaid, who looked an angel, and rush off to meet Elinor. But he did not wish to offend Miss Laidley, so he had to pass over the stories and flatter her, and finally plead an engagement. She was obliged to let him go, but she looked charming in her sudden pallor, which was not affected this time, and had great difficulty in not being absurd. She irritated him with a last taunt, and when he had gone she sat there in the summer-house and had three minds to make a tragical end to her romance—strangle herself with her lace shawl, or do something poetical and desperate. But strangulation would leave her black in the face, and there was no other mode of death convenient; so she sat and bewailed herself, and was very wretched, and sobbed in miserable earnest.

Rossitur made the best of his way to Alban Wood, and reached the house only to be informed that every body was out and might never return, for any thing the stupid new servant could tell. But Miss Grey had arrived—the stupid new man could assert so much, and Rossitur scribbled a hasty pencil note to say that he would call in the morning. It was all he could do. He did not know the Thorntons well enough to venture on a second effort that evening, and besides he thought from the abominable man's confused explanations that they had gone out to dine or commit some other fiendish absurdity to annoy him. He went away after charging Stupid to be sure and give the note to Miss Grey as soon as she returned. Stupid meant to do so—he had been engaged to fill a vacancy, and was so anxious to please and be retained that he committed numberless blunders, and naturally could not lose the opportunity at present offered of making a crowning one. He kept the note in order to have the satisfaction of handing it to the young lady herself, and the consequence was that, being dispatched on an errand by Tom as soon as the party returned from their walk, he forgot the scrap of paper and every thing connected with Mr. Rossitur, and hastened off to fulfill his mission and fall into new mistakes and heap added condemnation on his devoted head.

The evening passed quietly and pleasantly enough. In secret Elinor decided that Rossitur had not reached the hotel or obtained her message in time to come up to Alban Wood. She went to her room early that night, and shut Rosa out, because she was tired and wanted to make up for last night's broken sleep. She thought that she intended to go to bed, but after Rosa's maid had departed she sat in her white dressing-gown by the window and looked out across the moonlit shrubberies, as she had so often done during the preceding summer. She sat there until the associations of the place brought back restless fancies, and she shut out the clear radiance with a guilty sensation, relighted her lamp and brought herself down to the present. She thought of Leighton Rossitur—she remembered her decision, and she did not falter. She would be safest sheltered by his love. She recalled every kind thing he had ever done, dwelt on every noble word, and tried to believe him the real King Arthur. She would not heed the sorrowful feeling like that she had wept over in the woods on the day when she made her resolve. She was frightened by the nameless pang which had wrung her heart as she sat in the moonlight; she wanted to feel that her life was arranged—that some final step was taken, in order to have a prop whereon to steady her soul. She had done right; he loved her; she could not draw back, his affection would warm her heart at length—surely it must. Yet once more, at the thought of his love, the cold dread returned; she seemed to feel the clasp of his hand on hers, holding her fast, restraining her freedom. She called that fancy—an absurd whim to which she would pay no attention. She recollected that she had given him a new encouragement. By writing that one word on the card she had implied that she remembered what July was to bring and was not afraid. At the time she had not thought about the matter; it seemed of importance now. She had taken a final step. Well, she was glad—she could not hesitate if she would. She kept telling herself that she was glad until the night appeared to have turned chill and she wrapped a warm shawl about her and shivered. Yes, it was all settled—she should become Leighton Rossitur's wife. Only, just yet she could not have any love-making. She would write a letter: when he came for his answer she would put it in his hands and ask him to be generous and patient still; to be her friend and let her grow accustomed to this new aspect of life.

She sat down at the table and wrote her letter, and by the time it was finished she felt so tired that she was glad to creep into bed, and kept assuring herself that the sensation of relief came because she was at rest, at peace; it was all settled now. As she woke the next morning that letter was the first sight which met her eyes, and it reminded her that every thing had been arranged. She had nothing more to do—she would not even think.

Breakfast was late, but, late as it was, Rosa had not come down. "She is threatened with one of her dreadful sick headaches," Tom said; "she thinks if she lies still awhile she will be able to drive with you. Do you mean to go and see Mrs. Piffit?"

"Yes," Elinor replied, glad to be reminded of the business in hand and to have some engrossing occupation. "Tom, I feel savage. I am confident that I can frighten that dumpy little woman directly out of the village; but Mrs. Hackett says that Mrs. Ralston is quite as much to blame, and nobody could frighten her."

"Couldn't there?" queried Tom pensively.

"I never speak to her, any way. Somebody introduced her, but I never will do more than bow. She talks horribly about all women; and how she is to be silenced, goodness only knows."

"Queen Elinor," said Tom, growing suddenly grave, "you believe me honorable—you know I never talk about any woman?"

"You are perfect as far as that goes," returned Elinor.

"Then I will give you a charm that shall even subdue the Ralston, if you have an opportunity to employ it."

"What, Tom?"

"Look in her face and say these words—'A cottage at Vevay—a summer of roses—ten years ago—and Tom Thornton's compliments,'" said he slowly.

Elinor looked at him in utter bewilderment.

"Ask no questions," said Tom; "but I know you won't, nor will Rose. I have never said a word; there is no secret of mine, nor will my Rosa ever think so; but if the Ralston shows her fangs, do you mutter that spell, and I'll swear that you'll take yourself for a witch from its success."

Elinor repeated the words. "You are not laughing at me, Tom?"

"I am not. Do as you like; I am going to tell Rose just what I have you. I shall never open my lips again."

"Tom turned oracle," said Elinor; "I'll try it."

Tom made no answer; he rose from the table and went up to see how Rosa was, and Elinor soon followed.

Poor Rosa lay pale and miserable among the pillows. "I can't get up," said she piteously. "Elinor, Tom shall drive you down to the village."

"Can't," said Tom; "I am going trouting, and I've an engagement with Farnsworth. Elinor would not be so fiendish as to trouble these last days of fishing. Take the ponies and Cupid, my queen, and pass on 'in maiden meditation, fancy free.'"

"What does he mean about the Ralston?" asked Rosa. "He repeated the most absurd message and says he is done forever."

"Yes; he's mad, I think."

"No matter; use it if you meet her," said Rosa. "We know it isn't Tom's secret, that is enough."

Tom never opened his lips while they discussed the message, and looked perfectly blank.

"Oh, my wretched head," sighed Rosa. "I must lie here, Elinor, but it is a shame to let you go alone."

"Lie still, like a good girl; you can get up before I come back."

"Oh yes," said Tom, "I shall cure her because I want to go trouting."

"Indeed, you are not to wait," said Rosa; "just be off."

"Indeed I shan't, Miss Goosey."

Rosa began to declare that her head was better; but Tom, who was as anxious if her finger ached as though he were a bridegroom instead of a husband of ten years' standing, had no intention of leaving her.

"I shall drive the ponies in great state," said Elinor.

"Oh, they'll behave like lambs," replied Rosa. "Honestly, Tom, go and smoke a cigar, and if my head is not better I'll tell you; but if it is, I'll go to sleep and you may be off to Clive and the trout."

"A bargain," said Tom; "but if you fib to me you shall repent. There—one—two—no, that kiss was on your nose, so it doesn't count—two—three—aren't you better?"

Tom's kisses had not lost their potency although they were so frequent, and Rosa cried out—"Now isn't he good, Nelly? When I am sick I always say nice things to him because he is so kind; but oh, don't I pay him off when I get well!"

"You are a pair of spoiled children and twin geese," said Elinor.

"Jealousy—downright envy," vowed Tom. "You'd like to be a turtle-dove, you wretched creature, only you're a species by yourself—your mate was lost in the ark."

He sauntered off to smoke in peace, and Elinor sat by Rosa till she dropped into a slumber, then went to tell Tom that he was ordered out of the house, and prepared herself for her drive.

CHAPTER XXIX.

A LITTLE MISTAKE.

ELINOR had driven off on her errand, Tom had satisfied himself that Rosa slept and set out to find Farnsworth, after giving orders that no soul was to disturb the mistress of the mansion though it should get on fire, when Leighton Rossitur appeared, having ridden up from the hotel at the earliest possible hour.

As Stupid opened the door and beheld him he for the first time remembered the note, and straightway prepared a lie, which even Stupids can do with rapidity. Miss Grey was not in—Mr. Thornton was not in—nobody was in. Rossitur imperiously demanded if his message had reached the young lady. Stupid said there could be no doubt of that, for he had given it to Mrs. Thornton's maid.

"Go and see if there is a message for Mr. Rossitur," said Leighton, walking into the house in so determined a way that Stupid was glad to put wings to his flight. In searching for the maid he managed to upset several chairs and break a china vase, but those were trifling misfortunes. The woman had nothing for Mr. Rossitur. Of course Stupid did not betray his own lack of faithfulness: back he came to the impatient gentleman and said on his own responsibility that Miss Grey had gone somewhere, he thought with Mr. Thornton, and there was no message for any body.

Rossitur left the house in a furious passion. He forgot the really good, manly resolutions he had formed during the past months, forgot Elinor Grey's nobility of soul, and swore inwardly that she had been trifling with him and wanted to drive him mad. He was as insane as a jealous man in love alone can be. Rossitur's life and Rossitur's own nature made him think lightly of women in general, and now in his anger he remembered the venom which the mermaid, who looked an angel, had breathed in his ears, cursed her for the telling, and included Elinor in his animadversions against the sex. There certainly was cause for a hasty man to be filled with resentment. The book-keeper had forgotten to send the card to his room, so that he did not know of Elinor's message; she had disregarded his note—gone out without leaving any excuse for conduct that would have been discourteous toward the commonest acquaintance. Rossitur never believed in excuses either, and never, when he was angry, could put a favorable construction upon actions that appeared singular and wait until his friends might explain.

He could only think now that she had purposely insulted him, and for any thing he knew might have gone somewhere to meet that man Farnsworth. There was nothing he hesitated to think of any body when he was in one of his cold rages, during which he would never acknowledge himself in a passion at all. At such times a very fiend seemed to take possession of him, forcing him to indulge the most outrageous suspicions in regard to persons whom he really loved and honored, and making him utter bitter, horrible speeches which it was almost impossible for the most forgiving nature to overlook, as more than one woman linked with his past could have certified. When the devil left him he could scarcely be convinced that he had said or done such things, but while the fury was at its height he had a horrible pleasure in hurting himself by overwhelming his friends with abuse and insult. If at that moment he had met Elinor Grey, he would have forgotten what he risked and given her an exhibition of his temper which would have ended their acquaintance summarily, so it was fortunate that his course did not lead him near her.

He mounted his horse and rode away, neither thinking nor caring which road he took, making a tempest with his fancies which hid the brightness of the morning. The very sky looked black—he was cursing himself and Elinor Grey, and, more than either, Clive Farnsworth, whom at that moment he would have been willing to punish at the expense of every future hope. It chanced that as he spurred by Judge Hamlyn's gates the worthy old gentleman was emerging therefrom, and called out—

"Hallo, Rossitur! Are you turned into the Wild Horseman? Where are you going? Don't ride me down."

Rossitur checked his horse, and it being a peculiarity of his to be very pleasant to every body except the special objects of his rage, he returned the Judge's greeting with urbanity.

"Riding nowhere," said he; "running away from myself. How are you this morning?"

"I am as jolly as a crow," said the old Judge, who was the most charming man of near sixty that can be imagined; a lion in the court-room and the mildest, merriest companion out. "I'm going fishing. You must go with me. I want company because I'm a witty man and need somebody to laugh at my jokes."

Rossitur was willing; as well that as any thing.

"Turn up the avenue," said the Judge; "we'll leave your horse in my stables and find you a rod. I've my lunch in my basket, and there's enough for two, and here's a friend likewise," holding up a good-sized wicker flask that would have shocked a Son of Temperance or any other over-scrupulous individual.

Rossitur dismounted without more entreaty and walked along the carriage-road leading his horse, while the Judge trudged beside him in great spirits at having secured an agreeable companion. They disposed of Bucephalus, Rossitur was provided with the necessary implements of slaughter, and they retraced their steps. They crossed the road, struck down among the fields and made their way toward the brook, talking gayly, and, early as it was, Rossitur took a pull at the Judge's flask to see, as he said, if it proved worthy of the Judge's encomium. Strolling about the brook they met other fishermen, for that stream and its occupants were dreadfully tormented by people who ought to have had the sense to go off to the Adirondac mountains in search of great two-pounders, so that the poor trout in Alban Brook could have had a little good of their lives instead of perishing immature dwarfs.

They fished and they dawdled, they smoked and drank, ate and told stories, and about two o'clock the impromptu party was increased by the arrival of Farnsworth and Tom Thornton, attracted by the noise and jollity which had driven every trout with a grain of common sense in its head into the darkest shelter possible. The new-comers were greeted with acclamations; Tom Thornton was a favorite with every body, and there being no wives or maiden aunts near to frown, they were glad to assume the old terms of friendliness with Farnsworth.

"This is a pretty spectacle," exclaimed Tom.

"Here's a sight for virtue and morality! One judge, two counsellors, a fat bachelor, and a future president, sitting on the grass smoking, drinking, a pack of cards near, so much tobacco-smoke I thought the woods were on fire, and such improper talk going on that the very blackbirds have got their wings before their faces.

"Wings be hanged—virtue and morality be hanged too," cried the Judge. "Come and sit down and take a sip of this, and tell me if it wouldn't make an Irishman think it had been distilled in Elysium by the hands of St. Patrick himself."

Tom sipped and thought it would, and Clive took the assertion on credit, not favoring the national habit of early sipping. Salutations were exchanged; Farnsworth having seen Rossitur on the preceding day, and having known him of old in Washington, spoke cordially and did not notice the curt greeting which he received. Baskets were opened and successes compared, and Tom had the largest trout any basket could produce, whereat the Judge vowed he would sue him for trespass because the trout was caught in the part of the brook that ran through his land. Finally they agreed to try which of them could win the prize, and drew cards from the pack—first ace to take it.

"Spade!" shouted the Judge, at the second trial. "Ha, ha, Tom Thornton, lay that beauty in my basket."

There was a great deal of laughing and undignified merriment, then they sat on the grass and smoked and told remarkable stories, and Tom and the Judge kept the party in convulsions, as they usually did when they met. It was lazy weather—the shady spot was pleasant—there was no further hope of trout that day, so they took kindly to the *dolce far niente* style of business, and pretty much finished the portly flasks before they decided to break up the meeting.

Clive had been talkative and agreeable too; he was glad to forget the worry and suspicions of the past weeks in the genial companionship, and was half inclined to think that he might have been distressing himself about nothing, since the manner of his neighbors was so entirely unchanged.

Leighton Rossitur was moody one instant and almost boisterously gay the next. He had not drank enough to affect him—at least it would not have done so at another time—but perhaps in the excited state he was, it helped to make him more reckless than before and more desirous to give vent to the passion seething within. He laughed louder than any body at the Judge's stories, without having been able to follow them enough to catch the point; he said witty, absurd things, and was so brilliant that no one remarked his growing more contradictory and changeable.

It chanced that Clive had not actually addressed him many times—mere chance, for he liked Rossitur; but the talk was so general and fragmentary that it happened without his being conscious. Rossitur observed it, and he grew more furious as he watched Clive with his silent, secretive eyes. This man was jealous of him—he dared to be jealous of Elinor Grey—he with a wife, if she were his wife, whom he had picked up among the dregs of society, and perhaps was as eager for an occasion to betray his animosity as Rossitur himself. At a cooler moment Rossitur would not have insulted the woman he loved by a supposition like that, but the devil had a firm gripe of him and there was nothing too black for him to believe of the very mother that bore him. He purposely looked at Clive while asking some indifferent question; Clive, being at a little distance, did not observe that the remark was specially addressed to him, but sat playing with the handle of his rod and left some one else to answer. Rossitur could have taken his oath that it was an intentional slight; he had to pass his arm about the sapling against which he leaned and hug it firm and close to keep himself from making a spring at his enemy's throat and astonishing the party by a scene from a Corsican drama. He burst into a discordant laugh at some absurd speech Tom Thornton made, and began to tell an amusing story not in the slightest degree relevant.

Clive had not noticed that he was speaking, and broke in upon the first sentence by calling after the fat bachelor, who had risen and was prying about the trunk of an old hickory-tree and thrusting a stick into the den of some luckless squirrel. Rossitur stopped short.

"Go on with your story," said the Judge.

"I shall interrupt Mr. Farnsworth," returned Rossitur with elaborate politeness.

"I beg pardon," said Clive, roused to what was being said; "I did not notice that I interrupted you."

He spoke carelessly, but with good nature, supposing that Rossitur was only momentarily annoyed, as the most civil man may be when any body breaks the current of a good story. As he said the words, however, he caught Rossitur's glance and was at a loss to account for the steely glitter in his eyes.

"Come and sit down, you fat bachelor," called Tom Thornton. "How would you like a bigger animal than you to go prying about your den with a sharp stick?"

"A bigger animal?" quoth the Judge. "Then it would have to be a megalonyx or some exploded creature of that sort."

"Stop calling me nicknames," cried the fat bachelor plaintively. "I'm young and innocent, and I won't be contaminated by the immorality of you married men."

"Are married men ever immoral?" asked Rossitur.

Again Clive caught a look which pointed the words, but he forced himself to think that it was his own sensitiveness that made him do so.

"Prod that bachelor with a cane, somebody," said the Judge; "he is always in the way."

"He's so huge, poor fellow, he can't help it," returned Tom.

"Oh don't," sighed the fat man, who was the soul of good-humor; "I haven't my corset on to-day, that's what makes me look so."

They laughed, and said more absurd things, and the fat bachelor resumed his seat and tried to look injured.

"Now, Rossitur, tell your story," said the Judge.

"I have forgotten it," returned he; "you shall go unenlightened to your graves. It was a good one too."

"He hadn't any to tell," laughed Tom; "no man ever forgets a good story."

"You don't yours, Tom," squeaked the fat bachelor, "because you have just six, and you've told them till you know the whole lot by heart, and so does every body else."

"Prod that fat bachelor with a cane, somebody," ordered the Judge once more.

"Give him a drink," said Tom; "he means to be funny—take the will for the deed."

"Don't you be funny," added the Judge seriously, "or you'll have a fit or something."

"I won't be prodded with a cane," said the fat bachelor, "and I will have a drink; and you shan't abuse me, because I haven't my corset on."

"Talking of stories," said Rossitur, "did you read about that French chap who introduced a woman as his wife among all the great ladies at Rome, and they petted her immensely till somebody came on from Paris and recognized her as an opera *figurante?*"

The speech might have been accidental—Rossitur had lately arrived and might be ignorant of the scandal which made his words so unfortunate in that presence. Tom Thornton and the Judge both spoke at once and changed the conversation. Again Clive tried to make up his mind whether Rossitur meant to insult him or whether it was a careless remark which in his morbidness he felt might be thought applicable to himself; for he knew that if there had been gossip there was no story too absurd for repetition and belief.

"I suppose we ought to be getting under weigh," said Tom, after he and the Judge had effectually led the talk from dangerous ground.

The Judge acceded, for he wanted an opportunity to warn Rossitur of what was being said in the neighborhood. He liked Clive, had been charmed with Ruth, and had kept his stately wife from open outbreaks by his disbelief of the slanders. He did not dream that Rossitur knew of them and had it in his mind to insult Farnsworth, so he was uneasy until he could put him beyond the risk of saying any thing disagreeable. Rods and baskets were picked up and the party sauntered lazily toward the road, worrying the fat bachelor, who never heeded it, and discussing a variety of trifling matters. They came out into the field and had reached the fence and stood talking, when Clive chanced to dissent from some political assertion one of the counsellors made.

"He happens to be right, however," said Rossitur quickly.

"No," returned Clive, without an idea of giving offense, "he is entirely in the wrong; I have a volume of old state papers in my library which will prove it."

"Nevertheless, I must venture to persist in spite of Mr. Farnsworth's opinion, supported by state papers," said Rossitur in a bitterly ironical tone.

This was the third occasion on which by look or word Mr. Rossitur had almost insulted him ; beginning to feel certain that it could not be wholly accidental, Clive's own temper rose. "Your persistence will not change facts, Mr. Rossitur," said he politely enough, but in a tone w'ich showed that he did not mean to draw back from the ground he had taken.

"Nor will your assertion move them," said Rossitur.

"That is possible ; but as I can show the proof, why I repeat that the counsellor and yourself are mistaken."

"I dare say I am," said the counsellor hastily, made a little restless, as were the rest of the party, by the tone which the conversation was assuming.

"Easiest thing in the world to be mistaken," cried the Judge.

"Don't I know that ?" added the fat bachelor, executing a *pirouette ;* willing to be ridiculous if that would restore the general good nature. "I am always mistaken, and I am always positive —I like to be."

Every body laughed ; Clive recovered his equanimity and thought he had been to blame, and wished to avoid further discussion. But before any one could turn the topic Rossitur said with dogged quiet—

"I am never mistaken when I am positive, and in this case I am so. Mr. Farnsworth, you will have to admit that I am right."

"I shall admit no such thing," exclaimed Clive hotly. "We can easily settle which is right."

"Assertion is not argument," returned Rossitur.

"It must necessarily be a matter of opinion with each until we can get at proof," said Clive. "Now my opinion is not changed by your assertion, which, as you said, is not argument."

"Probably your opinion is valuable to yourself," returned Rossitur in a civil tone, with an insolent smile which belied his voice.

"Every man's is to himself, I suppose," said Clive.

"And some men's to no one else," retorted Rossitur, the inward fury growing hotter till he saw sparks dance before his eyes.

"Fortunately neither you nor I believe that of ourselves," replied Clive.

"Who does?" exclaimed Tom, like the others ready to break in and end the silly altercation. "I say, Judge, how will your hay look this season ?"

The Judge entered into an elaborate reply, but before he was half through he discovered that the two men were still talking. Rossitur had given vent to more bitter irony and Farnsworth had answered. There were several hot speeches on either side, then Clive, recollecting himself and the absurdity of allowing a quarrel to grow out of a trifle like that, said courteously—

"After all, Mr. Rossitur, it is too warm weather for discussions ; I move that we adjourn this."

"The better plan," said the Judge. "Quite too warm to have an opinion on any subject."

"Mr. Farnsworth insults me and then says we have talked enough," exclaimed Rossitur, not making any further attempt to restrain his passion.

"I certainly had no intention of insulting you," replied Clive, "and I am at a loss to see how I have."

"What did you mean by the known tendencies of Washington officials ?"

"Just what I said—you could not possibly apply it to yourself."

"Come, come, young men," cried the Judge, secretly uneasy but affecting to laugh, "not another word. You are probably both right and both wrong."

"And the matter is of no consequence either way," added Tom.

"If I was hasty I beg to apologize, Mr. Rossitur," said Clive.

Now under ordinary circumstances Rossitur was a man of polished manners, but, as I said, when he got into one of his cold rages he went insane, and he was so now. "I regard Mr. Farnsworth's apology as little as I do his opinion," he exclaimed. "Nor can the opinion of a man be very valuable who has been trying to imitate the French dancer's affair of which I spoke."

The words fell like a bomb-shell among the party—the Judge looked pale with horror— Tom Thornton grasped his rod tight in his hand —none of the spectators knew what to say.

It was well that Clive Farnsworth had reflected and was prepared for an emergency. His first impulse was to knock the speaker down, but quick as lightning came the thought that any act of violence would ruin Ruth. He said quietly—

"I do not understand how that can apply to me."

"The rest of us do, at all events," retorted Rossitur, "and I say it makes your opinion of no worth."

"A little explanation is necessary to make me understand," said Clive, keeping firm hold of his composure, recollecting that if he could pass this crisis without giving way to anger, he might crush at once whatever slander was abroad.

"There's no explanation wanted," cried Tom Thornton ; "Mr. Rossitur must have kissed the whisky-flask too often."

Rossitur paid no attention ; he had no objection to quarrelling with Tom Thornton, but he would finish this matter first. "I can make it clear," said he ; "I mean that is what you have been doing."

Farnsworth did give one bound toward him, momentarily forgetful of every thing but the desire to punish the insult, but the Judge stepped between and pushed him resolutely back. "Don't be a fool!" he exclaimed. "Rossitur, are you mad?"

"Let Mr. Farnsworth alone," cried Rossitur; "I am quite ready to support my assertion in any way necessary."

The Judge's common-sense proceeding restored Clive's reason. "The assertion is not applicable," said he, "therefore I have nothing to resent."

"It is a pity your neighbors could not be made to think so," sneered Rossitur. "They won't visit your house, and they give that as the reason."

"My house contains no inmate except my wife," said Clive, forcing himself to speak calmly.

"Who isn't your wife!"

Clive was master of the situation. He could afford to be calm—there could no imputation of cowardice or guilt attach to him now. "So people have been saying such things, have they, Judge Hamlyn?" he asked.

"Oh, there's been gossip," said the Judge in confusion. "There is about every body."

"And women will talk," said Thornton.

"And they have talked of my wife? Yes, I do know what gossips' tongues are. Gentlemen, there is no woman, your wife or mine, who escapes. Let me say only that I have one; that there is no cause for slander unless what I may have given by leaving her alone for a time, and she was noble enough to pardon my dishonorable treatment."

Rossitur's brain cleared—he saw what he had done in his passion. Now it was ten to one he was on the high-road to a duel; the loss of Elinor Grey and irremediable harm to half his future hopes would follow. He stood irresolute, longing to spring at Clive's throat, trying to restrain his rage.

"Those few words settle and explain every thing, Farnsworth," exclaimed the Judge. "I am glad you have spoken."

"The women are already ashamed of their nonsense," said Tom, "so let it die a natural death."

"Let it," returned Clive; "I am not at all afraid of being called a coward, and I have no intention of giving stability to the slanders by acting as if they were true."

"It only remains for Mr. Rossitur to apologize," said Thornton.

"One word, gentlemen," continued Clive. "You are my friends: I have to say that your wives and the wives of all of my neighbors must stop now and forever, or you must be responsible. I have denied the slanders and am ready to prove their falsity."

"As for my wife," cried the Judge, going back to his Constantia's first opinion, "she considers yours an angel."

"And so does mine," said Thornton. "But the gossip—which never was of any consequence—is killed already. Miss Grey heard of it, and as Mrs. Farnsworth was an old friend of hers she was able to set the female minds at rest."

"And no woman, if she were a queen, could have a higher title to respect than the friendship of Miss Grey," said the Judge, lifting his hat like a gallant old knight as he was.

The councillors agreed, the fat bachelor who hated to see people quarrel agreed, and they made a chorus of praise.

"Why was no man among my old neighbors enough my friend to come and tell me?" demanded Clive.

"Oh, it's so difficult to tell such things," returned Thornton. "It's all over, Clive. My wife just sent for Miss Grey, knowing that she could tell the women the rights of the matter."

"Not worth another thought," added the Judge; "nothing is so dolefully dead as refuted gossip."

Rossitur had stood silent—uncertain how to act. "Mr. Rossitur," said Clive, "in your anger you tried to insult me; it is impossible that I should insult my wife even by replying to your coarse speech—"

"Which he didn't mean," interrupted the Judge. "Rossitur is a gentleman—so are we all, I hope. I dare say he and I both tested the nectar too early this morning."

"Then he can say so," cried Thornton.

Rossitur glared; he wanted to quarrel with him now; but he was in a position which would make the blame recoil upon himself. "I don't need any man to teach me," he said haughtily. "If Mr. Farnsworth chooses to resent my words he knows his remedy—if he chooses to be content with my saying that I am satisfied, like these other gentlemen, and am glad my words need an apology, well and good."

"I do not choose to resent them," said Clive, "and I have given my reason."

"Which is enough," said Tom.

"Perfectly satisfactory," said the Judge, and they all repeated it. "Come, you two young fellows, just think no more about the matter. As for any talk of duels, I have only to say that if you were idiots enough to contemplate one, I and the whole neighborhood would manage to put a stop to it: don't intend to lose two good men for a little absurdity."

"And Mr. Rossitur's apology renders horse-whipping out of the question," said Thornton, unable to keep back that thrust.

"I don't think I am the sort of man that ever stands in danger of such punishment, Mr. Thornton," returned he. "Do you propose to transfer Mr. Farnsworth's quarrel to yourself?"

"Farnsworth is my friend and his quarrels are mine," returned hot-headed Tom.

"Thank you," said Clive, shaking his hand; "but I believe no one ever accused me of shrinking from my part."

"Hold your tongues, the whole lot of you," shouted the Judge. "You are three of the confoundedest idiots I ever saw in my life. The matter is ended. Come, I'm old enough to be umpire."

"No going back from your decision," cried the counsellors.

"Then, young men, shake hands and thereby own the matter is over and forgotten."

Clive held out his hand—Rossitur took it.

"That's all right," said the Judge.

"And now that it is over," added Tom, "I am glad it happened—it settled every thing."

Rossitur could have beaten his own head against the stone wall. It was the first time in his life he had done a really contemptible thing, and he had not been able to carry it off by making the consequences serious.

"It is getting late," said the Judge. "I move we go home. I say, Clive, my wife and I will be over to-morrow; she wants to see your new shrubs."

"Always happy to see you both," returned Clive.

"Any body going to invite me anywhere?" demanded the fat bachelor plaintively, to raise a laugh.

"I'll give you a dinner out of pity, you fat monster," said Tom.

"And I another," added the Judge.

"And Farnsworth, will you promise luncheons innumerable?" asked the bachelor. "I'm lone and little and—" They were all laughing, but his nonsense and their merriment were checked by a sudden clatter, rattle and bang.

Clive Farnsworth was close to the wall and first saw what occasioned the tumult. A close carriage drawn by two frightened horses which the coachman was unable to control in the least, some break in the harness having left the reins useless in his hands, was dashing at a fearful pace down the little hill. The speed of the animals increased with every bound, threatening imminent danger, perhaps death, to any occupant the vehicle might have. Quick as a flash Clive leaped over the wall and sprang before the terrified creatures brandishing his rod; they swerved and plunged aside—he caught the bits in a firm grasp, not stopping the astonished brutes by main force as people do in novels and nowhere else, but with happy presence of mind backing them till one of the fore-wheels caught between two friendly young trees which held horses and carriage fast. As he did this, a face appeared at the window—a woman's face, pale and tearless. It was Elinor Grey's.

The other men hurried to his aid; the driver, with his powers of action restored, sprang down from his box; the horses were quieted enough to be content with expressing their fears by a few snorts and kicks, and Miss Grey was helped out of the carriage.

CHAPTER XXX.

HOW THE ADVENTURE HAPPENED.

Elinor Grey drove down to the Lake House according to her intention; the long-tailed ponies submitting to her guidance with exemplary amiability and the tiger resting in state behind, with his buttons more prominent than ever. She went into the hotel, and while waiting in one of the great, glaring, uncomfortable parlors for Mrs. Piffit's appearance, she heard a weeping and wailing and great gnashing of teeth in the hall.

It was Eugenia Honora Arabella Dunlavy, the maiden who had subdued Mrs. Piffit on her arrival, that caused the tumult, for she had fallen upon another evil hour in a life replete with vicissitudes and misfortunes. Honora had been accused of theft by somebody not capable of appreciating her virtues or position, and had at first loudly asserted her innocence and threatened to take the law of the land against the person who had wronged a pure-minded young creature; but when the landlord was called up and the choice given her of restoring the stolen articles or being sent to jail, she concluded to produce them. At present she was prepared to leave the house: she had brought her trunk into the hall and was waiting for a porter to carry it out. She sat upon it with her feet on her bandbox and a small mountain of bundles in her lap, and having solaced herself with a private potation, was overcome by a sense of her afflictions, and to the amusement of the black waiters began keening as loudly and dolefully as if the trunk and the budgets were the coffins that held her entire family and she keeping a private wake over their loss. "Och, me charakter—bring me back me charakter! I'm a poor, lone gurl, and its a burnin' shame to trate me so. Oh, that iver I've lived to be suspicted—och hone! Oh, the wicked wurld!" Then she waxed indignant and shrieked—"I'll be down upon 'em. Is it me they'd accuse ;; born in the County Clare of a high family that ought to be at the queen's coort av me mother had had her rights! Projuce the slantherers and I'll crush them—oh dear, oh murther! oh the dirty Yankees!"

Somebody at that juncture seemed to be forcibly ejecting her from the hall, and her shrieks and her language were appalling, but as she was carried down stairs her voice rose in a last entreaty—"Me cha-rakter—give back me cha-rakter! A poor lone crayture, born in County Clare of a high family that ought to be at the queen's coort av me mother had her rights."

Elinor walked away to the inner room in hopes to get beyond the sound of the painful yet ludicrous scene.

In the mean time Mrs. Piffit was in a state of intense excitement and delight at this unexpected visit. She rushed into Mrs. Ralston's parlor to tell her that—"Miss Grey—hmf! hmf!—Secretary's daughter—come to call on me—dear friend of mine—hmf! hmf! How do I look?"

Now the Ralston would have given shekels

and gems to be on speaking terms with Miss Grey, and she told Piffit to make use of that parlor as if it was her own, because she was going out—meaning to come back and have an opportunity to meet the visitor.

Piffit was delighted, and could not wait to send a servant down to find Miss Grey. Away she hopped, sniffing and spluttering and beginning her salutations, according to her habit, long before she reached the person for whom they were intended, so that by the time her short-sight had discovered Elinor, she was panting and puffing in the most breathless manner.

"Miss Grey! How do you do? So glad! Heard you'd come—meant to call—very kind of you to hunt me up. Sit down—do sit down—oh no, don't! Come up stairs—got a private parlor—always like to be comfortable—never mind expense. How do you do? This way." She sniffed and hissed till Elinor expected her to suffocate and was obliged to follow without having been able to open her mouth.

The private parlor reached, Mrs. Piffit was so anxious to make her comfortable and do her honor that she pulled three arm-chairs toward her at once, and danced about like a magpie with a game leg, still shouting out broken words of welcome.

"So glad—dear Miss Grey—Secretary's daughter—such pleasure! Take this chair—no, this is better—private parlor—always do—never mind expense. Sit down—sit down—hmf! hmf! Chair easy—take another? Hmf! hmf!"

"Thank you, I am quite comfortable," said Elinor, finding an opportunity to speak as Piffit's voice at length sank into a series of sniffs from lack of breath. "I called to see you about a matter which I have very much at heart and—"

"So glad to help," broke in Piffit. "Anything I can do to oblige you, Miss Grey—notices—letters—you know me. Always ready to help. Tell me what you want—take some notes now so I won't forget." She pulled a stumpy pencil and a slip of brownish-white paper from her pocket.

"There is nothing to be written," said Elinor; "you may put up your writing materials, Mrs. Piffit."

Something in her tone startled Piffit, but she did not connect its import with herself. "What is it? What is it?" she sniffed. "So glad if I can do the least thing for you, Miss Grey; so much respect—not blind worshiper of position—got position myself, he! he! But Secretary's daughter—young lady of such celebrity! Oh, what is it?"

"If you will listen a moment I will tell you," said Elinor.

"Listening now—dying to hear. Any woman you want helped? Always stand by my sex—I'm a Presbyterian."

"You are right in part," continued Elinor. "I came to speak to you in regard to a lady."

"Husband been abusing her? Always do—nasty things—men, ugh! I'll expose him—tell me all about it—expose him as sure as my name is Piffit! Tell him I'm on hand—say

I'm after him—Mrs. Piffit, the writer—everybody knows me—hmf! hmf!"

Elinor saw that decided words alone would stem the torrent of ejaculations and inquiries. "It is not her husband who has done the wrong," said she.

"Who is it? Tell me quick! I'll help—Mrs. Piffit, the writer—who's abused her?"

"You for one, Madam," returned Elinor in her iciest voice and with a level glance from the gray eyes which one needed to be very frank and honest to encounter.

Mrs. Piffit sank back in her chair aghast, and comparison fails—there is no possibility of describing what her sniffs and puffs and strangled breathings were like. "Never abuse anybody," she squealed; "I'm a Presbyterian."

"Then I hope you will remember the virtue of charity," said Elinor.

"So I do—give lots—not a bit stingy—hmf! hmf!"

"I did not mean that; I meant charity in regard to believing and uttering slanderous reports about other women."

"Always do—always am," sniffed Piffit. "Somebody's been telling lies about me. Don't believe 'em, Miss Grey;—writers are always lied about. Never slander anybody—why, I'm a—"

"I want you to listen," interrupted Elinor frigidly.

"So I will—so I do—Presbyterian!" gasped Piffit, determined to finish her sentence if she choked in the effort.

"There have been injurious reports abroad in regard to a friend of mine and—"

"The wretches! Friend of yours? Ought to be burnt. Such a wicked world! I'll expose 'em—depend on me, Miss Grey. I'm Mrs. Piffit, the writer—I'll be after them."

Elinor perceived that she was losing her temper, and the only way to deal with the creature was to be outwardly self-possessed. "If you will be careful how you help such reports, I shall be satisfied, Mrs. Piffit," said she.

"Never said a word about one of your friends—never, Miss Grey! Somebody's been telling lies—I'll be after them."

Elinor went on, heedless of her interruption. "You have invented, or at least repeated, the most atrocious slanders in regard to Mrs. Farnsworth. I have come to tell you that she is my friend and to ask your proofs."

Mrs. Piffit did not attempt to interrupt; she gave one snort and fell back in her chair limp and terrified.

"You who are a writer, who talk so much about helping your sister-women, know better than any one what a serious affair a suit for slander and defamation of character is, Mrs. Piffit," pursued Elinor, taking advantage of her breathless fright and perceiving at once that the woman's cowardice would make the victory easy.

"I want your proofs—your sources of information—perhaps you will find it easier to give them to me here privately than in a court-room with newspaper people to take down every word."

"Oh, oh! Hmf! hmf!" squealed Piffit. "Never said a word—don't know Mrs. Farnsworth. Somebody's told stories—oh, oh! I'm a Presbyterian."

"Then the more shame for you to have been guilty of such wickedness," continued her judge. "It is useless to take refuge in denial, Mrs. Piffit; I warn you of that."

"Never said a word—oh, where's a Bible? Who said I had?" groaned Piffit, looking about with a vague idea of attempting her escape at least beyond the overpowering light of those eyes.

"Mrs. Hackett told me for one," said Elinor, "and is quite ready to persist in her assertion."

"Oh, oh! Never said any more than other people any way. Now do believe me, Miss Grey. I heard the stories; maybe I've talked, but I didn't mean to—oh, do believe me."

"I will when you prove that you did not invent the tales yourself," said Elinor.

"I never invent. Mean to be careful. Oh dear me, don't let any body sue me. I've got no money—oh, oh, oh!" Piffit fairly gave way at last, and cried like a dumpy wooden doll with a squeal in it, and sniffed and spluttered till any body outside would have thought a shower-bath was in active operation in the room. She was reduced to the precise state of distress and terror in which Elinor desired to see her plunged—the threat of a suit wherein she might lose money, moved Piffit's inmost soul. "Oh, Miss Grey, don't let 'em! Tell Mrs. Farnsworth I never did—didn't mean to, anyhow. I'm a sister-writer, like her husband. Oh, I'll go away—I ain't going to bear the blame. They've all talked—the whole of them—all the women in the neighborhood—"

"But unfortunately you have been very active, Mrs. Piffit," interrupted Elinor, "and the most venomous of the stories have been traced directly to you."

"Oh, what can I do? I won't be sued—I've no money—I'd go to jail first. I'm a writer—I can't bear such things. I'm a widow woman and a Presbyterian."

"If you did not invent these stories, from whom did you hear them?" demanded Elinor.

"I've said no more than the rest—I won't be browbeaten. Oh, it's a shame, when I'm a widow and a writer and a—"

"Woman who calls herself a Christian, and does work at which a fiend might shudder, under that holy name," said Elinor Grey, again interrupting and making Mrs. Piffit feel as if the voice was raining a slow shower of hailstones upon her.

"Oh, oh! Mf! mf! Sniff! sniff! Ugh! ugh!" Only these interjections can give the faintest idea of the noise which she made in her distress.

"Tears will be of no avail, Mrs. Piffit, at present," said Elinor; "when you have confessed you may weep. I hope they will be tears of repentance at your wickedness."

"I didn't mean to be wicked; do believe me, Miss Grey. I never made the stories up—she told me.—Oh Lord, now she'll sue me too—she said she would—oh, oh!"

Piffit was so near a fit by this time that Elinor thought a little relief might be offered and the desired information more quickly obtained. "Who threatened? Mrs. Piffit, if you will give me your authority for these slanders I promise to stand between you and harm."

"Honest? And I needn't pay? I shan't be sued?"

"I give you my word of honor."

"There, then! It was Miss Laidley—any way, the old yellow woman—and Miss Laidley made her tell. Call her an angel—angel of darkness—getting me into trouble—oh, oh!" And Piffit wept more quietly.

The Angel was at the bottom of the matter after all!

"Tell me exactly what she said, Mrs. Piffit," pursued Elinor. "The only way to clear yourself is to repeat word for word as you heard the stories."

"It was the yellow woman—Miss Laidley made her tell—said she was so innocent herself—don't let her sue me! Couldn't make out how the old brown thing knew—don't let that go against me! She mixed every thing up so—seemed to be a letter from somebody or she overheard something."

"Try and recollect what they said, Mrs. Piffit. Don't cry any more just now, if you please," continued Elinor with inquisitorial calmness, and Piffit was growing so much afraid of her that she dried her eyes and tried to check her sniffs while she told her story.

When she had finished she began to howl—"Don't let her sue me—you promised—I've no money—I'm a writer and a widow woman and a—" From force of habit she was going to add the claim to piety, but the inappropriateness of the word under the present circumstances struck even her, and she paused.

"You shall not be troubled, Mrs. Piffit," said Elinor. "But I warn you that you must tell no more stories, and you must inform your acquaintance here in the hotel that you were mistaken."

"I will, I will! I'm going away anyhow. Oh, Miss Grey, I never would have said a word; never do talk about people—that's my rule—been for years—"

"Be careful and not break it again," said Miss Grey.

"So glad it isn't true! What a wretch that girl is!"

"You will not mention Miss Laidley's name, remember that," said Elinor. "If you do, I retract my promise."

"Oh, good, Lord!" groaned Piffit, falling back in the chair from which she had partially risen. "I'll be deaf and dumb—I won't mention any body's name—don't want to speak again for a month. I'm going away—it's a nasty place and I won't stay. I've my duties; I'm a writer—I'm a Fashion Editor—Mr. Holly knows me—every body knows me—ugh, ugh, oh!"

She was sobbing bitterly again when the door opened and Jack Ralston's wife sailed into the room, determined to try if she could not establish a speaking acquaintance with Miss Grey. "Why, Mrs. Piffit!" she exclaimed in astonishment. "What is the matter? Oh, you have a visitor! Dear me, it is Miss Grey! I am happy to see you." She had not been young for the last seven years; perhaps in her girlhood she had been handsome, but now she was a bony, bold-eyed woman, who rouged beyond all decency.

Miss Grey rose to go, and gave Mrs. Ralston the coldest and most annihilating of bows; she would not speak—she had an unconquerable aversion to the woman—the bold eyes and the false mouth with its ghastly smiles filled her with loathing.

But Piffit shook herself and cried between her sobs—"You've talked too—you, Mrs. Ralston! Here, now, it isn't true! You're not to say a word more about Mrs. Farnsworth. We'll all be sued, and you'll have to sell your diamonds to pay."

Elinor had begun to move toward the door as Mrs. Ralston advanced, perfectly unconscious of her presence after that slight salutation.

The woman was filled with wrath at this treatment, and when Mrs. Piffit spoke, her crafty wit understood at once that the visitor had been trying to take the Farnsworth side; and since she could not conciliate Miss Grey she would show her that she was not to be intimidated or silenced. "What do you mean, Mrs. Piffit?" called she. "Are you speaking of that creature up at Clive Farnsworth's house? Then please not to name such people in my presence; I am a married woman, and no longer a girl, but I've some modesty left yet."

Elinor moved on toward the door.

"You'll be sued! You'll be sued—you'll have to pay!" howled Piffit, whose mind was most impressed by the loss which might happen to their pockets.

"I am quite able," said Mrs. Ralston. "I am not to be frightened or bought off. I shall say what I like. It is a shame for a creature like that to be tolerated in the neighborhood."

Still on her way to the door, Elinor reflected—this adder would be more venomous than ever if she were not crushed. Even to help Ruth, Elinor could not be on speaking terms.

"A bad, vile woman," pursued Mrs. Ralston.

"Don't, don't!" moaned Piffit. "You'll be sued—we'll all be sued—and I've no money, and I'm a widow."

"I shall speak my mind freely, here and everywhere," returned Mrs. Ralston; "I am not afraid, whoever may try to uphold the guilty wretch."

Elinor had reached the door—her hand was on the knob—Mrs. Ralston was in the middle of the room glaring at her. As she uttered those words Elinor ran back—it was so quickly done that it seemed to her after she had no will in the matter—she stood before the woman and repeated in a low, rapid voice—"A cottage at Vevay—a summer of roses—ten years ago—and Tom Thornton's compliments." She had not looked at the woman while she spoke; as she paused she heard a scream. The Ralston dropped on an ottoman, from there to the hearth-rug, and went off in hysterics, drumming her feet against the fender and groaning, while Mrs. Piffit howled a chorus in the easy-chair.

Elinor took one glance at the absurd tableau and ran away, fairly frightened at her own work. She had not had much hope in Tom's oracular words, and the overwhelming effect they produced was startling. She went down stairs and was met by the tiger, who told her that one of the ponies had cast a shoe and he had taken him to the blacksmith's for repairs. Elinor could not wait, and she sent him off to procure a carriage in which she might return without further delay.

As soon as she was on the road back, she forgot the closing scene of the tragical farce in thinking of Miss Laidley. The instant that Mrs. Piffit mentioned her complicity in the matter, and, indeed, showed that she was in reality the author of the slanders, a sudden light broke on Elinor's mind. Genevieve Laidley had read the letter from Ruth which lay in Elinor's writing-desk. That morning when she kindly sought for it in Coralie's absence she had taken the opportunity to examine the contents, having in some way discovered the secret spring which opened it. She had read that letter—had perceived there was some mystery—had been unable to penetrate it thoroughly, or had made her account purposely vague that in case of discovery the means by which she obtained her information might remain concealed.

Elinor thought of her with more pity than indignation; it was painful to be forced to believe any girl so false and contemptible. She tried to forget all about the miserable business and all the miserable people connected with it. She was tired after that subjugation of the enemy and wanted to get away even from herself, with the feeling of contamination which a pure woman must have when brought into actual contact with that which is mean and vile. She remembered the letter which she had written on the preceding night—she recollected that on the morrow Leighton Rossitur would come for his answer. She began to tremble a little and to feel her hands grow cold, but she assured herself that was ridiculous nervousness and she must effectually stop such folly or she should be taking to spasms and hysterical weaknesses before she knew where she was.

Yes, on the morrow he would come for his answer, and she was glad that the season of indecision was over—very glad. She repeated the words aloud as though her mind had been an unbelieving stranger whom she was determined to convince by her firmness and persistency. She thought how it would all come about. She should put the letter in his hands and go away; after reading it he would understand how shy she felt in the unfamiliar position, and with his usual generosity would spare her any exhibition of triumph—any love-making for a time—till she became accustomed to the new life, habituated to the idea that she was no longer queen of her soul, that with her own hand she had set a seal upon her freedom. But that last reflection was unfortunate; it made her head whirl and the absurd tremor come back, and she wanted to get on to the house to be relieved from her own society.

At that instant the carriage gave a lurch from a sudden bound the horses made; she heard a clatter among the harness—a shout from the coachman trying to control the animals by his voice, through which pierced a sharp fear and dismay—then a spring—a dash; she knew that the frightened creatures were rushing on at the top of their speed, and her mind quickly took in the full danger. She did not shriek or weep; she settled herself firmly in her seat and tried to be calm. At each instant the horses bounded more rapidly along. Through the open windows she could catch glimpses of familiar turns in the road, and the feeling came over her which is said to possess the minds of drowning persons. Like a landscape made plain to its slightest detail, her whole life swept before her, and, most vividly of all, she saw the group of maple-trees on the hill, where during the bright days of the past summer she had sat while Clive Farnsworth read his tragedy to her. She thought of Rosa and Tom—of Ruth—of those who would grieve for her—and then forgot every body else in the recollection of her father and the frightful agony in store for him. There had been broken prayers for relief mingling half unconsciously with those whirling fancies which seemed so long in their duration, but now Elinor only remembered her father—she only prayed that he might be helped to bear this blow.

A new rush and dash—the cry of many voices as it sounded to her—a sudden swaying of the carriage which she believed the commencement of its destruction—then she became conscious that the motion of the vehicle was checked, only the struggles of the horses shook it in their efforts to free themselves. She looked out of the window and saw Clive Farnsworth and fell back in her seat, for the first time faint and strengthless, yet with an undefined sense of safety and protection in his presence. She saw the group of men jump over the wall and hurry up; somebody opened the door—she heard Tom Thornton's voice cry, "Great heaven, Elinor, is it you?" She tried to rise, to speak, to put out her hand—she was not weak from fear or the reaction, she was only thinking of Clive Farnsworth's face as it met hers.

"Elinor, are you hurt?" Tom repeated.

Another face appeared at the door and Leighton Rossitur was uttering her name. She roused herself as if that voice had brought her out of a strange dream, brought her back to the real life. "I am not hurt," she said, somewhat faintly; "help me out, Tom."

Rossitur made an effort to be first, but Tom thrust him quickly aside, lifted Elinor from the carriage and seated her on a log with her back against the stone wall, almost beside himself with horror, and calling dismally, "Are you sure you're not hurt? Oh, Elinor, Elinor!"

The great strong fellow was tender-hearted as a woman, and he was very near crying, hanging over her, ordering the rest to bring a medley of impossible things, and vituperating the coachman and horses in broken sentences at which he would be the first to laugh when the excitement was over.

"I'm not hurt, Tom, I'm not hurt," Elinor said, but her head was still dizzy and she leaned against the wall, holding Tom's hand fast.

The Judge and the two counsellors and Leighton Rossitur and the fat bachelor were all about her, all suggesting remedies at once and being as helpless and absurd as men generally are in the presence of a woman who is faint or ill, but Clive Farnsworth was busy helping the coachman unhitch the horses from the carriage and did not approach.

Rossitur saw a little spring in the field—he ran to it—filled the cup of a brandy-flask with water and brought it to her. "Drink this, Miss Grey," he said, in a tremulous voice.

She opened her eyes and saw him bending over her; he was pale and agitated; she felt instinctively how he suffered, but the cold tremor came back and took away the faintness. She accepted the cup, drank the water and prepared to be sensible. She was not in dream-land—she was not killed—she was in the world, the dull, actual world, and this man who was to be the most prominent feature in her future life stood beside her. "I am quite well now," she said, looking about at the frightened group and managing a smile for their benefit. "I am not going to faint or make a scene. How do you do, Judge Hamlyn?"

The old knight caught her hand and kissed it and exclaimed, and they all exclaimed divers absurd things.

Elinor wanted to get away, to have a good cry, as the strongest woman would after such danger and excitement, but she was determined not to be a goose, so she braced herself against the wall and held Tom's hand close and tried to reassure them by her seeming composure. "You foolish old Tom," said she, with a poor little smile; "I am quite safe."

"I'd have dashed my brains out against the wall if any thing had happened," exclaimed Tom, with a suspicious gurgle in his throat. "What could I have said to Rosa and Mr. Grey?"

"I am glad to see you, Mr. Rossitur," continued Elinor, holding out her hand as he stood by her, while Tom gasped at the bare possibility of what he might have had to communicate to the friend and parent till he was more alarmed still.

Rossitur took her hand and tried to speak, but could only say, "I can't believe you are safe yet."

Some way, the chill which grew more perceptible and seemed creeping about her very heart, made Elinor calm and self-possessed. "Let me forget it," she said. "Don't you all look at me as if I was a heroine."

"But where are the ponies—how came you in this old trap?" demanded Tom.

Elinor attempted to explain, but he interrupted her. "Clive Farnsworth saved your life," he shouted. "We should have stood like a set of hounds and seen you killed. Clive, Clive, come and be thanked, you old hero!"

Elinor's fingers twisted themselves closer in his; she shut her eyes for a second, but opened them as Farnsworth approached and gave him her other hand. "I do not need to thank you," she said.

"You are safe, Miss Grey, that is enough," he answered.

Leighton Rossitur stepped back and leaned against the wall—he was shaking from head to foot.

"And you have saved my life," returned Elinor. "Thank him, Tom; gentlemen—tell him—" She broke off and turned her face away; she was less strong than she had thought.

"God bless you, Clive," cried Tom, fairly giving way to the suspicious gurgle in his throat.

"A man in ten thousand," added the Judge, "He has his wits always about him to help his courage."

The counsellors and the fat bachelor joined in the chorus.

"Don't make a marvel of me," said Clive, trying to laugh; "I was only nearer than the others—those trees caught the wheel and did the business."

Rossitur wished that their contention had ended in mortal strife, that they had rolled over and over on the grass, tugging at each others' throats. He would rather that Elinor Grey had been dashed to pieces—anything would be better than that she should have been saved by this man and he forced to stand by and hear him thanked and applauded.

"The first thing now," said Clive, "is to get Miss Grey on to Alban Wood. The Judge's house is near—we can find a carriage there." He spoke quietly and brought back the other men's wits by his practical suggestion. He wanted to end the scene, and it was with great difficulty he restrained himself from rushing away, no matter how odd the proceeding might appear.

This first meeting under such circumstances was doubly hard; to have saved her life and yet remember that she was as much lost to him as ever; that there was a whole world between them—and then he could have struck himself for the reflection, and kept his mind quiet by repenting inwardly—"Ruth, my wife, Ruth. I must go back to my wife."

The others seized on the suggestion he had offered—they could act if only somebody had head enough left to say what must be done. The fat bachelor and one counsellor started on a run down the hill with their coat-tails floating out behind—the old Judge was mingling congratulations to Elinor and praise of Clive—Tom had turned to the coachman and was relieving his mind by abusing him, and Leighton Rossitur leaned over Elinor, whispering—"Are you better? I am almost mad."

Elinor saw Farnsworth move toward Tom; she recollected that he was her preserver now; she wished, even while reproaching herself for her selfishness—she wished that Rossitur had been the man to save her, that it might have made a new bond between them. "I am well again," she answered. "Do not think about it."

"If I could have saved you!" he whispered.

"Yes, I should have been glad," she answered.

Rossitur caught the words—the color came back to his face. He should conquer—she was his—Clive Farnsworth might go his way for the present—he was victor after all.

"I couldn't help it!" they heard the coachman moaning in response to Tom's animadversions. "They got frightened at a dog—they bounced up like painters and them rotten lines broke. Why, I was jest as nigh killed as the lady—ye don't seem to think o' that."

"Don't blame the poor fellow," said Clive, "you unreasonable creature."

"Tom, let him alone," called Elinor; "he has been in as much danger as I, and he was a good, brave man not to jump from his seat and leave me."

"There!" cried the coachman, brightening up and rubbing his shoulder, which had received a bruise, "the lady understands—and thank you, ma'am, and I ain't one to shirk nohow."

"Tom," called Elinor again. When Tom came up she whispered a brief command, and Tom returned to the coachman, who was still holding the horses—transformed to lambs and ashamed of their late indecorum—with one hand and rubbing his shoulder with the other.

"The lady sends you this," said Tom.

The coachman forgot his hurt and grasped the reward. If he had been an Irishman he would have let the horses run away again while he went into ecstacies and invoked the saints upon her head, but being English by descent and New England by birth and breeding, he was able to preserve his equanimity. "And thank you," said he; "and the Lord knows I wouldn't hev minded being killed to save the lady—I wouldn't, gentlemen. I've driv horses all my life, and never had no mishap afore; but gosh darn it, who'd hev thought of them old sheep a runnin' away? Why, I've often driv 'em with my eyes shut."

"Keep them open hereafter," said Tom; "that's all."

"Ketch me a trustin' of 'em! Whoa, you old

catamounts! Wal, I guess the old rattle-trap ain't bruk. Ef you gentlemen'll jest help, we'll hist that hind-wheel out and I'll git on."

Tom and Clive aided him, but the wheel saw fit to part company from a carriage that got into such scrapes, so the old vehicle had to be left staring and yawning foolishly by the side of the road, while the coachman mounted one of the horses and road off leading the other.

"I think we had better walk on," said Elinor, longing to make some change.

But they vetoed that, so she sat still.

Clive was examining the carriage as if there was something very mysterious about it which engrossed his entire attention, and Tom and the Judge hovered between him and Elinor and began sentences to each which they never finished, and the remaining counsellor was reduced to a state of silent imbecility, so that Rossitur had again an opportunity to speak unheard by the rest of the party.

"I have been twice to call," he said; "I was wretched at finding you had left no message."

"I had not heard of your visits," replied Elinor. "Mrs. Thornton and I left a card for you at the hotel yesterday—didn't you get it?"

"No," Rossitur said.

If he only had!—Now he thought if he could have spared himself that scene with Farnsworth, and he remembered with sudden shame his own part therein. Not that he was sorry—his shame gave him a fresh desire to spring on Clive and grind his face down in the dust—but Miss Grey would hear of what had passed and it might make him trouble. What was he to say—how convince her that he had been provoked to madness—that he had not been mean and base? But there was no time to say any thing, for at that instant the long-tailed ponies and the basket-carriage appeared with Cupid enthroned on the cushions and handling the reins with dignified ease.

"Here's our basket, Elinor," called Tom; "we are all right now."

He ordered Cupid to stop and alight, and Cupid obeyed, his dignity lost in amazement at the sight of the group, with Miss Grey seated on a log and the cup of a brandy-flask at her feet. But nobody paid a due regard to Cupid's feelings by explaining the mystery, and he held the long-tailed ponies in wondering silence while Rossitur helped Miss Grey into the basket, and then he felt the tiger in his soul get ascendency over Cupid at an order from Tom. For Tom had lost his meerschaum pipe, and as he had been devoting his energies to its coloration during the past twelve months, and it was a present from his Rosa, he had no mind to lose it. Cupid was ruthlessly ordered to search every inch of ground between the road and the trout-brook and to bring back the pipe if he had any desire to breathe vital air longer, and was ignominiously banished down the path.

Tom took his seat. Rossitur kept his station to the last moment by Elinor, while the Judge uttered farewells, and the counsellor, grown imbecile under excitement, tried to smile. But Rossitur need not have feared that Clive would attempt to rob him of that last moment; he stood aloof, contenting himself with lifting his hat to Miss Grey and speaking from a little distance. As soon as the carriage drove off, he said—"I must say good-day, gentlemen—I am late."

He jumped over the wall on the upper side of the road, and took a hill-path which led into his own grounds, and the rest sat down to wait till the departed counsellor and fat bachelor should return, to be discomfited and enraged by discovering that they had had their pains for the satisfaction of giving their male friends an easy drive home.

Cupid, swelling with indignation and a sense of injury that might have moved Venus to sympathy for her son's namesake, took his way toward the trout-brook, and well-disposed as he was in general to his master, it was fortunate that nobody heard his remarks and opinions on that occasion. While he was searching about the bank, up came the ubiquitous Tad Tilman, the bad boy, who had been out on a trouting expedition of his own and had met with better success than the gentlemen, as was proved by the long row of speckled beauties that he had confined by their gills to a forked twig which he swung easily to and fro as he came up the path. "Hallo, what you at?" he called. "Why, if it ain't Buttons! What the dickens are you squatting and cavoorting round that way, like a lame rabbit, for?"

Cupid was in no mood to endure patiently that taunting name, which the ribald youth of the village had bestowed upon him, and he retorted—"Mind your business and I'll mind mine, scarecrow."

"I've finished my business," replied Tad good-naturedly; "so I'll help you about yourn."

"I don't want your help," said Buttons. "Just you cut your stick and let me alone; you ain't fit company."

"For Mr. Thornton's buttoned boy," said Tad. "You see I want to improve by your example, you young highflyer. My, Buttons, how red you be in the face!—how fat you do grow, Buttons! It's my belief you drink too much beer, Buttons—it's very swelling; you'll be getting the apoplex some day. Reelly now, Buttons, I shall have to speak to your marster—your marster"—here a whistle as if calling an invisible dog—"and have him provide you with a little sour wine to thin you out here and there. You're too fat, Buttons, and you're fat in the wrong places; you're lumpy. Reelly now, Buttons, ain't you ever afeered of bursing something?"

Buttons had not been silent during that harangue; he assailed the lean boy in violent language, and ended by calling him a sneak and a bully and a coward. Now it was only the week before that Tad had soundly thrashed two larger boys on Cupid's account, for Cupid was not courageous though he bristled well, and Tad felt

L

this conduct to be ungrateful ; moreover, the instant he caught sight of Cupid groping about in the grass he had known what he sought for and meant to put him out of pain.

"You're a sneak and a coward and a thief," said Cupid wildly.

"Wal," said Tad slowly, "I never stole any of your buttons at least. Maybe I'm a sneak, but all things considered, I wouldn't be the one to say it if I was you."

"Cock - a - doodle - doo !" squeaked Cupid. "Do you think I'm afraid of you ? Why you've been stealing fish out of Mr. Thornton's brook now."

"That's your marster you mean. My pooty Buttons, brooks is free in this land ; every thing is free axcept fat boys that button themselves to marsters. You're a gitting very red, Buttons, very red—take a fool's advice and don't bust nothing."

"I'll bust your head !" exclaimed the enraged Cupid.

"I wouldn't," said Tad; "you might want me agin to keep the butcher's boy off. You must learn to look round two corners, Buttons."

Cupid responded with such violent threats and gestures that Tad, though preserving his equable demeanor, laid his string of trout on the grass and said—

"Buttons, you've got a convenient spot about you that I axpect I shall kick in a minute. Buttons, wages and high living and fat is getting too much for you ; rcely, I shall have to speak to your marster about the sour wine ;—he's ben a good marster to you—here Cæsar, Cæsar, good dog !" followed up by a prolonged whistle.

Cupid's rage overcame his cowardice ; he dashed at Tad, who quietly stepped aside and Cupid, hitting his foot against a log, rolled over upon the ground.

"Why, Buttons," said Tad, "hain't you no more regard for marster's clothes than that ? I'm astonished at you ; I am indeed."

Cupid began to gather himself up, but Tad gave a warning shake of his fist that made him roll back.

"Lie still and rest, Buttons," said Tad, "and reflect—the tracts always tells us to reflect. I'm going to sing you a little song I composed about a boy with buttons, and at the end of each verse there's a chorus that you must sing."

"I won't—I don't know it."

"It's only 'Spare my buttons,' that's all. Now here goes—when I lift my hand so, you jine in—'Spare my buttons.' If you do it, we shan't fall out, but if you don't, I axpect there'll be a coolness between our families that'll be bad for the buttons. Now then !"

He actually sang several verses of a tuneful melody illustrative of the career of a fat boy who wore many buttons, and at the end of each couplet, by a shake of the fist, compelled Cupid to utter the chorus, which he did in a wail of mingled rage and fear.

"You're improving," said Tad, stopping at length ; "your voice is too much under your ribs, but by the time we've sung the whole two hundred and twenty verses, you'll come out as fresh as a cat-bird."

"Let me up—I want to go home," sobbed Cupid.

"You ain't rested yet; lie still, my pretty Buttons. Now I'm going to do a bit of conjurin'—I'm a dabster at it. Buttons, you was sent for marster's meersham pipe—you lost your temper instead of finding the meersham—when I come up you fell foul o'me, O Buttons. I'm going to smoke you now—it's the only way to save you. I wish I had a little saltpetre, but never mind. No, don't you stir, Buttons—I feel the sperit move me to do you a little good. I'll smoke, and if you're very quiet maybe I'll sing a little more." He pulled out of his pocket the pipe Tom had lost and a bag of tobacco, and made preparations to smoke.

"I'll tell Mr. Thornton you stole his pipe and was smoking it," cried Cupid.

"I'm free, Buttons; marster wouldn't mind a fellar-voter smoking his meersham. It's only them that's had liberty buttoned out on 'em as mustn't."

He lighted the pipe and smoked tranquilly for some time, making a sign with his fist whenever Cupid moved, which caused the luckless youth to crouch back on the ground, more subdued and crest-fallen than he had ever been in his life.

"It's gitting pooty late," Tad said at last. "Buttons, you take this pipe and this bag and carry 'em to your marster—you can give Mr. Tilman's compliments ; and Buttons, I axpect he'll lick you for being gone so long. I shall inquire, and if he hain't, why then, Buttons, on next Sunday afternoon I shall be leisuresome, and I'll give you the dod-derndest, all-firedest licking that ever a fat Buttons took if you show your face in the village."

Tad picked up his string of fish and walked away whistling Yankee Doodle, and Cupid brushed the stains off his plumage and made the best time possible home without stopping to look behind, registering a secret vow never to offend the bad boy again.

CHAPTER XXXI.

A TIMELY DISCOVERY.

By the time the long-tailed ponies had carried Elinor and Tom out of sight of the party, Elinor began to reproach herself with not having thanked Farnsworth, with having shown a coldness that must look like base ingratitude. "Oh, Tom," she said, "do you thank him. Tell him how grateful I am—tell him how papa—"

"Yes, yes, dear. Clive, you mean ? What a trump he is ! I tell you, Elinor, there's nobody like him. But you're sure you are not hurt ?"

"Quite sure. I don't think I was much frightened until it was all over," she replied.

"Clive saw the horses and was in the road and had stopped them before the rest of us had sense enough to know what was the matter," pursued Tom. "He's as brave as a lion. Any other man would have hesitated half a minute, and O Elinor, that would have been—Lord bless me, I daren't think!"

Elinor could not be sorry to get away from the subject; she wanted to forget Clive Farnsworth for the time.

"And to see his dignity during that quarrel," continued Tom, forgetting that he talked Sanscrit to her. "I tell you we all felt that he had true courage and respected him—"

"What quarrel?" interrupted Elinor.

"Oh, you don't know. I say, Elinor, that Mr. Rossitur of yours is an infernal villain—I always believed it—Rose too. I say he is—there!" fairly shouted Tom, giving way to one of his excitements.

"You must be crazy. What do you mean?" cried Elinor.

"I'd three minds to mash his insolent face myself," pursued he. "Clive would have murdered him like a dog only he has such good sense; and O Elinor, he has settled every thing—there'll be no more talk."

"Tom," she exclaimed, "if you don't want to drive me mad explain what you mean." She was shaking violently and deathly pale; Tom began to waste more time in self-reproaches.

"What an ass I am when you are so excited. There—I—"

"Tell me the whole story," said Elinor, in the old imperious tone.

"I will—that's better. You ought to know it. I won't keep that young devil's secrets for one—I say he is a villain."

"Do you mean Mr. Rossitur, Tom?" asked Elinor, in a voice slow and weak with sudden terror. "Did he quarrel with Mr. Farnsworth?"

"Yes, the rascal! Out with that slander point-blank! I tell you what, Elinor, if you ever had it in your mind, as Rosa feared—"

"Tom, if you don't tell me the whole story plainly, I'll jump out of the carriage and find somebody that will," cried Elinor.

"I'll tell you; sit still," exclaimed Tom. "Wait—let me see how it was. I needn't exaggerate—he behaved bad enough, the hound!"

Tom was frightened still by the recollection of Elinor's danger, he was full of wrath, and he had been made irritable beforehand. In the silent watches of the night, while he was sleeping the sleep of the just and dreaming that he was catching trout of fabulous dimensions out of a river of thick cream, Rosa poked him in the side with her forefinger and brought him away from his sport. She could not sleep, and she could not keep her fears to herself any longer; she had to tell Tom about the word Elinor had written on the card and pour forth her groundless aversion to Rossitur, which was the stronger because it had no foundation; and she would not permit Tom to go back in search of the trout until she had infected him with her dread.

Tom told the whole story, and did not spare Rossitur, although he tried hard to make his account scrupulously correct. "Now what do you think?" he cried. "Isn't the man a villain? Mustn't he, in spite of his graces and his pleasant ways, be a—well, I won't swear—a tremendous villain with a big blank before it, to speak of any woman like that—to give mouth to such suspicions?"

Elinor could not speak. The excitement, the danger, this new horror upset her completely, and she began to cry.

"Great heavens!" cried Tom. "You didn't care for him, Elinor?"

She shook her head and sobbed. "No; but, Tom—I was going to marry him!"

Tom nearly upset the basket with the bound he made, and the ponies started as if they thought Old Nick was driving them. "Marry him!" he faltered.

"I ought n't to have said it. I'm not mean enough to tell when men make love to me. But I am so surprised and bewildered, and you are like a good brother to me, Tom; only you must never repeat this even to Rose," sobbed Elinor, disproving her claims to being a resolute and strong-minded young female by weeping bitterly.

"Don't cry, dear," pleaded Tom; "you know I can't see a woman cry. There, just tell me—it will do you good, and even Rosa shall never know."

"He was so kind, Tom, and I was so lonesome; for I am a poor, weak idiot after all, Tom. He would wait—I was to give him an answer to-morrow—and O Tom! the letter is actually written."

"But it is not too late. You don't love him?"

"I see how wicked it would have been. I am so glad to be free! Oh, I'm a bad woman!"

Tom soothed her as if it had been his baby of a Rose instead of the stately Elinor who showed so unreservedly what a womanly creature she was under her pride. "You are saved any way," said he. "O Elinor, we may bless that quarrel. No wonder you believed in him—so smooth and specious—but he is not to be trusted."

"O Tom, Tom!" she cried, "is there no honor left among men? I am sick of every thing. Why, the whole world turns out false and black."

"No wonder you feel like that," replied Tom, "after these women's work and this added."

"But Ruth is safe now, that is one comfort," said Elinor. "With us and Mrs. Hamlyn to take her side, nobody will talk any more."

"They can't, you see. Clive owned there had been some blame—his, you know. I suppose he must have left her for a while or kept his marriage secret; but it is no matter what—they are all right now."

Elinor dried her eyes and was able to be quiet again, and as the keen pang of suffering at finding a friend whom she had trusted gave place to indignation, any hope for forgiveness to Leighton Rossitur passed away forever. "I am so glad, so glad," she repeated. "Tom, if I had married him and found too late that he was capable of a mean action, what should I have done?"

"Why, you'd have gone desperate. You couldn't have borne it as some women would. I tell you what, Elinor, I haven't brains to boast of, but I can read character a little, and I warn you that if you can't love somebody you had better live an old maid till you are a female Methusaleh."

"And so I will," said Elinor. "I am past danger now."

By this time they had reached the avenue leading to Tom's house, and there was no more conversation. Rosa was sitting on the piazza as they drove up and quite forgot the remains of her headache in the account of Elinor's accident and Clive's bravery, which Tom related at length. She hugged Elinor and praised Clive—she hugged Tom, and she was ready to scream at the bare idea of Elinor having been in such peril, and ran back to put her arms about her again and be certain that she had her there.

As Elinor would not go to bed they drank cups of tea, and Elinor lay on a sofa and the Doves rejoiced over her and talked, and Elinor had to tell how successful her efforts had been, and Rosa and Tom shrieked at the description of the final tableau. Then Tom must relate how well Clive had behaved in the affair with Rossitur, and Rosa belabored the culprit to her heart's content, and was in raptures when Elinor assented to her condemnation. While they sat there, the Idol's carriage drove up and the Idol and the Angel appeared, full of spirits, having decided to stop an instant on their way home from an airing.

Rosa told of Elinor's accident, and the Idol fired sesquipedalian words of horror, and the Angel did theatricals, and it was all as well done as possible.

Elinor had kept back the facts she had learned in regard to Miss Laidley; she never would reveal them except to the creature herself, and the whole thing had better be ended that day. After a little she said—"Genevieve, I want you to go up stairs with me, please—if Mrs. Hackett can wait."

She spoke so pleasantly that the Angel did not take alarm, and the Idol cried out—"If my time were Golcondas it should be at your disposal, dear Miss Grey. You are a heroine now; and oh, to think that our Apolloite should have been your preserver—your Atlasian shield —he has added new wreaths to his bays."

"And I want to show Mrs. Hackett the alterations we have been making in the greenhouses," said Tom; "so you young ladies can gossip as long as you like."

"Indeed we never gossip, Mr. Thornton," said the Angel. "Dear Elinor is too grand, and I am too much a child."

"The most artless blossom," cried the Idol as the Laidley followed Elinor out of the room. "It is beautiful to see them together; Miss Grey so peeress and our Angel so child-like— sweet comparison of lovelinesses. Oh, for a poet's lyre!"

"There's a liar in the case at all events," said Tom, and the Idol, as usual missing the point, assented rapturously.

Elinor led the way up to her dressing-room, and the Angel said —"I wanted to see you. It was so good of you to bring me here. Darling Elinor, I have such hosts of things to tell you."

"And I have something to say to you," replied Elinor very seriously; "I want you to listen with patience."

"Oh, dear me, is it any thing doleful?" cried the Angel, a little startled by Elinor's tone. "Don't tell me if it is—I can't bear doleful things. I'm a baby, you know. Besides, I'm nervous yet about your accident—see how my hand shakes. And Mr. Farnsworth saved you —isn't it romantic? Oh, I wish I could be run away with and have somebody save me."

"You must listen to me," said Elinor more firmly. "I have something very serious to say."

"I'll go off—oh, I won't hear serious things. Now don't look so severe. You're going to scold—I know you're going to scold."

"No, Genevieve," she answered sadly; "I am afraid scolding would be thrown away."

"Oh, I know it would! I should cry and forget all about it—I'm such a baby. There, darling Elinor, never mind the serious things. I want to tell you about—"

"I am in earnest, Genevieve," she interrupted. "I advise you to listen to me. You can be something besides a baby when you wish."

"I'm going to run away—I will!" cried Miss Laidley, inwardly frightened, but persevering in the infantile line. "I shall go down and tell them you wanted to scold me."

She rose from her chair, but Elinor laid a hand on her dress. "If you do go," she said, "you will force me to say these things before them all, and I have no wish to expose you, Miss Laidley."

"Expose me? What do you mean?" exclaimed the girl, forgetting her childishness and flushing into anger. "Let me tell you, Miss Grey, I won't hear such words from any body! You think because I am lonely and childish that you can trample on me, but I won't endure it."

Elinor waited patiently till she got through, then she said—"I have always been kind to you, Miss Laidley, but in this matter—"

"I shan't listen! Let go my dress!—Oh, be good! There, dearest, I was cross," she cried, going back to the old tricks. "Please don't scold—I haven't been in mischief. Indeed I'm a good little thing; and I love you so much, and I pray for you every night."

"Oh, Genevieve, stop," implored Elinor, sickened by the hypocrisy of those last words. "I have seen Mrs. Piffit to-day—she has told me every thing."

Miss Laidley sat down in her chair—she scented the full danger, but her wit was quick and her craft almost inexhaustible. She felt her heart thump violently against her side, but she controlled her face perfectly and said with a pretty wonder, "I don't know what you mean, Elinor."

Elinor was sick of dissimulation; she seemed to meet it at every turn, and it was impossible to endure any thing more that day. "Miss Laidley," she said quickly, feeling her own cheeks glow with shame for the girl who sat unmoved, "you may as well put aside these artifices. This is a painful conversation to me, but I shall go through with it."

"Quite in the dark am I," interrupted the Angel with a coo; "a babe in the wood, and you looking at me as fierce as if you were the wicked uncle in disguise."

"To enlighten your mind, let me tell you that Mrs. Piffit has confessed her share in the slanders about Mrs. Farnsworth, and has told me that they came from you."

"Then she is a false, wicked woman! I never told her a thing."

"But you made Juanita. Oh, don't prevaricate. If you could know how weary I am of deceit—how ready to believe you have not been deliberately malignant—I am sure you would be honest."

"Do you choose to believe Mrs. Piffit instead of me?" exclaimed Miss Laidley, doing virtuous indignation and injured innocence combined, in a way that would have been very effective under other circumstances. "I scorn to defend myself! I have loved you, Elinor Grey. I am your father's ward—a helpless, unprotected orphan. Insult me if you will—injure me if you choose—I am alone in the world." She buried her face in her hands and sobbed convulsively, while she cast about for some loop-hole of escape out of the dilemma.

"That very fact should have made you charitable toward other women," said Elinor; "your loneliness might have made you gentle to them."

"Father, father!" moaned Miss Laidley from behind her sheltering hands, "come and protect your poor Evangel—father, come!"

Elinor's hesitation to let the girl know how fully her baseness was discovered vanished before this last bit of acting, which did seem disgusting as well as wicked. "If that father can see you, Genevieve," she said, "think how he grieves to know you persist in this useless falsehood."

"Insult me—outrage me—I have no protector!" sobbed Miss Laidley. "Stab me to the soul! Oh, kill me, you cruel woman! A dagger in my heart would not hurt as your wicked words do."

"It is folly to prolong this scene," said Elinor. "You must understand that the utter falsity of those stories has been proved—you will disgrace yourself completely if you ever say another word."

Miss Laidley ceased sobbing and showed her face—the blue eyes were giving out their yellow sparks. "The stories were true!" she exclaimed. "Bah, Elinor Grey, you may hoodwink the whole world except me! They are true and you know it, and for some purpose of your own you want to uphold the vile wretch! Perhaps because you can't have Clive Farnsworth visit you unless you visit her."

Elinor was not angry—the girl was beneath contempt at that moment. "I am not surprised at such ideas suggesting themselves to your mind, Miss Laidley," she said, "and nothing could punish you so much as the fact of knowing, as you do, that they are miserably false."

"Perhaps!" sneered Miss Laidley. "Oh, Elinor Grey, I am childish and silly, but I am not blind."

"Young lady," said Elinor, "stop where you are. Not a word more—not a syllable of insolence further, or I will expose you unhesitatingly."

"What will you expose, pray?" cried Miss Laidley, still hoping that bravado would carry her through.

"You opened my writing-desk—you read a letter from Mrs. Farnsworth, misconstrued its contents, and made up this falsehood." Miss Laidley gasped and was silent; she had not expected this crowning blow, and her craft failed for an instant. "What your motive was I do not care to know," pursued Elinor; "whether to revenge yourself on me for some fancied wrong, or from pure wickedness, is no matter now." Miss Laidley had taken refuge in sobs. "Remember, I am not threatening idly. If you will be silent I shall not interfere with you, but if you persist you must bear the shame."

Did you ever see a rat in a corner? It flies about like lightning till it has tried every hope of escape, and failing, it makes a vicious dash at the assailant. There was no trace of the Angel left in the creature—she looked and acted exactly like the cornered rat. "Any way you would ruin that woman," she exclaimed; "if you told about the letter, every body would know the stories were true."

"I said you had misconstrued the letter. Mrs. Farnsworth alluded vaguely to some past trouble—her husband has to-day explained that to the satisfaction of the best men in the neighborhood; you are powerless, Miss Laidley."

Miss Laidley went into spasms without further remark. She tore the crocheted thing on the back of the chair to bits—she stamped her feet—she choked—she shrieked, and Elinor sat perfectly quiet and offered no assistance or intervention. At last Miss Laidley began to make dashes at the table-cover, and Elinor said, "I would not destroy any thing else—Mrs. Thornton may ask how it happened."

Even spasms had no effect, so the mermaid

came out of them and cowered down in her chair, a miserable, shameless culprit. "What are you going to do about it?" she asked suddenly.

"That depends on yourself."

"Oh, you hate me; so does Mrs. Thornton, the nasty cat; a pair of you! I'm younger and prettier than you, and you hate me and will be glad to do me harm in any way you can."

"I have no intention of saying one word, Miss Laidley, unless you compel me."

"A likely story! I'm not to be duped. Any woman is always glad to hurt another."

"Heaven knows in what school you learned such opinions," returned Elinor, full of horror and sorrow to think that a girl so young and fair could be hopelessly astray in every thought. "I only want you to promise me that not by word or look will you again try to prejudice any body against Mrs. Farnsworth."

"If I don't promise?"

"You will force me to tell the whole story, and oblige my father to throw up his guardianship."

"I don't believe he can. I won't have it!" cried she.

"You will find that it can and will happen."

"And if I do promise?"

"Then I promise to forget the whole business; and no matter what you may pretend to believe, you know that I always tell the truth."

"Oh yes; but that horrid Piffit will say I told her and set the Farnsworths and every body against me."

"There is no danger. I frightened her effectually; she will not mention your name."

"Oh, you dear Elinor," exclaimed Miss Laidley, brightening up, "that was so good of you; how thoughtful you are! There, let the whole thing go."

"You give me your word?"

"Yes; but you wouldn't take it. Gracious, I want to forget the whole business! That's the surest proof that I shall hold my tongue," cried she, in all sincerity and innocence this time.

"Let us both forget it," said Elinor.

Suddenly Miss Laidley turned into a penitent angel, and flung herself at Elinor's feet, writhing and sobbing. "I did look at the letter," she cried. "Oh, I'm so sorry—I've had no peace since. The desk came open in my hand and the letter fell out." Elinor did not mention the fact of its closing with a spring; it was useless to force her to more falsehoods. "I am so sorry. I love you, Elinor, I love you! Indeed I'm only thoughtless. You won't tell your father?"

"I will tell no human being."

"And you'll be good to me, and act as if you had forgotten, and not snub me; and you'll give me parties next winter?"

"I promise. I will forget if you will let me; at least neither by word nor look shall you think I remember."

"I don't care then. If you act just as usual I can forget all about it—that's my way—so it's all over."

Miss Laidley rose from her knees and flew to the glass, radiant, and began arranging her hair. "You haven't any powder? Never mind, I don't dare use it by day-light. My eyes aren't red?"

Elinor watched her in silent amazement: here was a new revelation of womanhood with a vengeance. The moment the fear of exposure was removed she cared no more about the matter—forgot her shame in exultation—and would never think about it any more, that was a literal truth: if Elinor gave the semblance of forgetfulness she would be content.

"But I say," she exclaimed, making the dimple in her chin deeper by pressing her little finger into it, "I do wonder you took all this trouble."

"What do you mean?"

"Why, I should have thought you would have been delighted to see Mrs. Farnsworth pulled to pieces, because he was an admirer of yours."

"They are both my friends, Genevieve. Don't try to talk about what you can not possibly understand," said Elinor with perfect good nature. She sat wondering whether the creature had any soul, any womanly sensitiveness, or was a mischievous Undine whom no spell had been able to give a spirit in keeping with her loveliness.

"I won't," said Miss Laidley. "I'm a funny little thing, now am I not? I sometimes wonder at myself. Let's go down stairs; I'm ready. Don't let them think we have had a quarrel, you dear, you. Is my new bonnet pretty? The Duchess gave it to me. Oh, Elinor, she gave me her emerald necklace! I never call her names now. I'm so glad you warned me. I should have missed such oceans of pretty things if I made her angry—the dear old soul."

Elinor followed her in amazed silence; and they were greeted by acclamations from the Idol, who had learned from Tom, not about the quarrel, but the fact that Clive had explained matters.

"Perfectly satisfactory," said the Idol.—Every body else would say the same, although the explanation had been so vague. But you see people are like sheep—they all jump one way—they only want somebody to jump first in the right direction.—"I am sublimated with delight!" continued she. "That lovely Heben and that adorable lord of the lute."

"You know, dear Duchess, I said all the while she was charming, and that I didn't believe a word, though I could not understand," cried Miss Laidley, completely transformed into an angel once more.

"Always, always, my precious," returned the forgetful Idol, and believed she was telling the truth.

Rosa Thornton made a private grimace at Tom; she said afterward she should have had a happening of some sort if she had not relieved her feelings in that way.

"Just think," pursued the Angel; "that abominable Piffit tried to make Elinor believe I told her those horrid stories."

"The reptile, the wretch!" cried the Idol.

"Yes, indeed; when she told you before me, and I couldn't half understand."

The Idol was furious, but Miss Laidley soothed her. "We must forgive her," she said sweetly; "forgive those who persecute us; I wish her no harm."

The Idol was enchanted; even Tom thought such entire innocence and sweetness must be natural, while Rosa, not to be deceived, swelled with wrath, and Elinor sat more bewildered than ever by the creature's assurance.

"Don't think about her, dear Duchess," she said, when the Idol flung huge anathemas at the absent Piffit; "I am glad she has told fibs and tried to injure me. I am certain now that I can forgive—we never can tell till we are tried, you know, Mrs. Thornton."

"No," said Rosa, and very uncompromising and unforgiving she looked.

"Upon my word," exclaimed Tom honestly, "there are not many girls who would bear it as well as you do, Miss Laidley."

Rosa annihilated him with a glance of unutterable contempt. Tom knew that he had been an ass.

"I do feel it," replied the Angel, with a tremor in her voice; "it makes me remember that I am a homeless, fatherless girl."

"My Angel!" cried the Idol.

"But I won't think about it," she continued. "I know you love me, dear Duchess, and so does Elinor."

Tom saw Rosa with a face of intense disgust making an effort as if to swallow something very nasty indeed.

"We'll never think about it again," said the Angel, seeing that she had blinded Tom at least, and not wishing to carry the matter too far.

The Idol rose to depart, and the Angel kept her quite in the background by her vivacity and sweetness. "Good-bye, darling Elinor," and she kissed her.

"The loving blossom!" cried the Idol.

"Good-bye, Mr. Thornton—I'll shake hands with you because I believe you do like me a little, if I am silly and childish."

"Indeed," said Tom, "I won't be slandered; I never thought you silly."

"And I like to be thought a child," cooed she.

"I know I'd like such a charming child always near," said Tom, quite subdued and shaking her hand warmly. "I hope you will come often to see us, and always be childish, Miss Laidley."

She beamed and went up to Rosa. "I won't offer to kiss you, because you don't like me a bit, dear Mrs. Thornton," said she archly.

"My sweet, what preposterousness!" cried the Idol.

"She doesn't," laughed the Angel. "Now be honest, Mrs. Thornton—do you?"

Rosa was a little taken aback, especially as she was in her own house, but she recovered herself. "I think you are very pretty, and the men think you are charming," she laughed.

"Now, you know in your heart you don't care a pin whether I actually like you."

"But I like you," said the Angel, "and I do want to be loved. I shall kiss your hand—oh, the pretty hand with rose stains inside!" and she kissed it in a very graceful way.

They departed after that; and when Tom returned to the room, Rosa exclaimed—"I give in! She did it well. Of all little imps that ever I saw, that Angel is the most cunning."

"Now, Rosa," said Tom; "I don't believe she's a bad little thing."

"Oh, my dear," returned Rosa, with contemptuous pity; "you are only a man;—you can't help being a dunce—one expects it. And it is fun to see how the Idol believes in her."

"Let the child alone," said Elinor.

"Child!" repeated Rosa. "Bah! That girl has lived five hundred thousand years, and she's the quintessence of every thing that's artful. You may be silent, you may deny it, but all heaven and earth wouldn't make me believe that she has not slandered Ruth Farnsworth worse than the others have all put together—there!"

Rosa retired from the subject with dignity, and requested that Miss Laidley's name might not be mentioned in her presence again that day, because it made her head dizzy to think about her.

After dinner Tom went over to Judge Hamlyn's place, according to promise, to make one at a euchre-party, for the rapid little game was among the Judge's weaknesses.

Rosa and Elinor would have the evening to themselves, and as Tom was taking leave and being absurdly funny up to the last, Elinor suddenly recollected that Mr. Rossitur would be certain to call before bed-time in order to inquire after her, and she was in no state of mind to see him. "We are not at home to any body, are we, Rose?" she asked.

"No indeed; not to the choicest ghost that ever Home called up," returned Rosa. "Tom, be sure and give orders; and O Tom, do dispatch that Stupid—I can't stand him about another week—I'd rather answer the door myself."

"And uncommon well you'd look," said Tom, "with a white apron and a frilled cap; and I'd be sure to make you say 'the master.'"

Tom departed and the ladies ensconced themselves in Elinor's dressing-room to be certain of security from any blunder Stupid might see fit to make.

It was still early when Elinor's suspicion was verified. Leighton Rossitur drove up, too anxious to wait, and confident from Elinor's manner when they parted that his visit would not be unwelcome. Unfortunately for him Elinor Grey had gone through a new experience since. Stupid was confident that he made no blunder this time—Mr. Thornton was out and the ladies had gone to their rooms. No, Miss Grey was not ill — only fatigued, and could not be intruded upon even with messages.

Rossitur had to make the best of it and be content to wait until the following day—the day to which for so many months he had been looking forward, and which now brought triumph so near. The man's will and love of success had a part in the smile which lit his face as he drove from the door. In his whole life he said to himself he had never failed, and he should not in this dearest, best aim. He had found the card at the hotel with that word written on it which puzzled Rosa Thornton and put her out of spirits, and it was intelligible to him — an omen of hope.

Presently Rosa's maid came up stairs and gave Elinor the card he had left. She glanced at the name and saw written under it—"To-morrow?" She too remembered what to-morrow was to have been, what it had so nearly brought, and shivered with the dread of an escaped danger, worse to contemplate than the death which had that morning seemed close upon her,

"Who is it?" Rosa asked.

Elinor told her, and absently twisted the pasteboard in bits and let them fall upon the floor.

Rosa was glad to go to bed early, for she had not entirely recovered from the effects of her headache, and Elinor was still more glad to be alone, that she might get through with the task before her and have done forever with the dream which during the long spring she had tried so conscientiously to cherish into brightness. She took out of its hiding-place the letter written on the previous night. The very sight of it made her tremble; she could not read it; she grew cold to remember that she could have made the open, honest avowal she had there done. She held it over the lamp-chimney until it took fire, and threw it down, looking on with a feeling of relief as the leaves curled and crackled in brief flame and lay a little heap of black ashes on the hearth. She could not have any interview with that man; she could not trust herself while her indignation and the pain of knowing herself deceived in a friend were so fresh in her mind. She wrote another letter: even that was a difficult business. Several times she was obliged to tear up unfinished pages, because her angry feelings showed themselves in some sharp sentence, and she wished the letter to be perfectly distinct and free from emotion of any kind, lest, noting that it had been written under excitement, he should hold fast to some hope. It was finished at last, put in the envelope and sealed, and she sat holding one of her old vigils until the clock struck twelve and Tom's step in the hall roused her. She went out and called him softly; gave him the letter, and begged him to see that it reached its destination at the earliest possible hour, and Tom carried it off in his hand with much silent exultation, for he felt certain as to the nature of its contents.

Elinor had done with Leighton Rossitur forever! She said the words over and over, and the thrill of joy at once more finding her freedom beyond danger warned her of the suffering she would have brought upon herself had it not been for this gracious interposition of some power higher than her own will. But all the while her heart ached; she was more alone than before. It was easy enough to forget the lover who proved unworthy, but it was sad to lose the friend in whom she had trusted.

CHAPTER XXXII.

THE LETTER AT BREAKFAST.

LEIGHTON ROSSITUR was never an early riser, and he liked to enjoy the idleness of his holiday to its full extent, so it happened that he was sitting in his own room, sipping his chocolate and enjoying the bright morning at his open window, when Miss Grey's letter was brought in. He recognized the superscription at a glance, and took the note eagerly. Its arrival caused him no alarm; he was not surprised that she had written and avoided an interview which her peculiar reticence made difficult to her. He had wakened from pleasant dreams, with the thought of the day full in his mind, and he was glad to be greeted by this epistle. He knew quite well what the pages would contain—she would trust to her friend. He should shield her and teach her to be grateful to the man who loved her. And she should love him !— his pale cheek flushed under that thought, and the bright smile curved his lip—love him with all her heart and soul, all her pride and strength, and that man whom he hated should see and writhe under the knowledge. Even with those feelings in his mind he could not keep away the baser emotion.

He held the sealed letter while he reflected. He was in no haste; it pleased his sensuous nature to enjoy this pleasure to the utmost. The pretty English envelope with the monogram in blue mediæval letters that nobody could have deciphered but the ghost of some old monk who had passed his monotonous years in illuminating manuscripts; the marked individuality of the hand in the superscription; the faint odor of violets which he recognized—he enjoyed the whole.

One of the eager impulses to which he was subject suddenly interrupted this slow tasting of anticipated happiness: he tore the envelope with reckless fingers to get at its contents, as he might some day have torn Elinor Grey's heart to get at its love, if Fate had not interposed. He glanced down the page; in his haste he had begun to read in the middle of a sentence; he started as if something had stung him, shook the letter out, and went back to the commencement.

"I have not forgotten, Mr. Rossitur, that to-morrow will bring the expiration of the term of waiting which you so generously offered to my hesitation. Believe me, during these long weeks I have never forgotten, and I have tried to act honestly. I can not marry you—I must write the words at once—easier for you in reading and for me in writing to have them over.

"I know now that for me to have decided otherwise would have been not only dangerous but an absolute sin, and you and I may both be thankful all our lives that I was guarded from committing it. I have no desire to write harshly, but this letter you must feel to be my full, unwavering answer. I can not marry you; because, setting aside the fact that my heart has never been touched by your generous devotion—and it has been very generous—I can no longer trust you as I have done.

"I have lost the friend in whom I believed. It is a little thing to see the lover go, but I can not easily forgive you that you have lost me my friend. When yesterday you so far forgot the commonest instincts of manly chivalry; when you insulted the name of a woman—not simply because she is dear to me, but because she is a woman pure and good—you broke the bond of friendship between us, and no human power can ever bridge the gulf.

"Forgive me if these last words are harsh; I would not willingly add to the pain you may endure by one severe expression, and it was for this reason that I avoided an interview. My temper is so hasty, and my indignation is so fresh in my mind, that I can not trust myself.

"Be you certain that years of reflection could not change my resolve. I must speak the whole truth—I must tell you honestly that I can not at present meet you with any appearance of toleration, and the kindly sympathy I might have felt for the man whose heart had gone out toward me is lost in my sorrow that the friend I trusted could have proved so ungenerous, in reality so unlike the person his gentleness to me had made me believe him. ELINOR GREY."

Rossitur read the letter through and let it drop on the table; his head sank upon his hands and he uttered one groan of exquisite pain. Verily the world had fallen at his feet; the element of baseness hidden under so much that was noble had worked this ruin. He sat for a time stupefied, then he started up with a mad intention of seeking Elinor Grey and overwhelming her with reproaches and threats—of finding Clive Farnsworth and tearing his heart out in his wife's presence. Then he fell back in his chair and covered his face with his hands and groaned anew. He looked up and saw the sunlight playing in at the window—the glass of summer roses which some soft-hearted chambermaid had sent up on the breakfast-tray—every thing as quiet and peaceful as before, and he marvelled. The world had fallen in ruins about him, and yet nothing was changed.

He sat there till the pain, the regret, were lost in a mad desire for vengeance, and he rose from that first season of reflection, which ought to have softened him, a worse man: harder, more unbelieving, and with every evil instinct in his nature strengthened and made active. At length he tore the letter in fragments, and that bit of violence was a momentary relief. He recognized that the light of common day was about him, and that life must go on with no glamour over it, at least for a season.

A great trouble ought never to assail one in the morning: it is made worse by the prosaic details of the hour. Rossitur had to come down from tragedy and finish dressing; to leave his room at the bidding of domestics impatient to get through their work. He did suffer, he suffered cruelly; but the sense of defeat, the rage, the desire for vengeance, in a measure supported him by their excitement and fury. He hurried out-of-door; she lounged about the veranda; he smoked; exchanged greetings with people who would speak cheerfully, and whom he must answer instead of knocking down; went through the variety of petty miseries we must in this world, and bore them as we must, though we may have come away from a murder or a mystery which shall cloud all coming years. He ordered a horse—at least movement would be a relief. He could gallop over the hills, and away amid their solitude he could be free to howl or curse or be insane in any manner the passing mood might dictate. While waiting for his horse he went up stairs again and paced back and forth the piazza, lighted numberless cigars and flung them away, and kicked every obstacle that came in his path, and was as absurd as any body is when nerves and sinews ache in sympathy with the heart. The sunlight was a curse; the green fields a desert; the world was at an end; and he could not get at that man and tear him as one wild beast tears another, because he must still live in this ruined planet, and he could not sacrifice every thing to this thirst for revenge. He might seek a quarrel with Farnsworth—might shoot him openly in a duel, or, better yet, spring on him in some lonely spot and grind his life out under a heavy heel, while his wife stood shrieking. He might do either of those things— he wanted to do both—and howl in the dying man's ear some vile slander about Elinor Grey: but he had to stay in the world, though it was become chaos. A coroner's inquest and a criminal's cell would follow the one assassination. If he shot him according to the code of murder, damnably called by a fine name, the consequences would be little less fatal. They would pursue him. If he sought public office they would stand in his way; political opponents would point him out to a crowd as an assassin, and everywhere he turned the infamy would follow. No, Clive Farnsworth must live, because the century is prosaic in certain matters, and though Tybalt and Laertes might slaughter their enemies and hope to hold up their heads after, if they were not cut off by a lucky thrust, Tybalt and Laertes of to-day must button their modern loose coats over their wrongs and curse in unadulterated and commonplace English, instead of brandishing daggers and bursting into blank verse.

Rossitur walked up and down and surveyed every side clearly enough; his selfishness controlled his passion, fierce as it was. He saw the children playing about the grounds and hated them for being merry; a group of men sat under the trees chatting and reading newspapers; the birds sang in the branches; the sunlight played and danced — every body and every thing united to be aggravations and abominations, and he cursed them from high heaven down. Presently from the corridor came sounds of wrath and distress—broken invective and dolorous sobbing—the first agreeable noises he had heard that morning, and he went to the door to see what mortal suffered and to enjoy the sight. In the middle of the hall stood Mrs. Piffit, her bonnet hanging down her back, the flat reticule on her arm, and she was assaulting a black porter who had her trunk on his shoulder and her bonnet-box in his hand.

"Set 'em down!" she shrieked. "Set 'em down, I say!"

"Lor bress ye, missis," returned the darkey, ducking and dodging, "miss de train, sure: ca'rage at de door and no time to lost."

"I won't go; I'll stay till I get my property! I'll rouse the house! Where's the proprietor? Set 'em down, I say!" The porter set down the baggage and stood rolling his eyes in wonder and delight, while Piffit danced about him. "Oh, my umbrella!" she cried. "I will have my umbrella! Somebody's stolen my umbrella! I set it against that chair while I ran up stairs, and it's gone. Oh, my umbrella!" Waiters began to gather—people opened their doors and came out—Piffit danced about and detailed her loss and was quite beside herself. "Where's the proprietor, I say? Call him. I've lost my umbrella! Call him, I say — maybe he stole it. Some of you stole it! I set it against that very chair. I will have my umbrella." The waiters expostulated — busy people said she ought to be put out of the house—Piffit only danced and shrieked the harder, growing more frantic each instant. "Call that landlord," she howled. "Fire! Murder! Thieves! thieves! I'll bring him. Fire! fire! fire!"

Out rushed more people; up they came from below in wild confusion, with the landlord at the head, to know where the fire was; and when it was discovered that the outcry was made by a mad-woman bewailing the loss of her umbrella, they fumed or laughed according as their tempers or their sense of the ludicrous happened to be most active.

Piffit flew at the landlord and seized him by the collar. "My umbrella!" she shrieked; "I will have my umbrella! Give it to me, I say."

"I haven't your umbrella," he answered, she shaking him so violently that the words came in gasps. "Why, let go—you're crazy!"

"No, I'm not. Somebody's stolen my umbrella—I set it against that very chair. Get it —find it. Fire! fire!"

"Get her a straight-jacket," said the crowd.

"Why, Madam," cried the landlord, extricating himself with the loss of an end of his neckerchief, which fluttered victoriously in Mrs. Piffit's hand, "I'll give you twenty umbrellas, if you'll only go."

"I won't go! I will have my umbrella! You're a set of thieves, the whole of you—landlord, guests, waiters and all. I'll take the law of the whole house!—My umbrella—I will have my umbrella!" She subsided for an instant into a storm of puffs and sniffs, and the landlord ordered the waiters to search in every direction for the missing article. "They'd better find it!" cried Piffit, with fresh energy. "Look in every body's rooms—pull the folks out of bed. I will have my umbrella! I'm Mrs. Piffit, the writer — I'll put you all in every paper, from Maine to Georgia—I'll show you up for a nest of thieves—umbrella—umbrella!" She paused again to sob and get breath.

"You have been a nuisance ever since you came," exclaimed the long-suffering landlord, roused to anger by the treatment he had received and the general confusion. "I only ask you to get out of the house; you may write what you please—only go."

"I won't go! I'll stand here till the Day of Judgment if you don't find my umbrella. Fire! fire! Murder! Thieves!" howled Piffit.

"For heaven's sake, Madam, hold your tongue," pleaded the landlord. "I'm doing all I can. I've got half the house hunting for your confounded umbrella."

"I won't hold my tongue! I'll expose you —I'm Mrs. Piffit, the writer. Oh, my umbrella!"

"Land's sake, ole Miss," spoke up the porter, who thought the exhibition fun beyond any experience on a Mississippi plantation, "don't take on so like all possessed; 'twan't only a nambarilly arter all."

Mrs. Piffit's wrath subsided in a passion of tears; she sat down on her trunk, perched her feet on her bonnet-box, and sobbed bitterly; for Piffit had one human weakness—she loved her old friend.

"'Twasn't only a nambarilly, arter all," repeated her sable comforter.

"It was more than an umbrella to me," said Piffit, weeping copiously. "It was a friend and companion—it shared my bed and my board."

"'Fore de Lord, it couldn't eat!" cried the Cloud.

"It might if it had wanted to and welcome: I wouldn't have minded the expense," sobbed Piffit. "I'm a lone woman and a widow. It walked with me—travelled with me—lay on the foot of my bed at night and was a protector to me—and now it's gone—ooh—ooh!"

That crowning elegy convulsed the listeners, and her dark consoler absolutely rolled over on the floor in an ecstasy of delight.

"Oh, you may laugh," sniffed Mrs. Piffit, brushing away her tears and going into a new access of rage. "You'll laugh out of the other side of your mouths before I've done with you.

I'll show you up—I'll make the papers ring. I'm Mrs. Piffit, the writer. I'll set Congress at you—I will have my umbrella! Fire! Murder! Thieves!" She fairly jumped up and down and shook her fists at the crowd.

At that moment one of the waiters appeared on the stairs carrying the green umbrella; but O, woful change! it bore witness to its sufferings since purloined from its loving mistress. Some mischievous child had seen and pounced upon it. It had been made a horse—it had been dragged through an opportune puddle—its stays were broken, its green dress was torn, and the muddy drops dripping from it seemed tears as the waiter held it aloft and it surveyed its mistress with its crooked handle. " Here's your umbrella," was the cry, and a heartless laugh followed.

Piffit sprang forward, seized her companion and hugged it to her bosom. She was past rage —she had no breath left; the sight of this havoc and ruin wrought on her trusty friend filled her with poignant grief.

" Carriage is waiting, Madam," said the landlord; "you've barely time to get down to the train."

" Leas' ways, ole Miss, yer's found de namharilly," cried the darkey, again shouldering her trunk.

Piffit sniffed and sobbed and held it fast. "Ten years I've had it, and it was as good as new," she moaned; "and now look at it!" She held it up, and a muddy tear oozed down the crook.

" Dat yere chile wants its nose wiped," suggested the negro.

" Get out!" cried Mrs. Piffit. "Go on! Let me get away. Oh, you're a pretty landlord—you're a sweet set! I'll show you up— I'll teach you! A nice house, where property isn't safe! I'll expose you—I'm Mrs. Piffit, the writer—from Maine to Georgia."

Her voice was heard all the way down the stairs as she trotted on, clasping the umbrella to her breast. She bounced into the carriage and the thoughtless umbrella brought her new trouble — it poked its crooked nose directly through the window.

"Dollar for that, ma'am," called the coachman.

" 'Pears like dat ar chile's 'spensive, ole Miss," said the porter. " Don't forget the conweyancer, ole Miss."

But he held out his palm in vain; Piffit only shook the umbrella at him furiously and was driven off. Up to the last moment that she was visible to the throng she was embracing her companion and holding it close. So Piffit was gone.

Rossitur stood in the door and watched the whole exhibition and laughed unrestrainedly; he enjoyed it the more because the woman's distress, though ludicrous and unreasonable, was genuine, and he was in a mood which made it a satisfaction to see somebody suffer—to soothe the gnawing at his heart with the sight of pain afflicting another. He went down stairs in search of his horse, and as he was mounting he saw Jack Ralston's wife come out and enter her stylish barouche, and if she could have heard the gentle message he mentally sent after her she might have been edified. Mrs. Ralston had an errand before her which was by no means a pleasant one, but which, after a night of sleepless terror, she had decided must be undertaken.

Elinor Grey, sitting by one of the windows of the breakfast-room at Alban Wood, saw Mrs. Ralston's carriage drive up, and instinctively drew back among the curtains to be concealed from view. She knew that the woman never ventured to pay Rosa visits, and when Tom from his easy-chair, hearing the wheels, called out to know who was coming, she uttered the name in a tone of horror, and Rosa repeated it with a little natural indignation added.

"Don't be excited, ladies," said Tom; "I prophesy that Mrs. Ralston's call is for your humble servant."

"At all events, she need not come to see me," cried Rosa.

"Bless me," said Tom; "you meet her at lots of places, and you invited her to a ball once."

"I did, to oblige Annie Ralston, but I never visit her, and barely speak. You know it well enough. You never said why, but you told me that was all I ever should do."

Tom did not have an opportunity to answer, for Stupid came in and verified his prediction. Mrs. Ralston wished to speak with Mr. Thornton an instant—her husband had been called back to town suddenly and had left a message for her to deliver. Would Mr. Thornton have the goodness to step out to the carriage, as she was in haste and had no time to make a call on the ladies.

"The impudence! A call on us!" ejaculated Rosa.

Tom made a month at her and went out of the room. Elinor sat still behind the curtains, and Rosa came and leaned over her chair.

They saw Tom approach the carriage—saw the woman's countenance, haggard in spite of paint, with the fierce eyes dimmed by a long night of terror, lean eagerly toward him, while he stood perfectly civil and indifferent. She talked rapidly—once clutched at his hand; they could tell by her face that she was pleading with much earnestness. Tom bowed—answered briefly — smiled, and looked entirely unconcerned.

"She's begging him to keep her secret," whispered Rosa; "but he'll never tell it even to me. She does not know Tom."

"And you would not hear it if he would tell," returned Elinor.

"Heaven knows I would not! It's not Tom's. I don't want to hear her name. How frightened she looks."

"It makes me sick," cried Elinor. "Oh the poor thing! Come away, Rosa—don't look."

They hurried from the window and were

standing at the further end of the room when they heard the carriage drive away with a great dash and whip-cracking, carrying off the woman who in spite of her splendor was more wretched than many a houseless beggar, "because her sin had found her out."

Tom came in, wearing his impassable expression. "Miss Grey," he said, "Mrs. Ralston desired me to offer you the most humble and entire apology—I quote her expression—for any word she may have said against your friend Mrs. Farnsworth. She begs you to believe that she will do every thing in her power to contradict the reports during the brief time she remains here."

Elinor was silent and Rosa exclaimed—"That is the last of the matter. Go on reading, Tom, we don't want to think of her."

Tom resumed his book, and during the rest of their lives there was never so much as an allusion to that secret in Mrs. Ralston's career, which some chance had exposed to Tom Thornton.

After luncheon Ruth Farnsworth drove over; so beautiful in her delight at Elinor's safety, so proud and happy that Clive should have been the one to save her, that Tom declared he lost his heart on the spot. Clive was not with her —he was busy with letters that day—he would not hear of her waiting until he should be at leisure, perhaps preferring to send kind inquiries, to be repeated in her graceful way, to trusting himself at Alban Wood so soon after a shock which made it difficult to settle down to actual life without a struggle. Ruth was so glad and happy, so radiant a sunbeam in her excited spirits, that when she departed Rosa was unable to say enough in her praise.

That evening Mr. Grey arrived somewhat unexpectedly, bringing Coralie and Hungarian Henry in his train, and Elinor thought she had never been so full of joy at seeing him. He had to be told of the accident, and was frightened out of his placidity at the bare recital. He kept her close by him for two hours after, appearing to think there could be no absolute safety for his treasure anywhere else. The next morning he would go immediately after breakfast to see and thank Clive Farnsworth, who could easily have dispensed with any expression of gratitude and devoutly wished that every body would forget the matter as soon as possible. But Mr. Grey would not forget, and he would consider Clive a hero to Ruth's intense delight, who thought him the most charming elderly gentleman the world ever produced, and could have listened to his graceful speeches all day, as indeed most people could.

After his return he was alone with Elinor and mentioned Rossitur's name, adding that he wished to see him. So Elinor had to say that the time of probation had come and passed. "And what did my daughter Elinor decide? Am I to lose her?" he asked.

"I am going to stay with you, papa."

Mr. Grey did not wish to lose her—he was glad there was no danger—still to a certain extent he was disappointed. She must marry some time—it was the destiny of woman—there was no man with whom in many ways an alliance could be so useful to Mr. Grey. "My Elinor has given the subject full thought, I know," he said.

"Indeed I have, papa. I tried to do right. Oh, you can't think what a relief it is to have it over—to be quite free again."

"Then certainly there is not a word to be said. I am sure you gave your refusal in the gentlest way."

"But I had to be decided, papa. I could not leave any hope."

"You were right. But I like Mr. Rossitur; I hope nothing will interrupt our friendly relations."

Elinor would not pain her father by telling him of the meanness which Rossitur had committed. Perhaps he was already sorry for it; she was glad now she had written instead of seeing him, because in a personal interview she must have plainly shown her contempt and wrath. She was glad to think he might be sorry—might have much in his character that was really noble—only the fact that there were such black possibilities too, would leave him worlds away from her forever. She would be civil when they met, and would not tell her father, and she was glad to leave the matter there; it hurt her to cherish harsh feelings against any body.

They met the next day but one at an impromptu dinner, as the Idol called it, given by her to honor the Farnsworths; and she had collected the chief of the Hamlyns and several of the chief among the magnates, and was in a seventh heaven of delight at Mr. Grey's arrival.

The Angel was also in ecstacies at the sight of her dear guardian; but though he was gallant and amiable as ever, the Angel knew that the scene so inopportunely interrupted could never be gotten up afresh. Mrs. Piffit had not ventured to leave any stings behind for her, therefore she escaped scot-free, and congratulated herself immensely thereupon. She told every body that Mrs. Piffit had tried to drag her into the matter, poor child that she was, who could not understand what the trouble meant; but her dear Elinor Grey had defended her. Most people believed her account, and she did the martyr very neatly, as she did nearly all roles she attempted, because—

"The serpent was more subtle than any beast of the field."

She had Juanita up before the Idol, and told her what wicked things Mrs. Piffit had said, and Juanita, having been previously instructed, rolled her eyes wildly and was proof that Piffit had once met her young mistress in the grounds and had begun to abuse every body, the bressed Senora Duchess included, and had been sent to the right about without scruple. The Idol praised her faithfulness, and gave her a gorgeous red dress and a yellow feather, whereat her young mistress was almost as much delighted as Juanita, because she had expected to be obliged to reward her fidelity herself. The Angel was at the dinner in the most bewildering toilette, and was an Undine and a seraph and every thing artful and bewitching added. She was enthusiastic over Ruth, and charmingly afraid of Clive because he was a genius; and Elinor felt at ease, since she knew that she would not dare let Ruth discover the scandal that had been crushed, and concerning which they had no care now except to keep her from knowledge of it.

The Farnsworths had arrived when the Alban Wood party entered; indeed, they were last of any body, for Rosa was never in a hurry and Tom was a hopeless dawdler. Clive Farnsworth was talking to stately Mrs. Hamlyn and watching Ruth, the centre of a little group of men—the old Judge chief among them—and thinking how lovely she looked and feeling glad and thankful at her safety, when he saw Elinor Grey come in. He did not cease his conversation; he gave one glance, then he looked at Ruth again till the mist had cleared from his eyes, and heart and brain were steady once more.

Leighton Rossitur saw her too as he leaned over Miss Laidley's chair; and though he had longed for this meeting, he felt at that instant as if he would be glad to get away. He delighted the Angel's heart by retaining his position and making her believe that her fascinations prevailed over the spell of Elinor's presence. The dreariest forty-eight hours that Leighton Rossitur had ever spent had been those since the reception of that letter. He had scarcely eaten or slept, and he had made a comforter of wine as much as he dared, not venturing to trust it too far, lest he should be led into some insanity which could not be retrieved. He had been in twenty different minds, and had resolved upon numberless plans of action, and was as far from finding any anchor with which to steady his senses as when the blow fell. He had been so certain of success—up to the latest moment every thing had appeared prosperous—and it was the first failure of his life. He had gone nearly mad, there was no doubt of that, and a soul in purgatory might have pitied his pangs, for he loved Elinor Grey with all the passion of his voluptuous nature. He was glad when the Idol's hurried invitation came; he should see Elinor; in some moods, the sight of her looking into his very soul with her eyes full of honest scorn would have been better than the misery of his solitude. That morning Mr. Grey had called on him, and had been so exactly the same as of old in his manner that Rossitur decided he could know nothing either of the season of waiting or its bitter end. He was pale and worn from lack of sleep, and feverish from thought and wine, but he controlled himself and listened eagerly to Mr. Grey's confidential talk, for the statesman had insensibly fallen into the habit of conversing

more freely with this young man than he ever had to any other, and he could hint plans to him which were best not exposed to "my daughter Elinor's" keen sense of honor and justice. Therefore Rossitur came to the Castle in that excitable state which made him unusually brilliant. He blazed all the evening like a meteor, and was the life of the party, and he whispered tenderer speeches than he had ever before offered to brighten the Angel's romance, and in a voice which thrilled her like shocks from a galvanic battery. He was not brought near Elinor before dinner, indeed he had nothing to do but whisper softly in the Angel's ear, for Mrs. Clive Farnsworth was made the chief feature of the occasion in a manner that would have goaded the Angel to desperation had it not been for him.

The Secretary had received a hint from Elinor, and he was surpassing the other men in his attentions, saying graceful things to Clive also, thanking him playfully as a public benefactor by his book, and something higher yet for having given him personally the happiness of meeting his lovely wife, his daughter Elinor's cherished friend. And the Idol beamed and fluttered, and stately Mrs. Hamlyn unbent, and the dignitaries generally so bowed before Ruth's shrine that she would have been nervous only Clive's smile assured her, and she forgot herself in thinking about him, and believing that she was courted on his account, because he was so famous and so grand that every thing belonging to him must be of importance. She talked just enough, and she talked well, and her poetry and her romances had taught her pretty phrases and wording of sentences, which never sounded studied from the fact that she employed them unconsciously.

The Bull not being in the home pasture, owing to the suddenness of the affair, the Idol requested her charming Secretary to play host, and to lead her sweet Cynthia of a minute, the brightest ornamentation among the bays of her Apolloite, in to dinner, because the feast impromptu was in her honor, as all must know. It came about that Elinor was paired off with some notable, and Rossitur fell to the Angel's share by a bit of previous diplomacy on her part.

Clive had not found an opportunity—no, that is not honest—he had been able to avoid speaking to Miss Grey until they came face to face in the general rising to go toward the dining-room. Ruth was close by, leaning on the Secretary's arm, and Elinor was glad to have her near. She held out her hand to Clive with frank cordiality, and said, "I have been talking to the best part of you," smiling at Ruth. And Mr. Grey leaned over to whisper—"I have not thanked you half enough. God knows I never can." Then, emotion being out of place, the line of march was duly taken up and the party gathered about the table.

"So blest to see these familiar faces of beloved friends gathered around my impromptu her romance, which was growing a very serious matter, but she believed that she was taking her hero away from Elinor Grey, and therefore her exultation equalled her happiness. Rossitur allowed her to think this—he wanted her to—and when she was most interested he told her that he must go. He was beginning to play the part which he had unconsciously acted toward her hitherto: he tantalized her with a purpose now, and made her romance more and more sensational by rendering her uncertain whether he cared for her or whether it must end with despair and death. He was going up to Lake George and the picturesque scenes about Champlain, and it was understood between him and the Angel that on his return he should join her at Saratoga. He hesitated and acted as though he was very anxious to meet her there, but was held back by some scruple. The Angel was more than ever convinced that a secret engagement existed between him and Miss Grey, and she never rested till she received his unconditional promise. He departed, and in spite of the incessant dissipation, the amusement every day and the opportunity of endless Germans every night, the Angel was restless. She assumed certain triumphal airs toward Elinor which amused Miss Grey and made her wonder in what petty craft the damsel believed herself to be victorious.

The Angel had a due share of admiration and a crowd of adorers, still Ruth Farnsworth was first, and that took the sweetness out of her cup. Nothing could be done unless Mrs. Farnsworth approved. She must decide whether the next day's party should be on the lake or a picnic in the woods; at the balls her favorite dances must be played; she must be the principal feature of every pleasure. Of course the guests took the tone adopted by the Alban Wood residents, classing the Secretary and his daughter thereamong, and Ruth's head might have been turned had she been in the least different from what she was. She never accepted the homage as a tribute to any charm of her own—she laid it at Clive's feet and made it a fresh offering of love and devotion. "My own darling," she would say, "I am glad they like me—it is for your sake." And he saw more and more clearly how pure the nature was that he had taken into his keeping—how free from the least tinge of vanity which even a noble-minded woman might have indulged at that time.

The Angel could not endure it long: she gave the Idol no peace until she persuaded her to be off to Saratoga. The good Idol was enjoying greatly what she called "this festal convivia," but she could not bear to disappoint her pretty blossom, and prepared to get under way. There came occasional letters to the Angel about this time, concerning which she made a profound mystery, only leaving it evident that she had one, and after receiving such epistles she always assumed a greater air of triumph toward Elinor Grey. For the letters were from Rossitur, and he could write remarkably well.

He call her his friend—his Consuelo. He hinted at a heavy cloud which hung over him, but he wrote very vaguely, and never committed himself. "The children of darkness are wiser in their generation than the children of light," and his letters were so worded that if vanity or pique should ever induce her to show them to Elinor, Miss Grey would only read therein the black anguish which filled his mind at her casting him off, and would understand that he had corresponded with this girl because her answers gave him tidings of the loved and lost, while the pretty phrases and poetical names were bestowed from the fact that he considered her a mere child. But the Angel treasured the letters; she would not have had Elinor know of them for the world. She believed firmly that Miss Grey loved Rossitur, and she feared that if a suspicion of this correspondence reached her she would force him back to his allegiance. So the Angel guarded her mystery; read the epistles again and again, wept over them, hid them in her bosom, slept with them under her pillow, and, with such force as her nature owned, she loved Leighton Rossitur. She was successful at length in forcing the Idol to carry her away under her wing; and as at the last moment one man offered his hand and heart, either from fancy or on account of her wealth, she went off with unalloyed delight, and the party in general missed her very little.

During this season Elinor and Clive Farnsworth were constantly brought into each other's society, but it was always in a crowd, and as neither sought any intercourse beyond the necessary civilities and appearance of cordial friendship, they were almost as far apart as they had been during the past months. I am glad that I have no sentimental episode to set down here; I am glad that there was not in the mind of the woman or the man a single thought which it was difficult to face in secret. The recent danger from which Ruth had escaped and of which she could never be conscious had made Clive's heart very, very gentle toward her. He did not allow himself lonely hours in which to grow morbid and visionary. He kept her by his side, he made her his companion in every pursuit, and out in the world he was busy watching that she was happy and so carefully guarded that the least shade of annoyance could not come near her. He simply kept self in the background—studied her pleasure—and that abnegation of self made him content in her happiness. I shall not tell you that the chance mention of Elinor Grey's name ceased at certain moments to thrill him to the heart's core, but he disregarded the weakness—he refused to yield. Sometimes when he looked up suddenly and saw her standing in the throng, so near and yet so far off, the mist would gather before his eyes and the lost life which never had any culmination would rise vividly before him; but to have mad thoughts pass through the mind is a very different thing from dwelling upon them. When such emotions troubled his quiet he went resolutely away to Ruth—he sought her beaming smile—he bent over her to hear some whisper of tenderness with which he might steady his soul and go calmly on again.

And Elinor Grey in her womanly purity had not even those feelings to contend against. He had literally no place in her mind other than as the friend who had saved her life, the man who had nobly redeemed his errors and who was the guardian of the girl she loved with a tenderness which we can only give those whom we have protected and helped out of suffering. Elinor was very lonely—life was very empty to her—but she was not mourning over any lost dream or shattered idol. She had acknowledged humbly to herself that her heart had gone out to Clive Farnsworth as it could never do toward any man again, but she put the memory aside and it ceased to have an actual part in her loneliness.

One bright sunset a party had been rowing over the pretty lake and had come back on shore and were roving about, climbing the steep hill to watch the sun go down, lingering under the pretenses with which people try to prolong a pleasant day. Elinor had slipped off from everybody for a few moments, and coming to a shady nook she sat down, as completely hidden from the rest as if she had been miles distant, but within reach of the merry voices still. She sat in the shadow looking out over the golden and green waters, up to the purple hills beyond, which were crowned with a line of white light like an ineffable glory. She thought sorrowfully that the scene was typical. As she sat in the gloom looking out at the sunlit waters, so her soul gazed out from among the shadows at the brightness which could never come near her life. It was a fanciful but natural thought, and she smiled at its morbidness, for, looking up, she saw the white glory crowning the purple hills, and remembered that thus from amid the darkness of this world may the soul gaze at the radiance that always streams down from the higher shore, if we would wipe our blinding tears away and search for it. As she thought, there was a step near, and before she turned her head she knew that Clive Farnsworth was standing beside her. He started a little—he had not dreamed of her being there—he too had strayed away for an instant's quiet. "Is it you, Miss Grey?" he said, with the slow, grave smile which had taken the place of youthful brightness. "If people talked as they do in books, I should say I almost fancied I had come on the guardian spirit of the lake."

"Only a very tired young woman," she replied, lifting her calm face toward him. "But look at those hills, Mr. Farnsworth; have you any comparison for that brightness?"

"I think it rests one to watch it," he said.

"If we could always look up—always remember the brightness is there—what a help it would be," Elinor returned softly. She told him part of her thought—not the sentiment which she had applied to herself, but of the likeness to human existence—looking out from among the shadows to the glory of the upper sky.

"And we feel it more and more as the years go on," he answered.

"Yes; that is the best of it."

"The best of it, as you say." He stood beside her and gazed up toward the dazzling radiance, and the tired face grew peaceful. It was the first time they had stood thus alone since that parting which was a final separation as far as the real life of this world might be concerned. They remembered the fact at the same instant; their eyes met, but the peaceful light was on both faces still, like a beam reflected from that heavenly brightness.

"I have had no opportunity to thank you," Clive Farnsworth said, "but I knew, Miss Grey, that it was not necessary. You have been loving and kind to my little Ruth; she is very happy now."

"If I have been allowed to help," replied Elinor, "you know that I am thankful—He has permitted me."

"Yes," Clive said, "I can understand and believe that now. I wanted to tell you so—I knew you would be glad."

"Very glad. My friends are so much nearer to me when they can believe this with me—it is such a rest. He keeps us—we are never alone, and the light is always there."

They were both silent for a little after that. I may safely say there was no human weakness in the thoughts which filled each soul.

"I read your book," Elinor said. "I am glad you wrote it. I wanted to blot out the title and have it—'Toward the Light.'"

"I tried to make it a good book," he answered. "I am not young enough to waste any more time or to write without a purpose."

"To live at all without a purpose soon ceases to have any charm," Elinor said. "It is very romantic and very pretty for awhile, but we soon learn how petty and selfish it is."

"And the melancholy and morbid feelings which looked beautiful grow very faded and tame," Clive said.

"Very faded. The most humiliating thing is that we find there has been no originality in them—everybody has had the same."

"Only you could not make any youthful dreamer believe that," he said. "And after all, I would not deprive youth of its romance."

"Nor I," said Elinor, "because you would take away its brightest charm. But I would try to direct it, to strengthen the character so that it might have no evil effect."

"Only nobody will try to help young people aright."

"No; older people seem to think the romance is to be laughed at or to be ashamed of, or they sneer from bitterness because their lives have lost even that glow."

"And it is so easy to sneer, and people are just as absurd in doing it as they were in the first folly—they think they have exhausted life and felt every thing."

M

"And have not lived enough to know the true light is there," she said softly, pointing toward the distance.

"'I will lift up mine eyes to the hills from whence cometh my help,'" Clive repeated involuntarily.

"'My help cometh from the Lord who made heaven and earth,'" added Elinor.

"Would they think we were making two dull sermons of ourselves if they heard us?" returned Clive with a smile, waving his hand toward the direction from whence the voices of their friends could be heard.

"Some of them might; we can pity them for it; their blindness or their inability to comprehend does not alter the beautiful truth."

"'Growing toward the light,'" he repeated, and again he looked out on the hills, and the peaceful smile softened his face still more. "I sometimes think," he said slowly, not turning away from the radiance, "that my life is very near its close for this world." Now he looked at her and smiled. "It is a weak thought perhaps—it may be only a relic of the old morbid fancies—but it comes to me so frequently that I can not believe it right to put it wholly aside."

"No, no," she said hastily; "I can not think so—for Ruth's sake, you know."

"Only we know Ruth would be cared for just the same. If I go, He will send other help."

"I forgot that; you see it is so hard to look up."

"I wanted to speak of this thought to you," he went on, "although it may be weak. I wanted to ask you to love her more and more, because she would lean entirely on you then as far as human sympathy is concerned."

Elinor Grey felt no sorrow; she was looking up too. If his thought were true she could not regret that he might go away.—Life here seems so poor when we gaze over yonder; not with sickly longing to be away from care, but content to remain while there is work to do; only ready to hear the call, ready to give free vent to the gladness.

"I know what you would be to her," Clive said.

"I would try."

"Yes. I have told you now; that was all. It may happen that in the whole course of our lives I should have had no other opportunity, and I wanted to say this."

"I am glad to accept the trust," she replied.

They stood there, looking away from each other, not because there was any pain in either heart, but each wanted to watch the brightness and remember whither it led.

After a time Clive said — "Thank you. When the thought comes now I shall be quite at rest."

"Since whichever way it may be will be right," Elinor answered.

He bowed his head. I think if he had been dying and she had come to hear his last words, both would have had very much the same feeling they had at that moment. It was not grief,

it was no relapse into weakness; their minds were steady and calm, but it seemed a very solemn season to them, and they knew that this meeting and parting was like death, like something holier too. It was as if he had been dead and his soul for a brief space was permitted to come back and be visible to her and look straight at her soul beyond all mortal disguises.

"There is nothing else," he said gently; "I am at rest now."

She gave him her hand quietly and he held it an instant in his own, and without another word they turned back to the world. The first to meet them was Ruth, her cheeks blushing with roses and her eyes like twin stars. "Everybody is going," she said. "I am so glad I found you together. You never have a chance to talk and get well acquainted. Oh, Elinor, you can't know me really if you don't know Clive; I'm only a bit of him, after all."

They could both smile at her and love her and be glad that she should meet them thus.

"I know Clive very well," Elinor answered, for the first time calling him by that name. She was smiling still, and kept the action from appearing strained by a quiet playfulness. She took Ruth's hand and laid it in her husband's. "When I think of one I think of both," she continued softly; "Ruth and Clive—they make but one friend to me."

There had been seasons, there might easily be again, when that incident would have caused Farnsworth the keenest anguish, but he did not suffer now. Though she called him by the familiar baptismal name, and he remembered that it was the first and last time in all their lives that she would ever call him thus, he did not suffer. A few moments longer they stood there, and the conversation floated back to every-day subjects, as was wisest and best. Presently the rest of the party came trooping up; it was growing late, and though poetry and admiration of nature are very well in their place, every body had exhausted them for the time and wanted to get back to dinner, which I suppose would have been equally the truth if they had all been Longfellows or Mrs. Brownings.

CHAPTER XXXIV.

THE INCONSIDERATE HOSTESS.

The days went pleasantly on past the middle of July, then Alban Wood emptied itself of guests, the other houses followed the example, and every body rushed away through the hot summer glare in search of the purgatorial pleasures of watering-places.

The Angel had been enjoying a season of unbroken delight at Saratoga. The Idol humored every whim in the most amiable way, and the more whims the Angel had the more charming she thought her. Wherever she moved people bowed down before her and yielded to the spell of her witcheries or to her golden charms, and all she cared was to have the admiration; she did not trouble her angelic mind about the motive.

Her romance had reached its culmination—she was mad for Leighton Rossitur.—I employ the word advisedly, pink-and-white seraph though she was.—He played his part most skillfully, and enjoyed the refuge from dismal or wicked thoughts. He wanted her to love him; if the blackest possibility must be realized, and he found there could be no hope of a restoration to Miss Grey's favor, he would marry Genevieve Laidley because her wealth would afford him a life of luxury and be an invaluable aid in his wish for political advancement. If her heart—supposing that she had one—chanced to be broken in the game, he would care as little as the Angel herself would have done in a similar case. So he acted his *rôle* well; making her believe that he was partially engaged to Elinor Grey, had been before he knew and loved her. Now he was held fast; he could only wait till he learned whether he might consider himself honorably released.

The Angel would have had little sympathy with such scruples, only if he had not clung to those chivalrous safeguards there would have been no secret and no mystery, and losing those concomitants, her romance would have lost half its charm. He did not tell her outright that he loved her; he kept his full power by letting her think he was constantly on the verge of doing so. He called her his Consuelo, his Genevieve, and did melodrama in a style which delighted her and amused him sufficiently in the need he felt for constant excitement. He brought about meetings at impossible hours and places, and he raved like Claude Melnotte. Once when they were on the lake in a boat he dropped the oars and caught her in his arms, crying dismally that they would at least die together. A cruel Fate kept them asunder here—he could not live without her—she should die with him. At first she shrieked with delight, then she shrieked with actual fear; he looked very pallid and wild, and no wonder, for he had been drinking all night; but she recovered herself and did her part with great spirit. They must live—they must not tempt Heaven. He saw it in that light too, and came down from tragedy to sentiment, and moaned like a Bedlamite in Owen Meredith's choicest stanzas; and she wept bucketfuls of tears. Her emotion made him relapse into momentary frenzy; he seized her hand and swore he would kill her then and there if she did not vow never to marry any other man, and dictated a horrible oath which she mouthed after him with great relish. That over, he flung her from him and beat his forehead with his fists—it did ache dolefully, which was not surprising. He threw himself on his knees and tilted the boat dreadfully, called himself a fiend, a base wretch, and many other unpleasant names, and begged her to forgive him. Then she forgave him in blank verse; then

he cursed fate—the world—all things; then he cheered up and called her Consuelo, his love, his dove, his star! Then they went ashore and found the Idol and a good dinner, and their appetites were wonderfully sharpened by the recreation, which was a blessing, for their insides needed wholesome food very much. The Angel had been living on trash for a fortnight, and he had been pouring wine and something more potent into an empty stomach till it was a marvel the coats had not dissolved entirely.

But in spite of indulging in midnight orgies, in spite of doing absurd drama with the Angel, Rossitur never forgot his grief or his rage: one or the other was uppermost in his soul all the while. He was not afraid of acquiring the habit of unlimited drinking—he could indulge for a month whenever he pleased, and forget for two years after that he had ever cared for the excitement—and his frame was so wiry and muscular, notwithstanding his seeming delicacy, that the occasional excesses did him no apparent harm. When he was tired of alternately sending Miss Laidley up to paradise or down to black misery by his changeable moods, and discovered that it would not be safe to pursue the unlimited drink business any longer, he announced to her that he was going away. Duty called, etcetera! His was a hard, uncongenial life, but he would not murmur. Only Consuelo must remember him. He should find her out soon again—he should come back to look in her eyes and see heaven once more—but now he must go. Even in the anguish of parting—and he did it in a way that would have made his fortune on the stage—he was careful not to commit himself; he could not speak—he was not yet free—but she must know that his heart would linger there; and in her excitement she was ready to offer him herself and her money, but she did not. He broke off in a passionate speech—rushed to the door—came back; he groaned—he ranted—and this time the poor miserable little Angel got so much in earnest that she almost fainted. He uttered her name in a despairing baritone; he caught her in his arms; he kissed her till he took her breath away—he had no objection to doing that because hers was a pretty mouth to kiss and he did not commit himself by any amount of osculatory practice to which she would submit. He strained her to his breast; he swore she was his soul's bride, and dared her to wed another, promising if she did to dye her bridal robes with the hated rival's blood at the altar. He kissed her again, flung her from him, and dashed out; and she actually believed herself dying and loved him, and he went off to keep a crowning revel. Before the morning dawned, had any woman accustomed to seeing him as he appeared in society looked at him with a wine-glass in his shaking hand, his wavy hair falling about his pale face, his voice harsh with coarse jests, she would certainly have thought that she saw some evil spirit who had assumed his likeness.

When he had gone, the Angel grew restless

again. She wanted to be off to Newport; her darling Duchess must send and have the cottage there put in order; the doctors advised sea-air for her chest—and the Angel coughed piteously. The blessed old Idol consented, and proposed that they should leave at once and spend a few days at the Castle, and see what their friends were doing. The Angel was ready for any change that could be snatched at without delay, so down they went to the Castle, they and a troop of men-servants and maid-servants, and clothes enough to have filled twenty arks like Noah's, and twenty arks they had to hold them. But behold, when they had reached the Castle the neighborhood was a desert. The Hamlyns were gone; the Thorntons and the Greys had set off to the Green Mountains, meaning to see Canada and the Thousand Islands and other lovelinesses before they returned; indeed, every body was absent. No, the Idol to her delight learned that the Farnsworths were at home. Ruth had preferred staying quietly in her beautiful house to any trip whatever, and Clive was quite willing to gratify her.

The Angel wanted to depart without so much as unpacking a single ark, but this time the Idol had to insist on a little opportunity to get her breath before starting on a fresh chase. She was a large body, and large bodies can not be expected to move with the celerity of celestial creatures burdened with only enough semblance of mortality to confine their soaring souls. It is doubtful, however, whether the Angel would have permitted this delay with a good grace, or indeed have permitted it at all, had not the Idol showed her an order that was going down to Pinchon for two heavenly ball-dresses for a young seraph, and given her a set of sapphires on the spot. So the Angel said—"Oh, of course we will wait, darling Duchess; I am so glad to have you a few days all to myself."

"Thanks, love. Indeed, the cottage will not be ready this week—people are so dilitative; and the hotels are crammed with odious creatures. Besides I think I am not quite well, sweet—I have a dull pain in my head, and my limbs fairly pain me when I walk.

"Oh, you'll be quite well in a day or two, sweet Duchess. Don't think about it; so bad for nervous people, you know," cried the Angel, never interested in other people's maladies.

The Idol had excellent health; she admitted that it was preposterously good; and she did not fancy herself ill now, and had no intention of complaining. "We will drive over and see the Farnsworths, love, to-morrow," she said; "but, really, if you will excuse me, I think I shall siesta for a space—my head is too painful."

"It will cure you to sleep," replied the Angel as sagely as if she had been a female physician with the pretty feminine accompaniments of a scalpel in her belt and the odor of pills about her garments. "I would offer to read to you, but you will be better alone and quiet."

"It will pass briefly, I doubt not," said the Idol. "Amuse yourself, sweet pet—read—

drive—while away the dreamy hours as may please your exuberant mind."

She took her aching head away to her bed-chamber, and when she was gone the Angel executed a pas seul before the mirror expressive of delight, and did it so well that it was a pity there was no one to admire. She hoped devoutly that the Idol's head might continue to pain her until they were ready to depart. She was not fond of her own society; but it was better than the Idol's, unless while she was in the act of bestowing presents. So the Angel slept a great deal—she had a happy faculty of curling down in easy places and sleeping peacefully at will; she devoured great quantities of trash; she read a new foreign novel the name of which I will not mention; she wrote letters to Rossitur; bemoaned herself loudly when she was tired of other amusements; and managed to get rid of the time.

Two days passed, and the Idol's headache seemed to increase rather than diminish; and when she did force herself to sit up and try to entertain her guest, it would have filled a boa-constrictor with compassion to see how ill she looked and how determinedly she fought against her sickness. But the Laidley was another sort of serpent, and she was touched with no compassion whatever. Indeed, she thought the old thing was trying to be hateful: probably she had overeaten herself. The Angel, by the way, thought that after an hour's picking at jelly-cake, cold paté, cream, ripe plums, bonbons by the box, and other trifles too numerous to mention. On the third day they drove over to the Farnsworths, and to the Angel's joy the pair were out. She had no desire to see either of them. She was growing exasperated under this seclusion; bear it any longer she could not and she would not. A journey somewhere should be undertaken if the Idol died on the road; in fact, that would be romantic; and the Angel fancied herself doing grief over her sweet Duchess's death-bed to the admiration of sympathetic strangers. She had driven several times to the village—she had hunted in vain for an adventure. There was not a male biped who could be transformed into a temporary prince or troubadour, and the Angel began to feel that life was a burden, to have longings to fly at the Idol and peck her, and to nip old Juanita privately by way of consolation. She assured the Idol that she was better, and the Idol smiled in a very ghastly fashion, and tried to have faith in the opinion so confidently asserted and followed by such tender epithets. The Angel would not say a word about departing that day, but on the next go they must; in what direction she little cared. She would not be mewed up in that trumpery Castle any longer for all the ailments that ever troubled a legion of dumpy duchesses. What did the vicious old grimalkin mean by such conduct? Was she to be treated in this way? She asked these questions of Juanita, in a great rage because the Idol had been obliged to go to bed on their return from the drive. Juanita was unable to give satisfactory answers, although she fully agreed with her young mistress, who flung a few choice flowers of rhetoric at her head and boxed her ears for talking when she had no business; and that was the sole relief she could find.

But she was tired of being alone, and wanted Juanita to flatter her since there was nobody else to do it; and Juanita, marking that, seized the opportunity to turn sulky and sat rubbing her ear, which still tingled from the pressure of the Angel's white hand. The Angel had to coax her with sugar-plums, and finally the well-mated pair sat on the floor and ate sweets, and Juanita told her how lovely she was, and invented praises from innocent people, and then diverged to ghost-stories, for which she and her mistress had a weakness, and frightened them both so successfully before she got through that they screamed like two eagles when one of the servants chanced to pass the door. This was after dinner, at which the Idol forced herself to appear and had gone to bed again convinced at last that she was ill, and promising her maid, who had been getting more frightened ever since the attack commenced, that in the morning she would permit a physician to be sent for if she were not materially better.

"Don't be alarmed, sweetest," she said to the Angel, trying to be playful and kind, till the Angel was mentally reminded of a sick porpoise attempting to disport itself in the sun, "I shall be well on the morrow—I am never ill."

"Oh, don't be! I should go mad at once!"

"Sweet sympathizer! No, no; fear not."

"I should die too, and Mr. Hackett would have to be sent for," cried the Angel, remembering him at a juncture like that.

"Oh, dear man, he has no leisure to attend to sick people. He is very kind—but, love, ours is a union of mind and matter—yes, yes! He is the soul of goodness, but he is always down among those dreadful B.'s, you know."

"What bees?" asked the Angel.

"That dreadful slang phrase they have in Wall Street, love—Bears and B.'s, you know."

"No, I don't. Bees, bees! How funny!"

"Never mind, love; that is the initial. I can not bring myself to repeat their indecorous phrases."

But the Angel was determined to make her utter the word, just by way of gratifying her ill-humor. "I'm going to ask every body what it is," cried she, in her most childish voice; "so you had better tell me."

Now the Idol could not divest herself of the idea that there was great indelicacy in saying leg, bull, or go to bed; and being ill, she was quite fretted by her Angel's persistency. But she had no peace till she had pronounced the improper word, and then her head ached worse than ever. "I shall retire," she said, "and seek oblivion on my couch. Adieu till to-morrow, sweet pet."

"Mind you are well then, dear Duchess, or I'll never forgive you."

"Oh, I shall be quite restored—val—val!" and the Angel privately tittered to see that she appeared more and more like a sick porpoise as she tried to be at ease.

"And oh, sweet Duchess!"

"Yes, love?"

"Don't dream you hear a B. crying boo! boo! at another B., and frighten me by crying out like a P. P.," called the Angel.

"Playful love! You try to make me forget my ills," said the Idol. "But what is P. P., sweetest?"

"Ah, I'll not tell you," said the Angel, archly; "I have my secret now."

The Idol's head seemed splitting and she had to depart without more ado.

"What is P. P.?" asked the Angel, going before one of the mirrors and imitating the poor Idol's wavering gait. "Why, puffy porpoise, ponderous princess, pompous Pandora, pawky primper, pernicious pug, and five hundred other nasty things; and you're every one of them, you old turkey, you!" And having relieved her feelings somewhat, the Angel went off to bed in her turn.

But before the disrobing operation commenced she had her little difficulty with Juanita, and the candy-eating and ghost-story telling followed, so that by the time she was ready to seek her virginal couch the delicate Angel was frightened half out of her wits. She made old Juanita lie on a rug by her bedside, and the brown animal, able to sleep in any position, wrapped herself in shawls and blankets and crouched down, her wild eyes shining and rolling in the lamp-light, for neither of them had courage to go to bed in the dark. Miss Laidley was horribly afraid, but after her face was safely muffled in the counterpane so that she could not have seen a whole troop of ghosts had they appeared, she could not resist frightening herself worse by forcing Juanita to relate another story more horrible than those which had preceded. Juanita was trembling in every withered limb, and consequently told the tale with great spirit; and when she reached the culminating point of interest—"And jes, as de clock struck twelve dere was a step in de hall—one—two—and de door opened and dere a figure stood all in white—" the clock in the dressing-room beat the fatal chimes and the Angel cowered lower in the bed with a smothered shriek which old Juanita echoed in such dismal tones that any body overhearing might have thought the luckless Angel was being devoured by an ill-regulated hyena with a morbid taste for young and tender flesh. The Angel scolded her for having terrified her, and Juanita had to disregard her own nervousness and soothe the fair creature as well as her chattering teeth would permit.

At length, after a great many false starts and numerous rousings of her brown guardian, the Angel went off to dream-land and Juanita followed: of course not into the paradise where the pretty Angel would be borne with her thoughts like white lilies, but into such lower realms as Morpheus may be pleased to reserve for animals of her calibre. How long they had slept neither could have told—it seemed to the Angel that she was only dropping into a doze, though in truth she had been slumbering peacefully for hours—when they were called back simultaneously to the dangers and troubles of waking existence by loud knocks on the door and a mournful outcry. The Angel uttered one prolonged shriek, thinking that the ghost had certainly come at last, and Juanita, responding with a howl, sprang upon the foot of the bed, and forgetful of her duties as guardian to a seraph, dragged the coverings ruthlessly off her in a wild effort to shroud her own shaking form.

The knockings continued; Miss Laidley recognized a voice—if it was a ghost it spoke in the tones of the Idol's maid—and her rage at Juanita's selfishness and presumption helped more than any thing else could have done to bring back her senses. "Get up, get up!" she exclaimed—and there was a sound as if her two fairy feet came in heavy contact with Juanita's woolly head—"go to the door, I say."

"Oh, please, Senora mia — oh de Lord! Please, young mistress! Lie still—it's a bogy —oh, don't stir!"

"If you don't get up I'll take you down to Cuba and sell you and have you whipped to death," cried the Angel; and Juanita, though born as free as Miss Laidley herself, had unlimited faith in her mistress's power and believed that she could do any thing she pleased.

She got off the bed, materially assisted by another push from the fairy feet, groaning a chorus to the knocks and calls which still went on without. "Young Senora'll be cut up," she cried. "Juanita's not feared for herself, but she's feared for young Senora;" and her chattering teeth made her voice resemble that of a long-armed ape more than ever.

But the Angel was past fearing ghosts; the pleasure of scaring Juanita out of her senses checked that dread, and she imperiously reiterated her command with worse threats than the one she had uttered about the selling of the brown carcass to be murdered by inches somewhere in the depths of Cuba. Juanita muffled her face in a shawl and sought blindly with outstretched arms for the door, nearly upsetting the table and banging her shins, which were the most sensitive portions of her anatomy, either mental or physical, against all sorts of opposing objects in a way which caused her to emit strangled squeals from beneath her head drapery. She found the door at last and unlocked it; the Angel sitting up in bed saw the Idol's maid rush in followed by another servant, both bearing lamps, half dressed, and in great excitement.

"*Madame se meurt! Madame se meurt!*" shrieked the Frenchwoman, waving her torch and nearly making a conflagration of Juanita and her shawl.

"Oh, Miss Laidley, Mrs. Hackett is a dyin',"

echoed the chambermaid in the vernacular.

The Angel darted out of bed and began to scream; old Juanita rolled herself closer in her shawl, not daring to look out in spite of the ghosts having familiar voices, and howled like a dog baying the moon. The concert executed by the four would have driven an entire flock of spectres back to the Stygian pools, convinced that the lowest realms of Pluto were not disturbed by such diabolical sounds.

"*Que faire ? Je perds la tête !*" moaned the Gallic female, forgetting her limited knowledge of English altogether in her terror.

"Don't know what on airth to do, none on us," added the chambermaid. "The housekeeper ain't tu hum, and the men's all struck of a heap. She'll die! she'll die!"

"*Oui, oui,*" cried the Frenchwoman, grasping at the English words. "She'll died, she'll died!"

Another howl from Juanita — shrieks and symptoms of hysterics from the Angel.

"I believe it's striped fever," moaned the chambermaid; "and that's the truth."

"Striped fever?" echoed Miss Laidley. "Oh, what's that? Does it kill people? Will I catch it? Let me out of the house! I won't stay to be killed—let me out!"

"Land's sake!" exclaimed the chambermaid. "You can't go and leave the poor woman to die alone?"

"I don't care how she dies!" shrieked the Angel, unable to think of any thing but fears for herself. "I wish she was dead! Why didn't she tell me she was going to have some dreadful thing, so I could get away?"

"Wal, if that aint the beat!" exclaimed the chambermaid, somewhat restored to her senses by this exhibition of character. She was native-born and seldom demeaned herself by performing domestic duties, but the housekeeper had persuaded her to come for a few weeks to take some vacant place. "Here Frenchwoman," she continued, "stop your mung duing and come along back. We'll send down to the village fur a doctor, and we'll put ice on her head, and that's all we carn do.' We've ben acting like fools, but my grit's up now and I ain't a goin' to let nobody die while I can help it."

"Is she very sick?" demanded Miss Laidley.

"She's a lunacing awful," replied the damsel. "The Frenchwoman come and woke me up so sudden I lost my head like, but I've found it now;" and she shook the organ in question, surmounted by the most wonderful tower in the shape of a night-cap that ever woman wore.

"*Que faire, O mon Dieu ! La bonne maitresse ! Mais c'est a fendu le cœur ! Elle vous appelle, Mademoiselle ! Mais venéz pour l'amour de dieu.*"

"Oh shet up!" exclaimed America, shoving her lamp under the frightened creature's nose. "None of that furrin gibberish now—jest talk a Christian tongue or don't say nothin'."

"She says Mrs. Hackett wants me," groaned Miss Laidley. "Oh, I can't go—I never do go near sick people."

"There hez to be a beginnin' to most things," replied the chambermaid, "and you carn't begin this younger. Why, come along; it ud melt a heart of stun to see her. I jest looked in, and there she lay with her face like fire, a screechin' like mad. This bawlin' furriner skeert me so that I was a fool too, and we come a yowling here instead of standin' up to our dooties."

"I know not the zootics," moaned the Frenchwoman. "*Madame se meurt!*"

"I shouldn't think yew did," exclaimed America addressing the waiting-maid, but eying Miss Laidley wrathfully, and glad to give vent to her emotions by abusing her fellow-domestic. "Now come along back and talk sense —no more gibberish. Will you come with us, Miss Laidley?"

"Oh, I can't—I don't know what to do. I am ill myself—oh, I am dying!"

"Wal, I guess you'll hev to put it off ef you want any attention," returned the native. "Some folks has one way and some another, but ef I was a young lady of name and fortin' I don't think I'd stay in my room and let a female what had loaded me with trinkets die like a dog. Come along, furriner."

"You are an impudent creature!" cried Miss Laidley. "How dare you speak like that? Do you suppose I'll be insulted by a servant?"

"Oh, there, land's sake, that upsets the bilin'!" cried the damsel, roused to desperation. "Hold this lamp, furriner. My forefathers fit and bled on Bunker Hill, and I ain't a goin' to be called a sarvint by nobody."

"Help, help! She'll kill me!" screamed the Angel, running behind the bed.

The Frenchwoman and Juanita, not half comprehending what had been said, howled more hideously than ever. The damsel's sense of the ludicrous overcame her rage, and she shook her cap-tower with laughter.

"I ain't a goin' to tech you," said she; "but remember, I'm nobody's sarvint! I come here fur a few weeks jest to oblcege. But here we be a wastin' time. Will you go or not?" Miss Laidley cowered behind the bed and made no answer. "Then come along, furriner. You'n I'll try what we can do. I ain't afeared of striped fever now."

"Oh, what is striped fever?" cried Miss Laidley, emerging from behind the bed.

"I dessay you'll find out, mum," returned the chambermaid. "They've got it awful all about. I hope you won't hev it afore mornin', fur we'll all be busy—but folks is tuk suddin'. Anyhow, you've got that ar yaller varmint to help you. Striped fever? Some folks says typhis; but up to our place we allers said striped, and I allers will."

"Typhus fever!" shrieked Miss Laidley, quite insane now. "Let me out of the house! Why, it's sure death! Let me out!"

"Pretty sure, mum, and you can't outrun it; but the side door's unlocked if you wish to try. Come along, furriner."

"Oh, don't go—don't leave me! Stay here and I'll give you a new dress—I'm very rich—I'll give you six!" exclaimed Miss Laidley.

"I've heerd of promises afore," returned she. "Dooty calls and I obey—twenty new dresses wouldn't keep me. Mebby I'm rough, mebby I'm a sarvint, but I'm made of flesh and blood, and I've got bowels, and that carn't be said of every body, ef they be pooty and rich. Come along, furriner."

The Frenchwoman and Juanita had stood stupid while the dialogue continued, occasionally throwing their heads back and uttering a simultaneous howl, but as the energetic damsel dashed out with her cap-border shaking, the Frenchwoman followed in blind obedience to the stronger will, and Juanita, concluding it was to be a grand rush somewhere for safety, darted after them. The Angel caught her in the door and dragged her back, pulled her down on the carpet and sat upon her, in order to make sure of not being quite alone, while she shrieked and moaned and beat tattoos with feet and hands upon any portion of Juanita's person that chanced to be uppermost.

There was a good deal of confusion in the house by this time, for the whole troop of servants had been roused. Some of the men had gone with all speed to the village in search of doctors, and the chambermaid was making herself of great importance, and did manage to do several little things for the poor Idol, who lay upon her bed raving with delirium and calling piteously on her sweet Angel to come and help her out of some danger. "It would melt stuns!" exclaimed the chambermaid, wringing a cloth out of ice-water and laying it on the Idol's forehead, while she addressed the group of helpless women about her. "Stuns? Yes, it would soften amadantines and nanycondys to see and hear the poor creetur, and there that young nimp sticks in her own room and won't stir a peg nur lift a hoof. Why, she ort to have a disease as much wus'n striped fever's striped fever's wus'n the measles." The listeners agreed unanimously in the sentiment, for Miss Laidley was no favorite among them.

The Idol lay there, and in spite of her wealth and grandeur many a poor creature in the humblest station would have been better cared for than she during a few hours. The house was full of servants, but the under ones were mostly Irish, the others French or German; the housekeeper was absent, the major-domo had gone on to Newport, so there was nobody to display a grain of sense except the native chambermaid. The Irishwomen were ready to collect about the bed and howl, but the French and Germans, with the exception of the bewildered waiting-woman, were so appalled by the direful name the native gave to their mistress's malady that they ran away from the part of the house where she lay in wild confusion.

The Angel sat upon the struggling Juanita,

who, nearly smothered, only gave vent at intervals to strangled squeaks and spasmodic twitches, and loudly the Angel bewailed her fate. "I shall die! I am very ill! I want a doctor! Oh, they've left me here to die alone! Oh dear, oh dear!" The words "striped fever" had filled her with such terror that in spite of the after-explanation she could not help believing the Idol had been seized with some mysterious and infectious disease, which would communicate itself to her without loss of time. Seized with fresh horror, she jumped off Juanita and ran to the light to look at her arms. "Oh, I believe the stripes are coming out on me," she moaned. "I'm dying—I'm dying!" Juanita sat up and shook herself, and drew several deep breaths to relieve her stomach, which had been so long oppressed by the Angel's weight, and began to howl again. "The old wretch!" vituperated Miss Laidley. "She did it on purpose—she's murdered me! I hope she'll die twenty times! Oh, why didn't I go with Elinor? Here I am left to die by myself."

"O young Senora, don'tee, don'tee," pleaded Juanita. "Fever won't touch you; it'll catch Juanita fust—allays takes brown folks fust. Oh, de Lord, de Lord!"

"Does it?" cried Miss Laidley, her terror brightened by a ray of hope. "Are you sure it does?"

"It allays does. Old Juanita'll die. Oh, de Lord, de Lord!"

"But you don't feel sick, do you, Juanita? You haven't got it—so I'm safe."

"Juanita feel berry sick," groaned the old woman, crouching on the floor and swinging her short body back and forth—"berry sick. Oh, de Lord, de Lord!"

"If you dare to get the fever I'll kill you!" shouted the Angel furiously. "I'll take you to Cuba—I'll have your flesh torn off with red-hot pincers! Get up, you old devil, get up!"

"Oh, de Lord, de Lord! Oh, my stomaco!" cried Juanita, making fierce gripes at the organ in question with her claw-like hands.

"Oh don't die—please don't," sobbed Miss Laidley. "I'll give you a new turban if you won't—I'll give you a new gown."

Juanita sat upright and clutched the organ. "Gib 'em now, young Senora," she said, like a wise magpie. "Mebby old Juanita be better then."

In her fright Miss Laidley ran to a wardrobe and pulled down the first dress she laid hands on, caught up a blue scarf that had been the chief longing of Juanita's soul for weeks, and flung them toward her. "Take them, take them," she cried. "I'll give you every thing I have in the world if you won't be sick, dear Juanita. Come to the light and let me see if you have stripes on your arms." Juanita bundled the treasures under her dress and approached the table, baring her witch's arms to her mistress's eager gaze. But the brown shrivelled skin was uniform in color. "There's nothing the matter, you old cat," shrieked Miss Laidley; "you

only wanted to frighten me! Oh, I'll have you beaten! You shan't keep the things!"

"Such dre'ful pain here," moaned Juanita, pressing her hands hard against her food-casket once more, and skilled in theatricals from long watching of her mistress. "Dre'ful pain! Stripes all inside, young Senora, and dat's wust. Oh, old Juanita'll die, she'll die!"

"Don't, don't die," sobbed the Angel, frightened again and reduced to abject submission. "There's some wine in the closet—the Duchess brought it up when I was sick the other day. You shall have some—I'll get it. Don't die, dear old Juanita, and leave your poor little mistress who loves you so." The promise of the wine induced Juanita to postpone the death-struggle, and the Angel hurried to unlock the closet and produce the bottle. "Drink it, drink it!" she cried eagerly; "it is sherry. You'll be well after, I know you will." Juanita, anxious to live a little longer as a special favor to her beloved Senora, did not wait to pour the wine in a glass, but raised the bottle to her lips, threw her head back, and allowed the contents to gurgle down her throat, while she kicked her feet in ecstasy, and the Angel, thinking the movement caused by a spasm of pain, was more alarmed than before. "Are you better—has it done you good, Juanita dear?" she asked tearfully, when Juanita removed the bottle from her lips to get a little breath.

"Some good — little better," replied she, smacking her lips, but holding fast to the bottle. "Mebby old Juanita won't die jes' yet, but young Senora must be good. Stripes all inside and dey might bust out and young Senora ketch 'em."

"Go away—get out of the room! I won't catch them," moaned the Angel. "Oh, you wicked old woman!"

"Young Senora mustn't be frightened," said Juanita, beginning to roll her eyes more wildly than usual and to speak a little thickly as the fumes of the golden cordial mounted to her brain. "Jes' keep quiet, young Senora. Mebby old Juanita can get to sleep, and then she won't die."

"You shan't go to sleep! I won't be left alone."

"Oh! oh! dese stripes," moaned Juanita, smiting her stomach with one hand and raising the bottle with the other. "Wuster and wuster, young Senora—mustn't let 'em break out."

There were new sounds in the hall. The men had returned in hot haste, bringing every physician that could be knocked up in the neighborhood, and the disciples of Esculapius, astonished at this meeting of the clans, glared wrathfully upon each other and were inclined to go away individually because so many had been called. Fortunately a noted physician from town chanced to be staying at the Lake House, an acquaintance of the Idol's, and on his appearance the lesser lights paled and he went to work like a sensible man. The Angel heard the tread of feet, the rushing to and fro, and thought the Idol must be dead, or that the demons who ruled the fever were coming in a body to attack her. She bundled herself into a wadded dressing-gown and got her feet in a pair of stockings and slippers. "I won't stay another minute in the house," she screamed; "I shall die here! I won't die—I can't die!"

"Don'tee, don'tee, young Senora," grunted Juanita, who had nearly finished the bottle and was too comfortable to remember the stripes variegating her interior and threatening to break out if she was crossed. "Don'tee, don'tee. No fever here. Let old Duchess debbil die. Can't come here—yah, yah!"

"You're drunk. You'll kill me!" shrieked Miss Laidley. "Help! help! Come somebody! I'm dying—Juanita's murdering me! Help! help!" She caught a blanket from the bed, wrapped it about her, and ran out into the hall in a paroxysm of terror which for the time made a veritable lunatic of her.

Juanita dropped the bottle, after draining the last drop, and staggered on behind, echoing her mistress's cries without knowing wherefore, hiccuping and sobbing in a maudlin way. They encountered the native chambermaid with a pitcher in her hand, which she nearly dropped in her enjoyment of the spectacle. "Is she dead?" cried Miss Laidley. "Let me out! I won't stay! Is she dead?"

"Wal, not to say as yit," replied the chambermaid, who had been relieved by the doctor's assurance that, although very ill, the patient was in no immediate peril. "She's alive yit; but law, this striped fever is turrible! I hope yew wun't ketch it; fair-haired folks allus hez it wus'n others—I'm dark myself."

"Oh, let me out!—let me out! Call the doctor! Tell him I'm dying! Say it's Miss Laidley the heiress—I'll make him rich if he'll come and cure me."

"Bery rich, young Senora," grunted Juanita. "Bring doctor."

"Doctor's got his hands full now," responded the damsel with grim delight. "Miss Laidley the hairess'll hev to put off dyin' jest at present. The doors is all onlocked ef ye want to get out, but you'd better heel it nimble or Striped'll ketch up with ye."

Miss Laidley gave another shriek and darted down stairs, Juanita tumbling after, and the grim damsel set the pitcher on the floor and shook herself in silent mirth. She waited until the outer door banged behind them, then she flew down and fastened every means of ingress and returned chuckling to her duties.

Miss Laidley had dashed out at a side door, and she ran to the back of the house, too frightened to do more than gasp, seeking some place of shelter, while Juanita followed with unsteady steps, grunting brokenly — "Don'tee, don'tee, young Senora. Old Juanita keep Striped off—dar, dar!" An out-building in which fire-wood was stored chanced to be the first refuge Miss Laidley discovered in the darkness: she ran in and cowered down in a corner

and went off in veritable spasms. Old Juanita, stumbling along in her wake, happened to fall on a pile of shavings, and the bed being soft and warm she soon went to sleep and left her mistress to her fate. When Miss Laidley could think or cry out again, she heard a horrible sound like the growls of a wild beast which filled her with dread. "Juanita!" she shrieked. —There was no response — the growls grew louder. — "She's gone—I'm all alone! Help! help!" shouted the Angel. But nothing answered save the echo of her own voice and the ominous sounds. She shrieked again with no better success; she moaned, she sobbed, she had convulsions, and when she was nearly dead with terror and cold she rolled over on the pile of shavings and lay there. When day-light roused some of the men her cries were overheard. They ran to the spot and discovered the Angel moaning among the shavings and Juanita snoring in blissful unconsciousness near at hand, unseen by her mistress, who had believed herself alone with some terrible enemy. She was carried up to her room, and Juanita, effectually roused by having a pail of water poured over her head by the native chambermaid who came out to look after them, was able to assist in getting her mistress in bed. The chambermaid was sleepy and had no pity to waste on the suffering Angel; indeed, reckless of consequences, she did not hesitate to overwhelm her with reproaches and to tell her that what she had endured was a judgment on her cruelty, and added, as a final blow, that she was certain to catch the striped fever now in its most malignant form. Miss Laidley had no strength to answer, and the damsel having no faith in hysterics, and small pity for convulsions, ruthlessly dosed her with valerian and brandy and left her paralyzed by that last threat, which she followed up with— "I'll look in agin if I hev time'n, remember jest to see whether you're dead or not—so good-bye."

The Angel fell asleep from sheer exhaustion, and Juanita, curled up like a dog on the floor, slept off the confusion left in her senses by her unaccustomed libations. The doctor had gone away at length, promising to come back soon and bring a nurse, and as the housekeeper would return that day, the servants recovered their sanity in the morning light and went about their duties with tolerable regularity. In the mean time the native chambermaid watched over the bedside of the Idol, who had become more composed and dozed a little at intervals, but was very, very ill.

CHAPTER XXXV.

TWO WOMEN.

EARLY that morning one of the Castle servants, dispatched upon some errand, chanced to encounter a man employed on Clive Farnsworth's place, and gave him an account of his mistress's illness. The news was brought to

Ruth by her staid housekeeper soon after breakfast. Clive had gone out on some business, the breakfast having been hastened on his account, and Ruth could not wait for his return. Under ordinary circumstances she could never undertake the least thing without consulting him, but the tidings filled her with grief and she could not delay an instant. She must go over to the Castle, for the idea of poor Mrs. Hackett lying unattended, unless by frightened domestics and a helpless creature like Miss Laidley, inspired her with horror. She was certain that Miss Laidley must have been at her bedside all night, and would know nothing about illness, and Ruth was a born nurse. She must go at once, and the carriage was ordered in great haste and a note scribbled to Clive, that he might be made aware of what had happened.

Ruth had heard there was fever in the village, but the fear that it might be infectious did not deter her for an instant. If she had been going to certain death it would have been as impossible for her to hesitate or think about herself as it would for the Angel to have forgotten her own precious safety and behave with decency and composure. She drove over to the Castle, and neither the doctor nor housekeeper having returned, she was met by the Goddess of Liberty, who shoved the Frenchwoman aside and told her story clearly, feeling with the first glance at Ruth's face that she had at last encountered a woman blessed with a little common sense.

"Can I go up?" Ruth asked, when she had finished her account. "I know Mrs. Hackett well. I shall not disturb her, and I am accustomed to sick people."

"She was a dozin' when I came down," replied the chambermaid, "but the minit she wakes up I'll tell her, and precious glad I shall be to hev a little help frum somebody with a head-piece on their shoulders."

"Is Miss Laidley lying down?" asked Ruth.

"Yes'm, she's laid down, she has," returned Liberty with emphasis.

"Poor thing," said Ruth, "she is worn out, I suppose; one night's watching is hard on any person not accustomed to it."

"Wal, yes," replied the native with grim but unbounded delight, "I believe a body may say she watched all night—yes. Oh, mebby you're afeared of fevers too, mum, and this is what we call, over our way, striped."

"Striped fever? I never heard of it," said Ruth in amazement.

"Wal, I s'pose the more geological name is typhis," returned the native; "but where I was rose they called it striped, and I do as folks did where I was rose."

"Typhus fever," said Ruth; "oh, the poor thing! I am glad I came. I have seen a good many cases of it, and I shall be glad to help you till the nurse comes."

The Goddess of Liberty gave her an approving scowl. "You ain't like our young hairess," said she. "I thought she'd a died with fright."

"She is very fond of Mrs. Hackett."

"Wal, she mought be, 'nd she moughtn't. Anyhow, she wished her dead, and run out and sot all night on a pile of shavin's, and that drunken yaller catamount along with her; an' she's in bed this blessed minit, 'nd well I dosed her with valerium and old cut-your-eye, fur where I was rose we don't hev much pity fur hystrikes, I carn tell you." The young woman uttered her speech volubly, and before Ruth could answer, went on—"Riches don't make a lady, and a person may be young and well favored, but that don't hender their bein' snakes; and ef ever I see a snake, and a cold-blooded one, it's that young hairess."

"You must not speak in that way of any guest Mrs. Hackett may have," said Ruth, with her gentle dignity. "I will go up and see Miss Laidley, if you will be good enough to show me her room."

"I will and glad to. I know a lady when I see her, and you're one, born, rose, and edicated," cried the native, determined to finish the expression of her opinions. "I never was called a sarvint afore, and it's what I shan't bear, and so I told her. I came here to obleege—jest for a few weeks, 'cause the housekeeper's a friend of mine, an' 'twasn't suspected the madam or that young sarpint—hairess—would come back; but I'm no waiter."

"You must not be angry because Miss Laidley in her fright—"

"Oh, law, I mind her no more'n a muskety! I'm of New England extract—I was rose partly there and partly in Herkimer county—and I've teached school in Pennsylvany where I went to stay with an aunt of mine, an' I expose I've ketched some of their unorthographical expressions; but I know a lady, and you're one—there!"

She wheeled about and showed Ruth the way to the Angel's room, and when Ruth entered Juanita sat on the rug rubbing her red eyes, the Angel woke, recognized her visitor, and began to sob and shriek with delight. "Have you come to take me away? Oh, you darling creature—I love you so! I am almost dead! The poor Duchess is ill—I got fastened out-of-doors by a wicked wretch who ought to go to prison. Oh, take me away! I shall die—I can't die here!"

Ruth comforted her and tried to make her somewhat reasonable, but that was never the Angel's forte. "I heard of Mrs. Hackett's illness and came over to see if I could help in any way," she said.

The Angel was smitten with a new fear. "Have you been in her room? Do you want to give me the fever?" she shrieked. "Oh, you heartless creature—a poor young orphan like me!" Ruth hastened to re-assure her. "Then take me away—take me to your house—I won't stay here! Somebody must telegraph to my guardian—he shall come after me. He and Elinor are cruel wretches to desert me in this way," moaned the Angel, too thoroughly alarmed to try to hide her selfishness or make it interesting.

"My husband will send a dispatch to Mr. Grey," Ruth said. "You shall go to our house if you like, Miss Laidley."

"Yes, let me go at once. I'd go anywhere to get away! Take me right away, you darling."

"I must see poor Mrs. Hackett first—she is very ill. I must stay with her till a nurse comes and her husband can be sent for," Ruth said.

"Then you'll come and give me the fever! Oh, they'll kill me—every body wants to kill me!" sobbed the Angel.

"You can go back in the carriage," continued Ruth; "I will have you made comfortable, and you shall not see me until there is no danger. But indeed, Miss Laidley, the fever is not infectious in the way you fear."

"Oh, yes it is. I should be sure to get it—I am so delicate. I must go away — I can't wait."

"As soon as my husband comes," Ruth said, "you shall go. You had better have a cup of tea now and get dressed."

"I will. Oh, you must take care of me—I'm a baby! It is cruel of my guardian and Elinor to expose me to such things. Don't leave me —stay here by me."

But Ruth was roused by such mention of Elinor and said, "I must go to Mrs. Hackett; she needs me."

"So do I," sobbed the Angel; "I'm a great deal sicker than she. I've caught my death of cold, and I've the fever besides."

Ruth ordered Juanita, who was still stupid from her late revel, to get her mistress some tea, and having done every thing she could to comfort Miss Laidley, went away to the Idol's chamber. The poor Idol was awake and rational for the moment, and so glad to see Ruth that it was pitiful. "You idolizable Cynthia!" she cried, employing the huge words still from force of habit, "I can not thank you. Dear friend, I am so ill—but I trust it is not serious."

"You must lie quiet and try to sleep," Ruth said. "I am going to sit by you."

"So good! And have you seen my poor Angel? Don't let her come in, for she is so nervous and delicate," said the thoughtful Idol. "I ought not to let you stay."

"I shall not go away if you send me," Ruth said pleasantly, and by this time the Idol was glad to lie still.

Ruth threw off her bonnet, and in ten minutes, without making the least bustle, she had effected a total transformation in the appearance of the room. The disorder had vanished, the light was properly shaded, an open window made a pleasant coolness, and the Idol was refreshed by having her face and hands bathed in cold water and her bed so softly arranged that she fell asleep with some broken words of thanks on her lips. When the doctor arrived he told Ruth that he had telegraphed for Mr. Hackett and a nurse, and Ruth, hearing that there was not a fit one to be found in the neighborhood, assured him that she should not leave her post until proper assistance arrived. The doctor glanced about the transformed chamber, looked at her, and he knew that she was capable of fulfilling the task she had undertaken. "You must tell me just what to do," Ruth said, "just how ill she is, and then you may trust me. I am accustomed to the care of sick people."

The doctor could have worshiped her, for he had been at his wits' end. They left the native chambermaid in possession for the time, while he went away with Ruth to explain matters thoroughly. "My dear lady," said he, "you take a great load off my mind."

"I am anxious to do all I can," Ruth answered. "Mrs Hackett is so entirely alone, in spite of this houseful. She is an old friend of my husband's too."

The doctor was very desirous to learn who this pretty, unselfish creature was, and he asked in the suavest way, that, as he said, he might know by what name to address his fair coadjutor.

"I am Mrs. Farnsworth," Ruth answered.

The doctor nearly whistled—he had heard the dying whispers of gossip on his arrival. "I know your husband well, dear Madam," he said. "I can not refuse your aid — but indeed, you must be very careful. There is no positive danger of infection—"

"I am not in the least afraid, Sir," interrupted Ruth. "I will be careful, but I can not leave her."

"Why, Madam, you are—you are an angel!" cried the doctor enthusiastically, and Ruth laughed.

She made him explain exactly what she was to do, and he was to come up again that day. The fever was not typhus, it was some peculiar type of disease such as occasionally rushes through a neighborhood. A good many people were coming down with it, though how the poor Idol should have been so quickly seized was one of those inexplicable things which even physicians can not throw light upon. The doctor said he feared that the fever was going to prevail to a considerable extent, and would perhaps become an epidemic among the poor people in a village on the opposite side of the lake, but there was little danger to be apprehended in Mrs. Hackett's case. "I think it right to tell you these things, Madam," he said, "so that if you have any fear you can leave the house at once; and if you did nobody could blame you—nine women out of ten would go."

"Oh, what will those poor people do over in South village?" cried Ruth, not hearing his last observation. "Can't something be done at once? I wish you would wait till my husband gets here. Some plan must be settled on. It will be terrible!"

The doctor thought she was beyond angelic now, and he promised to wait and see Mr. Farnsworth, and consoled her by saying that while he remained in the neighborhood he would do every thing in his power.

"If it can be kept from spreading among those poor creatures!"

The doctor said it was only in ill-ventilated dwellings, and among those who were less cleanly and well cared for than they ought to be, that the fever was likely to prove fatal, and the South village, as it was called, was a cluster of Irish shanties, rum-houses, and other fungus growth that had sprung up during the past year. A tunnel was being excavated for a new railway, and the work had brought its usual accompaniments of a hurried hamlet which looked like booths erected for a fair, and misery and drunkenness and like horrors.

The Idol woke and began to moan, and Ruth returned to her bedside, bathed her forehead again, fanned her and soothed her, as only one woman in a score can quiet a sick person. The doctor went down stairs to await Farnsworth's arrival and to meditate upon the beauty and virtues of Farnsworth's wife, and to think, very justly, that any body who could look in her face and not feel she was every thing that was pure and lovable, must have a mind so hopelessly contaminated that nothing but a vigorous scouring with some sort of mental soda could afford it the least benefit. It was not long before Clive arrived in hot haste, having heard of the spread and nature of the fever, and quite beside himself at the idea of Ruth exposed to danger. He was ready to blame the doctor, of course, because it is natural for any man to blame somebody when trouble arrives, but the doctor cleared his skirts by declaring that Mrs. Farnsworth was in the sick-room when he reached the house, and could not be induced to leave her post, although he had told her of the possible danger. "And, Sir," cried he, "I took the liberty of telling her that she was an angel, and I repeat it to you, Sir—an angel, no less! Most women would have left Mrs. Hackett to the care of servants and thought it right."

"But I can't have my wife run such risks," returned Clive. And Ruth, having heard of his arrival, entered the room as he spoke the words, and coming behind him, laid her hand softly on his shoulder and said—"Dear old Clive, there is no danger;, if there were you would not let me run away from so plain a duty." Clive put his arm about her and held her fast.

"Did I say she was an angel?" cried the old doctor, blowing his nose till it sounded like a trumpet. "Bah! there must be female angels too good to be sent on errands like the male ones mentioned; and she's one of them—come down for your special benefit, Sir—that's what she is!" and he blew his trumpet again.

"You see I must stay, dear," continued Ruth. "The room is well aired—there is no danger. I think the fever is very like that I helped in once. But oh, Clive, something must be done for those poor people in South village! Do help them! If the fever gets there, think of the misery."

"Yes, yes, only don't be distressed."

The doctor held out both hands in an appealing way. The gesture said plainly—"There is no comparison for this woman; I want one and can't find it." And he sounded his trumpet a third time. You see the old doctor, in spite of his oddities, was a favorite physician among delicate women who had on velvet and could scarcely breathe common air, and he was so accustomed to selfishness that it bewildered him to see this young creature, rich and elegant, ready to believe that she had strength to help herself and other people into the bargain.

"Mr. Hackett is certain to be up before night," Clive said.

"Oh yes," returned Ruth; "don't think about that any more, dear. But you will see to-day that something is done to warn those poor people?—and the doctor will help." They both promised her, provided she in her turn would not think and be disturbed. "And Miss Laidley! O Clive, I forgot poor Miss Laidley," Ruth exclaimed. "She is frightened almost to death. It seems she got fastened out of the house in the confusion and stayed all night in a shed."

"How came she out?" asked Clive.

"I think in her alarm—" Ruth did not care to finish her explanation, because it would have been an exposure of the young lady's selfishness.

"She ran out," added the doctor; "of course she did. Nine people out of ten would have run at being told that there was an infectious disease near. It seems that young woman who is here 'to obleege' for a few weeks, frightened them all by calling it starred and barred fever—no, striped."

"Miss Laidley can return in the carriage," continued Ruth. "I think the doctor had better see her first, she is so nervous. I must go back to Mrs. Hackett now. Good-bye, Clive."

Clive followed her into the hall to beg her to be careful, and to hold her close in his arms for a moment with an undefined but poignant premonition of danger. She whispered a few cheering words and ran away, and he went back to the doctor to await Miss Laidley's appearance. Ruth had sent her word that she could leave the house, and that Mr. Farnsworth was waiting for her. So the Angel got out of bed and put by her fright long enough to dress herself becomingly. She would have done that if she had been struck with death, and would have been divided between horror of the summons and a dread that she might have to go before assuring herself that her corpse would be picturesquely attired. She descended upon the gentlemen, very pale, sobbing and trembling anew, and fancied herself looking lovely, and she was; but they had the remembrance of another type of woman fresh in their minds, and were not much touched by her weakness and her tears as they might have been under other circumstances. "Oh, Mr. Farnsworth!" she cried, rushing up to him and snatching his hands. "You have come to take me away! Bless you—heaven bless you, my preserver! I am ill—dying! Oh, let me go at once!"

The doctor rubbed his hands and nodded approval; that was the sort of performance he expected from fragile creatures at an extremity like the present, and he was glad to have his experience put straight again, for Ruth had upset all his theories.

"You can go at once, Miss Laidley," Clive answered. "My wife has told me that you have been much alarmed."

"Ill—dying! A fiendish woman drove me out of the house in the middle of the night. Somebody ought to punish her. Oh, if my papa were living! But I am a helpless, desolate orphan. Oh, father! father!" She went through the old scene, striking an attitude and flinging her arms aloft, and as the sleeves of her dress were loose, her arms showed to good advantage.

Clive retreated and the doctor whispered in his ear—"I say, she does it very well—very well. Now that's the sort of thing I understand and expect. Lord bless you, if it was her dear papa sick up stairs, she'd be for running off all the same."

"Take me away, take me away!" moaned Miss Laidley, noticing the whispers, and thinking that her point, as the actors say, had been more appreciated than it was.

"As soon as you please," said Clive. "My wife—"

"She mustn't come near me," interrupted Miss Laidley, forgetting every thing again in fears for for her own safety. "She shan't come —she'll poison me! She must fumigate herself, or whatever it is—I won't be killed!"

"We will do our best to preserve your life," returned Clive, too much disgusted to be more than civil. "By the way, Miss Laidley, this gentleman is Dr. Aldrich. I dare say he can recommend something to help your nervousness."

The Angel stretched out her hands to him in mute appeal, as she might have done if she had been on a burning roof or a plank in mid-ocean, and he had appeared to save her. The doctor felt her pulse, and mixed some sugar and water for her and said flattering things, and she soon felt strengthened. She began to tell them how much she had suffered, how six times she had tried to get into the chamber of her darling Duchess and thrice she fainted on the threshold—her spirit was brave, but ah, she was so frail! Thrice that evil woman had pushed her back, and then had driven her from the house, and she wandered about in the grounds, alone, deserted, till morning came and some Samaritan found her stretched lifeless upon the turf.

"The most affecting thing I ever heard," exclaimed the doctor, who had listened to the story already as rendered by the chambermaid, and so took it at its proper value. "The woman ought to be gibbeted."

Miss Laidley was so much encouraged by his sympathy that she heightened her account with a few more details. "I knelt on the damp earth beneath the casement of my dying friend and prayed. I believed that our souls would go out together—it was all I asked."

"Beautiful!" said the doctor. "It is as romantic as a novel; but much more real and touching, much more."

Clive thought she had gone far enough, and advised her to get her bonnet on and depart—every moment spent in the house was running a new danger.

"Let me go!" she cried, in a tremor again. "I'll be ready in an instant. Oh, let me get away!" She darted out of the room and the doctor nodded his head many times and rubbed his hands in glee.

"I've seen a great many of them do that sort of thing," said he, "but she beats Vestris—perfect! And to see her get frightened in earnest every few minutes, and stop lying to own her fears and show her selfishness. It was perfect, Sir, perfect."

"It was disgusting," said Clive, who had a bad habit of speaking his mind when roused.

"Nonsense, nonsense," returned the doctor. "She must behave according to her gifts. Can't expect all women to be like that angel of yours, Sir. According to her gifts she acts; and by Jupiter, she acts well! It's a pity she's rich; she'd have done wonders on the stage."

"Most people consider her a pretty, thoughtless child," said Clive.

"Of course they do; so they ought. But I'm a doctor, and you're a writer—we see a little closer. Bless you, she's delightful! Why, she'll do an amount of mischief in this world that is refreshing to think of," replied the physician. "In a decorous way; she hasn't stamina—not blood and bone enough to get beyond that."

Miss Laidley came back followed by Juanita, and the old doctor felt her pulse again, and told her what a fragile flower she was, and she beamed. "Did the medicine help you?" he asked.

"Oh, so much! It must have been very powerful. I thank you—I shall think of you as my preserver." The doctor was a picture. "And oh, Mr. Farnsworth! I want to send a telegram to my guardian: he must come for me," she continued.

"I will go down to the village myself if you will give me his address," replied Clive. Miss Laidley wrote it on a slip of paper, and wrote the message also, not stopping to count the words, because she recollected that Farnsworth would have to pay for it. "Doctor," continued Clive, who felt that he could not endure more of her society just then, "perhaps you will have the kindness to go to my house with Miss Laidley while I attend to this. The carriage can take you down to the hotel after, and I'll drive down in your trap."

The doctor was quite ready to study this peculiar phase of human nature a little longer, being given to odd theories, so he expressed the pleasure he should have in serving the young lady. Miss Laidley gave him one of her sweetest looks, for she thought him much more impressionable than Clive, and the doctor thought, "If she only had more stamina—more blood and bone! But the acting is good, and in theory she must be immense. What a course of foreign literature she has gone through—bless the little dear!" He saw Miss Laidley safe in Farnsworth's house, and recommended her and Juanita, whom he felt certain was a brown ape gifted with the faculty of speech, to the housekeeper's best care, and went back to the hotel to await the train which ought to bring the Idol's other half and a nurse.

The Bull arrived sorely dismayed, for he was fond of his Idol in his way, and was divided between grief at her illness and distress at leaving Wall Street in a critical juncture. He brought another physician and a brace of nurses, and Clive thought he could take Ruth home, but the Idol, still partially astray in her mind, conceived an aversion to both nurses and would not permit Ruth to leave her. The Bull was helpless as a spring calf, and could only wander about the house and bellow mournfully. Clive was forced to yield to Ruth's importunities; she could not be heartless·enough to go away, and he could not wish her to, anxious as he was. He drove home to tell Miss Laidley that his wife could not return, and being too much engrossed by his fears for her to pay the Angel much attention, she determined to do something annoying if she could. She was seized with scruples—impossible for her to remain there, in the absence of the mistress of the house, if he did. She was an orphan—an unprotected child —she must be very cautious in the merest trifles. Clive was only too glad of an excuse to get back to the Castle, and departed without wasting many words upon her. He kept the Bull company nearly a fortnight, for the Idol's illness had taken too firm a hold to be easily subdued, and she would allow no one but Ruth to attend upon her. So Ruth stayed, and did not take leisure to think she was a heroine or to think about herself at all. Once during that time the Bull made a rush down into Wall Street to see that affairs were prospering, but the rest of the period he lowed sorrow-stricken about the home pasture and threw himself helplessly on Clive for society, and the two animals, having no more sympathies or ideas in common than a bovine monster and the fabled Pegasus would have had, were both of them in distressing case by the time the sojourn was ended. Miss Laidley's dispatch had been speedily answered, and her guardian found her an escort without being obliged to journey back himself, so she and Juanita and her wilderness of trunks departed. She would not go to the Castle for an instant— left a brief note for Ruth and hurried off in great delight, so full of the new scenes and possible adventures to which she might be going that she never so much as remembered the Idol and her illness.

The blessed old soul could sit up at last, and the Bull and Clive were admitted into her room when she was for the first time lifted out of bed.

It was ludicrous and yet touching to see her gratitude to the husband and wife, and weak as she was she would articulate immense phrases that burst out like spent cannon-balls. "I have no syllableization!" she cried. "Apollo, Apollo, my heart pants for expressiveness and finds it not! Thank her, my husband—go down on your knees to her!" The Bull mumbled a few words, but was very much out of his element, and so confused by the request that Ruth took pity upon him and talked in his stead. The Idol promised that she would not be selfish any longer—on the next day they might return home. They must sleep under her roof once more. Ruth should go to bed and have a long rest— no, even in her weakness she was not guilty of saying "go to bed." "Morphean garlands shall strew her couch," said she. "But remain—when I wake in the gloom I must be cheered by remembering that my dwelling is guarded by her presence." She kissed Ruth, she wept over Clive, and they had to force her to lie down and be quiet, lest she should do herself harm. "And I have been trouble enough," she said, submissive as a child, "so I will obey."

She was able to see them before their departure the next morning, and could utter more thanks and call down more blessings on their heads. She spoke kindly of her absent Angel, but it was plain that she was much hurt at her not having left a message in her haste, though Ruth good-naturedly excused her. "Yes, yes," said the Idol, "she is young—youth is effervescing! But you, dear lady—there are no words." She was strong enough to be indignant at a new performance of Mrs. Piffit's which the Bull related to her. Piffit had besieged his Wall Street stable and told him she was his wife's friend, and forced him to take her money to invest in some wonderful speculation of his which she had heard talked about till she forgot her usual prudence. Clive laughed at this last effort of the Piffit, but was glad to cut short the farewells and get Ruth away.

They were once more in their own house; and though Ruth was very pale and completely worn out, she insisted that it was only fatigue that ailed her. She would not go to bed, and she would sit by Clive and talk and be cheerful and try to forget the dreary ache of body and nerves in her joy at being home again. She was saying, "I am so glad, so glad—" when the dizziness and weakness asserted itself, and she sank fainting in the arms of her terrified husband.

CHAPTER XXXVI.

ONE TOO MANY.

Our party of travellers were stopping on the shore of Lake Champlain for a few days when the news from Miss Laidley broke in upon their enjoyment, and plans for her joining them had to be arranged. Rosa spoke aloud the secret sentiments of each member of the group, bewailed this intrusion, and called the Angel an ungrateful little monster for deserting the Idol in her sickness. But there was nothing for it only to wait there until she could reach the place, and a more lovely spot to rest in during the golden summer days can well be imagined. They were established at a hotel near Burlington in Vermont, on the banks of the beautiful lake. Back of them stretched the range of the Green Mountains; in front, away beyond the bright waters, the grassy plains, and the waving woods, rose the lofty peaks of the Adirondacs, so glorious in the changing light that it was like a glimpse of the Delectable Hills to watch them. The sunsets were so gorgeous that it seemed heaven itself opened in full splendor—the grandeur and yet exquisite loveliness of the view fairly intoxicated one's senses with its beauty.

Elinor Grey revelled in the beauty of the spot, and her companions were congenial associates. Such days as they had! The rides among the hills; the sails on the lake; the dinners over at that old farm-house on the opposite side where there was a bevy of pretty girls; the freedom; the sense of renewed health and vigor—they all enjoyed it immensely. And into the midst of their pleasure must come the shadow of the Angel's arrival; and as Rosa vowed, "it was too bad." "One so seldom has a happy week," she declared; "and to have this spoiled by that little cat! You need not look shocked, Mr. Grey—you need not try to frown, Elinor—you hate it as much as I do. I wish she was back in Jamaica. She's an angel, and I wish she was up in purer air. I've a mind to cry! I'll bite her if she attempts to kiss me!"

"Go it, gentle woman," cried Tom.

"And all her graces—bah! Her nerves and her sorrow—we shall have the whole. The outrageous little pigeon, to run off and leave the poor Idol! Oh dear me, life is a burden."

"And you are out of breath, fortunately," replied Elinor. "Submit to fate with becoming fortitude, my Rosa."

"Not when it comes in the form of Miss Laidley," she averred. "Never mind! I'll mimic her; I'll be as wicked as she is—no, that is impossible; but I'll do my best."

"And we can ask no more," said Mr. Grey, laughing, who in his heart had never quite forgiven his ward for having so nearly made a fluffy, disjointed idiot of him.

"There is one consolation," cried Rosa; "we all know her thoroughly. She can't do any mischief; Elinor has conquered her in all sorts of quiet ways."

"Let us hope, then," said Mr. Grey, "that she understands—' Una salus victis, nullam sperare salutem;'" and he was one of the few men who can quote the classics without being absurd. I think it was the way in which he took out his snuff-box carried off the quotations.

"She understands it if it is any thing wicked, you may be sure," returned Rosa. "There! I won't say a word more. Don't all look shocked. When she comes I will be very sweet to her, but she shall not torment us, and she shall not make us change our plans."

Miss Laidley arrived in due course, and verified Rosa's prediction about her nerves, her sorrow, and all the rest. There was nobody whom she could hope to fascinate, and she proved a nuisance, always wanting to do the very thing that was most inconvenient and most opposed to the others' wishes. But even Rosa bore with her patiently enough; when the Angel was too annoying she mimicked her, and when she was poetical she solaced herself by private grimaces at Tom. (Let me remark, in passing, that the amusement which children call "making faces" may not be elegant, but it is a wonderful relief to the feelings. Just try it when somebody bores you. Pretend to hunt for something in a corner, any thing to get your back toward the bore, and then go through the performance. You can return to your seat and endure like a Christian after. I was staying one summer in the country, and was dreadfully persecuted by a solemn man who would come to see me, and who would prose, till, if I had not made faces, I should inevitably have burst a blood-vessel or split his head. As it was, I put a box on my table that had a glass in it, and every now and then I solaced myself by a series of grimaces, which refreshed me as much as an hour's gymnastics would have done. I kept charmingly civil; and I like to be civil—except when my temper's up. But on a luckless morning some fiend of a chambermaid put away the box. The solemn man appeared, and he was a more outrageous bore than ever—he was ten bores rolled into one. Civility deserted me: I made a horrible face directly in his; and, thinking it was no use to be careful after the ice was broken, I treated him to a delightful bit of my mind. He went away and abused me worse than most people did, and they in general abused me enough; but he was a solemn man and a pious, and wanted to do his duty—how he did give it me behind my back!) But they all bore the infliction of the Angel's presence with a better grace than she did what she called "a horrid waste of time." They went to Canada; strayed about quaint old Quebec, steamed to Montreal, saw Montmorency, and floated down the St. Lawrence among the Thousand Islands, and every body enjoyed it except the Angel. Even old Juanita chewed bark and kept her composure, and was glad she seldom had to be alone with her mistress; and she certainly had reason to congratulate herself upon that fact, for, when any opportunity to vent her feelings did occur, the Angel pinched and pulled her to such an extent that Juanita's arms and neck seemed dotted with small rainbows. The old witch, however, had her share of craft and cunning; she made the Angel observe how thin the partition walls were, and after that if her mistress, rendered desperate by the ills of life, appeared inclined to seek a little consolation in tinting and tattooing her brown flesh, Juanita would utter loud lamentations, and as Elinor's room was on one side of Miss Laidley's apartment and Mrs. Thornton's on the other, the unfortunate girl was deprived of her last resource. She was very severe in her strictures upon the careless mode of building houses prevalent in the land, and in sharp whispers reproached Juanita bitterly for her selfishness and insubordination; but Juanita rubbed her spotted arms ruefully, and rolled up her eyes in mingled entreaty and warning. She was blindly attached to her mistress, as a dog sometimes is to a cruel master, and when there was no avoiding the pinches she took them as a part of this world's experiences; but when thin walls and near neighbors offered a prospect of relief, Juanita could not resist taking advantage of it. The Angel thought her conduct in keeping with the dismal era upon which she had fallen, and pitied herself as the most unfortunate seraph breathing, with a quartet of horrid people at hand to annoy her, and no speedy means of relief visible—not the ghost of a flirtation to be got at. She kept a close lookout upon such travellers as appeared, but there was nothing to reward her. Several times parties of men bound for the Adirondacs came, but they only stayed over night, and when the Angel had caught sight of some man among them who looked worth dressing for, she had exerted herself to go down stairs to breakfast in a picturesque costume, and found to her disgust that the whole set had gone off at some preposterously early hour, too anxious to reach the region of primeval forests, with their attractions in the way of hunting, even to wait for a second glance at her. One man did come and stay several days—a raven-haired, melancholy man, with a charming pallor of visage and a long mustache, who did nothing but stare at her whenever she appeared. The Angel began to meditate ways and means of acquaintance—having decided from his looks that he was an Italian exile, in better circumstances, evidently, than the generality of those devoted heroes, for he dressed well and had horses and servants—when Tom Thornton innocently spoiled her dawning poem by pointing him out to Rosa in her hearing and giving his history. He was a Jew clothes-merchant, who had made an immense fortune, softened his original appellation of Jacob Jacobs into Jaccopo Jacopi, cut the synagogue, and went further than old Shylock in his dealings with Gentile dogs, being not only willing to buy and sell with them, but to eat and drink and even to pray with them, if that could have helped him to cultivate their acquaintance, though the habits of most of them gave no opportunity to practice that particular grace. The Angel liked nature in books, and could quote whole cantos of Childe Harold, and give you any amount of Manfred you might desire, but this realization of poetry was not in the least to her taste.

The *Herald* informed her of the recovery of Mrs. Hackett, and announced that she had gone on to Newport, and the Angel tore the paper in bits and stamped on them in her rage at having spoiled her own pleasure by her fright and selfishness. But there was nothing impossible with her! She actually wrote the Idol a long letter full of sympathy. She would never have left her darling Duchess, but the physicians ordered her away. Now she was pining and desolate among her friends, kind as they were. Nobody but her sweet Duchess understood her; she should droop and fade and float off to the Better Land if the Duchess did not summon her. Her chest was weak—these northern airs were killing her—but she could not alarm her guardian; she could not selfishly ruin the pleasure of her companions, who were too happy to notice how ill she was—an illness induced principally by her sufferings on account of her darling Duchess. But she would not repine. She could die! She was a lonely little thing whom no one would miss! Better that she should go and join her lost parent in the Elysian Fields! In fact, that was what she wanted—she had only written to bid her beloved Duchess farewell before increasing weakness rendered this last act of friendship impossible. She should bless her with her latest breath and then fly away, away! All this and much more, on numberless tiny sheets of tinted paper, with legions of exclamation points like pigmy sentinels, and every other line underscored. Broken sentences which implied that death was near; but she would not detail her sufferings—every thing that was touching and sweet.

The Idol received the letter, and forgot the slight soreness that had been in her mind. Indeed she reproached herself bitterly for having had the least doubt of her Angel. She wrote, begging her to come; she wanted the whole party—but at least she must have her Angel. Some acquaintances whom they encountered were bound for Newport, so the Angel and her brown familiar were put under their care, and she departed rejoicing; and truly her departure was a great relief, though only the incorrigible Rosa avowed it openly.

I must leave them here to pursue their journey in peace, and go back to other scenes. I hope you have not forgotten to be sorry for the distress in which we left Clive Farnsworth and the black terror which filled his heart.

CHAPTER XXXVII.

THE GODDESS OF LIBERTY.

I LEFT Ruth fainting in Clive's arms as a preparatory step toward illness and death. You thought so, you know you did; you foresaw how the romance was to end—of course you did. Now she did not die, she was not even sick, and after frightening Clive out of his wits, she recovered from her swoon and was very much ashamed of herself. I broke off abruptly, having reached a sensation, and put a brief chapter of suspense between it and the explanation, because that is according to the rules of high art; and do you think I wish you to go on with events happening in regular and natural sequence, and have you say that I do not understand high art? Now the truth must come out. Ruth was not ill, and after resting a few days was as bright as ever. But you thought she would die; you thought he would marry Elinor Grey—don't be aggravating and deny it; and I have shown that I know how to make the most of a sensation, and am as highly artful as any nine-hundred-pager among the craft.

Notwithstanding the efforts Clive and the old physician made, the people in South village could not be persuaded to forswear the uncleanliness and misery in which they had been reared in their native lands and had brought with them over the sea. Were they to be taught by Yankees and made to wash themselves in a free country? Not a bit of it! They expressed as much contempt for the Yankees as their betters do, and, when the trouble came, were as glad to howl and be helped as their betters are when they get into difficulty.

Am I never to flutter the star-spangled? If any body in England reads this, why—whisper—it is only another specimen of high art! If any body in America reads this, why—very loud—I am not one to truckle to foreign weaknesses; I'll make the eagle scream—hurrah! In the mean time I add—this to myself—O Brother Jonathans and John Bulls! there is a good deal to admire in you both; nevertheless, O Britannia and Columbia! you are the silliest, conceitedest old mother putting on virtuous airs, and the most boastful, outrageous child; together the most arrogant pair that ever deafened the ears of the whole world with incessant self-glorifications, backed by a lion that has lost several of its best teeth and an eagle that needs to have its tail-feathers viciously pulled.

The fever skipped about a little on the side of the lake where the hotel stood and frightened such guests as were let into hasty departure. After a few days of intense heat and breathless nights, in which a damp, miasmatic fog rested on the waters, the demon made straight across and attacked the ready victims. They did suffer terribly, poor things. Scarcely a foul, ill-ventilated cabin from which the moans for some lost one were not going up to Heaven, and may be Heaven hears the moans of the dirty and miserable as easily as those from fresher lips. The wretched creatures suffered much, and would have suffered more had it not been for Clive Farnsworth and his Ruth. There were not influential people enough left in the neighborhood to prevent any real good by a fit of philanthropy. The directors of the railway behaved as the directors of most railways, whether proposed or finished, do in this land: that is, like abominable brutes, who ought to be strung in rows on the tallest trees from the Atlantic to the Pacific, and compelled to hang there heads

downward through all eternity, with the shrieks of their countless victims forever ringing in their ears.

I can not say that Clive might not have been inclined to think he had fulfilled a fair share of his duty by affording liberally the means to make the unfortunate creatures comfortable, but Ruth could not be satisfied with that. As long as any sanatory measures could be taken she insisted on going with Clive to see that they were carried out—that is, if what was the sweetest form of pleading could be called insistence—and her persuasions moved the reckless Celts more than all the advice and hygienic precautions Clive and the doctor could lay down.

"You see, dear," she would say, "they don't half know their own danger. If we just drove over again to be certain that every thing is being done."

"I will go, Ruth; there is no need to expose you further."

"But there is no risk, Clive; if there were, you couldn't be cruel enough to go and not let me share it."

When the fever did attack the place, and both saw how much there was to be done, neither had any mind to keep aloof. Ruth's presence was like a blessing in every house; the people used to say that the sick always mended after her visits. "Oh, yer honor," said an old man to Clive, "just the sound of her voice seemed to take away the pain." A poor little lame girl in whom she became greatly interested, one day whispered to Farnsworth—"Don't you believe she's the Blessed Virgin, Sir, come down for a little out of pity, because we suffered so?"

The violence of the disease soon spent itself, thanks in a great degree to the vigorous measures that had been commenced almost at the first alarm; the dead were buried out of sight, and the sick returned to strength and the ordinary hardness of their lives. When there was nothing to be done, and no danger of having to spend any money, the directors called a meeting and appointed men to go up and find out if it were true that the laborers were menaced by an epidemic, and passed such fine resolutions that when the newspapers reported them every body was greatly impressed by the kind-heartedness of those great men, who, in spite of their camel-loads of wealth, were certain to pass easily through the needle's eye. The residents of the neighborhood came pouring back when they were convinced that they did not endanger their precious lives thereby, and, to Ruth's wonder and annoyance, persisted in regarding her as a heroine. The Idol kept writing astounding letters to every body, relating again and again that Mrs. Farnsworth had preserved her from death, and setting the seal in the minds of the readers to Ruth's claims to heroineship.

The housekeeper at length came to Ruth with a request that she would go down to the village to see the bad boy of the neighborhood, Tad Tilman, who had fallen very ill. His aunt had besought her friend Mrs. Sykes to ask this

N

favor of her mistress, because Tad insisted that he must see her, and would allow no one in the house any peace until she was sent for. Mrs. Sykes looked upon Tad with horror, and had no doubt whatever in her own mind that he was "possessed," and, as she was wont to say with an awful shake of the head, "Not by one—" leaving a blank for the word devil which she thought wicked utterance from other than the lips of preachers or deacons in meeting—"but by a Legion! There is such and we know it, and I'm afraid to think what would become of all the pigs, far and near, if what's in that boy could be driven out." With the prospect of such misfortune to the neighboring swine in case the boy should be freed from the control of his unpleasant familiars, and such sentiments as she entertained toward him personally—sentiments which she had not kept for private contemplation, but had many times felt it her duty to repeat to Tad with variations when she encountered him at his aunt's house, which in spite of their mysterious awfulness had small effect upon him, inured as he was to being told that he was the most depraved of sinners, to being prayed over and wept over and groaned over in the family circle, to being set up as a target in meeting for the deacon to fire reproofs and warnings at, to being exhorted in mourning and solemn tones as to the place where he would go if he did not mend his ways, and encouraged by the information that there seemed no hope of his being able so to do if he wished, whenever a select knot of his worthy relative's friends met for a religious tea and an afternoon's consideration of the wickedness of the world and the probability of its speedy destruction—it was natural that Mrs. Sykes should prefer her request with a good deal of hesitation. Indeed she went about so much, made so many apologies, ran the beginnings of such opposite sentences together, and was so incoherent and mysterious that Ruth for sometime was at a loss to understand whether therewas somebody sick or some strange apparition had appeared in the meeting; whether some dark calamity had befallen the pigs or the sinners, or whether private trouble had assailed Mrs. Sykes herself, and she had come to seek sympathy and advice. She gained a faint perception of the good woman's meaning at length, and asked—

"Is it that little Tilman boy who is sick?"

"Yes, ma'am; and as I was a sayin'," replied Mrs. Sykes, going off again into regrets at troubling her mistress about such a reprobate; mingling a description of his aunt's anxiety and a compendious history of the boy's misdeeds from his cradle up, in happy disregard of nominative cases and personal pronouns.

"You say he wants to see me, Mrs. Sykes?" inquired Ruth when there was an opportunity given by the housekeeper's being forced to draw a little breath into her exhausted receiver.

"Yes, ma'am," she answered, hurrying a rush of air in, which hissed in her pipes as if hey were hot, "and if you could see how worked

up his poor aunt is; and no wonder, with the trial that boy's been, and she a prayerful woman, ma'am, and a strivin' after mortifications if ever a woman did; not a bit set up, but jest layin' that boy afore the deacons and askin'— though it wasn't no use, for it did seem as if the more was done the worse he got—and you couldn't believe if I was to tell you, ma'am, how they've wrastled over him and he a goin' on in the old way; as Elder Mosely has said to him many a time, dancin' on the brink of the pit as it were—in my hearin'—"

"I am sorry he is sick," interrupted Ruth; "I doubt—"

"And nobody can blame you, ma'am," interposed Mrs. Sykes; "and I don't wonder you feel so about goin', and I didn't expect, but asked because his poor aunt was so worked up."

"I was not going—"

"Excuse me, ma'am, for interruptin', but I must say in self-excuse I know'd you wasn't, I couldn't expect you would, and I can't blame you and nobody couldn't. I've only wondered at your goodness in tryin' to have him help among the flowers, and him a standin' on his head for an aggravation to me, like a piny with the root up, when you'd gone into the house."

"I shall go to see him this morning," said Ruth; "you misunderstood me. I have found him very obliging and industrious."

"Wal, ma'am," replied Mrs. Sykes, looking much relieved, "it'll be a kind act, and it'll be like you; and who knows?—a body must always hope for a sinner as long as he's left within the hearin' of grace; of course when once they've gone beyond it, why then we know where they've gone, and it's a comfort to us feelin' that we've warned 'em and wrastled with 'em—"

"Yes, I will go," Ruth interrupted, not being so much at ease as Mrs. Sykes under the form of theology that left a person with a true Christian spirit so confident in regard to the final destiny of sinners, and so comfortable in the belief that the "wrastlin's and warnin's" had been a complete fulfillment of duty. Mrs. Sykes, after expressing her sense of her mistress's kindness, and uttering a few more moans over the depravity of the lost child—for in spite of her remark about his being still within the reach of grace it was evident there was no possible loop-hole for him in her view of the matter—retired to pursue her contemplations in private. It is very probable that her fears for the sick boy diverged into doubts where her master and mistress were concerned, for she often indulged in such, as was natural, since they must be in a good deal of danger while they went to that church which had a painted window, and the still greater enormity of a flower-wreathed, candle-decorated altar, and where they offended Heaven by repeating prayers out of a book.

When Clive was ready to drive out with Ruth on her daily round, she told him about poor Tad's illness and request, and begged him to take her to the house at once. Clive had a liking for the boy, and always enjoyed the stories of his misdeeds, not possessing a well-regulated mind. " Poor little fellow," he said, " how he must suffer now he is entirely at the mercy of his relations and the deacons."

" He is such a bright, quick little fellow," Ruth answered ; " we used to hold long talks while he helped me among my flower-beds. Clive, if he gets well, couldn't you have him sent to school ?—Why, what are you laughing at, you bad boy ?"

" Only this is the forty-fourth small individual whose future you have asked me to take on my hands during the last fortnight," replied Clive.

" Not so bad as that," rejoined Ruth, laughing too. " But, Clive, I do feel so sorry for the poor children."

" And you shall help all that come in your way in every possible manner, I promise you," said he.

" You good Clive !"

" Yes, it is I who am good," he answered, laughing again, yet moved by her unconsciousness ; " you have nothing to do with it, of course ; you never want to help people."

" You are not to tease, Sir. But isn't that the house ?"

" Yes, I think so ; I shall go in too. I have a decided weakness for Thaddy and his diabolical propensities."

So the groom had an opportunity to drive the horses up and down the street and know himself an object of admiration to all the youthful females in that neighborhood, while Clive followed Ruth into the house. They were met at the door by a tall, scraggy young woman with her hair in curl-papers, who began to exclaim at sight of Ruth—" Why, dear me—Miss Farnsworth ! Do come in ! I declare, I'm ashamed to ast you into such a poor place. I didn't axpect to see you here, I'm sure ! I see you up to Miss Hackett's, if you don't disremember." In fact, the scraggy damsel with horns protruding over her temples was no other than the Angel's enemy of that dreadful night when the Idol's reason went overboard.

" Mrs. Sykes told me," said Ruth, " that Thaddy Tilman was very sick and wanted to see me."

" Wal, ya'as, he's ben proper bad. I wouldn't have had you troubled on no account, but Aunt Prudence she youmors him, and he's dreadful youmorsome. I'm sure it's no place to ast you into." At this moment she became conscious of Clive's presence—her faculties before that had been concentrated in the contemplation of Ruth's hat ; she started back with a mysterious sound in her throat, and appeared to have some idea of concealing herself behind the door. " If it aint Mr. Farnsworth too !" she exclaimed, making a grab at her self-possession and dignity, determined to be equal to the occasion. " Wal, this is onaxpected. I declare, Thaddeus is a lookin' up." She gave an engaging giggle, and added to Ruth in a painful whisper that

must have been audible across the street, " Deary me, to think o' my bein' ketched this way—in my old dress and my hair—" That last reflection was so appalling that she broke off in dismay, put both hands on her horns and cried shrilly—" Aunt Prudence ! O Aunt Prudence !"

At the imperative summons, down stairs came a meek, watery-eyed old woman, who had witnessed the arrival from an upper window and been hesitating about making her appearance. " I'm so glad to see you," she said in a little trembling voice, " I don't know how to thank you."

Here the scraggy damsel cut her short, desirous of showing that she was perfectly aware what was proper on an occasion like the present. " This is Miss Farnsworth, Aunt Prudence," said she, taking one hand from her horns to wave it in the air, " and this is Mr. Farnsworth, though I hain't the pleasure of an acquaintance " —removing the other hand to wave at him, forgetful of the spiral decorations—" but Miss Farnsworth I see up to the Castle when I were there fur a week to obleege. They've come to see Thaddeus. I'm sure I didn't axpect company and me such a figger ; but sickness in the house and all, I hope it won't be noticed." Here she clapped both hands to her horns again and tossed her head at Clive with another giggle. " I'll jest let Thaddeus know," said she ; " no more on us had better be took by surprise, though it mightn't be so onsupportable as it is to some ;" and here, perceiving that Ruth had begun to make inquiries of the old woman about the sick boy, and that Clive was looking at a flower-pot in the window, the damsel retreated hastily, not so much to warn Tad as to have an opportunity of enduing herself in a new pink gown and removing the obnoxious horns.

The room was so clean and tidy that it was a relief after the abodes of misery Ruth had seen among the foreign population in South village, and the woman herself seemed a meek, kind-hearted body, very grateful for the visit, but inclined at once to become lachrymose on the subject of her nephew, not so much where his illness was concerned as in fear for the soul somewhere hidden in his fever-consumed little frame. There was a piteous creak in her voice too, evidently an affair of long habit, which made Clive think she had been repressed and overcrowed by her husband and the scraggy damsel, as well as alarmed by the theology she had heard from the deacons. " He wanted to see you so much, and he thought "— the last " he " referred to her husband—" mebby it was a sign sumpthin' was a workin' in him "— now she meant the boy again. " The dear knows we've wrastled with him, and since he's ben sick we've had Deacon Spriggins reg'lar every day ; but he's a cur'us boy, though good to his old aunt I can't but say."

" You have had a doctor, of course," said Clive.

" Wal, no, we hain't ; you see he was on'y

took day afore yes'day—was it day afore yes'-day? no, 'twas the night no, 'twarnt, wal, anyhow I thought mebby he'd git on, and Granny Cumber she's seeh a doctor herself, and she's give him a powerful lot of yarbs, and he's had four doses o' calomel and castor-ile."

Taken in connection with her previous remark, which however she had intended to apply to his spiritual condition, this was too much for Clive's gravity, and he retreated to the window and the friendly flower-pot.

"You must have a doctor," Ruth said; "and oh, don't give him any more calomel."

"Wal, when I was a gal," replied Aunt Prudence, "calomel and jollip was thought could cure a'most any thing, and Granny Cumber she sets great store by 'em."

"But in these fevers," pursued Ruth, "you need to keep the strength up as much as possible.—Clive, please tell Jones to drive round for the doctor at once, do."

Clive went out and dispatched the man on his errand; when he came back, Aunt Prudence was in the midst of a dismal account of a meeting they had held the night before in that very room, and growing tearful over Tad's refusal to permit Deacon Spriggins to go up and pray with him. Indeed it appeared that when that worthy gentleman got to the head of the stairs and tried to point out to him the fearful state of his soul, considering the life he had led, Tad refused to listen, and assailed that precious disciple with vituperative epithets which had filled the minds of the listeners with horror, and convinced the deacon that the case was even more hopeless than he had believed.

"I do hope the poor boy was out of his head," said Aunt Prudence, wiping her eyes; "but husband he's quite discouraged, and Miss Sykes an' Granny Cumber, they seemed actilly afeared it wasn't so much the fever that's goin' round as raal possession. It was awful when he called the Deacon a shad-bellied, stiff-necked old Nicodemus!"

Clive exploded, and Aunt Prudence held her apron fast in her hands and stared at him. "You must not let any body worry him now, Mrs. Tilman," he said; "the thing to do at present is to take care of his body. I think you had better put the meetings aside till he is better."

Aunt Prudence, accustomed to be regulated in her opinions by those of the person speaking to her, was wonderfully consoled. "I was sayin' that to husband," returned she, "and now mebby, when I tell him you advised it, he'll think so too. He's raly discouraged, and indeed, Taddy's ben a great trial to him, very headstrong and consaty. I know he's a bad boy, but he's allays good to me, and I've ben mebby too youmersome to his faults, 'cause he's an orphing and not my own flesh and blood, though I didn't want him to know no difference."

"I'm sure you have meant to be good to him," Ruth said, to comfort her; "I think he is fonder of you than of any one else."

"I have tried," she replied in her meek croak;

"and though he was husband's nevvy, they couldn't seem to agree, and it's ben a massy your gettin' him up to help in your garding. Ever sence he was took he's ben a beggin' to see you, and so at last I thought I'd ask Miss Sykes to tell you."

"I am very glad you did," returned Ruth. "May we go up stairs now?"

Aunt Prudence dried her eyes on her apron again and led the way to the chamber where the sick boy was lying. "Taddy," said she, in that unearthly whisper certain people think it proper to employ in a sick-room, and which is enough to make the blood of a giant, sound in wind and limb, run cold- "Taddy, here's Miss Farnsworth and her husband too, come to see you."

The boy raised himself on his pillow, his face and eyes burning with fever, and held out his hand to Ruth, while the muscles of his hard young mouth worked convulsively under a smile of welcome.

"I'm sure you're obleeged to 'em, Taddy," said Aunt Prudence, in the same torturing under-tone.

"For the land's sake, speak out!" poor Tad fairly shrieked. "I'd rather hear it thunder than the way you all go a whispering around. Oh, Mrs. Farnsworth, my head does ache so, and they won't let me alone! They're a groaning over me, and a praying over me all the time, and when they ain't at that they're a dosing me with calomel; I can't stand it!" Ruth sat down by him and with her usual dexterity had his pillow smooth and his hair out of his eyes in no time. "I'm so dry," said the boy, "and they won't give me no water."

"I've brought some lemons," Ruth said; "you shall have some lemonade at once.—It will be good for him; see how parched his lips are," she added to Aunt Prudence.

"Wal, ma'am," returned the poor woman, too much accustomed to being pushed about by her husband and his niece to think of opposition, "I s'pose you know best, but Granny Cumber, she said, in her day cold water wasn't never giv—"

"Granny Cumber's an old fool!" interrupted Tad, in another nervous shriek. "Did she expect me to drink hot water? Here I am a burning up! Oh, Mrs. Farnsworth, they'll kill me if they can, I do believe."

"Oh, Taddy, don't!" pleaded Aunt Prudence. "You know how anxious we be. Your uncle prayed and prayed last night. Oh, my poor boy, if you would only—"

"Shet up!" howled Tad. "I tell you I won't have briny hell poked down my throat any longer—I'm sick of it! I've heard nothin' else sence I can remember. I'd rather the devil had me and be done with it! Aunt Prudence, if you don't be still I'll jump out of the window." The poor frightened woman began to groan, and Ruth, glad to get her out of the room under any pretext, sent her down stairs for sugar and a tumbler. "Oh, I'm so tired," moaned Tad, with difficulty repressing a sob, "and my head aches so. And all these messes make me so sick. Oh, Mrs.

Farnsworth, if you'd please heave 'em away—they smell so!"

There were several bowls and cups on a stand by the bed, and Clive examined the contents of each with much curiosity. One bowl held water that looked as if there had been ashes stirred in it; a few bits of blackened bread were floating about on the top. "Now what do you suppose this may be?" he asked Ruth.

"It's crust coffee," said Tad, who was intently watching him. "Old Granny Cumber said I might drink that, and it tastes just like mud and sawdust."

"Out of the window it goes, Thad," said Clive, to the boy's great delight. "And this?" he continued, taking up a cup that contained a slimy liquid, with something curled up in the bottom that closely resembled a fat yellow worm.

"That's slippery ellum bark," explained Tad, "'cause my mouth was sore. It's so nasty! If you'll only throw it out afore Aunt Prudence comes." Clive emptied the slime and the wormy-looking coil out of the window in disgust. "There's enough more," said Tad. "Oh, pitch 'em out! There's snake-root, if I had the colic; and there's water off biled cod-fish; and there's more yarbs and bitter things than 'ud kill a horse."

Clive was astonished and vexed at the array of nauseous doses, which were new to his experience, but Ruth had seen too much of the agreeable compounds bestowed on sick persons according to the old-fashioned mode of nursing among country people, to be surprised. "They shan't give you any more such things," she said; "the doctor that is coming will leave you little powders that have no taste, and you shall drink all the water you want."

"You're good to me," faltered Tad, beginning to choke. "Oh dear, I thought they never would send for you! They've cat-hauled me about till I feel as if I was on fire and every bone in my body sticking into me wrong, and that old Spriggins a praying over me; oh, how I do hate him!"

These last words were heard by Aunt Prudence as she entered the room armed with the sugar-bowl and a pitcher, which she nearly dropped in her dismay that the visitors should have had such personal knowledge of her nephew's depravity. "Oh Taddy, Taddy, don't!" she groaned. "He's such a good man!"

"Then I want to be bad!" shouted Tad. "If he's a going to heaven I won't—that's flat! I've had enough of him here. He's tormented me all my life, he and uncle Josh 'tween em, and told me I was bad and a child of the devil, and accused me of everything that was done wrong in the neighborhood till I don't care. I mean to be bad — I want to be bad — and I'll break old Spriggins's head with the shovel if he sets foot up here agin!"

The boy was becoming greatly excited, and Clive had seen too much of the fever not to know that he was very ill, so he was ready to obey Ruth's little signal, which he understood perfectly to mean that he was to take the old woman away and give her a little wholesome advice on the necessity of the patient's being kept tranquil. He asked her to go down stairs with him, but when they reached the sitting-room there was no opportunity to deliver the lecture, for behold there was the scraggy damsel prepared to entertain him, and meek Aunt Prudence slipped away into the kitchen to cry by herself.

The young woman was arrayed in a pink gingham gown, so shiny and stiff that it looked as if it had been cut out of pasteboard; the obnoxious curl-papers which had before made a horned animal of her, and caused her such anguish of mind, were removed from her hair, which now depended in long ringlets on either side of her face; but from having been taken out of their wraps too soon they were languishing and evinced a tendency at the ends to spread into untidy little tails in a weak-minded fashion not in keeping with the young woman's general appearance; while the mass of hair at the back of her head was drawn into a marvellous structure like a fortification, topped by a large comb with a silver-washed back, with three green glass eyes in it that blinked insanely with the rapid motions of her neck. She was seated in a rocking-chair of the uncomfortable wooden species yclept Boston, with perpendicular rods for a spine that bulge out in the wrong place and whirl in just where they ought not, so that sitting therein is painful to a bony person and unpleasant to a timid one, from the fact that the rockers are usually so put on that one must sit rigid to avoid being tilted forward on one's nose or keeled in the opposite direction in a fashion that, if picturesque, is not proper.

The damsel rose as Clive appeared and began volubly—"I hope you think Thaddeus is likely to chirk up pretty soon, Mr. Farnsworth, though he looks dreadful meachin' to be sure. Is Miss Farnsworth up stairs?" It seemed probable that she was, as she must have passed through that room to get out of the house, unless she had made her exit as Tad often had done at night when he wanted to play with the boys or do something equally atrocious and wicked, by the window and a ladder. But the damsel paused for no reply; she had had time after the robing process to collect her faculties; she knew that her duty now was to make conversation, and she was able to do her part. "It was very kind of you both to come," continued she; "I wasn't for sendin' myself—I'm not one to curry favor—but I'm glad and obleeged, because I'm not above ownin' a kindness as many is, although I'm not one to forgit my rights and my doos, and well I know we don't live in a furrin land of oppression where the rich and great preys like salamanders on the honest poor, though not that you'd ever do it, I'm ready to certify if a certifier was necessary, for well I know your name, by sight too, and I've cried over your books till my eyes was like red flannel, nor your wife either, I'm sure, for I see her at the Castle and a coincidence she was to that young hairess, the like of which I never thought to meet, and blushed to own the claim of sect, scrouged behind the bed and Miss Hackett a callin' fur her in tones that might have softened stuns and nanycondys.''

She paused with a great flourish of her head that sent the curls flying out as if they had been miniature specimens of the serpent she mentioned under a name of her own coinage; and Clive, with an eye to business, seeing the possibility of future "copy" in encouraging her to talk, was so bland and bowed so politely that the damsel was in a flutter of delight. She could not decide on the instant whether he was most like Lord Mortimer in the "Children of the Abbey" or the hero of a sensation story which she had lately devoured with much interest, wherein the said hero was first presented to the readers in a deer-skin frock, popularly supposed to be the legitimate dress of hunters, backed against a tree with several knives in one hand, a revolver and rifle in the other, talking exalted blank verse to a band of desperadoes, a score at least, from whom he had just rescued the heroine of the tale, who clung to his shoulder while he brandished the weapons and spouted the poetry.

"But do set down, Mr. Farnsworth," said the young woman, reserving her decision for a lonely hour, and offering him the rocking-chair. But Clive, being acquainted with the style of seat, had no mind to put himself to the torture of its embrace, so he sat down on a lounge near the window, and the damsel resumed possession of the rocker, managing the monster with much skill, sitting erect as if her back had been of the same material as the chair, with her hands folded in her pocket-handkerchief and the toes of her shoes turned up in a virtuous and strong-minded manner. "I do declare," she continued, with a giggle and a flutter, "in the topsy-turvyness there's ben no nettequette at all, not that there's any body to think of it in this house except myself, but dear me, Aunt Prudence—oh, she's gone into the kitching—it's quite confusing, I'm sure—if your lady was here I'd git her to mention—"

"You are Taddy's sister, I suppose," Clive said, catching her meaning.

"I am," replied she, with another flutter; "his sister Amanda."

"Thaddeus and Amanda," said Clive involuntarily.

"Yes," returned the damsel, shaking her curls; "I thought they'd strike you—Thaddeus of Warsaw and the Children of the Abbey! My mar was a great romancer, Mr. Farnsworth, and they was her favorite works, but the dear knows, I'm sure if you'd been a writin' then it's out of your books she'd have took names, fur they're so sweet; though of course it's ridic'lous to talk about your writing then."

Clive smiled his gratitude at such praise of his stories, and Amanda, a little embarrassed but determined to make the most of the opportunity, had so many things she wished to say that she could only flirt her handkerchief and giggle.

"I see you are fond of flowers," Clive said, pointing to the crooked, thorny cactus in the window, stretching out claws as if it wanted to pinch somebody.

"And birds, and books and scenes, and above all poetry," said Amanda. "Ofen and ofen I set in the twilight and repeat verses till Aunt Prudence thinks I'm quite moonstruck. I think Astronomy is such a beautiful study; I attended a course of the geological development of the heavens last winter—it is so elevating."

"It is," said Clive.

"I'm of opinion, Mr. Farnsworth, that the female mind carn't be too much cultivated, and I don't believe you're one to contradict or undermine, though many men would."

"Not I, believe me," replied Clive.

"I was sure of it," said the damsel. "Not that I wish to see woman shoot beyond her native spire—far from it; strong-minded I am not, though I know my rights and doos, and that we're not in a land where kings and rampart lions sway and roar, and when I'm roused I speak, and roused I was that time at the Castle."

"Indeed," said Clive.

"I was, and so I'd wish to say to Miss Farnsworth, fur her opinionation is one to crave, and I never shall deny I was so excited by the conduct of that hairess, who's a Pompadore at heart if ever there was a Pompadore or doress, it doesn't matter which, fur facts is facts whatever their gender may be. I mebby said more than was consistent, though if ever I dragged her through the hall or pushed her out-of-doors, as some has spread stories that was only too glad from envy, though she must have started 'em, is as false as the Allohorn, and if ever she and I do meet, tell her so I shall."

"I am quite certain you meant and did every thing for the best," remarked Clive.

"It's a great relief to have your vote," Amanda answered, "for you, Mr. Farnsworth, are one to feel and know, and what a village like this may say I'm not one to care nor hold my head no lower, though I must say, mebby that hairess would be disappinted to find she didn't injure me with all her tales. I'm very glad to afford the explanation, and Mrs. Hackett too, as I've thought several times of writing her a letter, but word of mouth from you will be easier."

Amanda was interrupted by the appearance of the physician at the open door, and was soon left to reflect with satisfaction upon the mingled dignity and ease with which she had supported her part in the late interview, and a gratified smile wreathed her thin lips as she twined the ends of her ringlets about her fingers and tried to coax them into shape. It struck her too that she had been decidedly happy in her little effort at the poetic, which was a new style for her to adopt, she having hitherto adhered rather to the strong-minded genus; it had been the inspiration of the moment, and Amanda permitted the smile to soften her severe lips more and more, as she thought of the effect she must have produced on the author.

CHAPTER XXXVIII.

A FAULT PHOTOGRAPHED.

WHEN Tad found himself alone with Ruth he appeared more composed, and having drank some lemonade and had his face and hands bathed with fresh water, he lay back on his pillows with a long sigh of relief.

"This is a great deal better, isn't it?" Ruth asked in her cheerful voice, which of itself was a comfort and help after the mournful whispers of Aunt Prudence which had echoed about him since the fever began, varied by his uncle's squeaky admonitions and the deacon's nasal menaces. "A good deal better, Thaddy."

"I guess it is! I don't feel as if I was burning up any longer, and its sumpthin' to get them nasty doses out of sight."

"You shan't be troubled with any more."

"I do' know what to say; you're so good to me, Mrs. Farnsworth," returned Tad, with another suspicious twitching about his mouth; a sign of agitation neither his uncle nor the deacon had ever been able to bring by their lectures. "I tell you what, I'm a pretty tough one, but I ain't an ongrateful cub, whatever old Spriggins says, and I shan't forget this."

"You must not think about Mr. Spriggins, nor any body now," returned Ruth.

"Deacon Spriggins!" amended Tad with wrath and scorn, unmindful of her counsel. "A pretty one he is! He'd better be a thinking of the measly pork he sold, and the son he turned out-o'-doors for learning to play on the fiddle, than come a talking through his nose at me."

"You must not think such harsh things, poor Thaddy," said Ruth; "he meant to be kind."

"No, ma'am, I don't believe he did. His looks is enough: he's long and lean, and crooked in the wrong places, and his nose is like a hook; and I can't stand him," added Tad with feverish energy.

"I shall ask your aunt not to let him or any one come up here till you get better," returned Ruth; "she will take care of you. I am sure you like her?"

"Oh yes; Aunt Prudence is real good when old Josh ain't pecking at her; but he tells her how bad I am till she gets scairt, and then she shakes her head and cries, so it's worse'n their preaching."

"She won't do any thing now to distress you," said Ruth; "she is too sorry for you and too anxious."

"Why, am I so sick?" asked Tad quickly. "I aint going to die, be I?"

"Oh no, my boy; not that; but this fever is severe while it lasts."

"Sometimes I've thought I would not care if I did die, when they hectored me so," said Tad. "I'd have gone off somewheres long ago, if it hadn't a ben for Aunt Prudence."

"That would not have been right, Thaddy; it would have made her unhappy. When you get well, Mr. Farnsworth will see that you go to school; you would like that, wouldn't you?"

"Yes, I would, if it wasn't like the schoolteacher's mussing here—every body here seems agin me and I'm agin every body, and I jest believe its half 'cause Josh and Deacon Spriggins goes about groaning over me and standing up in meeting to pint me out."

"When you get well you must try not to give them any cause."

"Oh, they don't want no cause, Mrs. Farnsworth, they don't; they're causes enough for theirselves, and they're both that set in their way they wouldn't believe I was any better if I went to be a missionary. I guess they'd say I wanted to get out where I could eat up babies and be a New Zealander."

"You may not be a missionary," said Ruth, smiling, "but I am sure you mean to grow up a good honest man and do right."

"I do' know," replied Tad wearily; "the righter I try to do, the wronger I get. Sometimes I a'most think I'm what they say."

"I suppose they think you unruly and mischievous, but you must show them you don't mean to be any more."

"No, 'tain't that," said Tad, putting his hand to his throbbing forehead; "they think I'm lost, that's what they say; that I ain't elected—and oh, dear me, I didn't care nor want to be; and if I wasn't, how could I help it? They keep saying I'm born to be damned, and then tell me it's my fault, but how can I be to blame if I was born for it?"

The poor little victim to Calvinistic creeds looked as much confused and troubled as many older and wiser persons have done under those perplexing dogmas, and Ruth wishing he could be kept from any thought, still felt that she could not leave the poor boy alone with his dark fancies. "Thaddy," she said, "the blessed Saviour died for all of us, he pitied us so; and he is just as sorry now, and just as ready to help us—don't think of any thing but that."

"They never talked that way to me," returned Tad; "they don't say much about the Saviour anyhow—it's always Jehovah and the God of Battles; and they talk as if he was always mad and hated us."

"But you know he must love us, Thaddy, when he came down and died on the cross for us."

"Tell me about it," said Tad.

"My dear boy, surely you have read—"

"Oh yes; I've learned lots of verses at Sunday-school, and Uncle Josh reads the Old Testament every night, and picks out all the blood and thunder places; but jest tell me, please—mebby it'll make me quiet so's I can sleep. I know what the words say; but tell me they mean it, you know. I don't see how He can love me if I am born to be damned whether or no."

"My child," said Ruth, "we have nothing to do with such thoughts; the Saviour wants you to be good and obedient and cheerful."

"Cheerful?" repeated Tad. "That's laughing; and the Deacon and Uncle Josh says it's wicked, and when they talk about heaven they groan so you'd think 'twas worse'n the bad place they want me to go to."

"But heaven is every body's home, Thaddy; we all want to go, and to do the best we can, so that we may not be too much out of place there."

"But," said Tad, going straight back to the idea that had most impressed him after those years of gloomy teaching, "if some are elected to go to hell, how can they help it?"

"Nobody is, Thaddy. Jesus died for every body—all the world—you and me; he wants every one in heaven."

"Does he?" asked Tad, with a certain inflection of doubt in his voice.

"They baptize little children that they may be his children," said Ruth

"I was vaccinated," said Tad hesitatingly, but offering the suggestion as if he thought it might be the next best thing. "The Deacon's sort, they don't baptize children as I know; you have to wait till you get a new heart, and if you die afore that, you burn. Where be you to get one, and how can you if you was elected to belong to Old Scratch afore you was born? Predestined and fore-ordained—O Mrs. Farnsworth! they're jest like two bells ringin' in each ear, and I do' know what they mean unless they're big doors to keep folks in the dark. I pretended I didn't care," continued he, unable to keep silent now that the restraints were broken; "I've bin bad, but I couldn't help thinking. Many a time when I've gone and stole old Spriggins's apples, jest to make him and Josh mad, I've set down and wondered why I was born if I was to be cuffed and huffed and put on here, and then burnt forever down in the pit. And you see I can jest remember my mother, and what she whispered as I set on the bed when she was a dying—'Thaddy, I'll wait for you in heaven;' and I loved her, and now they say I can't go where she is." He clenched his hands over the bed-clothes and the tears oozed slowly from his eyes; he was a reticent, hard-headed creature, but there were great capabilities for loving in his heart, which, finding no vent, had centered about the memory of that lost mother.

"You can go where she is, Thaddy; all you have to remember is to do the best you can each day, and ask the Saviour to lead you on the road to heaven, for there is no one knows it but him, and he wouldn't have come down to die for us if he had been willing to leave a portion behind forever."

"If I could only think of something pleasant," said Tad; "but they say God is mad at me, 'and they say I'm possessed, and sometimes after they've prayed and howled and worried me

I've come up here to bed in the dark, and I couldn't lay still, and I've wished I could be good, and then felt wickeder than ever, and bumped my head agin the wall, and tore the clothes, till I didn't know but I was crazy."

It was very difficult to know what to say, but those simple words revealed a kind of suffering so strange and terrible to come near one so young that they fairly tortured Ruth's heart. "See here, Thaddy," she whispered; "if you could think of Jesus—could remember that he loves you; that even if you seem alone he is beside you; that he would no more let any thing evil come near than your mother would have let some wild animal when you were a baby—if you could think that while he is all-powerful and good he was once a little boy like you; that he knows exactly how you feel—"

"Oh, it would be so good," interrupted Tad. "Tell me more—make me think so."

Ruth wore about her neck a slender chain, and attached to it, hidden in her bosom, was a little gold cross. She did not know how to argue—she could not tell what more to say; she took off the chain and held the cross before him. "See, Thaddy," she said; "Jesus died on a cross for us; if I put this about your neck, couldn't you remember more easily, when you felt its touch, that he loves you?"

"Oh, they say that's what the old priests and nuns have," replied Tad; "ain't it wicked?"

"It can't be wicked, my child, when it is a sign of what he did for us—when we can't look at it without remembering that Jesus loves us."

"Let me wear it," said Tad; "you won't think I'm so much worse'n any body, will you, ma'am?"

"No, indeed I will not, Thaddy. Does your head ache yet?"

"It feels as if it would split; but I don't mind it so much now."

"I think I hear the doctor," Ruth said.

"Oh," exclaimed Tad quickly, "I hain't half said what I wanted to. There's sumpthing I wanted to tell you, Mrs. Farnsworth, 'cause if I should get side of my head, or—or—you know—"

"What is it, Thaddy?"

"Ain't they coming up stairs? I can't tell you now; oh, please, ma'am, won't you come again?"

"I will come every day while you are sick, Thaddy."

"Then to-morrow, please—'cause I want to tell you; and you won't let any body know?"

"Certainly not."

Clive came up with the doctor and Thad had no opportunity to say any thing more, but Ruth answered his anxious look with a smile that assured him she would not forget her promise. Aunt Prudence was summoned and made to understand about the medicines that were to be given, and, to Tad's delight, she was strictly forbidden to administer any other remedy than those left, or to vary in the slightest degree from the rules laid down.

"And if old Granny Cumber comes," said Tad, "she's to be punched on the head, and Deacon Spriggins worse yet."

"No one shall disturb you, my little fellow," the doctor promised, "although we won't resort to such harsh means."

"Oh, I hope Taddy don't mean it, I hope he don't," said Aunt Prudence in a pathetic voice.

The doctor took her into another room and so thoroughly impressed upon her mind the necessity of being cheerful, and forgetting for the present that the sick boy had any thing but a body, that she came back wearing a poor attempt at a smile, and she trusted that the exigency of the case would be an excuse for what she could not help thinking the sin of being any thing but lachrymose and doleful when there was illness in the house. As Ruth bent over Tad to speak a few parting words of comfort, and to reiterate her promise of coming again on the morrow, he whispered—"I guess I ain't possessed, anyhow, for the doctor left just such looking medicine as he did for 'Melia Bump when she had the fever—I'm a going to sleep."

The namesake of the remarkable young woman that dwelt in the Abbey and was exposed to such harrowing adventures, wherein her hair was never rumpled and her white gown never soiled, was stationed in the room below to utter her farewell thanks to Mrs. Farnsworth, and show Clive that at least one member of that household was acquainted with the forms of ceremony fitting the occasion. "I'm sure Thaddeus'll be dreadfully chirked up by your visit, Miss Farnsworth," she observed, "and I suspect he'll be more reformable, though reely they have aggravated him unintentional, and I couldn't much blame him when he called the Deacon shad—shad—bosomed." This elegant rendering of the phrase which Aunt Prudence had repeated in Tad's honest English caused Clive new satisfaction. "Your good gentleman and me had quite a spell of talk," she continued, and I mentioned about that hairess, which I could wish you to repeat to Mrs. Hackett if you'd be so good. I'm sure your kindness to Thaddeus, lemons and jelly and all, which I've took out of the basket you brought and it's in the phitton now, as your driver calls it, is what would move a harder heart than mine, for I am not adamantines for which I'm thankful, though I may not be a hairess, and know my rights and doos, as I shouldn't scruple to tell her wherever we met if she was forty hairesses with feelin's like stuns, for my fathers fit on Bunker Hill and the flag of the free is as much my dowry as hern."

She drew herself up with extra rigidity, satisfied that her peroration had sounded like a Fourth of July speech, and that she could not increase its effect. She courtesied to Clive with great state, tempered by an engaging smile, and her pasteboard dress creaked in unexpected places, and she was altogether such a mixture of embarrassment and determination to support the dignity she felt proper to her, and so self-complacent at her success, that Clive vowed,

after, she only needed the cap of Liberty on her head to be complete.

The next day Ruth went to the house unaccompanied by Clive, much to the disappointment and indignation of the scraggy damsel, who had put on the pink gingham dress, arranged her hair in stiffer ringlets, and perched the three-eyed comb higher on the fortification, in the hope of another interview with the author. Still she was gracious to Ruth, and took a long survey of her hat, wondering if it would not be possible for her to construct a head-gear in imitation of it. She really was grateful too on Tad's account, for she was fond of the boy in her prickly, uncomfortable way, and had watched by his bed nearly the whole night, as wakeful and grim as if she had been a gray owl and he an unsuspicious chicken upon which she meant to pounce as soon as there was no danger of interference.

Tad had been freshened and brightened by Amanda's own hands in expectation of this visit; she had rubbed his face with a coarse towel till he looked as if spotted with scarlet rash, had combed the ends of his hair into his eyes and bolstered him up on the pillows in an uneasy attitude, all of which performances Tad, softened by his illness into letting his natural heart have sway, had tried to bear with composure, knowing that she meant to be kind; but the final shake with which she settled him, after rubbing his nose upside down and bringing the water to his eyes by the contact of stray locks, caused Tad to utter an immoral—"Gosh dern it, Amandy, you needn't haul me inside out as if I was an old flour-bag."

And Amanda answered with much dignity—"Cursin' and swearin' stuns is bad enough when you're in health, Thaddeus; but stretched where you be, I'd ruther see you thinkin' of your latter end."

"Oh, you git out," said Tad. "But there, Amandy, don't be blowy; I didn't mean it cross."

Ruth's opportune arrival put an end to the dialogue, and the damsel, after giving a laboredly correct account of his symptoms and conduct during the night, and taking mental notice of Ruth's dress, retired with the remark that she would peregrinate down stairs and so be ready to assault the physician on his arrival. Ruth had her little comforting talk to Tad, then seeing that the matter about which he had wished to speak lay heavy on his mind, and that he hesitated over its utterance, said kindly—"Now, Thaddy, you had something to tell me. There is nobody here; you can tell me any thing, you know."

"Yes, ma'am, I believe I could," returned Tad; "and I know you ain't a going to blame me, for I didn't mean to do no harm, only you see she went away afore I could make up my mind to let her know how it happened."

He looked very anxious in his desire not to be blamed, so Ruth said in a general way—"Yes; I am certain of it."

"I declare," said Tad, "I'm gitting as foolish as 'Mandy and Aunt Prudence, a beating round the bush. See here, Mrs. Farnsworth, it's about something I've got that belongs to Miss Laidley; you know, the gal that was up to the Castle."

"Something that belongs to her, Thaddy?"

"Yes'm, and I'll tell you how it happened, for you won't breathe it, and I ain't a feller to let out secrets, do you think I be?"

"I am sure not," said Ruth.

"I know'd you'd think the best you could of me," returned Tad, with a gratified smile; "you ain't like Uncle Josh and old Spriggins, allays ready to believe the worst of a chap. You see, it was give to me by a man at the hotel to carry to her—law, I've been mail-carrier for half the fine folks hereabouts, I have—and I meant to carry that as straight as I had other things to her, but it was awful rainy and I fell in the mud and it got all stained—"

"And you were afraid to give the note?"

"I pulled it out of my pocket and see the enveloper was all sticky, and I tore it off, only meanin' to save the letter, and it wasn't a letter, and it was muddy and I come home with it, a thinking I'd let it dry, but indeed I didn't want to be mean."

"Of course not, Thaddy; and you were afraid to give her the note after that?"

"It wasn't a note," said Tad, in a whisper; "it was a photography; it was—hern and—"

"Oh, if that was all, Thaddy, I will take it and send it to Miss Laidley with an explanation."

"Yes'm," said Tad, but with hesitation. "You see, it wan't hern alone. But there, it's the on'y way. Mrs. Farnsworth, it's hid in the bottom book in that ere little chist in the corner, if you'd please to get it."

Ruth searched the receptacle to which Tad pointed, evidently the stronghold of his treasures, for it contained a singular medley of objects, with a few dog-eared pamphlets under the other rubbish. "That's the book," said Tad, as she lifted up a yellow volume the cover of which was decorated with a marvellous woodcut. She carried it to him, and on his shaking the leaves out fell a card photograph which he picked up and handed to her. Ruth looked at it and gave a little start of surprise. The likeness of Miss Laidley was excellent, but in spite of its excellence had probably not been intended for general distribution among her friends, inasmuch as it represented her with her head reclining on a gentleman's shoulder, her wavy tresses mingling with his dark whiskers, her eyes raised to meet those of the male image which regarded her with an expression that, in spite of its intensity and the undeniable beauty of the orbs, might not have been agreeable to all women.

"Ain't she pretty?" said Tad, breaking the silence.

"I suppose it is some one whom she is going to marry," returned Ruth.

"Wal, not axackly, I guess," said Tad, with a little chuckle which he turned into a cough.

"That feller's Mr. Jack Ralston—I know him like a book"

"I think you must be mistaken, Thaddy," returned Ruth; "I never saw Mr. Ralston, but he is—"

"Married; oh yes'm! That's him! Bless you, he was allers sending notes to some— That hain't nothing to do with it."

"No," said Ruth, laying the photograph, face down, on the counterpane. "I am sorry you kept it, Thaddy."

"Oh, so be I! It's been like a nightmare to me; but afore I could make up my mind she was gone, and Mr. Ralston he was gone, and there it's laid, till I fell sick. I got to thinking if I should die no knowing what would become of it, and I jest made up my mind to git you to take it."

There seemed no way of avoiding the commission, distasteful as it was, although the picture did not strike Ruth in the way it might have done many people; she only thought it had been some freak of Miss Laidley's in keeping with her childishness and the heedless actions of which she had heard so much. "I will take it," she said, "and will write to Miss Laidley exactly how it happened."

"If you would, please! Tell her I didn't go to do it, and I'd rather have broke my leg. No matter what old Spriggins says, I never was mean, and I'd cut my tongue out afore I'd tell a thing; but you see here I am, and you'll do it better'n I can."

"It was taken for sport, probably," Ruth said, "when there was a party sitting for pictures."

"He give it to me the day afore he went off," observed Tad, "and told me to be awful particular not to let any body have it but her, and to hand it to her when she was alone out in the grove, where I allays give her things that was sent. I do' know but I ought to send him back the money he give me, bein' as I didn't do it."

"I think you may keep the money," Ruth said, "and there is no explanation necessary where Mr. Ralston is concerned; but, Thaddy, another time don't hesitate. She would not have been angry if you had told her it was an accident."

"Oh, wouldn't she!" cried Tad. "I seen her git mad at her old woman onct, and she boxed her ears. But there, it's off my mind now and I'm as sorry as I can be, if you'll please to tell her, and that nobody knows about it but you and me."

"I certainly will, Thaddy; don't let it trouble you any more," Ruth said, noticing that his excitement had brought up his fever to a pitch which made the pulses in his temples throb painfully.

Ruth's opinion in regard to the taking of the photograph was more correct in its leniency than yours or mine might have been, for we are given to harsh judgments in such cases, and should be inclined to believe that a young woman who would sit for a picture of herself, leaning on a married man's shoulder, might be induced to go very far; and we should have been as much mistaken in this particular instance as Jack Ralston himself was. The affair happened during the Angel's first visit at the Idol's house in town. She had a serious flirtation with Jack, during the course of which, as I have mentioned, she contrived to keep that demon of jealousy, Mrs. Jack, quiet and amiable. Miss Laidley had not the slightest objection to Jack's being in love with her, and he was greatly taken for the time; she enjoyed hearing him bemoan his fate and descant upon the tortures he endured in his ill-assorted marriage. All that was like the things people did in modern novels, and had a spice about it wanting to the ordinary flirtations with men in a state of single blessedness. Jack had teased for her picture; he wished her to have it taken on a plate with his, that each might possess a souvenir of those weeks in which her society had brightened his life. Now Jack's friend, the fat bachelor, among other harmless attempts at killing time, had studied photography, and had an apparatus set up in his rooms from which he turned out very creditable pictures. Thither Miss Laidley consented to go one day, near the close of her visit, when she had begun to get a little tired of Jack's devotion, accompanied as usual by Juanita. The bachelor was prepared for their call; he was a little surprised to see how unhesitatingly Miss Laidley allowed Jack to exhibit his devotion before a witness, but he went about his task with the discretion of a plump partridge. Jack was hard to suit where the attitude was concerned: they would look so stiff sitting side by side; he must get on one knee and she must let him hold her hands. He was not unwilling that the Angel should go as far as she would before the fat bachelor, for Jack had taken fresh hope within the past few days, and thought his success was likely to be worth more than it ever would be. In the whim of the moment the Angel leaned her head on his shoulder and they were photographed, and that incident, which Jack, as any man would, thought a grand step gained, was the closing scene of their flirtation. Miss Laidley fluttered gracefully on to safer ground in her intercourse, and Jack Ralston never got another bewildering shower of yellow sparks out of her eyes.

When she met him again in the spring the picture she was determined to have, and persuasions failing, coolly told him she would go to his wife with a literal account of the whole affair if he did not restore it. "Every body knows how heedless I am," said she, cooing, "and oh, won't your dragon give it you well!" Jack actually believed she would keep her word, and he came out of that adventure with the admission to his friend the fat bachelor, that, well as he knew women, that girl was a fresh revelation. The pair wondered a good deal about the matter, and discussed a variety of theories in regard to it, which I may omit here, but as both were honorable men in their way where women were concerned, the history of the picture was never divulged. Before Jack left the Lake House he thought it best to restore the photograph, for fear Miss Laidley should absolutely bring his dragon down upon him. He had employed Tad, knowing from experience that he was a trusty messenger, and poor Tad had fallen in the mud, and being afraid to offer the soiled card lest the fact of his having torn it out of the envelope in his alarm should meet with suspicion and contumely, had suffered more than any body from a consciousness of misconduct.

Now to the boy's great relief the photograph was safely consigned to Mrs. Farnsworth's keeping; he had made a full confession which at least met with credence from her, and Tad could lie back on his pillows and regard this illness, in spite of the aching limbs and throbbing head, as more agreeable than the usual sandy desert of his life, since it brought Ruth's comforting presence. She was very kind to him while his sickness lasted, visited him often, sent him refreshing delicacies, and took care that his old enemy the deacon was kept aloof. Indeed, when Tad grew better and could get about he was rather inclined to look back on that season as the pleasantest he had ever spent, nor did Ruth's care end here. A comfortable home was found for him at some distance and he was sent to school, and Tad improved so rapidly in many respects that Aunt Prudence was greatly rejoiced, and even Uncle Josh and the Deacon were inclined to think there might be a faint hope for him; a hope which they considered wholly due to their "wrastlin's and warnin's." Mrs. Sykes shook her head and sighed, but hoped he might do better in a doleful tone which proved that she feared this apparent improvement was only another wile of the Evil One, who wanted to get a firmer gripe on the degenerate boy.

About this time came the meeting of delegates for a new Congressional nomination. Clive had paid little attention to the matter, and was at first somewhat astonished and in doubt when he learned that his party had again put forward his name as their candidate. Still it was not a case that admitted of much hesitation; the duty seemed plain enough, so he told the leaders frankly that if the people saw fit to elect him he would serve them to the best of his ability, beyond that he did not greatly concern himself.

The summer passed. Clive and Ruth made several trips to places of interest, but for the most part lived quietly in their home, into which no new shadow seemed inclined to intrude. Ruth was a little troubled by the possession of the photograph, and any species of secret which she could not confide to Clive, but she did not like to send it while Miss Laidley was flitting about, lest it should fail to reach her, and as Clive expected to go to town in the autumn, and she knew the Angel would be there, she decided to leave the card safe in its hiding-place until she could give it into the owner's fair hands and make her little explanation. Autumn came; the only incident was the election, and at this contest Clive's majority was so overwhelming there could be no pretext for any annoying circumstances such as had followed the former one. The Thorntons were back at Alban Wood for a few weeks, but after the election Tom could listen to Rosa's request that they might go to town, as Elinor Grey was to be there for a time. Clive was detained in the country, and the photograph still troubled Ruth's conscience, though she rested in the hope of seeing Miss Laidley and restoring it to her before she went on to Washington; these weeks of delay having made it more difficult than ever to write and explain.

CHAPTER XXXIX.

HOLLOW GROUND.

MATTERS of importance—political matters of course, Elinor knew—made it necessary for Mr. Grey to sojourn in New York for a season, and she was glad to be there since he must; but I really think if it had not been for that inducement the incomprehensible young woman would have preferred the unmitigated dullness of Washington, which would not waken to life until the approach of the coming session of Congress.

The Idol had reached town and brought the Angel in her train, for after the Newport trip they had paid a variety of visits together, and the Angel was again a guest at the Murray Hill mansion. The Idol was still very fond of her "gushing innocent," though she recalled periods when, if Miss Laidley's claims to angelic perfections had not been so thoroughly established, she might have thought her not a little selfish and exacting. She was glad to have her pet with her, but expected that Miss Laidley would be anxious again to join Elinor and her guardian. She was undeceived, however; the Angel was seized with scruples before they arrived in town. " I can not think a hotel life *convenable* for a young girl, dear Duchess," she said; "you can't fancy how I dread it! No chaperone, no one to tell me what to do. Elinor is wise and lovely, but she is not you, sweet Duchess; she doesn't mind a hotel herself, but then she is so much older than I—she has such discretion. *Hélas*, if I should do something very heedless, and people made ill-natured remarks about me, I should die at once—I am so sensitive." It was not to be permitted that she should be put to any such risk; she was implored to accept the Idol's hospitality a little longer, and gracefully consented, to the wrath of the whole domestic staff, from the chief butler down to the lowest scullion, for whatever their mistress's faith in the Angel might be, they were unanimous in their opinion, expressed in various languages, that " she was a nasty young minx and her old yellow servant no better than a witch."

Mr. Grey was more overpoweringly attentive than ever to the Idol, and held many secret consultations with Pluto. It seemed to Elinor that there was a change in her father; she could scarcely have told in what it consisted; perhaps it was only one of her fancies. He was much occupied, surrounded by New York politicians who came in swarms like the locusts of Egypt (it may be added that they resembled the locusts also in the fact that they seldom leave a green thing where they alight), and weighty matters of business pressed heavily on the minister. The presidential term would close a year from March; the whole country was already preparing for a grand convulsion; party spirit ran high, and various names were beginning to be trumpeted about as probable candidates. Though the reigning President might from the popularity he enjoyed during the first half of his term have confidently expected a renomination had he desired it, there was a powerful clique of men of his own party who had become his mortal enemies, and these men were secretly gathering nearer and nearer Mr. Grey. It was necessary for him at length to return to his post, and Elinor found herself once more settled in Washington; for the first weeks free from the encumbrance of Miss Laidley's society, as that young lady still lingered in the Idol's temple, perhaps because she hoped to make Rossitur anxious for her arrival, perhaps because she had a little mischief on hand that needed present attendance.

Washington was not yet fully alive; it gave at intervals feeble starts toward consciousness, but they were spasmodic and soon died away; moreover a certain pretty letter informed the Angel that Leighton Rossitur expected to come to town before a great while. So the Angel stayed, wheedled the Idol out of more presents, pulled Juanita's wool a good deal, the partitions in the Idol's palace being very thick, unfortunately for Juanita, and no hope of her wails piercing the heavily-curtained doors; occupied herself with such flirtations as fate threw in her way, and growing very restless because Rossitur did not make his appearance. That astute and somewhat unscrupulous young gentleman had not entertained the slightest idea of so doing, but it did not suit him that Miss Laidley should enter Washington until he was certain what terms he stood on where Elinor Grey was concerned.

Those weeks of waiting had been very long to him, and at their close he was no more resigned to lose his dream of happiness than he had been when the cloud broke. Since his return to the Capital he had tried to occupy himself with his duties, but they appeared more irksome than ever. His mind was a battle-ground for such hosts of contending feelings that the daily routine of business was an almost insupportable drag. He loved Elinor Grey still, loved her with a passion that was akin to hate in its fierceness, and he felt that if she could any moment be in his power, body and soul, it would be difficult to decide which would be uppermost. The dissipation in which he had freely indulged during those miserable weeks in the summer had left traces such as no similar indulgence had ever done. He had a new craving for excitement and stimulant, and though he constantly assured himself that when his mind was at rest either way, when the victory was gained or defeat accepted as inevitable, he should regain the old power over his appetite, he could not at this time restrain the feverish restlessness that forced him to seek a comforter in wine and led him, O Cornelia, into many strange scenes and through divers interesting experiences.

But Elinor Grey had returned and he was sorely in doubt what step ought to be taken first. One thing was evident, Miss Laidley would be an unendurable nuisance just yet, and might do some harm besides, therefore a fresh letter went to her address containing a fresh promise and several prettily-worded paragraphs about the dreariness of the world while he travelled it beyond the light of his Consuelo's smile. Before he had seen either Elinor or Mr. Grey, Rossitur was helped toward a plan of action by the appearance of a scout from the party of New York politicians, who knew the terms upon which he stood with the minister, and made choice of him as an assistant for coming negotiations. That he had been so confided in made a new bond of intimacy between him and Mr. Grey, and their first private conversation was turned to the best use by Rossitur, who bore his part so well that Mr. Grey said to Elinor that evening—

"I saw Mr. Rossitur at the Department." Elinor was only civilly interested. "You told me that your decision was made, my daughter Elinor—"

"And unalterable, papa," interrupted she, not able to remember good manners sufficiently to let him finish his sentence.

"So I suppose," returned Mr. Grey blandly; "that is, I am not supposed to know any thing about the matter. I hope, however, that your resolve will in no way interrupt our friendly relations; indeed, it is due to yourself that it should not; and besides, in the position which he occupies it would be a real inconvenience to me."

Elinor could not tell him that she had no faith in Leighton Rossitur, that she believed him unscrupulous and false, because in reality she had not sufficient grounds whereon to base the assertion. The conduct which had lowered him in her eyes might have been the result of an ungovernable temper rather than a sign of a mean, coarse nature. It might be, but she could not believe it was, although she would not injure him in her father's esteem while she had only her own intuitions as a reason. For her part, she would have much preferred to regard her acquaintance with him as an episode done with forever, but it was in the books that she should not so conduct herself, and when she recalled his goodness and devotion she was sorry to find that time had not softened her judgment. On their first meeting the old sensation of personal repulsion came back as she looked in his pale, worn face, yet the sadness in it might have moved her had her perceptions been less keen; they were stronger than her desire to be gentle and forgiving, in spite of her resolve.

Some adventurous spirit had taken the initiative in the way of an evening reception, and thereat she encountered Rossitur. He made no effort to approach her until such time as he could address her a few moments unheard. "I did not know whether I might venture to speak to you," he said after the first words of greeting.

If they were to meet and exchange conversation, Elinor had no mind that it should be on this footing. A constant humility on his part, and the opportunity of referring at will to that which was past and gone, was a kind of intimacy that would be more unpleasant than frank, cordial intercourse. She did not reply to his remark.

"May I hope that we are friends?" he asked.

"Certainly, Mr. Rossitur; that we may remain so, we will not talk about the past."

"Only you will let me say this—this one thing."

"Do you not think it would be better to leave it entirely alone?" she asked coldly.

"I am not going to weary you with protestations, Miss Grey; what I must bear, I bear. I shall not parade my sorrow; but, in justice to myself, I must tell you how bitterly I repent those hasty words that lost me your esteem."

"I am very willing to believe they sprang from temper, not deliberate wickedness," she replied. "It is like my frank, honest friend of last winter to make the confession."

"Thank you for those words," he said; "I shall not worry you any more; you have given me great comfort."

He saw that he had done the best possible for himself, and that matters for the present must rest where they were. He sat and talked cheerfully to her, and she tried to think he was what he appeared, open and impulsive, and succeeded but poorly; while in his heart the fierce emotions seethed, and he realized that he hated her with a hate which proceeded from a love so mad that he would have perilled his soul to gratify either the tenderness or the desire for retaliation. After that they met frequently, but it was always in the presence of others, and Elinor could avoid any conversation beyond that which was intended for the ears of the whole world. She owned to herself that he behaved like a man of generous nature in unhesitatingly accepting his part, and that it was due to him no one should perceive any change in her conduct from that of the previous winter. But she could not trust him; she could not believe that either his penitence or his patience was real, and the personal repulsion grew so strong that she fancied she could tell the instant he entered a room and was watching her. She commenced the season by avowing a resolution not to dance;

he had been her most frequent partner formerly; she would not give occasion to remark by declining to permit him that pleasure now, but the idea of having her hand in his made her absolutely sicken with an undefinable thrill, so she announced her resolution and persisted in it.

Elinor at this time saw less of her father than ever before; he was at the Department, or the house was filled with guests, or they were out in the world together. The whirl of gayety was his desire; he requested Elinor to give numerous entertainments, and in what she termed her morbid moods it almost seemed that he did it to avoid being alone with her. When Miss Laidley heard of the gayeties, she appeared upon the scene at once; and naturally, after her arrival, there was no peace whatever. She was inclined to be affectionate to Elinor, because in her heart she believed that she was wreaking vengeance by carrying off Leighton Rossitur. He often asked himself why in the name of every thing that was common sense, according to his creed, he did not ask her to marry him. Her wealth would afford him a life of complete ease and luxury, and he so loved both; would help him far on in any political ambition; and he cursed himself for a trifling idiot when he questioned and knew what held him back. He could not give up the hope that had taken such root in his soul; he could not believe that Elinor was irrevocably lost to him. In every scheme of Mr. Grey's or of the clique who were rallying about him, Rossitur kept looking forward to see if a chance might not arise which could be turned to his advantage. He knew how absurd and imbecile it was, but he could not help waiting to discover if some move would not in some unheard-of way place the minister in his power, so that he might claim Elinor as the price of his discretion. He laughed outright in bitter scorn of his own insanity at expecting to live an incident out of a novel, but the thought would constantly come back. Therefore Miss Laidley was still kept in suspense, and in consequence her romantic dreams knew no diminution in interest. She believed that he loved her; he did not hesitate to tell her that in the most impassioned language at every opportunity. Between his gradual admissions and her own fancies, she came to think that he had never been able to free himself from his entanglement with Elinor, and that he could take no decisive measures because there was some political project in which he required Mr. Grey's support.

The Angel cordially detested her guardian whenever she thought of her failure in that little plot to delude him into making a moaning monstrosity of himself, therefore the idea of suddenly springing a mine on both him and Elinor was highly agreeable to her. She felt that she was living a plot, and playing an exciting game, so she was constantly interested. When the moment of success arrived, Mr. Grey would discover that he had been outwitted—he was of course aiding Rossitur because he expected and desired him to be his son-in-law—and Elinor's heart would be

wrung by seeing her lover borne off in triumph. There was nothing solid whatever to make the basis of that belief, but it was none the less clear to the Angel on that account. What political end Rossitur might have in view she did not know or think, but out of his artful revelations and her skilled imagination she built up a magnificent structure that was a perfect labyrinth, wherein she played hide-and-seek with antagonists who were quite unconscious of her Cretan maze and her well-played game. She wanted some place where she could meet Rossitur without fear of Elinor; he wanted that too, therefore she began to cultivate Indiana Tallman with assiduity, thinking to make a little side annoyance for Elinor, while pursuing those grand schemes against her peace.

Mr. Grey, in the midst of his occupation, was very anxious that every thing should be done to please his ward and make her comfortable, yet it seemed to Elinor that he positively disliked her: not that in word or manner did he show any thing but gallantry and respect, still she fancied that she perceived a great change. Miss Laidley did not think about it; as I have said, from the day she arrived she was carrying out imaginary plots and counter-plots against Elinor and her guardian, and was so enveloped in mysteries that she was excited and happy. Old brown Juanita was always creeping about on some spying expedition which the Angel believed had an important aim, and was the carrier of so many secret billets that she became quite a contraband post-office, delighting in the secrecy as much as her mistress. It seemed a scarcely supposable case that if Elinor loved Rossitur ever so madly, and was wrung by jealous pangs which made her watch Miss Laidley as vigilantly as that damsel believed, she would, in her desire to discover whether letters passed between the Angel and Rossitur, covertly follow Juanita out of the house or assault her in the hall to obtain such missives by physical force. But Miss Laidley chose to believe there was danger of such attempts, and the artifices to which she and Juanita resorted to hide the notes were worthy the heroine and waiting-maid in an old-fashioned comedy. One morning the epistle was concealed among the knots of wool under the brown witch's turban; the next it was wrapped in tissue paper and placed in her shoe; sometimes sewed in the lining of her cloak or rolled in the form of a miniature cannon-ball in a layer of sheet-lead, and being held in her mouth, so distended her wrinkled cheeks that she looked as if gagged, and went about for hours after with a metallic taste on her tongue which was sickening. The getting her out of the house each morning was a performance that exercised all Miss Laidley's powers and afforded an unfailing gratification. First, the Angel went down stairs and sent every servant likely to approach the hall on impossible errands, then she peered into the room where Elinor sat and quickly retreated, then she returned to the head of the staircase and whispered to Juanita to run for her life, holding her back to give an infinity of last directions, while Juanita rolled her eyes, and, if she chanced not to be gagged, responded in unearthly gasps that could be heard as far as a sharp wind, or if she were leaded and loaded, so to speak, up to the muzzle, contented herself with winking fiercely and making frantic gestures which would have qualified her to take the part of chief lunatic in a mad-house. Having watched her down the steps, Miss Laidley flew to an upper window to see whether Elinor rushed into the street after her and to be certain that if her destination was southerly she started due north, so that any spy of Miss Grey's who might be in waiting would be neatly puzzled. No matter whether the notes were for Rossitur or Indiana Tallman, or for some secret despairing swain who excited a temporary interest, the same ceremony in sending them was preserved, and the reception of the answers was carried out with as much form. Juanita would enter the house as cautiously as if she had been a burglar with designs on the plate-chest, and Miss Laidley, hanging over the banisters while the brown familiar panted up them, would wring her hands, and at every sound utter strangled squeaks expressive of her fear that the jealous Elinor was hidden in some corner, ready to spring with ten extended fingers upon the messenger. Juanita was caught in the Angel's grasp, hurried into her rooms, the doors locked, and the Angel would cry—"Quick, quick! Give it to me! Hark! was that a step? Don't open the door—on your life—silence!" Juanita would relate what perils she had run, what escapes had; tell of an imaginary man in a Spanish cloak who dogged her, and a sepulchral-voiced woman, with her face hidden in a veil, who boldly attacked her. She discovered that when she narrated a fable unusually wild and improbable Miss Laidley was so delighted that she sometimes gave her a reward on the spot instead of the old promises, and Juanita possessing a talent for histrionics like her mistress, entered magnificently into her part and made her points in a very melodramatic manner.

In the mean time, the rush of gayety went on, and Elinor in her undefined anxiety about her father would have given much to stop quietly at home and leave Miss Laidley to waltz from house to house under Mrs. Copeland's guidance. But her father had requested that she would be very careful to keep her popularity in the ascendant, so she endured the miseries of party-going and party-giving, and between her restlessness and her duties had little thought to give the tremendous mysteries which Miss Laidley lived about her.

To Mr. Grey, those were the most anxious weeks that he had ever spent, and as he reviewed his position, it seemed scarcely credible that such a strange jumble of actual power and daily dread of consequences, such opening hopes of new position and advancement, standing side by side with such possibilities of abasement and shame, could be real. There were more frequent communications than ever between him and the Bull, but they were growing of a different nature from those of the previous summer and autumn, when every thing had prospered and promised so goldenly. The scheme on which Mr. Grey had built much was a failure —the Ship Canal was a bubble of the past, and several measures upon which he confidently counted had been hardly dealt with at the hands of Congress; and the Bull, as much deluded as himself, had made several wrong moves which had shaken the stock-market like an earthquake and startled him into the knowledge that he was not infallible. It was too late to retreat; he was pushed on by the force of circumstances and Mr. Grey was pushed on with him, ignorant of the extreme peril in which Pluto stood, but understanding enough to be full of harassing fears which went beyond the dread of mere pecuniary ruin, went beyond the dread of injury to his political reputation, if indulgence in stock-gambling could be supposed to injure that.

There was something behind it all. No wonder he avoided being alone with Elinor; no wonder he never had leisure to talk with her, as in the happy times gone by, of his ambitious hopes, and hear her aspirations and delight at his increasing popularity. Why, it was the dread of being considered in her eyes capable even of a weakness that had led him into the maze: a request to her would have kept his feet at least in tolerably straight paths, certainly free from any trouble or the worst but what would have been confined to herself and him, and he had not been able to make it. He had not been able to cast the slightest shadow over her hero-worship, and when the need of assistance was absolute and stringent he had taken his fatal step. It was a temporary thing; the next week perhaps, certainly the next month, would not only right his affairs, but leave him with a private fortune secure which would amply atone for a lack of further advancement in political life. Connected with that, too, there were new complications and fresh doubts, which, after they were stripped of their speciousness, amounted simply to these questions: Should he be true to the policy of the President, which from the opening of the Administration he had encouraged—true not only to the leader, but to the personal friend of long years—or should he desert him, and placing himself at the head of the Chief's enemies, sweep triumphantly into office on his downfall?

The measures which had excited the hatred of the party must soon come up; they could not be longer delayed, nor did the President shrink from the part he had resolved to perform. Congress was against him it was believed, though the matter had not reached a vote; for in his indecision Mr. Grey had secretly been fighting like a tiger against the efforts of the opposition leaders to force the President into action. The great body of the press was howling against him, and the people were in that undecided state where either way he was likely to meet with blame, although in the end he would be sure to have right on his side, and be remembered as an unwavering patriot, probably when the recollection could do him no more good than the sun that might shine over his grave. To turn Mr. Grey had been the object of the New York politicians and their coadjutors in all portions of the country, and the bribe was not a small one. They wanted the President to find himself paralyzed by the opposition of his right arm, the Cabinet, but they wished the blow to strike him at the last moment, when he could not pursue his course without ignominy, or retract without being covered with opprobrium for his cowardice. Mr. Grey's reward for carrying out their plans was to be the candidateship at the coming Presidential contest. If nominated, there was no doubt of his election; the party was powerful, and dissension in the opposite ranks was leading to the breaking up of the old platform, the downfall of which would cast a host of men opposed to either extreme into its numbers.

Of these things Elinor was in ignorance, for Mr. Grey knew very well that in her mind there could be no room for doubt; she must be left unadvised until the storm burst. If he became a secret traitor and an outward patriot, he must trust to her being still sufficiently blinded by her love to accept his course as forced upon him by the exigencies of duty alone. He did doubt and he did debate the matter uneasily; not perhaps so much in a conscientious point of view as from the fear whether, with the Presidential chair gained, he might not, before the term of his office expired, find himself so bound up with the party who would have bought him in, that his light would go out in a darkness which could never be lessened. He could not help feeling to what end their course pointed—how surely and insidiously the very foundations of peace and liberty were being undermined by their machinations. The question was whether, if he gained the coveted honors, the consummation for which they were striving could be staved off during his four years of supremacy, and he be left with a record that would bear inspection. With all these plans and plots working in his brain, to be tormented about Wall Street; to have on his mind one ceaseless recollection which proved his nature kindred to the men who at this juncture were causing odious paragraphs in the newspapers and seeking shelter from their crimes across the sea, was enough to make him feel at times that the whole thing must be a bad dream. And this danger run that he might keep his elevation in Elinor's esteem! Verily, those were not pleasant days to Mr. Grey, and, to add to the annoyances, his health during the past months had not been free from grave causes for alarm when he had leisure to study it.

Rossitur was beside him during these weeks of mental questionings—Rossitur with his plausible sophistries, his silken way of making things smooth, and his faculty of giving so fine a name and appearance to doubtful matters that they wore a lustre which concealed their original base metal. He was just now back from a hurried visit to New York, and he had seen the Bull, for Mr. Grey's transactions with him were no more a secret to Rossitur than these political moves. Indeed he had been a friend of Pluto's long before Mr. Grey knew him, and ever since he had held any position which could give him a clue to secrets worth having he had not scrupled to employ the power in Pluto's service. It never occurred to Rossitur whether there was any thing derogatory in this; plenty of other men did it; any way he wanted money, and had nearly as extravagant tastes as Mr. Grey himself, so he had fallen into the habit. On his return he did not tell the Secretary what he believed, from a variety of circumstances which had come to his knowledge, to be the fact, that Pluto was tottering on the verge of a precipice over which he might go in splendid ruin; on the contrary, he gave the most hopeful account, and to Mr. Grey, who was no business man, it did appear incredible that any real danger could menace his Wall Street champion.

Rossitur knew a great many things that he was not supposed to know—the Secretary's weakness for cards and the fact that he was most awfully dipped in Pluto's speculations; but his penetration showed him there was something lay heavier on Mr. Grey's mind than the fear of pecuniary losses or the dread of blowing himself up among the fireworks of the politicians, and Rossitur meant to discover what it was. A couple of emissaries had come on when Rossitur returned, with new treaties for Mr. Grey, and he desired Rossitur to be his agent in the business as he had in a great measure been throughout. Rossitur was going to meet them that morning, and he and the minister sat discussing the points upon which he was to touch, the way in which evasion was to be employed here, a meaning look there, an oracular answer at another point, for what Mr. Grey wanted was to hold aloof still and not compromise himself while it could be avoided. He had been very careful, and the whole affair was much more a secret than he dared to hope: there was not so much as a written note to bring up against him in case the matter came to nothing. Rossitur had been invaluable, and indeed it was a relief to Mr. Grey, with those diverse questions on his mind, and that dreary dull ache which had taken up its abode in the back of his head, to have somebody with whom he could talk freely and whose art in making the doubtfullest subjects presentable was unequalled.

"I don't think I'm quite clear about the last," said Rossitur suddenly, leaning back in his chair and holding the pencil, with which he had been making notes on a bit of paper, in his hand. "I think I must give something satisfactory in the way of reply on that."

"How satisfactory?" asked Mr. Grey.

"I ought to have said decided."

"Ah! but, my dear friend, that is just what I don't want to do. To make it satisfactory and not decided is the very thing; the more time gained, the better."

"It needs one of your smooth, flowery periods," said Rossitur, laughing.

Mr. Grey gave several general hints as to the manner and method, but Rossitur still looked a little doubtful. The Secretary wheeled his chair to the table and wrote down several heads that must be touched upon, and elaborated answers in his graceful, easy style, while Rossitur leaned over him and read the page. "The very thing," he said, "and diplomatic enough in all conscience. I will copy it outright."

Mr. Grey took a pinch of snuff and surveyed the paragraphs, well satisfied with their appearance. Rossitur hastily copied the page, put up his tablets and moved toward the hearth where Mr. Grey was standing. "Just tear up that specimen of my chirography, please," he said with a smile.

Rossitur, before he had fairly begun to speak, threw a fold of paper on the coals. "There it goes," he answered; "I have burned it." Mr. Grey turned and saw it blazing on the grate and nodded his head; but the paper was one containing some lines of figures that Rossitur had taken up from the table—the page which the minister had written was hidden in his breast-pocket.

"I think we have made every thing satisfactory for the present," Mr. Grey said, watching the paper burn and blacken to a shrivelled tissue which made a frantic effort to fly up the chimney and fell back in ashes, as one's best hopes often slip down from a short flight.

"Yes," Rossitur said, "but I tell you honestly, Mr. Grey, one way or the other, your decision will have to be made before many weeks. Falcon himself will come on, and there is no parleying with him; he will know where he stands with every body."

"A coarse man," Mr. Grey said; "I often wonder at the power he wields, and the strangest thing is it is not confined to his set in New York; it spreads far and wide."

"We can at least say for him that he is faithful to his enmities," said Rossitur; "he does hate the President with a bitter hatred, and so he is certain to serve you. He and his party offer you every security; you can't fail. I own I only wonder at your hesitation."

If Mr. Grey had spoken frankly he would have admitted that he had also many times wondered since the first glimmer of the project was made known to him in the autumn, but I may say here what one could not say in history, because in novels we often tell truths the writers of history are ashamed to state through a fear of being considered puerile—his daughter stood in the stead of a conscience before Mr. Grey; his love for her was the one pure light of his life, and he had not yet seen how he was to make his course, if he yielded to the bribe, clear in her eyes. There was too the dread which I have already mentioned, that if elected he might not be able to keep aloof during his administration the catastrophe for which he felt that party was secretly working. The better reason for hesitation was one of which he could not bring himself to speak, but he did mention the latter and Rossitur had a quick answer for that.

"When you are President, if you find that the leaders of your party desire to carry out ends which they had kept secret from you, cut adrift from them. You don't want re-election, I fancy; you can afford to be patriotic."

"And I should be, Rossitur, if the case I am supposing arose."

"Very right, Sir; but that is a thing a long way in the future; let us leave it there."

"Let us leave it there," repeated Mr. Grey, musingly, not thinking of the future, but of his conscience in the form of Elinor. It was a plausible sophistry to offer. With his far-sightedness he foresaw the danger that might menace the country if this unscrupulous party brought a man into power who would favor its machinations; therefore he heroically threw himself into the gap at the expense of appearing a traitor to his old friend, trusting to time and the patriotism of his motives to set him right.

He remained looking in the fire, and Rossitur, covertly regarding him, knew that his thoughts had left the subject altogether and slipped away to other questions or regrets, nearer and more oppressive. The keen-eyed watcher was not deceived; Mr. Grey was thinking of the other side of his life, that which had nothing to do with political aims or greatness, the weaknesses which had brought him such losses at the card-table and the visionary turn of mind which had led him so deeply into Pluto's schemes, and into schemes of which Pluto in his practicality did not approve, although, having stated his objections, he was willing to be the agent therein. His thoughts dropped lower than those plans which had glittered so brightly a few months since—dropped down to a level which he could not bear to contemplate, and from which he was daily hoping to be released by some favorable turn in Pluto's fortunes. He had been led to commit his fault by the need of a moment: a large sum must be raised on the instant to make the future secure, and Pluto, overburdened, turned to him; he had supplied the necessity, and since that he had known no peace, trusting each week that he should be able to set himself right, and seeing the poor round of days give place to fresh ones, still fettered by that loathsome recollection.

"I think," said Rossitur carelessly, as he took out his cigar-case, "our tremendous old Bull is getting straight again."

Mr. Grey did not exactly start, but there was change enough in his demeanor to make Rossitur sure he had hit the ground of his moody reflections. "You have no doubt?" he asked.

"Oh, no; I told you how clear he made it. Wonderful head on those very high shoulders.

O

Will you smoke? These are your favorite Reginas." But Mr. Grey had a pinch of snuff in his fingers; he watched Rossitur placidly lighting his Havana, apparently not intending to follow up his chance remark. "These are hard lines for those fellows in Wall Street," Rossitur added, blowing a series of white rings with great skill into the air and regarding them as if his life held no more important thought. "My own opinion is, there will be a terrible crash within the month. The houses already down make a fine beginning, and those men take a panic like scarlet fever."

"Our friend Hackett stands on a very different basis from the greater portion of them."

Rossitur made another white ring and sent a small cloud through it with the dexterity of a conjuror. "Very different," he answered, and he thought if Mr. Grey knew exactly what he had learned during his visit to New York the bland minister might not regard the difference as being in Pluto's favor.

"You impressed upon him the importance of those last securities being returned to me with the least possible delay?" Mr. Grey asked, finishing his pinch of snuff.

"Oh, yes; he mentions it in your letter. I should say this last turn in Dove Island stuff would give him control of any amount of the ready.—I forgot you detest slang."

"I forgive it," said Mr. Grey, smiling, "in consideration of the good news it conveys of our friend. I should be sorry to see his ship strike a rock; indeed, as you know, I have been of some little assistance to him; I may say I should be sorry to meet with any loss myself."

Rossitur knew him for the very coolest hand he had ever encountered, but that touch did strike him as sublime—the man must be accustomed to showing his thoughts to each other in full dress. When Rossitur knew that he was heavily involved—when there was between them the not altogether creditable secret of aiding the Bull's apparent gift of second-sight by any amount of private information—it certainly was stupendous. But there was more back, that was what filled Rossitur's mind; an anxiety which he had not probed, and which went beyond the fear of money losses. If he only had the clue to that in his hands he might make a reality of the absurd fancy which he had indulged of humbling Elinor through his hold upon her father. He blew another ring of white smoke, and before it broke welded a fresh one to it in a very artistic manner, and as he lazily watched the pair melt into one and float off in a wide, eccentric circle over the minister's head, he observed—

"What a fearful jar it would have made if Pluto had chanced to smash. It would have been like an earthquake."

This time Mr. Grey did start; the idea of what would have stared in his face had that calamity arrived was too horrible. He took out his snuff-box; in an instant he was himself again, but Rossitur's eyes were too quick to be

deceived by the ease of his manner or the natural languor of the tone in which he said—

"An earthquake indeed; it would have made the whole Board totter, I fancy. At what hour were you to meet those men?"

"Twelve," replied Rossitur, looking at his watch; "almost that now. I must be off. Well, I believe I am prepared at every point for the encounter."

"I think so. I may not be here when you get back; I promised to see Sloane's Committee to-day," Mr. Grey said, rising as Rossitur did and standing with his back to the fire. "You dine at Count Treville's, don't you—his day, I believe?"

"Yes; I shall see you there," Rossitur said, and after a little more indifferent conversation went out.

Mr. Grey walked up and down the room in silent meditation, and it was a worn, troubled face that he carried, apparently forgetful of the committee which awaited him, or the business close at hand that might easily have had a claim on his attention.

Rossitur hailed a carriage and drove off on his mission, biting the end of his cigar viciously between his teeth, and at last taking it out of his mouth to mutter—"There's where it is, you old fox—some move you've made in that Wall Street business. I fancy I shall see bottom before I am through. Turning off the talk with questions about dinners! Bah! do you think I'm a mole?"

He threw his cigar out of the window and flung himself back in his seat, staring moodily before him and thinking the wild thoughts that had been so long in his mind, and finally settling his reflections wholly upon Elinor Grey, and that love which was hate, and that hate which was the most burning portion of his mad love.

CHAPTER XI.

KINGS AND QUEENS.

THE season hurried on and bore every body near the consummation of their destinies, whatever that consummation was to be, and with several of those with whom I have to deal it remained doubtful where it would leave them.

Leighton Rossitur was helping Miss Laidley live her romance, still insanely looking forward to some event which should place Elinor Grey in his power, and in the life outside of that he was serving to the best of his ability that party which had bought him; he had been bought for a special purpose, that in regard to Mr. Grey, and he was doing them good service.

The Idol came to Washington when the season was at its height, and her grandeur was beyond any thing that even she had attempted in previous days. Some accommodating widow who owned a stylish house and had money enough to make her a lawful prey for fortune-hunters, though her years might have taught her discretion if they ever did teach any body that apocryphal virtue, saw fit to fall in love with a scape-grace sufficiently young to have been her son, married him and bore him off to Cuba as a fit resting-place during the brightness of the honey-moon. She was an acquaintance of the Idol's, and the Idol being aware of her intended folly, engaged the house for a couple of months, and when the well-mated couple departed in search of happiness, came on to dazzle Washington, bringing her retinue with her and even various fresh decorations for the mansion, that it might be made more worthy to be her shrine. She gave dinners, she gave balls, and the expense she was at could only be equalled in the Arabian Nights, or in a country gone mad after speculation.

Indiana Tallman and the Angel had become such fast friends, and the Banger had been so obliging in regard to the yielding up of her library as a whispering-ground for Miss Laidley and her supposed adorer, so faithful a confidante every way in the Angel's numerous plans, that she felt she ought to have a little return; something more tangible than the vague and magnificent promises which the Angel lavished upon her as freely as she did on the rest of her friends. Indiana desired to go to the Idol's balls, and the Idol did not wish her to display herself thereat, so the Angel, with a view to future whisperings in the friendly seclusion of the library, had to be mediator and soften the Idol. That was not a difficult task, in spite of the good soul's aversion to the Banger; Miss Laidley, having brought the matter artfully into the conversation, had only to embrace the Idol and say—

"For my sake, dearest Duchess, for my sake!"

"My love, any thing that I can do for you is a guerdion to me; but that odious woman—how can you tolerate her?"

"Oh, indeed I only feel sorry for her because she can't be agreeable. That is a gift; you must know that, sweet Duchess, you who have it in such perfection. I'm such a foolish little thing! I can't bear to see any body disappointed—and she must feel heart-broken at not being invited. If you would, for your poor little Angy's sake, who hasn't many pleasures, who can't often do the least thing to make any human being happy."

"Enough, my pet—she comes; sweet child, ever filled with sympathy for others! But I would not see you intimate with her."

"Mercy, no! I never go there, hardly, only she begs me sometimes, and—she was very kind—but no, I won't tell that, because it would seem like praising myself."

"To me you may confide it," returned the Idol, "who understands your gentle spirit. What kindness could she do you?"

"Only I wanted to give a lot of money to a poor family without any body knowing it, and she helped me. I wouldn't tell any one but you; don't think me vain."

"So like you! Ah, it is rejuveniscence to watch such purity!"

"They were orphans," said the Angel, plaintively; "how could I help pitying them? Four helpless young creatures, with only a lame, feeble elder sister to care for them." She began the falsehood without having any idea whither it would lead her, but the lame sister presenting herself to her imagination, she could not help elaborating the picture. The Idol was touched and wanted to aid the distressed family also. "But they are gone," continued the Angel; "they had some relatives in Kansas, or somewhere—I sent them off so happy. And you will invite that dreadful Tallman woman? I want every body to have pleasure. Isn't she just like a giraffe, dear Duchess? I always have a fancy when I look at her long neck that she must have her luncheon put at the head of the stairs, while she stands below in the hall and stretches up to it. Oh, that's wicked! Never mind, I didn't mean it; and since we are going to be good to her we may laugh a little between ourselves."

She went off satisfied with her success, not only because it was for her interest to oblige Indiana, but she liked to think she turned people about her finger, and sought the Banger to describe the absurdities of the Idol and amuse Indiana by imitating her walk and exaggerated speech. "The nasty old thing made me give to one of her charities," said she; "a large sum too, for some abominable orphan family with a lame sister; but I couldn't refuse, because I wanted to keep her good-natured."

In certain ways the Banger was as much duped as any body by the Angel, and having conceived an intense hatred to Elinor Grey, was ready to believe the stories Miss Laidley told of her tyranny, and was always persuading the victim to take some decisive steps which should make Miss Grey's evil conduct publicly known. The Banger's husband and the minister were no longer friends; something the Californian had wanted for somebody was in Mr. Grey's gift and had been refused; as it was to have been for the gratification of one of the Banger's favorites, naturally she was furious, and strengthened the anger of her spouse by her outcries. The rumors that Mr. Grey would probably be a nominee for the Presidency nearly drove her mad; the thought of seeing his daughter queen it at the White House, Indiana felt was more than she could endure; if the reality ever came to pass, she really must die outright. It was not to be expected that her wishes could have much effect; if he did become a candidate she could not go about the country on electioneering tours, but it occurred to her that she might plant a thorn in his side which would prick him severely when the electioneering duties should be undertaken by other people. The Banger knew very well that if she could persuade Mr. Grey's ward to leave his house and seek her protection, the fact could easily be published far and wide, and would make a beautiful handle whereon to hang the blackest aspersions when the speech-making days arrived. Not only against him; Miss Grey's name would be dragged into the affair, and she had heard too many "stump" orations in her time not to know how ruthlessly opposing politicians would assail it, and how it would be bandied about by coarse men in a fashion that would be worse than death to a delicate-minded woman.

The bare idea was delightful to Indiana; she fancied the things that would be written and said, the cutting paragraphs and the miserable jokes, and she felt that she could cheerfully give her right hand to do so much for her country in her day and generation. Consequently she helped by every possible means to keep alive in Miss Laidley's mind the fiction that Elinor was in love with Rossitur and secretly devoured by jealous pangs of the most poignant sort. But although the Angel would have been delighted with the notoriety arising from an open quarrel with her guardian, and would have enjoyed acting the scene to the utmost, even to the extent of rushing in her stockings at midnight to the refuge of the Banger's arms, she was sufficiently afraid of Rossitur to hesitate. She was still too doubtful of the extent of her power over him to run any risks of spoiling her romance and mystery, so she contented herself with pouring the recital of her wrongs into the Banger's ears, and being as annoying to Elinor as circumstances would admit. Indiana was too energetic and impatient to be satisfied with such half measures, and vowed that Miss Laidley should do something desperate and absurd; if in the end that young female's reputation was injured thereby, the Banger could not help it; any means was justifiable which could bring calumny against the Greys; the matter became a patriotic scheme and not a private vengeance, and Indiana felt that she was working for her country and her country's good.

At length events that had been looming in the distance gathered into the near horizon and made ready to burst, and in a degree, Elinor Grey's own conduct helped to precipitate the storm. The Idol gave a grand fancy ball, an affair so magnificent that it seemed even she could never go beyond the triumph of that night. All the world was there; the Banger was an Eastern queen, of what country or age did not appear, and wore an old mixture of dress, something between that of a ballet-dancer and a Russian empress. The Angel was sylph-like in a gauzy raiment, and Elinor, who had gone about for days loathing the thought of the whole thing, made herself beautiful in a costume that she chanced to have by her, which it seemed a mockery to put on, remembering how and when she had worn it across the sea at a ball while balls were pleasant to her and there was an agreeable excitement in investing herself in its loveliness. She was firm as ever in her resolution not to dance, and the night was as dreary to her as if she had been a ghost compelled to do penance by haunting scenes that had once had a charm for her. She could not forget how the worn, strange look in her father's face had deepened during the past days, or rid herself of the feeling that some great trouble was close at hand which any moment might reveal. The sensation came with her to the ball and took the sparkle out of the scene, seeming to endue her with an inner sight which made her see how listless and tired most of the faces looked, in spite of their smiles and gaudy trappings. The Idol herself was Queen Elizabeth for the occasion, and the splendor of her toilette might have satisfied the overblown tastes of that royal old virgin, who has been raved over in history, paraded in novels, swept in gorgeous pageants across the stage, and represented at fancy balls till one is sick of the very thought of her, and has an unchristian hope that some old Papistical reprobate like Philip the Second is tormenting her without mercy in a very hot purgatory at the present moment. Mr. Grey was there in a dress that made him look as the Idol said more like "Richaleo" than ever, for the fiat had gone forth that nobody, whatever his or her quality might be, must appear unless in some species of costume similar to the garbs in which people made themselves uncomfortable centuries ago.

It was as idiotically stupid as fancy balls invariably are, no matter where given. The women went about encumbered by stiff draperies or discomposed by a lack of them; the men dropped plumes off their hats as if they had been a collection of ostriches at the moulting season, and the bashful man, who had held Elinor's bonquet on one memorable evening, dove among people's feet impressed with the idea that every plume he saw on the floor had just dropped from his beaver, and sticking them in the gold band without looking, was remarked at one time to have no less than eight feathers of different hues fluttering over his head.

"I don't see that old deaf woman," said Indiana, as the Angel and Rossitur stood by her for a moment; "I expected her to be here masquerading in the white opera cloak and blue feathers."

"Here comes the Idol," said Miss Laidley; "I must ask her."

The Idol, for the time her gracious Majesty of doubtful memory, sailed up so magnificent that the sight of her lacerated the Banger's feelings and made her long to throw decency to the winds, to assault the Idol and scatter her decorations and pull her hair down. The Angel propounded her question, but the Idol could not tell whether she was there. "I am sure," said she, "I would have asked her if I could remember her name. She is well connected, you know, though peculiar; but indeed, I should have been at a loss where to send her a card."

"Oh, round the corner; people always do," said the Angel.

"Artless prattler," said the Idol, and Indiana laughed so at a private *mone* of the Angel's that Rossitur roused himself from a gloomy con-temptation of Elinor Grey in the distance and asked of whom they were speaking.

"The old deaf woman; I never can recollect her name," said the Banger.

"I told Queen Elizabeth she ought to have sent an invitation round the corner for her," added the Angel.

"Further than that," said he.

"Why, she comes usually," observed Indiana, "whether she is invited or not."

"She may come now," returned Rossitur, "but I suppose it would be a long journey. I wonder if she would bring her ear-trumpet."

"What do you mean?" asked Miss Laidley.

"Why, she's gone round the last corner," said Rossitur.

"Deceased?" cried the Idol in horror, while Indiana and the Angel laughed heartily.

"At last," said Rossitur; "it was supposed that she would have gone long before, but Death couldn't make her hear."

"Oh, jest not upon such a theme," said the Idol, and rustled away, while the others stood laughing at her.

Rossitur was in a mood to say or do any thing; he had already many times found his road to the punch-room, and he delighted the Banger with his satirical speeches, and entranced the Angel by his whispers as they flew through the dance.

Elinor Grey stood about and walked about, and listened to absurd speeches and made answers that were equally unmeaning, until she could endure it no longer. Wherever she moved she felt Leighton Rossitur's eyes following her, till she had an absolutely superstitious tremor come over her. She would have been glad to go away, but she knew if she did her father would accompany her, and as he seemed sufficiently amused with a bedizened foreign embassadress who looked like some strange bird with a hooked nose, ugly feet, and brilliant plumage, stupid from long confinement in an aviary, she would not be unnecessarily selfish.

Up in the region of the dressing-rooms there was a small chamber where card-tables had been set out for the convenience of elderly people who might get tired of having their toes trodden upon in the ball-room. Elinor found her way thither; fortunately it was empty. To watch a large portion of mankind absurd in fancy-dress had proved more attractive than whist to the elderly people, and they were enduring the corn-trampling somewhere below with such equanimity as long experience might have given them. The bronze woman holding a torch at the end of the sofa, and the monstrosities depending over the card-tables, had all the gas turned low, and the shade, after the glare of the apartments she had left, was particularly acceptable. Elinor closed the door and sat down on the couch with a sensation of relief, and the bronze woman eyed her curiously; indeed as the light from the torch flickered about her face she seemed to wink with her left eye, and there was a grin on her mouth which reminded Elinor too much of brown Juanita to be agreeable. She turned her back on the inquisitive Moorish female with an irritated feeling as if something alive and sentient were watching her, and sat looking straight before her, wondering from whence proceeded the restlessness which had beset her for weeks and kept growing more strong. The change that to her vigilant eyes was apparent in her father, despite his labored affectation of his usual manner; the rumors which had come to her, she scarcely knew how, that he too was likely to turn against the President, which rumors she treated with scorn, while concerning them for some undefined reason she could not bring herself to speak to him; all these things troubled and perplexed her. At the same time, her faith in her hero was so entire that she would not admit to her own mind the possibility that he might err even in judgment, and altogether she wondered at the varying fancies which oppressed her peace, and demanded sternly why it was that she could never let herself be at rest. She tried to think that the fears and uneasiness were wholly caused by her alarm about her father's health, concerning which she had many times essayed to question him, but had been obliged to cease because he so evidently was annoyed by her solicitude, the possibility of ill-health being a weakness that Mr. Grey never could bear to contemplate or hear mentioned.

The opening of the door made Elinor look up; Leighton Rossitur stood on the threshold, and in her nervous state it seemed as if he were the living realization of all her vague fears. He uttered a little exclamation at the sight of her, though he knew very well that she was there and had followed for the express purpose of speaking to her alone, with what intention or to what end he could not have told. The passion in his soul made him absolutely mad to-night; he could not longer support the *rôle* of patience and humility which he had been enacting during the past weeks. He had noticed Elinor go out, had seen that the Angel was safe in the arms of a Highland chief with false calves to his legs, doing double time to a fast waltz tune, and had followed Elinor, determined to speak, to force her to answer, if it were only to meet her scorn and wrath—any thing to break the ice of decorous indifference which she had kept between them. She saw him standing in the door-way and had that quick thought about his being the embodiment of some approaching evil, then declined to take such a stilted view of his importance and gave a little gesture of annoyance at the intrusion.

"Miss Grey!" he exclaimed wonderingly.

"I believe it is," she answered, trying to speak with civility.

"I was so astonished that I thought it might be fancy."

"I think I must look tolerably real in this stiff dress," she replied; "and seeing me here, considering that I have been in the house these two hours, can scarcely be a matter for astonishment." She could not help it; she was vexed at his words, which had been meant to imply that his fancy expected her at all seasons and beheld her in all places.

"I beg your pardon," he said drearily; "have I offended you?"

"Not in the least, Mr. Rossitur; I am tired and I dare say rude," she answered, wishing she had restrained her first speech, yet extremely annoyed by his melodramatic starts and the deep gloominess of his voice and aspect.

"In the old days you used not to think it necessary to apologize to me for any exhibition of your real feelings," he said, with an inflection upon the personal pronoun that irritated her afresh.

"I thought we had gone back to the oldest possible days," said she, touching her dress; "I'm aged two hundred years and more, and you to the full as old, I am sure."

"If I were to judge by my feelings," he said, "I might have been old when the pattern of these dresses was new."

He was gotten up in some sort of black-velvet costume that might have answered for Hamlet or a tragic Spanish cavalier; any way it was very becoming, heightening his natural pallor and giving him the look of some character of romance, which had filled the Angel's soul with delight. His appearance did not strike Elinor in the same manner; she thought as he stood there that he would have answered for a handsome Mephistopheles. She did not answer his last remark, and remained waiting for him to bow and go away, but he kept his position.

"You look very tired," he said softly, in the voice that had once sounded kind and earnest to her, but only seemed artificial and importunate now with its low, pleading tone.

"I am," she replied; "as you go back, please don't say to any one that I am here; I really want to rest before enduring the glare down stairs again—I was nearly suffocated with the heat."

The hint was politely enough delivered, but plain as it was it did not have the effect of sending him away. Her words and manner, her evident effort to be courteous, filled him with a hot rage, and at the same time her pale beauty, increased by her costume, brought the passion up hotter than ever as he looked at her leaning languidly back in the shadow. With a quick movement he closed the door and advanced a few steps toward her. He did not know what he meant to say, whether to plead or upbraid, but her name broke from his lips with a smothered vehemence that was positively startling in its unexpectedness—

"Elinor! Elinor!"

She drew her head slowly back in the old proud way he knew so well, and regarded him with a quiet fixedness that was more overwhelming than the angriest reproof could have been.

"You let me call you so once," he exclaimed; "O Elinor, Elinor!"

There was real suffering in the voice, yet it seemed to her that she could detect the smothered rage under that imploring sound. "If I did once allow it," she said coldly, "the recollection shall help me to think this was a lapse of memory, not an intentional fault."

"For God's sake, don't speak to me in that tone!" he cried. "Can't you see that I am almost mad?"

After the variety of things in regard to him and Miss Laidley which had come to her knowledge of late, this last appeal sounded like a bit of repulsive acting too unworthy to be gently met. "That I may not think you wholly so, Mr. Rossitur, have the kindness to go away," she said.

"Have you no pity, no heart?" he exclaimed. "You sit there like a beautiful statue and know you are crushing my heart in your hands, and are utterly unmoved."

"I beg your pardon," she could not resist saying, "I have nothing in my hands but my handkerchief."

The instant the words were uttered she felt that they were ungenerous and was sorry, but the Angel by incessant repetition had so disgusted her with every exhibition which looked like private theatricals that she was difficult to move where she doubted the sincerity of the speaker as she did his. Rossitur gave a short, bitter laugh; even in his excited state, with his brain whirling from passion and wine, he could control himself enough to know that he had been making a spectacle of himself.

"You are right enough to sneer at my high tragedy," he said very quietly, "but it is scarcely generous, Miss Grey, for you know that if it is absurd it is terribly earnest to me."

"If so, I am sorry for my words," she answered. "Please go away now, Mr. Rossitur."

"Let me stay a moment—give me a moment," returned he.

"Not for conversation of this sort," she said; "it is worse than useless, and as painful to me as it can be to you."

"How do you mean useless?" he asked.

"I think you know, Mr. Rossitur."

"I know that to speak to you at all, to hear you speak even those cold words, is heaven to me," he said rapidly, in a voice that carried the ring of truth in it. "I have suffered so! These weeks have been torture to me. Let me speak now. If ever man atoned for a wrong, I have. Elinor, Elinor, look at me! Don't sit there like a block of marble! Tell me there is a little hope left—give me the faintest safeguard against utter misery and desperation."

She was moved now, and very sorry for him; the scene was inexpressibly painful to her, but his face and voice showed too plainly what terrible earnest he was in for her to remember aught but her pity. "If I could say any thing that would be a comfort, Mr. Rossitur," she replied, "believe me, I would do it, but I can not—"

"You can give me a hope," he interrupted.

"You know that it is impossible; I beg you for both our sakes to say nothing more, to let this subject end forever."

"I can't be silent any longer, Elinor—I must call you so this once—I have waited till I am almost mad. I thought you would relent; I thought, knowing how I suffered, you would pity me."

"I do," she said, "but I told you that my decision was irrevocable. O Mr. Rossitur! I could not have made my meaning more plain—you understood it so—you could not have helped it."

"All for a few angry words! You are so unforgiving that you break my heart as a punishment for giving way to a fit of temper."

"Not for that; you know there was another reason; I told you that though I was angry at the time, there was another reason. I do believe that you are sorry—I have no unkind feeling toward you."

"Then retract your resolution."

"You know I can not."

"Why?" he asked sullenly.

"You know why," she answered. "Mr. Rossitur, it is cruel to yourself and me to force me to say things that sound harsh. I entreat you to end this conversation here."

"I must speak. I must—"

"No," she interrupted kindly, but in a firm voice, "I can not hear you—I beg you to be silent. You force me to tell you that unless I need run no risk of similar scenes in future, we must be strangers."

"And this is the end!" he exclaimed. "You take my heart for a plaything—for months you amuse yourself with my devotion—you let me be your blind slave, and when your caprice changes, you coolly tell me that I must submit without a word."

The gross injustice of his speech stirred an angry emotion in Elinor's mind, but she controlled it ; she saw that he suffered greatly, and believed that the words might have been wrung out of his suffering and would be repented after without reproof from her. "If I am to blame," she said, "I beg you to pardon me. You know, when you reflect calmly, that I dealt honestly with you from the first. I did not treat your love lightly."

"You allowed me to lavish it upon you; you gave me hope."

"Oh, look back, Mr. Rossitur, and in justice to both see what the truth was. I told you that I could not think it right to permit you to care for me, to hope, and you said then—" She hesitated in compassion ; she could not bear to wound him by recalling the difference between his generous protestations of that time and his persistence now.

"What did I say?" he asked in a voice so harsh and stubborn that her pulses quickened again.

"I think you must remember, Mr. Rossitur."

"I choose to hear you say it: so much you owe me."

"Sir," she said, "I owe you nothing when you address me in that tone—not even an answer. Since you will hear me repeat it, you said that so far from being unjust I was generous, because you must love me." She began angrily, but his face changed so under her words, the hard smile turned to a spasmodic trembling of such exquisite pain, that her voice faltered over her last words.

"I did love you ; I do!" he groaned.

"And I ask you to forgive my share in your unhappiness," she said. "I was wrong to be persuaded ; I ought not to have allowed you to wait, but you do know that I meant, that I tried to do right."

He raised his eyes toward her with a strange look and said—"You would have married me if it had not been for that accursed day's work —that one day." She did not answer. "That was your reason," he continued ; "own it."

"I shall not deny that it was one reason, Mr. Rossitur, but there was a stronger still."

"What was it?"

"I gave it to you at the time."

"I want to hear it again. I have a right to ask and I will!" And his voice more than his words stung her pride like a blow.

"I did not love you, Sir!"

He gave an odd, panting breath and pressed his hand hard against his chest, but again he regarded her with that defiant smile. "And now," said he, "you hate and loathe me."

"I am going away that this conversation may end before I do," she replied, moving toward the door.

"Elinor, Elinor!" he repeated in a voice of such wild entreaty that she could no more have left him without another attempt to soften his pain than she could have left some drowning wretch to drift off a plank before her eyes without making an effort to aid him.

She went toward him, holding out her hand with such truth and earnestness in her face that a noble-minded man, remembering how conscientious she had been from the first, would have been at once subdued. "Let us part kindly," she said ; "let us part friends—only I think, Mr. Rossitur, that it would be better for us not to meet for some time to come. In your heart, you must do me the justice to own that from the beginning I tried to be perfectly frank and honest ; you must know how I suffer in your suffering, and reproach myself for having consented to delay my answer."

She told the truth and he knew it: she had been more generous to him than to herself, for in her dread of making him unhappy she had come very near wrecking her own peace. He knew that, but at this moment his demons had full possession of him and he could only feel horrible wrath at the consciousness that he had lost her, that this conversation was the seal to the defeat which he had refused to accept, and that if he had only worn his mask one day longer in that past summer she would have been his.

He looked at her as she stood holding out her hand, and returned her glance of sympathy with a regard which revealed his emotions. "I do not forgive you!" he exclaimed; "I will not take your hand! If these were my last words, I would pronounce you a false, perjured woman!"

"They are your last to me," she said, walking toward the door again, more astonished by such fierce capabilities of rage than angered by what he said.

He was too insane to reflect; the tornado was sweeping over his soul in its full fury. He stepped suddenly between her and the door with a gesture that was a menace. One woman would have been frightened, another enraged; Elinor stood still and looked at him in a kind of wonder if it could be real that an insult had come so near her pride and the life that to its minutest detail had ever been guarded by such knightly courtesy. "They are not the last!" he exclaimed; "I have more to say, and you shall hear! I said you were a false, perjured woman — doubly so — you loved Clive Farnsworth."

She was looking at him still, and the expression of cold surprise on her haughty features did not change. "It might have been," she said slowly; "he was a gentleman."

Rossitur's two hands crossed each other and tugged at the lace about his wrists, tearing it into tatters; it was like looking into fire to look in his eyes, and his voice was like nothing human. "I have shown you how I can love—I will show you how I can hate, Elinor Grey! This shall fall on your father's head. I hold that in my hands which I will use if it ruins me body and soul—which shall show him a paltry trickster, trying for office by selling his friend. Go, tell him I said so!"

"You shall tell him yourself," said Elinor. "You have been insolent, but I would not willingly expose a disobedient greyhound to the punishment of the lash. Let me pass."

Quick as the insane fit had come it died under her icy words. "Oh, I must be mad!" he groaned. As he moved aside, she swept past him out of the room before he could speak again, if indeed he could have found any words. In the hall she encountered Miss Laidley rushing along with her gauzy draperies flying out like a cloud.

"What have you been saying to Mr. Rossitur?" she demanded. "You have been talking to him ever so long. You disgraceful creature, shutting yourself up in a room with any man at this time of night!"

"Be quiet," was all Elinor answered, in the subdued tone and with the impatient feeling she would have had toward a pug dog that insisted on barking inopportunely.

"I won't be quiet! I'm not a bit afraid of you—not a bit! Every body knows how you have treated me and is talking about it. I don't mean to endure it any longer."

Elinor passed on without reply; as she descended the staircase she saw people standing at the foot, but apparently no one had heard Miss Laidley's remark, though it had of course been intended for the public benefit—no one unless it might be the Banger, who was coming up the stairs and treated herself to a malignant sneer which Elinor unfortunately did not observe, and Indiana was more angry still to think that her facial contortion had been wasted.

Elinor wanted to get home, and tried to make her way through the crowd in search of her father, stopped each instant of course, and compelled to take somebody's arm in the crush. In the entrance to the ball-room she found him, but before she could speak he bent over her and whispered—"I am obliged to go away; I have had a telegram of importance."

She looked at him and saw that he was very pale, but the light touch of his hand on her glove warned her that was not the place to make any sign. "Let me go too," she said.

"I can not stop; I'll send the carriage back. You must not go; it is early yet."

He was perfectly composed, but there was something in his eyes Elinor had never seen there before, the meaning of which she could not read; it struck her like a strange fear and horror which was reflected in her own heart. But she was leaning on the arm of somebody, and somebody was leading her on, and the crowd pushed along more thickly, and the music sounded again, and it was no time to think or feel.

For Mr. Grey to get out of the house and into his carriage was like the work of a dream, but it was done in a quiet manner that arose from habit. He had been fearfully anxious all day; in hourly expectation of a telegram from New York, and had left orders with his faithful Henry that if any came it was to reach him even at the ball. There had come a message and Henry had managed matters with his customary tact. He had gone to the house, and being on confidential terms with the Idol's chief retainers, had told one of them that he must see his master, and the man, not surprised that the statesman should be troubled with business at any hour or in any place, had put Henry in the empty supper-room and succeeded in informing the minister that he was wanted. Mr. Grey left off flattering the jewelled embassadress and got into the supper-room and read his letter, written in a cipher that was only too plain. There had been another grand crash: the bursting up of a projected telegraphic line somewhere in the West. Some lucky sinner had decamped with money enough to gild his sin and wretchedness in a foreign land, and Pluto had to give the news, because the sale of Mr. Grey's shares had been a thing under negotiation; but there was nothing to sell now.

Mr. Grey sat in his private room writing letters to be sent by the earliest train, looking back over the events of the past year, and feeling the back of his head swell and throb as if the pain that had been abiding there for weeks found the quarters too confined and had gone to work at the outer walls with a hammer and chisel, to make a breach in them preparatory to enlarging the domicile. He was glad to go to bed at length and get away from thought. Pluto still had great hope: this must be the last blow; if so-and-so happened, something wonderful would be the result, and if it did not, the storm could be weathered by keeping sails close. In short, Mr. Grey's head, never of the clearest where the details of business were concerned, though he had a great faculty for seeing in theory how visionary successes might be arrived at, was completely muddled, and he could only leave things where they were and cling to the belief that no irremediable evil would arrive.—We never any of us believe there can.

CHAPTER XLI.
THE MIDNIGHT EXODUS.

As Elinor passed down stairs Miss Laidley hurried into the room where Leighton Rossitur still stood trying to realize that he had at last leaped the final gulf, and that its blackness swept between him and every hope or dream which was worth rescuing from the poor wreck he had made his youth. She rushed up to him and exclaimed—

"What were you saying to Elinor?"

He could have felled her to the floor, the sight of her was so odious to him at that moment. "Nothing," he said.

"You were; she was here ever so long! I will know! I'll not be treated in this way by you or her any longer."

To have told her what a miserable, transparent, abominable compound of idiocy and artifice she was, would have been a great relief, but he had been sufficiently sobered by Elinor Grey's last words to regain a slight possession of his senses. The fullness of defeat had come; at least he need not throw aside the promise of ease and wealth offered by Miss Laidley's romance. "I hear your favorite galop," said he; "come and dance."

"I shall not," she replied; "I'll not be treated like a child any longer! What were you saying to that woman?"

"I will tell you all about it to-morrow," he urged.

"I shall not wait! I'll never speak to you again on earth if you don't tell me this minute," exclaimed Miss Laidley.

He had a mind to tell her to go—to lose every thing; but he made a wonderful effort and said—"I told you I must have one conversation with her."

"You are always talking to her," retorted Miss Laidley, and it was doubtful whether jealousy or curiosity was the stronger emotion in her mind. "You take every opportunity in spite of the things you say to me—things I'll not believe."

"I never shall again," he answered; "you may be certain of that."

"Have you quarrelled with her? Did you tell her that you hated her?" demanded Miss Laidley eagerly.

"Yes, I did," he said between his clenched teeth.

"I am so glad, so glad!" she exclaimed.

He could have found a sweet enjoyment in choking the life slowly out of her as she spoke; but one is not permitted such modes of relief in this prosaic age. "You ought to be satisfied," he answered; "I did it for you."

"Is every thing over?"

"Every thing."

"I wonder if you ever cared for her?" questioned Miss Laidley, somewhat annoyed at his not acting the scene with more spirit.

"You know that from the moment I saw you first I have been your slave," he said, and the words were so difficult of utterance that he could scarcely restrain himself from rushing out of the room.

"You have given me very little reason to believe it," pouted she.

"Great heavens! Genevieve, what more would you have?" he exclaimed, trying to make a show of earnest. "I have been on the verge of madness—ready to cut my throat because I could see no way out of the toils—because I thought you were lost to me—and now you can say such things? Oh, these hearts of women —bah!"

That sounded more like the speeches to which she was accustomed; the sneer at the close had its effect. "Ah!" said she.

"Now you reproach and suspect me," he continued; "I might have been prepared for it! Fool that I was to trust any woman."

"No, no; you may trust me—you know what I feel!"

He might as well end it—as well secure his prize then; but oh, how Elinor Grey's face came up and looked at him across the gulf! He had not much more faith in a Hereafter than he had in things human and mundane, but at that instant there was a quick thought in his mind of something he had read years ago —was it in the Bible?—of some soul in torment looking up at the happy spirits in heaven; so he, out of his hell, looked across the impassable gulf at the image of the woman he had loved and lost. Only the lightning-like fancy of an instant that is so long put in words, then he was holding Miss Laidley's hands and saying—

"Tell me that you love me, Genevieve."

"Have I not told you already?" she asked.

"That you will marry me?"

Those last words were such as she had been eager to hear for weeks and weeks, but to play the coquette was absolutely necessary even when her feelings were more deeply interested than they had ever been in her life. "Ah! that is quite another thing," she said, drawing back.

Rossitur could bear nothing more; it had been horrible to try to make love to her at that moment; to be treated to such baby play was more than he could endure. Ten to one if she felt the power in her own hands she would draw back; she was no more to be trusted than a young kitten with some stray drops of tiger-blood in its veins; any way he had borne all he could for that time. He flung out his hands with a tragic gesture of repulsion and exclaimed in a hollow voice—"Genevieve, farewell!"

"Leighton, Leighton!" she cried; but he was out of the room, and when she reached the door had disappeared wholly.

With the fear that she had lost him came back her love and romance in full force, and she was dashing herself on the sofa in a paroxysm of despair when the Banger looked in. "All alone, my dear?" she asked. "Where's the Black Knight?"

"Gone!" moaned the Angel. "He has left me forever!"

"Nonsense!" returned Indiana. "Have you been quarrelling?"

"I said such cruel things to him," sighed the Angel, "and now he is gone—gone forever. *Hélas, mon rêve, mon bonheur!*"

"Well," exclaimed the Banger, "if you do let Elinor Grey get him after all that's been done you're a greater fool that I took you for! Why, that man is worth twenty of the ordinary sheep girls have about them." The Banger prided herself on her straightforwardness, and blunt speech was as much her forte as sentiment was the Angel's.

"He's gone—gone—*ah, ma jeunesse!*" moaned Miss Laidley.

"Not so far but he can be found," replied Indiana, whose consolations were not offered with sufficient poetry to be satisfactory to the Angel. "Do you know what he had been saying to Miss Grey?"

"They quarrelled, and he told her that he hated her," replied the Angel, composing herself in a new attitude of misery.

"So far, so good. But what did you act like a fool for just after it? You must have, you know; tell me what he said."

"He asked me to be his wife."

"Very well; you want to be, and you mean to be, don't you?" questioned the terrible Banger.

"I love him," sighed the Angel, behind her fan.

"And if you marry him, you stand as good a chance as any girl I know of being embassadress or ruling up at the White House," said Indiana. "I don't talk much poetry, but I talk sense, and call things by their names, and I know the world. I tell you that man will go very far—very far."

"He is so noble, so handsome," sighed Miss Laidley.

"What did you say to him?" demanded Indiana sternly, not to be turned from her purpose of being practical.

"I answered him evasively—with a jest. Oh, what made me—how could I? *Cruelle; cœur de marbu!*"

"Because you're a woman," said Indiana, "and women must upset their milk-pans just as the cream has risen. Well, what did he say then, if I must get it question by question as if I was pumping it out of you?"

"He only said—'Genevieve, farewell!'" quoted the Angel, imitating his tragic gesture and falling back on the sofa with another moan.

"Oh! merely a lovers' quarrel," said the Indiana with strong-minded contempt for such weaknesses; "I dare say he has gone off in a rage, but he'll come back soon enough."

"If Elinor does not come between us again! Oh, what shall I do? She is capable of murdering me; you don't know how violent she can be! When I passed her in the hall she called me dreadful names."

"Do?" cried Indiana, in a voice that sounded as if it came from a throat of brass, and with a look that would have answered for the queen of the Amazons. "Why, come to my house and marry Rossitur before she has time to make you more trouble. I wouldn't stay under the same roof with her another night if I were you."

"But couldn't Mr. Grey make me go back or keep my money?" demanded Miss Laidley.

"No; didn't you show me a copy of your father's will? The moment you are married your husband can claim your fortune—Grey is obliged to give it up. I tell you plainly, Genevieve, if you don't want to lose Rossitur—if you really love him—"

"As my life," broke in she; "better, far better!"

"Then you had better show it by taking some step in earnest, instead of quarrelling and doing high tragedy."

"I will do what you tell me," said Genevieve, who was always somewhat awed by the Banger's thews and sinews, and thought that where there was so much physical force the counsel offered must be proportionably valuable. "Advise me—I will obey."

"You won't," returned Indiana with a sneer; "you'll go back and be pushed and browbeaten by Elinor Grey, and let her marry Leighton Rossitur before your eyes, while you wring your hands and moan."

"I'd stab her to the heart first!" cried Miss Laidley.

"That's pretty—in a play," said Indiana.

"Oh, what shall I do? what shall I do?" moaned the Angel. "I am the most wretched, helpless creature in existence."

"If you will follow my advice, I'll give it," continued Indiana; "but I don't intend to waste my breath on a girl obstinately determined to let her peace be ruined by the haughtiest woman that ever tried to walk over every body's neck."

"I will follow it—I promise—I swear!" cried the Angel.

"Don't; I never believe a woman under oath."

"Ah, you can jest when my heart is breaking."

"Ta, ta; broken hearts have gone out. I can't cry with you, tears are not in my line; but I can help you. Do you come home with me—"

"But my clothes—all my things!" interrupted Miss Laidley.

"Bless me! money bought them, money would buy more," replied Indiana; "but there's no talk of losing them that I know of. You don't suppose people in the Greys' position are going to be put in the papers for keeping a woman's duds?"

"Well?" questioned the Angel submissively.

"For the matter of that, we'll drive round that way; get what you want for morning, and have Juanita pack the rest up. I'll wait in the carriage while you do it."

"But if they stop me—if they try to lock me up?"

"Then you scream till you rouse the street. I'll bring help enough, I promise you. I'll teach that old smooth-tongued Secretary and his touch-me-not daughter!" exclaimed the courageous Banger.

The matter began to present itself in the light of an adventure to the Angel and pleased her accordingly. "I will do as you tell me," she said; "you are my only friend."

"Very well; now get up, shake your dress out, come down stairs, and behave like a sensible girl," replied Indiana, who had no mind to lose her due share of the festivities, and was in high spirits at her success. "Give me a woman that can show a little courage and I'll go through fire and water for her."

"I have no heart to dance, to be gay," sighed the Angel.

"You don't dance with your heart," retorted Indiana.

"Ah, how hard and stern you are," shivered Miss Laidley; "you can bear every thing; you are always ready to act; you are granite—*les nerfs d'acier*."

"I represent common sense and you romance, that's all. Romance is very well, but it would be apt to go to the wall if there weren't a few people like me left in the world," said the Banger, speaking as if she were one of the last survivors of a race of Anakims or other rare creatures of a superior mould to ordinary human nature. "Hark! Good Lord! they're going in to supper and here we are wasting our time."

She seized Miss Laidley by the arm and rushed her down stairs, captured some luckless man and forced him to make way for them among the motley groups that were streaming into the supper-room, for the Banger required a good deal of solid food to keep her powers of practical judgment in working order. One of the Angel's victims saw her and was happy to take charge of her and she was led along in the wake of Indiana, who, clutching her prisoner, looked as warlike as if she were marching in her regal robes at the head of an army and panted to meet the foe. Genevieve glanced about for Rossitur, but he was not to be seen, therefore she thought she was like the heroine of a novel, standing flower-crowned with death in her heart, and was so intensely wretched that she enjoyed it thoroughly. By and by Elinor came up to her and the Angel shrank visibly from her touch and was minded to quote in an audible whisper something

about a basilisk—not that she knew what the animal might be—but had no opportunity.

"The carriage has come," Elinor said quietly, instead of muttering imprecations or displaying a dagger as the Angel would have preferred. "Are you ready to go, Genevieve?"

It was aggravating to be brought down to such common ground when she was giving free rein to her fancy. "No, I'm not," snapped she, forgetting to answer after the models afforded by numberless heroines with whose expressions she was familiar and often employed with good effect.

"Go!" repeated Indiana, overhearing, and speaking with a large bit of *paté* in her mouth; "of course the poor child doesn't wish to be dragged away yet; she is young enough to enjoy the thing."

"I will send the carriage back for you, Genevieve," continued Elinor, without noticing the Banger.

"I will see you safe home, Miss Laidley," interposed the Banger fiercely, nearly choking herself in her rage that she could not force Elinor to be conscious of her rudeness.

"Oh, I don't wish to make any body any trouble," said the Angel in her most martyr-like voice.

"It will be no trouble to me," cut in the Banger; "I may be unpolished, but I am not selfishness incarnate."

"Oh, no, no, thank you, Mrs. Tallman," returned the Angel, in a timid way. "Dear Elinor, if you wish to go, of course I am ready—I would not make trouble for the world."

"I will wait for you," said Elinor, seeing that Miss Laidley had a disposition to make a scene, and that the Banger asked nothing better than to help her.

She went directly away to avoid further discussion, and endured patiently another two hours, while the Angel waltzed and flirted with scores of men and indulged in dark thoughts and smothered sighs under laughter, and was in an agony of happiness that would end in a fit of hysterics before she could get back to the level of ordinary life. At last Elinor thought she had waited long enough, and meant to go unless Miss Laidley was desirous to stay and see the gas put out, but as she was about seeking her, the young lady came up and said rudely—"You needn't have waited to watch me; you'll gain nothing by it; I am going back with Indiana Tallman."

Elinor bowed courteously, asked somebody to see that her carriage was called, and made her way to the dressing-room, wondering how much longer it would be necessary for her to endure these daily increasing impertinences. She had not complained to her father because the annoyances were so petty that she had been ashamed to cry out under them, as she would have been ashamed under the prickings of a gnat, but of late the young creature had been worse than a whole swarm of the musical insects. She did think that when Miss Laidley's majority arrived, which it mercifully would in the course of a few months, she should be justified in announcing that the same roof could not cover her and that restless specimen of the angelic race any longer. She drove home and forgot Miss Laidley in the remembrance of the inexplicable trouble she had seen in her father's eyes. Henry was up and met his mistress, as wakeful as if all the poppies in Persia could not surprise him into slumber.

"Do you know whether my father has gone to bed?" Elinor asked.

Henry was certain that he had. He begged to inform Mademoiselle that Monsieur had been oblige to answer some dispatches; had requested a cup of tea, and desired that he might not be disturbed.

She had seated herself in one of the reception-rooms to hear these details, and as Henry finished the Banger's carriage drove up. The Hungarian flew to open the door for Miss Laidley before any impatient ring from a cross footman could disturb his master. The Angel, between her trouble about Rossitur, her fatigue, Indiana's sneers and persuasions, and the hysterical emotions which had become a positive disease with her, was ready for a scene of the most sensational kind.

"Mademoiselle is still down stairs, Mees Laidley," said Henry, who to the Angel's disgust always gave her that commonplace designation in contradistinction to the title which he bestowed upon his mistress.

"Where is she?" asked the Angel.

Henry waved her toward the reception-room and she dashed past him before he could get to the door, which with his usual exalted manner he would have flung wide open for her passage. "What are you waiting here for?" demanded she, sweeping up to Elinor. "Do you want to spy and watch me always?"

This was too much in keeping with Miss Laidley's manner and tone during the past fortnight to excite any surprise on the part of her listener. "I believe I shall say good-night, Miss Laidley; it is very late," said Elinor, rising.

The Angel stood still, not knowing exactly how to continue, since her opening attempt at a scene had failed signally. "I am absolutely afraid to sleep in the house with you!" she exclaimed, bursting into hysterical sobs. "I believe you mean to murder me this night, and have laid your plans."

Henry had remained in the hall waiting for the young ladies to go up stairs that he might put out the gas and make all things secure, and naturally stood open-mouthed at that remarkable speech. Elinor walked toward the door without making any reply.

"Help! help!" cried Miss Laidley. "She's going to lock me in here! I won't be locked in! Help! help!"

Scenes equally exciting Elinor had so often passed through that she was not in the least alarmed for Miss Laidley's sanity, as a stranger might have been by her words and gestures.

"Henry," she said calmly, "go to Juanita's room and send her down."

The Hungarian rushed noiselessly away, discussing in his mind whether the young heiress was a little *tocquée* or *grisée*—he thought in French, and I put the words in that language because the last was not a pretty term to apply to an angel; but that wicked old Henry had known human seraphs of high degree capable of such very queer freaks and indulgences that he sometimes held improper thoughts in regard to them and their actions.

"I won't be left here with you!" cried Miss Laidley. "You shan't kill me! What are you hiding your hand in your dress for? I believe you've a dagger there! Do you mean to stab me?"

"Don't scream, please," said Elinor; "my father is probably asleep, and you would not care to treat him to one of these scenes."

"I would! I will! I won't be murdered! Scenes, indeed! Am I to be stabbed without resistance? Help! help!" repeated Miss Laidley, making a rush forward as if she meant to tear through the halls and rouse every sleeper in the house.

"Positively, Genevieve, if you don't stop this instant I will lock you in here," said Elinor, losing patience; "you are too absurd."

"Wretch! Fiend! Vile murderess!" moaned Miss Laidley, giving full vent to her hysterics, and rapidly getting beyond power of self-control. Elinor was afraid of her getting out on the staircase and screaming till every soul under the roof would be wakened and rush down in terror that the dwelling was on fire at least. She wanted to keep her where she was till Juanita appeared, trusting that the old woman could soothe her as usual, and having compassion enough on the girl to desire that she should not make herself utterly ridiculous in the eyes of the servants. "Hush, I beg; Juanita will be here in a moment," said she.

"Let me out! Let me out!" screamed Miss Laidley, making a dash at her as she stood in the door-way and pushing her aside with such violence that she hurt her.

"Miss Laidley, this is insupportable," exclaimed Elinor, putting her hand out to prevent herself being jammed against the door-post.

Miss Laidley bounded aside and managed to tear her gauze raiment to a deplorable extent. She ran through the hall and flung open the outer doors, and Elinor, beginning to think she had gone mad at last, ran after her and tried to hold her back from rushing down the steps. "Mrs. Tallman! Mrs. Tallman!" called the Angel despairingly. Elinor became conscious that the carriage was still before the entrance, and that the Banger's head was thrust out of the window. She comprehended at once that the whole scene had been arranged between the pair, released Miss Laidley, and stepped back into the vestibule. "Mrs. Tallman!" cried the Angel again. "Help! help!"

The Banger, who had been eagerly waiting

for some catastrophe, was overjoyed at a sight like that. Out of the carriage she sprang, up the steps she flew, dashed into the vestibule and clasped Miss Laidley in her arms, exclaiming—
"You are safe—I am here! What does this mean? Miss Grey, I saw you push this unfortunate creature out-of-doors."

"Look at my dress," sobbed Miss Laidley; "she has almost torn it off me! She pushed me and struck me—I do believe she had a dagger in her hand! Take me away—if you have any mercy, take me away!"

"At once; come, poor child," returned Indiana. "Miss Grey, I leave explanations for tomorrow."

In spite of her anger the absurdity of the whole thing struck Elinor so forcibly that she laughed. "I hope Miss Laidley has them to offer," said she. "Excuse me if I close the doors."

"Not on me!" cried the Banger. "You can't frighten me! I'll call my servants. You can't shut me in your murdering house!"

"I should be sorry to do so, Madam," said Elinor. "Good-night, Miss Laidley; of course you must consult your own pleasure whether you go or stay." She walked back through the hall, and meeting Henry and Juanita on the stairs, bade him follow her and motioned the old woman to go on. The end was not what the Angel had expected; both she and the Banger felt a good deal sobered by finding themselves clasped in each other's arms in ball-dress and standing in a windy vestibule at that time of night with no enemy to confront.

"You must go with me, my love; you can't stay in this house," said the Banger in a high key.

"Oh, take me away, take me away!" sobbed the Angel.

"What's matter — what's matter?" cried Juanita, running to them. "Come in'e house, young Senora—catch'er death. Come to Juanita, poor dear—got'e nerves again?"

"It is not a case of nerves, my good creature," said Indiana, "but of fright and ill-treatment. Look at her dress, half torn off her."

"Oh, de Lord, de Lord!" groaned Juanita. "Come in, young Senora, come in. Oh, de Lord!"

Miss Laidley gave free vent to her sobs, and Juanita, not knowing what to make of the scene, or what she was expected to do, stood muttering and flinging her arms about.

"Go pick up your mistress's cloak," said the Banger; "that has been torn off her too. Come, my poor child; I couldn't answer to my conscience if I left you here alone; Heaven only knows where this would have ended if I had not chanced to wait, stopped by a foreboding of evil."

"Oh! oh!" sobbed Miss Laidley.

"De Lord, de Lord!" muttered Juanita, conscious there was a play being acted and certain that her mistress expected her to take a part, but from not having been instructed at a loss how to perform, so she danced about and uttered monkey cries.

"The cloak!" ordered the Banger, and Juanita ran and picked it up from the hall floor where the Angel had thrown it, and wrapped it about her mistress.

"My servants witnessed the outrage," said the Banger, in an elevated voice; "when witnesses are needed they will be ready. Come, love."

"She tried to murder me," gasped the Angel. Oh, my clothes—I can't leave my clothes," she whispered.

"I'll bring some in a bundle 'fore morning," hissed Juanita; "I'll get out'e window."

The idea struck Indiana as a telling one—she to rescue the sufferer and the faithful serving-woman to follow in the late watches of the night, escaping at the risk of her life from the house, with a change of apparel for the mistress whom she idolized. The coachman and footman seated on the box had not the slightest idea what was going on, only that their mistress and the young woman seemed in a "great twitter" about something when nobody was visible. "James!" called Indiana. James sprang from his perch and opened the carriage door; the Banger perceiving there was no hope of Miss Grey's re-appearance, and no design on that lady's part to notice them in any way, led the moaning Angel down the steps and they entered the carriage and were driven off, obliged to look to the telling of the story for success. Juanita flew up stairs to her mistress's rooms and bolted the doors upon herself; Elinor sent the stupefied Henry down to settle matters for the night, saying only—
"See that Juanita goes early in the morning to Mrs. Tallman's with some clothes for her mistress."

"Certainly, Mademoiselle," Henry answered.

Elinor's first thought was to waken her father and tell him what had happened, but it could do no good, and she would not disturb his rest. By morning Miss Laidley would probably have returned to her senses. She knew that the Banger would spread the most horrible reports abroad, but after all, Miss Laidley, in decency and out of regard for herself, must either return to the house or go back to Jamaica. Her father would arrange it—this time she could not spare him the annoyance—but indeed the whole thing was too miserable to think about. It had been an evening of such disgusting events; as the recollection of them came up, Elinor's cheeks burned to remember the words Leighton Rossiter had dared to utter. Of that scene she must also tell her father—at least so much as would convince him concerning the man's real character. The coarse threat he had employed she would not give a place in her mind; it was too contemptible as applied to the parent whom all her life she had regarded as much removed from the weaknesses of ordinary natures as if he had been a god. That he had anxieties which he concealed from her she was certain, though of what nature she could not divine. Perhaps only the troubles inseparably connected with his duties; and that made her reflect that unless Miss Laidley chose to come to her senses and show the falsity of the reports by returning to the house, there might be no end to the gossip, the newspaper hints and allusions which would be spread from Indiana Tallman's stories. Indefinitely she connected Leighton Rossiter with this matter too; she was confident that he had been holding a secret correspondence with Miss Laidley, and probably by his conduct had excited her to this last step. But the whole matter was a weariness, and of no importance beyond the fact that it might annoy her father; what her own share in the reports would be she could not pretend to care, other than as it made an added annoyance for him.

She went to bed at last and fell asleep. Having of late somewhat relaxed her rigid discipline in regard to hours, Coralie, the devoted, peeped in, and seeing her asleep did not disturb her. The consequence was that she did not wake till what she deemed a preposterous hour, and summoning the maid desired her to go at once and beg her father not to leave the house until she had spoken with him. The first thought in her mind had been Miss Laidley's performance, for the young woman had haunted her dreams and acted melodramas in costumes that varied with every move she made, while Indiana Tallman looked on approvingly from a lofty throne where she sat with a square gold tower on her forehead for a crown, wearing a harlequin's dress instead of the regal robes which might have been expected to accompany the chair of state and diadem. Leighton Rossiter had been there too—it was Rossiter, but it was Mephistopheles also—and very handsome he looked, only Elinor saw that he had a forked tongue as he laughed at Miss Laidley's antics. The Idol was there; the old deaf lady who somebody had told her was dead was present, lying in her coffin, and by mistake the coffin was taken for a supper-table, and the corpse sat up, a grinning skeleton, and pointed at her father who suddenly appeared on the scene. He was so white and changed that at first she hardly knew him, and then she was thrown into an agony of terror by his clinging to her and imploring her to save him from a gulf that opened where the ball-room had been, looking down which, she saw only a horrible blackness, from whence came up the sound of the waltzes the orchestra had played. It was all as mixed and absurd as dreams usually are after excitement, but somehow it made Elinor shiver to recall it, and, plainer than any sight, she beheld her father's white face as his head sank on her shoulder in that helplessness which, in her dream, she had heard a voice from the black gulf call a living death.

In answer to her request, Coralie said that Mr. Grey had already departed. He had risen earlier than was his habit and gone out directly after drinking his coffee, and had desired Coralie to say to her mistress that he was so much hurried by business he could not wait to see her. If Mademoiselle pleased, Hungarian Henry wished to speak with her as soon as she could conveniently so far honor him.

Elinor was annoyed at this fresh delay, and in doubt what course to pursue in regard to Miss Laidley. "Bring me my chocolate and tell Henry to come up," she said, when the toilet process was over and she had at length established herself before a sunny window in her dressing-room.

Henry appeared, taking advantage of the opportunity to bring the chocolate himself, for he and Coralie were always waging an amicable warfare as to which should have the felicity of ministering to their mistress's wants.

"Coralie said you wanted to speak to me, Henry," said Elinor, as he set the tray on the table before her.

"Since Mademoiselle is so good. If she pleases, the waiting-woman of Mees Laidley left the house by a back window, and it was open till the cook went down stairs."

"Do the servants know, Henry?"

"No, Mademoiselle; I said nothing about the mulatto, though the moment they told me I knew it was her work and not a thief's. If Mademoiselle pleases, she came back quite early, and as good luck would have it, I saw her first."

"Did she say why she went out?"

"To carry clothes to the Mees, she said. At present she have made up the boxes of the Mees, and is clamoring to have them taken down stairs and put on a coach that has come."

"Very well, if Miss Laidley has ordered her to do so."

"It was why I wished to speak to Mademoiselle."

"Did you tell my father that Miss Laidley had gone home with Mrs. Tallman?"

"Pardon; I was not able. Monsieur sent me out with letters that no other might deliver; Monsieur had borne himself away before I was of return."

It was a very tiresome piece of business altogether, and really there seemed nothing to be done at present. Her father would be back in the course of the morning, and he alone could go and learn what might be the meaning of this remarkable conduct on Miss Laidley's part. "You will say to the servants, Henry, that Miss Laidley has gone on a visit to Mrs. Tallman," was all she said.

"I have made so already, if Mademoiselle pleases."

"Thank you; that is all, I believe."

He bowed and retired, a statue of propriety to the last, but as soon as he had seen Juanita and the boxes safely out of the house, he and Coralie fell into a wonderment and discussion that they would not have betrayed to the inferior domestics for the bribe of twin annuities. Coralie had kept watch over Juanita from the moment of her return, to see that she did not talk to the other servants, though what was the matter neither she nor Henry had the least idea. To speak of the matter to Miss Grey was something neither would have dreamed of doing, so they went about devoured by a very natural curiosity, and only able to decide that Miss

Laidley must have had a worse fit of lunacy than usual.

"She must have been ill to the utmost when she could rend her robe," said Coralie, when Henry described the state it had been in. "Many of the hysterics I have regarded her do, but the robe was well defended at the worst."

Henry did not hesitate to confide his suspicions that she had indulged too freely at supper, but Coralie being young yet, and not having such experience as the Hungarian, was somewhat shocked thereat. However, they united in the opinion that she was a small deviless of the most atrocious description, and that the patience with which Mademoiselle had supported her follies, retaining them even from Monsieur himself, was a proof of goodness such as no human creature except their ravishing Mademoiselle could have exhibited.

CHAPTER XLII.

MARRIED LIKE A HEROINE.

THE night had not been the bearer of fairy dreams to Mr. Grey, nor had his bed been of roses, though, metaphorically, he had during his whole life been much accustomed to strewing his couch therewith. The time was come when he must take a stand and deliberately choose whether his place should be by the President's side or chief among the ranks of his enemies. His plans had been kept sufficiently secret for him still to stand upon apparently open terms with the President, but it was impossible that this state of affairs should continue longer. The malcontents believed themselves sure of him, the time had come when they desired him to act, and the pledges he held were such that to take no positive step toward their ranks would bring the fury of the whole set upon him. In joining them the promise of success was as certain as any human event could be, but still the remembrance of that daughter who stood in the place of a conscience kept between him and the ability to be at rest. Many times he had gone over the sophistical view of the case which had presented itself to him during that conversation with Rossitur; he had prepared a series of fine-sounding periods with which to convince Elinor that his course was that of a true patriot; had even thought that to his old friend the betrayal might be softened by offering his conviction that he must step forward and accept the hands of the plotters in order to save the country from the full effects of their evil designs. But when he had gone the round, and elaborated every point, it was no easier to do than before. It was not long since he and Elinor had been dining alone with the President, and during some discussion, in answer to those sweetened persuasions of Mr. Grey as to the expediency of temporizing and awaiting the course of events, the old man had persisted in his opin-

ions, and Mr. Grey had seen by Elinor's kindling face how she honored his courage and shared his belief. He recollected how at some speech of hers his old friend's hand had been laid caressingly on her head as it so often had in her childhood, and he exclaimed—"Ah, Mr. Grey, whatever befalls you, here is your comforter; and, unlike most women, she knows on what her sympathies are based." Perhaps that was the last time they three would ever hold such friendly talk, and Mr. Grey wondered if the tender words the old man had spoken, and the confidence he had expressed, would be one of the prominent recollections in Elinor's mind should he be forced to tell her that he had left his friend to bear the tempest alone. Any day, almost any hour, might force him to a decision; if certain proposed measures came up before the House, the next Cabinet council might show the President that even in that circle he stood surrounded by opposition, and Mr. Grey might go forth, certain one day to stand in that very room holding the reins in his own grasp, a perjured man to his conscience.

Down from those doubts and waverings he had come in the stillness of the night to sharper stings, more present troubles, growing out of those business dealings with Pluto, and his miserable secret with himself. But the dismal news the Bull had sent was softened by an exposition of his hopes and arrangements, for the man still believed in his own powers and the possibility of tiding over the peril. He wanted now the earliest information possible of the report concerning a certain bill that the Senate had placed in the hands of a committee; to be certain whether it would be rejected or passed when it was brought up, as it would be very soon. What he asked was a little start of Wall Street in general, that he might know whether the great heaps of stock were to be called in or dexterously disposed of, or in some way transformed before the result should be common property. The means thus placed in his hands would help him very far along; Mr. Grey's anxiety should be set at rest.

Driving toward the Department, Mr. Grey's carriage was recognized and stopped by some messenger who had a note for him which he had been charged to deliver with all speed; as the carriage was driving on again Mr. Grey caught sight of Leighton Rossitur descending the steps of his hotel. "The very man I wanted to see," said he, as Rossitur approached in answer to his gesture; "I was afraid you would not be on hand. I have forty different things to do at once."

Rossitur had seen him and come up with something of a tumult in his heart, but Mr. Grey's manner and words proved that he was still in ignorance of the scene of last night. Did Elinor mean to keep his threat a secret? Had she thought it too contemptible to repeat? Those were his first thoughts; then he steadied himself and tried to appear as usual, which was not easy, as it would not have been for any man who had only found time to wash his face after a night's revelry. "I suppose I can help you with a few of the forty; but you are very early," he said, "or I am very late."

"I am early," Mr. Grey answered, opening the carriage door. "But you don't look well this morning; did you keep up the ball too long?" he continued, as they drove off.

"Dancing till near day-light, and having some work to do after, is not likely to make a man wear the look he would wish preserved in his portrait," said Rossitur, laughing.

"Not exactly," replied Mr. Grey absently, looking at the note he held.

"How are the ladies this morning?" Rossitur asked, desirous to discover whether Elinor had withheld any revelation or it had been postponed from lack of opportunity.

"Still in bed and asleep, I fancy," replied Mr. Grey; "at least neither of them were visible when I left the house."

"And no wonder," Rossitur said, glancing at his watch. "I think you can not have had much sleep yourself."

"I am greatly perplexed, Rossitur," said Mr. Grey. "Here's a note from Falcon—he got here last night. Those men have a meeting this morning and they insist on my coming."

"The conspirators calling for Cataline," returned Rossitur with a sneer; he could not keep the words back. Mr. Grey never gave way to temper, but at that malapropos remark he put the note in his pocket and took out his snuff-box. "That is," added Rossitur, so quickly that it seemed the continuation of his first sentence, "according to the view you will take of the case. Now, you know, I think the President a miserable old fogy, without brains enough to discover that what he calls patriotism is tyranny and hard-headedness, and I only wonder that you have hesitated so long about playing the part of Brutus."

Mr. Grey took a pinch of snuff and endeavored to forget the former unfortunate comparison, which was very unlike Rossitur. "I have avoided meeting them in full conclave," he said.

"Yes; and they begin to complain loudly. I assure you I had great difficulty in keeping the red-hot ones quiet yesterday."

"I owe you much for all your trouble and patience in this business," said Mr. Grey; "I could not have kept matters undecided so long without you; but you won't find me forgetful, Rossitur."

"There is no need to assure me of that, Sir," Rossitur answered, and thought — "I'd like to see you try it, even if dame Elinor tells her tale." Then in the same breath he added aloud, "I do assure you, Mr. Grey, it will be simply impossible to hold off any longer."

"I know, I know," he answered hastily. Then the knowledge that of all the world this was the one man to whom he could speak freely, made him add, "But this is a weighty matter, Rossitur."

"It is as clear as a map, Sir! They are bound to support you, and there isn't another man in the country so certain to run in on their platform."

"I was not referring to that," said Mr. Grey; "the doubt of success has not kept me undecided; I want to be certain that I am right."

Now Rossitur did not believe that any human being would have such scruples at a time like the present, nor had the minister stated the feeling in his mind fairly; what he wanted was to hear Rossitur's specious arguments repeated, that they might come to him like an echo of public opinion, wherewith he could strengthen his courage to face his friend and his conscience —that is, Elinor—with the truth.

"If the President persists in that Spanish business, you can't stand by him," Rossitur said.

"And he will," replied Mr. Grey.

"Then that settles the whole and makes your course perfectly plain. Your decision will be forced upon you, and after that he can't be in any way a question in your mind. The voice of the people, Sir, must go with you, and you will only be praised, as you ought, for having tried so faithfully to cure his blindness and obstinacy."

The carriage stopped at the Department as Rossitur finished his little speech and he followed Mr. Grey into the private rooms, smiling at the false ring of it, and the Secretary's willingness to accept it for the silver voice of Truth's trumpet. "Are you going to Falcon?" he asked.

Mr. Grey was breaking the seal of a note that had been handed to him as he passed through the offices, and began to read it without having heard the question. The letter was from the President, asking for a private interview without delay; not an official message from the Chief Magistrate to his minister, but a few honest lines from the man to his trusted comrade. The rumors of Mr. Grey's defection had reached his ear and he asked him to answer; he wanted before the Cabinet meeting took place on the morrow to know upon what he had to depend. He would not believe that the counsellor whom he had summoned to his side, that he might have not only the support of a political coadjutor but the advice of a friend, was about to desert him, seduced by the bribe of the chair of state that had proved so thorny a seat to himself; but he desired him to come that they might converse freely together and see exactly where they stood.

Mr. Grey read his letters and said—"Falcon must wait; they must put off that consultation till to-morrow."

"Really, Mr. Grey—excuse me, but I do not see how you can ask further time—every moment is precious now."

"I can't meet them this morning," he replied, in a voice that showed more irritation than he often displayed. "The French dispatches are in—I have to go to the President."

"Do you wish me to see Falcon?"

"No, I will write. Stay a moment."

He stood thinking; somebody tapped at the door. It was a message for Rossitur—two letters. One he put in his pocket after glancing at the superscription; as he opened the other he said—"This is from Hackett;" and glancing down the page, added, "he wants to know about the bill."

"Ah! that is what I wanted you to do for me," returned Mr. Grey. "He is greatly put about—the committee will certainly bring in their report before night. If you will find out what it is to be and which way the Senate will go—Simmons will tell you; get to him if he is in the committee-room, find out to a certainty, and telegraph."

He had forgotten the minister in those other anxieties, and Rossitur, curious to see how much he could be moved, said—"My opinion is, that if he can't stand up to this he'll go over the bay."

Mr. Grey's face, though firm and cold as ever, looked as though something had suddenly flung a pale shadow across it. "You've no news that I have not heard?" he asked, yet with a kind of denial of the interrogatory in his tone.

"No; I was only speaking my thoughts."

"But you brought every confirmation of success yourself from him," said Mr. Grey, looking up with sudden sternness, as if wondering what this unusual manner might mean. "A downright failure to him would be next to impossible; you might almost as well expect Wall Street to sink bodily."

"That is true," Rossitur answered; "I spoke carelessly. Well, Sir, I will attend to all that business; there is nothing but to send him the figures one way or the other. I'll get at Simmons."

"That is all; there is no doubt the bill will pass—he seems provided for either way; what he wants is correct information in advance. I confess I don't quite see how all his plans hinge."

"I imagine that no created being but a New York broker could," replied Rossitur.

"I dare say not. Any way, I am thankful he is righting; I was exceedingly anxious for a while."

"And a few extra hundred thousands will not come amiss toward election time," said Rossitur, laughing.

Mr. Grey glanced at his watch; it was almost the hour the President had appointed; he must go. He was strangely beset by a feeling of haste, a sensation such as we have often in dreams; trying to think how he was to bear himself in the interview; if the best thing to do was so far to admit that he was wavering as to ask till the Cabinet council for time to deliberate; he was worried beyond measure by the Plutonian dispatches, and his desire to impress upon Rossitur the necessity for expedition and exactness, without betraying his great anxiety.

"If you will write Falcon I shall be obliged," said he. "Write in your own name as usual; say that to-morrow you will be prepared to give a definite answer. That ought to be satisfactory."

"Yes; but it will have to be given then."

"Very well, very well. And, Rossitur, you will see Simmons at once; there is no telling but the bill may come up to-morrow."

"I will do it; you may depend upon me."

"Yes, I know; an error now might be fatal to him."

"It might—to him," returned Rossitur, curling his mustache. "There shall not be any. Is that all?"

"Yes, I believe so. Upon my word, Rossitur, sometimes I wish that I had kept the embassy and stayed away from all this rush and worry."

"You are not thinking of Wall Street now, I suppose," replied Rossitur; "you mean political worries."

"Of course," said Mr. Grey, giving him that half-wondering look again.

"Still," pursued Rossitur, "after the first open step, it will not be unpleasant looking forward to the next inauguration day."

"And yet that will be only the beginning of the real trouble," said the minister; "those men are a set of harpies."

"Yes," replied Rossitur lightly, "but one can't quite go in for the Idol's dream of bliss—being a shepherd with a crook."

They both laughed a little; Mr. Grey was unlocking drawers and looking into them in search of some papers he wanted. "Ah, here," he said, "just enclose these to Hackett; they ought to have been sent several days since."

There were a few more hurried questions and answers; Mr. Grey's time was up and he took his departure. Rossitur sat down at a desk, wrote a note to Falcon and dispatched it by one of the messengers. It was necessary then to go in search of Simmons. Oh, the papers for Pluto! He took them out of the drawer which Mr. Grey had left open; they were not of a nature, of course, to tell him any thing that he was not to know; there was nothing to do but enclose them in an envelope. He was not thinking much of what he was doing; his hand trembled and his head was dizzy, though he had made his breakfast off two cocktails to steady himself. Business of any kind was a burden which caused him to curse it, instead of laying the blame of its heaviness on his own folly.

He was thinking of Elinor Grey and the overpowering scorn which had flashed upon him out of her eyes; he was madder under that reflection than from the effect of his night's revel. He thought that when she did make her revelations there was an end to personal friendship between himself and Mr. Grey. If the Secretary accepted the Falcon proposition, neither he nor the party could throw him, Rossitur, over; if he did not, his anger was a matter of no moment—he would go out of power with the present Administration. It was all disgusting; political advancement a miserable humbug. He would take a foreign appointment—if Mr. Grey became President he could not refuse him that, whatever his feelings might be; he would ac-

P

cept it and get out of the turmoil of the next four years, which would be better avoided by a man who had a whole political life before him. He would marry Genevieve Laidley, and her money would gild the foreign life in which he could deaden the sense of disappointment and defeat. Her name reminded him that a note from her lay in his pocket. How he sickened at the recollection of her while thinking of Elinor Grey, and that which he had lost. The varying emotions concentrated in a fierce rage against the woman who had overwhelmed him with her contempt. He hated her with the hate of a fiend; at that instant he would have sold his soul for revenge upon her. He remembered how during those weeks of waiting he had solaced himself by the thought that if the worst came, and he was obliged to accept his dismissal as final, in some way he would have vengeance; it was to have been made ready for his hand to deal if he desired. The crowning abasement had smitten his plans and he was powerless to touch the woman who had humbled him. Why, what a pitiful dreamer he was!—what a wretched driveller!—only fit to rave and tear at his own heart, instead of having the means of reprisal in his clutch. But he had no time to spare for reflection; he must curse himself and admit that he was powerless. No turn of events now could give him the least hold upon her; she had gone completely out of his world—no, worse than that, she had convicted him of baseness and cast him so far below her height in her scorn that he could not reach up to her level again. Curses, treble curses on her, himself and fate! Ah well! he must leave it there and send off those letters to Hackett and hunt up Simmons.

He went back to the papers. A memorandum upon one of them caught his eye; he started at it—muttered something—suddenly flung the document on the table and started to his feet as a man might who had been groping about in the dark and had caught a glimmer of light in the distance. He opened other drawers and examined the papers they contained; he searched in a private desk of his own for certain memoranda that he had made in regard to diverse matters which had come to his knowledge in helping Mr. Grey in that business; each thing the merest trifle by itself, but linked with things discovered at other times, equally trifling in themselves, the whole made a copy that was plain to him. Scraps of information in regard to the investments of Miss Laidley's fortune; notes concerning a score of apposite details. He was unfolding them—peering into them—recalling Mr. Grey's excitement—words Pluto had let fall, puzzling at the time—suddenly coming upon that which made the whole, conversation and papers, clear to him, though they would have been heathen hieroglyphics to another. He stood there breathing hard—not seeing the place or aught about him—not summoning the image of the man whose steps he had tracked at last—in fancy standing before Elinor Grey, confronting her with his tale, changing that

look of scorn into humiliation and fear. He understood every thing—that a downfall to Pluto was ruin to Mr. Grey; that it was Genevieve Laidley's money he had used in the recent strait. Fool that he had been, with his previous information, not to have comprehended at once; with his knowledge of what the stocks belonging to her were, with those fatal letters several times written upon his notes, to have needed this last clue—why, the wit upon which he prided himself had grown dull indeed. No matter; before now the revelation could have done no good—he must have waited; nay, it had come at the most fitting moment, as if Destiny had desired to put revenge in his hands. He, scorned, defeated, made to know that he was stripped of the last shred of his false colors, his baseness fully comprehended—and this in his hands—the vengeance he had sworn should be his if the culmination of events showed him that his love was slighted—nay, a sharper sting than he could have hoped for! And this whirl in his brain—these fierce thoughts tugging like hot hands at his heart—O Elinor Grey, Elinor Grey!

He sat down and took out of his pocket the letter Miss Laidley had written. It was full of contrition for her cruel words, begging him to forgive and come to her; telling him that Elinor had so ill-treated her in Mrs. Tallman's presence that this good friend had taken her out of the house in the middle of the night. Now she was frightened nearly to death and implored him to come; she would do whatever he told her; there should be no hesitation, no delay; she loved him, heart and soul; only he must come at once—come before her guardian could get there. He crumpled the letter in his hand and laughed aloud. More revenge: a bitter, biting wind of gossip to fan the flame of ruin. Wait, let him look clearly. He had wanted to see Elinor Grey in the dust at his feet: the thunderbolt that should strike her was in his own grasp. He walked up and down the room —came back—took up the papers Mr. Grey had left, and glanced carefully down his own notes and ciphers. Gradually, as if some unseen hand had mapped it out upon the pages before his eyes, the course became plain. If Pluto passed this danger Mr. Grey was safe; those stocks had been used as a temporary help, they would be replaced on the first occasion offering. If Pluto failed suddenly, with a terrible crash, which Rossitur knew he had been so near doing, Mr. Grey was powerless to hide the defalcation only until his ward reached her majority. If she married, he could not conceal it for a day. By the terms of her father's will her husband could demand on the instant the rendering up of the guardian's trust.

Wait! Was it not all arranged—had he any thing to do but follow the pointing of Fate's finger? Miss Laidley was more likely to marry him in secret, at an hour's notice, than if she were given time to get weary of her novel by an engagement. She would snatch at any chance so romantic as an elopement; the wilder the reason given for its necessity the more eager and excited she would be. If Pluto failed the money was lost—half her fortune; but there were four hundred thousand dollars left—that amount left and the power to call Mr. Grey instantly to account. Rossitur knew well what Miss Laidley's fortune was; he knew the exact terms of the will—Indiana Tallman had once shown him a copy of it. Why, it was ruin inevitable and of the most horrible kind; a story to be a theme for tongues and books during years to come—a man within a step of the Presidency proved an untrustworthy guardian to an innocent girl! And all to come home to Elinor Grey—to smite her pride in one fell swoop —the daughter of a man so disgraced that he could never hold up his head again. If old Hackett failed! Every thing turned upon that. If one error occurred now, if there were one false step, Hackett must fail; he was so cramped and encumbered that in spite of his wide-spread resources he must go overboard if a fresh blow struck him too suddenly for him to be prepared. If he failed, and at one swoop the news of the broker's downfall and a letter from his ward's husband, demanding the instant delivery of the charge in his hands, came upon Mr. Grey, where was Elinor Grey then? With time given she might help him. Well, that would be ruin to her. But there should be no time; the ruin should come like lightning, and Elinor Grey know that he had kept his oath, that he had shown her how he could avenge.

The moments were passing. The shock that should let the tempest burst, he saw what it must be; he could not think of that, only of his revenge. He scribbled a passionate note to Genevieve Laidley; he told her that if she did not desire to be parted from him forever she must be prepared to act at once according to his decision. He could not explain; they were beset by dangers and wily foes; within two hours he would be by her side. He sent the note, seized his hat, and before his brain had done reeling he found himself in the Senate room. Every thing was dolefully quiet there, and matters proceeding with their usual dull precision. Some old venerable was speaking upon some subject, his spectacles on nose, and a flag of foolscap with piratical-looking black lines on it in his hand. Only a decent number of Conscript Fathers were present. One Senator was nodding behind a newspaper, perhaps he had been among the illustrious shades at the Idol's ball; another was absorbed in rapt contemplation of his own boot-heels; two or three were gathered in a knot about one desk and were evidently listening to and telling funny stories in turn; several sat upright and resignedly despairing in their places; others looked miserable in other attitudes, but miserable enough all such as made a pretense of listening looked, while the merciless old soul that had the floor droned on with his—"And thirdly, Mr. Speaker, and lastly, Mr. Speaker." But nobody was deceived by that lastly, which was the three hundred and fourteenthly at least; not a Senator present goose enough to have any faith therein, while the foolscap fluttered in fresh folds. But he did stop unexpectedly—as if he had not been sufficiently wound up. The dozing Senator shook himself; the admirer of his own boot-heels put them out of sight for future contemplation; the story-telling men stopped in the exercise of their talents; two or three Romans who had been out imbibing morning potations appeared; two or three others straggled in from somewhere else, looking as seedy as if the somewhere had been a place they ought not to have been at, and the Speaker rapped lustily for order. More noise; more debate; a trio of men eager to catch that functionary's eye that they might shout "Mr. Speaker," and he avoiding such catastrophe with the dexterity of long practice; cries of "Question, question;" really some hope of an end to something.

There Rossitur stood till the room and its occupants reeled before his eyes, and the rows of faithful guardians of the public weal seemed to be trying to dance jigs on the ceiling, and the hum of voices was like a loud wind in his ear. What was he there for? why was he waiting? He felt dizzy, he wanted air; why wasn't he off? He captured a wandering Roman: where was Simmons—in the committee-room? Yes, he was there safe enough, and thither Rossitur went, wondering why he could not make haste, why he was held as by a nightmare. Mr. Grey's potent name brought out the desired man. He could give a certainty as answer: the bill was sure to come up at once and to pass, there was no shadow of doubt; there were names, any thing to oblige Mr. Grey, and Simmons not asking or caring for reasons. What more was Rossitur waiting for? Something tugging at him on every side till it seemed to him that he must be staggering like a drunken man. He ought to be in the telegraph office. It was only a matter of sending a couple of figures—it was like making 14 instead of 24—that was all he had to do; those operators made such blunders every day. Simmons going off; something stronger pulling and dragging at Rossitur; Elinor Grey's eyes full of scorn gazing at him and through him as they had gazed on the preceding night, blotting out every thing but the hate and his oath. He was out of the anteroom, he was in the air; it was all like a nightmare still. The next thing he realized he was making his figures; perhaps he should wake before he finished writing the address of Hackett's purblind old clerk, superannuated long ago, whose name even was forgotten in the office, but who could faithfully discharge the part assigned to him. The heading written—the figures; Rossitur was watching the preparations for their being flashed over the wires. He had swallowed a glass of brandy, the nightmare oppression was gone, it seemed to him that his head was perfectly clear; he was like a man under the control of hasheesh rather than the influence of drink. So much of his work done, and he had simply telegraphed the truth—"Doubtful." How long to be so was another matter. After all, he had done nothing. Were he brought face to face with Mr. Grey and Pluto, at the most he had only blundered in a figure ; not he either. There was nothing to think about ; a wrong—a crime was different from that. He might not have been able to forge a name ; there would have been a deliberation about that from which even in his frenzy he would have recoiled. This was an error, no more than that. He could not realize any reality in the matter, with hundreds of miles between him and its consummation. When the Caliph in the Eastern story cut the rope he was safe in his luxurious chamber, beyond the power of feeling what he did. Coil by coil it swept away underground ; miles, leagues. He could not hear the great stone drop ; the horrible death caused by the fall could not be his causing.

Rossitur had more brandy, then he drove to the Banger's house and was received by that strong-minded female, who informed him that Miss Laidley had cried herself to sleep an hour before.

"Did she get my note?" he asked.

"Yes ; it was a little comfort to her, and glad enough I was when she went to sleep. I never had any nerves myself, and I don't know what to do with the young females of this generation. Nerves, indeed ! What you want in this world is blood and bone !"

"She wrote me so confusedly," Rossitur said, "that I could make nothing of it, beyond the fact of your having brought her away from her guardian's house in a strange way—"

"In the dead of the night," broke in the Banger ; "with her dress half torn off her by that amiable Miss Grey ; and if the story isn't spread far and wide, my name is not Indiana Tallman."

Now furious as Rossitur was with Elinor Grey, he could not be idiot enough to believe the narrative with which Indiana followed up her exclamations, but he chose to think that he did for the moment and lashed himself into a new rage ; that was easy enough to do. "The hell cat !" he exclaimed.

"Exactly what she is," replied the Banger approvingly, "That's the most sensible word I've heard you speak in a month, and if it would be any relief to swear, don't let my presence stop you. There's nothing abominable but I could hear with pleasure about that creature—with her airs and her queening it."

Rossitur laughed bitterly. "I think there's a little blow in store for her," said he.

"What is it? What do you mean?" demanded the Banger.

Rossitur collected his senses ; it would not answer to be premature in his exultation. Surely he had not drunk enough to be an ass ; if any thing, he needed more to steady himself. "This," of course ; what you're saying."

"Oh ! Now look here, Rossitur," said Indiana. "I'm a woman of sense and decision ; what I think I say, and when I have to act, I act. I hate shilly-shallying."

"So do I," said Rossitur.

"Humph !" retorted she. "Well, never mind ; only I must say I think you've done a good deal of it during these last weeks."

"It has been forced upon me, Mrs. Tallman."

"Perhaps it was. No matter ; there's one thing certain now : if this girl goes back to Mr. Grey's house you'll never get her—witch Elinor will see to that—and I shouldn't think you were the man to throw away near a million when it's between your fingers."

"I am not likely to be thinking about the money—"

"There," interrupted the Banger, "that'll do ; keep that for Genevieve. I represent Common-sense ; I've no taste for heroics whatever. I should call you a fool if you didn't think about it."

This style of dialogue was very disagreeable to Rossitur at that moment. He could easily work himself into a theatrical enthusiasm and make mad love to the Angel, but he did not wish to be brought back to the commonplace. "Let me see Genevieve," he said ; "please tell her I am here."

"Of course," returned the Banger ; "I'm not an ogress. I brought her for you—I like you ! I dare say ten years ago I might have loved you, as so many of these women have. Bah ! I'm not afraid to call things by their names —I'm Common-sense."

Rossitur thought of something she was more like, but he could not mention it ; besides she looked very far off, the room seemed to grow larger ; through the rattle of her voice he heard the click of the telegraph wires, he saw Elinor's face changing from pride to fear ; heard, saw, and felt as he had once done when the revelations contained in a wonderful book made him essay the power of the strange Eastern drug.

"Good gracious !" exclaimed the Banger. "You are as pale as a ghost, and your hand shakes like a leaf."

"I am a good deal excited by this news."

"You must drink a glass of wine," said the Banger, who prided herself on always having her wits about her. "When I say wine, I mean brandy ; wine's cat-lap, where real benefit is to be done. Come into the dining-room ; I dare say luncheon is up." She took him into the dining-room, poured him out brandy in a way that proved she understood the need of a good deal of a good thing being necessary, and while he drank it and forced himself to eat a crust of bread, she went on : "I have been expecting old Grey here all the morning. I wish he'd come ! I'd like nothing better than to tell him what I think of him and his daughter. I'd shake his blandness and his smoothness and his hypocrisy—I've no patience with it !"

"He doesn't know Miss Laidley has left his house ; I saw him early this morning."

"Very well ; he'll find it out soon ! Let him come to me—let Madam Elinor come if she likes! I think I am Indiana Tallman—I believe I am acquainted with myself," said the Banger, with a fine show of scorn and irony.

Yes, he would find it out soon; that reminded Rossitur there was no time to be lost. He wanted to be married before the news from Wall Street could reach Mr. Grey; that and the tidings that he was required to deliver up his trust must come together.

"Will you tell Genevieve I am here, Mrs. Tallman? Indeed I can not wait; there is a great deal to be done. Let me see her, then I'll explain every thing to you."

"Act first, explain after," said the Banger, who thought that sounded as pithy as one of Solomon's proverbs. She rushed away—that is the only expression which gives an idea of her style of locomotion—to rouse and prepare the angelic martyr, and very soon the fragile creature was arrayed and established in the Banger's dressing-room.

She was pale and trembling, very much frightened, very much in earnest; but even her deepest emotion had such a leaven of romance about it that it was like a play. She had been afraid Rossitur was gone forever, and she loved him more wildly than she had ever done; she was in mortal terror lest her guardian should come and force her back; she was enough excited by sal-volatile, laudanum, and every other species of restorative that the Banger had recklessly poured down her throat each time in the night she opened her mouth for a hysterical shriek, to be ready for any thing that resembled an adventure.

"Genevieve! Angel!" cried Rossitur bursting into the room, and had her in his arms, calling her by every tender name, and pouring out a flood of lofty rubbish. But there was method in his madness, or rather the instant his lips touched hers he was not mad at all, except to think that this girl was in his embrace instead of the woman he loved and feared. It was a very dull business the love-making, and he was thankful for the fresh stimulant the Banger had offered. He went through the necessary scene with due spirit, and still with that hasheesh-given power to see and hear so much at once; scenes and faces far away were a fuller reality to him than the actual surroundings.

Genevieve told him that she loved him, that she would live or die for him as he saw fit, and he had to explain that if she wished to live with him there was no time to be lost. They were in imminent danger of being separated forever; if she were once back in Mr. Grey's power there was no hope for them.—Never! She would stab herself first!—There was a way: they must be married at once secretly.—An elopement? a secret marriage? Genevieve was delighted with the idea.—Very rapidly but clearly he laid out his plans. They would go to Europe.—Another charm! but most delightful it was to be like one of the stolen matches in books.—They could not sail just yet; indeed, he had an important plot against Elinor to carry out.—Here he grew very vague and more melodramatic.—They

would hide themselves for a few days in a house near the city owned by a friend of Rossitur's, which fortunately at this time had nobody but the servants in it.

The truth was, Rossitur had no idea of sailing until what was left of her fortune should be in his power; the concealment in the friend's house he proposed because it would please her fancy and he wished to be on the ground when the disaster reached Mr. Grey. The Angel was in a state of excitement too intense to think collectedly about any thing. Rossitur went to Indiana and unfolded his designs, which met with her warm approval. There was not much to arrange; he had only to go in pursuit of a clergyman and of the friend who owned the house he wanted and get his possessions packed. If Mr. Grey appeared while he was gone, the servants were charged not to let him in; he was to be told that Mrs. Tallman and Miss Laidley had gone out to drive and would not be back till dark. The Banger would have preferred to meet the guardian if he did come to claim his ward—her soul was eager for a fray—but Rossitur showed her the necessity of deferring it until matters were made secure. He hurried away to find his friend, who was happy to oblige him and cared very little whether he wanted to take a wife or somebody else to the house that had held more than one inmate, and wherein Rossitur himself had mingled in revels which perhaps he would not care to recall as he led his bride over its threshold.

Married in church Miss Laidley would be—the runaways in English novels always were—and in a white dress; fortunately the latter need was easily supplied from her countless stores. Rossitur returned with every thing prepared. A messenger had been dispatched to the house with orders to have it in readiness, and the trusty group of domestics were too much accustomed to hasty descents upon the quiet of the domain not to be prepared. A clergyman had been warned, and luckily, for appearance' sake in Miss Laidley's eyes, his church was a sombre, shadowy place that made one shiver. The Angel was dressed when Rossitur arrived, so lovely in her nervousness and her rich satin which she had had made from some caprice and never worn, that under the influence of more potations in order to Rossitur he had not done so ill for himself. Little short of half a million was not to be despised; he could afford to give the rest for his revenge. As the click of the telegraph wires sounded anew in his ears he began to be fiercely glad. There was great haste and confusion; not that there was the slightest reason, but such attendants seemed necessary to a secret marriage, and Juanita and the Banger flew about discoursing in unearthly whispers that would have been more in place in Mrs. Ratcliffe's Castle of Udolpho than in a modern dwelling.

The wretched travesty of romance and a runaway marriage took its course. The pair stood in the shadowy church and uttered those vows, awful in their solemnity, with about as much thought as nine couples out of ten do in this remarkable age. Genevieve kept glancing nervously about, expecting each instant to see her guardian appear with a troop of myrmidons at his back—having last seen him at the fancy-ball, she pictured him in the attire he wore there—but no such interruption occurred. The Banger and Rossitur's friend were the only spectators besides Juanita, and they were neither of them people likely to be moved by the impressiveness or the romance. The Banger was thinking how delightfully she had punished the Greys; the reckless-faced man was thinking what a deuced good thing Rossitur had made of it, and wondering whether he was the sort of fellow likely to be useful when another fellow's debts became so pressing that little luxuries like secret houses, and unlimited poker, and race-horses, and other healthful pleasures should be difficult of obtainment.

They were married. As they turned from the altar the bride flung herself on Indiana's Spartan breast and murmured her thanks, whispering for the fiftieth time that day that the instant she reached New York there would be sought a gift, the splendor of which, great as it might be, could feebly express her love and gratitude. She did this because people are true to their characteristics even in the agitation of being married or dying, and gave way to fresh tears. Then she looked about again for her guardian in mediæval costume, followed perhaps by men with halberds; then up rushed Juanita to kiss her hand and chatter like an aged monkey troubled with colic. There were hurried farewell words; attempts at pretty speeches from the reckless man, which seemed damp and limp, and smelled of cigar-smoke and juleps and a gambling-house; then Rossitur hurried her impatiently down the aisle and their three companions followed.

It was not an enlivening sight as they reached the church porch to see a hearse, followed by a short train of mourning-carriages, drive up and their vehicles forced to give way thereto; a typical show of how every thing, even weddings, must give way to the grim Summoner. It really appeared for a moment that the marriage and funeral trains were about to meet; the coffin be carried into the church past the bride coming out. Genevieve shrieked aloud and shrunk back, and the Banger whispered to the reckless-faced man—

"Good heavens! how unfortunate."

"Ya-as," drawled he, not to be disturbed or surprised; "they're not going in that, are they?"

It appeared there was some mistake. Out rushed the man who had been helping the clergyman get his robe off, and interchanged a few words with the driver of the hearse, while Rossitur drew his new-made wife back into the vestibule and she hid her face in his bosom, too sorely frightened for an instant to remember that there was a tragical romance about the encounter. The hearse and funeral-carriages drove slowly on, the hearse creaking somewhat as if it had expected to engulf new victims in its maw and felt a sense of injury in not being permitted, while the mourners stared at the bridal-party over the handkerchiefs, which they had remembered somewhat late to put up to their eyes.

"It was a mistake," whispered the sexton to Mrs. Tallman and the reckless man; "twasn't our funeral at all! Belongs to a Baptist meeting-house round the corner. Some folks can't even go out of the world straight."

"Who was it, anyhow?" asked the reckless man.

"Upon my word, I forget the name. It's an old lady every body knew—I've seen her lots of times; deaf as a post. Odd, I—"

"Why," whispered Indiana, "it was old Mrs.—what was her name?—that always came to parties. I heard last night she was dead."

"Trying to get in where she had no business to the last," returned her companion. "Upon my word, that's being consistent; now, isn't it? Ruling passion strong in etcetera, isn't it?"

"Hush!" said Indiana.

The hearse and the carriages disappeared round the corner; and as the meeting-house was near, probably that was the poor deaf lady's final mistake in a world that had been for so many years little more than an immense cavern of indistinct noises to her. It was to be remarked that she could not get her name pronounced even at the last juncture in which it was likely to come up. The relations in the carriages were bestowing original and unpleasant epithets upon her, none of which could have been put on a visiting-card or a coffin-plate, because they had discovered that the little hoard to which they had looked forward during the long siege of shouting themselves hoarse at the end of her ear-trumpet, and sometimes getting puffs of snuffy wind in their eyes when she blew through it instead of spoke, as was her habit in moments of agitation, had been disposed of beyond their reach years and years ago, and there was nothing left unless it might be the blue feathers and opera-cloak; and even those treasures were at the scourer's and his charges must be paid before they could be got out of his possession.

Rossitur had much difficulty in soothing Genevieve, who was quite upset by the mischance and looked as if she expected to see her bridegroom turn into a grim skeleton and force her into the hearse, like a modern version of the melancholy fate that befell Imogen the Fair. Juanita began to wring her hands and moan, but her the Banger quieted by a fierce look and a private pinch so sharp and artfully dealt that it proved she must have been in the habit of practicing on some unfortunate. The reckless man caught her at it, and wondered if it was the tough skin of the Californian she had nipped till she reached that perfection in the art, and he was so charmed with Juanita's grimace and bound that he wished he might put her in a cage and keep her down at the secret house as a rare specimen of the gorilla tribe, to amuse his varied guests. The poor bride was comforted at last and persuaded to look up; her fright had been earnest, therefore she came quickly out of it and was prepared to rush to the other extreme and be recklessly gay. They were in the carriage at length and dashed off at full speed, and Juanita followed in a vehicle loaded with trunks and packages, so much bewildered by the hurry of the whole thing, the awful mystery, and the crowning misadventure, that she did nothing but utter monkey cries in the solitude of her carriage and brandish a bronze paper-cutter which she had concealed in her dress and carried to church as a neat and useful weapon wherewith to assault the guardian if he made his appearance.

It was late in the day before Mr. Grey returned home, and Elinor was uncertain what to do, having twice driven to the Department and been unable to find him. His interview with the President was long and not satisfactory to either, though they had come to no open rupture; Mr. Grey had stood firm on the ground that he must have time for reflection, and uttered several eloquent periods about not being able to force his sense of duty to bend in obedience to the dictates of friendship, to which the old lion had listened with a grim smile. After that there had been several committees to meet, and diverse troublesome affairs. When he returned to his office there was a telegram which the Bull had sent off on receipt of his morning's tidings, and it said a few words which meant "I am all right," which was such a weight off the minister's mind that the declining day seemed to brighten.

Elinor went into the hall to meet him as he entered the house, drew him into the library, and said—"Papa, Miss Laidley is gone."

She told her story from beginning to end, briefly and clearly; never repeated a statement or rambled in any way, which was wonderful for a woman. The matter was annoying, but it did strike Mr. Grey as very absurd, and his spirits were so much elevated by the telegraphic message that he laughed a little.

"She wants a scene," he said.

"But what is to be done, papa?"

They decided that the best thing would be for him to write a kind note to Miss Laidley, saying that he would see her that evening, and plainly pointing out to her how much annoyance she would bring upon herself, as well as him, unless she returned. Henry was dispatched with the missive, and, as it chanced, met the Banger herself entering her house on her return from the church. He gave her the note and she handed it back with the information that there was no longer any lady owning the name upon the letter—Miss Laidley was married to Mr. Rossitur, and gone.

Henry, never to be betrayed into so weak an emotion as surprise, only said—"Where shall I tell Monsieur they are gone?"

"You shall tell him to find out by his diplomatic skill," said the Banger, "and give him my compliments and congratulations."

Indiana thought she had been sarcastic and went into the house triumphant, and Henry, having called her by a very long name in his native language—a sign of anger with him—and by an appellation in French which I must not write, though people are permitted to say peculiar things in that language which our national modesty could not suffer in the vernacular, and having rounded his interjections by a third terse English word which was more expressive than the others, returned to Mr. Grey. He delivered the Banger's exact message, with an apologetic wave of the hand, as if to intimate that nothing but a desire to make matters perfectly clear could have induced him to repeat it, and left the father and daughter looking at each other in silence.

"Not a word to say?" asked Mr. Grey, smiling.

"I don't think I am astonished," Elinor replied.

"I believe she has done us a favor," said he. "But it seems like a dream. I saw Rossitur this morning. Why, my dear, I did not imagine he was looking in that direction."

"It is in keeping with his character," returned she; "his duplicity is only equalled by hers."

"It is a good thing for him," pursued Mr. Grey; "but why they need have made an elopement of it puzzles me. Nobody would have wished or been able to hinder their marriage."

"My dear father!" expostulated Elinor, "when you know Miss Laidley so well! Why, the mystery is what pleased her; it explains her going off last night and every thing else."

"And prevents any annoyance for us," said Mr. Grey, "which will be an annoyance to that strong spirit, the Tallman."

"Poor girl, she is to be pitied," said Elinor. "Papa, that man's conduct is inexcusable—after your confidence."

"I am not prepared to say. Don't be shocked, my daughter Elinor; if she would have the romance, what was he to do?"

Henry tapped at the door again and came in with a letter for Mr. Grey. It was from Rossitur—a resignation of his position; on the other half of the sheet a few hurried words to say that within a very few days he could offer full explanations. Mr. Grey, remembering the telegram, the certainty that all was right, could smile again and let Elinor read the note.

"You don't know him, papa. Let me tell you—"

"To-morrow; forgive me, but let us forget the whole thing for the present; I am tired. Let me see—haven't we some people at dinner?"

"Yes, papa; the Hewlands and General Mansfield."

"I suppose we need not go in mourning because Miss Laidley has eloped. The story may as well be told to-night as ever."

The guests came, and several of them having heard already the rumor of the elopement, which the reckless man was frantically spreading about in his desire to be first to tell the tale, were anxious to listen to the unvarnished story, and the bride might have been disappointed could she have known how little surprise her romance excited, and not flattered at the remarks concerning its being in accordance with their ideas of her character in its useless mystery and theatrical gloss.

Every now and then Mr. Grey repeated to himself the mystic words of the message, and was so brilliant and gay that he charmed the whole circle into thinking that delightful as he had always been, he appeared to have developed new powers in the art of being agreeable.

CHAPTER XLIII.
THE DARK HOUR.

THE next morning, after her father had gone out, Elinor had leisure to perceive the new sense of quiet that pervaded the house, and to find a great enjoyment therein. No monkey cries from Juanita in contention with the other servants about something in which she had no business to interfere; no rushing in of the Angel, overpowering from high spirits or a sudden revulsion toward spasms; and no whispered confabulations between mistress and attendant on the staircase or in the halls or any other place where they would be likely to attract attention. It was delightful to sit down and enjoy the freedom, and Elinor was glad also to remember that Leighton Rossitur had passed entirely out of reach of her life. The feeling of insecurity which the sight of him had given her for weeks; the vague fear, which her pride would not permit her to own, that in some secret way he was trying to disturb her peace through his influence upon her father—all this was gone, and Elinor could breathe freely. By the contrast, she comprehended how oppressive the neighborhood of those restless spirits had been, the while a certain commiseration for both, knowing them as she did, mingled with her sensations and kept her from any harsh recollections toward either.

In the course of the morning the Idol drove up to the house in great excitement, having heard the report of Miss Laidley's elopement, and fearful, if it were true, which she would not believe, that some annoyance might have been caused Elinor and her father. She met Elinor with outstretched hands, exclaiming — "My adorable Miss Grey, is it veritable—has she gone? I would not credit it, though my informant said she had it from Mr. Hilton—that sad man—who witnessed the ceremony."

"It is true," replied Elinor calmly, escaping from the embrace, which owing to the Idol's heavy draperies was a somewhat suffocating operation, and settling her visitor in a chair.

"Gone?", repeated the Idol. "Married to Mr. Rossitur?"

"So he wrote to my father."

"But I can not elucidate," exclaimed the bewildered Idol. "Why elope? What prevented a reasonable and decorous marriage, proper to her station as the ward of our Richalooan minister?"

"That I am unable to tell you," Elinor answered. "You know Miss Laidley was fond of romance ; she may have thought the ordinary course on such occasions too tame and hackneyed."

"I am so grieved, so disappointed in her! My dear, it was so inappropriate—a style that is obsolete. Why, my love, clopements have not been fashionable for the last twenty years."

"Perhaps she wished to revive the fashion."

"Such ingratitude to your noble father—such duplicity ! And I thought her the soul of innocence and truthfulness ! You must be shocked and pained beyond measure."

"I am sorry to appear hard-hearted, Mrs. Hackett," said Elinor, "but personally I can not pretend to feel any regret. I suppose the step will be the cause of much gossip, but I fear that in the end it will recoil more upon her than any one else."

"Indubitably," replied the Idol. "They told me that dreadful Tallman woman had aided, and was attempting to say that you and your father's persecutions were the cause."

"I should doubt any of our friends easily crediting that statement," Elinor said with a smile.

"My love, it was too puerile to repeat—not worth an answer. But give me the details. You know, my sweet Miss Grey, it is not idle curiosity on my part ; you know my affection for you, my admiration for your transcendent parent ; and I was very, very fond of her—I grieve, my dear."

Elinor told her what she knew, beginning with Miss Laidley's return from the ball and plunging into a frenzy which ended in her leaving the house guarded by Indiana Tallman, who played the part of St. George rescuing the Angel from the claws of the dragon. There was nothing approaching acrimony in Elinor's account, but it was only justice to her father that the story should be told exactly as it happened ; besides she had no wish to hear Miss Laidley accused of any thing beyond flightiness and a somewhat exaggerated love of scenes.

The Idol could not so easily forgive the very apparent effort to make mischief, and she had possessed such faith in her Angel that she was deeply shocked and grieved, only able to relieve herself by long and amazing quotations which were supposed to be Shakespeare or translations from the classics ; but whatever they might have been originally, they were transformed in true Plutonian style. She would not leave Elinor alone, persisting in her belief that she must be unstrung after such excitement ; and as Elinor knew that she could not gratify the good soul more than by allowing her to remain, she was willing enough to accept her society. But unmitigated wonder and bewailing became somewhat tiresome, so she led the conversation to other topics and the Idol regained a moderate degree of composure, though broken at intervals by renewed exclamations and blank verse, when such poesies as seemed applicable to the late adventure recurred to her mind.

"My love," she said, after having indulged in a reminiscence of one of Juliet's speeches, which, if she had known it, suggested the idea that in her mind she regarded Mr. Grey as a kite or a vulture, "do you know the Farnsworths are coming to the Capitolian shades?"

"Rosa Thornton wrote me that they were to be here for a week, but she did not say when. I am glad."

"They come instantaneously. I had a missive from the dear wife of the poet. I had taken the liberty—but it matters not. I only meant they are so kind, she is such an angel—no, I shall eschew that word henceforth; it will awaken echoes in my soul of that which is past and ne'er may be again, howe'er ye wreathe the fragile bowl, as says the poet."

She had completely lost the thread of her remarks in that species of parenthesis, and looked bewildered; to afford her a little light, Elinor said—"You had a letter from Ruth."

"Ah! yes. In answer to my request—they are so very kind. I told her I could venture to trouble her, knowing the urbanity of her heart; and indeed, my love, she is indeed—I lack words—Elysian—the very term, and he is such an Apolloite, so bayed with fresh laurels—I jubilate to reflect upon them." Elinor was glad to have Ruth appreciated, though she might have bargained for the praise to be chanted in a more intelligible strain. "She indited me a letter so sweet, to say she had heeded my slight request. This dreary winter, my love—one could not help remembering those wretched beings in South village—I say it not for glorification of self, you will be my sponsor."

"I know you do not," Elinor said, nor did she; certainly the Idol had not neglected her stewardship where charity was concerned.

"Thanks; always wide-seeing, always Olympian in your judgments—what says the poet?—and sermons sparkling in her mind like stones that run in brooks and good in every thing. And that fair Hebean creature does so much—never weary—never oblivious of common mortality in the pyramidical shrine wherein the poet's love enwraps her." This last burst was so fine that she was a little astonished at it herself and paused for breath. "Excuse me," she said, "but that theme always inspires me. When I dilate upon her devotion during my illness—her serenity of patience and her cornucopia of wisdom—I am overpowered."

"You can not think too highly of her," Elinor said.

"No, no; feebly my wildest praise could syllable ecstatic lays, as warbles the song-bird—is it Mrs. Hemans? And they are coming—such joy to greet their garlanded brows! My love, I must devise some tournament to do them honor."

"I think they both love quiet."

"Yes, yes; but the world craves its meed. Ah! fame and state are only gilded jailers after all."

It was a somewhat heavy morning to Elinor, but at least there was a sincerity under the Idol's grandiloquence and absurdity which was a relief after the unmitigated selfishness and transparent hypocrisy with which she had been so long housed. She congratulated her visitor on the success of her ball, and the Idol went off in explosions of thanks, admiration of her, praise of the good-nature of her friends in general, and regrets that she had not known the Farnsworths were coming that she might have deferred her festivities. She stayed to luncheon, and some delicacy on the table reminded her of the Angel, who had been fond of it, and she leaned back in her chair and apostrophized the dish in a strain, which she believed to be something Shakespeare had said, so wild and incoherent that Henry had some difficulty to preserve his equable mask and not appear to see or hear any thing beyond his immediate duties.

Long before the usual hour of her father's return Elinor heard his voice in the hall and hurried out to meet him, for though his improved appearance the evening before had made her hope that her late fears were without foundation, it required little to rouse them anew. "Are you ill, papa?" she asked. "Why, how pale you look!"

"I believe I am not quite well," he said, and the admission was almost unheard of with him. "I have come back to rest, for we have a Cabinet meeting to-night and I must get rid of this languor."

Elinor was alarmed at his appearance, but he would not suffer her to think that any thing beyond fatigue ailed him. He was however sensible of very strange feelings; the ringing which had been in his ears for weeks, the peculiar sensation in the back of his head, now a numbness, now a sharp pain that spread and tingled to his very finger-ends, had so much increased that he found it insupportable torture to go through with his routine of duty, and, after making sad confusion in every thing he attempted, had been obliged to return home. He had a horror of illness, and could not bear to admit that it might come near him or that the years had left him less strong than in his youth, therefore he treated Elinor's fears lightly.

"I think instead of lamentations," said he with a smile which only made his face look more worn and ghastly, "you might congratulate me on having leisure to sit with you, my daughter Elinor; it will be like old times."

"O papa," she whispered, "Mrs. Hackett is here—too bad!"

Mr. Grey was very glad to hear it, he would have returned an hour before only he had sat waiting in the hope that he should receive tidings from Pluto, and had been made so anxious by their non-arrival that he was forced persistently to repeat the satisfactory telegram of the

previous day to keep down the throbbing in his
head which the least indulgence in thought increased till it made him blind and sick. "I
will go in and see her," he said; and putting Elinor's hand on his arm with the old caressing
tenderness, he led her into the room where
the Idol was ready to greet him with her usual
fervor.

"This is a startled pleasure," she said; and
by consulting a mental glossary which the Idol's
friends needed to keep open while listening to
her conversation, he decided that she must mean
unexpected.

He said complimentary things to her according to his wont, and allowed her to give free
vent to her surprise in regard to the elopement,
which he was still inclined to regard as a matter for amusement. He listened and talked,
and though each moment of delay in discovering whether she had news from her husband
was mental and bodily agony, the habit of self-
control and concealment was too strong to be
outwardly shaken. Not till the fitting opportunity offered, and only in the most natural manner, to evince simply a friendly interest in Elinor's eyes, did he say—

"Mr. Hackett was quite well when you heard,
I hope."

"Indeed," replied the Idol, "I have had no
tidings in several days; I expected letters this
morning. Mr. Hackett is so hurried—so overwhelmed—so deeply buried in the busy mart."

"I regard him as a second Atlas," said Mr.
Grey.

"Thanks; he needs an Atlasian brow indeed
to bear his weight of occupation. But though
so much engrossed, he is always thoughtful, always attentive. I marvel that I have at least
no hasty message."

"You will doubtless receive letters to-day,"
returned Mr. Grey.

"Oh yes; I should be absolutely alarmed
else."

"I dare say the last mail brought them,"
continued he; "I will send some one to your
house that you may have them at once."

The Idol could not hear of his taking the
trouble, and Elinor wished that he would not
protract her visit by removing the only reason
she could have for a speedy departure, but he
persisted in his gallant way. "The soul of
thought ever," said the Idol, as he rang and
ordered Henry to send to Mrs. Hackett's house
for any letters that might have been brought
since she came out. "The very essence and
aroma of delicate · attention in every slightest
act. Ah! admirative Crichton, how you unfit
us of the fragile sex for the society of common
mortals."

He would answer blandly, and appear perfectly composed, and Elinor watched him with
growing fear at the increased pallor which gathered over his face, certain that he was very ill,
but obliged to seem unconscious lest she should
annoy him. The message sent, he grew horribly anxious; the moments dragged like lead-

on weights through the heaviness of his brain,
and the outpouring of the Idol's talk sounded
like a torrent; the numb sensation crept slowly
about his head, dissipated at brief intervals by a
stinging pain that quivered like a snake down
the spinal nerves. Henry opened the door
again and advanced with his customary deliberation; there was a letter on the little salver
which he held, and the sight brought back the
quick pain with such violence that fiery sparks
absolutely danced before Mr. Grey's eyes.

"For Mrs. Hackett?" he asked.

"Yes, Monsieur;" presenting his offering to
that lady. "It did not come by mail; a special messenger was just of arrival at the house."

Mr. Grey sat still, holding his snuff-box in
his hand; not a muscle of his face changed, not
a quiver was apparent.

"A special messenger?" repeated the Idol,
not in surprise but pleasure that her husband
showed so becoming a sense of their dignity,
being somewhat forgetful thereof, as a rule, in
his daily habits. She held the letter in her
hand and regarded it with a satisfied smile,
while Mr. Grey remained motionless, conscious
that if he so much as stirred a finger he should
snatch the packet from her hand and tear it
open. "So weighty a missive," she said complacently; "I can not think what it may contain;" and instead of breaking the seal to find
out, she smiled at Mr. Grey in majestic surprise.

"I somewhat expected letters from him myself," Mr. Grey could not help saying; "there
may be something enclosed for me."

"Pardon," said the Idol, taking that opportunity to be playful, which, considering Mr.
Grey's feelings, was about as opportune as if she
had held a grinning skull in her hand and was
jesting over it. "Then I shall transgress the
laws of etiquette and ascertain its contents.
What says the play?—By thy leave, waxen—
Cleopatra says it, does she not?"

Elinor was looking at her father in vague
wonder. He sat motionless, intently regarding
their guest. Mrs. Hackett opened the envelope
with graceful deliberation and drew out two
letters, one of which was sealed. "Ah! this
must be for you," she said, glancing at it.
"Why, there is no superscription—that careless, busy man!"

Mr. Grey tried to speak, but his lips and
throat were so dry that not a sound escaped his
mouth.

"Your letter will tell you what it means,"
said Elinor impatiently, filled with an inexplicable dread.

"Of course; how trivial in me to hold it and
marvel," returned the Idol, laughing. "Ah,
Mr. Grey, the fragility of the sex—what says
the poet?" She unfolded her letter; the room
was so still that the folds of the thick paper rustled strangely as she shook them out. "The
unintelligible callifery," said she, laughing again
and holding up the sheet. "Quite Egyptian
anagrams, I protest."

Would she never read it? would there never be an end to this horrible trifling? The fiery sparks danced before Mr. Grey's eyes—the stinging serpent coiled down his spine—a rigid band of pain wrapped its fetters across his forehead; Elinor watching him—out of the great sympathy of her love having the torture reflected in her own heart; the Idol smiling and unconscious.

"Now for the world of Wall Street, for Augean labors and traffic's busy mart," said the Idol. "Another realm I view, as some minstrel sings, and this is our Open Sesame." She began to read; spelled out the first almost illegible lines; stared up from the page with a look of utter bewilderment; read on a little further, and fell back on the sofa with one sharp cry that smote Mr. Grey's ear like a knife—"Ruined!"

Elinor sprang to her feet and hurried toward her; Mr. Grey tried to get off his chair and sank back helpless—he could not speak.

"Ruined!" repeated the Idol, and still her voice had in it only the ring of stupefied incredulity.

"You must have read it wrong," Elinor said.

"It can not be! it can not be!" exclaimed the Idol in a changed tone. "Wait—let me read again—wait!" She peered at the page anew, and for the third time the dreadful word broke from her lips, not in wonder, not in blank stupor, but in a passionate sob that was agonizing. "Ruined! It can't be—it is not true! Read it, Miss Grey; I can't see—the lines dance before my eyes. Speak, somebody—say it is not true!"

Elinor took the letter and read the page which told the truth in a few brief, despairing sentences.

"What does it say?" cried the Idol. "It is not true—I read it wrong—it is not true!"

"My poor friend!" was all Elinor could articulate. The Idol cowered lower and covered her face with her hands, trembling as if afraid to look up and realize the truth. "Father," said Elinor, still reading, "this other letter must be for you; he says he encloses one. Oh, Mrs. Hackett has fainted." As she dropped the letter and turned toward the unfortunate woman she heard a voice, so sharp and strange that she would not have recognized it as her father's call—

"That letter—bring me that letter!"

She caught up both letters from the floor and ran toward him. "Father!" she gasped in sudden terror, for the white face in which she looked might have been the despairing lost ghost of the face she had all her life seen so smiling and so proud. "Father!"

"Hush!" he answered in the same unnatural voice; "the letter!"

She put the two in his hands; the touch of the paper was like a tangible proof; the realization of the horror brought a sort of strength. "Stay with her," he said, rising slowly and painfully.

"O father, what is it?" she exclaimed, catching his icy hand.

He shrunk from her touch; a strange fear came across the horror in his face. "Stay with her," he repeated; "I'll come back—I want to read it alone."

She cried out again—his gesture and the wild entreaty in his glazed eyes stopped her—she allowed him to pass from the room. She looked and saw Mrs. Hackett still lying with her white face on the arm of the sofa. Elinor ran toward her, raised her up, got some water and sprinkled upon her forehead, eagerly trying to bring her back to consciousness that she might follow her father.

"Did I read it? Is it true?" gasped Mrs. Hackett as she opened her eyes.

"I fear there is no doubt," Elinor said.

"Read it again—every word!"

Elinor read the page slowly and distinctly and the the poor Idol burst into a paroxysm of grief.

The tale was told with terrible brevity and distinctness; the wretched man had written it as soon as he could recover from the first prostration of the blow. If he had given the details of the day they would have been brief enough, but he did not. Before noon he had received the telegram Leighton Rossitur had sent, and busy had every body connected with the establishment been, calling in and buying up a certain stock that the absolute control of it might be in Pluto's hands before the action of the Senate could inform others of its value, and as each messenger returned Mr. Hackett felt a new glow in the consciousness that the crisis was passed—he was saved. Up to four o'clock a hurry and rush of business, then he was able to go home, and in the solitude of his great house sit down and think that he had once more steadied himself on his height and saw the way clear to new successes. It was not of course that this one venture, immense as it was, could by itself have ruined a man of his resources, but for the past year, while apparently on the highest pinnacle of its splendor and security, Pluto's pagoda had been troubled by underground rumblings and premonitions of an earthquake. He had grown daring from the very fullness of good luck; he had only needed to touch a scheme to make it brighten into a glorious fruition, until he could entertain no fears. It had been a year of wild speculation; during the past weeks the reaction had begun: houses crumbling about him; men of unblemished reputation detected in gigantic frauds: this bank crashing under its load; that telegraph company a failure; projected railways falling in hopeless confusion; a chaos of misfortune which swept Pluto along; two colossal defalcations on the part of men whom he had trusted added, until ruin seemed inevitable, till with the new hope he saw how other matters might be arranged, and knew that if he could pass this danger, destiny would once more be in his own hands. The peril was over; he beheld his course clear now. It was over, and his dazzling triumph would not have a shadow. He sat in his room, rubbing his forehead with a dusty silk handkerchief and indulging in a feeling of exultation such as he had not known in a long time. A newsboy under the window calling out an Extra *Herald*—reading scraps of news by way of attracting attention—"Extry *Her'ld!* European war—great victory of the—" The voice died away to rise in new sharpness with, "Bill passed the Senate!" The sharp, boyish voice came up into the room where Pluto sat, and made him start to the window and listen breathlessly. Again it came—"Bill passed the Senate!" He got to the bell, pulled it wildly, and ordered the servant to bring him the Extra. He was in the room again alone—in his chair—glaring at the leaded column—reading the words over and over. In the distance came back the echo of the newsboy's voice—"Bill passed the Senate—bill passed!" The paper fell slowly from Pluto's hand—he understood at last. There had been an error; he knew that he was ruined.

The Idol listened to the letter, and amid her sobs cried—"I can not believe it! I should sooner have expected the end of the world! Ruined? Why, he was worth millions! Mr. Grey, Mr. Grey! Where is Mr. Grey?"

"Oh, what has happened to him? Tell me!" demanded Elinor.

"Where is Mr. Grey?"

"Gone; he would not let me follow—gone to read this letter. What was it?"

"I know not; my heart will break! I fear he is involved—I know so little of the business! O Miss Grey, it can't be—we're not ruined—oh, oh!"

Elinor had made her drink some water and opened a window to give her air. "I must go, Mrs. Hackett," she said; "I must find my father."

"Yes, yes; I must go too," said the Idol, trying to recover herself and proving by the effort that she was a woman of sense under all her follies. "I can not believe it—ruin for us—for you—for so many!"

"Was my father engaged in those speculations?" Elinor asked.

"I fear it—I know so little! Oh, forgive us, Miss Grey! Don't blame my husband—promise that."

"You know I should not, whatever came. But I can think of nothing only my father now. I must go."

"Yes, I won't keep you. Tell him— I do not know what I say! It must pass—it must be a temporary trouble. I want a carriage. I must get back—I must start for town."

"There is a train in an hour," Elinor said. She went out and ordered Henry to send for a carriage, came back and helped Mrs. Hackett to get on her bonnet and cloak.

"I must be mad," moaned the poor Idol; "we must all be mad—dreaming. It is not us —we did not read it! Oh, the letter!" and at the sight of it lying at her feet on the carpet she jumped back as if it had been a snake.

Elinor had few words; she tried to comfort her, to say it was perhaps not so black as Mr. Hackett feared; but could see nothing, think of nothing except her father's white face and the sound of that unnatural voice.

"It can not be, it can not be!" the Idol moaned one instant, and sobbed piteously the next—"Get me a carriage—let me go—ruined, ruined!" The carriage drove up; she flung herself upon Elinor in a convulsive embrace, uttering broken words which sounded like no human language whatever, but were pitiful to hear.

"I would go with you," Elinor said, "to the house, but I can't leave my father—"

"Go to him, go to him! You shall hear from me—forgive me! Oh, my poor husband —I am afraid I have been too worldly! All that wealth—it can not be gone—oh, it must be some frightful dream!"

She was out of the house at last, and Elinor went up stairs in search of her father. She found him in his dressing-room, his chair close to the fire, and he lying back with his eyes closed, a look in his face, a stillness in every limb so like death that Elinor softly opening the door and catching sight of him, called in terror —"Father! father!" At the sound of her voice a quiver passed through his whole frame; he put up his hands, as if to keep her back—not in pain, not in trouble alone—with a gesture of absolute fear, and groaned aloud. Elinor was on her knees beside him; clasping his hands and exclaiming—"Father, father, look up—it is Elinor!" He only shrunk back in his chair and groaned again. "Have you lost by this, father? If you have, it is only money. Father, look up—speak to me."

"Only money?" he repeated in the same unnatural voice which had so frightened her before, a voice that did not seem to be his, that spoke without any volition on his part. "It is honor—life! Go away—go away—I can not look in your face."

She tried to think. He had not injured her personally; he had no control whatever over her fortune, it was not in any way in his hands. "What is it?" she cried. "O father, tell me! You used to say there was no secret between us! Do you want money, father dear? There is mine—all, all; only tell me what it is!"

His wild eyes glanced over the table at his side; his hands clutched Mr. Hackett's letter—not that—snatched at another—a letter Henry was receiving at the door as he passed through the hall and had given him. He pointed to the sheet—he tried to speak—there was only a faint discordant murmur in his throat.

"You want me to read it?" asked Elinor. "I saw hers; I know what it is, father, I know."

"Not that," he gasped; "the other.

She saw the letter at which his shaking finger pointed, seized it, looked at Rossitur's name at the end, and read the page. A brief, civil letter, with an undercurrent of doubt that was very insulting. It said that he was about to sail for Europe; by the terms of the will left by his wife's father, her fortune must be at once transferred from Mr. Grey's hands. He desired to hear from Mr. Grey immediately; the lawyers would wait upon him. His haste must excuse the brief notice; he knew of course that, with Mr. Grey's rigid integrity, the delivering up of the seals of guardianship would be the merest form in the world, but it must be distinctly understood that not even twenty-four hours' delay could be permitted; important affairs made it necessary for himself and wife to depart at once.

"Let him have what he asks on the instant, father," said Elinor, and as the words left her lips a new fear started up in her heart at the sight of his face.

Mr. Grey did not speak; he had put one hand between his face and hers; the strange attitude, the same gesture of shrinking and entreaty which had so bewildered her before. All her life long this man had been her idol—a doubt in regard to him had been as impossible as a doubt of her religion—but now, in spite of herself, as she read that letter and looked at him, a perception of what he had done crept over her. An instant's whirl in her brain; she was beside him again, her arms about him, straining him to her in a wild gush of tenderness; not like the love and veneration for the father she had so loved, but such pity and tenderness as she might have felt had their positions been reversed and she the parent first made cognizant of her child's error. "Don't shrink away, father," she pleaded; "let me whisper! If it was hers—if you needed hers—tell me, father."

She heard the broken murmur—"It was hers!"

"But my fortune is safe; we can pay it. Try to tell me. Don't think of any thing only that it is a trouble we must share together. We must act at once, you know; only tell me how much and what we must do."

The numbness and deadness was creeping closer and closer to his vitals like the chill of death; he could only say with a great effort—"In that safe—the papers."

She understood; she was to read the papers therein. She kissed his forehead and ran to the safe. It was locked. "The key—I want the key, father."

He fumbled in his pockets and produced a small key; she took it and unlocked the miniature safe, such as is sometimes used for jewels and valuables of small compass. She would not look toward him again; she sat down on the floor and turned her back that he might have a little time, and pulled out the files of papers until she came upon what was needed to make the matter clear. She understood what he had done; he had used the shares of stock and Government bonds invested for Miss Laidley to the amount of almost four hundred thousand dollars. She sat still for a few moments —not thinking of the blow—not remembering

that a few paces from her sat her shattered idol in the dust of his discovered criminality—only trying to collect her senses, to see how to act. Her fortune would exactly cover the amount. Nearly half of it was already invested in the same bonds, the other was in a condition so that it could be transferred at the briefest possible notice. She rose from the floor, put the papers in the safe again and locked it, doing it all with a strange methodical quiet as if there had been something dead in the room and she was afraid of disturbing it. She went back to her father; he had not moved, he was lying in the chair still with his eyes closed.

"Listen, father," she said. "It is only to write a letter—I will send at once to Mr. Gresham—by the time they can get to New York your lawyers will have every thing in readiness." He moved his head a little, but did not open his eyes. "Did you hear, father? Oh, look at me, please. Father, you frighten me! It is all over—never to be thought of again. See, I am going to write now; I can send it by one of Mrs. Hackett's men. Only look up—only say you love me and we will have no more trouble."

He rested his two hands hard on the arms of his chair to steady himself and sat upright, not looking at her, and speaking thickly in a broken voice. "I loved you so—I was drawn on and on. I could not bear to ask your help—I needed your love more than the world's esteem. Look at me now—my daughter Elinor—my daughter Elinor!"

The familiar name she had heard uttered in pride, in exultation, in tenderness! To hear it now in that abject supplication—to see him shrinking and quailing before her! She put her arms close about him again—she soothed him with loving words. "You were ill, father, before this came. I will finish the letter, then you shall go to sleep and forget it. I love you so, father! We have been so much to each other all my life, but I never loved you as I do now—father, dear father!"

There was a faint dew in his glazed eyes as they turned heavily toward her, but the numbing pain was growing so acute that it was difficult for him to move. "I have ruined you," he said; "every thing I had is gone too."

"It doesn't matter. Father, we have each other, and we have something left. Listen: the amounts I had laid by out of all those dividends —I meant to use them for the hospital—they will be for us, father; a great deal—quite enough." He could not answer; he could only let her lay his heavy head back against the chair and kiss him, as she said—"I am going to write my letter now; rest, father."

She thought him stunned by the sudden shock; perhaps to know the letter written and sent would help him more than any thing else. She sat down at his writing-table and wrote her clear, imperative wishes. When the epistle was finished and sealed she looked at her father again; he was watching her with a regard so piteous that it rent her very heart. She kissed his forehead softly, saying—"I will send the letter at once. I'll be back in a minute."

He held fast to her hand and tried to say something; the muscles of his face worked convulsively, his breath was labored and heavy; she began to fear for the physical effects of this terrible blow and to remember the signs of illness she had for days dreaded. She went out and found Henry; bade him take the letter himself, and be certain that some one among Mrs. Hackett's people whom he could trust took charge of it. On the way back he was to call for a physician; she could not bear the responsibility any longer. When she returned to the dressing-room her father was lying on the sofa; he opened his eyes as she entered and begged her to give him a glass of wine. After drinking it he appeared revived, but with renewed strength came added capability of realizing what had befallen him, and where he had fallen before the eyes of the daughter he adored. Elinor comprehended his emotions; she could not be certain what to say or do, lest in her very desire to be of comfort she might hurt him, so she sat holding her cheek against his, hoping that he would fall asleep. Presently he turned his face a little and said abruptly—"That villain has done it on purpose." She knew that he meant Rossitur. Then came to her mind that menace he had uttered on the night of the ball, so haughtily rejected then, but since the experience of the past hour grown into a possibility which tore at the very springs of her life, yet which must be mentioned lest some other blow should strike her father in the dark.

"The other night he was in a great rage," she said; "at Mrs. Hackett's ball; and he said something which angered me, but I would not mention it. Has he any hold over you—any paper?" It was very difficult to put the question, but it must be done, and she could only use the plainest, briefest words.

"Hold—paper?" he repeated, pressing his hand to his forehead.

Elinor took his nerveless fingers in one of her hands and laid the other lightly on his head. "Try to think, father," she said softly.

"There can't be any thing," he answered with an effort, "unless about the Falcon party; did he mean that?"

"What is it, father?" she asked.

"Oh, you don't know; that was another secret. Child, child, I can't think—I can't act—you must do both."

"Tell me what you mean, father; don't try to explain much—I shall understand. The Falcon people wanted you to do something?"

With the numbness always increasing, sinking nearer his heart, rising higher and higher in his brain, it was not much trouble to confess. He could not realize indeed that it had been so completely a secret; he only knew that she must be told; she must act—he was done. Not that he thought he was near death—he had no defined feeling—only he had nothing more to do; Elinor must act

"They wanted to oppose the President—I was to be at the head of the party. It was only to go against his measures," he continued ramblingly; "somebody said it would be like Brutus; who said that?"

Elinor understood; he had been tempted to desert his friend in the storm; she saw what means had been employed. "Does the President know, father?"

"No. He heard I wavered—we talked yesterday. I will have to be decided to-night. I must go with him or side wholly against him—is it time to go?"

"To-night?"

"Yes, yes; the meeting, you know—I must be there. I am very tired—let me go to sleep—it isn't time to go."

Oh, this last was not to be borne! How was she to appeal to him—how be cruel enough to rouse him from that slumber? But his honor! To-night—and he looked so ill! If he should have a long sickness and those men compromise him while he was helpless!

"Father," she said, "father!"

He roused himself at her call. "My daughter Elinor!" Oh the pitiful, child-like pleading in the voice.

"Father, you will not desert the President, no matter what is offered; he is right."

"The head of the party," he said brokenly; "I should be certain of election. What did Rossitur say about Cataline? He meant Brutus."

Filled with alarm at this change, this wandering—mad with the thought what use might be made of his name while he lay powerless in his sick-chamber, Elinor was forced to rouse him again. Useless to argue; whatever it was that ailed him, it was that which would not permit him to reason; she could only hope to gain his consent to her line of action. She had to speak several times before he opened his eyes. He only roused up at the tender repetition—"Father, dear father!" He smiled faintly, and looked at her with some show of understanding. "You won't desert your friend," she said; "you will have me write and tell him so; say that for a little you may have been in doubt, but that you are convinced he is right—whatever comes, you are by his side; that you are too ill to be at the meeting, but you send this answer for him, for his Cabinet, for the whole world." The fire flashed into her eyes for an instant, the animated ring strengthened her voice and seemed to animate him.

"Write, write," he said, with sudden eagerness; "I will sign it. For the whole world—yes—quick, quick!" He raised himself feebly, but she gently laid his head back on the cushions.

"Lie quite still," she said; "when I have the letter ready you shall sign it; you can sleep after that."

He made a gesture of entreaty and lay watching her as she sat down at the table and wrote; something of the animation roused by her voice kept the stupor back for a little. Elinor wrote very rapidly, glancing now and then at him, resolutely keeping back every fear, every feeling except the present duty; conscious only that whatever came there was her whole life in which to mourn, but that the one proof she could give of her love was to act now. It was a noble letter, written in Mr. Grey's best style, only with less ornament than he employed, but it was no place for that. It said frankly that he had for a season hesitated, that while believing the President right he had thought it might be better to temporize, but he was convinced that he had been in error. No matter how fiercely factions might rage, no matter how much for a period even the verdict of the people, blinded by the insidious eloquence of partisan leaders, might be against him, time must prove that the President had been dictated in his course by the purest, the most patriotic motives. Through all, in all, he should find Mr. Grey by his side; if it came to pass that for a season they two stood wholly alone to battle the tempest, they would trust to the future and to God to make their actions clear. He was still lying with his eyes fixed upon her when she finished; she sat down by him again and read the letter.

"Is it what you wanted, father?"

"If it pleases you," he answered in a voice so low that she had to bend over him to catch the words. "It is all I can do—broken—disgraced. O my daughter Elinor!"

She dared not agitate him by giving way to her emotions; she said very quietly—"Always my love, my pride, father! See, I am going to wheel this little table to the sofa; I will hold you up while you sign the letter."

He allowed her to raise him—held the pen to the line where she pointed and wrote his name. "I did not desert him," he said feebly; "I have done something for honor—for you—I—" The pen slipped from his hand—he fell heavily back against her—there was a quiver through his whole frame, then he lay like a weight of lead in her arms, and as she shrieked for help Henry opened the door.

"Is he dead? is he dead?" she asked in an awful whisper, as the man laid the motionless form on the sofa.

At a glance Henry saw what had happened—Mr. Grey was stricken with paralysis.

"What is it, Henry?" she asked in the same tone.

He told her quietly; he had sense to know it was best.

"Won't he ever move again?" she questioned in that whisper which was worse to hear than a shriek of mortal agony.

"Indeed, indeed, he may yet get well, Mademoiselle—they often do. The doctor is down stairs."

She made a motion to have him called; she knelt by the couch and looked into the still white face; she thought there was some sign of recognition, of entreaty still in the dim eyes. "It is Elinor, father," she said, "your Elinor."

Henry came back with the physician; his experience had made him too well-skilled in the human face not to know that the only kindness he could show Elinor Grey was to spare her many words. "I shall ask you to go down stairs," he said after a few questions, "while we get him in bed. You shall come back very soon—you shall stay by him," he added, answering something in her eyes.

"Will he know me?" she asked, as they reached the door. "Can he hear me?"

"He will doubtless be able to speak in a few hours; it is the suddenness that makes it so terrible. The sooner he is undressed and in bed the better. You shall be called."

Mechanically obedient, Elinor turned to go—saw the letters on the table—took them all—kept in her hand the one she had written and went down stairs. She was so stunned that she could not feel acutely. The letter must be sent—must reach the President before the meeting — but whom could she trust? She went into the room where they had been sitting when Mrs. Hackett read her fatal news; the associations of the place broke the icy spell; she could weep and get rid of that strange sense of oppression. As she sat there she heard the door-bell, heard voices in the hall, and recognized one as Clive Farnsworth's. The letter—instantly she thought of that. She went out. He was standing there talking to the servant; at sight of her in her livid pallor he came quickly forward.

"They tell me your father is very ill," he said, not waiting to utter words of courtesy.

"It is—it is paralysis," Elinor answered; she was so cold and still that a stranger might have thought her almost unmoved. How well he knew the agony she was suffering.

"Is there any thing I can do?" he asked.

"Yes—this letter; it is very important it should be in the President's hands before night. If you could—"

"I will give it to him myself; I will go at once. You understand—I will put it in his own hands."

"Yes; thank you. Where is Ruth?"

"At the hotel; we came this morning. I called to leave some letters the Thorntons sent. Would you like to have my wife come—are you alone?"

"Yes; all alone."

"I will take your letter and then go for her."

"Yes—thank you," in the same difficult voice. "It can not be made too public—let it go in all the papers at once; if you will say that to the President—my father wishes it."

Clive tried to utter a few comforting words, but it was very hard to find them, looking in that white face on which the work of the morning, closed by its last terror and grief, had left the worn appearance of a long illness. He hurried away, and she went slowly up stairs again. Clive Farnsworth performed his promise to the letter, then he returned to the hotel intending to take Ruth to Elinor, but he found her so feverish and ill that he knew it would not be safe.

She had taken a severe cold while in New York, and they had deferred their journey several days on account of it, but she had seemed so much better that they came on at her plea, for she was certain that the milder climate would relieve her at once.

CHAPTER XLIV.

RUTH'S VICTORY.

ALL night Elinor watched by her father's bedside; a portion of the time alone, for she had that feeling many of us have known in the course of our lives, since illness and death will come into the most carefully-guarded homes, of wanting her loved to herself. The physician remained until late; after he had gone, Elinor desired Henry to go to bed, overcoming his plea to stay with the assertion that he would need to husband his strength, as the regulation of every thing must devolve upon him. The nurse who had made her appearance was a quiet, motherly woman, who had the sense to perceive that the greatest kindness she could do the lady was to sit in the dressing-room and leave her alone by the sick man, for there was nothing to be done except administer the medicines at regular hours.

Mr. Grey lay like a dead man; only the labored breathing showed that there was any life in the rigid form. He seemed to sleep at intervals, occasionally opening his eyes with a blank stare which changed to anxiety and fear until Elinor's voice re-assured him, at the sound of which a painful smile would hover over his lips. There Elinor sat and watched, with no room in her mind for any thought but her love. The great shock of the day had no place in her reflections; it never would have. The last blow, this terrible and sudden breaking of strength, would in one way be a merciful prevention. She would always believe that the conduct which proved her hero so miserably human had been brought about by the gradual approach of this stroke; that for weeks, may be months, the cloud had been slowly drawing over his mind, dimming his perceptions, and she would never hold him accountable for this fall.

Late in the night he woke with gasping for breath, followed by a great effort to speak, but it was a long time before he could articulate. Elinor bent over him whispering gently, and at length the troubled smile came back like a flickering light to his face; bending her ear close, she caught the murmur—"My daughter Elinor!" The old, old words that under his pride and error had rested close upon his heart—the one pure watch-word in his devious course. After that his mind wandered a little, more as it might between sleeping and waking than from the effects of delirium. She distinguished several broken sentences; at last she heard Rossitur's name pronounced. That reminded her there was one thing left undone. In his hands remained a paper, if his words had been true, of what nature she could only imagine; it might

afford him the means of working some harm, leaving some stain upon her father's memory. For Elinor knew that henceforth to the world he could never be any thing more. However the illness might terminate, though speech and recollection and the power to move might come back, she realized that as far as a part in the world's course was concerned her father's life had come to an end. She had lost every thing remaining to her in one heavy blow. The hope which might have made her womanhood beautiful had long since died out, almost before she was conscious of its brightness. Every aim and dream had been bound up in her father's career, and there he lay, helpless, shattered, and it seemed to Elinor that her life had come to an end with his. The horrible sense of loneliness, which even in the first bitterness of grief made itself felt, darkened the room like the visible shadow of the inexorable visitant who could not be far off. In losing her father she lost her all; scarcely a human being in the world besides in whose veins ran blood kindred with her own. Her love had been not only the deep tenderness of a daughter, but her ambition, her pride, had centered in him; the strongest powers of her nature had there found their vent. She had nothing besides him to love; other women of her age had mothers, the sweet influence of family ties; she had nothing but him, and a few hours or weeks, at the utmost, might leave her wholly alone. She could only cling fast to the thought poor ignorant Mrs. Olds had once uttered—"God never forgets." She said it over and over; she made it a supplication for help, for resignation, every thing for which she could wish to pray, and her heart could steady itself upon no other prayer; it is so difficult to be still, to have faith in such an hour.

The long night came to an end. With a dull wonder Elinor saw the slow dawn peep in at the closed curtains and recognized that another day had begun. During her watch it had seemed that each moment must cause some vital change; now, weak and exhausted, she comprehended that it was only continued anxiety and suspense. The nurse came again and urged her to lie down, employing the sole plea that could have produced any effect: "You will need all your strength, ma'am; he may be sick a long, long time; you mustn't use it up in the beginning."

It had seemed to her that she was to lose him instantly—that night had looked like the last; there was a kind of hope in the counsel offered. She allowed poor Coralie, who had risen at the break of day, to lead her to her chamber, and once in bed she slept for several hours. When she was up and dressed again Coralie told her that the doctor had come and was holding consultation with two physicians who had accompanied him. She set Coralie to watch that he might not leave the house without her seeing him, and having tried to drink some tea and eat a few morsels, went down stairs and wandered desolately about in the rooms which looked so changed that it appeared impossible only a few hours had elapsed since the black trouble swooped into them. The news of Mr. Grey's illness had found its way into the morning papers—side by side with that last letter—and the house was besieged by inquirers, though, thanks to Henry, people were answered and sent off without Elinor's ears being tortured by the sound of bell or knocker.

After a time Ruth Farnsworth came and Elinor could see her; there was scarcely another woman, besides Rosa, whose presence would not have been absolute martyrdom. Ruth did not attempt to console her; she held her fast in her arms and let her gasp a few dry sobs that were more painful than tears, she told her how often such attacks were recovered from, and thanked her for seeing her. Elinor sat down with a pitiful quiet which she forced herself to preserve lest her last strength should give way. She saw that Ruth looked feverish and unwell, and her throat was so much affected by her cold that her voice was husky and painful.

"But it is nothing," Ruth said; "I shall nurse myself diligently for a day, and I shall be well then. I think I can help you, Elinor, if you will let me come; I am accustomed to sick people, you know. Clive says we'll not go away till Mr. Grey is better." Elinor could feel that she was not entirely alone; the dear sweet face was full of sympathy, and the cheerful, hopeful words were a great comfort. "Clive has telegraphed to the Thorntons," Ruth added. "We knew you could not think of it, and you want them."

"You are very good to me," Elinor answered.

It wrung Ruth's heart to see her patience and humility. In her mind Elinor had been elevated so far above common mortals that it was dreadful to think of the trials which assail others coming near her. "If we only could do something," she said. "But at least you know we share your trouble; it's better than being alone, dear, if we can't help."

It was better; much better. They sat there and talked for some time, and the companionship was good for Elinor. The doctors were still up stairs; there was nothing for Elinor to do, and Ruth knew that it was better for her to be kept occupied even by conversation which might be a little irksome than to be sitting solitary in the oppressive stillness of those great rooms. A photograph of Miss Laidley which graced one of the albums on the table brought up her name, and Ruth told Elinor that she had a reason for wishing to see that beautiful runaway, and was sorely puzzled how to do it.

"They are gone," Elinor said.

"No," replied Ruth; "Mr. Hilton told Clive—it was a secret he said, but he told it, though of course Clive did not ask. They are near the city; in a house that belongs to Mr. Hilton."

Elinor remembered what Rossitur had in his possession and shivered, recalling the hate in his face on that night of their last meeting.

"What is it?" Ruth asked. "Elinor, don't think about them. It was not right of Miss Laidley; but she is so thoughtless."

"I was not thinking of that, Ruth."

"Something troubles you, Elinor. Oh, if you could tell me—if there was any thing Clive or I could do!"

"I don't think there is," she replied; "I don't think any body— Indeed, you must excuse me; I don't quite know what I say, my head is so dizzy."

Ruth drew the poor aching head on her shoulder. All her life Elinor had been supporting somebody; it was very pleasant to be petted now. "Elinor," she whispered, "I—I never told Clive even—but I have something to give Mrs. Rossitur which—I mean I think she will be obliged, and want to thank me. If there is any thing you want done, I might ask her while she is softened—or him."

A favor of them? No, Elinor felt that if the paper held what might prove her own death-warrant she could not beg of them. It might be something that could cause only rumors or annoyance; neither could ever affect her father: for herself she could bear. She was crushed and humbled, but she could not think that a debasement such as that could be right for her even if it could be of any avail.

Ruth comprehended that whatever Elinor wanted she would die ten thousand deaths before she would ask a boon at the hands of that man or his wife. If the face had been that of the famed Grecian statue to which it had so often been compared, there could not have been less show of feeling. "I don't know what it is," she said, fearful to venture, yet unwilling to leave the subject till she discovered if any effort could be in her power; "but, Elinor, if, without telling me, you could let me know whether there is any thing I might do."

"Thank you, Ruth—nothing. I did not hesitate to tell you. Mr. Rossitur I believe holds a paper which I should be glad to have. I shall never ask for it; no, I could not if it were to save my life. I— There, don't let us talk about it; only I did not wish you to think I could not trust you."

"I should not. But I must ask you—it's wicked to trouble you now—but tell me, would it be wrong for me to go to the house and give what I have to Mrs. Rossitur? It has worried me so."

"Certainly not," Elinor said.

"I don't want a secret from Clive, but I'm afraid if I spoke he would object, and I can't keep it any longer. It's nothing of so much importance, but I must give it into her own hands and explain why I have kept it so long."

Those people lingering near? What did it mean? why had Rossitur concealed himself and his wife in this strange manner? Could the paper be something of vital importance, which in the state of her father's brain had only left a vague anxiety? was he waiting to deal some final blow? Elinor's face grew more ghastly as those thoughts rushed through her mind, and

Q

Ruth, seeing it, knew that in some way her peace depended upon getting possession of the paper. She made no further allusion to the matter, and as they very soon heard the doctors descending the stairs, Ruth rose to go.

"I will come back," she said, "dear, dear Elinor." She kissed her and went away, seeing the consulting physicians pass out of the house, while the other went into the apartment where she had left Elinor. Henry was in the hall. It occurred to Ruth to ask him a question—he might know where Mr. Hilton's house was, and now she had a double anxiety to find her way there. Henry did—he always knew everything—he had learned through Mr. Hilton's man that the newly-wedded pair were hidden within the pleasant shades.

"I want to see Mrs. Rossitur," Ruth said; "Henry, if you will please tell the coachman where to drive. Is it far?"

It was not far—not an hour's ride. There would be plenty of time; Clive would be out all the morning. Poor little Ruth got into the carriage, and Henry gave the man directions where he was to go, and it might not have been agreeable to young Mrs. Rossitur could she have heard the whispered answer of the coachman—

"Ho, that 'ouse—know it? Bless your eyes, I've drove Mr. Hilton and his hopera dancers down lots o' times, and I've seen sights there—"

"Chut!" interrupted Henry. "Mr. and Mrs. Rossitur are there; you must drive this lady down."

Ruth leaned back in the carriage as it drove off, somewhat frightened at what she was doing, but certain that it was right. To have a secret from Clive filled her with a sentiment of guilt, but this had been forced upon her, and from the first she had decided that she must be silent. If she told him that she had something Miss Laidley left in the country he would have proposed her sending it, and Ruth knew that she should never forgive herself if it chanced to fall into wrong hands and brought its owner any trouble. There was nothing for it but to go herself—to see Mrs. Rossitur and leave the picture—she could afterward tell Clive where she had been and her reason; he would not be angry, she knew; he would only praise her when it was over. It seemed a long, long drive to Ruth; several times she grew so nervous that if the recollection of Elinor's face had not come up she might have been tempted to order the man to return. At length the carriage drove in at a pair of open gates, and looking out of the window she saw they were approaching a pretty cottage, which in the summer must be wholly concealed from the road by its grove of trees and tall thickets of shrubbery.

The coachman got down and rang the bell. Ruth was standing on the steps when the door opened and a female servant confronted her, evidently much astonished at her appearance. "I want to see Mrs. Rossitur," said Ruth, summoning her courage; and seeing by the woman's face that she was about to deny the presence of that lady in the house, she added, "She is here, I know. Tell her Mrs. Farnsworth wishes to speak with her a moment; she will see me."

"Good gracious!" exclaimed a voice, and the Angel, who, roused by the unusual sound of the bell, had been leaning over the banisters in hopes something fresh in the way of romance was about to happen, rushed down lovelier than ever in a blue morning-dress, pushed past the servant and dragged Ruth into the hall. "Why, Mrs. Farnsworth," she exclaimed; "I never was so astonished! How did you discover we were here? We've run away, you know—I suppose it's all over the country—but how did you find out where we were?"

Ruth waited till they were in the drawing-room and the door closed, then she said hastily —"You must excuse me—"

"Oh, don't say a word," interrupted Mrs. Rossitur, who was blooming and in high spirits; "I am so glad to see you. Isn't this a pretty room? There's the sweetest little conservatory back—is it not romantic? We are hidden here just like people in a novel; but we're going to-morrow—I am so glad! Do tell me what people say! When did you come to Washington?"

"Only yesterday; I have seen scarcely any one."

"There have been ever so many paragraphs in the papers," Genevieve continued; "have you seen any of them? But of course—ça va sans dire. There was a long letter from somebody yesterday in the Herald—the lovely heiress, the ward of—such hints and romance and— I wonder what I did with the paper? I had it here."

"I saw the letter," Ruth answered, marvelling at Mrs. Rossitur's delight, for while reading the gossip she had pitied the poor girl and thought how wretched the notoriety would make her.

"Wasn't it charming?" cried Genevieve. "I always said I would not be married in a prosy, dozy way. I wore a white satin, high neck—it was like what they call a special providence, my having it made—and there was such haste and secrecy — ciel, how nervous I was! But how did you find us out?"

"I wanted very much to see you," Ruth said, evading the question.

"You dear little thing! I suppose you like romance too and wanted to see how I would look after being run away with. I am happy as a queen—it's like a novel exactly. But I am glad we are going away—I know I should get dreadfully bored here. I am such a sensitive creature—I must have change and excitement, else I get nervous—"

"I was afraid you might think my visit an intrusion—"

"Now don't make excuses," broke in the Angel; "I am delighted to see you—Leighton will be too. He's busy now—old Frost, the lawyer, came a few moments before you; they're in the dining-room."

Ruth had no desire to see Mr. Rossitur; she wanted to get away; she was anxious to tell her small secret, and hesitating how to begin for fear of Genevieve's being distressed by her knowledge.

"I mean to tell Leighton you are here," said the Angel; "may be it will hurry that nasty old Frost a little."

"No, please," returned Ruth; "I came—I wanted to see you—"

"Of course you did or you wouldn't have come, you darling! Oh, I must show you the house—there's such a romance. Some man loved a woman whose husband treated her dreadfully—she was to run away and stay here till she got a divorce and could marry the man she loved. Poor thing, she was killed—on a railway or something. Isn't it delightfully romantic? Every time I am alone I think she is going to appear, and I scream." The story was based on a vague account Rossitur had invented to satisfy her questions, and she embellished it with her usual talent. Then she flew off to something else. "Your coming will make Elinor Grey furious—horrid thing!"

"I wanted to see you about a little matter," Ruth went on rapidly. "I have something of yours that I wanted to give you."

"Of mine?" repeated Mrs. Rossitur "What on earth is it? You dear, little, mysterious *chouette*, what on earth is it?"

"It was given me a good while ago," Ruth proceeded; "you must excuse my having kept it. I should have sent it by mail, but we were expecting every week to come, and I thought you would rather I gave it into your own hands; I meant to do right."

. "Why, what can it be? I shall die of curiosity if you don't tell."

"A—a picture," faltered Ruth.

"Whose picture?" asked Genevieve, for with her customary recklessness she had forgotten the matter, which had caused her a good deal of uneasiness while the incident was fresh in her mind.

"It is your own," Ruth said.

Genevieve began to laugh. "Oh, you dear innocent bird—you can't be used to subterfuges! You wanted to see me and I don't wonder; I am always *jolie* about people who do any thing out of the common way. It doesn't need any excuses. I tell you again I'm delighted—*voila*. You know we are going to Paris? I do hope the elopement will get in the French papers. Fancy how it will make me stared at and talked about."

Her levity was incomprehensible to Ruth, but she could not wonder concerning it until she got the secret off her mind. "Please to listen," said she earnestly.

"*Madonna mia!* how serious you look," cried Genevieve, laughing again. "Heavens! you've not come to read me a lecture for running away and having a secret marriage? Oh you sweetness—you unsophisticated love—*une vraie princesse de fée!* I vow I must call Leighton."

She was rising, but Ruth caught her dress. "Please don't," she said; "wait a moment. You don't quite understand. It is—the—the picture that little Tilman boy was to bring you—that's what I have."

"O the blessed Saints!" exclaimed the Angel. "I had forgotten it! Give it to me—give it to me."

Ruth took the photograph out of her pocket, carefully sealed in a letter envelope. Mrs. Rossitur seized her prize, tore off the wrapper, gave one glance at the picture to be certain it was the one she now remembered with such unpleasant sensations, and with another cry, half fear, half acting, enjoying the scene in the midst of her fright, as she must any thing like a mystery, ran to the fire, held the card in the blaze till it almost scorched her fingers, then threw the blackened fragments under the grate. "If Leighton had seen it he would have killed me—he's the only human being I ever feared a bit," she exclaimed. "How did you get it?"

"The boy gave it to me—"

"The little wretch! He ought to be burned alive."

"No, no—wait. He was not so much to blame. He was very sick and thought he might die; he begged me to give it to you and say he never had told any body else. He dropped it in the mud and did not dare take it at the time; then he said it was so pretty he kept it to look at because he didn't know what else to do with it."

"Well, it is burned now," said Genevieve, with a flutter of relief. "So he kept it because it was pretty—the little goose! But it was only nonsense—you must not think it was any thing else."

"I am sure it was not," Ruth said.

"He wanted me to sit for it—I did not reflect—I am so heedless—such a baby! Oh, your husband'll not tell?"

"He does not know—indeed I never mentioned having seen it to any human being," replied Ruth, and the Angel, notwithstanding her very limited faith in the protestations of most people, saw that she was telling the truth. "I never looked at it after; I sealed it up and was only waiting an opportunity to give it to you; I felt guilty at keeping it so long."

"You're a darling," cried Genevieve, kissing her enthusiastically. "I adore you! When I get to Paris I'll send you the loveliest bracelet! I shall not forget—I'm the most grateful little thing in the world—all heart! I feel things too much."

"You need not be grateful," said Ruth; "I only did what was honest."

"What a quaint creature—you dear Red Riding Hood—honest! But I tell you what, lots of women would have done something spiteful in your place. I know them—nasty cats! Bless me, if Elinor Grey had laid hands on it!"

"Indeed, indeed, she would not have made you any trouble."

"Oh, I don't know—she was so jealous.

Horrid dragon she is, with her airs and graces—but you're a love! Why, I would do any thing in the world for you—sell my soul to please you! Oh, what can I do? Tell me something I can do."

Ruth, with the recollection of Elinor's words in her mind, answered quickly—"You can do something if you will."

"Oh!" said the Angel, and her countenance fell; she had not expected her pretty gush of gratitude to be taken so literally; "but you see I'm shut up here—hidden. When I get to Paris—oh, you'll see, when I get to Paris!"

"There's a paper of Mr. Grey's that your husband has," said Ruth.

"How do you know?" cried Genevieve. "Are you an artful thing after all—pretending to love me and be kind? Did Elinor get you to do this?"

"No, no; but she's in such trouble—I thought perhaps you would persuade your husband to let me have that paper."

"I'll not do any thing for Elinor or him either—I hate them both! She's a deceitful, treacherous creature, and he—"

"Oh, don't you know that Mr. Grey is very ill—dying?"

"Dying?" repeated Genevieve, always frightened at that word. "You don't mean it—you say it to terrify me."

"Indeed I do not; I thought you might have seen it in this morning's paper. He had a paralytic stroke yesterday, and there is no hope of his recovery."

"How dreadful!" exclaimed Genevieve with a shudder, a good deal frightened and shocked. "Have you seen Elinor?"

"Yes; she doesn't know yet that he can't get well, but the doctor told my husband last night."

Genevieve shivered from head to foot and grew pale; her dread of death was so excessive that to have it come near any one she knew filled her with terror. "Don't tell me," she pleaded; "it frightens me! Why, he was as well as we are—don't tell me."

"But I know you will be sorry for Elinor in her trouble."

"Oh, yes, I am; but then she has such nerves—she is iron. Why, I should have dropped dead! I fainted six times when poor papa—Oh, don't talk about such horrors."

"But if you could get me that paper—if you know about it."

"Yes, I know; Leighton came across it this morning while he was sorting his letters—his things are all here—and he showed it to me. It isn't much—just some memorandums in Mr. Grey's writing—but he said when the election came—" She checked herself, remembering that he would be furious at her revelations. She could not think that it was a matter of much importance; at another time the fact that she could annoy Elinor or her father by keeping it would have made her resolute not to give it up, but she was softened and alarmed by this sudden news concerning him.

"She did not know I meant to ask you," Ruth proceeded. "But she seemed anxious; and when you said you were so much obliged to me for bringing the picture I thought perhaps you would let me have the paper."

Genevieve leaned back in her chair, clapped her hands, and burst into a fit of laughter that astonished Ruth. "Well, you are the most innocent little thing," she exclaimed. "Why, where were your wits? You might have held fast to the picture and driven your own bargain—threatened me with going to my husband if I did not give up the paper."

Ruth's eyes widened with wonder. "You are jesting," she said; "that would have been very mean and base. The picture was yours and I had promised to restore it. I had no right to use it in any way."

"Ah, mais c'est trop fort!" cried Genevieve. "You are too good for this world, that's clear; fit for what the Idol calls the forest of Ardent—that blessed old dunce! Why, don't you know any other human being would have forced me to do what was wanted?"

"I think not," said Ruth gently; "I hope not. But now that you know Mr. Grey is so ill, you will let me have it. You would not keep back any thing that could ease his mind when he is dying."

"Don't speak that dreadful word," exclaimed Genevieve, shivering again; "it almost gives me a spasm. I'll get the paper—you may have it. Wait here—it's of no importance, really."

"But very little things are of importance when one is ill," Ruth answered, following up her advantage. "If you could see him—"

"Oh don't, don't—you'll make me scream—I can't think about it! I'll get the paper—bless me, any thing!—wait."

She flew out of the room, and Ruth sat uttering mental thanksgivings over this unexpected success, so overjoyed at the thought of being able to relieve Elinor's mind in any way that she regarded the childish bride more leniently than ever. Mrs. Rossitur made sure that her husband was still closeted with the lawyer, then up stairs she sped and sought the paper. She had been leaning over Rossitur as he arranged his desk and remembered where he laid the note in an envelope by itself. She took it out of the box, arranged the other letters again, and ran down to Ruth, holding up the coveted treasure as she entered. "There," she said; "now am I not a good little thing?"

"I can't thank you enough," exclaimed Ruth, seizing it and at once sealing the envelope.

"Why, what are you doing?" demanded Genevieve.

"I have sealed it."

"But you haven't looked at it—read it."

"It is not mine," Ruth said, pressing the edges hard together and placing the letter carefully in her pocket.

"Of all the odd creatures I ever saw you are the oddest," exclaimed Genevieve, and her surprise was the most genuine sensation she had felt in many a day.

Ruth had accomplished every thing for which she came, and more than she had dared to hope, and was eager to go.

"Do stay," said Genevieve; "I want you to see Leighton, please."

"I can not; my husband would not know what had become of me; besides, I am not well."

"You don't look well," returned Genevieve, for the first time observing that, having as usual been too full of herself to notice the appearance of her visitor. "How heavy your eyes are, and you are very pale, and so dreadfully hoarse."

"Yes; I have a severe cold, but I think it is better this morning, only my throat is exceedingly painful still."

"Oh, good gracious! I hope I'll not get it. I'm so sorry I kissed you. Why didn't you tell me?" cried Genevieve.

"I do not think I am infectious," replied Ruth, laughing. "Now good-bye. I hope you may be very happy."

"I shall be—no fear! I suppose Elinor is furious. How she must want to tear my hair! She was mad in love with Leighton, but he never cared for her and he let her see it."

"Poor Elinor has no thought for any body but her father," Ruth answered gravely, flushing a little.

"Peutêtre! However, I'm not revengeful. I forgive her—I can afford to; I got the best of her every way. Good-bye—I'll not kiss you. Tell every body how happy I am, and that we are off for Paris." She kept stopping in the hall for last words; the opening of a door made Ruth afraid of seeing some one else; she hurried out of the house and was driven away.

"Who the deuce was that, Angel?" asked Rossitur, coming into the hall.

"A visitor—you'd never guess," replied Genevieve.

Mr. Frost was taking his leave; when he had gone Genevieve put her arm coaxingly in her husband's. "Well," said he, "we can be off to-night." She cooed with delight. "Every thing is ready;" he continued; "we shall have to stay in New York—"

"O Leighton," she interrupted; "Mr. Grey is very ill."

"Yes, Frost told me."

He had been utterly confounded by the news the lawyer brought; information that Mr. Grey's lawyers in New York would put him in immediate possession of his wife's fortune—no attempt at delay or compromise. He could not understand it; he knew that Pluto had failed, and at the moment when he expected to taste his revenge came this message delivered to the lawyer by Miss Grey in her father's name. He only knew that he had been overreached; in some manner Elinor had done it; her fortune must have been in a state to be rendered more quickly available than he had supposed. But his rage and wicked resentment had been a good deal checked by the news concerning Mr. Grey. He had no wish to fight a dying man; it was not pleasant to face the reflection that his seizure was caused by the bad news—that some time he might have to face the recollection that he had on his soul not only one man's ruin but another's murder. He did as most people do—he did not think. Pluto was going to make shipwreck any way—he was virtually bankrupt weeks before; Mr. Grey had been threatened a long time with that attack; what folly to be frightened at himself; he was not fate; he had done nothing in reality.

"Who was that went out?" he asked.

"Mrs. Farnsworth," replied Genevieve.

"In the name of goodness! what brought her?"

"She wanted to see me—of course."

He looked puzzled. "Did the Greys send her?" he asked.

"Certainly not! There he is out of his head or worse, and— Why, she wanted to see me. Are we really, really going to-night?"

"Yes; there is nothing to stop for."

"I must have Juanita put up what things are out," said Genevieve.

"And I must finish sorting my papers; old Frost interrupted me."

"I'll do it, dear," said Genevieve sweetly.

"No, thanks, pussy," replied he, laughing: "you would get them in such confusion I should never find any thing again."

She was frightened at the probability of his discovering what she had done, still she had acuteness enough to reason that he was less likely to be violent than if they had been longer married; besides, she saw that he was greatly shocked by the news about Mr. Grey. Things must take their course—in certain ways she was a thorough fatalist. They went up stairs, and Genevieve flitted about instead of summoning Juanita while Rossitur collected the remainder of his papers in order. He heard her talk—he answered her pleasantly enough—the spell of her youth and her prettiness was fresh upon his sensuous nature, but that was not an agreeable half-hour to Rossitur. He was glad to chatter —to get away from the image of the dying man which kept rising in a ghastly manner. Revenge did not taste so sweet as he had expected; it was all different. He had thought to have Elinor appealing to him for mercy—for a little time; here every thing about the money was straight enough. It looked ugly — the click of the telegraph sounded in his ears. Curse it, a man was not to be haunted in broad day-light with sights and sounds that were fancy after all! He stopped in his employment, went down into the dining-room and drank a glass of wine—he had already taken several since the news reached him—and came back to jest and laugh with his pretty wife and shut out every thought besides the golden fact that the wealth and luxury he had craved were at length in his grasp.

Genevieve was unusually playful and bewitching, but she was very nervous and could not help bringing on the discovery she dreaded.

"Where did you lay that paper of Mr. Grey's?" she asked, bending over his chair as he examined the desk.

"Here," returned he, lifting some letters. "No—why—"

"What is the matter?" she asked, as he began pulling the papers out.

"It is gone!" he exclaimed; gave one more search, glanced up at her and cried out—"You gave it to that woman."

In an instant Genevieve was on her knees before him, clinging to his hands, sobbing, half acting and half terrified. "I could not help it! She said he was dying—I could not refuse! Leighton, darling, don't be angry—remember that he is dying."

It was fortunate for her that he did remember it; fortunate that something had been all the morning stinging him like an awakened conscience; that in his swift thought while he sat gazing down at her with a look she had never before seen in his face he remembered there were certain restrictions upon a portion of the wealth which he wanted to coax her into removing; that the influence of her delicate loveliness had not had time in the least to pall upon his changeable nature.

"Leighton, Leighton!" she sobbed, made wholly earnest by that black glance. "Say you forgive me! Oh, you'll kill me if you look like that! Any way, that nasty Elinor had to beg for it—that's some comfort."

It was a little; besides, the paper could only have been made an annoyance at the time of an election; Mr. Grey was past suffering from such trouble now. He restrained himself, raised Genevieve and kissed away her tears. "I am not angry," he said.

"Sure—will you forgive me?" she pleaded.

"Yes; but, Genevieve, don't you ever so much as peep among my papers again." There was something in the voice that, following the look which had been in his face for an instant, gave Genevieve an internal shiver; she comprehended that she had found her master.

"I never will," she said humbly, without trying to make a bit of a scene. "Don't be angry—I do love you."

In a short time they were laughing and talking gayly; she looked so fair as she hung about him that he could not feel harsh toward her. He was not sorry, in spite of his hate for Elinor, to think that his conscience was somewhat lightened in regard to the dying man. As for fully crediting his wife's story, he did not; he knew her too thoroughly for that; he was not willing to lose an opportunity of showing her that he understood her perfectly, and that she might expect the myriads of artifices she always had on hand to be read at once with as much ease as this.

"Angel," said he.

"Yes, love."

"Tell me the truth; what made you give up that paper?"

"O Leighton, when I told you! Don't talk about it any more—you said you forgave me."

"So I do, chick; but what little hold had Farnsworth's wife on you that enabled her to do the business?"

"Hold? What an expression! Indeed, Leighton, this is really insulting," said she, drawing her head away from the hand which was playing carelessly with her hair, and looking virtuously hurt.

"Now, Angel," said he, laughing, "don't you do the injured virtue dodge too strong or I shall believe it is something of consequence; too much indignation is always suspicious."

"Oh, you dear, you wouldn't believe any thing cruel of poor little me, I am sure."

"No; but what did she offer in return for the paper?"

"Oh, you wicked thing, with your suspicions always ready!" cried Genevieve, re-assured by his good-nature.

"Yes, I know. Just tell me; you can call me names after," said he, giving her hair a little pull.

"Ah, you hurt me! There, I'll call you all the loves and goodies in the world, if you'll let me get up. There are so many things to do. Where is that dreadful Juanita?"

"Never mind Juanita," returned Rossitur, laughing still, but detaining her as she tried to rise from the arm of his chair. "I say, what did she give?"

"You persevering, atrocious—— O Leighton, I shan't be ready!"

"Plenty of time, dear; there are always trains, but the reason for confession can't be passed over."

"Oh, I've bitten my tongue! Please let me go! Dear me, Leighton, you've a dimple in your chin—I never noticed it before—let me kiss it."

"To kiss a dimple in my chin is reserved for a well-behaved, straightforward little Angel," said he, holding her hands. "Now confess, witch."

"There, then—a letter I left in a drawer at her house, from that foolish Walters," said Genevieve suddenly. "I was afraid you would be angry, so I was glad enough to get it."

"Honor?" said Rossitur.

"Yes, indeed—honor! I don't fib—look." By good luck she had such a missive in her pocket; she had found it among some scraps she was burning that morning, and remembered now to make use of it. She held up the letter —sure enough, there was Walters's signature. "Now are you satisfied?" she asked.

"Perfectly! No thank you," as she offered to let him see more; "I don't want to read the trash."

"He wrote beautiful letters," said Genevieve indignantly; "and he was crazy about me."

"I dare say. I just wanted to make you own up. I thought such disinterested conduct on your part must have some righteous motive at the bottom."

"But you're not angry?"

"Not a bit. The paper wasn't much. Let it go; I never could use it now. But you did confess, eh?"

"Yes; you bad thing—always getting at the truth in spite of me! I think I hate you—only I love you." She kissed his hand and went off carolling a merry song, in high delight to think that not only was the matter safely settled, but that she had the best of it—she had deceived him, after all.

They started for New York that night, and on meeting the lawyers Rossitur found every thing straight. He could not tell how it had been brought about, only he felt that by some means Elinor Grey had made his treachery useless. They sailed in a few days for France, both so full of excitement at the change and novelty brought into their lives that real happiness would have looked very tame by the side of it. Before leaving town the Angel sent a gift to the Banger by express—omitting to pay the charge of carriage. The present proved to be a gold pencil-case, at sight of which the Banger was in a tremendous rage. She lavished a few wild flowers of prairie rhetoric upon the head of the absent seraph, but finally laughed at her own discomfiture, and revenged herself by exhibiting the souvenir to her visitors and telling the story of Mrs. Rossitur's meanness, which was a great satisfaction.

CHAPTER XLV.

GOING AWAY.

ON reaching the city Ruth drove to Mr. Grey's house, and Henry, seeing her anxiety, did for her what he would not have done for any other woman in Washington—went up to let his mistress know that she was there.

Elinor came down stairs, whiter than ever if possible, but very calm. The physician had told her the truth. Her father might live only a few hours; the feeble thread of life might be spun out for a few weeks, even months, but there was no hope. The moment Ruth looked at her she knew that Elinor had heard the verdict, but she did not intrude with ill-timed sympathy.

"I have that paper," were the first words; "I have seen Mrs. Rossitur—she gave it to me herself." Elinor could scarcely credit the fact even when Ruth placed the envelope in her hands. "I told her you did not know I meant to ask. She was sorry about your father. Look at it—to be certain."

"He had but one," returned Elinor, shrinking from a perusal of the lines. She opened the envelope, ascertained that the paper was in her father's writing, and put it away. "I can't say any thing," she went on in a cold, hollow voice; "but you know how I thank you."

"Don't, Elinor, don't. Think what I owe you! O my poor dear, if I could comfort you—if I could bear your pain!"

"You are a good woman, Ruth; God bless you!" Ruth clung to her; they both sobbed a little, but were soon quiet again. "There is no hope," Elinor whispered; "you knew it."

"The doctor told Clive. O Elinor, I can only say what you said to me—it was such a comfort—God never forgets."

"Yes—only I'm so blind and deaf." She shook from head to foot, but repressed her emotion and said, "You look very ill, Ruth; go home at once and to bed."

"I shall be better to-morrow—it's only my cold," Ruth insisted. "I am so glad that is settled."

"But you ought not to have gone, you were too ill. If I had to think you made yourself worse by trying to do me a favor—"

"No, no; I had to go—it was for Genevieve herself—but it's over. I'll not keep you now; to-morrow I shall be able to come and help you. Be sure to expect me."

A few loving words and they parted. Elinor followed her into the hall; as Ruth looked back, something made Elinor go up to her with an outgush of feeling at variance with her usual reserve and clasp her again in her arms. "God bless you!" she whispered.

"And you," returned Ruth. "It seems wicked to think of myself now, but O Elinor, I have been so happy, and your coming was the commencement; it seems like your work."

She went away and Elinor returned to her lonely watch. Late that night Tom and Rosa arrived, and their presence was a great comfort.

When Clive returned to the hotel toward evening he found Ruth lying on the sofa in their gloomy parlor. He entered so softly that she did not hear the door open, lying in a sort of stupor which would neither release its hold nor allow her to fall asleep. He was startled by the deathly whiteness of her face and stood irresolute, not certain whether she slept. Some strange perception of his presence, of which she was always conscious, made her lift her eyes. He hurried forward and she tried to raise herself and greet him with the familiar smile.

"Don't stir," he said quickly; "my darling child, you are worse."

"No, I think not," she answered slowly; "my head aches frightfully and my throat is very painful. If I could only get to sleep I should be better." He leaned over her, laid her head gently back on the pillows, smoothing her hair from her face, and again she looked up and smiled. "Thank you," she said; "I believe your very touch makes me better at once." Her voice was husky and broken, and he could see that the effort to speak caused her intense pain.

"I ought not to have left you," he exclaimed, in sudden self-reproach; "but you seemed so much better this morning."

"Yes; I thought it was all over. Indeed, Clive, I am not really ill. I went out; I suppose that has irritated my throat."

"I wish I had begged you to stay in the house."

"I wanted to see Elinor so much, Clive," she said, getting hold of his hand and speaking with her eyes closed, though the smile of content was on her lips still. "Poor Elinor! She ran after me and kissed me—I am glad."

She was stopped by a cough, not violent, but accompanied by such struggles for breath that Clive was greatly alarmed. "You must let me call Dr. Meadows," he said.

"I don't believe it's worth while, Clive; if I could sleep, I should be quite well. Why, you don't think I am very sick, do you?"

"At least he can give you something to relieve your throat and make you breathe more easily."

He insisted, and, as ever, she was ready to comply with his wishes, though she could not believe there was much the matter; the very nature of the insidious disease which held her in its clutch rendering her unconscious of her state. Clive went out and dispatched a messenger for the physician, requesting him to come without delay, and with each instant his anxiety increased. He was not in the least accustomed to sickness, and Ruth had always been so well and active that it appeared impossible any serious illness could have seized her, but the white face and the heavy eyes, so changed except in their look of love, terrified him beyond measure.

"Come and sit by me," Ruth said feebly, as he returned to the room, and again he took his station by the couch.

"You mustn't try to talk, dear," he said; "I think it makes your throat worse."

She shook her head. "I'm sure I am better now you have come," she answered. "I want to tell you—please, Clive, don't think it was wrong."

"What is it? You couldn't do any thing wrong, childie."

"My Clive!" touching her lips to the hand she had once more taken and was holding on her heart. "I went to see Mrs. Rossiter—I had something of hers she left in the country."

"My little one, that long drive! How wicked I was to leave you."

"Don't, don't!" she returned, becoming excited at once, the ill effects of which were apparent in her breathing. "Please never think that—it makes me worse than any thing—promise."

"Yes, dear; only be quiet."

"I was so well—I didn't think it could hurt me. There was something Elinor wanted, too—a paper. She didn't know I meant to get it—but I did." She stopped; her respiration was so difficult that he raised her head on his shoulder, supporting her in his arms. "This is better—it rests me," she whispered. "I'll be well to-morrow. My dear old boy, he looks so frightened."

It was no marvel that the color left his face and the dark terror crept into his eyes; the possible nature of her illness had occurred to him—that dreadful malady which he knew only by name, which he could hardly utter in his thoughts. He listened eagerly for steps; the doctor ought to have come, but Ruth was lying quite still and he could not disturb her by getting up.

"Clive," she whispered; "I told Elinor how happy I had been—when she came back to kiss me. We are so sorry for her, Clive."

"Yes, my little one."

"So happy," she continued, going back to the words she had spoken and nestling closer to him. "Clive, it can't be wicked! Oh, if I had been in heaven all this last year I couldn't have been happier."

"My little Ruth!"

"I like to be that," she went on, in the same slow whisper; "to be like a child—to be spoiled—O my Clive!" She was stopped anew by that painful cough, which hurt her so much that in the effort to repress it she seemed suffocating. Clive got a glass of water and held it to her lips; she tried to swallow a little, shook her head and signed him to take it away.

At that instant there was a knock at the door, and Clive opened it to find the physician standing there. A few whispered words passed between them, but they heard Ruth's voice in a hoarse whisper—"Clive, Clive!" The instant she could not see him she became uneasy, trying to lift her weary head and look about.

"Yes, dear," Clive said, hurrying back. "It is the doctor, Ruth; he will give you something to relieve your throat at once."

The whiteness of her face was broken now by twin spots of crimson that had risen in her cheeks, making its lividness more striking, and her eyes were bright with fever through their heaviness. The doctor followed Clive and stood beside her—she motioned him to bend down. "Tell Clive I am not very sick," she said. "It is only my throat, and as if there was a great weight here," laying her hand on her chest. The doctor touched her forehead lightly, felt her pulse, and saying something about a severe cold, asked her to let him see her throat. As he laid her head back on the pillows, and she closed her eyes, Clive looked at him and read the realization of his worst fears in the grave face. "Tell him I shall be better to-morrow, please," Ruth said without opening her eyes, but searching for Clive's hand. The physician made some slight answer, sat down at a table and took out his case of tiny vials. He came back bringing a wine-glass which held some drops of a dark-colored liquid diluted with water.

"The doctor wants you to take this, Ruth," Clive said. She looked up obediently, let him raise her head and tried to swallow; the effort brought such acute pain that she uttered a little cry. After the convulsive breathing grew easier Clive laid her head down again, and whispering that he was going for something in the next room, motioned the physician away.

"Tell me at once," said he.

"It is diphtheria, Mr. Farnsworth."

"Is there any hope?"

"It would be only cruel to deceive you—I fear not."

Clive stood still while the physician summoned assistance and called for the dismal paraphernalia of requirements, the bare sight of which is such a horror to any body that has watched in a sickroom where the fearful malady held sway.

"You must tell her she is very ill and not to be frightened at what we do," the doctor said.

Clive went back; she was lying motionless; the stupor was coming over her again—the doctor signed Clive to rouse her. "Ruth," he said, trying to make his voice calm and natural, "I want to lift you up—the doctor has to do something to your throat."

The change in his voice pierced through the dull weight on her brain; she looked up wildly. "Am I so sick, Clive?"

"We hope you will be better soon. You must be patient, even if he gives you great pain —it is for me, Ruth."

"For you, Clive, for you."

I need not and I can not detail the suffering of the next two hours, and, most moving of all, Ruth's fortitude, her thoughtfulness for Clive even then. Every thing had been done; a friend of Clive's stopping in the hotel had heard of Ruth's illness and come at once. They had worked over the sufferer with the patient energy of desperation—there was nothing left in mortal power.

The last attempt had been so excruciating that the stupor following lasted longer than any time before. She was lying back in Clive's arms, such a heavy, lifeless weight; suddenly she opened her eyes. "I'm not dying, Clive," she gasped; "I'm not dying?"

It was half an exclamation, half an inquiry. He could not speak—could only hold her fast to his heart as she repeated his name. He saw the doctor look at him—then he and the lady attendant went softly into the adjoining room and left the husband and wife alone. Clive knew what he meant.

"Did they go out, Clive? Are we alone?"

"Yes, Ruth."

"If I'm dying, tell me, Clive—I can bear it from you." There was an instant's hush; her labored breathing had grown so quiet that Clive could hear the ticking of his watch. She waited a little. His very silence answered her question. He felt her shiver slightly, felt the hands that held his tighten their grasp, then relax—he saw her lips move and caught the broken words of prayer. "God knows best," she said faintly; "he has been very good to us, Clive." With perfect submission she had borne every trial in the years gone by—with the same sweet patience she yielded to this last fiat. "Don't let them try any thing more, Clive," she said; "it only hurts me—let me stay alone with you."

"O my God, have mercy!" broke from his lips.

"Don't, Clive, don't! Put my arm over your neck. My Clive, I have been so happy." She was forgetting the pain, death itself, every thing, in her desire to comfort him. "Always remember that, Clive—perfectly happy. Don't shiver, dear, don't sob. I shall not be far away —think of that, Clive. I didn't want to die—I was so happy here—but God knows best—say it, Clive, say it." Oh, he could not say it. With his agony, his remorse coming up afresh, so little time given for atonement, how could he yield? "Say it, Clive," she repeated.

As her lips again feebly framed the words, he forced himself to repeat them with her—"God knows best."

"That is right, Clive," she said; "it will be easier now. O Clive, just before we came from home I dreamed an angel appeared and told me I must go, and I saw you and was so full of pain to leave you, and then—I don't remember what I saw, but I knew it was right and best, and I was at peace—as I am now, Clive." He wanted her forgiveness once more—the re-assurance of her happiness, but he could not bear to ask, lest he should trouble her. "Not a cloud, not a break," she said. "Clive, God has been so good—he gave me a foretaste of heaven here. Kiss me, Clive—hold me close." She lay still in his arms for a little, then she went on—"I tried to pray—I have asked God not to let me be wicked—I am going to him—it can't be wrong to give you these last moments—hold me close to your heart, close." If he could have done so, or have gone forth with her—his Ruth, his little Ruth! "You'll not be dreary when you think about me, Clive — you will know I am happy. Kiss me, Clive. It seems very light—is it day already?"

"No, dear."

"The light—look, Clive—the light!" Her head sank lower on his shoulder—her eyes were raised — the glory which she saw, invisible to him, was reflected in her face. "Do they want me, Clive?" she whispered. "It is not far—so bright, so bright. Your name last—I love you, Clive."

A sudden relaxation in every muscle of the slender frame—the head drooped lower—all was still. "Ruth, Ruth!" he called. There was no response. He looked and saw that he held in his arms only a still white form. Ruth could not answer him any more—she had gone forth with the angels.

CHAPTER XLVI.

THE TABLES TURNED.

THE panic in Wall Street, which had been spreading for weeks, was deepened by the failure of Pluto's house; trouble and dismay brooded over the great city that has no medium in any thing, knows only the extremes of reckless prosperity and overwhelming disaster. Mrs. Hackett reached her home to find it a howling wilderness of confusion, and Pluto so desolate under the shock that the full truth impressed itself upon her. Up to that moment she had tried to believe that there was some hope; it seemed impossible that actual ruin could have befallen them, for however much she might talk in her poetical moments of theirs being a union of mind and matter, the Idol had unlimited faith in his powers and what she was wont to term his "fisical genius." The morning after her arrival she sat alone in her dressing-room. Pluto had departed to survey his countless wrecks and try to steady his senses sufficiently to see what was to be done next. The Idol was almost surprised to find her magnificence still about her; she had gone to bed so completely crushed that she would not have been astonished to have wakened in some barren hovel, or at least in some such plain, out-of-the-way abode as that in which she and Pluto had commenced their career, a whole life back, a life which had been forgotten for years before opening success taught her to aspire.

With all her follies, the Idol was not a fool, and she was generosity and justice personified. She and Pluto had held a long conversation before they slept, and it was a little comfort for her to know that she could do something. There had been investments enough made in her name during the past years to have contented a score of families with moderate desires—stocks and bonds, and tenements of every description, besides the great palace in town, with its regal chests of plate, and the Castle up in the country, which for dimensions and splendor might have satisfied an exiled sovereign as a retreat; indeed, in the point of warmth and modern comforts it was decidedly preferable to the old chateaus where those uncrowned unfortunates usually find shelter. It was something to feel that she could help Pluto in any way; he was only overwhelmed, not crushed; her counsels, fervent if very ungrammatical in her excitement, her faith, strong as ever in his genius, expressed in Spenserian stanzas without the rhymes, had helped to restore his courage; he wanted now to free his name that he might begin another career. The Idol was ready to give every thing she held in her right—houses, bonds, jewels, the very shoes off her feet; unlike many women in her situation, who in such emergencies rumor reports to have gone about in dashing new carriages to receive the condolences of their friends.

The Idol sat with her breakfast before her, but the chocolate was poison, the French roll dust and ashes, the variety of delicacies with which her servitors had tried to tempt her appetite, gall and bitterness. She was busy thinking that perhaps she should be obliged to drink corn coffee out of a tin mug and stir it with a pewter spoon, and she glanced at the array of Sèvres china and gold breakfast-service, and felt that it was hard. There was a loud ring at the door-bell—it seemed to the Idol that it had rung unceasingly since her return, though out of the host that had feasted in her halls, and danced or been trodden on, according to their age, in countless Germans in her ball-room, there was not a soul to come near her in her loneliness. People are so sorry for their acquaintance in misfortune — words would be a mockery, calls an insult, therefore they are careful not to intrude. Not only a ring at the bell, clamorous, vicious, and prolonged, but voices in the hall so loud, and one at least so sharp, that it pierced even to the Idol's chamber. The door of her dressing-room opened, a servant looking bewildered and frightened, dishevelled as to his hair and disarranged as to his attire, as though he had just had very much the worst of it in a hand-to-hand combat, appeared, saying confusedly—

"It ain't my fault—she will come in."

"Of course I will," squealed a voice from the head of the stairs; "that's what I've come for. Here, you, get out of the way!"

"I can't see any body—I will not see any body," groaned the poor Idol, rising hastily from her chair.

In spite of her assertions, in spite of new protestations from the dishevelled domestic, there was a rush of female garments, the unlucky retainer was swept aside as by a wind, and amid a shower of puffs and sniffs Mrs. Piffit danced into the room, snorting—"Of course I'll come in! Get out of the way! Can't see me—won't see me? I'd like to catch her at it! I'm Mrs. Piffit, the writer—go where I please—say what I like. Keep me out, indeed!" She stopped to catch breath and confronted the Idol with fresh sniffs and a fire of furious winks. The servant seemed to think he had done his part, and retreated to enter into an examination of the injuries he had received from Piffit's claws, whose first greeting had been a box on his left ear, followed by a vigorous poke in the region of his liver.

"What do you want?" exclaimed the Idol. "How dare you force yourself into my room in this way?"

"None of that," wheezed Mrs. Piffit; "none of that. I want my money—I will have my money—give me my money!" In her struggle with the servant her bonnet had fallen back—the flat reticule hung on her arm—in one hand she held the green umbrella, arrayed in a new dress, and as she spoke she pounded the floor with its foot, like a dingy enchantress trying to raise diabolical aid. "Give me my money," repeated she; "I will have my money!"

"I haven't your money," cried the Idol, her wrath giving way to a kind of terror at the spectacle before her; for the stumpy woman so puffed and blew, there was such menace in her look, such vigor in the way she pounded the floor, that it was enough to have troubled a clearer head than the miserable Idol could that morning boast.

"You haven't my money? Don't dare to say it! It's here and I'll have it — I'm Mrs. Piffit, the writer—never say isn't to me. I told him I would! The nasty brute tried to stop me —wouldn't let me up. I choked him — I'd have choked a legion such; yes, I'd have done it if they had been a legion of Bulls and Plutos instead of flunkies!" shouted Piffit, giving a sounding thump with the umbrella, then holding it up suddenly so that the beak glared wrathfully at the Idol, and it seemed no longer a simple shelter from rain but a hideous-faced demon which she had suddenly conjured to her assistance.

"What do you mean? What do you want?" groaned the Idol, falling back in her chair.

"My money! my money! my money!" howled Piffit, with three upright leaps and three flourishes of the green demon that were appalling. "Your husband has it! I've been to his office, and been, and been, and he's never there. I've sat on the door-step and yelled till the policemen came and all Wall Street was looking on; now I'm here, and I won't go till he gives it up. Where is he—where have you hidden him? Bring him out—let me get at him! I'll teach him—I'll broker him—the wretch, the beast, the swindler!"

The Idol's amazement and fear were lost in anger. "Don't you call my husband names," she exclaimed, "or I'll have you sent to the station-house."

"Me? Have me sent to the station-house?" sneered Piffit. "He! he! That's good—I like that. Me! Mrs. Piffit, the writer! It's your husband ought to go if he had his dues—yes, to Sing Sing. I'll expose him—I'll put him in every paper from Maine to Georgia! I'll not be bought off—I want my money!"

Stunned by the noise the woman made, for her poor head was aching dreadfully, exasperated by the insulting intrusion and conduct after so many years of power and smiling faces, the Idol made a dash at the old majesty and stately words. "Oh," she exclaimed, "you—you—Polyglot of a woman—away! Leave my presence—I command ye."

"Polyglot? No sense in it—means about languages," sniffed Piffit. "You're ignorant—that's what you are; you don't know one word from another—ignorant." Then her sneer changed quickly to wrath. "Order me out? Don't you dare! Try to put me out—just try! Lay a finger on me—shake one at me—I'd like to have you! I've got a policeman round the corner—told him where I was coming—said I wanted my money, and if I didn't come out he might know I'd been murdered by the wretches that had stolen it."

"Will nobody come?" moaned the Idol, feeling herself terribly helpless while the beak of the green demon menaced her. "Haven't I a soul left to protect me from this brutal woman?"

"No, you've not—they don't dare! Let me see 'em try! I'd—I'd umbrella 'em, as sure as my name is Piffit."

"Oh, the inhuman creature," groaned the Idol.

"Don't creature me!" shouted Piffit, growing more belligerent as the Idol shrank from her fury, after the habit of poltroons. "I'm no creature—I'll not be creatured—I'm a woman, and a writer, and a Presbyterian, and every thing that's an ornament to society. It's you're the creature—wearing stolen finery—living on the subsistence of widows and orphans! You're no better than he—you're worse, I believe. Oh, ain't you ashamed of yourself, sitting there tricked up in your gewgaws, with your rings, and your silks, and—and your hair combed." The state of Mrs. Piffit's own tresses at that time, and most others, afforded ample reason why she hit upon that precise matter as a source of peculiar insult and aggravation to injured widows and orphans. "A pretty thing it is!" cried she, sniffing anew. "A sweet spectacle you are for a lone widow woman who's been tricked and gulled and cheated—you, with your rigs and jigs and your hair combed! Why, give me my money! I'll not be put off—I will have my money."

The Idol did remember now what Pluto had related as a good joke during her illness—the appearance of Mrs. Piffit in his office, announcing that she was a friend of his wife and her determination to make an investment in some scheme of his that had struck her fancy.

"My husband means to pay every body," gasped the Idol; "indeed he does. You will be paid—only wait."

"Paid!" echoed Piffit, in profound scorn. "Wait?" she repeated, changing her tone to one of angry inquiry and showing the beak of the green demon to the Idol again, then bringing the point on the floor with a louder bang. "I'll not wait—I'll have my money! Tell me to wait? Oh, you monster! It's enough to cheat men—but a lone widow, hardly out of black for her husband! Oh, if he was alive! But I'm not to be trampled on—I'm not to be put off! My money, my money!"

"You'll get it, you'll get it," sighed the Idol.

"As sure as my name is Piffit I will! I've an article all ready for the papers. You'll catch it—with your dressing, your balls, your jewels, and your teetotums, and my money paying for it! I to toil like a galley slave! I to write books, and memoirs, and poems, and plays, and you to roll in luxury on the proceeds! Oh, you shameless woman!"

"She will drive me mad," sobbed the Idol.

"I mean to—I want to—it's my way; I'm Mrs. Piffit! I tell you, I'll not leave this house without my money! Oh, let me have it—I don't mind taking it in diamonds," she added, suddenly changing to a kind of ferocious entreaty. "Part of it—I can't lose it—part—I'm a lone woman and a widow."

"Indeed, indeed, I am sorry," faltered the Idol.

"Then show it," said Piffit; "prove it. Don't have bowels of brass and a back of iron—it's against the Bible. I could quote you twenty texts, only they've gone out of my head. You take warning. Remember Ananias and Sapphira, and Lot's wife, and Pharaoh, and the children of Israel in the wilderness."

If the Idol could have thought at all, she would have deemed the fate of Lot's wife preferable to that she was enduring, and the most dreary waste ever trodden by the stiff-necked tribes an agreeable place of refuge if it could have relieved her from the presence of this woman. "Oh," she cried desperately, "if you know the Bible so well, you might have a little mercy—it says you must."

"And it says the Devil can quote Scripture," returned Piffit. (Then in a wheezy aside that was involuntary, "No, it was Shakespeare said that; but she don't know.") "And don't quote the Bible to me—it's not for such as you. It's to be mentioned in meeting and on Sunday, you wicked, papistical, Episcopalian, Saint-day-worshiping abomination, you! Go and hear Elder Smithers—he'll teach you religion! He can twist Scripture for you! He'll show you what perdition is and endless punishment too! Get his tract about—"

"I'll not have any body's tracts," sobbed the Idol; "I'm not a New Zealander to pick my enemy's bones."

"You are," said Piffit; "you're worse—you pick the bones of the widows and orphans. That'll tell you. Why, it shows up such as you —ten pages close print! Tells what's under this very Murray Hill with its fashion and its wickedness, and the fires and the imps only held down by the houses of his own congregation, standing up like golden posts to light the world."

"I don't want to hear," moaned the Idol; "go away and let me alone. Smithers, indeed! I'd rather be smothered."

"You'll be worse than smothered," howled Piffit, with an awful shake of the demon. "You'll be burnt, every one of you, you set of Diveses; and all the Lazaruses you've cheated and despised, looking down at you out of Abraham's bosom."

"Oh, this dreadful woman," groaned the Idol, wringing her hands, "Pietro! James! Hortense! Come and take her away."

"They'll not come," returned Piffit; "you're deserted in your day of judgment—you're like the Flood people calling to Noah, you diamond-necklaced iniquity, you! Come?"—and up flamed the wrath again—"I'd like to catch 'em at it! I'm a lone woman and a widow, but I've my umbrella—come?" She levelled the umbrella at every point of the horizon in rapid succession, made fierce dashes at unseen assailants, and ended with a shake of its beak at the Idol, and her face was so hideous, and her gestures were so fierce, that the Idol became convinced she was in the power of a mad woman and fell back in her chair quite exhausted. "Give me my money," said Piffit; "that's what I want— my hard-earned fortune. I'm not to be put off —I'm not to be deluded—I'll have no more words."

"No, no," pleaded the Idol; "no more words."

"You want to force me into silence," cried Piffit, "do you? I'm to be cheated, and robbed, and ruined, and not tell my wrongs? I'll tell them to all New York—I'll yell it at all the corners of the streets—I'll put it in the papers— I'll translate it into German—I'm Mrs. Piffit, the writer!"

"My husband only wants time," sighed the Idol.

"Don't tell me what he wants!" shrieked Piffit. "Time! He's had time to ruin me— isn't that enough? Now I know what your sweetness last summer meant—loving me so—flattering me—"

"I couldn't bear you," broke in the Idol, for this new taunt could not be borne.

"You wanted my money," pursued Piffit, heedless of the interruption. "You wanted to cheat me—to draw me into the vortex—that's what your invitations and your luncheons meant."

"I never invited you," retorted the Idol, roused to frenzy. "You pushed yourself into the house—you would come."

"And I've come now," said Piffit, nodding her head with energy; "and it's for my money, and I'll have it."

"You'll get it. Don't you hear me say all my husband wants is a little time—only a little?"

"Don't talk to me about time!" cried Piffit. "It's eternity he'd have to be thinking of if he had his deserts—and a halter, and every thing in the way of punishment that can be found in this world, or over the best of tracts told about in the next."

"Don't talk so horribly, don't," pleaded the Idol. "Time, time!" Amid her fright and confusion the habits of years held their sway, as they must over all of us; she remembered dimly some famous dying-speech somebody put in the mouth of Queen Elizabeth. "Millions of inches is a single money in time," she gasped frantically.

"Don't talk rubbish," sniffed Piffit. "That's rubbish. Your head always was upside down, and you always talked wrong end foremost."

"Millions of inches," the Idol was half unconsciously beginning again, but Piffit stopped her.

"Didn't I say that was rubbish? An inch of time, indeed! No, no; I'll not give you a barley-corn's length—you've had ells already. A pretty use you'd make of time! You want to get off to Europe with what you can save, with your plate and your jewels! I know—a secret flight is what you're at—in the night—no, no."

"I don't want to go anywhere—I only want to be left alone."

"I'll never leave you alone!" shouted Piffit, waving her umbrella. "Here I am—here I stay till I get my money! Touch me, put me out, if you can! Just so much as finger me, if you dare!" Once more she broke off in her threats to make entreaties, as the thought of losing her cherished treasure wrung her soul. "Why, I can't lose my money; try and let me have it. I can't lose it; I've toiled for it, slaved for it night and day, nobody knows."

"You shall have it; you shall."

"Then give me a pledge," said Piffit, looking about in search of valuables which might secure her against loss.

"I'll give you any thing, if you'll only go away."

"I'll take it," cried Piffit, "if it's salable and good security. Watches, jewels— Here, I'll take it in spoons and forks," continued she, noticing the specimens of plate on the table. She caught up two gold tea-spoons and bit the bowls to ascertain their quality. "They're solid—give me enough of 'em and I'll be satisfied." She leaned the umbrella against a chair, set the flat reticule on the table and opened its rapacious-looking mouth, and the Idol, seeing her apparently determined to take instant possession of whatever she could lay hands on, tried to think of some way of getting her out of the house, even if she carried every valuable it contained along with her.

"How much was the amount?" she asked. Several times she had been on the point of inquiry, but Piffit bewildered her by her noise, and her increasing fury had made her think the amount must be so large that she had not before gained courage to put the question. "How much was it?"

"Seven hundred dollars!" cried Piffit.

"What?" demanded the Idol, in an altered voice.

"Seven—hundred—dollars!" repeated Piffit with a groan, not observant of the changed voice, and forgetting that the sum was not so large to every body as it looked in her own eyes. "I can prove it. I've the papers—the receipts and every thing—here in my bag. I'll show 'em to you! Oh, I can't lose my money! I'm a lone woman and a widow—I'm a writer, and more sensitive than ordinary people. Only pay me—pay me—I'll take any thing!" She broke off to hunt in her reticule for the proofs of the transactions which had taken place between herself and Pluto, while the Idol sat recovering rapidly from her fright, and going straight over to a state of feeling that might have startled Mrs. Piffit had she been aware of the revulsion. "Seven—hundred—dollars," Piffit was saying again. "It's a good deal of money! I'm a lone woman and a widow—nobody to bring any help but myself. I've got the papers here—I'll show you that it's all straight."

Had she, the Idol, who for many years had been seated on a pedestal so lofty that she could see the whole world at her feet, she whose words had been listened to as if they were oracles, before whom people had bowed with 'bated breath, actually been insulted and browbeaten for that pitiful sum? It was too much! Even in her ruin, to be brought face to face with such petty miseries was not to be borne. Seven hundred dollars! And she had been thinking of thousands upon thousands; partly from considering the magnitude of her husband's failure, partly from Mrs. Piffit's earnestness. Why, she had nearly twice that sum lying in the little bronze chest that set on a carved bracket by the chim-ney—a miracle of workmanship in which she kept money and private billets. With the means of relieving herself at once from this abominable persecution, she had allowed the fiendish creature's insolence to frighten and overpower her, and out of the goodness of her heart had felt distress at the widow's loss, in spite of all that harsh language. The while she indulged in these reflections, Mrs. Piffit hunted and muttered over the reticule, peering into its recesses and occasionally croaking like an ill-conditioned old raven with soiled plumage—"Seven hundred dollars! A good deal of money. Seven hundred—" Ending each time with a prodigious sniff and an internal rumble.

The Idol rose with much of her majesty restored, swept up to the bracket, unlocked the bronze chest, and took out seven crisp, fresh-looking bank-notes. Piffit, squinting at her with one eye, saw the action and snorted loud.

"Why, you had the money all the time!" she exclaimed, divided between pleasure at the prospect of speedy payment and a return of wrath at the idea that the Idol had meant, if possible, to avoid giving up her private hoards. "You had it all the time!"

The Idol swept toward the table again, holding the notes in her hand, and regarded Piffit with mingled dignity and disgust. "Of course I had that contemptible amount by me," she said; "but how could I suppose any human being would conduct himself—or herself—" she was composed enough now to strain after correctness of speech—"as you have done for so miserable a trifle?"

"Trifle!" sniffed Piffit, dropping her voice to a whine. "It may seem so to you who've been rolling in wealth—"

"Wrung, I think you observed, from toiling widows and orphans," interrupted the Idol loftily."

"Oh well, I don't know what I said; but it's a great deal of money to me—I work hard. Why, just the running up and down stairs at the newspaper offices is ruin to shoe leather and ankles."

"Why did you not name the sum at first?" continued the Idol. "How dared you come here and conduct yourself like—like— I have no comparison for such actions."

Mrs. Piffit was wonderfully soothed by the sight of the bank-notes; she began to feel new respect for the Idol since she saw her able to pay, and was only afraid that she might lose her beloved money after all if the stately lady grew too angry. "Don't bear malice," she sniffed; "it's unchristian."

"Do not venture to utter more of your hypocritical counsels," exclaimed the Idol, warming rapidly. "After your conduct, your language, to call yourself any thing but a heathen—yes, the most abandoned of Patagonians in some desert isle—would be preposterous."

"Now don't call names," said Piffit, trying to restrain the courage she felt oozing out at her finger-ends; "that's actionable, remember, and it isn't lady-like. I know—I've written a book on etiquette."

"Peace, woman!" returned the Idol. "Produce your papers and your proofs, and leave my presence."

"I only want my money," whined Piffit; "I'm a hard-working—"

"Evil-tongued woman," added the Idol. "I would not have stabbed my worst enemy when in misfortune, as you have done, for millions, no, not for continents of gold!"

"I didn't mean to be violent," pleaded Piffit; "I suppose I was a little excited. You mustn't mind it — writers always are. I'm alone in the world—I have to keep a sharp lookout. Here are the receipts—look." She spread the papers on the table, and fearful lest it should be a trick of the Idol's to get them in her own possession, held fast to the precious documents with one hand—a very fat hand, with ink-spots on the nails, and a general appearance of having suffered from the lack of soap and water since Piffit's fears of expense had been roused.

The Idol glanced disdainfully at the records. "Write a fresh receipt," said she, "stating that I have reimbursed you; yonder are chirographic implements."

"Yes, yes," said Piffit, snatching up the papers, which had already assumed the brown and glutinous appearance all things did that were engulfed in the flat bag, and she wrote the receipt with alacrity, pulling over it a great deal.

The Idol handed her the money and took the documents. She was enough herself now to wish to end the scene in an imposing way; there was some undefined thought in her mind as if she were a great queen who had lost crown and throne and was ordering a treacherous parasite from her presence. "Go," said she, pointing her finger toward the door; "your sight is pollution—your voice more loathsome than the groaning of the fabled fiends on Thessalonian heights."

Piffit was struck dumb by this sudden end of her troubles; the consciousness that the money was absolutely warming her palm, filled her with a delight which went straight to her soul.

"Go," repeated the Idol, "spectacle of Medusean horror, go!"

"I'm going," sniffed Piffit, "I'm going."

The Idol rang the bell. Mrs. Piffit made a dash at the reticule, and as she did so something rattled in its interior. To her horror she saw that while brandishing the gold spoons one of them had fallen into the gaping mouth, and the Idol saw it too—she would not have been human if she could have refrained from torturing her enemy a little after the recent scene. "A theft—a robbery!" she exclaimed. "You abandoned woman, you force yourself into my house, you insult me, and while doing it you purloin my plate! My servant is a witness—he can behold it," she continued, waving her hand toward the man who opened the door.

"I didn't—I didn't—it dropped in!" howled Piffit.

"Dropped in!" repeated the Idol with withering scorn. "Do gold tea-spoons fly about like winged butterflies? Woman, you are discovered—exposed—prepare to meet thy doom!"

"Let me out!" snarled Piffit. "Here's the spoon. I didn't want it—didn't know it was there. Let me out!" She threw the spoon on the table, caught up her bag again and turned to go.

"If I sent you away under the guidance of the officers of the law, I should but treat you as you deserve."

"Oh, don't," sobbed Piffit, cruelly frightened. "I didn't mean to take it. A mistake's a mistake the world over—any body may make one. Let me go! I'm sorry I said any thing —I ask your pardon—oh, dear me, don't!"

"This is a change of tone indeed," pursued the Idol. "No more taunts, no more Titanic insolence? My faithful retainer saw you cast the valuable from the bag where you had concealed it. Ha, woman! what says that brazen forehead now?"

"I'd rather give up the money," shrieked Piffit. "Let me go!"

"To assail me in the sanctuary of my Penadians—to purloin golden treasures—"

"I didn't—don't say such things! Why, you'd ruin me! I wouldn't steal—I'm a widow, and a writer, and a Presbyterian!" And Piffit began to sob in terror and anguish.

"Madam," returned the Idol, "your conduct has prepared me to believe any thing, every thing that is atrocious of the three characters."

"O Mrs. Hackett, I'm so sorry! I didn't mean what I said—I've always had the greatest respect for you! I've written you scores of notices—I said from the first I knew you'd pay, that Mr. Hackett was the most honorable man alive and so were you—oh, oh!"

"Your praise would be only added calumny," replied the Idol; "take not my husband's name upon your lips."

"I won't, I won't—I'll do just what you want. If you like, I'll write a notice and say it's all a lie, that he hasn't failed at all. Don't be revengeful—there's a hereafter— No, no, I don't mean that—you wouldn't be—you're above it. O Lord! I don't know what I mean." She broke down and cried like a fat baby, sobbed and kicked, and her late antagonist, the footman, regarded her with a grin of delight which at another time would have roused her to fury. "O Mrs. Hackett, let me go! You're a lady, by birth and station—you wouldn't harm a lone woman! I'll promise any thing—I'll do any thing—I'll go down on my knees to you—oh, oh!"

"Enough," said the Idol; "kneel not to me. Relieve me of your presence—depart! James, see that woman out."

Mrs. Piffit gave a bound that no startled gazelle ever equalled, dashed past him and was down stairs like a flash. The permission to go had been so unexpected that she could not credit its reality, and once out of the house she flew down the avenue at a pace which made several policemen look inquiringly after her, and caused much amusement to those she met, rushing on with her umbrella over her shoulder, her petticoats flying, the great tears still on her face, and her machinery working with a piteous creak. It was not until she was out of the neighborhood, had turned down a side street, and gained the friendly shelter of an omnibus, that she began to feel herself free from peril. For days after she kept close at home or went out in odds and ends, by way of being disguised, and thereby made herself more noticeable, but the Idol never dreamed of molesting her further. It was said that the adventure taught Mrs. Piffit a little discretion, but much Mrs. Piffit could not learn. Wherever she may be, she is undoubtly in pursuit of a man in hiding, or helping some unfortunate woman to make herself notorious, or composing paragraphs to injure somebody who has been silly enough to do her a favor; but wherever she is, or whatever doing, be sure the flat reticule is hanging on her arm and the green familiar reposing by her side, and we will leave her in their company with resignation and composure.

———◆———

CHAPTER XLVII.

WINDING UP THE THREADS.

CLIVE FARNSWORTH had gone away over the sea, to seek in distant lands the peace which must come after the first violence of the shock that brought back his remorse had passed, and he could remember that he had been allowed to make expiation for his sin. Ruth's last words would recur to his mind and help more than any thing to give him quiet — she had been happy.

For several weeks Mr. Grey lay upon his bed with little or no change visible; it seemed that each fresh day must carry hence the poor life on its close; but after that period, he began unexpectedly to mend. He could sit up, could be moved from room to room, could talk, and show pleasure in Elinor's presence. She knew this was only a brief respite, mercifully given that she might have time to grow accustomed to her desolation, but she was grateful for it. His mind was much impaired, or rather his memory, for his conversation was usually agreeable; but he retained such vague recollections of the past year that they caused him no trouble. He often talked to Elinor as if they were living in the years long gone, still he did not regard her as the child she was at that time. She was every thing to him—hands, eyes, judgment; his deference to what she might think best in the veriest trifle connected with his meals,. was touching and painful. The Thorntons remained with her and shared her solitude; and as spring came on, and he grew so much better, it was proposed that he should be taken to Alban

Wood. The physician thought the change might be of benefit, and Mr. Grey showed great satisfaction at the proposal. They made the journey by easy stages, stopping in New York for a long rest and fresh medical advice, which could give no hope. Mr. Grey's life was at an end; how long this feeble semblance of existence could be kept up was doubtful. There they were in the quiet of Alban Wood, and Elinor watched over him, comforted by Tom and Rosa's companionship.

The scenes which had preceded that attack had no place in her mind; any fear of the least stain upon her father's memory had passed away. That letter had gone over the length and breadth of the land; even those censors of the press most opposed to the President had nothing but honorable mention for the last act of the statesman whose career had so suddenly and mournfully terminated. Ere autumn, Mr. Grey had gone beyond the reach of blame, if it had been likely to assail him; gone beyond the reach of praise, that would once have been so sweet, for his death was followed by honors and lamentations which knew no stint, but they could not move him then.

He had been failing more and more for weeks; one bright midsummer morning, when the breeze and the sun and the songs of birds streamed in at the open windows, Elinor sat by his bed, holding his hand fast in hers, and feeling the nerveless fingers grow colder, as he drifted slowly out toward the ocean beyond. "Father," she said softly; "father." He raised his eyes and looked at her; the old smile played across his lips, and once more they framed the familiar response—

"My daughter Elinor!"

With that purest utterance his heart had ever known, the head turned on the pillow, the smile remained fixed, and while Elinor sat watching for another movement, Tom Thornton drew her gently away. Mr. Grey had gone, and perhaps to the angels, who judge more clearly than we, every feeling, every expiation had gathered in the utterance of that name which had been his religion.

Elinor Grey remained at Alban Wood. It was understood that it was her home now, and they were all glad to have it so. Elinor told her friends only that the greater part of her fortune had been lost in some unexpected failures, but there was enough left to satisfy her moderate wants, and she had no intention of paining them, or making herself absurd, by starting out in search of a mission. Faithful Henry entered Thornton's service, and Coralie clung to her mistress; it was like keeping something of the old life to have their faces in sight.

The months passed till it was a year from the events of the last winter I have described—swept on till another midsummer came. The career of Pluto is matter of history; I need only tell you that by the close of that year and a half he was far on the road to new successes, which in time became so great that, having gone over to the Bears in disgust at the conduct of certain Bulls at the period of his failure, he waxed the most tremendous Grizzly that ever walked down Wall Street, and terrified the Bovines more by his growls than ever he had the Bruins by his bellowings before his transformation.

The Idol stood by him with unfaltering devotion; gave up every thing she owned—jewels, palace, castle—and found much satisfaction still in weighty sentences and misquoted blank verse. Before he left for Europe, Clive Farnsworth took time to remember her misfortunes and place his house at her service for the summer, insisting so urgently upon her occupying it that she could not refuse; so to her great delight she was near her chief favorites still. A proud and happy Idol was she, when with her own hands she was able to refund to Elinor a portion of the lost money, and to give the assurance that the restoration of the rest was only a matter of time. Indeed, her admiration of Miss Grey knew no bounds and was ever on the increase. The nearer the old wealth and station she soared, the more heart-felt her esteem and gratitude became.

"I know humanity," she was fond of saying; "I have seen the hollow leaves fall from my summer-trees at the breath of adversity, but I heeded not—my soul was stayed on other steeps than they! The Thorntons rank loftily in my mind, but when I regard Miss Grey, and compare her with the rest of the world, I cry—'Lo, Hyperion to a Satire!'"

Leighton Rossitur and his wife remained in Europe—I think it doubtful if they ever return. Perhaps it may be thought that it was not poetical justice to have given them both their wishes, but I do not know that a worse punishment could have been meted to either. Rossitur had the wealth he craved, but, from his habits of self-indulgence, so far from being a stepping-stone to influence and power, it would prove a weight that must drag him surely down. Useless to return for the present, he knew, so far as political aims were concerned. The Falcon party hated him with a bitter hatred, believing that he had willfully aided in their deception, and they would effectually close the way to advancement in that direction. He stayed where he was, and in a whirl of excitement and recklessness tried to destroy such memories as stung his soul, and rapidly burned out the last promise of his youth. As time went on, people returning from Europe told Rosa Thornton incredible tales of the madness of husband and wife, and that, among other fancies, both had developed a passion for gambling which was the theme of every tongue even at Baden.

The Thorntons. Ah! I am glad to come back to the midsummer, and leave them with their happiness increased by a new hope. No wonder looking into Rosa's eyes was like looking into heaven; no wonder Tom walked about on air, and acted as if he had unexpectedly been declared emperor of all dream-land—there was

going to be a baby! There had been one child born, years before, but they never spoke of it, never until now had they been able to allude to it even to each other. Rosa had met with some accident, and the poor infant only came into the world for a week of pain, and went back to heaven. But now Rosa was strong and well—there was to be a baby!

I am aware that we are an essentially modest people; never in conversation, never in books, do we so much as allude to babies before their birth, but there was always a slight twist in my moral anatomy, and I did not inherit a fitting share of the national modesty, so I must tell you about this baby, this unborn baby. My story will not go on to the period when the mystery became an established fact which might be proclaimed aloud, concerning which, five minutes before such consummation, not even a woman's own grandmother would for the world have appeared conscious that any thing was the matter, no, not if she had borne a baker's dozen of children in her time, triplets on more than one occasion, and counted her descendants by scores.

When they came to compare notes, it appeared that Rosa had rather set her heart on a boy who should have Tom's eyes, and Tom had thought he could be satisfied with a girl who should possess dimples like Rosa's, so they looked a little blank at each other when the private speculations were brought to light. Then that insatiable monster, Tom, by way of settling the matter satisfactorily as he said, absolutely had the hardihood to suggest twins, and was properly put down by Rosa. Indeed, she vowed that if he did not stop his nonsense in regard to every thing—leave her to eat, sleep, and walk in peace, and cease looking at each indigestible morsel she coveted as if it were rank poison, and wherever she moved, wincing as though the ground was a succession of pitfalls—she would not have any baby at all, just to punish him. Tom, knowing her to be a woman of resolution, though matters had gone rather far for such a declaration to be very terrible, was quite appalled, and for the rest of the day went about as meek as Moses, to the wicked little woman's silent but intense delectation. So they dreamed on into midsummer, a year from the time of Mr. Grey's death; and Elinor could find pleasure in their happiness, for her grief had not been selfish.

Clive Farnsworth had returned from Europe the previous autumn. He had taken his seat in the House and distinguished himself by several powerful speeches and a line of conduct that won the highest encomiums from those whose approval was worth having. It was some time now since Congress adjourned; the Idol had months before given up Farnsworth's house, but Clive did not come back to the old place, which, as Rosa said to Tom, looked as if it were waiting for him. He did not come, and however much the Doves might wonder in secret, to Elinor they were silent, though she forced herself often to speak his name with praiseworthy composure.

Until now she had not thought much: there had been many things to occupy her; but now that womanly heart of hers would talk at times about its little story, and the heavy trouble through which she had passed had left the haughty will so much softened that she could not always shut out its whispers as she might once have done. She was alone much of the time as summer advanced, and the confinement of the house was irksome to her; she rode about the picturesque hills or wandered among the shadowy woods, and tried to convince herself that she was very ungrateful not to be content, since life had so many blessings left; but though she succeeded in filling her mind with a proper remorse for the unthankfulness, the restlessness would not leave her. At last, when she could no longer avoid reflection, she knew that Clive Farnsworth would never come to her. The love of a brief season had died out as was natural; he saw her as she was, a hard, imperious woman, not fitted to retain any man's affection.

Time went on to a day that could now be an anniversary in Elinor's mind, which would grow, she believed, one of those holy seasons such as so many of our wasted lives keep, we who have seen the brightness of our youth go out. She left Rosa and Tom quite to themselves that day, and they were those rare creatures who could let a friend alone. She had been out of the house all the afternoon, and now, in its late brightness, she was sitting on the hill, in the shadow of the very maple-tree where Clive Farnsworth had read to her for the last time. In certain ways that season appeared very far off, but sitting there in the stillness, her heart would not allow her to think of all she had lived through since then; it would make its whisperings heard and tell her its story. She must rouse herself and go away before that vision

R

died out in pain. She rose, glanced lingeringly about, and as she looked down through the winding aisles of the wood, she saw Clive Farnsworth coming toward her. He was by her side, holding her hands, calling her name.

"Elinor! Elinor!" The reality which she had been endeavoring to face was gone forever—her heart's dream was the actual. "I have come back, Elinor," he said hurriedly; "are you glad to see me?" She tried to speak some words of welcome. "Do you know what day this is?" he asked. "I waited for it—I was afraid to come—but I could not bear the suspense any longer. Elinor, I love you with the old love grown so much greater and holier that I think it must redeem a little of my unworthiness. I have tried to atone for the errors—the sins—I have thought the blessing our pure angel left with me might have helped me in your sight. Elinor, I have come back—must I go away again?" He had spoken rapidly; as he ceased he loosened his clasp of her hands, but she did not withdraw them—they lay, trembling a little, in his own.

And Clive Farnsworth was answered.

Till the glory of the sunset swept about them in its dazzling radiance, they stood in that quiet spot, and then remembered that it was time to go. As they turned to walk down the hill, Clive checked the hand he held; she glanced up at him inquiringly.

"It seems like a dream, Elinor," he said. "From the first moment I looked in your eyes, I loved you. Tell me — you have not told me — when your heart first had a place for me?"

She gazed honestly in his face and said—"From the moment I looked back in yours."

For a little time they stood there together, silent under that great wealth of happiness, then went slowly forth into the sunshine—never to lose its blessed radiance.

THE END.